STRAY BULLETS ®

STR
BU

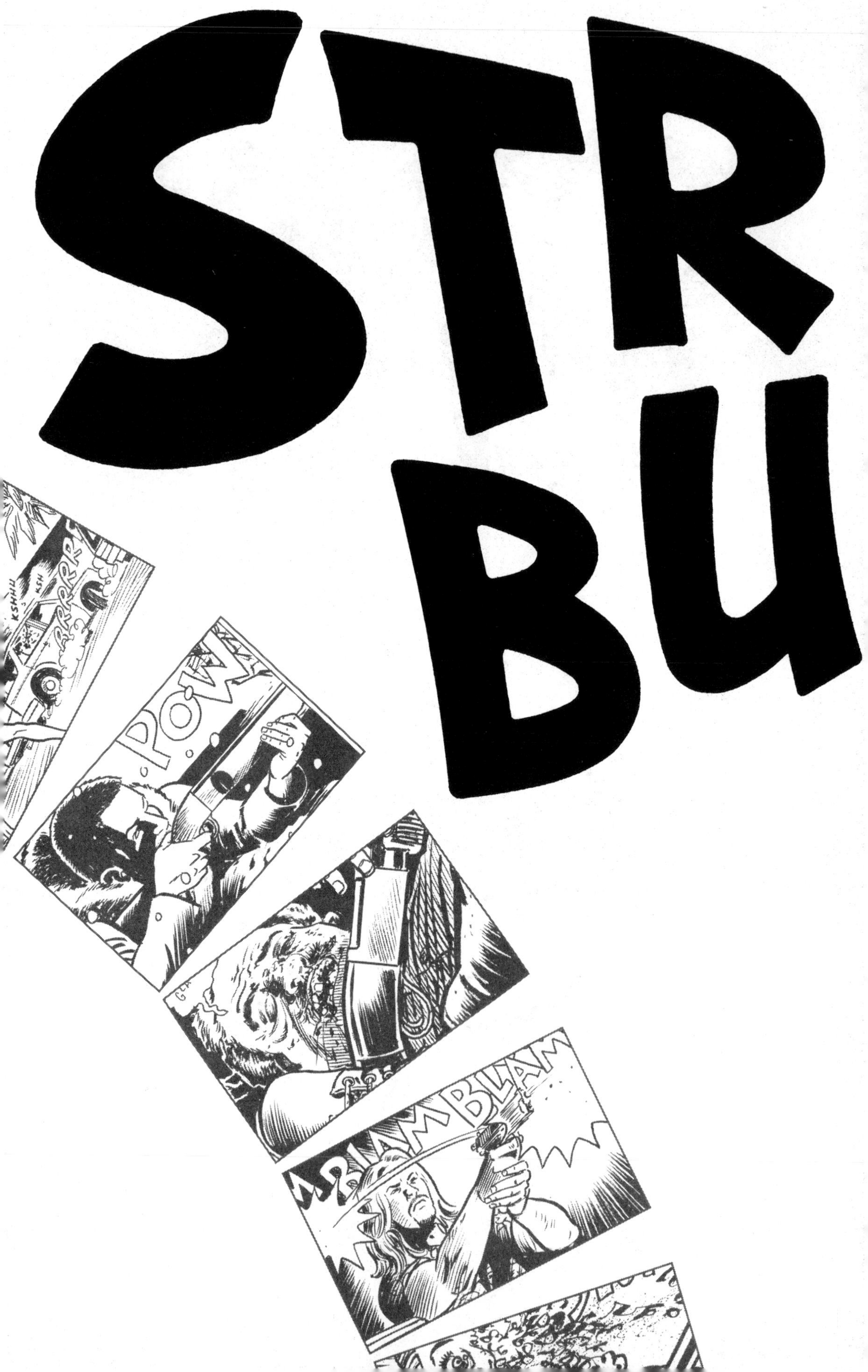
POW
BLAM

AY
LETS

PART FOUR

"THE SALAD DAYS"

by
DAVID LAPHAM
MARIA LAPHAM

STRAY BULLETS: SUNSHINE & ROSES, PART 4

by
DAVID LAPHAM

•

PRODUCED AND EDITED BY
MARIA LAPHAM

AN 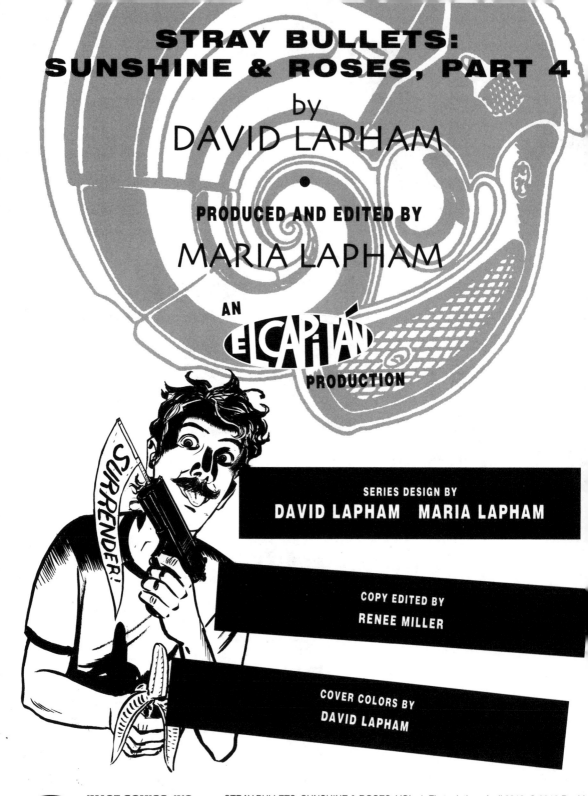 EL CAPITÁN PRODUCTION

SERIES DESIGN BY
DAVID LAPHAM   MARIA LAPHAM

COPY EDITED BY
RENEE MILLER

COVER COLORS BY
DAVID LAPHAM

® **IMAGE COMICS, INC.**
Robert Kirkman—Chief Operating Officer
Erik Larsen—Chief Financial Officer
Todd McFarlane—President
Marc Silvestri—Chief Executive Officer
Jim Valentino—Vice President
Eric Stephenson—Publisher/Chief Creative Officer
Corey Hart—Director of Sales
Jeff Boison—Director of Publishing Planning
        & Book Trade Sales
Chris Ross—Director of Digital Sales
Jeff Stang—Director of Specialty Sales
Kat Salazar—Director of PR & Marketing
Drew Gill—Art Director
Heather Doornink—Production Director
Nicole Lapalme—Controller
IMAGECOMICS.COM

STRAY BULLETS: SUNSHINE & ROSES, VOL. 4. First printing. April 2019. © 2019 David and Maria Lapham. Published by Image Comics, Inc. Office of publication: 2701 NW Vaughn St., Suite 780, Portland, OR 97210. The chapters in this book were originally published as issues #25-32 of the comic book STRAY BULLETS: SUNSHINE & ROSES. El Capitán and the El Capitán logo are registered trademarks ® of Lapham, Inc. No part of this book may be reproduced in any form, or by any means, electronic or mechanical, without the written permission of the publisher and copyright holders. All characters featured herein and the distinctive likenesses thereof are trademarks of David and Maria Lapham. The stories, characters, and events herein are fictional. Any similarities to persons living or dead are entirely coincidental. For information regarding the CPSIA on this printed material call: 203-595-3636.

ISBN: 978-1-5343-1046-9   PRINTED IN THE U.S.A.

CONTENTS

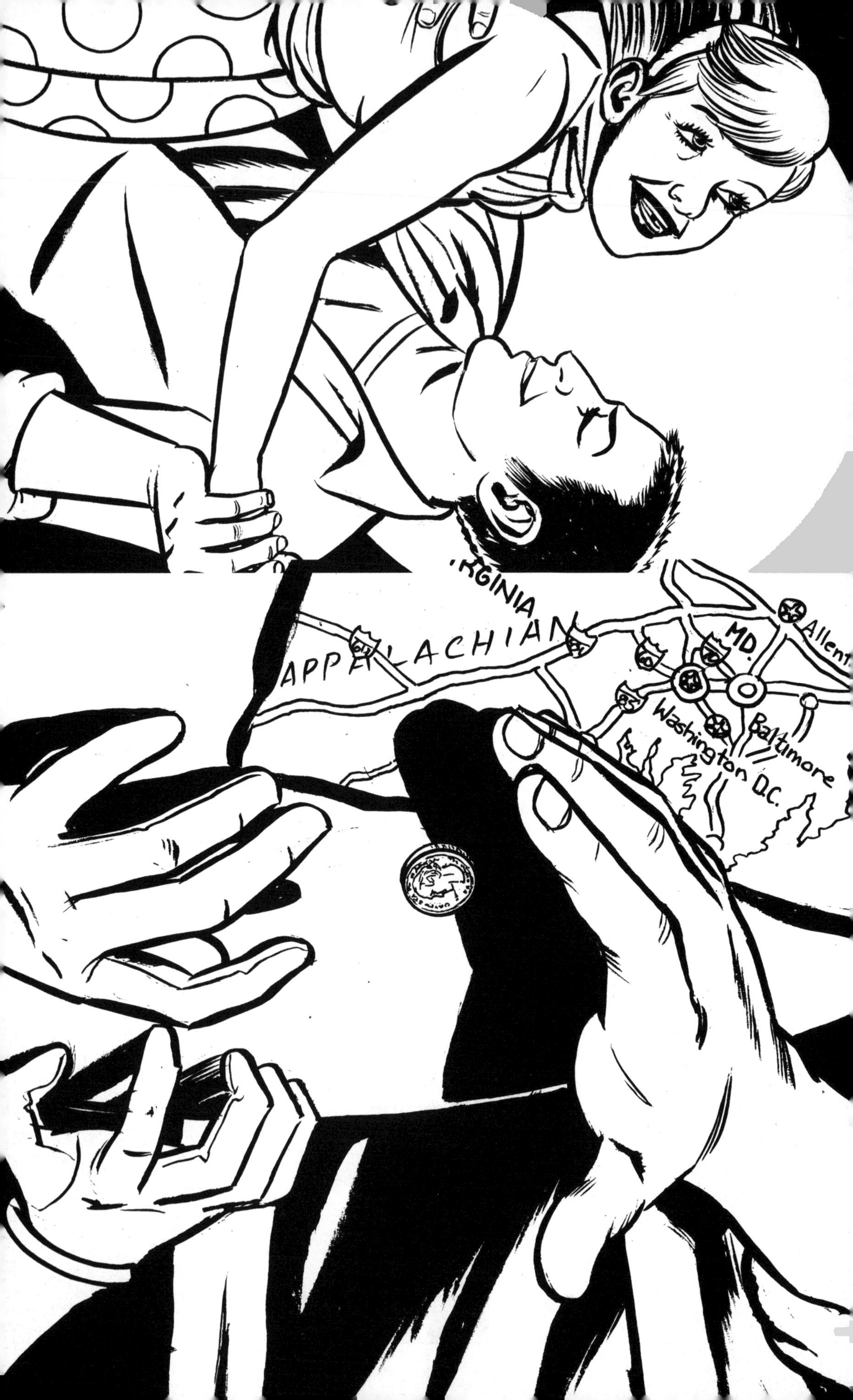
MD.
Baltimore
Washington D.C.

STRAY BULLETS

"We'll deliver our own fucking message."

"THE SALAD DAYS"

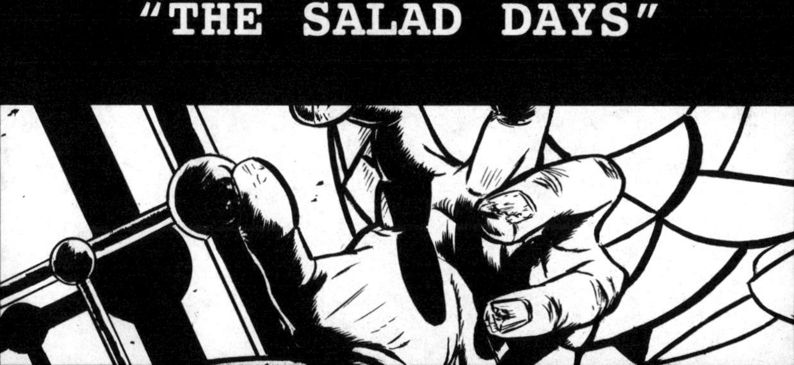

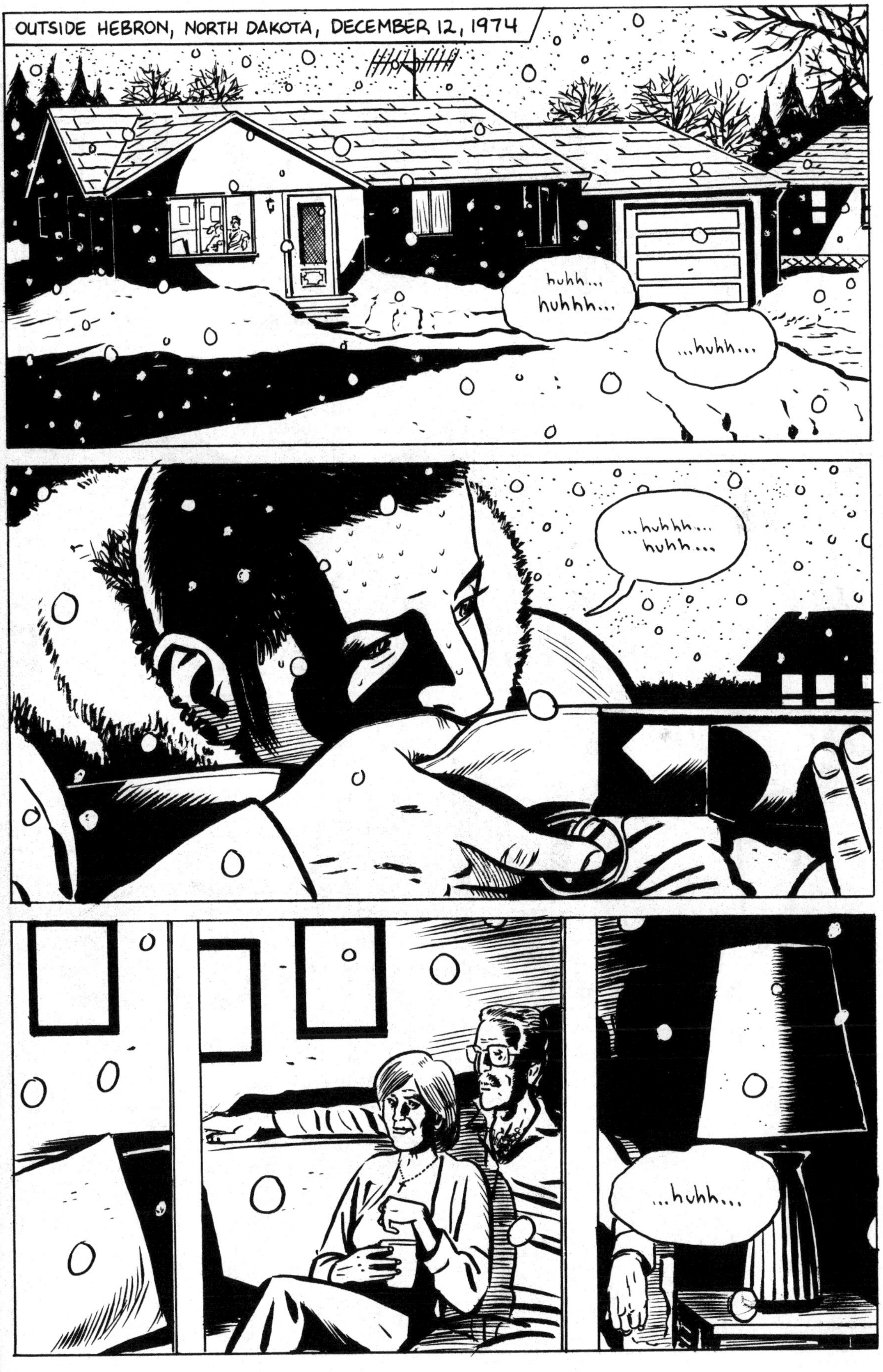
OUTSIDE HEBRON, NORTH DAKOTA, DECEMBER 12, 1974
huhh...
huhhh...
...huhh...
...huhhh...
huhh...
...huhh...

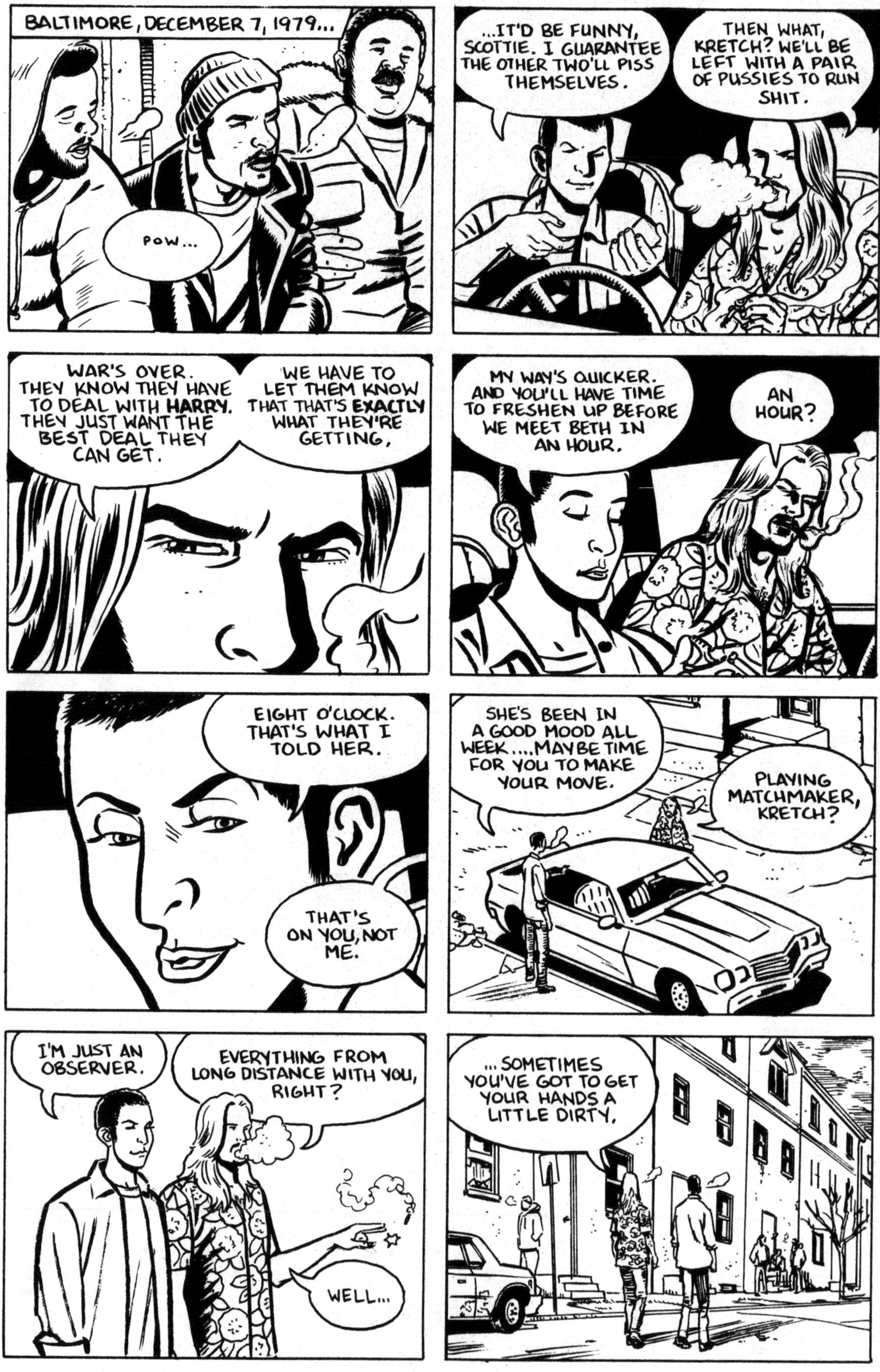
BALTIMORE, DECEMBER 7, 1979...
POW...
...IT'D BE FUNNY, SCOTTIE. I GUARANTEE THE OTHER TWO'LL PISS THEMSELVES.
THEN WHAT, KRETCH? WE'LL BE LEFT WITH A PAIR OF PUSSIES TO RUN SHIT.
WAR'S OVER. THEY KNOW THEY HAVE TO DEAL WITH HARRY. THEY JUST WANT THE BEST DEAL THEY CAN GET.
WE HAVE TO LET THEM KNOW THAT THAT'S EXACTLY WHAT THEY'RE GETTING.
MY WAY'S QUICKER. AND YOU'LL HAVE TIME TO FRESHEN UP BEFORE WE MEET BETH IN AN HOUR.
AN HOUR?
EIGHT O'CLOCK. THAT'S WHAT I TOLD HER.
THAT'S ON YOU, NOT ME.
SHE'S BEEN IN A GOOD MOOD ALL WEEK.... MAYBE TIME FOR YOU TO MAKE YOUR MOVE.
PLAYING MATCHMAKER, KRETCH?
I'M JUST AN OBSERVER.
EVERYTHING FROM LONG DISTANCE WITH YOU, RIGHT?
WELL...
...SOMETIMES YOU'VE GOT TO GET YOUR HANDS A LITTLE DIRTY.

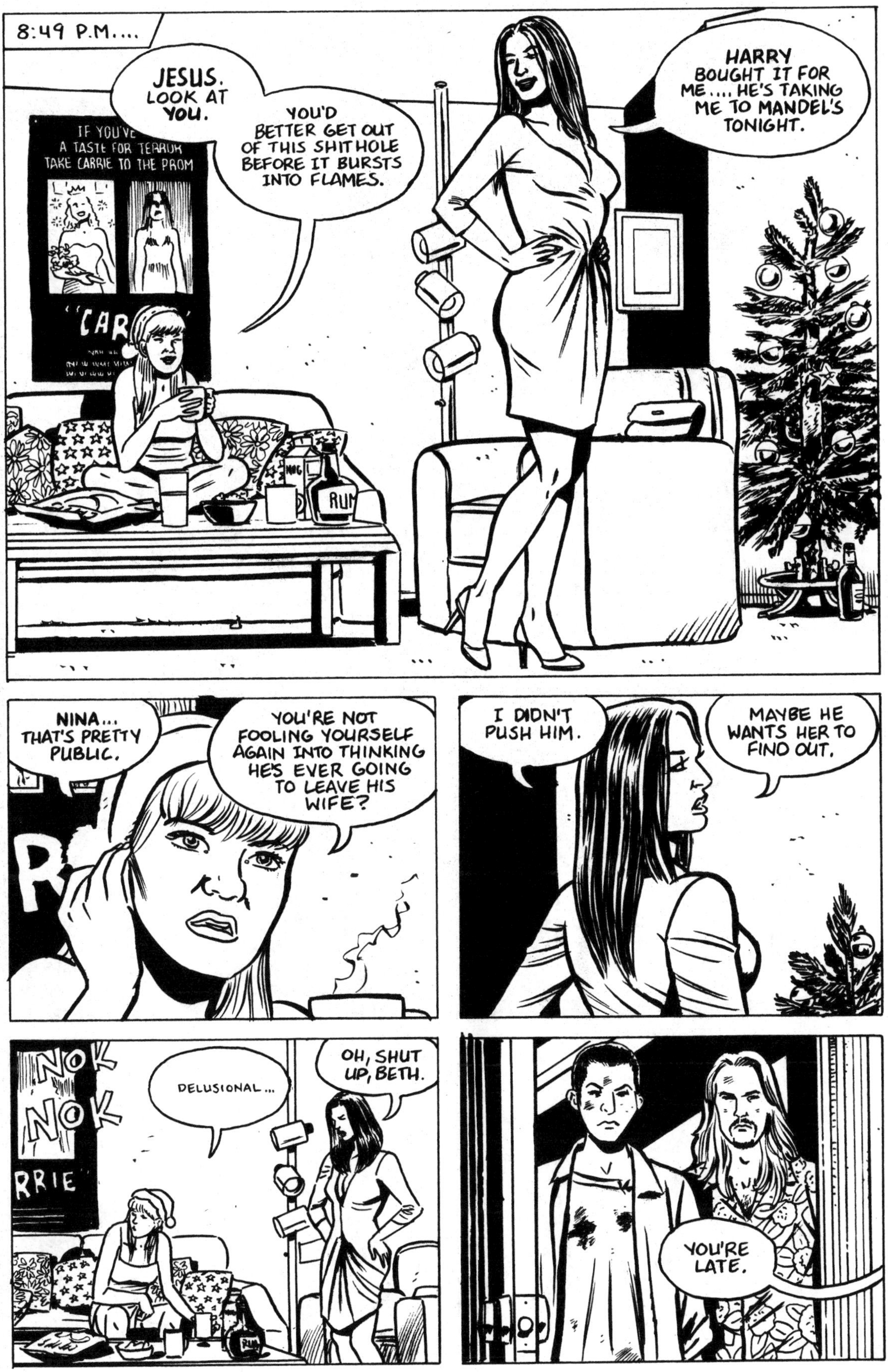
8:49 P.M....
IF YOU'VE
A TASTE FOR TERROR
TAKE CARRIE TO THE PROM
JESUS. LOOK AT YOU.
YOU'D BETTER GET OUT OF THIS SHITHOLE BEFORE IT BURSTS INTO FLAMES.
HARRY BOUGHT IT FOR ME.... HE'S TAKING ME TO MANDEL'S TONIGHT.
RUM
NINA... THAT'S PRETTY PUBLIC.
YOU'RE NOT FOOLING YOURSELF AGAIN INTO THINKING HE'S EVER GOING TO LEAVE HIS WIFE?
I DIDN'T PUSH HIM.
MAYBE HE WANTS HER TO FIND OUT.
NOK
NOK
DELUSIONAL...
OH, SHUT UP, BETH.
YOU'RE LATE.

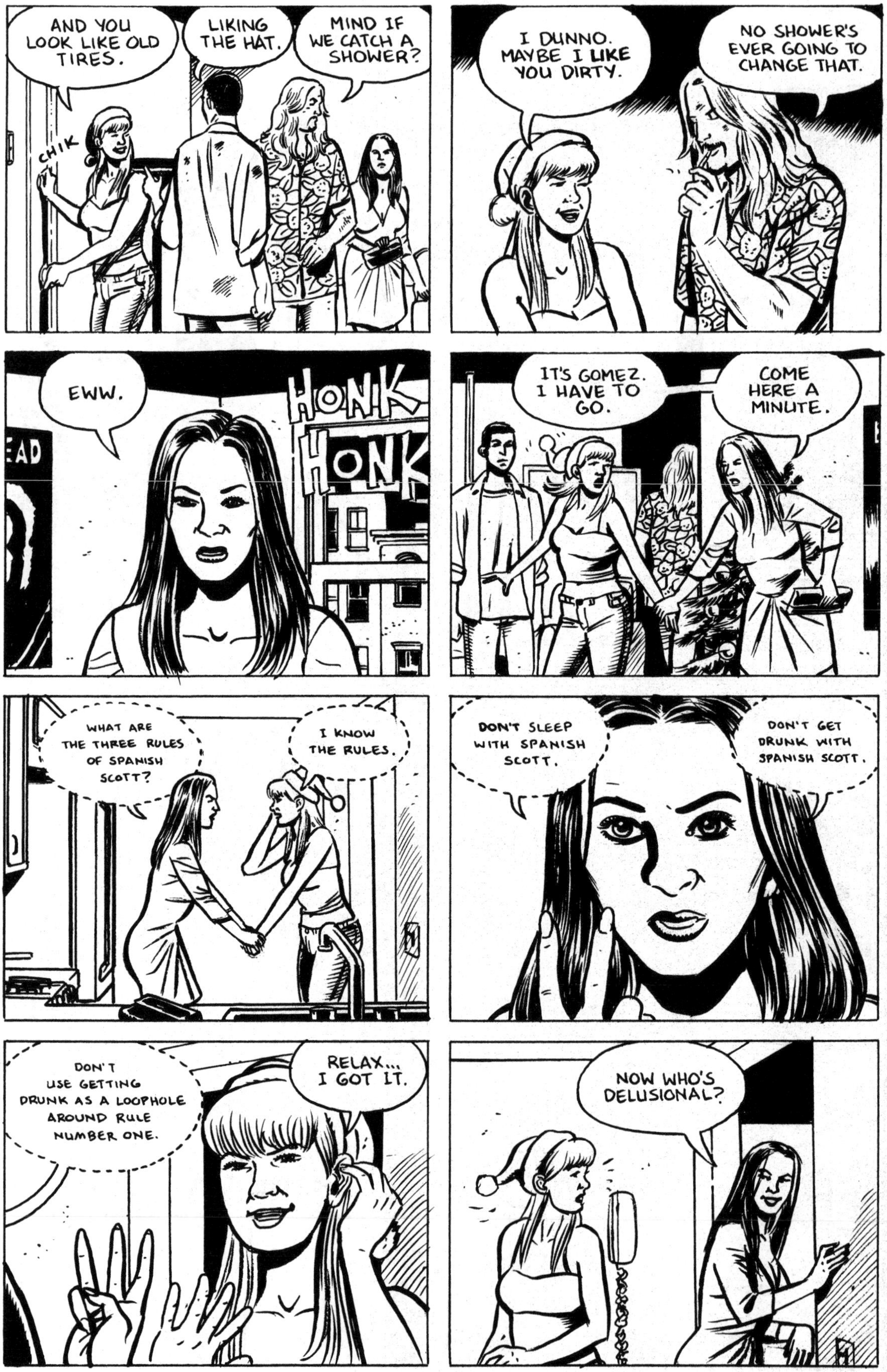
AND YOU LOOK LIKE OLD TIRES.
CHIK
LIKING THE HAT.
MIND IF WE CATCH A SHOWER?
I DUNNO. MAYBE I LIKE YOU DIRTY.
NO SHOWER'S EVER GOING TO CHANGE THAT.
EWW.
HONK HONK
IT'S GOMEZ. I HAVE TO GO.
COME HERE A MINUTE.
WHAT ARE THE THREE RULES OF SPANISH SCOTT?
I KNOW THE RULES.
DON'T SLEEP WITH SPANISH SCOTT.
DON'T GET DRUNK WITH SPANISH SCOTT.
DON'T USE GETTING DRUNK AS A LOOPHOLE AROUND RULE NUMBER ONE.
RELAX... I GOT IT.
NOW WHO'S DELUSIONAL?

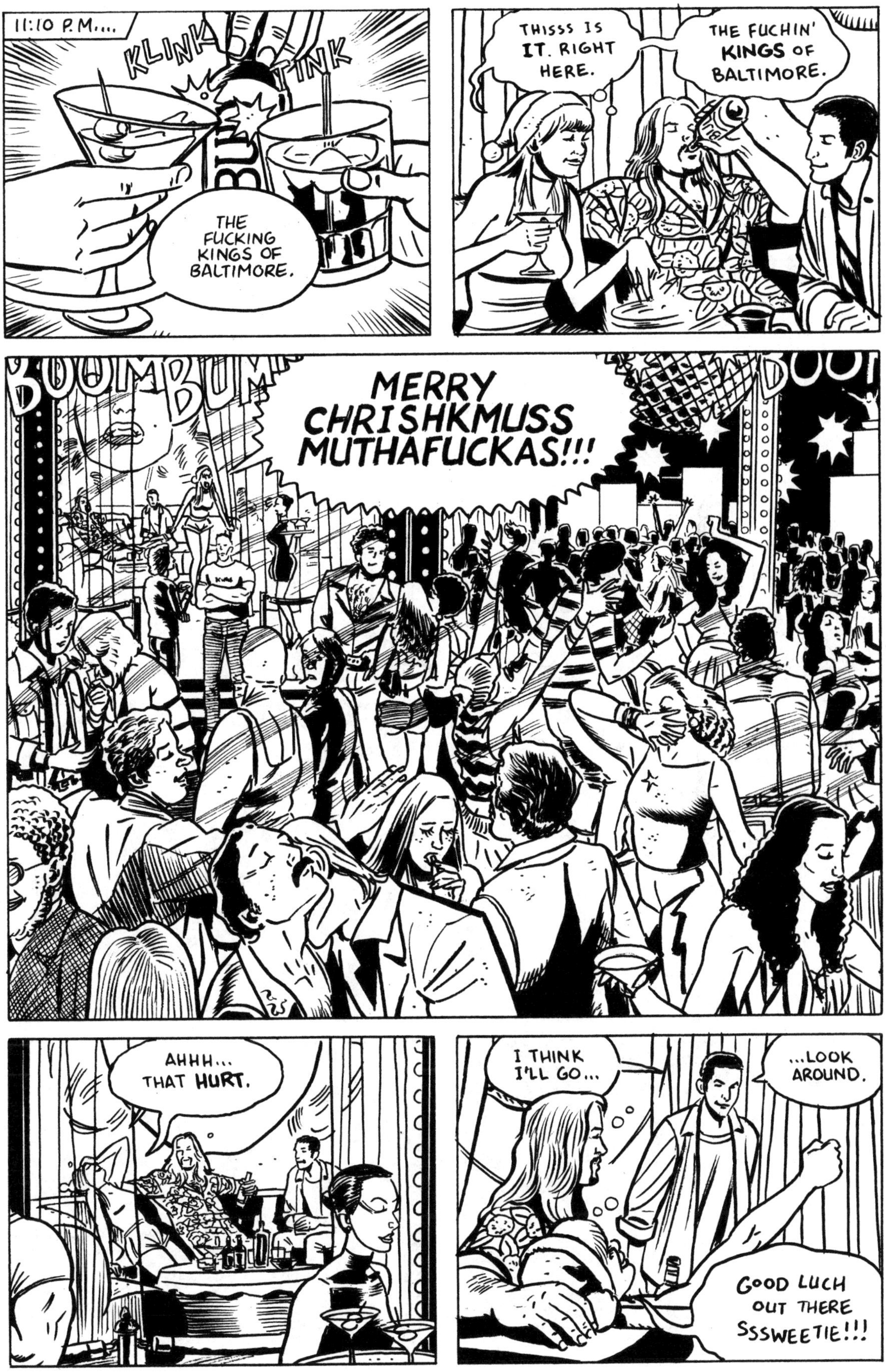
11:10 P.M....
KLINK
TINK
THE FUCKING KINGS OF BALTIMORE.
THISSS IS IT. RIGHT HERE.
THE FUCHIN' KINGS OF BALTIMORE.
MERRY CHRISHKMUSS MUTHAFUCKAS!!!
AHHH... THAT HURT.
I THINK I'LL GO...
...LOOK AROUND.
GOOD LUCH OUT THERE SSSWEETIE!!!

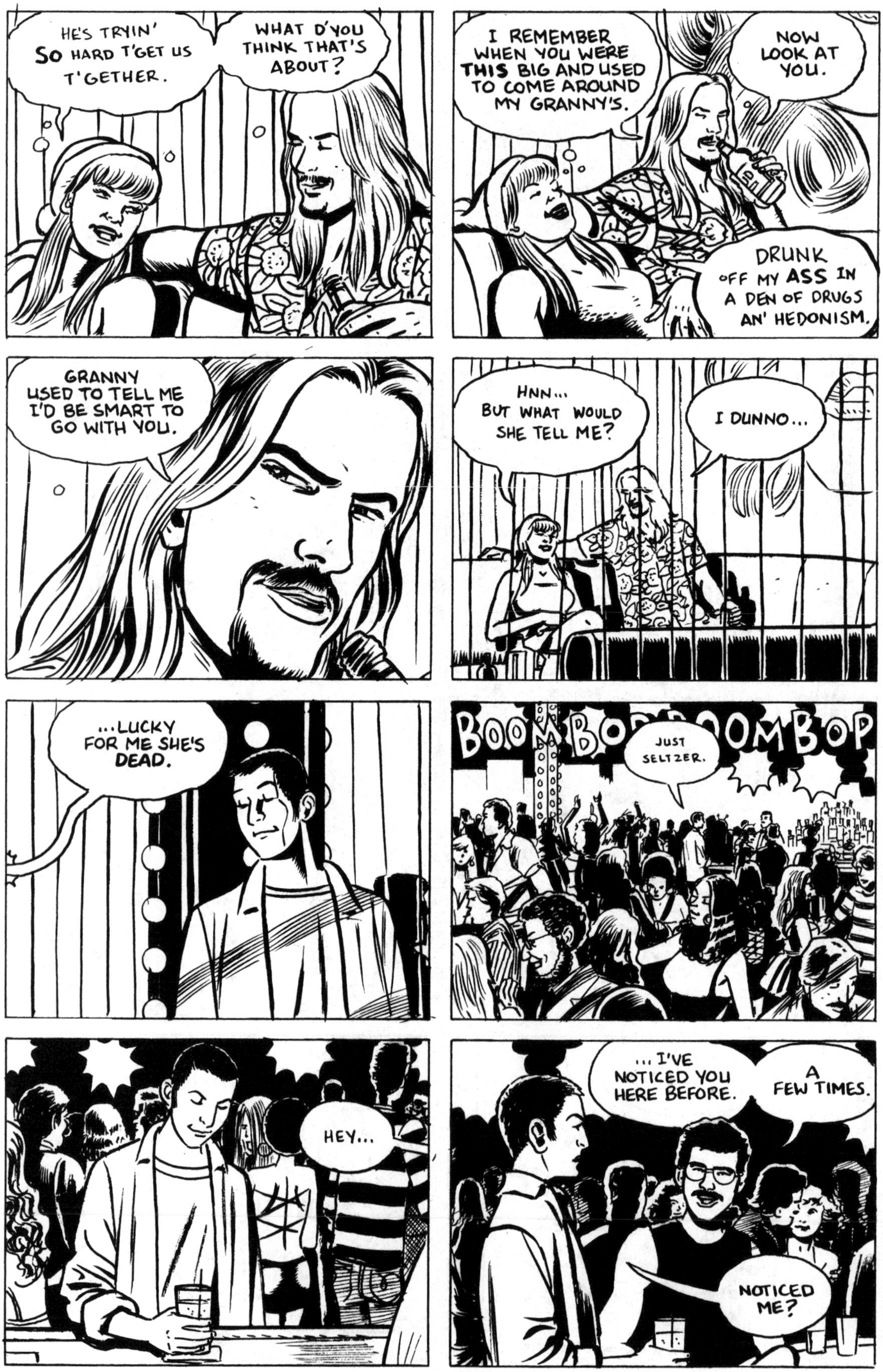
HE'S TRYIN' SO HARD T'GET US T'GETHER.
WHAT D'YOU THINK THAT'S ABOUT?
I REMEMBER WHEN YOU WERE THIS BIG AND USED TO COME AROUND MY GRANNY'S.
NOW LOOK AT YOU.
DRUNK OFF MY ASS IN A DEN OF DRUGS AN' HEDONISM.
GRANNY USED TO TELL ME I'D BE SMART TO GO WITH YOU.
HNN... BUT WHAT WOULD SHE TELL ME?
I DUNNO...
...LUCKY FOR ME SHE'S DEAD.
BOOMBOPBOOMBOP
JUST SELTZER.
HEY...
...I'VE NOTICED YOU HERE BEFORE.
A FEW TIMES.
NOTICED ME?

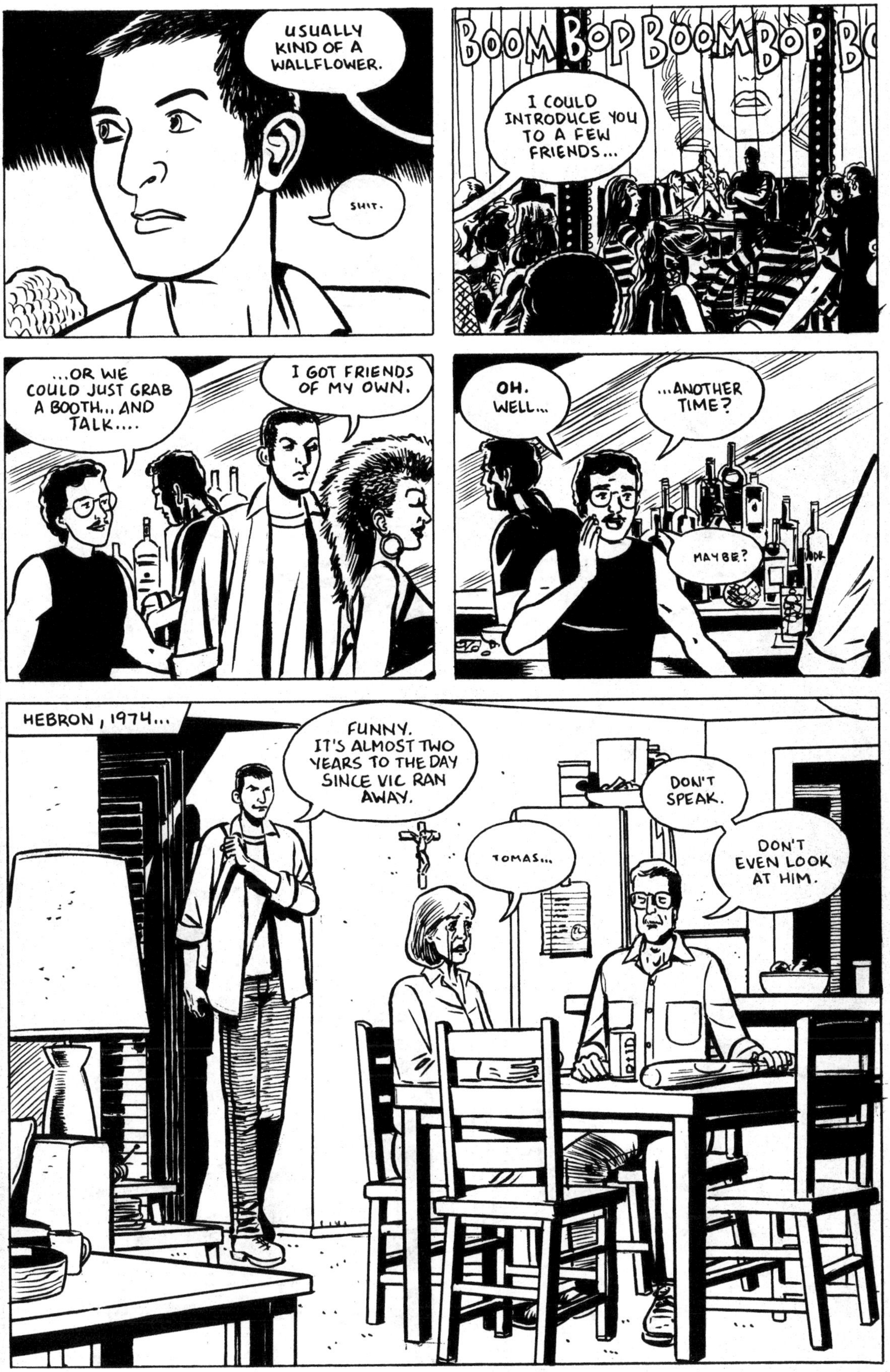
USUALLY KIND OF A WALLFLOWER.
SHIT.
BOOM BOP BOOM BOP
I COULD INTRODUCE YOU TO A FEW FRIENDS...
...OR WE COULD JUST GRAB A BOOTH... AND TALK....
I GOT FRIENDS OF MY OWN.
OH. WELL...
...ANOTHER TIME?
MAYBE?
HEBRON, 1974...
FUNNY. IT'S ALMOST TWO YEARS TO THE DAY SINCE VIC RAN AWAY.
TOMAS...
DON'T SPEAK.
DON'T EVEN LOOK AT HIM.

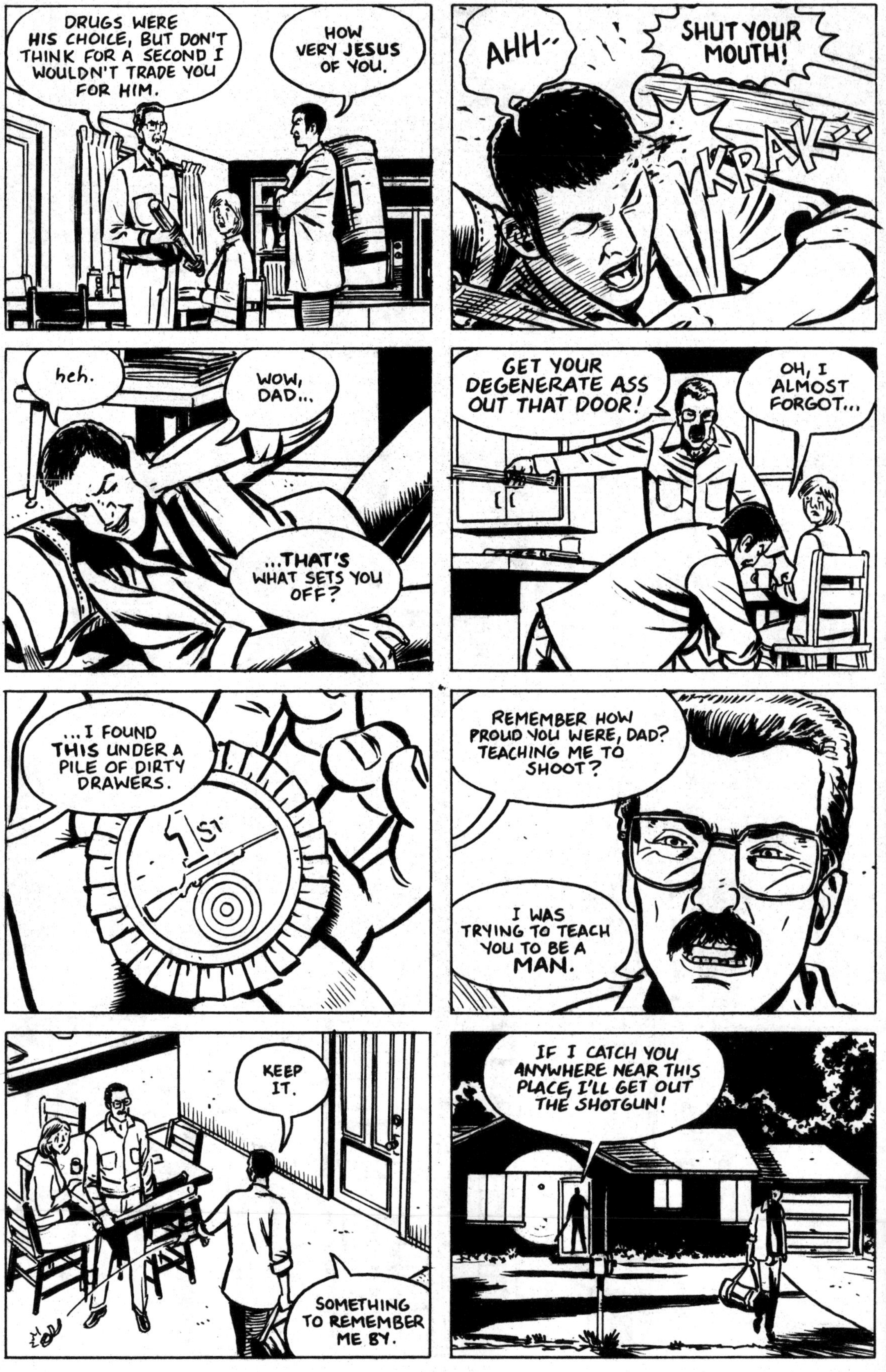
DRUGS WERE HIS CHOICE, BUT DON'T THINK FOR A SECOND I WOULDN'T TRADE YOU FOR HIM.
HOW VERY JESUS OF YOU.
AHH--
SHUT YOUR MOUTH!
KRAK--
heh.
WOW, DAD...
...THAT'S WHAT SETS YOU OFF?
GET YOUR DEGENERATE ASS OUT THAT DOOR!
OH, I ALMOST FORGOT...
...I FOUND THIS UNDER A PILE OF DIRTY DRAWERS.
1ST
REMEMBER HOW PROUD YOU WERE, DAD? TEACHING ME TO SHOOT?
I WAS TRYING TO TEACH YOU TO BE A MAN.
KEEP IT.
SOMETHING TO REMEMBER ME BY.
IF I CATCH YOU ANYWHERE NEAR THIS PLACE, I'LL GET OUT THE SHOTGUN!

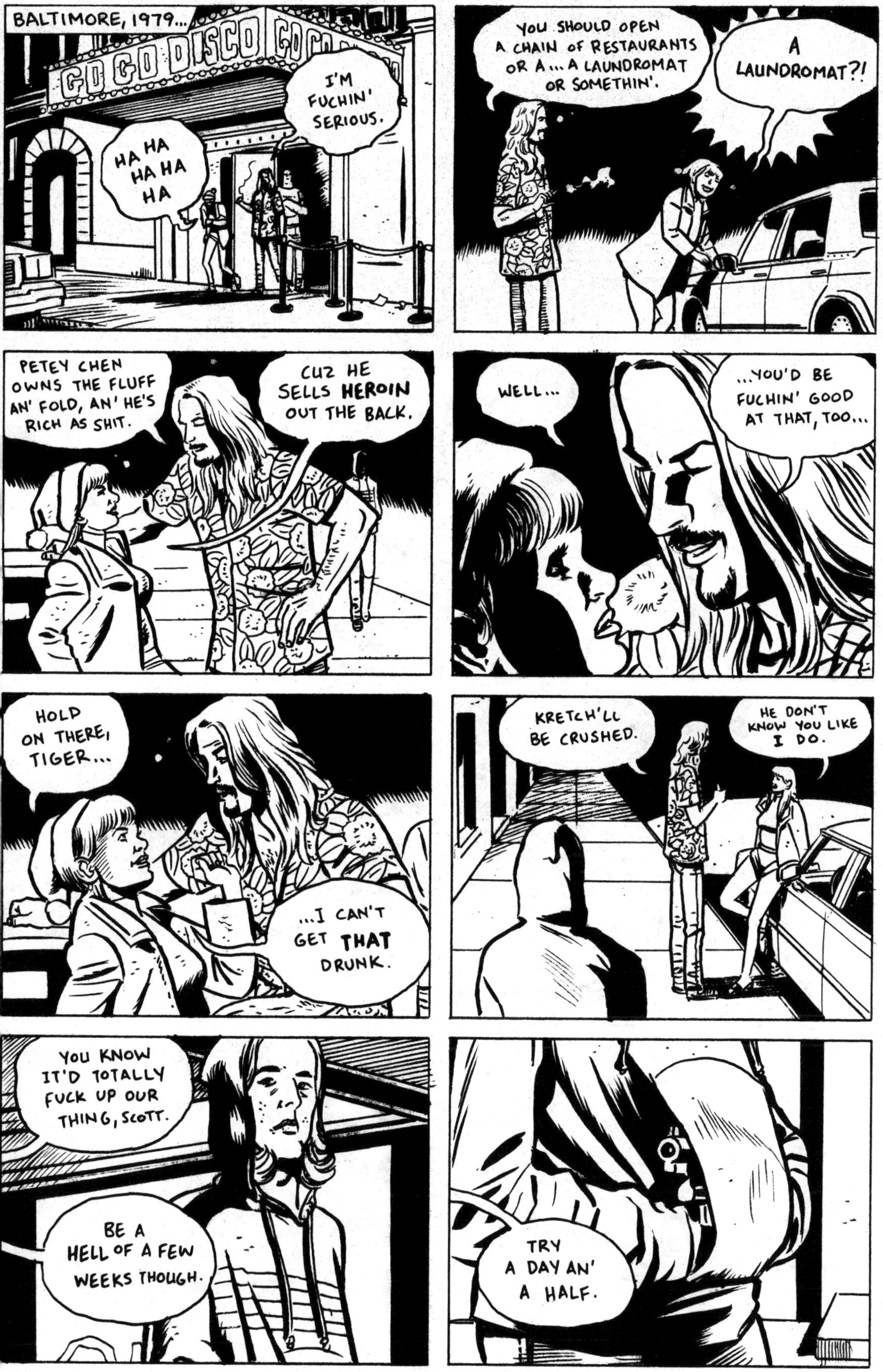
BALTIMORE, 1979...
GO GO DISCO
HA HA HA HA HA
I'M FUCHIN' SERIOUS.
YOU SHOULD OPEN A CHAIN OF RESTAURANTS OR A... A LAUNDROMAT OR SOMETHIN'.
A LAUNDROMAT?!
PETEY CHEN OWNS THE FLUFF AN' FOLD, AN' HE'S RICH AS SHIT.
CUZ HE SELLS HEROIN OUT THE BACK.
WELL...
...YOU'D BE FUCHIN' GOOD AT THAT, TOO...
HOLD ON THERE, TIGER...
...I CAN'T GET THAT DRUNK.
KRETCH'LL BE CRUSHED.
HE DON'T KNOW YOU LIKE I DO.
YOU KNOW IT'D TOTALLY FUCK UP OUR THING, SCOTT.
BE A HELL OF A FEW WEEKS THOUGH.
TRY A DAY AN' A HALF.

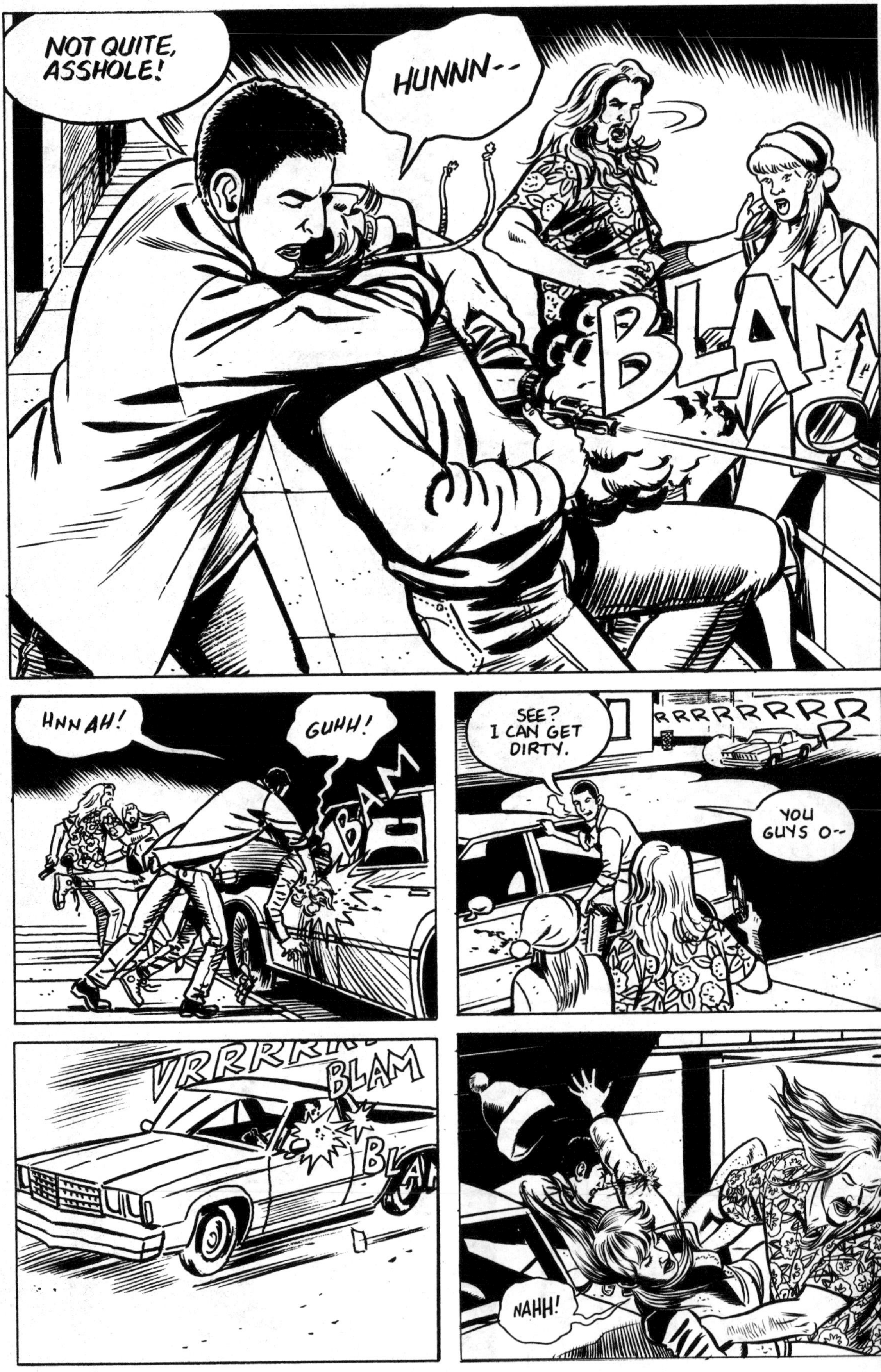
NOT QUITE, ASSHOLE!
HUNNN--
BLAM
HNNAH!
GUHH!
BAM
SEE? I CAN GET DIRTY.
RRRRRRRRRR
YOU GUYS O--
VRRRR
BLAM
BLA
NAHH!

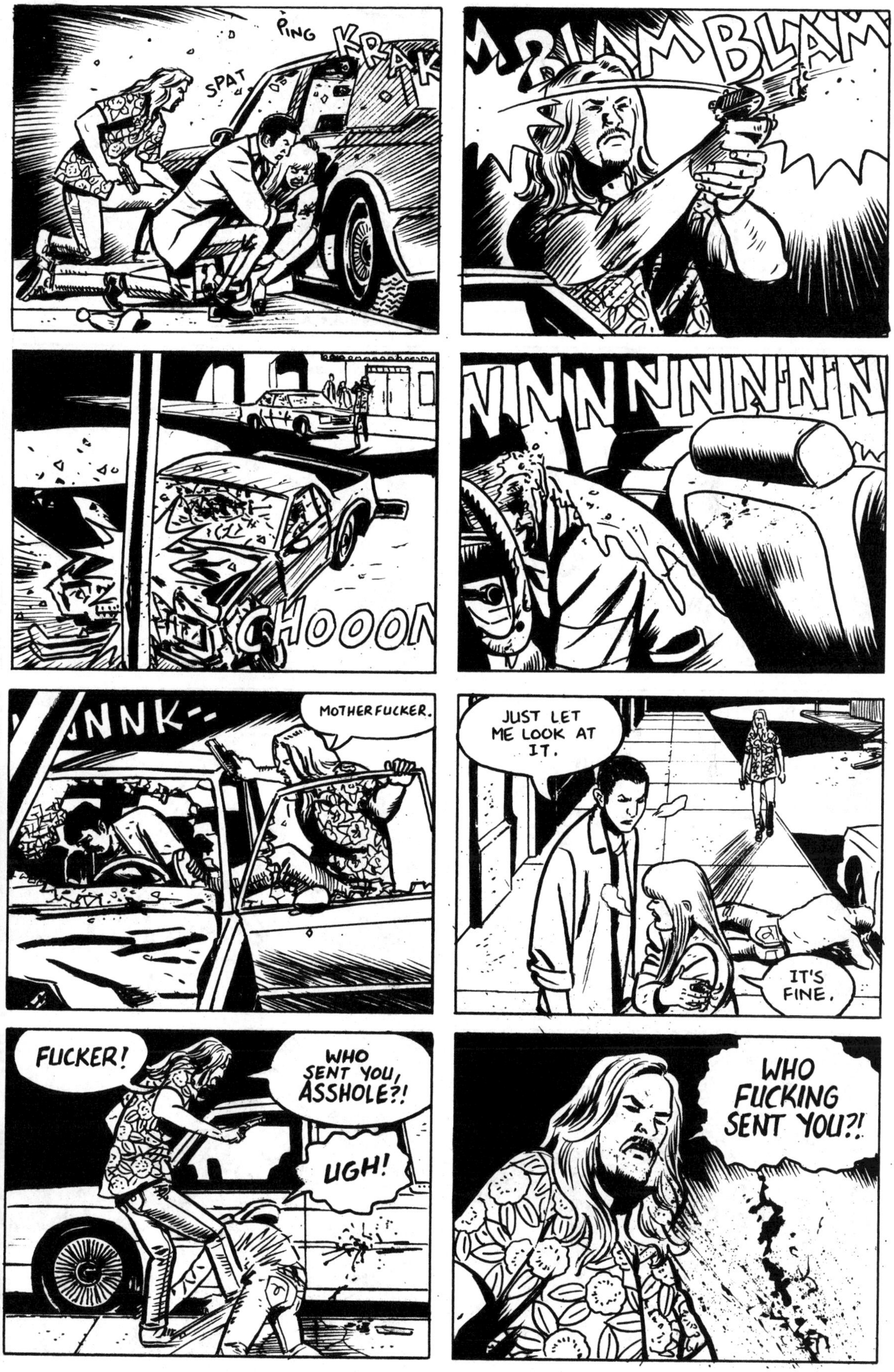
PING
KRAK
SPAT
BLAM BLAM
CHOOON
NNNNNNNN
NNK
MOTHERFUCKER.
JUST LET ME LOOK AT IT.
IT'S FINE.
FUCKER!
WHO SENT YOU, ASSHOLE?!
UGH!
WHO FUCKING SENT YOU?!

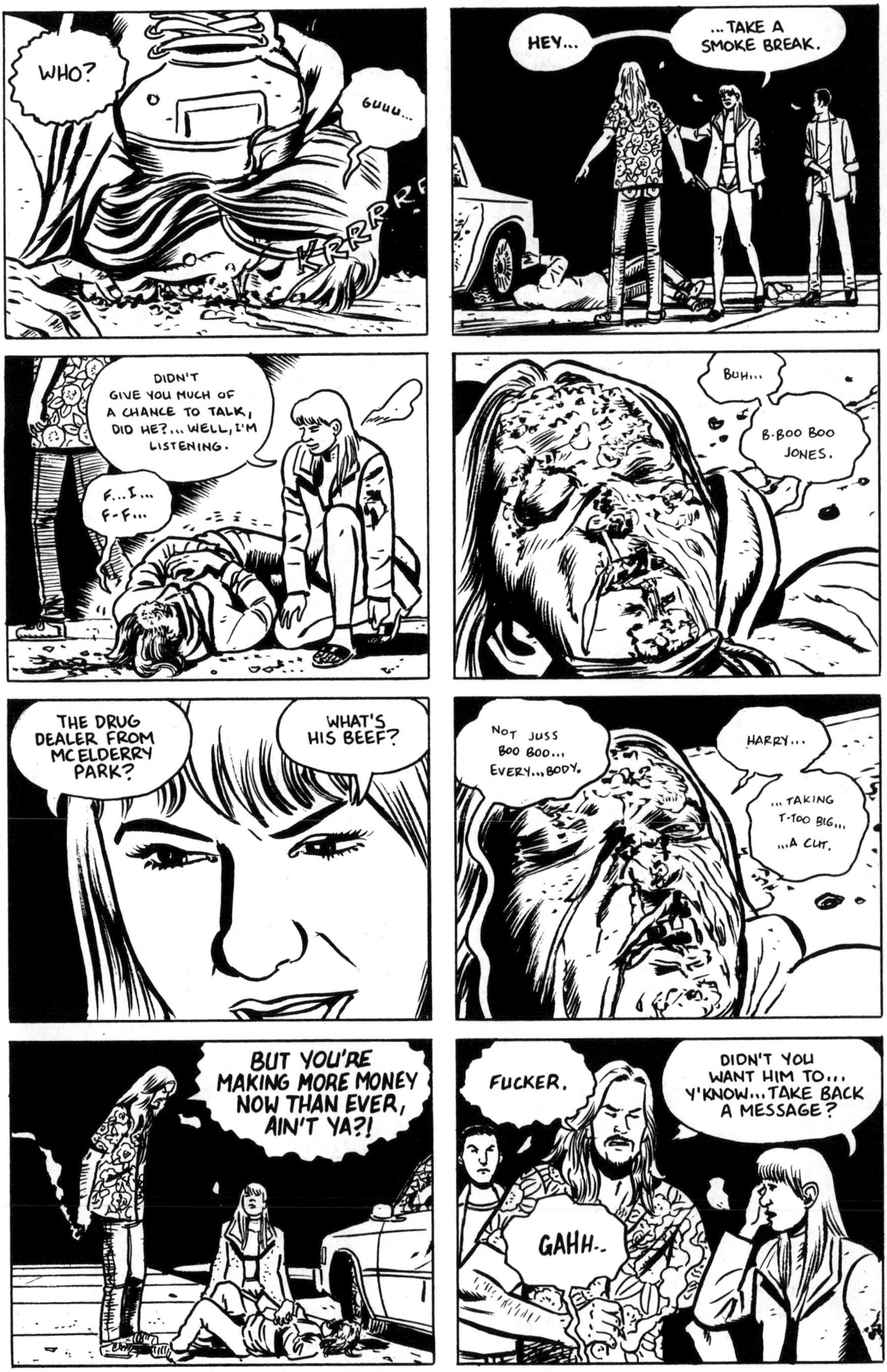
WHO?
GUUU...
KRRRRR
HEY...
...TAKE A SMOKE BREAK.
DIDN'T GIVE YOU MUCH OF A CHANCE TO TALK, DID HE?... WELL, I'M LISTENING.
F...I... F-F...
BUH...
B-BOO BOO JONES.
THE DRUG DEALER FROM MCELDERRY PARK?
WHAT'S HIS BEEF?
NOT JUSS BOO BOO... EVERY...BODY.
HARRY...
...TAKING T-TOO BIG... ...A CUT.
BUT YOU'RE MAKING MORE MONEY NOW THAN EVER, AIN'T YA?!
FUCKER.
DIDN'T YOU WANT HIM TO... Y'KNOW...TAKE BACK A MESSAGE?
GAHH-.

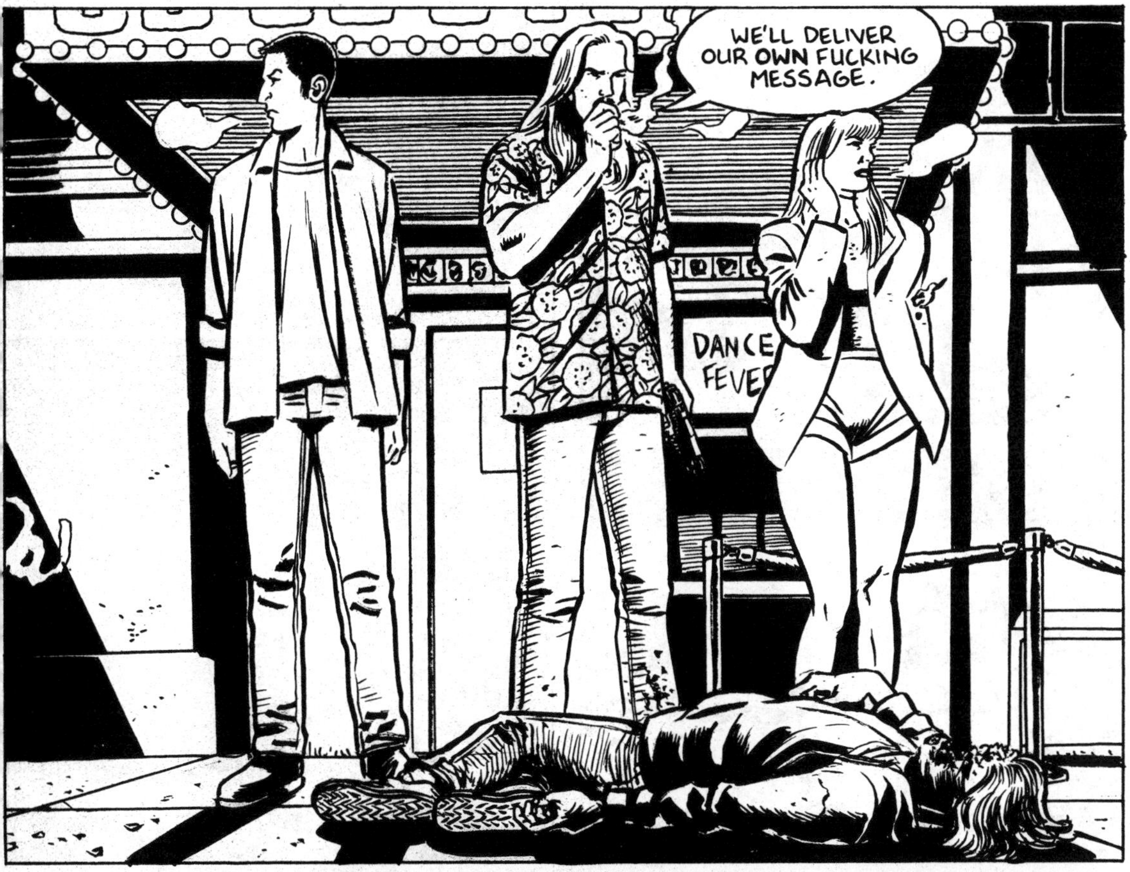
WE'LL DELIVER OUR OWN FUCKING MESSAGE.
DANCE FEVER

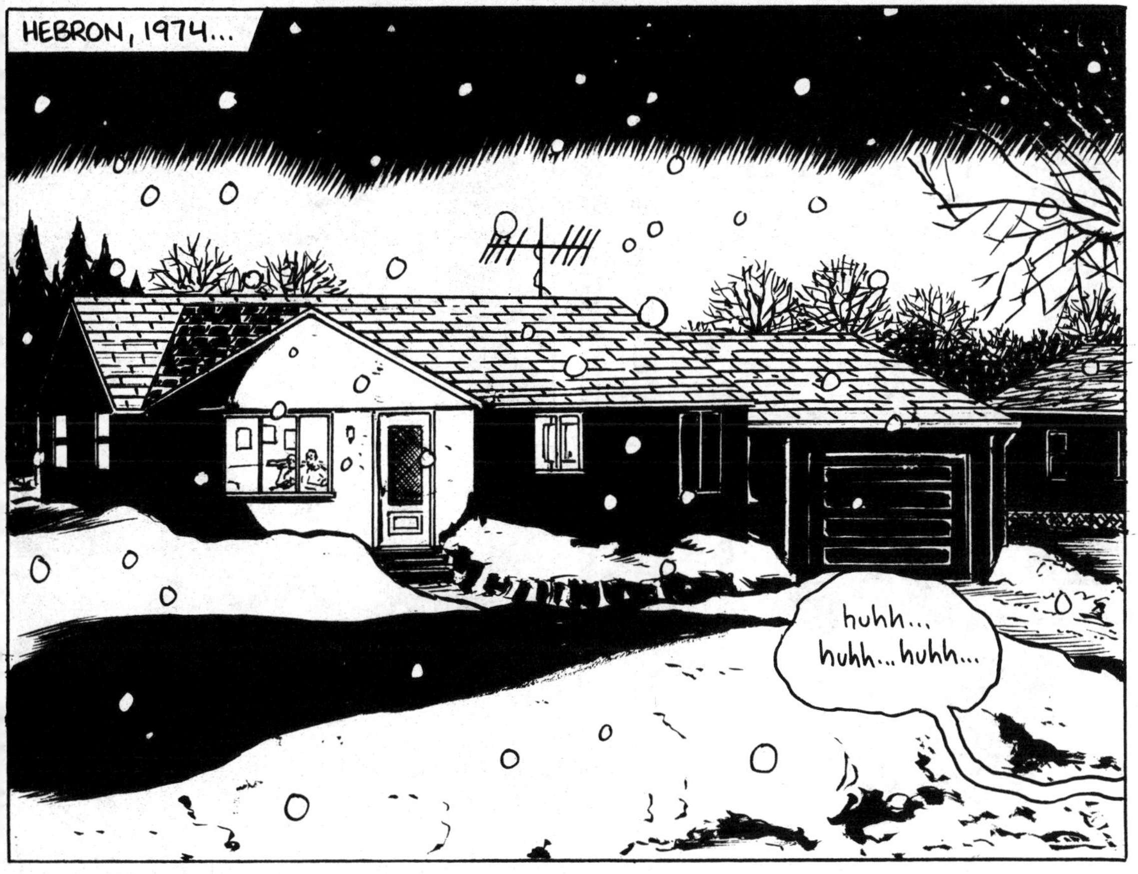
HEBRON, 1974...
huhh... huhh... huhh...

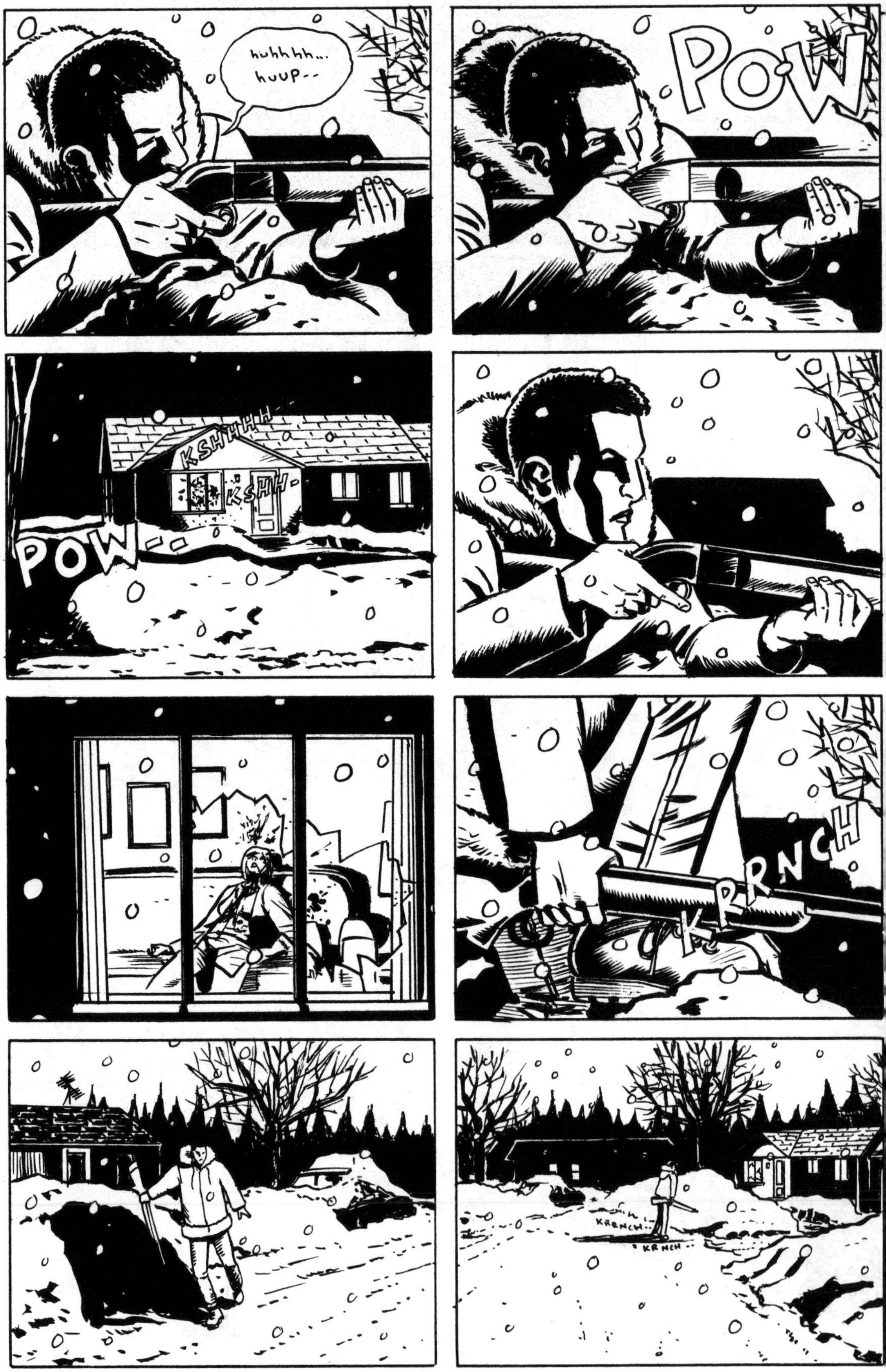
huhhhh...
huup--
POW
KSHHHH
KSHH-
POW--
KRRNCH
KRRNCH..
KRNCH..

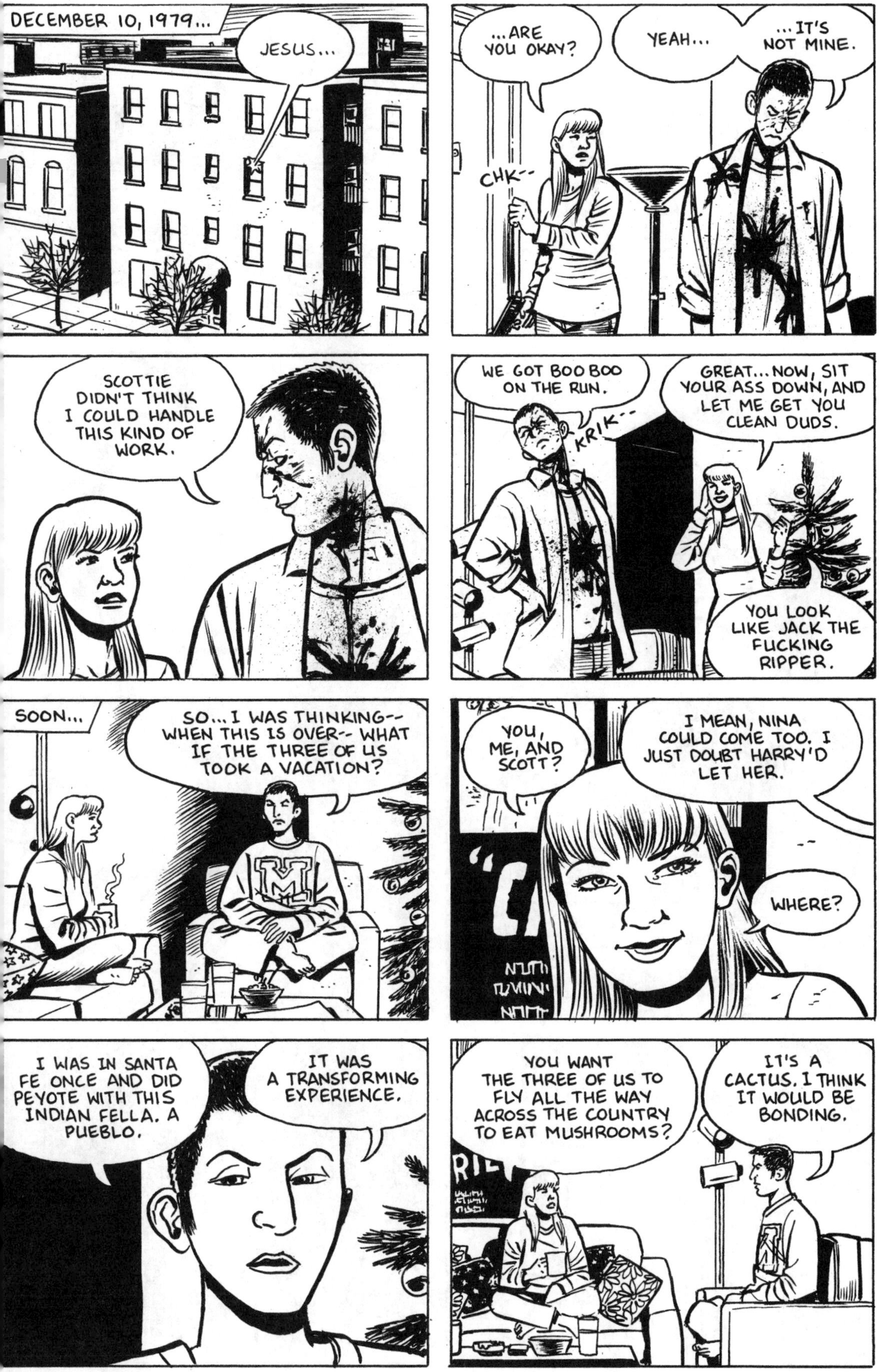
DECEMBER 10, 1979...
JESUS...
...ARE YOU OKAY?
CHK--
YEAH...
...IT'S NOT MINE.
SCOTTIE DIDN'T THINK I COULD HANDLE THIS KIND OF WORK.
WE GOT BOO BOO ON THE RUN.
KRIK--
GREAT... NOW, SIT YOUR ASS DOWN, AND LET ME GET YOU CLEAN DUDS.
YOU LOOK LIKE JACK THE FUCKING RIPPER.
SOON...
SO... I WAS THINKING-- WHEN THIS IS OVER-- WHAT IF THE THREE OF US TOOK A VACATION?
YOU, ME, AND SCOTT?
I MEAN, NINA COULD COME TOO. I JUST DOUBT HARRY'D LET HER.
WHERE?
I WAS IN SANTA FE ONCE AND DID PEYOTE WITH THIS INDIAN FELLA. A PUEBLO.
IT WAS A TRANSFORMING EXPERIENCE.
YOU WANT THE THREE OF US TO FLY ALL THE WAY ACROSS THE COUNTRY TO EAT MUSHROOMS?
IT'S A CACTUS. I THINK IT WOULD BE BONDING.

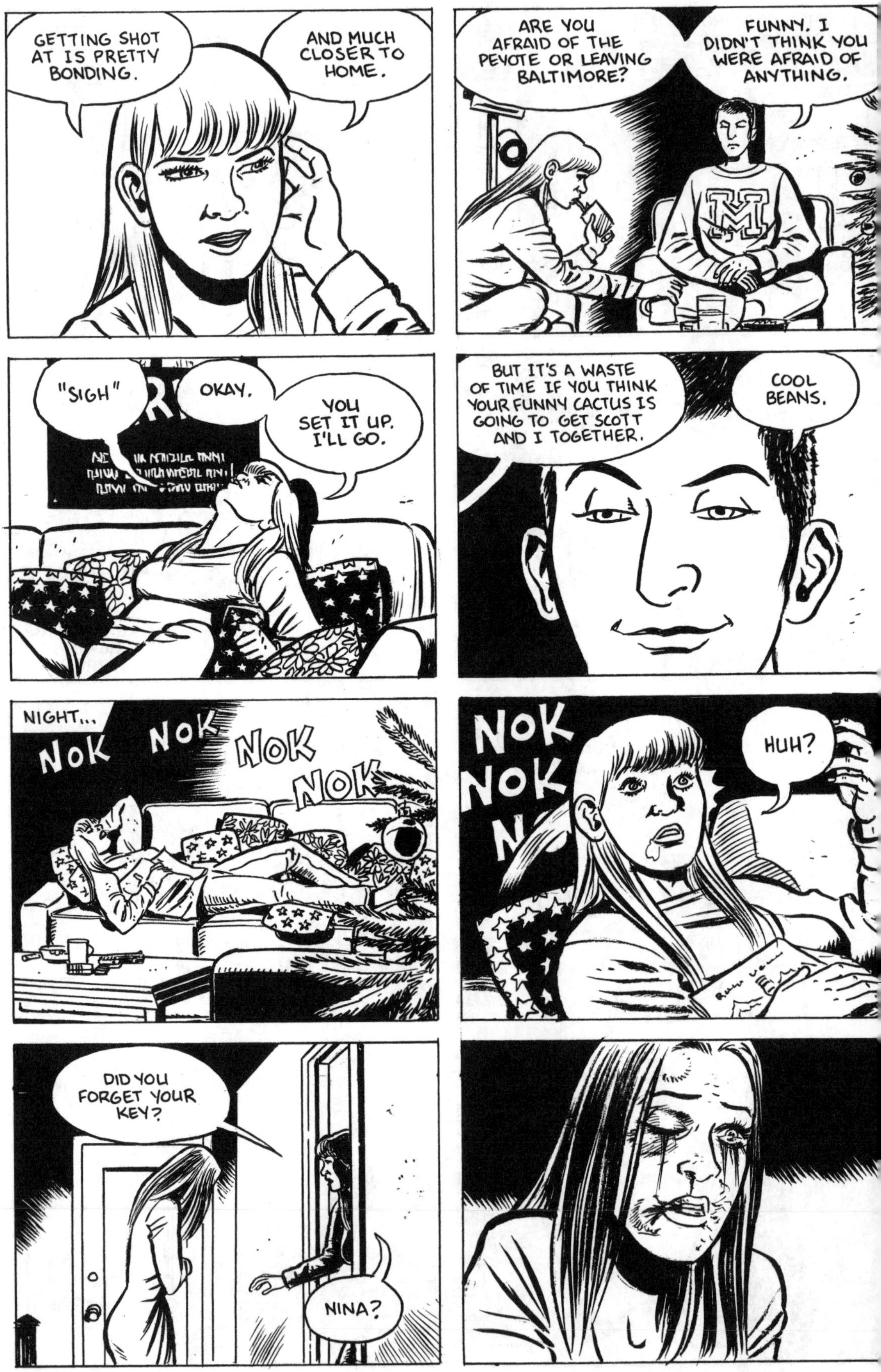
GETTING SHOT AT IS PRETTY BONDING.
AND MUCH CLOSER TO HOME.
ARE YOU AFRAID OF THE PEYOTE OR LEAVING BALTIMORE?
FUNNY. I DIDN'T THINK YOU WERE AFRAID OF ANYTHING.
"SIGH"
OKAY.
YOU SET IT UP. I'LL GO.
BUT IT'S A WASTE OF TIME IF YOU THINK YOUR FUNNY CACTUS IS GOING TO GET SCOTT AND I TOGETHER.
COOL BEANS.
NIGHT...
NOK NOK NOK NOK
NOK NOK
HUH?
DID YOU FORGET YOUR KEY?
NINA?

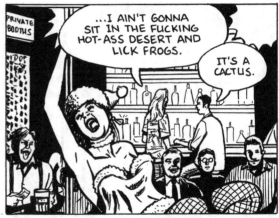

COCK'S CROW LIVE NUDE

BENTLEMEN'S CLUB BOOM BOOM

NO WAY, KRETCH...

PRIVATE BOOTHS

...I AIN'T GONNA SIT IN THE FUCKING HOT-ASS DESERT AND LICK FROGS.

IT'S A CACTUS.

BETH SAID SHE'S IN IF YOU ARE.

NNN... SOUTH BEACH IS MORE MY SPEED.

MY INDIAN FRIEND SAID THE BEST SEX HE EVER HAD WAS ON MESCALINE.

YEAH?

COME ON, SCOTTIE, IT'D BE GOOD FOR US. I REALLY THINK WE CAN DO BIG THINGS TOGETHER.

Y'KNOW, IF I WANTED AN ANNOYING LITTLE BROTHER...

...I WOULD'VE FUCKED MY MOTHER....

BOOM BOOM BOOM

FUCK OFF.

SPEAK OF THE DEVIL.

HEY! GOOD NEW--

SCOTT, WE NEED TO TALK, RIGHT NOW.

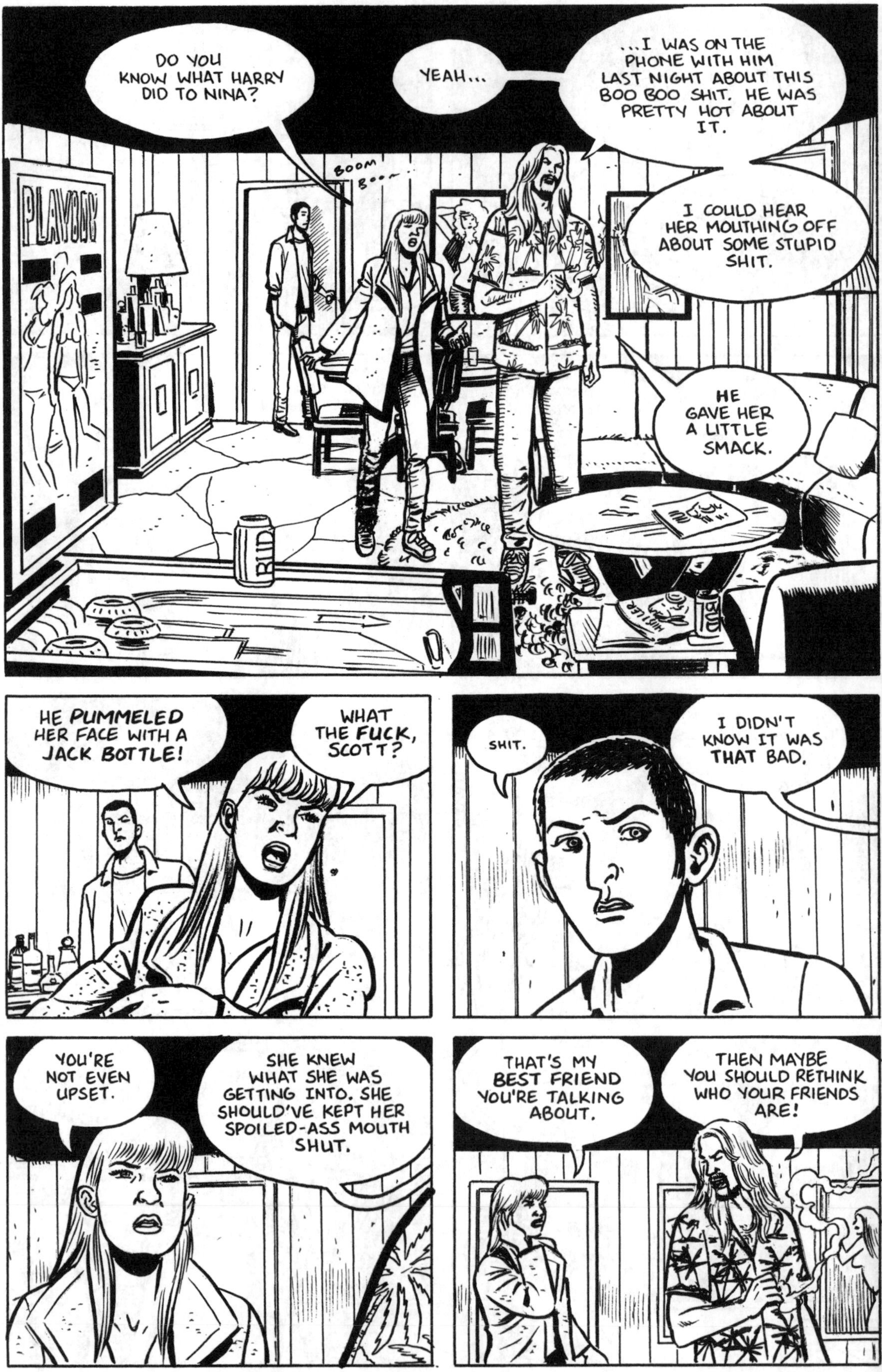
DO YOU KNOW WHAT HARRY DID TO NINA?
YEAH...
...I WAS ON THE PHONE WITH HIM LAST NIGHT ABOUT THIS BOO BOO SHIT. HE WAS PRETTY HOT ABOUT IT.
I COULD HEAR HER MOUTHING OFF ABOUT SOME STUPID SHIT.
HE GAVE HER A LITTLE SMACK.
HE PUMMELED HER FACE WITH A JACK BOTTLE!
WHAT THE FUCK, SCOTT?
SHIT.
I DIDN'T KNOW IT WAS THAT BAD.
YOU'RE NOT EVEN UPSET.
SHE KNEW WHAT SHE WAS GETTING INTO. SHE SHOULD'VE KEPT HER SPOILED-ASS MOUTH SHUT.
THAT'S MY BEST FRIEND YOU'RE TALKING ABOUT.
THEN MAYBE YOU SHOULD RETHINK WHO YOUR FRIENDS ARE!

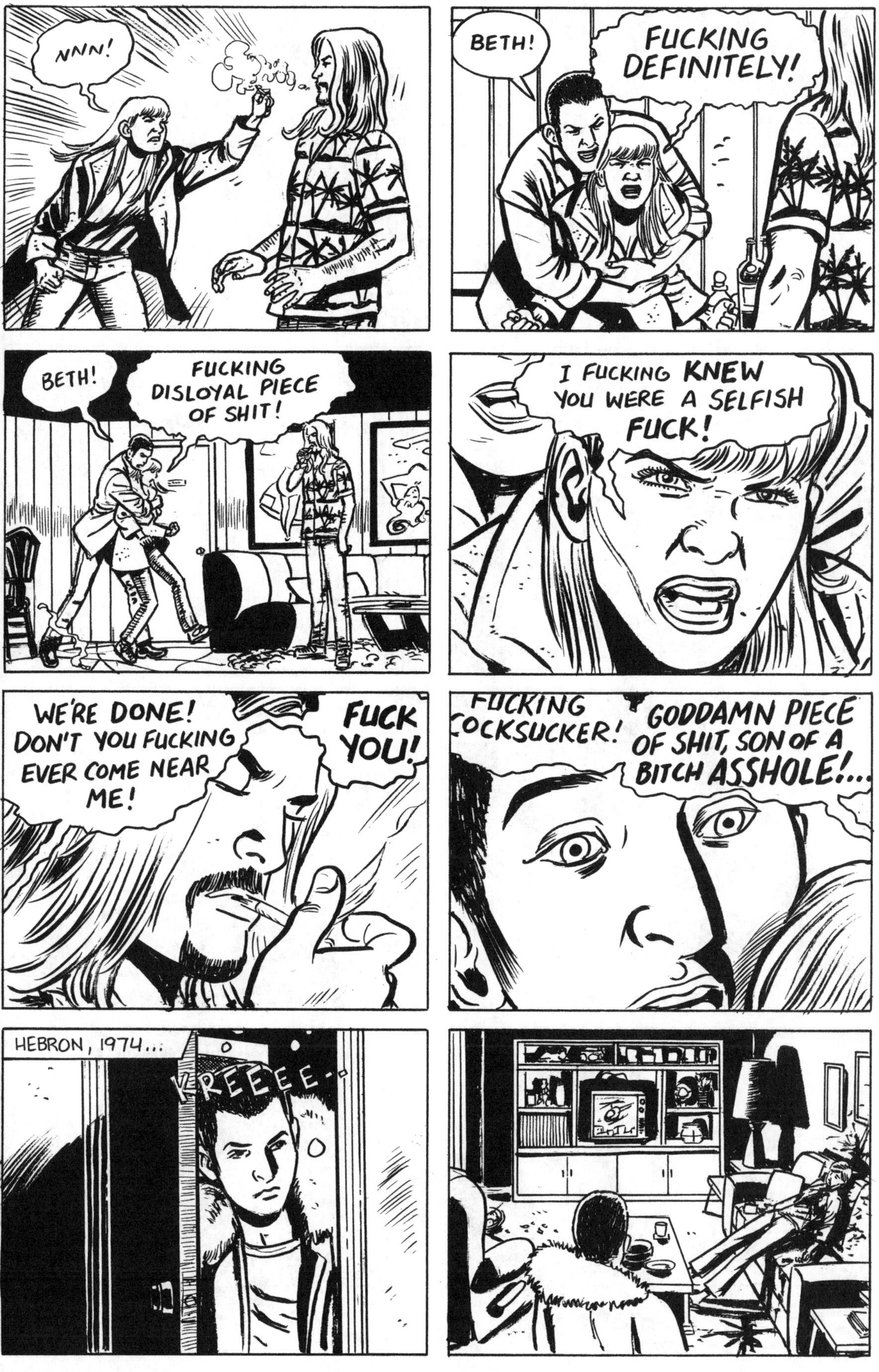
NNN!
BETH!
FUCKING DEFINITELY!
BETH!
FUCKING DISLOYAL PIECE OF SHIT!
I FUCKING KNEW YOU WERE A SELFISH FUCK!
WE'RE DONE! DON'T YOU FUCKING EVER COME NEAR ME!
FUCK YOU!
FUCKING COCKSUCKER!
GODDAMN PIECE OF SHIT, SON OF A BITCH ASSHOLE!...
HEBRON, 1974...
KREEEE...

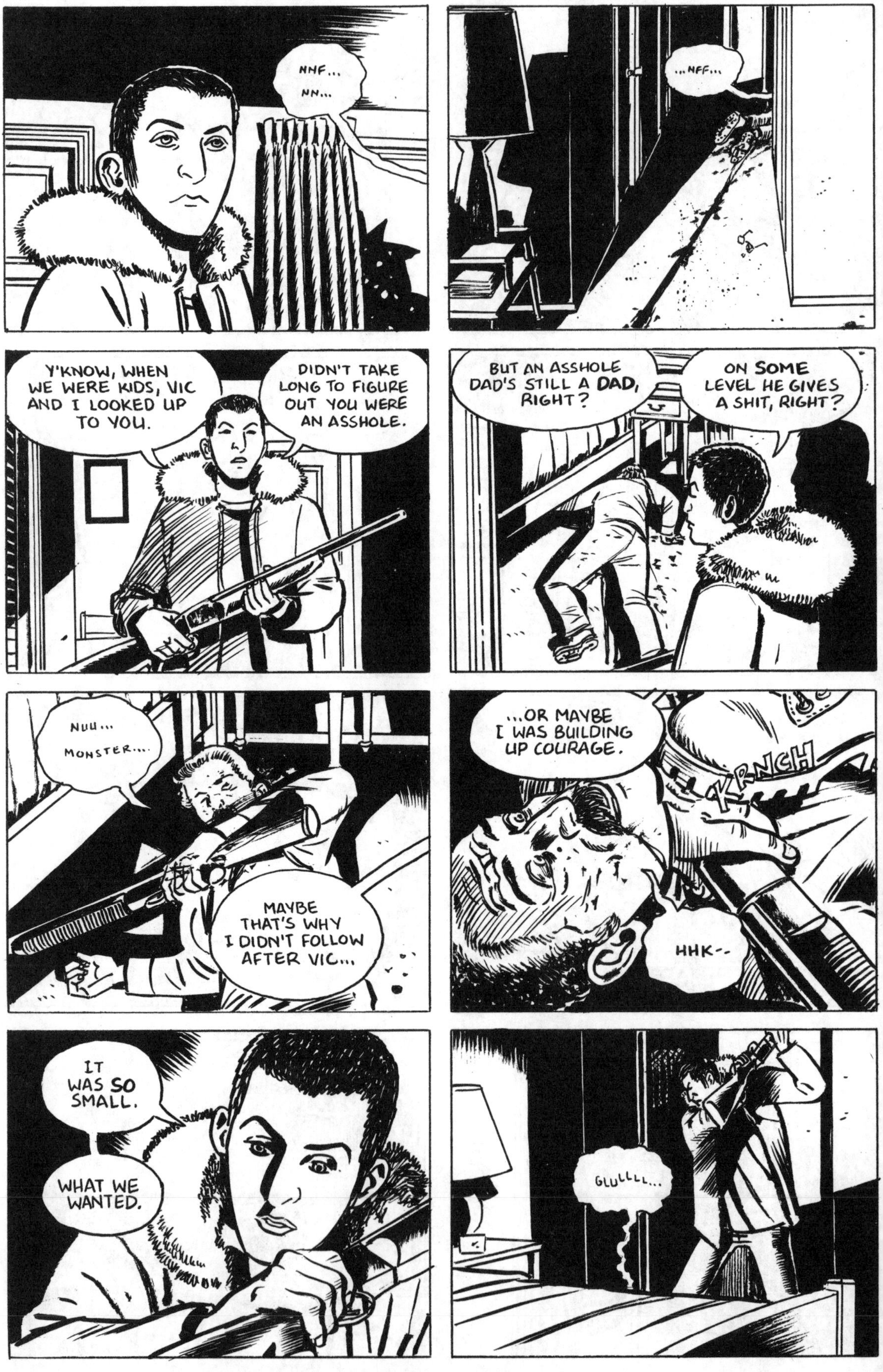
NNF...
NN...
...NFF...
Y'KNOW, WHEN WE WERE KIDS, VIC AND I LOOKED UP TO YOU.
DIDN'T TAKE LONG TO FIGURE OUT YOU WERE AN ASSHOLE.
BUT AN ASSHOLE DAD'S STILL A **DAD**, RIGHT?
ON **SOME** LEVEL HE GIVES A SHIT, RIGHT?
NUU...
MONSTER...
MAYBE THAT'S WHY I DIDN'T FOLLOW AFTER VIC...
...OR MAYBE I WAS BUILDING UP COURAGE.
KRNCH
HHK--
IT WAS **SO** SMALL.
WHAT WE WANTED.
GLULLLL...

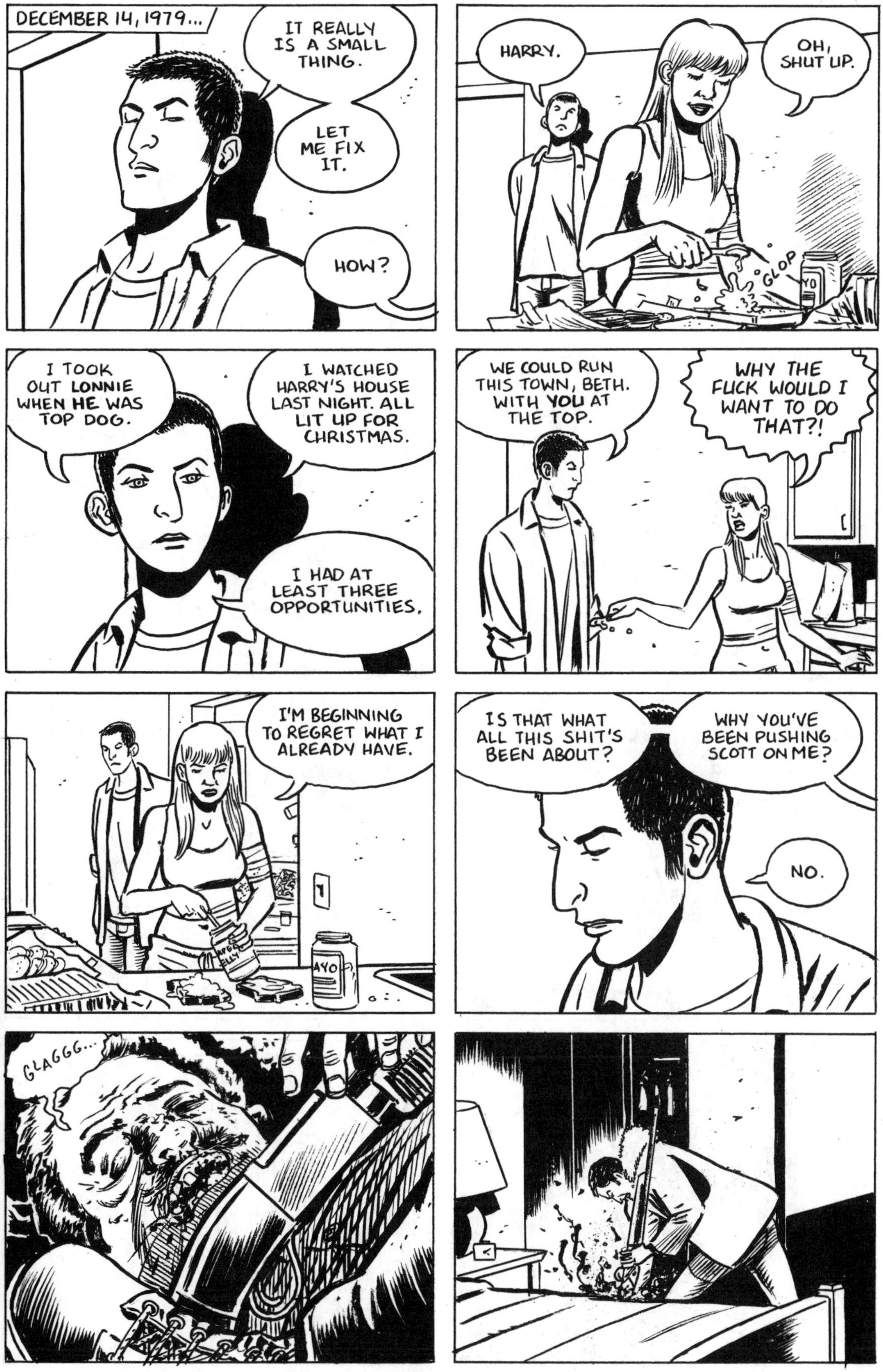
DECEMBER 14, 1979...
IT REALLY IS A SMALL THING.
LET ME FIX IT.
HOW?
HARRY.
OH, SHUT UP.
GLOP
I TOOK OUT LONNIE WHEN HE WAS TOP DOG.
I WATCHED HARRY'S HOUSE LAST NIGHT. ALL LIT UP FOR CHRISTMAS.
I HAD AT LEAST THREE OPPORTUNITIES.
WE COULD RUN THIS TOWN, BETH. WITH YOU AT THE TOP.
WHY THE FUCK WOULD I WANT TO DO THAT?!
I'M BEGINNING TO REGRET WHAT I ALREADY HAVE.
IS THAT WHAT ALL THIS SHIT'S BEEN ABOUT?
WHY YOU'VE BEEN PUSHING SCOTT ON ME?
NO.
GLAGGG...

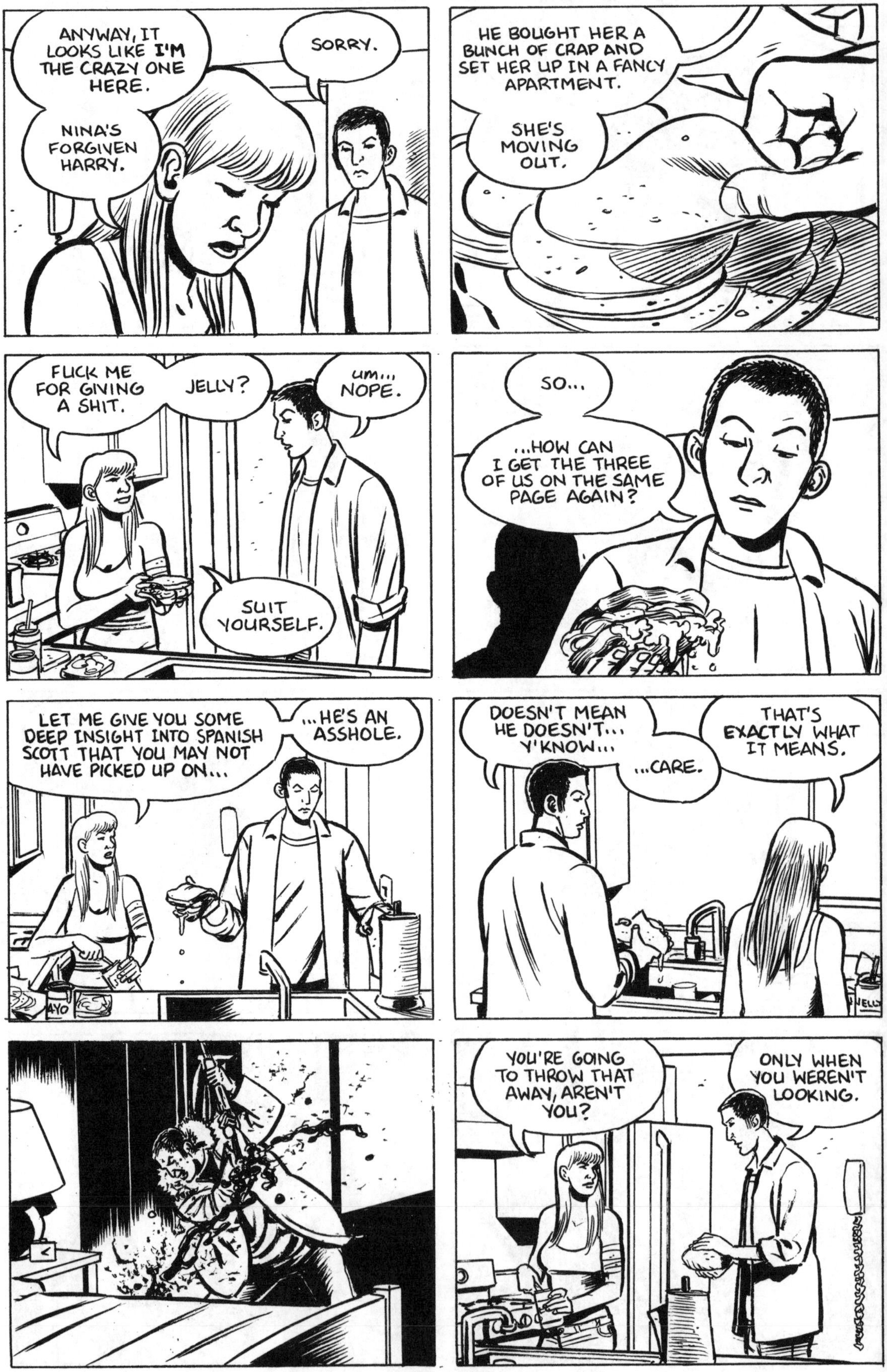
ANYWAY, IT LOOKS LIKE **I'M** THE CRAZY ONE HERE.
NINA'S FORGIVEN HARRY.
SORRY.
HE BOUGHT HER A BUNCH OF CRAP AND SET HER UP IN A FANCY APARTMENT.
SHE'S MOVING OUT.
FUCK ME FOR GIVING A SHIT.
JELLY?
UM... NOPE.
SUIT YOURSELF.
SO...
...HOW CAN I GET THE THREE OF US ON THE SAME PAGE AGAIN?
LET ME GIVE YOU SOME DEEP INSIGHT INTO SPANISH SCOTT THAT YOU MAY NOT HAVE PICKED UP ON...
...HE'S AN ASSHOLE.
DOESN'T MEAN HE DOESN'T... Y'KNOW...
...CARE.
THAT'S EXACTLY WHAT IT MEANS.
YOU'RE GOING TO THROW THAT AWAY, AREN'T YOU?
ONLY WHEN YOU WEREN'T LOOKING.

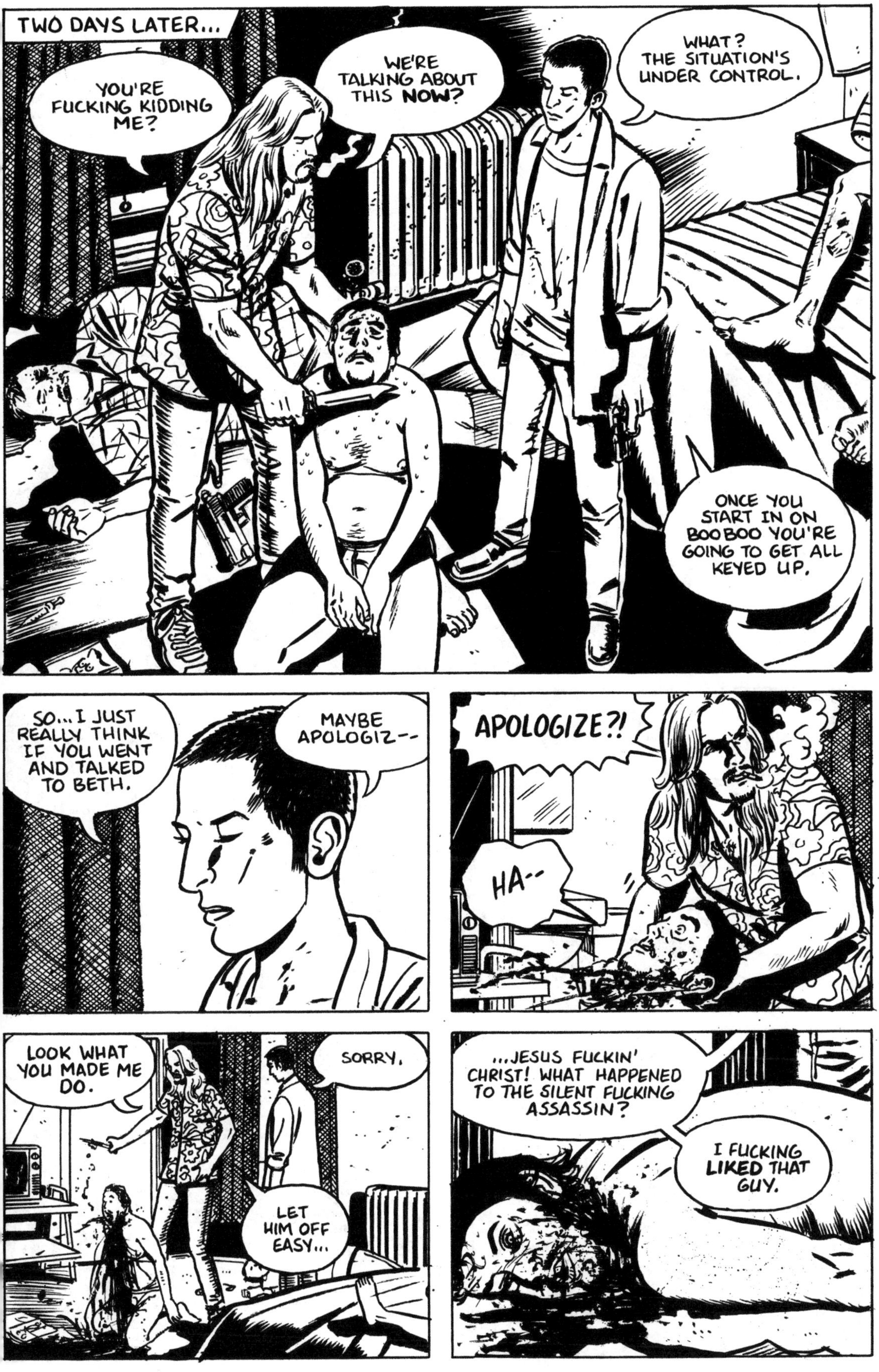
TWO DAYS LATER...
YOU'RE FUCKING KIDDING ME?
WE'RE TALKING ABOUT THIS **NOW?**
WHAT? THE SITUATION'S UNDER CONTROL.
ONCE YOU START IN ON BOOBOO YOU'RE GOING TO GET ALL KEYED UP.
SO... I JUST REALLY THINK IF YOU WENT AND TALKED TO BETH.
MAYBE APOLOGIZ--
APOLOGIZE?!
HA--
LOOK WHAT YOU MADE ME DO.
SORRY.
LET HIM OFF EASY...
...JESUS FUCKIN' CHRIST! WHAT HAPPENED TO THE SILENT FUCKING ASSASSIN?
I FUCKING **LIKED** THAT GUY.

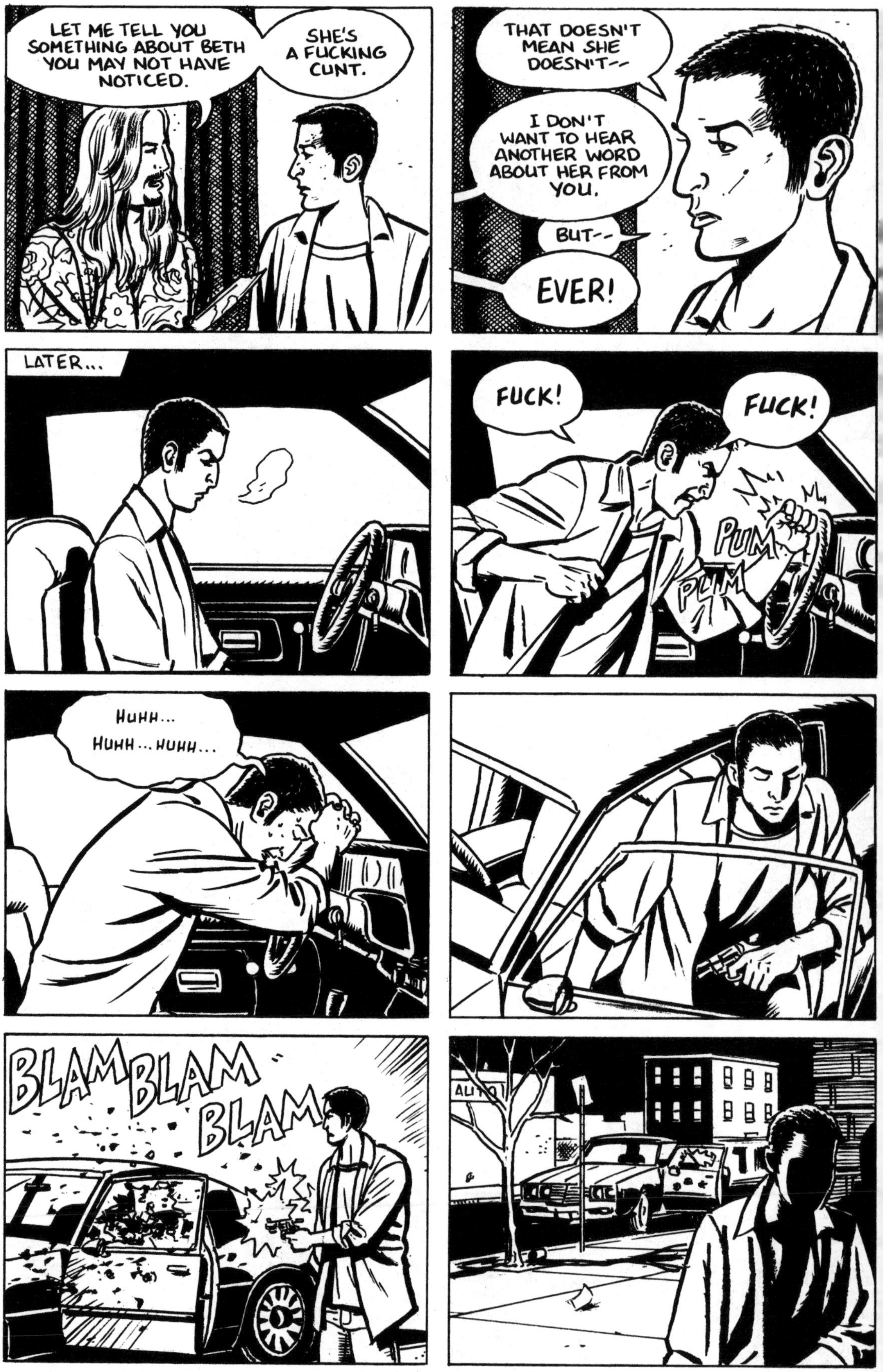
LET ME TELL YOU SOMETHING ABOUT BETH YOU MAY NOT HAVE NOTICED.
SHE'S A FUCKING CUNT.
THAT DOESN'T MEAN SHE DOESN'T--
I DON'T WANT TO HEAR ANOTHER WORD ABOUT HER FROM YOU.
BUT--
EVER!
LATER...
FUCK!
FUCK!
PUM
PUM
HUHH...
HUHH... HUHH...
BLAM BLAM
BLAM
AUTO

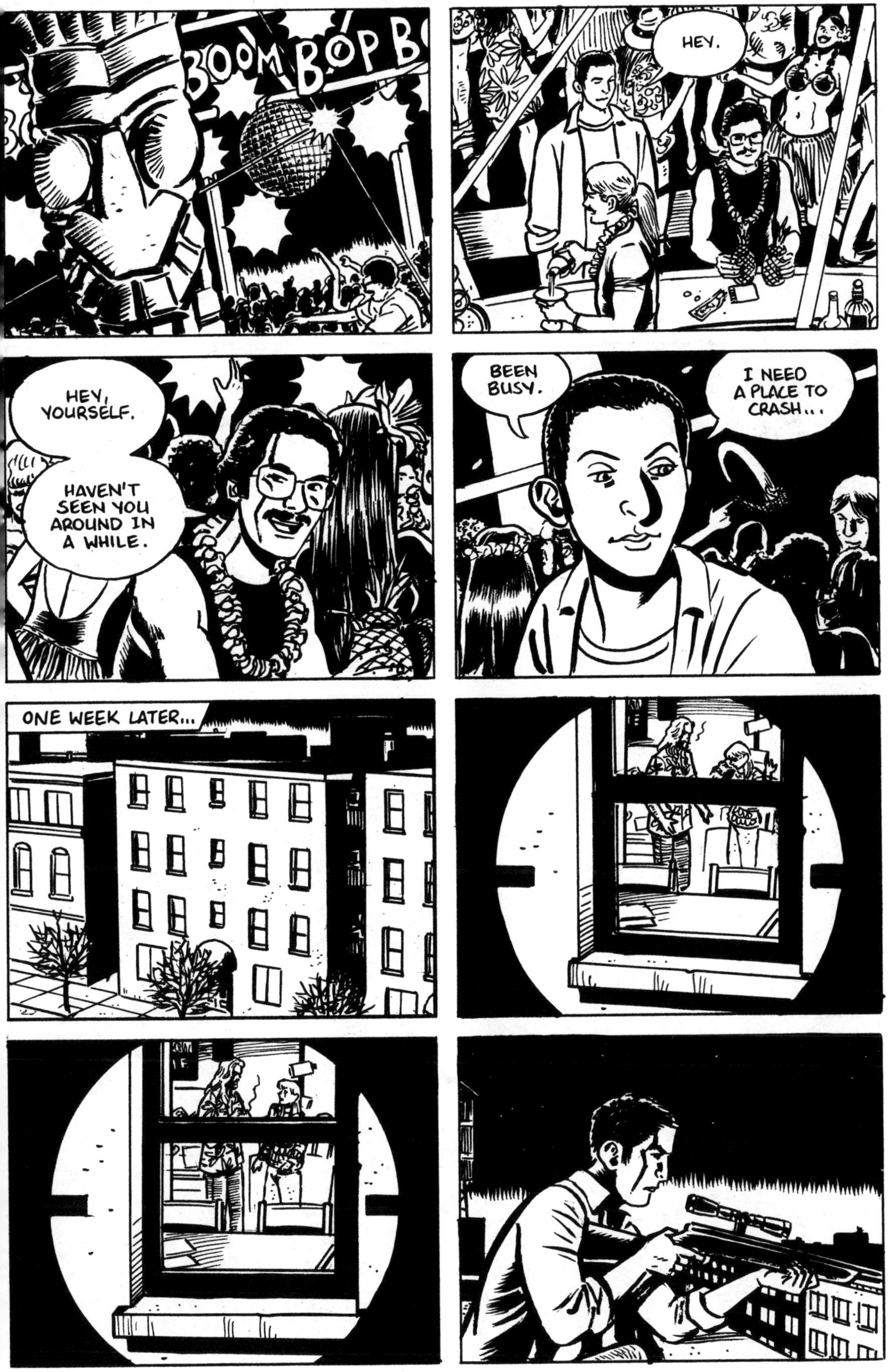
BOOM BOP B
HEY.
HEY, YOURSELF.
HAVEN'T SEEN YOU AROUND IN A WHILE.
BEEN BUSY.
I NEED A PLACE TO CRASH...
ONE WEEK LATER...

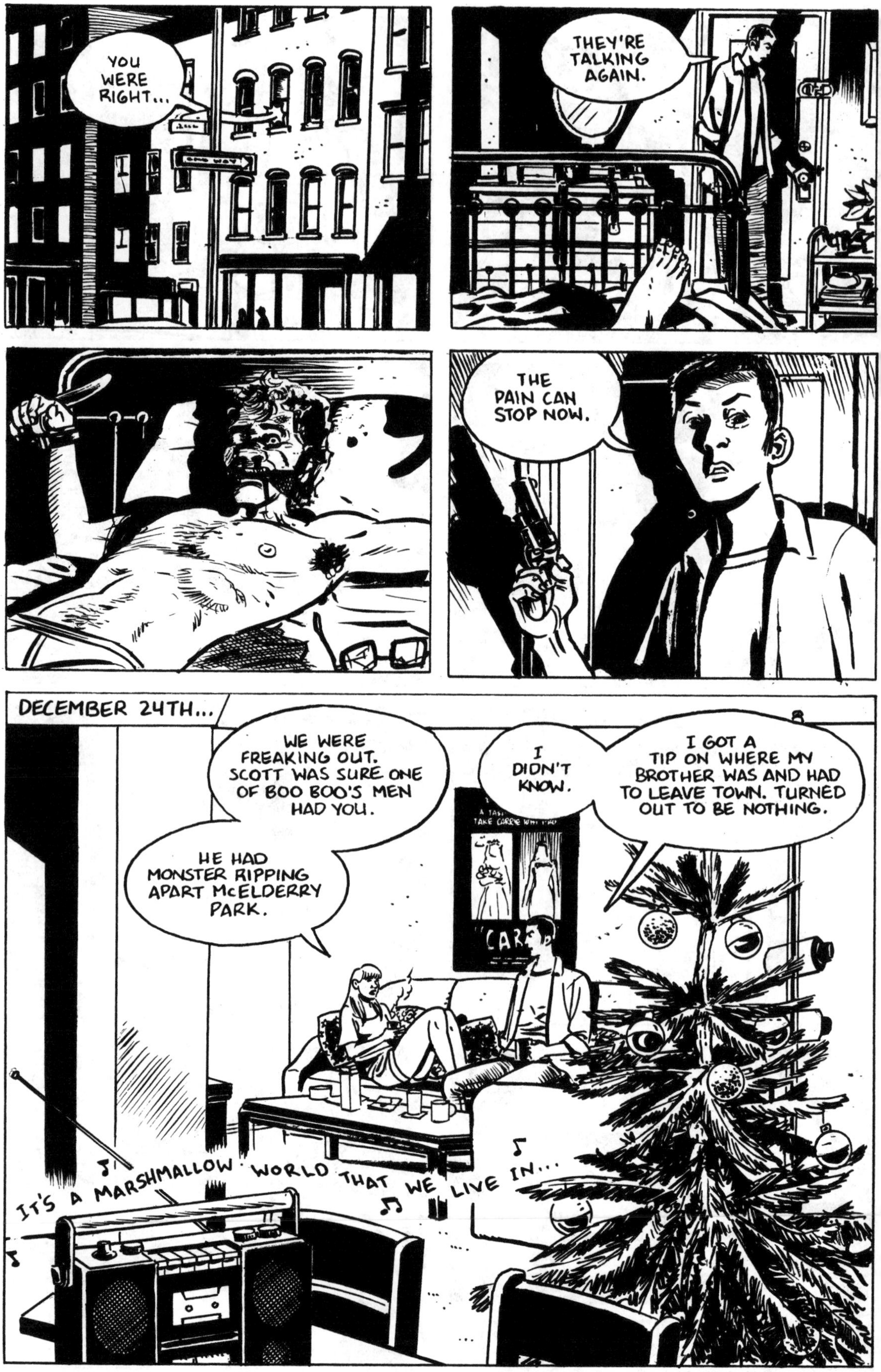
YOU WERE RIGHT...
THEY'RE TALKING AGAIN.
THE PAIN CAN STOP NOW.
DECEMBER 24TH...
WE WERE FREAKING OUT. SCOTT WAS SURE ONE OF BOO BOO'S MEN HAD YOU.
HE HAD MONSTER RIPPING APART McELDERRY PARK.
I DIDN'T KNOW.
I GOT A TIP ON WHERE MY BROTHER WAS AND HAD TO LEAVE TOWN. TURNED OUT TO BE NOTHING.
IT'S A MARSHMALLOW WORLD THAT WE LIVE IN...

I DIDN'T FUCKING KNOW YOU EVEN **HAD** A BROTHER.

HE COULDN'T HANDLE MY DAD'S SHIT, GOT HOOKED ON HEROIN AND RAN AWAY.

MY DAD AND STEP-MOM DIDN'T CARE. I WAS ANGRY FOR A LONG TIME UNTIL I REALIZED I WAS REALLY MAD AT MYSELF.

I WATCHED IT ALL HAPPEN AND DID NOTHING.

I LET HIM DOWN, BETH.

I FEEL LIKE I'M DOING THE SAME TO YOU AND SCOTTIE.

JESUS CHRIST...

...HERE

YOU COULD USE THIS,

FLY AIR

AIRLINE TICKETS 43771761

AIRLINE TICKETS 43774146

AIRLINE TICKETS 4377542

FLY AIR

SANTA F

39 SE

NM

CALL YOUR INDIAN FRIEND.

MERRY FUCKING CHRISTMAS, KRETCH.

THREE?

YEAH...WELL... WE CAN ALL USE AS MUCH BONDING AS WE CAN GET.

NOW I'M GOING TO POUR US SOME EGG-NOG, AND WE CAN TALK ABOUT MY NEEDING A NEW ROOMMATE.

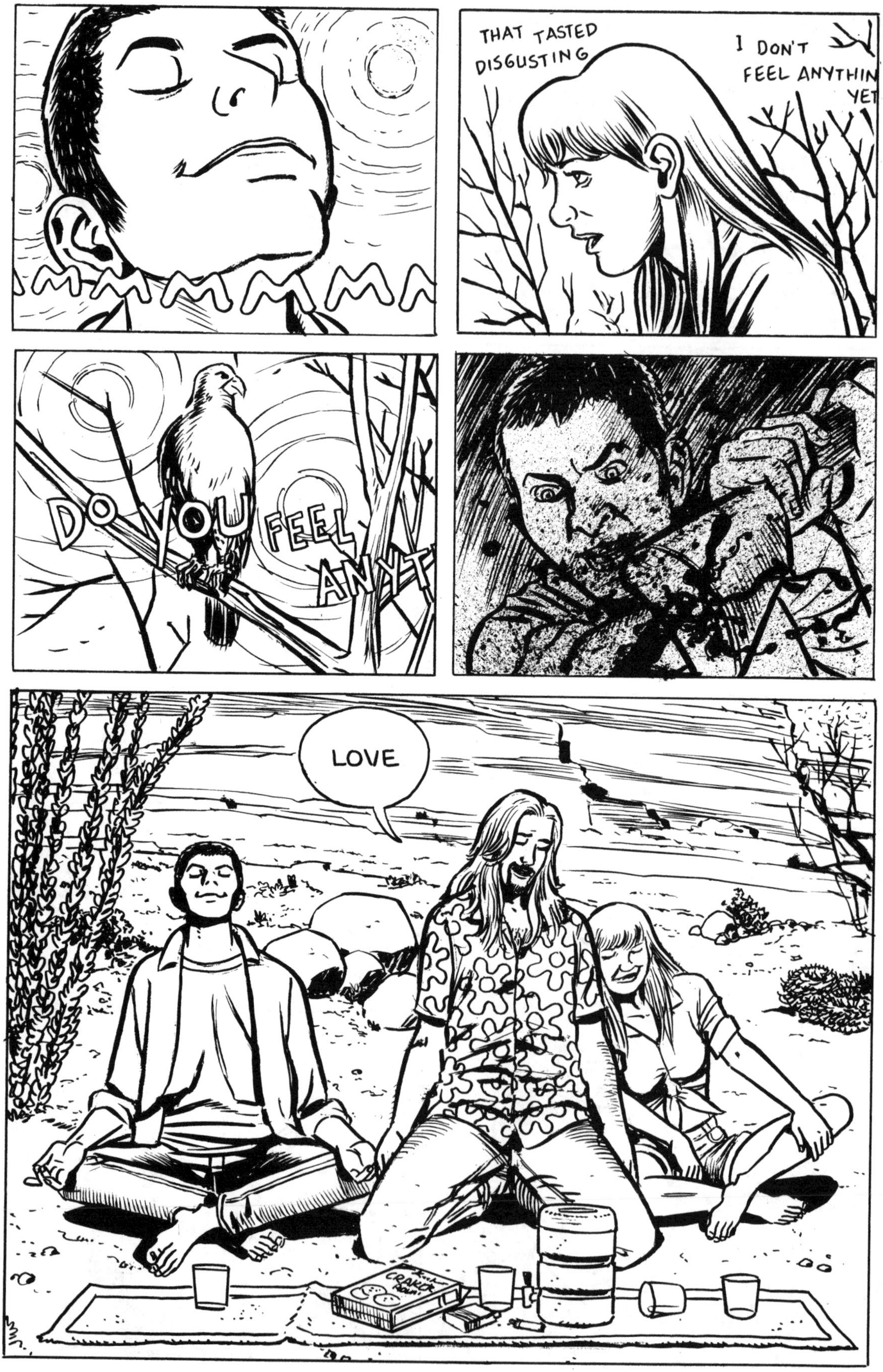
MMMMMM
THAT TASTED DISGUSTING
I DON'T FEEL ANYTHIN YET
DO YOU FEEL ANYT
LOVE

THE END...

2

"PAHT–NAHS"

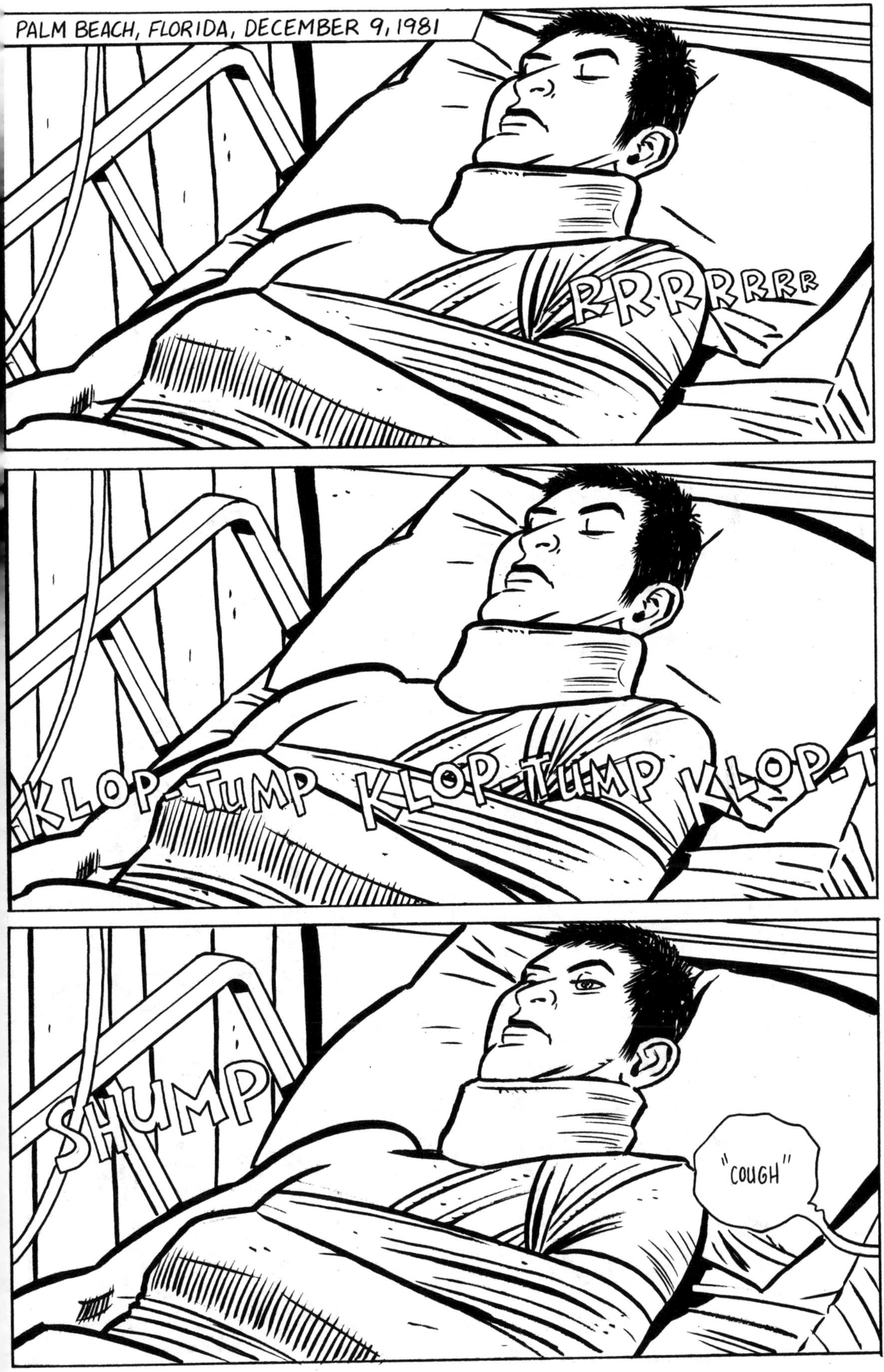

PALM BEACH, FLORIDA, DECEMBER 9, 1981
RRRRRRR
KLOP-TUMP KLOP-TUMP KLOP-T
SHUMP
"COUGH"

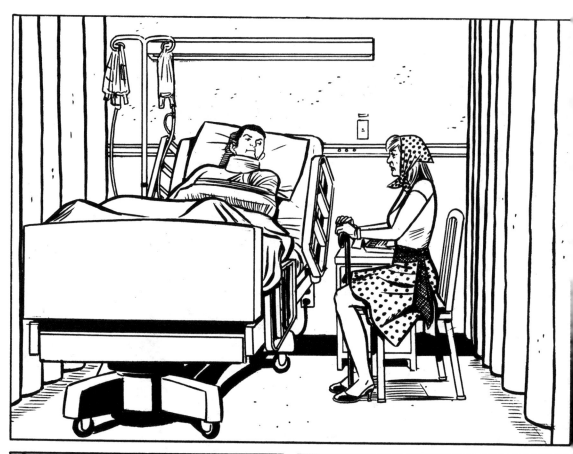

YOU'RE BETH'S MOM, RIGHT?

AHH-NEE.

AAHN-NEE.

SO, WHAT'S WITH THE...?

'AD A...

...STROKE.

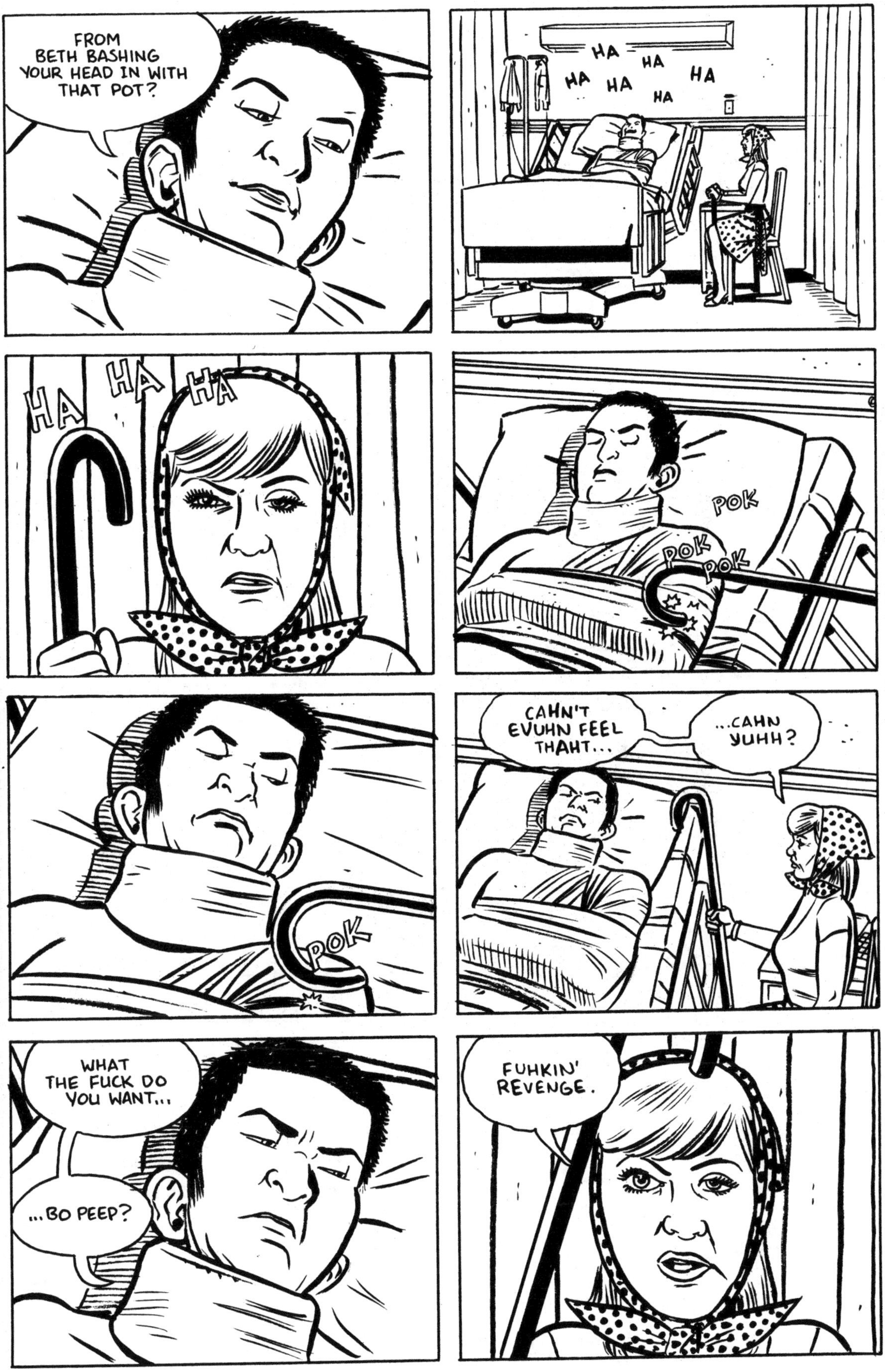

FROM BETH BASHING YOUR HEAD IN WITH THAT POT?
HA HA HA HA HA HA
HA HA HA
POK
POK POK
POK
CAHN'T EVUHN FEEL THAHT...
...CAHN YUHH?
WHAT THE FUCK DO YOU WANT...
...BO PEEP?
FUHKIN' REVENGE.

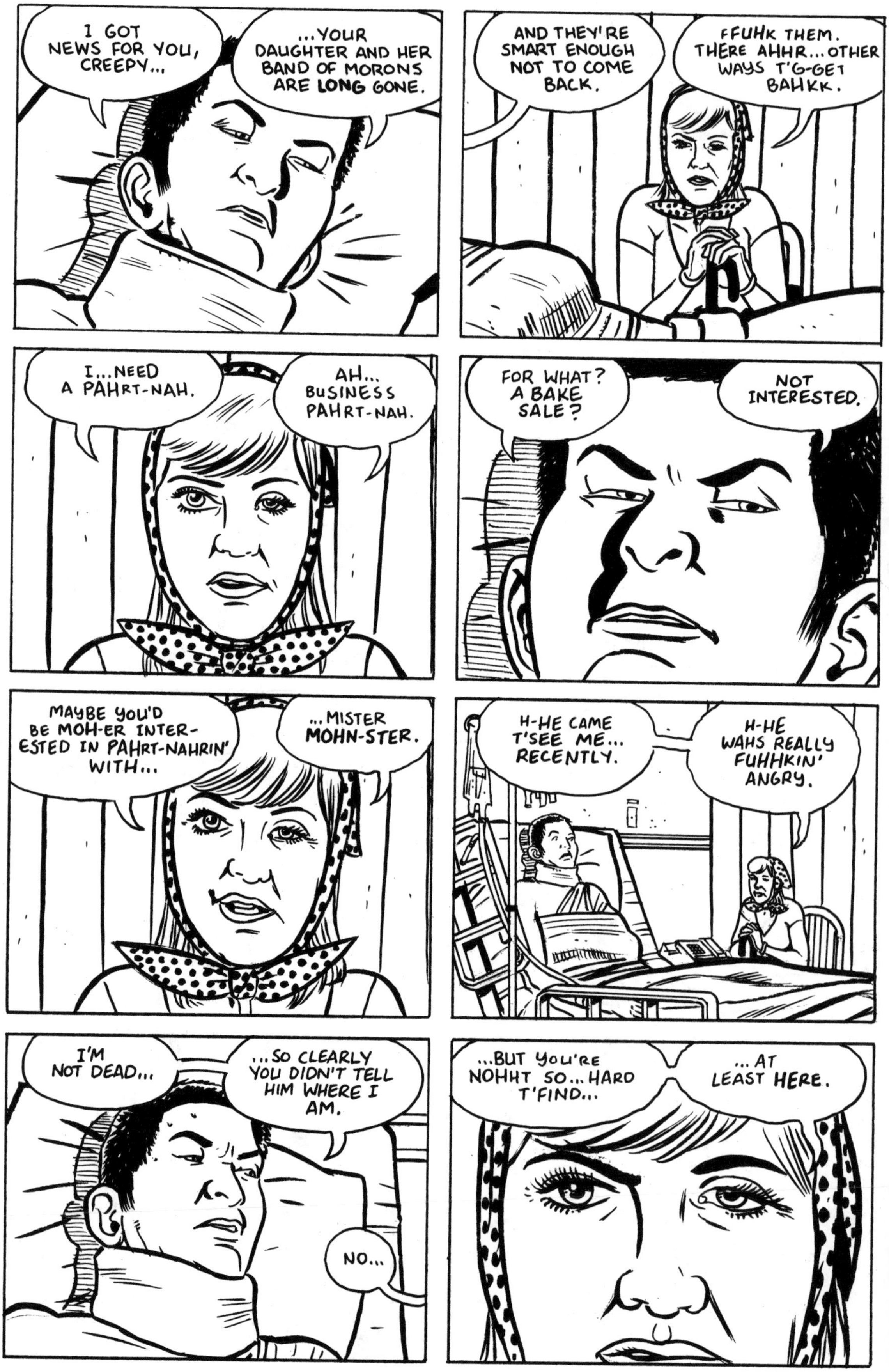
I GOT NEWS FOR YOU, CREEPY...
...YOUR DAUGHTER AND HER BAND OF MORONS ARE LONG GONE.
AND THEY'RE SMART ENOUGH NOT TO COME BACK.
FFUHK THEM. THERE AHHR...OTHER WAYS T'G-GET BAHKK.
I...NEED A PAHRT-NAH.
AH... BUSINESS PAHRT-NAH.
FOR WHAT? A BAKE SALE?
NOT INTERESTED.
MAYBE YOU'D BE MOH-ER INTER-ESTED IN PAHRT-NAHRIN' WITH...
...MISTER MOHN-STER.
H-HE CAME T'SEE ME... RECENTLY.
H-HE WAHS REALLY FUHHKIN' ANGRY.
I'M NOT DEAD...
...SO CLEARLY YOU DIDN'T TELL HIM WHERE I AM.
NO...
...BUT YOU'RE NOHHT SO...HARD T'FIND...
...AT LEAST HERE.

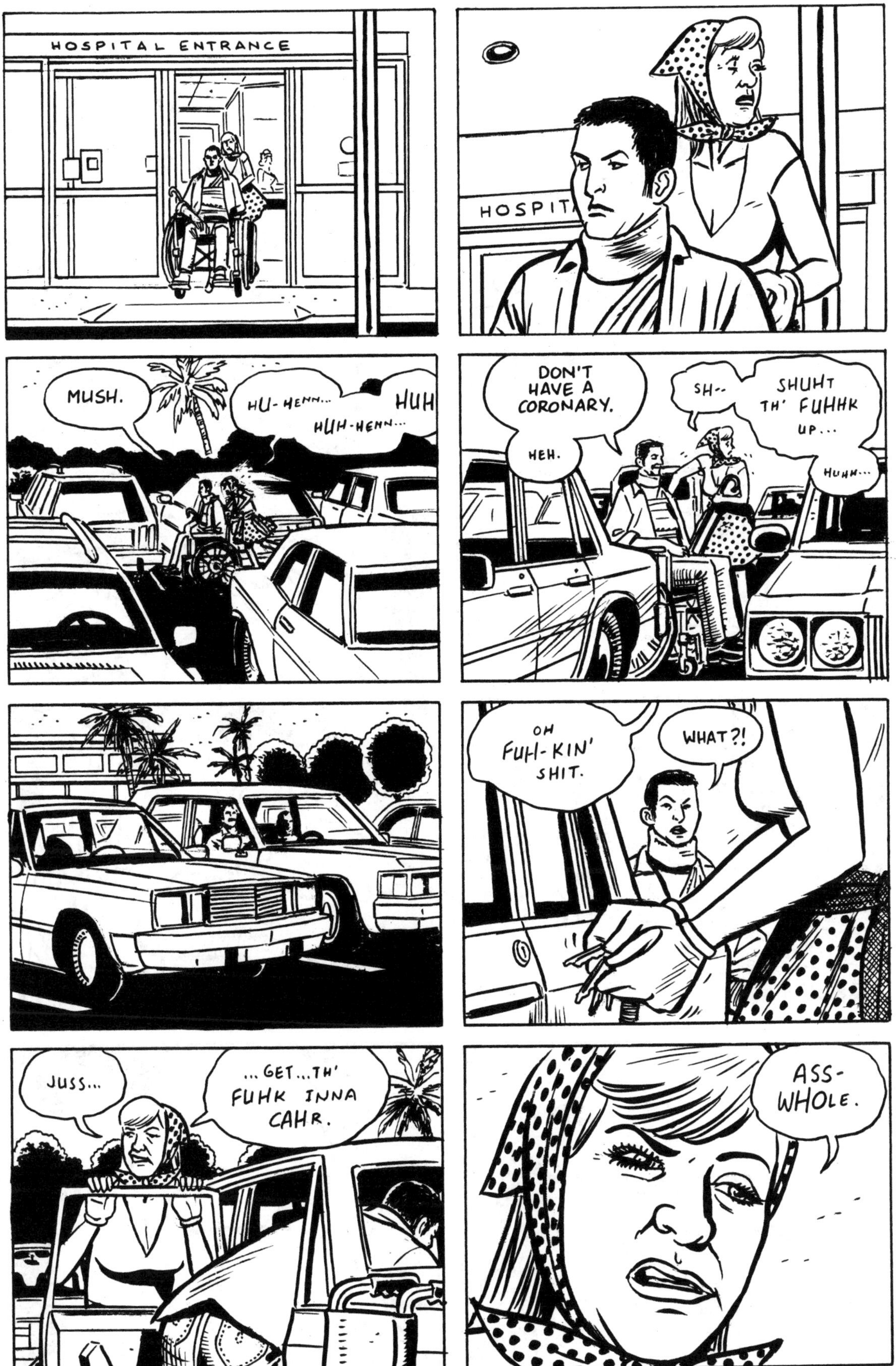
HOSPITAL ENTRANCE
HOSPIT
MUSH.
HU-HENN... HUH HUH-HENN...
DON'T HAVE A CORONARY.
HEH.
SH--
SHUHT TH' FUHHK UP...
HUHH...
OH FUH-KIN' SHIT.
WHAT?!
JUSS...
...GET...TH' FUHK INNA CAHR.
ASS-WHOLE.

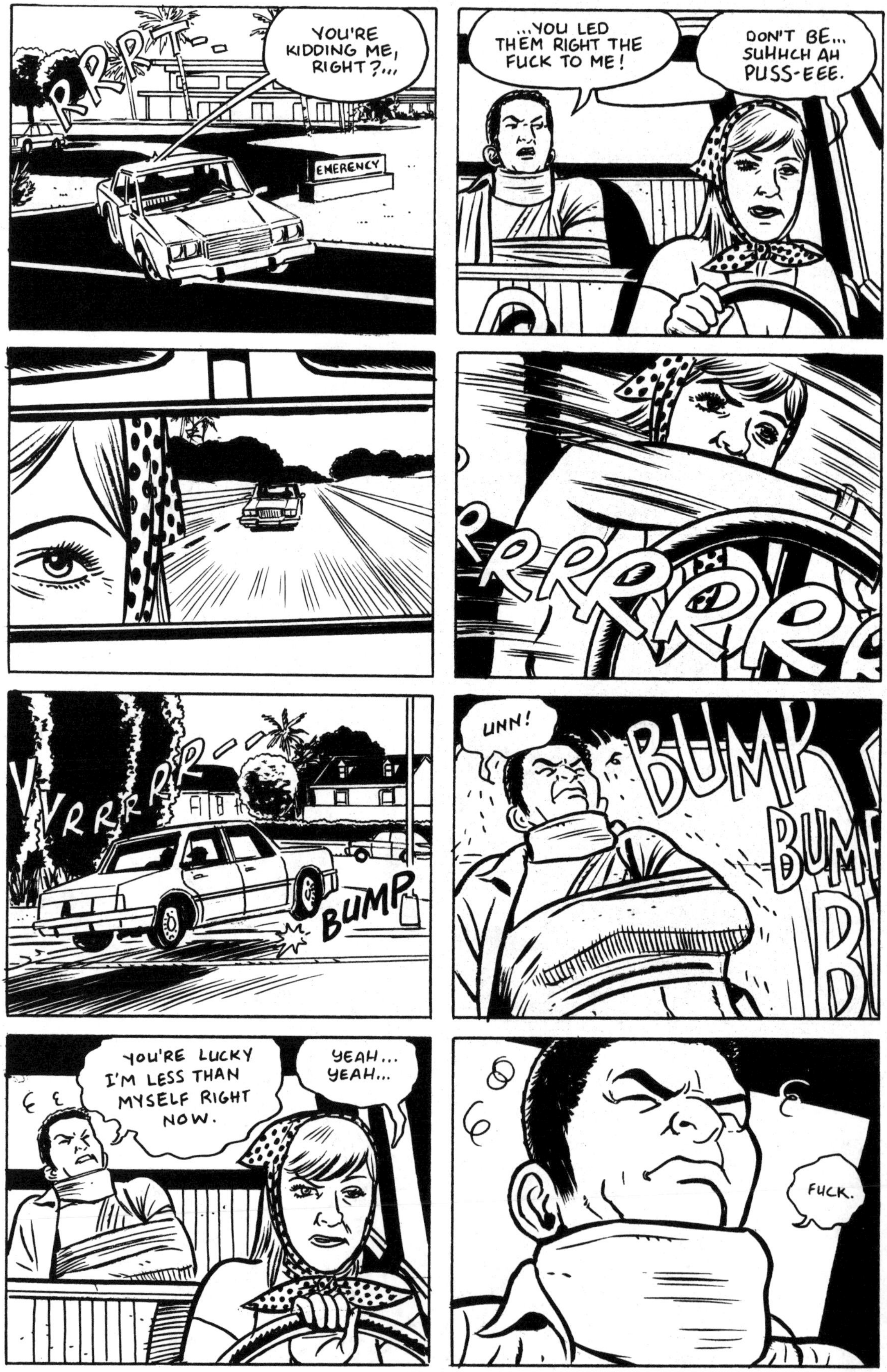

RRRT-
YOU'RE KIDDING ME, RIGHT?...
EMERGENCY
...YOU LED THEM RIGHT THE FUCK TO ME!
DON'T BE... SUHHCH AH PUSS-EEE.
RRRRRR
VRRRRRR-
BUMP
UNN!
BUMP
BUMP
YOU'RE LUCKY I'M LESS THAN MYSELF RIGHT NOW.
YEAH... YEAH...
FUCK.

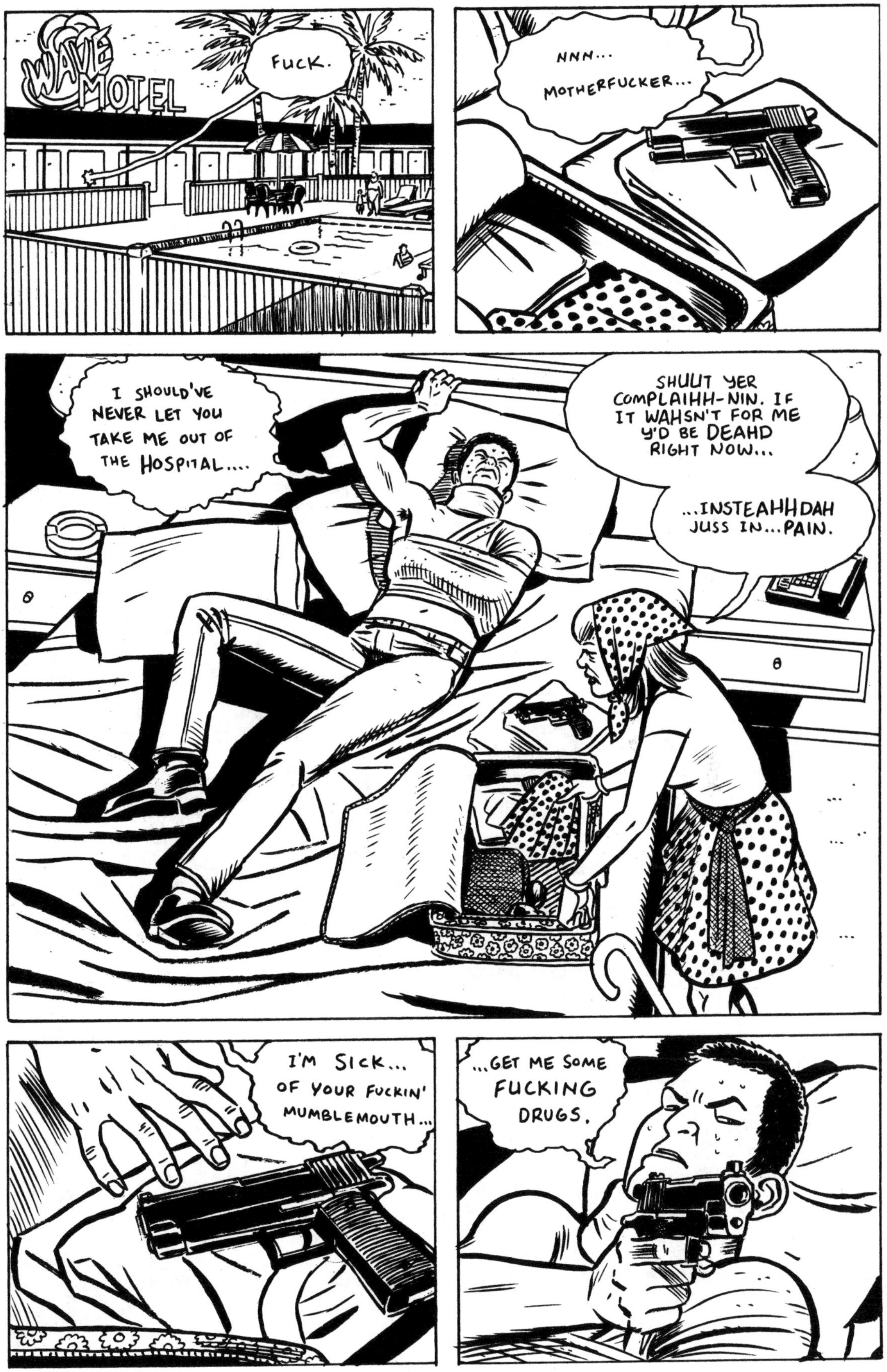

WAVE MOTEL
FUCK.
NNN... MOTHERFUCKER...
I SHOULD'VE NEVER LET YOU TAKE ME OUT OF THE HOSPITAL....
SHUUT YER COMPLAIHH-NIN. IF IT WAHSN'T FOR ME Y'D BE DEAHD RIGHT NOW...
...INSTEAHHDAH JUSS IN...PAIN.
I'M SICK... OF YOUR FUCKIN' MUMBLEMOUTH...
...GET ME SOME FUCKING DRUGS.

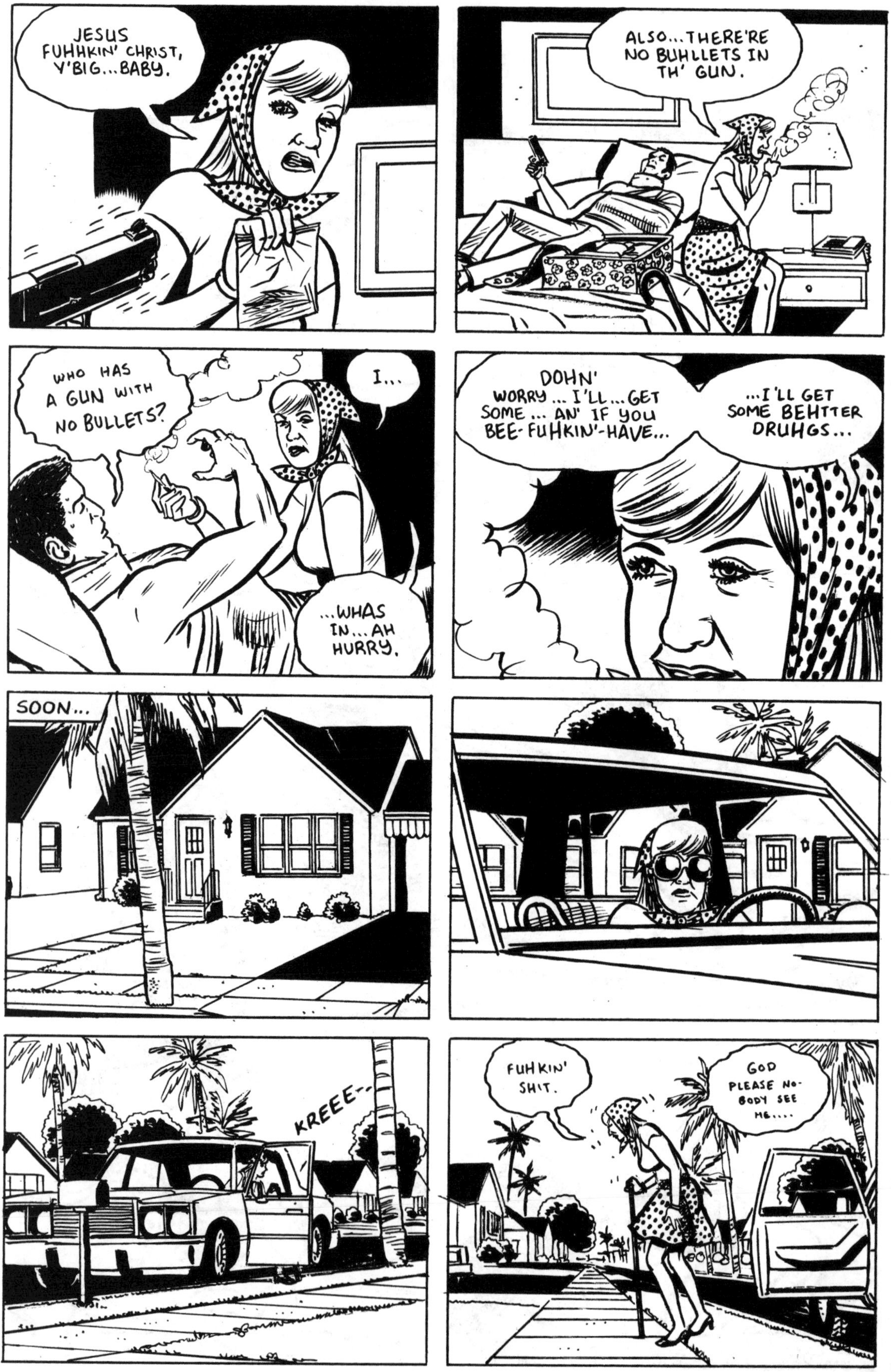
JESUS FUHHKIN' CHRIST, Y'BIG...BABY.
ALSO...THERE'RE NO BUHLLETS IN TH' GUN.
WHO HAS A GUN WITH NO BULLETS?
I...
...WHAS IN...AH HURRY.
DOHN' WORRY... I'LL...GET SOME... AN' IF YOU BEE-FUHKIN'-HAVE...
...I'LL GET SOME BEHTTER DRUHGS...
SOON...
KREEE--
FUHKIN' SHIT.
GOD PLEASE NO-BODY SEE ME....

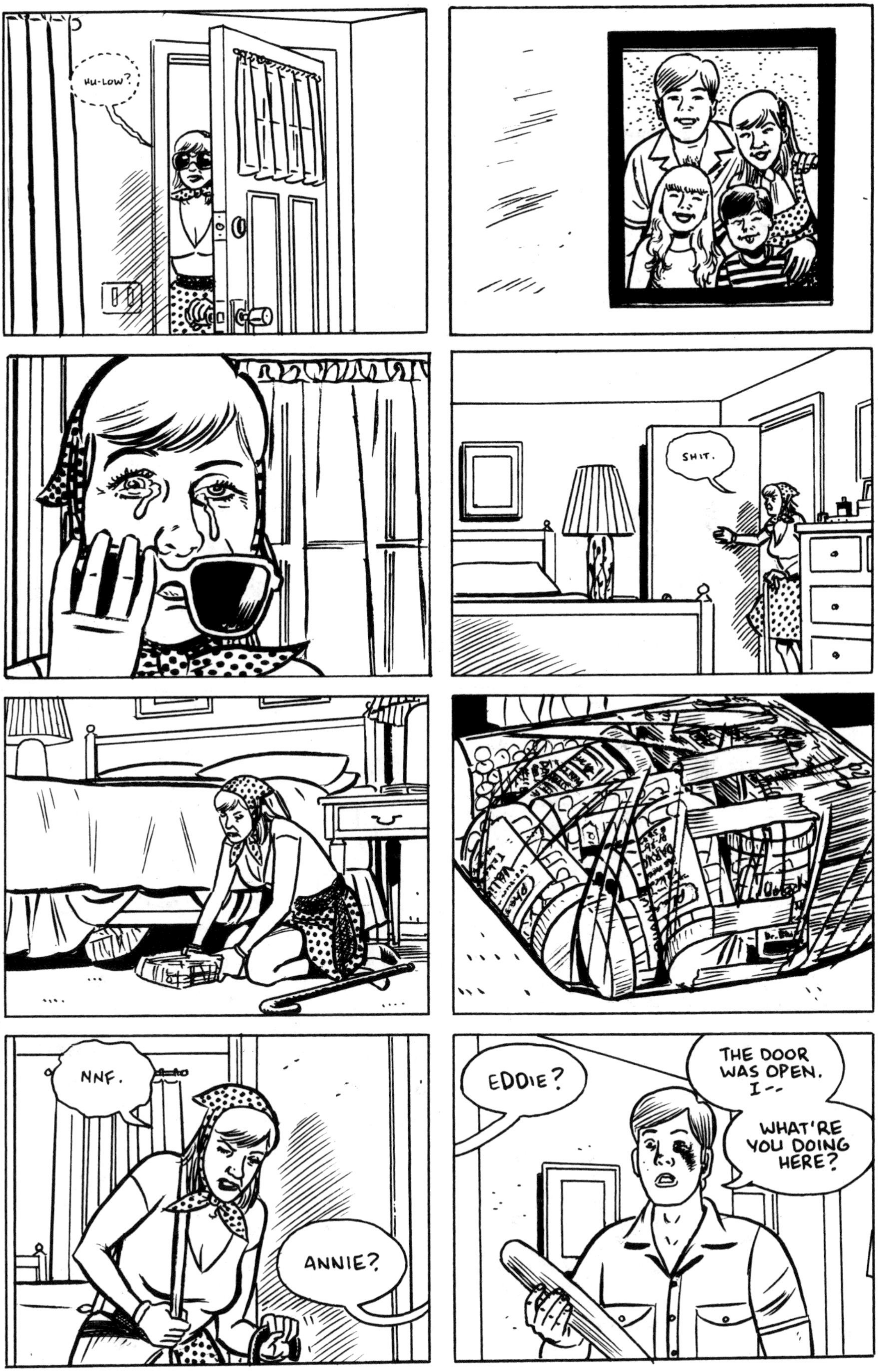
HU-LOW?
SHIT.
NNF.
ANNIE?
EDDIE?
THE DOOR WAS OPEN. I --
WHAT'RE YOU DOING HERE?

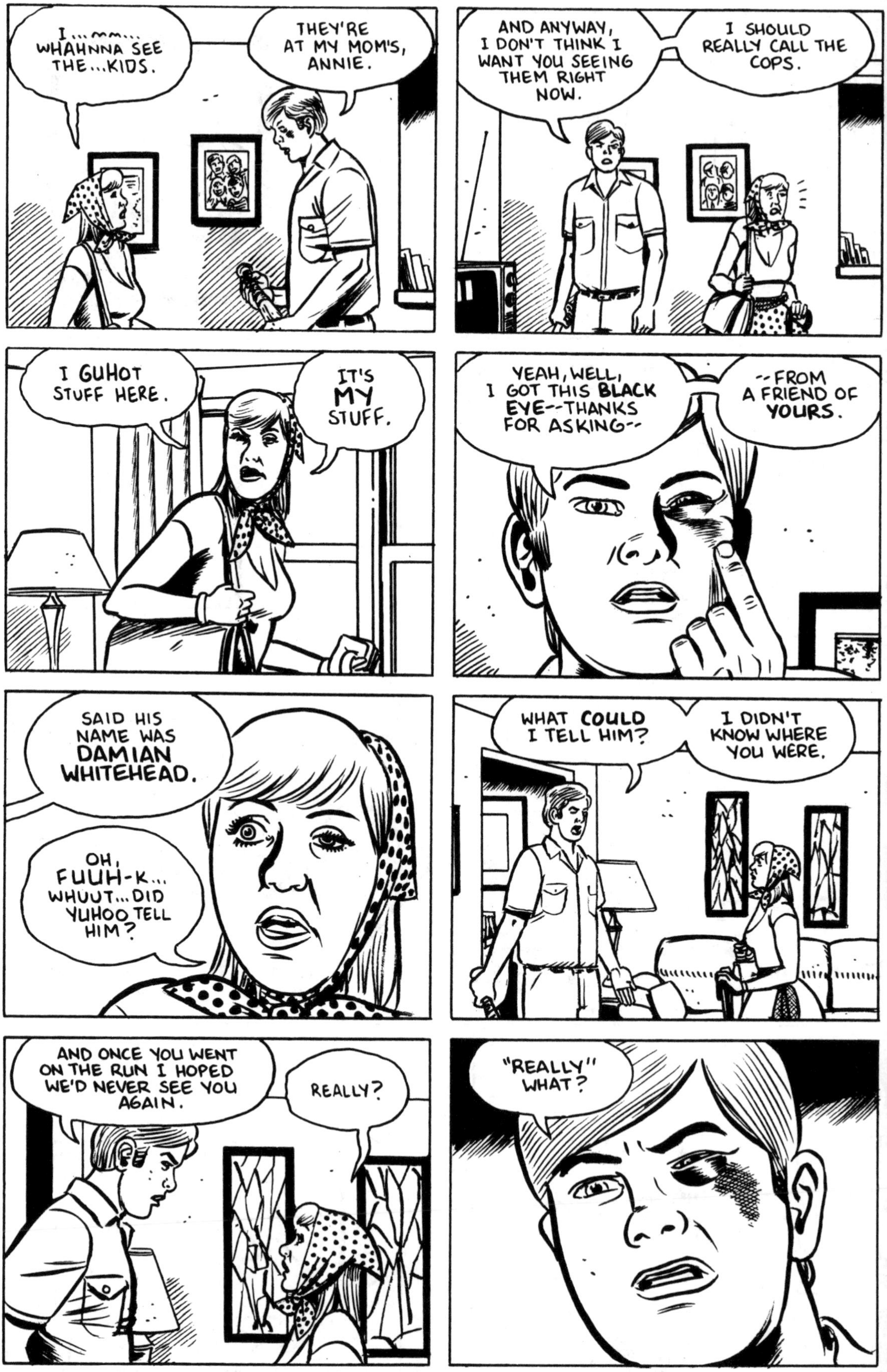
I...mm... WHAHNNA SEE THE...KIDS.
THEY'RE AT MY MOM'S, ANNIE.
AND ANYWAY, I DON'T THINK I WANT YOU SEEING THEM RIGHT NOW.
I SHOULD REALLY CALL THE COPS.
I GUHOT STUFF HERE.
IT'S MY STUFF.
YEAH, WELL, I GOT THIS BLACK EYE--THANKS FOR ASKING--
--FROM A FRIEND OF YOURS.
SAID HIS NAME WAS DAMIAN WHITEHEAD.
OH, FUUH-K... WHUUT...DID YUHOO TELL HIM?
WHAT COULD I TELL HIM?
I DIDN'T KNOW WHERE YOU WERE.
AND ONCE YOU WENT ON THE RUN I HOPED WE'D NEVER SEE YOU AGAIN.
REALLY?
"REALLY" WHAT?

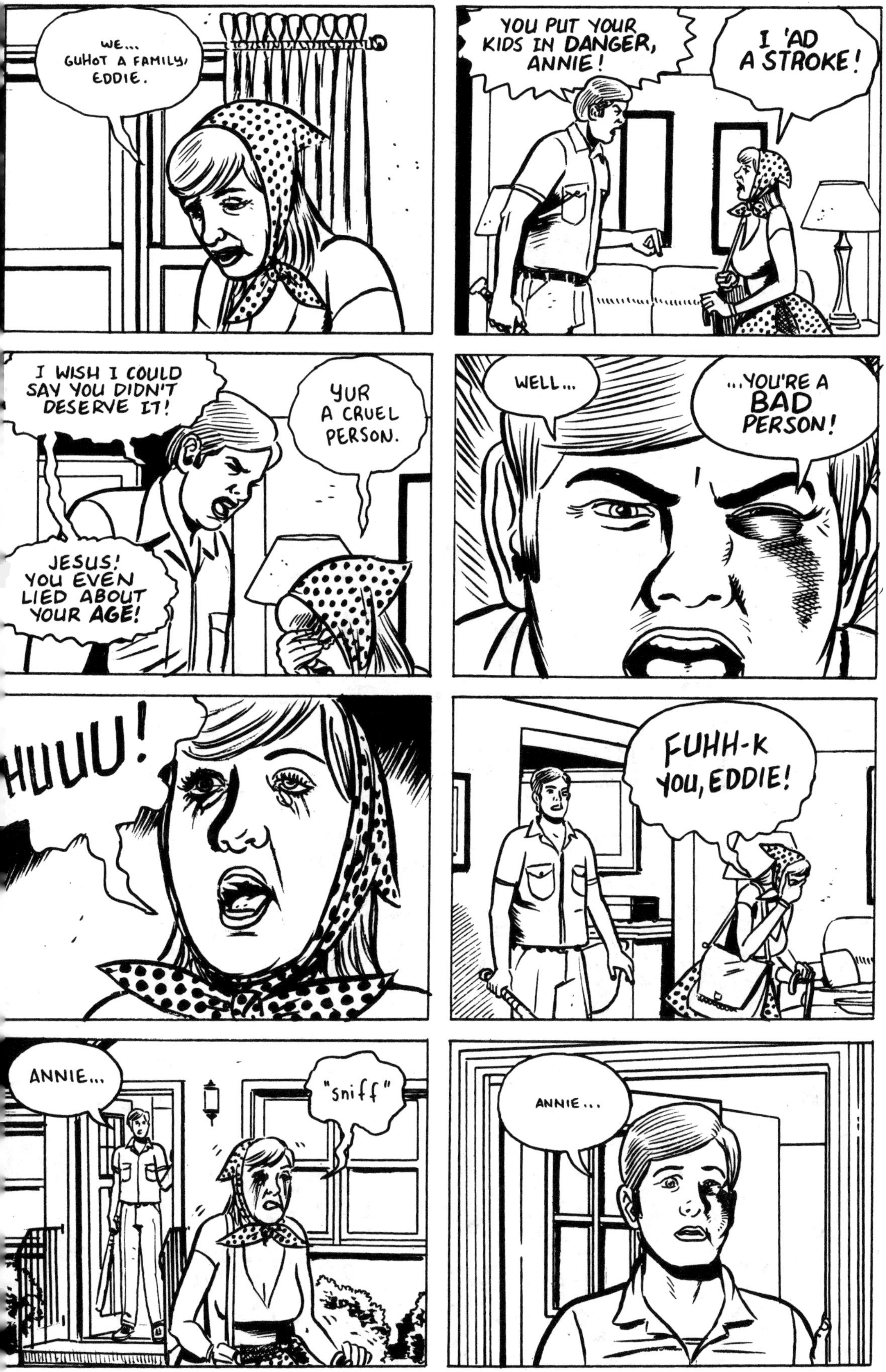
WE... GUHOT A FAMILY, EDDIE.
YOU PUT YOUR KIDS IN DANGER, ANNIE!
I 'AD A STROKE!
I WISH I COULD SAY YOU DIDN'T DESERVE IT!
YUR A CRUEL PERSON.
JESUS! YOU EVEN LIED ABOUT YOUR AGE!
WELL...
...YOU'RE A BAD PERSON!
HUUU!
FUHH-K YOU, EDDIE!
ANNIE...
"sniff"
ANNIE...

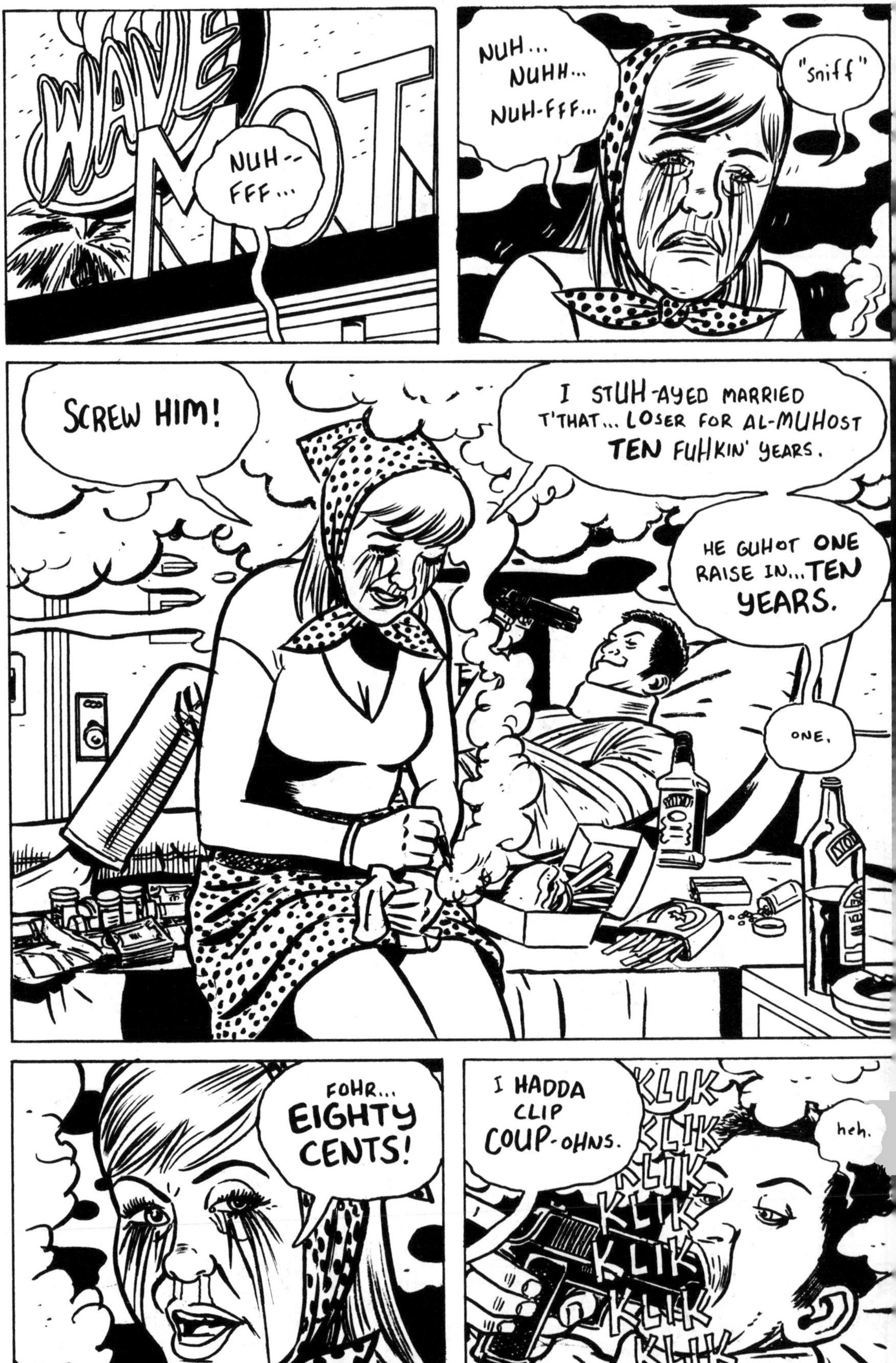
WAVE
MOT
NUH--
FFF...
NUH...
NUHH...
NUH-FFF...
"sniff"
SCREW HIM!
I STUH-AYED MARRIED T'THAT... LOSER FOR AL-MUHOST TEN FUHKIN' YEARS.
HE GUHOT ONE RAISE IN... TEN YEARS.
ONE.
FOHR... EIGHTY CENTS!
I HADDA CLIP COUP-OHNS.
KLIK KLIK KLIK KLIK KLIK KLIK KLIK
heh.

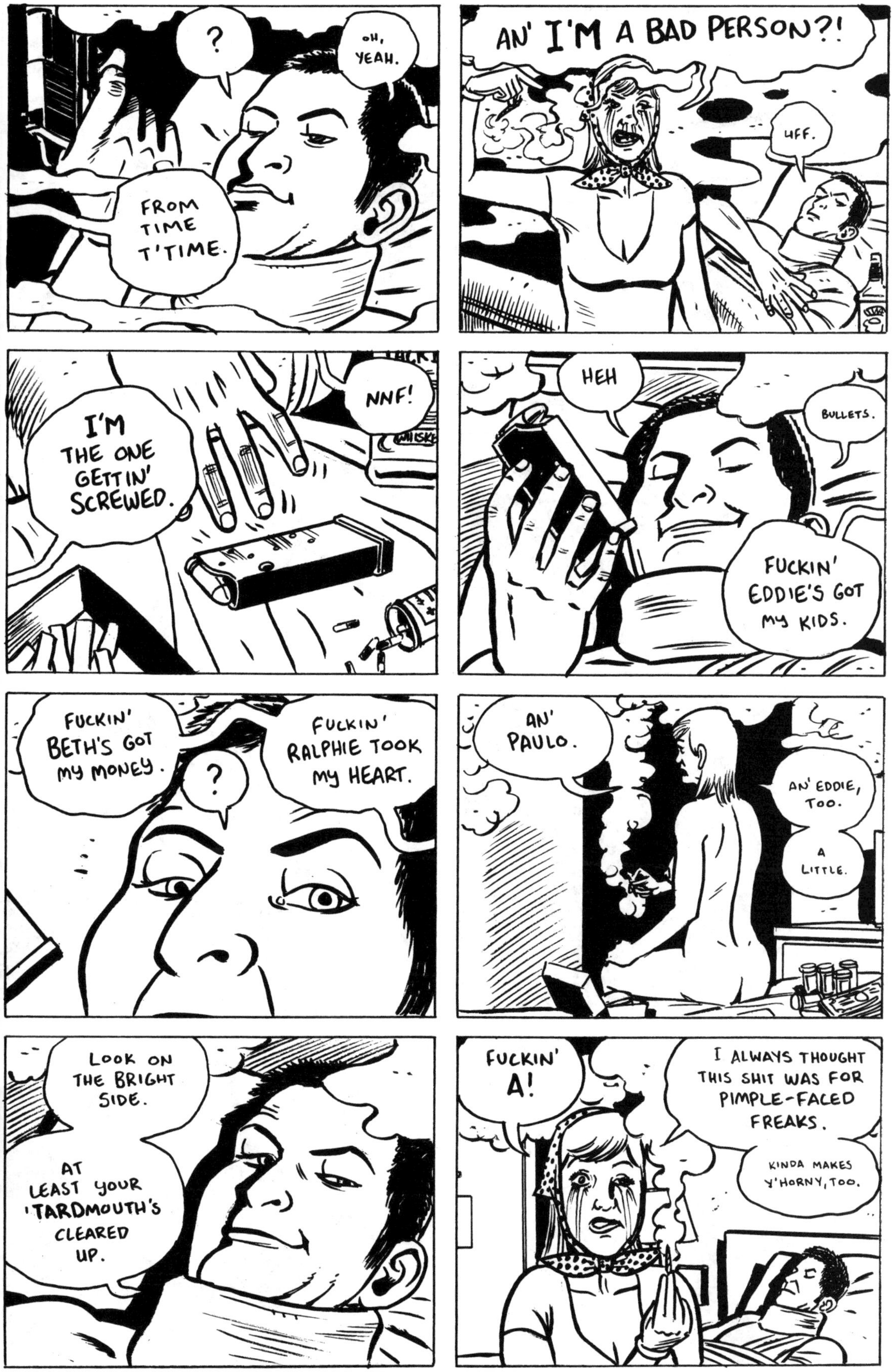
?
OH, YEAH.
FROM TIME T'TIME.
AN' I'M A BAD PERSON?!
UFF.
NNF!
I'M THE ONE GETTIN' SCREWED.
HEH
BULLETS.
FUCKIN' EDDIE'S GOT MY KIDS.
FUCKIN' BETH'S GOT MY MONEY.
?
FUCKIN' RALPHIE TOOK MY HEART.
AN' PAULO.
AN' EDDIE, TOO.
A LITTLE.
LOOK ON THE BRIGHT SIDE.
AT LEAST YOUR 'TARDMOUTH'S CLEARED UP.
FUCKIN' A!
I ALWAYS THOUGHT THIS SHIT WAS FOR PIMPLE-FACED FREAKS.
KINDA MAKES Y'HORNY, TOO.

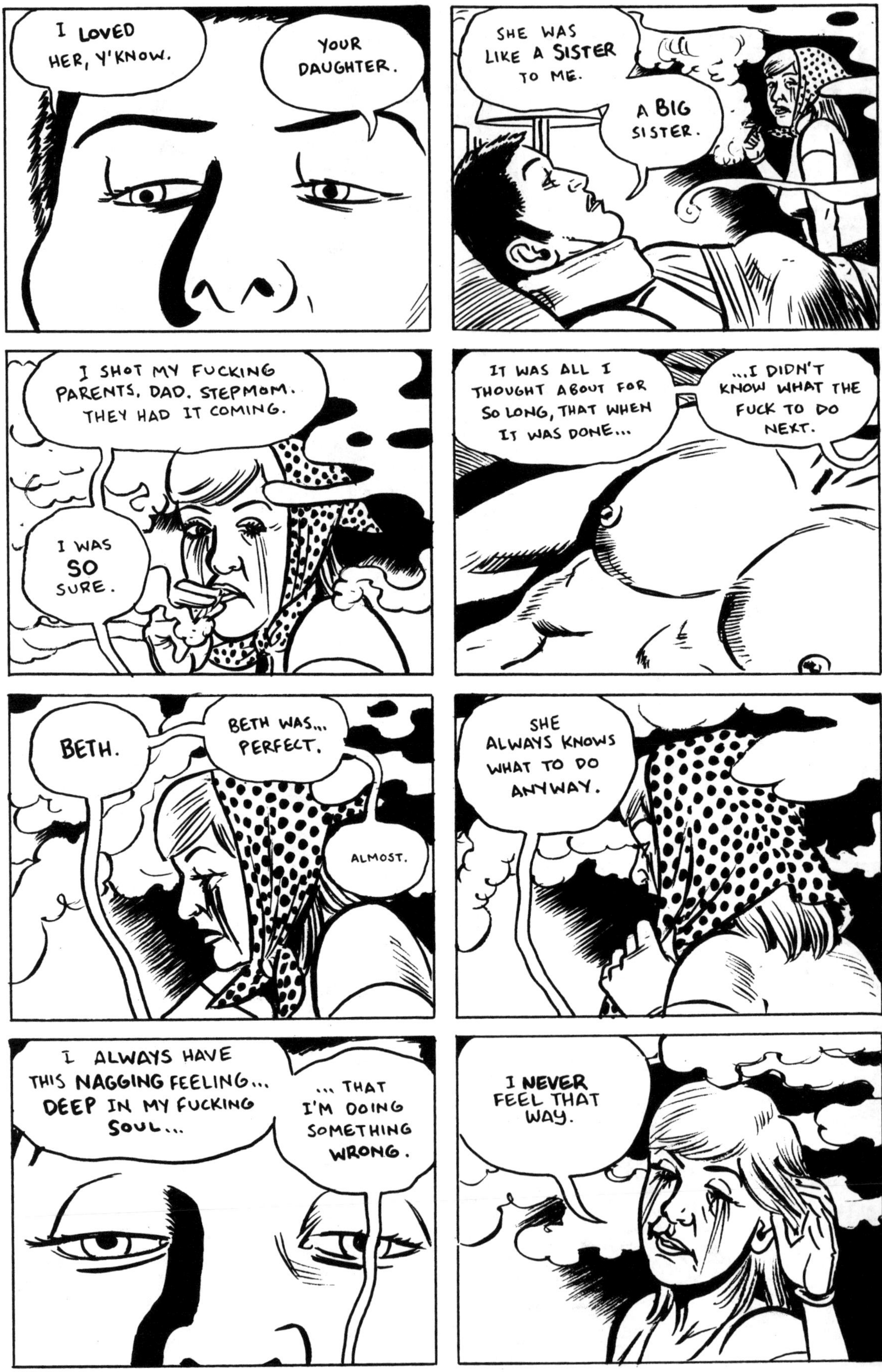
I LOVED HER, Y'KNOW.
YOUR DAUGHTER.
SHE WAS LIKE A SISTER TO ME.
A BIG SISTER.
I SHOT MY FUCKING PARENTS. DAD. STEPMOM. THEY HAD IT COMING.
I WAS SO SURE.
IT WAS ALL I THOUGHT ABOUT FOR SO LONG, THAT WHEN IT WAS DONE...
...I DIDN'T KNOW WHAT THE FUCK TO DO NEXT.
BETH.
BETH WAS... PERFECT.
ALMOST.
SHE ALWAYS KNOWS WHAT TO DO ANYWAY.
I ALWAYS HAVE THIS NAGGING FEELING... DEEP IN MY FUCKING SOUL...
... THAT I'M DOING SOMETHING WRONG.
I NEVER FEEL THAT WAY.

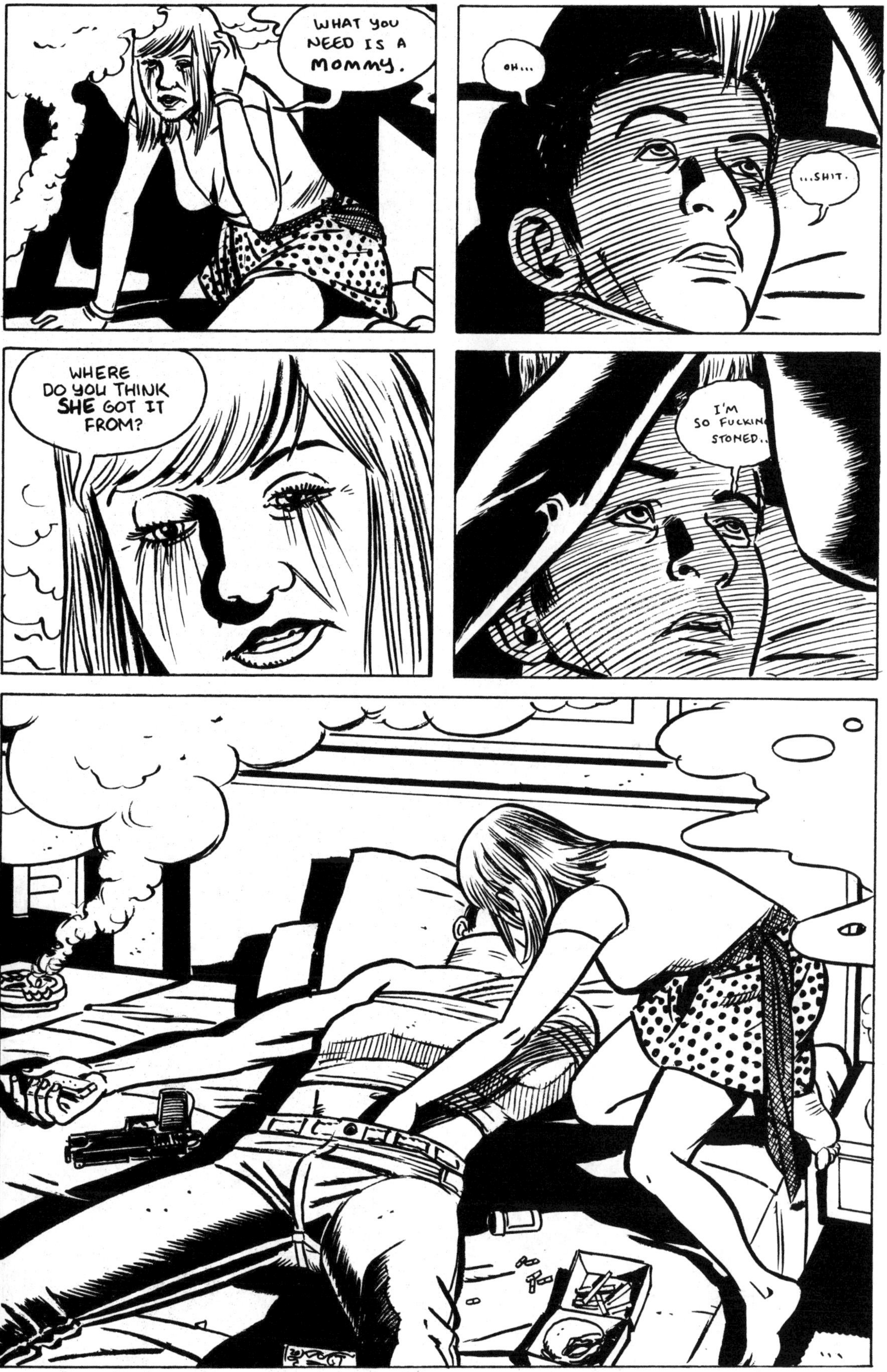
WHAT YOU NEED IS A MOMMY.
OH...
...SHIT.
WHERE DO YOU THINK SHE GOT IT FROM?
I'M SO FUCKING STONED...
...

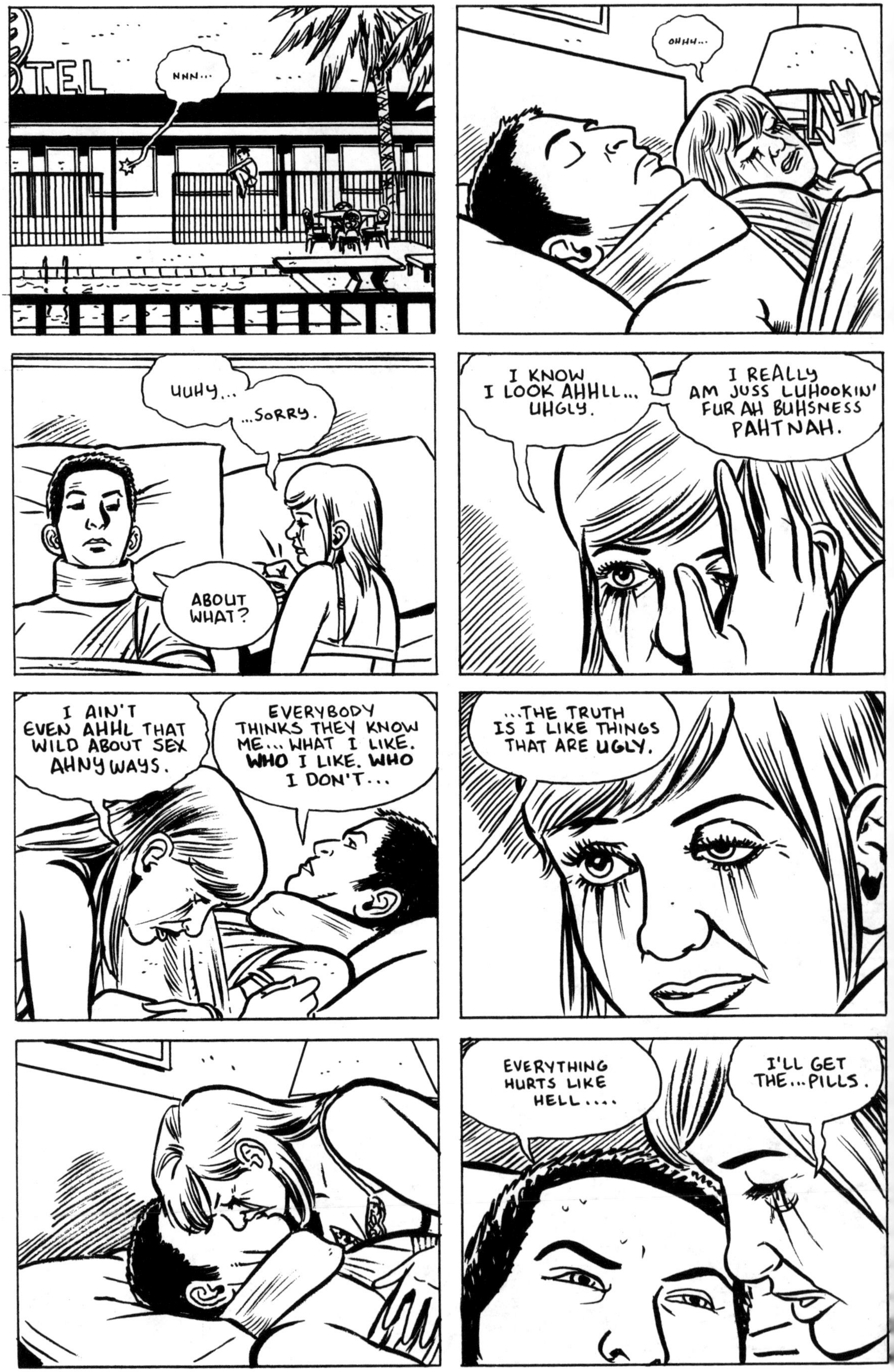

OTEL
NNN...
OHHH...
UUHY...
...SORRY.
ABOUT WHAT?
I KNOW I LOOK AHHLL... UHGLY.
I REALLY AM JUSS LUHOOKIN' FUR AH BUHSNESS PAHTNAH.
I AIN'T EVEN AHHL THAT WILD ABOUT SEX AHNYWAYS.
EVERYBODY THINKS THEY KNOW ME... WHAT I LIKE. WHO I LIKE. WHO I DON'T...
...THE TRUTH IS I LIKE THINGS THAT ARE UGLY.
EVERYTHING HURTS LIKE HELL....
I'LL GET THE...PILLS.

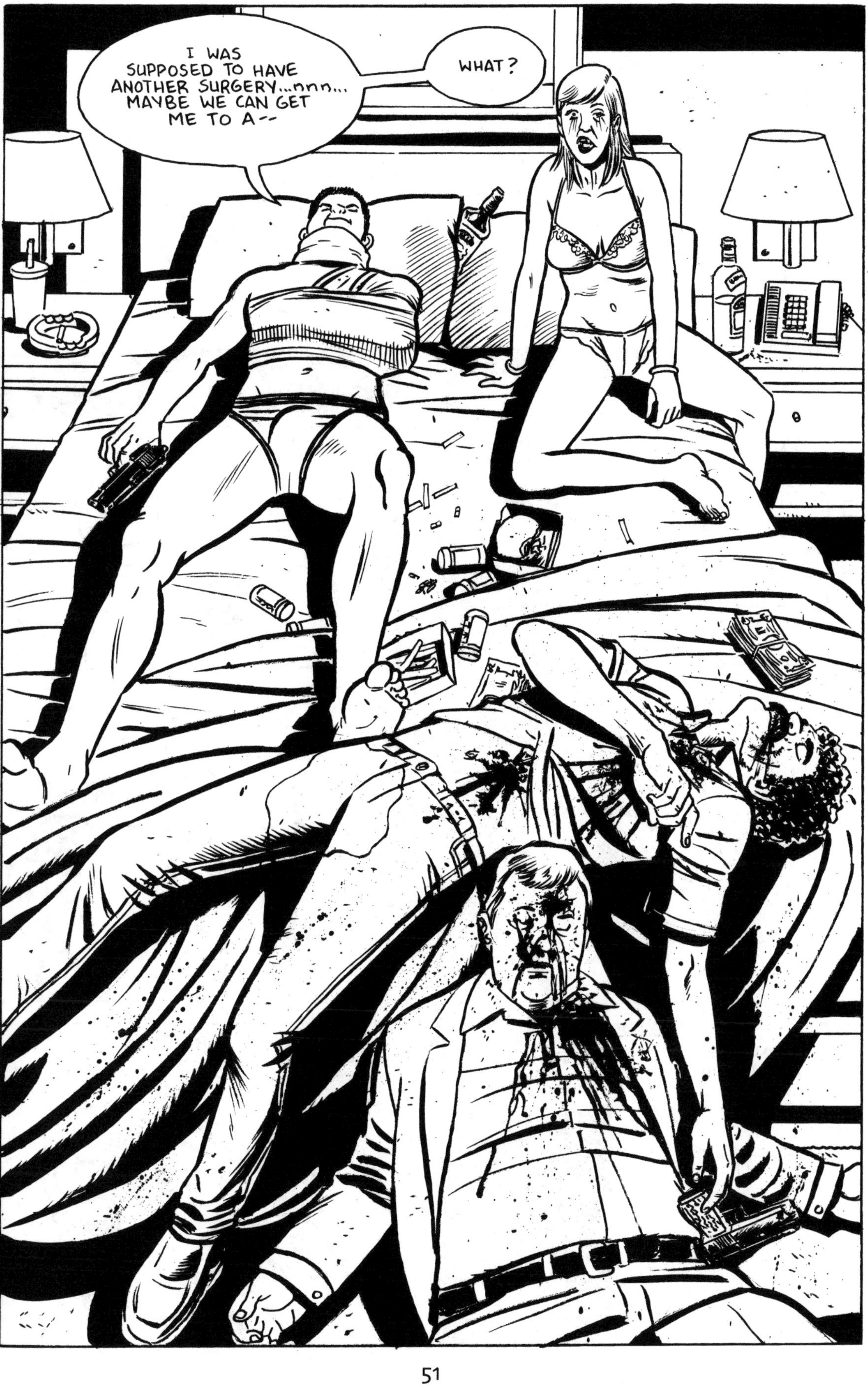
I WAS SUPPOSED TO HAVE ANOTHER SURGERY...nnn... MAYBE WE CAN GET ME TO A--
WHAT?

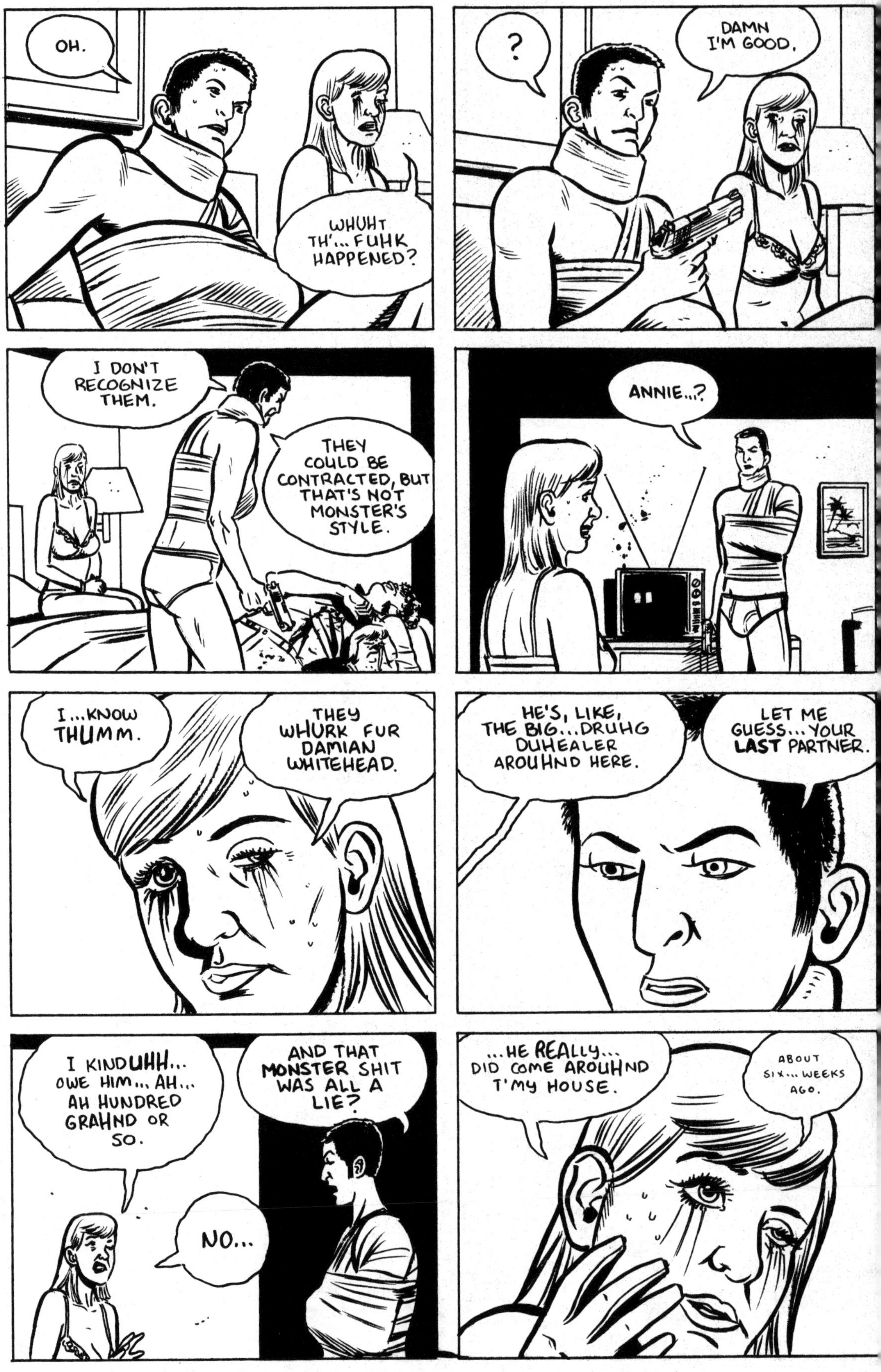
OH.
WHUHT TH'...FUHK HAPPENED?
?
DAMN I'M GOOD.
I DON'T RECOGNIZE THEM.
THEY COULD BE CONTRACTED, BUT THAT'S NOT MONSTER'S STYLE.
ANNIE...?
I...KNOW THUMM.
THEY WHURK FUR DAMIAN WHITEHEAD.
HE'S, LIKE, THE BIG...DRUHG DUHEALER AROUHND HERE.
LET ME GUESS... YOUR LAST PARTNER.
I KINDUHH... OWE HIM... AH... AH HUNDRED GRAHND OR SO.
AND THAT MONSTER SHIT WAS ALL A LIE?
NO...
...HE REALLY... DID COME AROUHND T'MY HOUSE.
ABOUT SIX... WEEKS AGO.

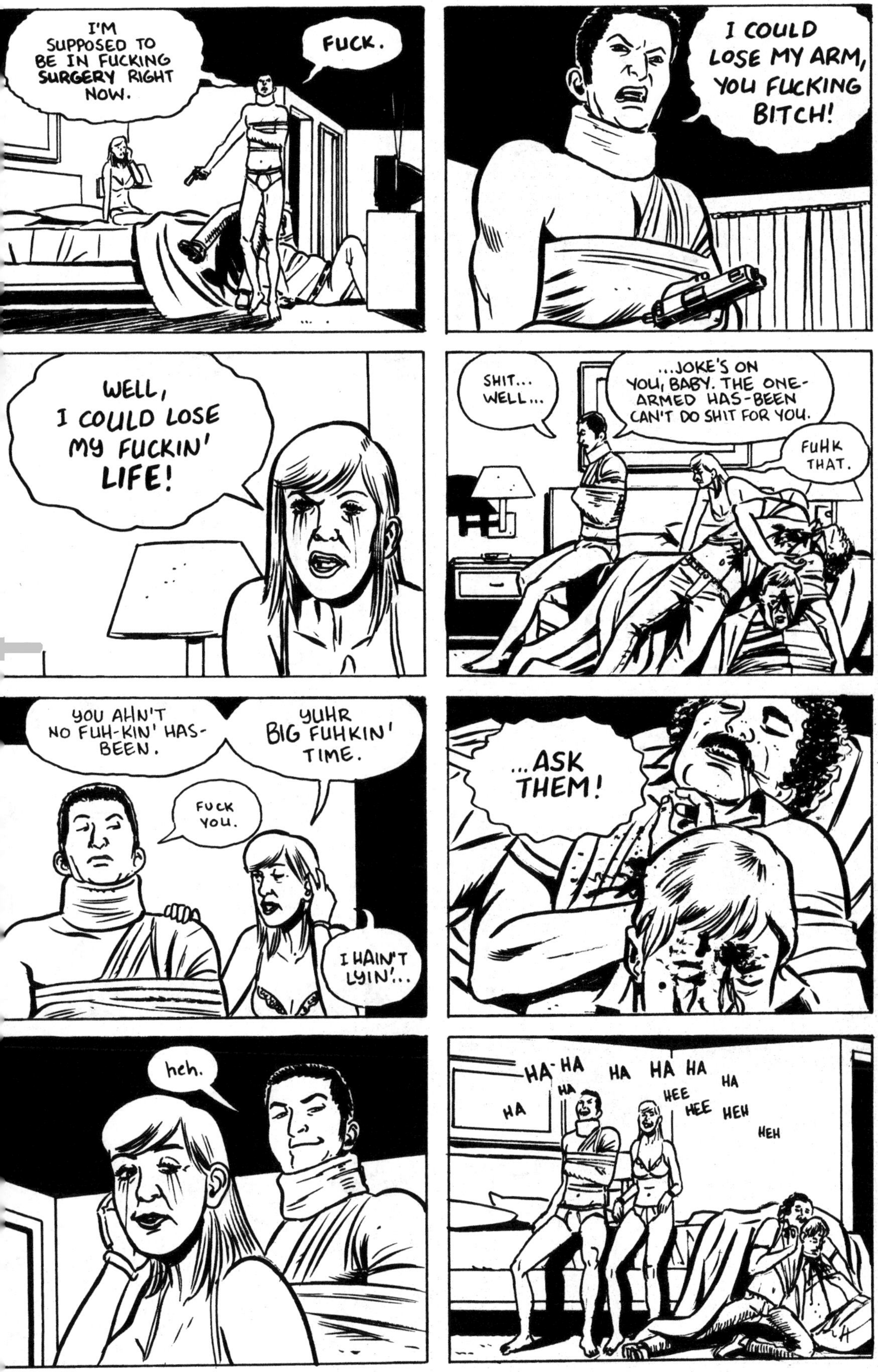
I'M SUPPOSED TO BE IN FUCKING SURGERY RIGHT NOW.
FUCK.
...
I COULD LOSE MY ARM, YOU FUCKING BITCH!
WELL, I COULD LOSE MY FUCKIN' LIFE!
SHIT... WELL...
...JOKE'S ON YOU, BABY. THE ONE-ARMED HAS-BEEN CAN'T DO SHIT FOR YOU.
FUHK THAT.
YOU AHN'T NO FUH-KIN' HAS-BEEN.
YUHR BIG FUHKIN' TIME.
FUCK YOU.
I HAIN'T LYIN'...
...ASK THEM!
heh.
HA HA HA HA HA HA HA HA HA HEE HEE HEH HEH

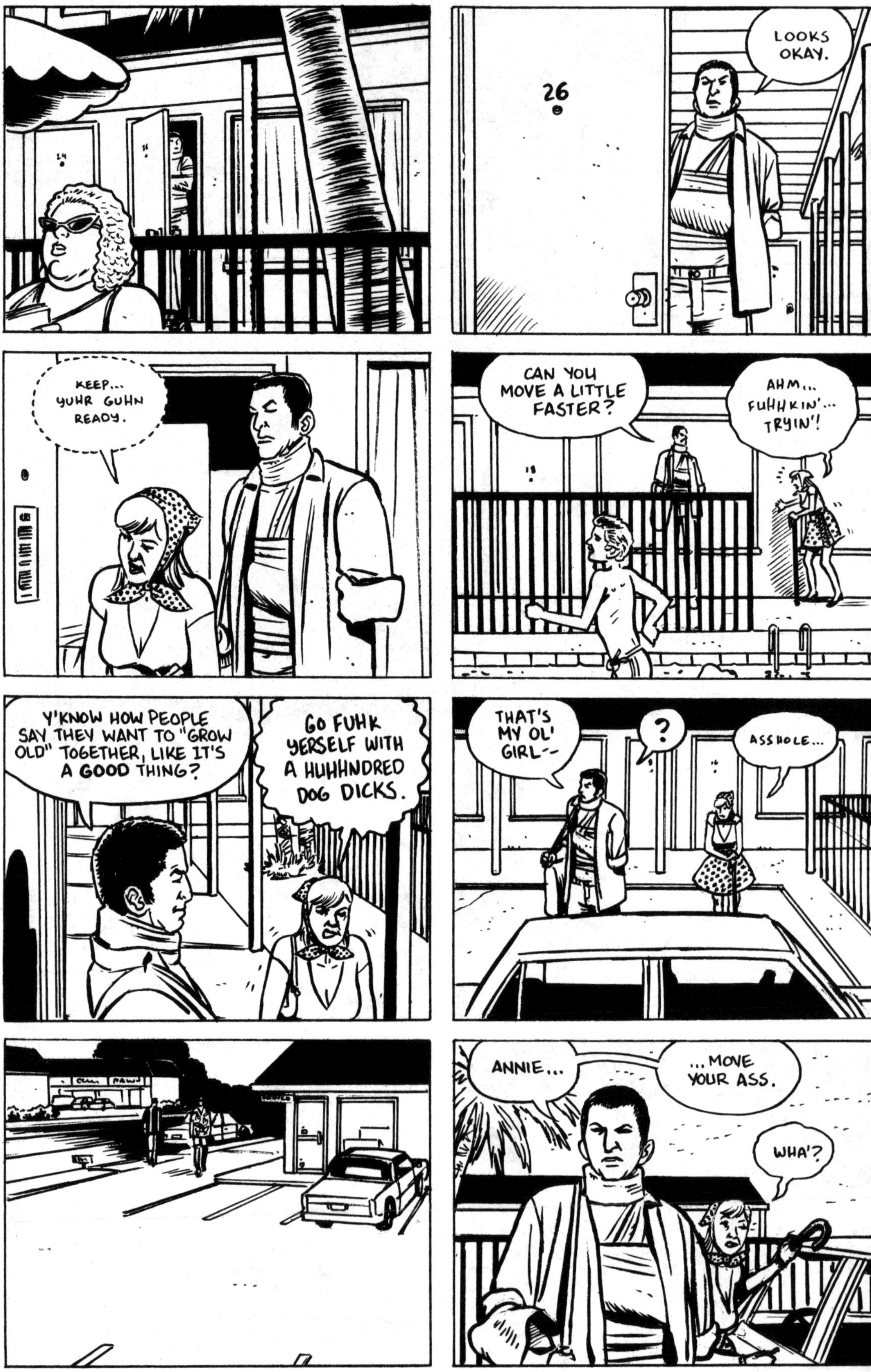
LOOKS OKAY.
26
KEEP... YUHR GUHN READY.
CAN YOU MOVE A LITTLE FASTER?
AHM... FUHHKIN'... TRYIN'!
Y'KNOW HOW PEOPLE SAY THEY WANT TO "GROW OLD" TOGETHER, LIKE IT'S A GOOD THING?
GO FUHK YERSELF WITH A HUHHNDRED DOG DICKS.
THAT'S MY OL' GIRL--
?
ASSHOLE...
ANNIE...
...MOVE YOUR ASS.
WHA'?

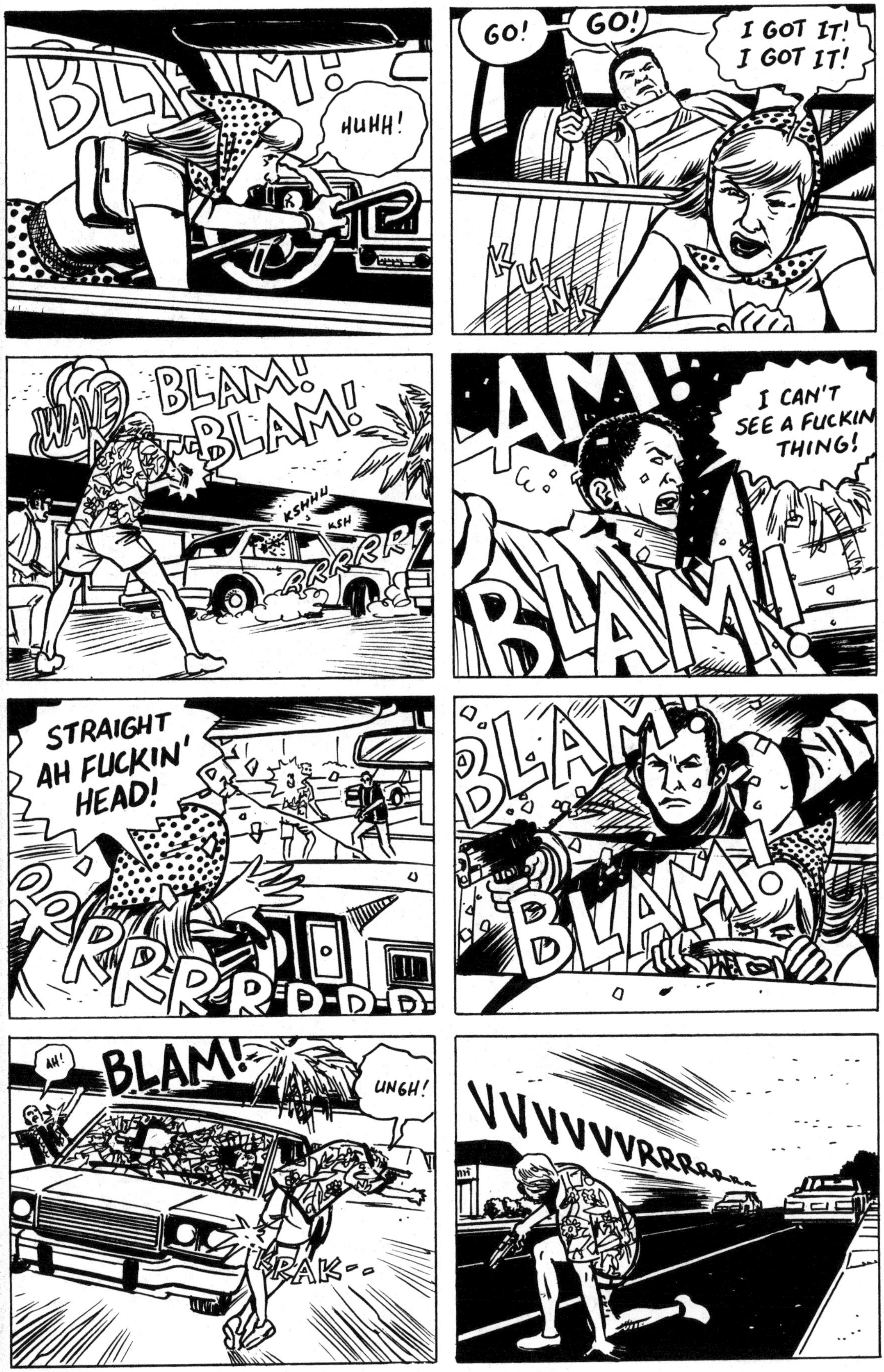
BLAM!
HUHH!
GO!
GO!
I GOT IT! I GOT IT!
KUNK
WAVE
BLAM! BLAM!
KSHHH
KSH
RRRRRR
I CAN'T SEE A FUCKIN THING!
BLAM!
STRAIGHT AH FUCKIN' HEAD!
RRRRRRRDDD
BLAM!
BLAM!
AH!
BLAM!
UNGH!
KRAK
VVVVVVVRRRRrrrr

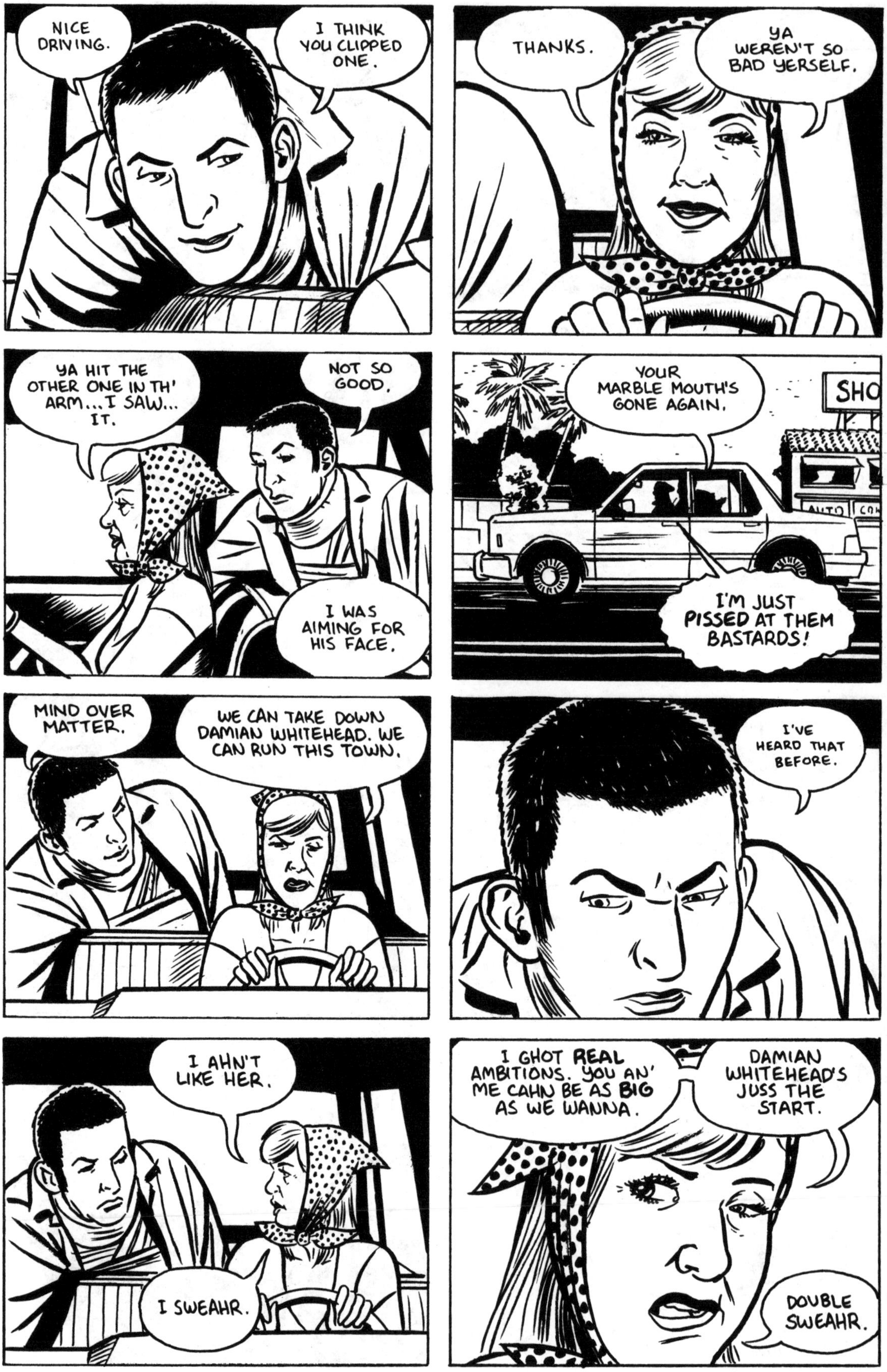
NICE DRIVING.
I THINK YOU CLIPPED ONE.
THANKS.
YA WEREN'T SO BAD YERSELF.
YA HIT THE OTHER ONE IN TH' ARM... I SAW... IT.
NOT SO GOOD.
I WAS AIMING FOR HIS FACE.
YOUR MARBLE MOUTH'S GONE AGAIN.
SHO
AUTO
I'M JUST PISSED AT THEM BASTARDS!
MIND OVER MATTER.
WE CAN TAKE DOWN DAMIAN WHITEHEAD. WE CAN RUN THIS TOWN.
I'VE HEARD THAT BEFORE.
I AHN'T LIKE HER.
I SWEAHR.
I GHOT REAL AMBITIONS. YOU AN' ME CAHN BE AS BIG AS WE WANNA.
DAMIAN WHITEHEAD'S JUSS THE START.
DOUBLE SWEAHR.

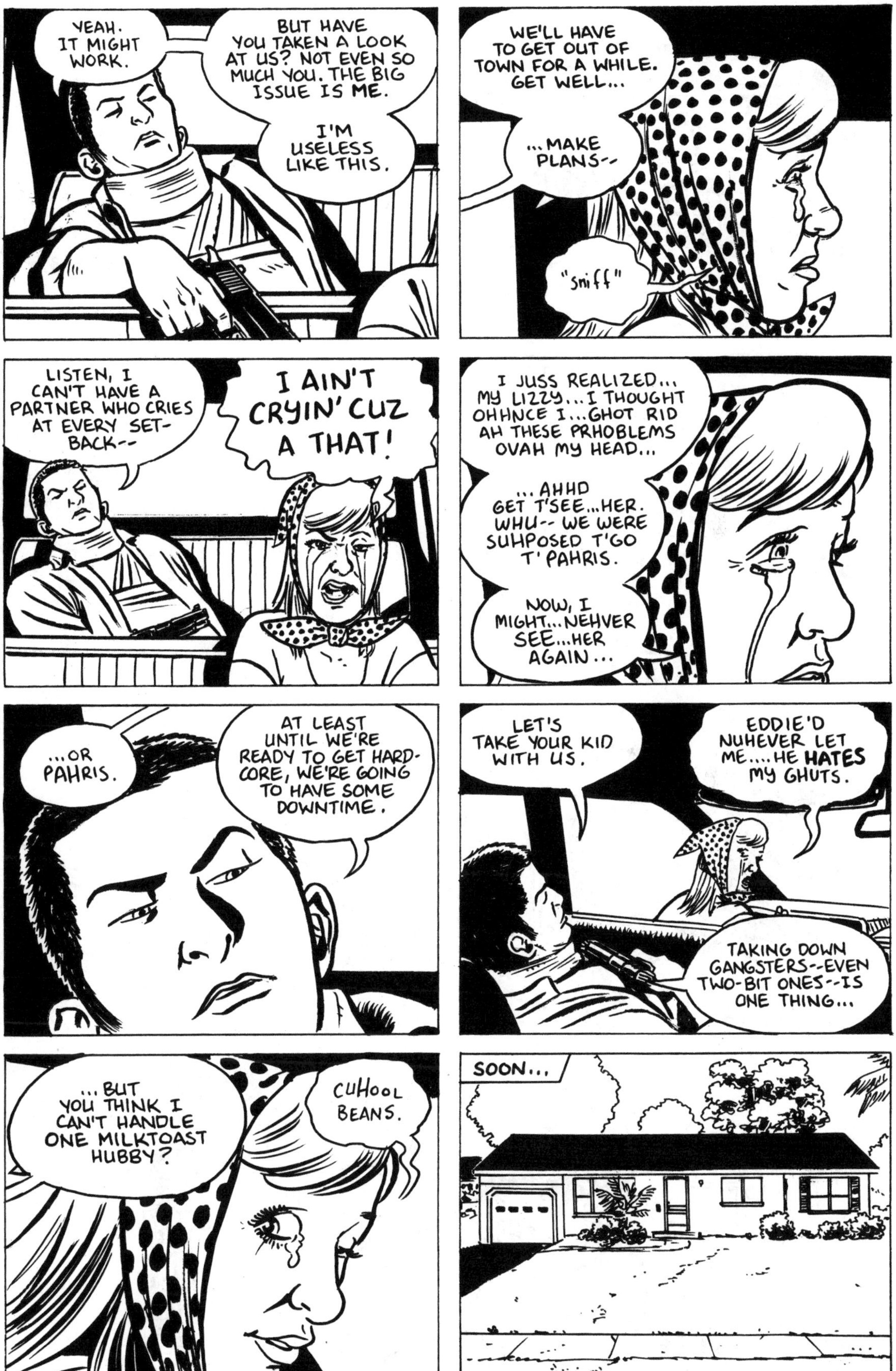
YEAH. IT MIGHT WORK.
BUT HAVE YOU TAKEN A LOOK AT US? NOT EVEN SO MUCH YOU. THE BIG ISSUE IS ME.
I'M USELESS LIKE THIS.
WE'LL HAVE TO GET OUT OF TOWN FOR A WHILE. GET WELL...
...MAKE PLANS--
"sniff"
LISTEN, I CAN'T HAVE A PARTNER WHO CRIES AT EVERY SET-BACK--
I AIN'T CRYIN' CUZ A THAT!
I JUSS REALIZED... MY LIZZY...I THOUGHT OHHNCE I...GHOT RID AH THESE PRHOBLEMS OVAH MY HEAD...
...AHHD GET T'SEE...HER. WHU-- WE WERE SUHPOSED T'GO T' PAHRIS.
NOW, I MIGHT...NEHVER SEE...HER AGAIN...
...OR PAHRIS.
AT LEAST UNTIL WE'RE READY TO GET HARD-CORE, WE'RE GOING TO HAVE SOME DOWNTIME.
LET'S TAKE YOUR KID WITH US.
EDDIE'D NUHEVER LET ME....HE **HATES** MY GHUTS.
TAKING DOWN GANGSTERS--EVEN TWO-BIT ONES--IS ONE THING...
...BUT YOU THINK I CAN'T HANDLE ONE MILKTOAST HUBBY?
CUHOOL BEANS.
SOON...

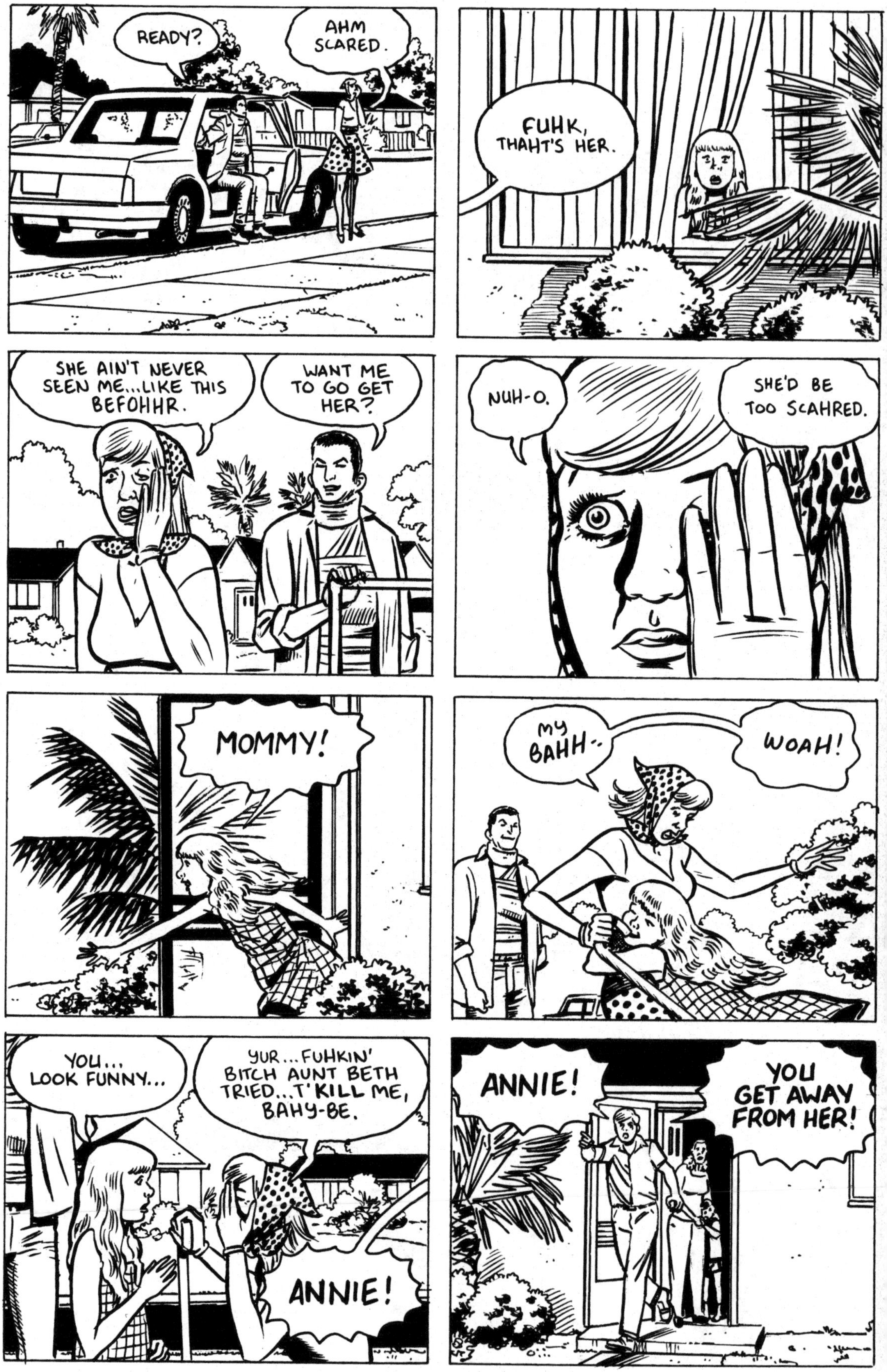
READY?
AHM SCARED.
FUHK, THAHT'S HER.
SHE AIN'T NEVER SEEN ME...LIKE THIS BEFOHHR.
WANT ME TO GO GET HER?
NUH-O.
SHE'D BE TOO SCAHRED.
MOMMY!
MY BAHH-.
WOAH!
YOU... LOOK FUNNY...
YUR...FUHKIN' BITCH AUNT BETH TRIED...T'KILL ME, BAHY-BE.
ANNIE!
ANNIE!
YOU GET AWAY FROM HER!

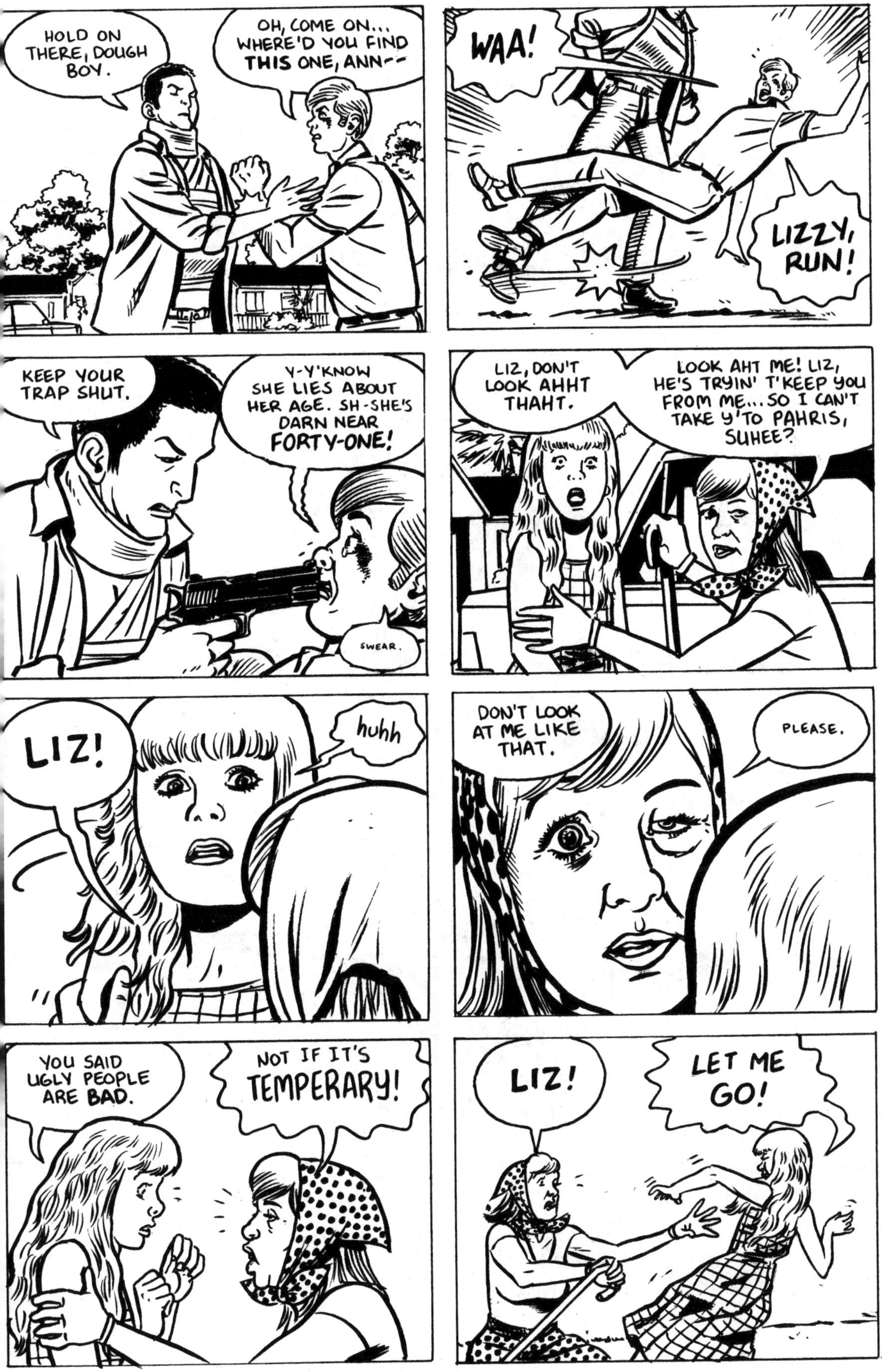
HOLD ON THERE, DOUGH BOY.
OH, COME ON... WHERE'D YOU FIND THIS ONE, ANN--
WAA!
LIZZY, RUN!
KEEP YOUR TRAP SHUT.
Y-Y'KNOW SHE LIES ABOUT HER AGE. SH-SHE'S DARN NEAR FORTY-ONE!
SWEAR.
LIZ, DON'T LOOK AHHT THAHT.
LOOK AHT ME! LIZ, HE'S TRYIN' T'KEEP YOU FROM ME... SO I CAN'T TAKE Y'TO PAHRIS, SUHEE?
LIZ!
huhh
DON'T LOOK AT ME LIKE THAT.
PLEASE.
YOU SAID UGLY PEOPLE ARE BAD.
NOT IF IT'S TEMPERARY!
LIZ!
LET ME GO!

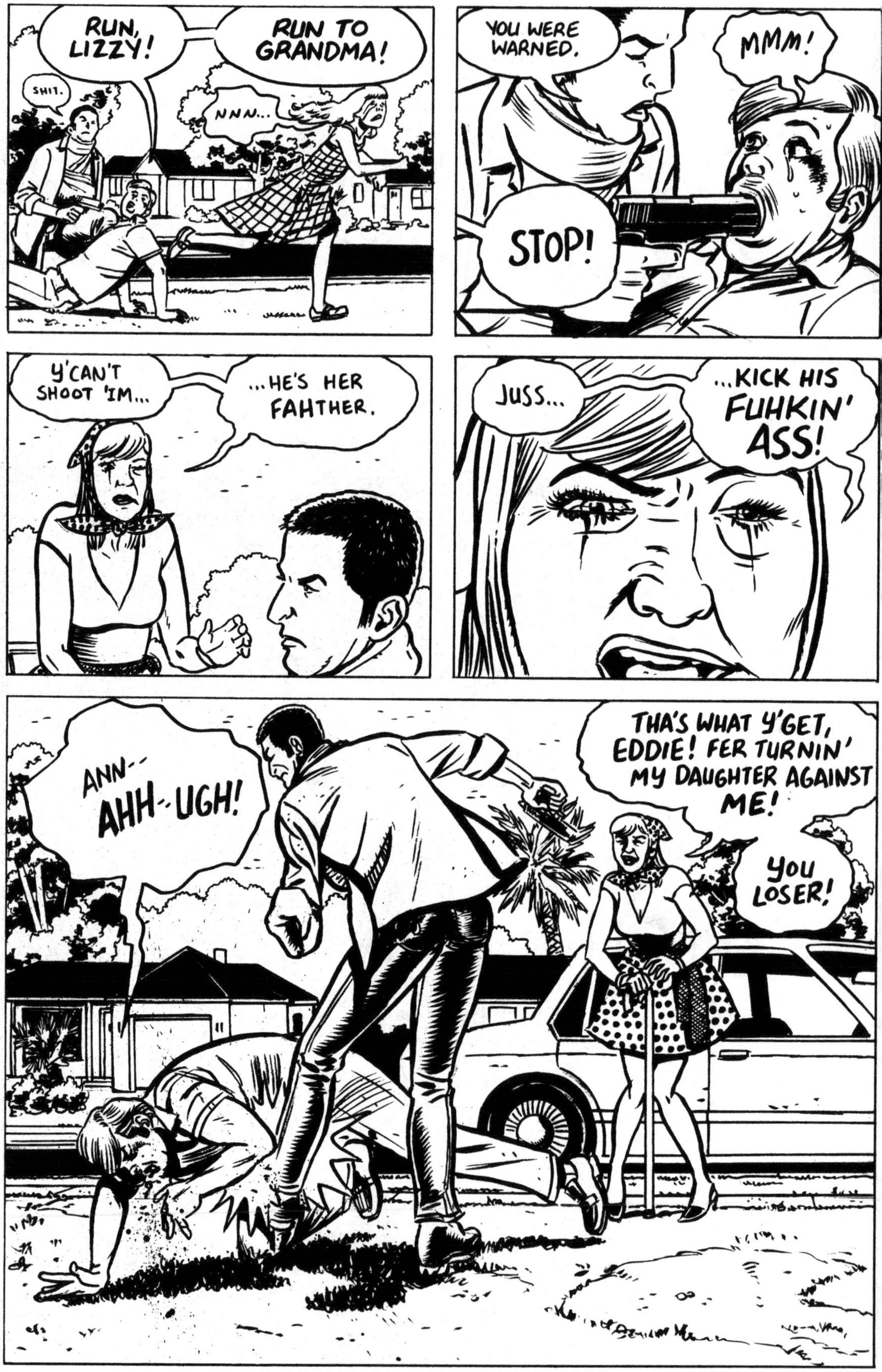
RUN, LIZZY!
RUN TO GRANDMA!
SHIT.
NNN...
YOU WERE WARNED.
MMM!
STOP!
Y'CAN'T SHOOT 'IM...
...HE'S HER FAHTHER.
JUSS...
...KICK HIS FUHKIN' ASS!
ANN--AHH--UGH!
THA'S WHAT Y'GET, EDDIE! FER TURNIN' MY DAUGHTER AGAINST ME!
YOU LOSER!

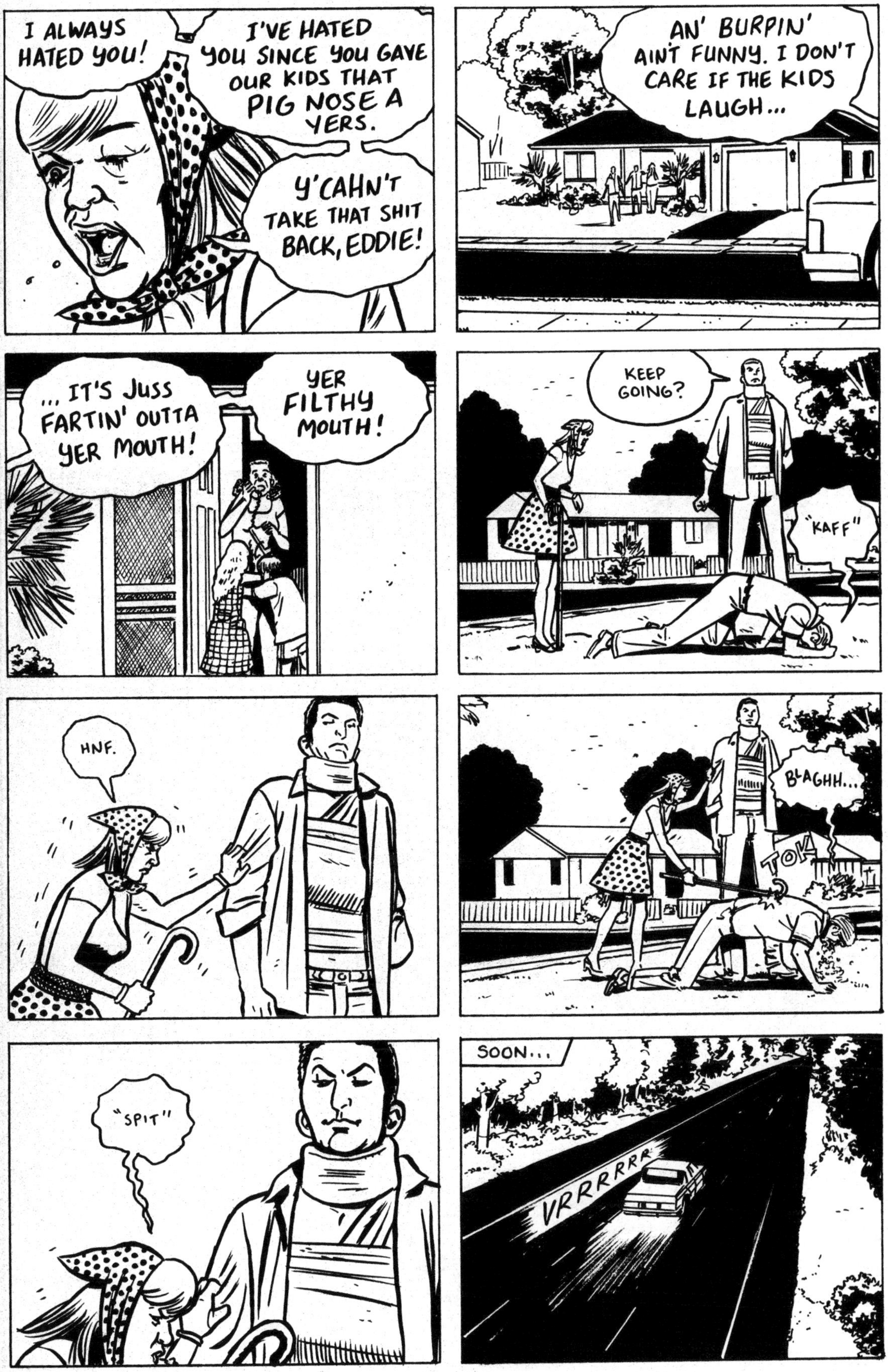
I ALWAYS HATED YOU!
I'VE HATED YOU SINCE YOU GAVE OUR KIDS THAT PIG NOSE A YERS.
Y'CAHN'T TAKE THAT SHIT BACK, EDDIE!
AN' BURPIN' AIN'T FUNNY. I DON'T CARE IF THE KIDS LAUGH...
... IT'S JUSS FARTIN' OUTTA YER MOUTH!
YER FILTHY MOUTH!
KEEP GOING?
"KAFF"
HNF.
BLAGHH...
TOK
"SPIT"
SOON...
VRRRRRRR

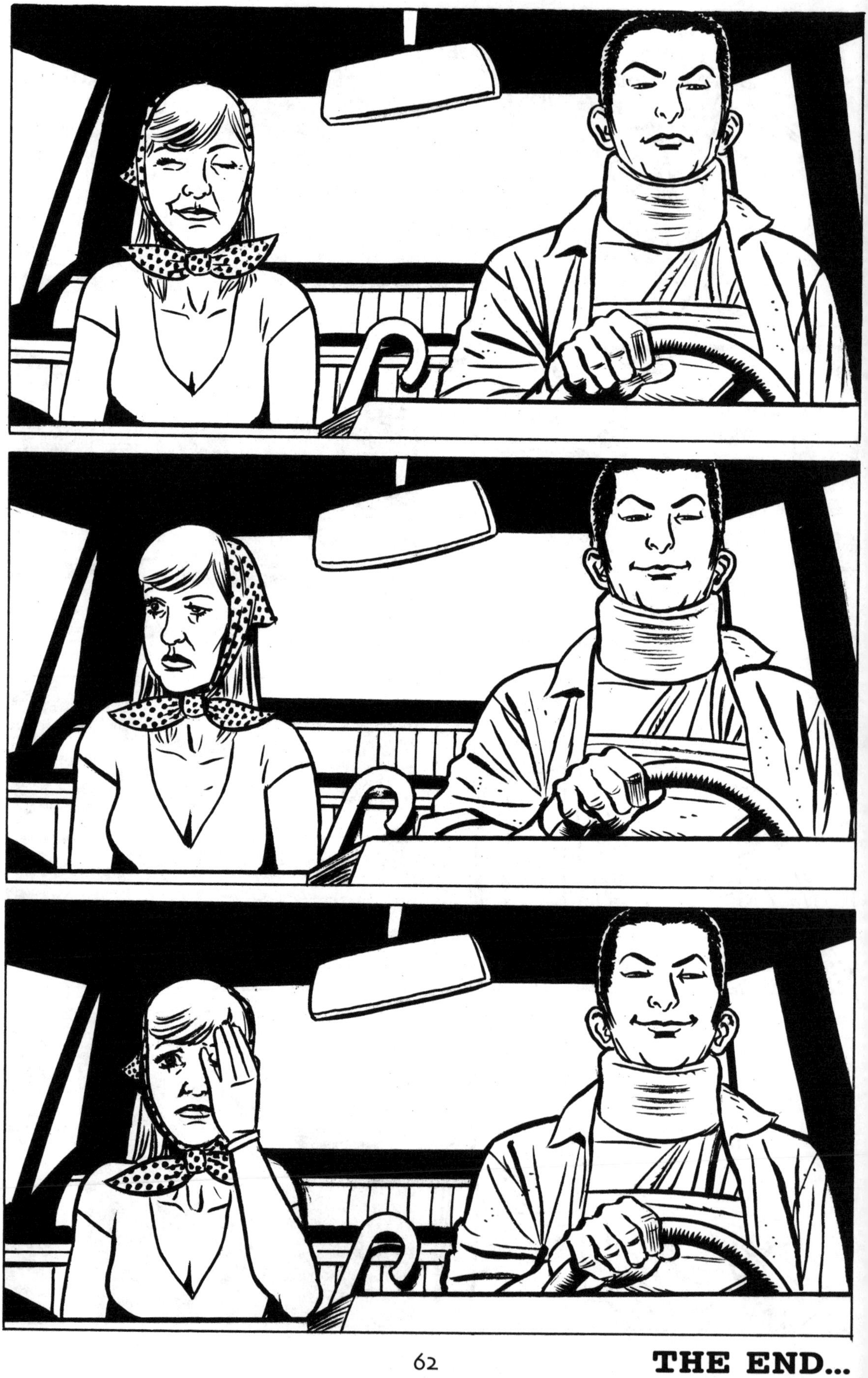

THE END...

3

"PRETTY ON THE INSIDE"

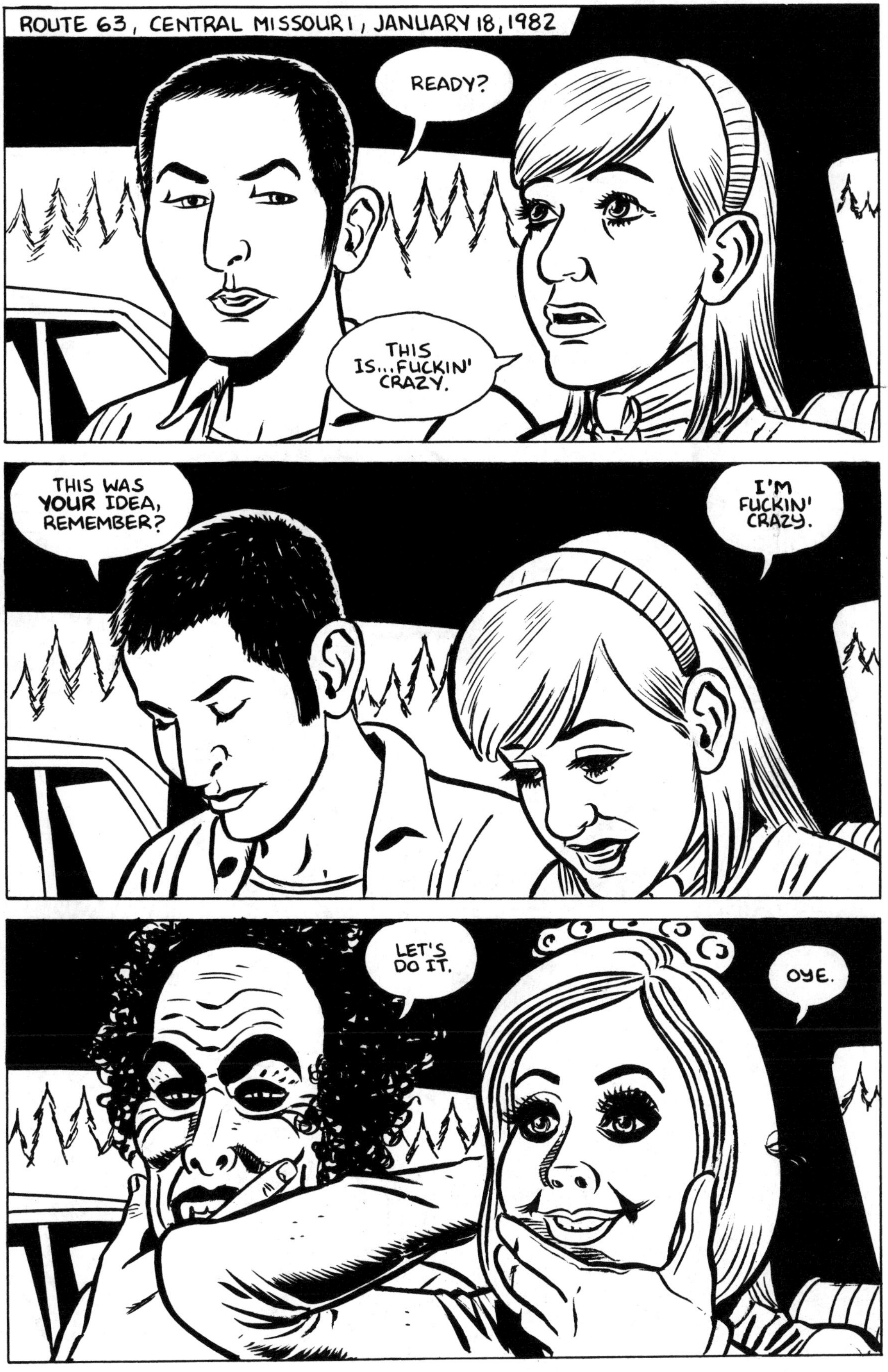
ROUTE 63, CENTRAL MISSOURI, JANUARY 18, 1982
READY?
THIS IS...FUCKIN' CRAZY.
THIS WAS YOUR IDEA, REMEMBER?
I'M FUCKIN' CRAZY.
LET'S DO IT.
OYE.

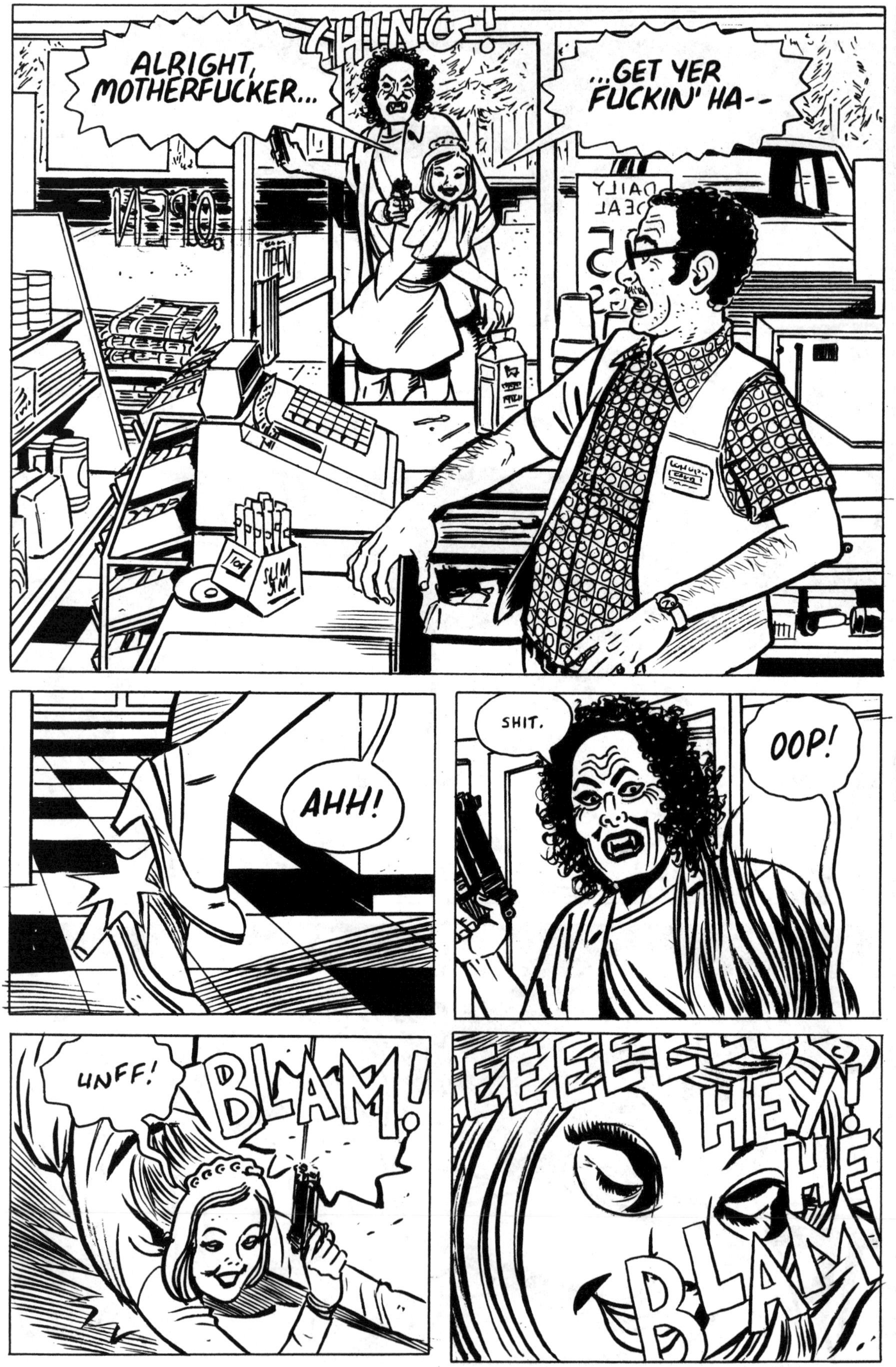
CHING!
ALRIGHT, MOTHERFUCKER...
...GET YER FUCKIN' HA--
AHH!
SHIT.
OOP!
UNFF!
BLAM!
EEEEEE
HEY!
HE
BLAM

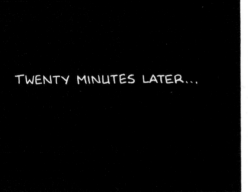

TWENTY MINUTES LATER...

THAT WAS ALMOST FUNNY.

SORRY.

OH, YEAH.

EXCEPT FOR THE PART WHERE YOU SCARED HIM SO BAD HE WENT FOR HIS GUN, AND I HAD TO BLOW HIS BRAINS OUT.

DON'T GET ME WRONG, I ENJOY KILLING AS MUCH AS THE NEXT GUY...

...BUT IF WE'RE GOING TO GO ON A COAST-TO-COAST MURDER SPREE, WE MAY GET MORE FAMOUS THAN WE'D LIKE.

I SAID I WHUS SORRY!

IT'S FINE.

3:23 A.M....

KRUNCH

RUMMMM

KRAK

KRNNCH

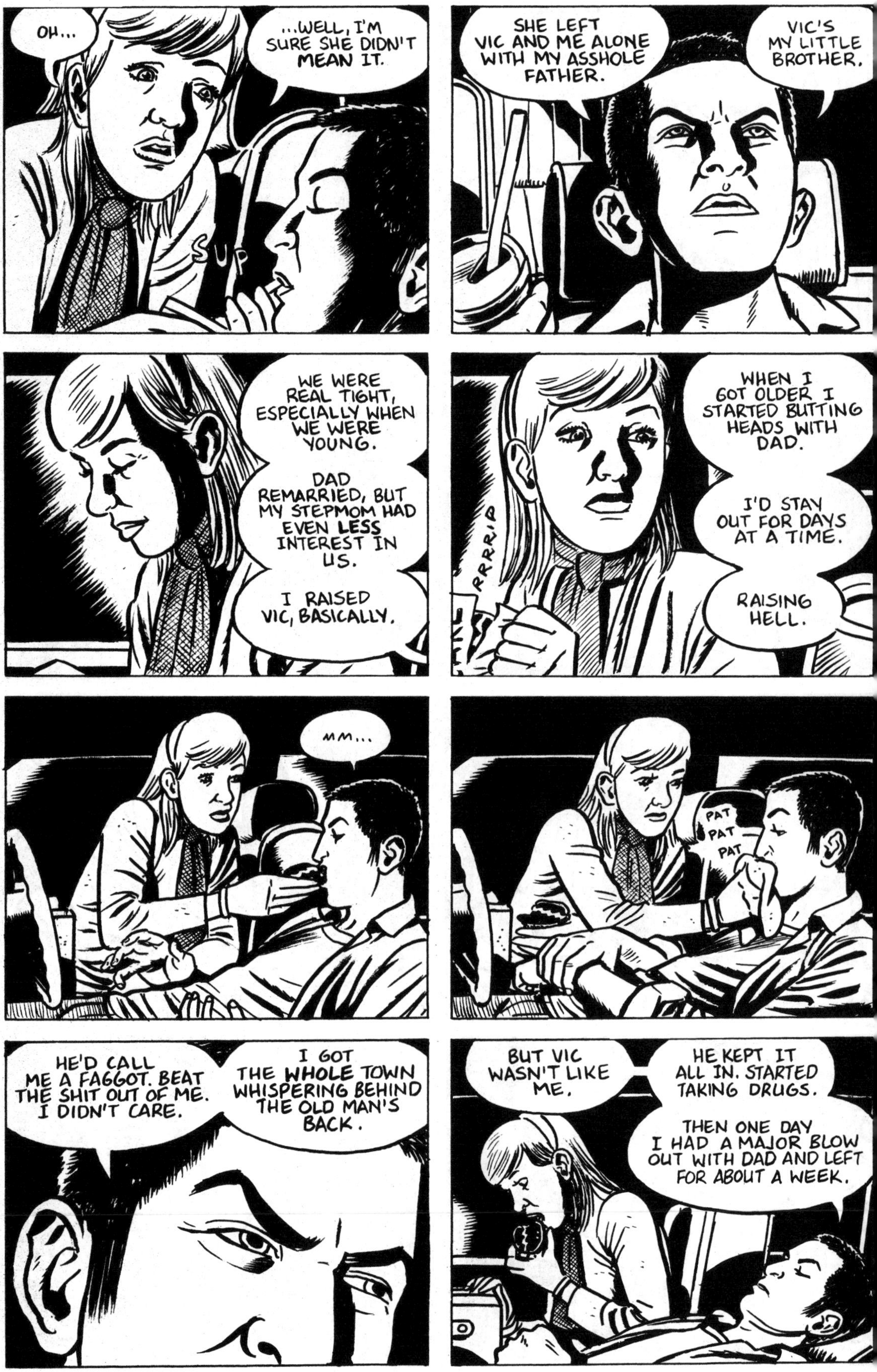
OH...
...WELL, I'M SURE SHE DIDN'T MEAN IT.
SHE LEFT VIC AND ME ALONE WITH MY ASSHOLE FATHER.
VIC'S MY LITTLE BROTHER.
WE WERE REAL TIGHT, ESPECIALLY WHEN WE WERE YOUNG.
DAD REMARRIED, BUT MY STEPMOM HAD EVEN LESS INTEREST IN US.
I RAISED VIC, BASICALLY.
WHEN I GOT OLDER I STARTED BUTTING HEADS WITH DAD.
I'D STAY OUT FOR DAYS AT A TIME.
RAISING HELL.
RRRRIP
MM...
PAT
PAT
PAT
HE'D CALL ME A FAGGOT. BEAT THE SHIT OUT OF ME. I DIDN'T CARE.
I GOT THE WHOLE TOWN WHISPERING BEHIND THE OLD MAN'S BACK.
BUT VIC WASN'T LIKE ME.
HE KEPT IT ALL IN. STARTED TAKING DRUGS.
THEN ONE DAY I HAD A MAJOR BLOW OUT WITH DAD AND LEFT FOR ABOUT A WEEK.

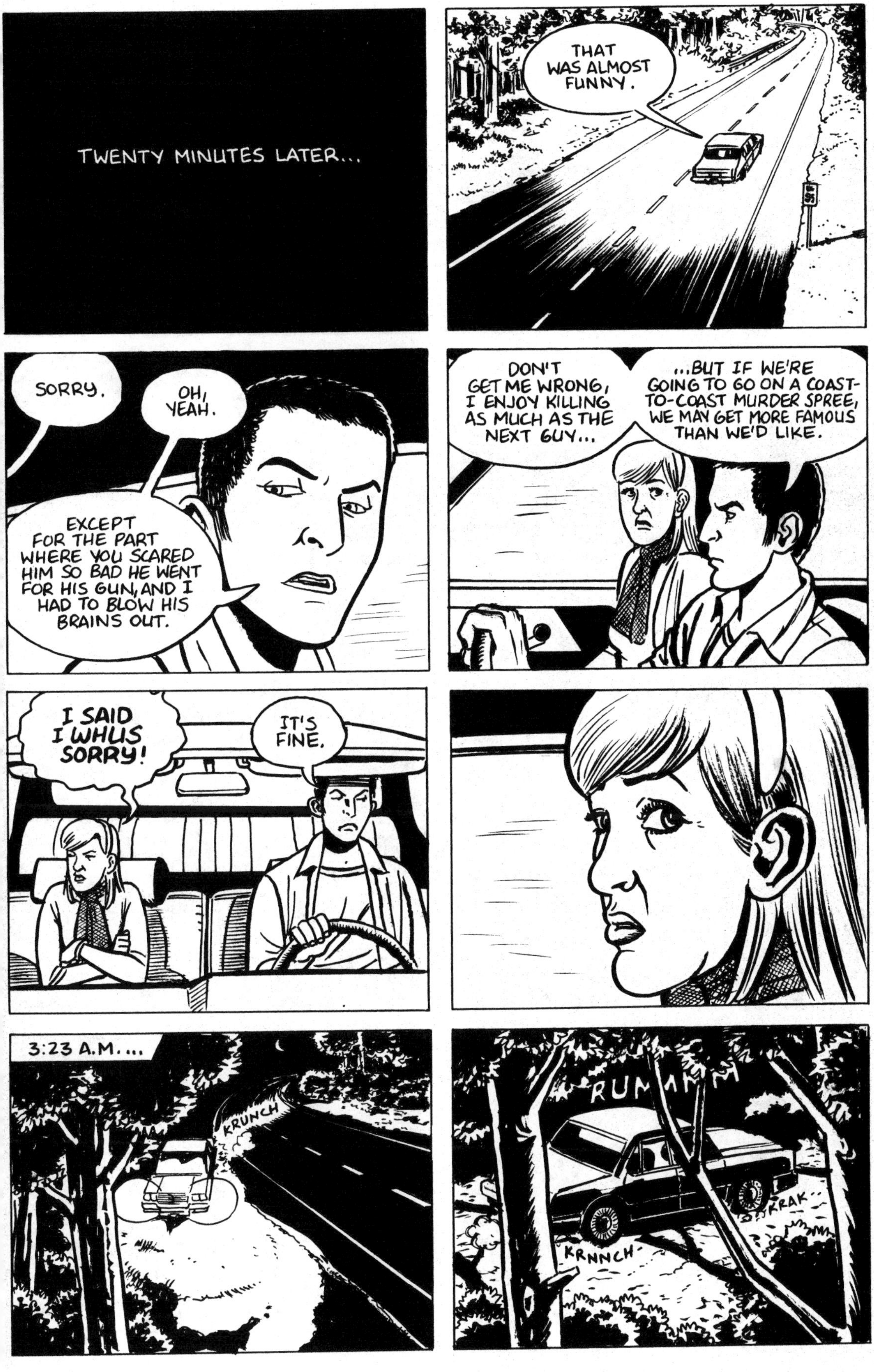
TWENTY MINUTES LATER...
THAT WAS ALMOST FUNNY.
SORRY.
OH, YEAH.
EXCEPT FOR THE PART WHERE YOU SCARED HIM SO BAD HE WENT FOR HIS GUN, AND I HAD TO BLOW HIS BRAINS OUT.
DON'T GET ME WRONG, I ENJOY KILLING AS MUCH AS THE NEXT GUY...
...BUT IF WE'RE GOING TO GO ON A COAST-TO-COAST MURDER SPREE, WE MAY GET MORE FAMOUS THAN WE'D LIKE.
I SAID I WHUS SORRY!
IT'S FINE.
3:23 A.M....
KRUNCH
KRNNCH
KRAK

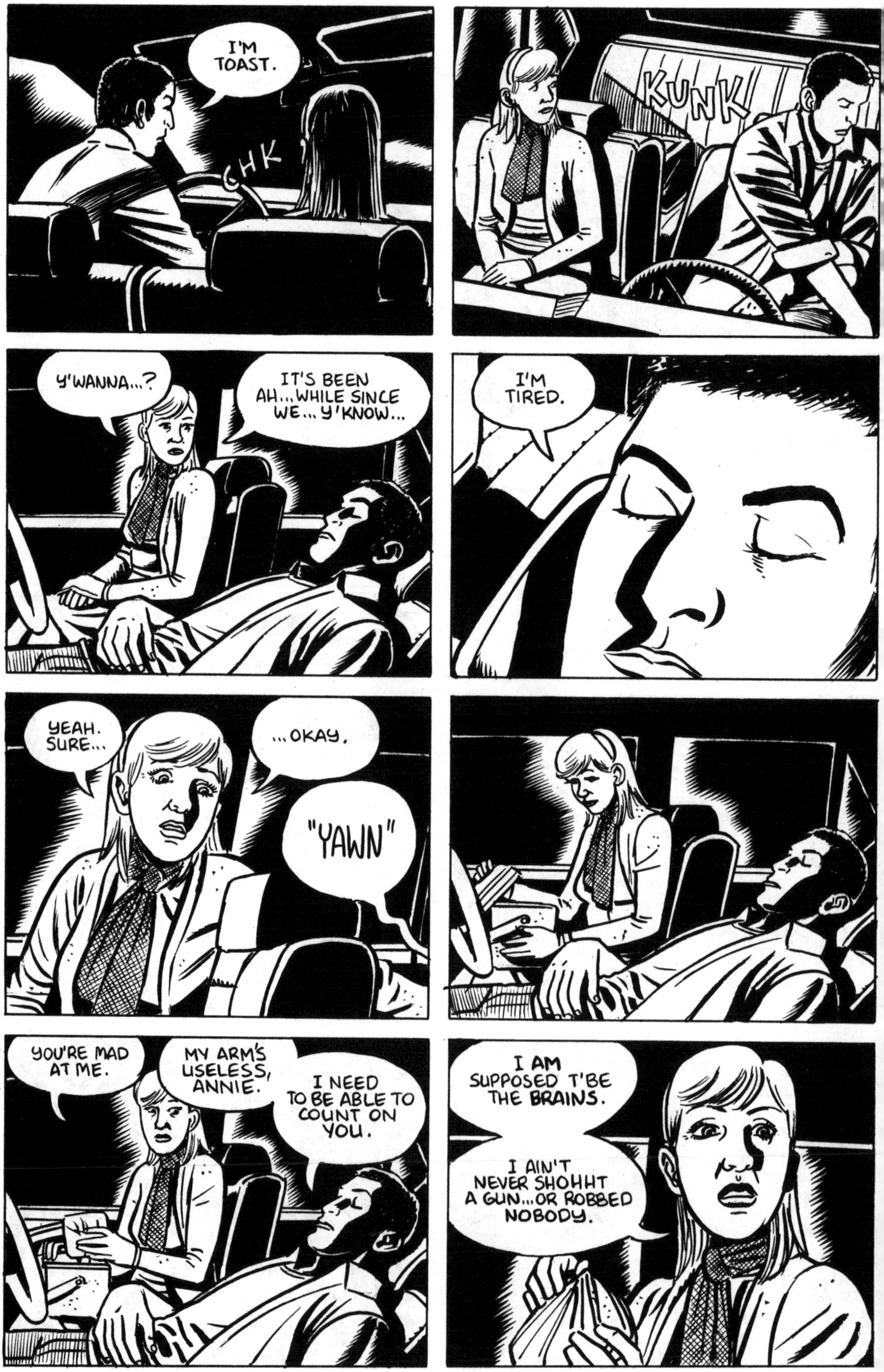

I'M TOAST.
CHK
KUNK
Y'WANNA...?
IT'S BEEN AH...WHILE SINCE WE... Y'KNOW...
I'M TIRED.
YEAH. SURE...
...OKAY.
"YAWN"
YOU'RE MAD AT ME.
MY ARM'S USELESS, ANNIE.
I NEED TO BE ABLE TO COUNT ON YOU.
I **AM** SUPPOSED T'BE THE **BRAINS**.
I AIN'T NEVER SHOHHT A GUN...OR ROBBED NOBODY.

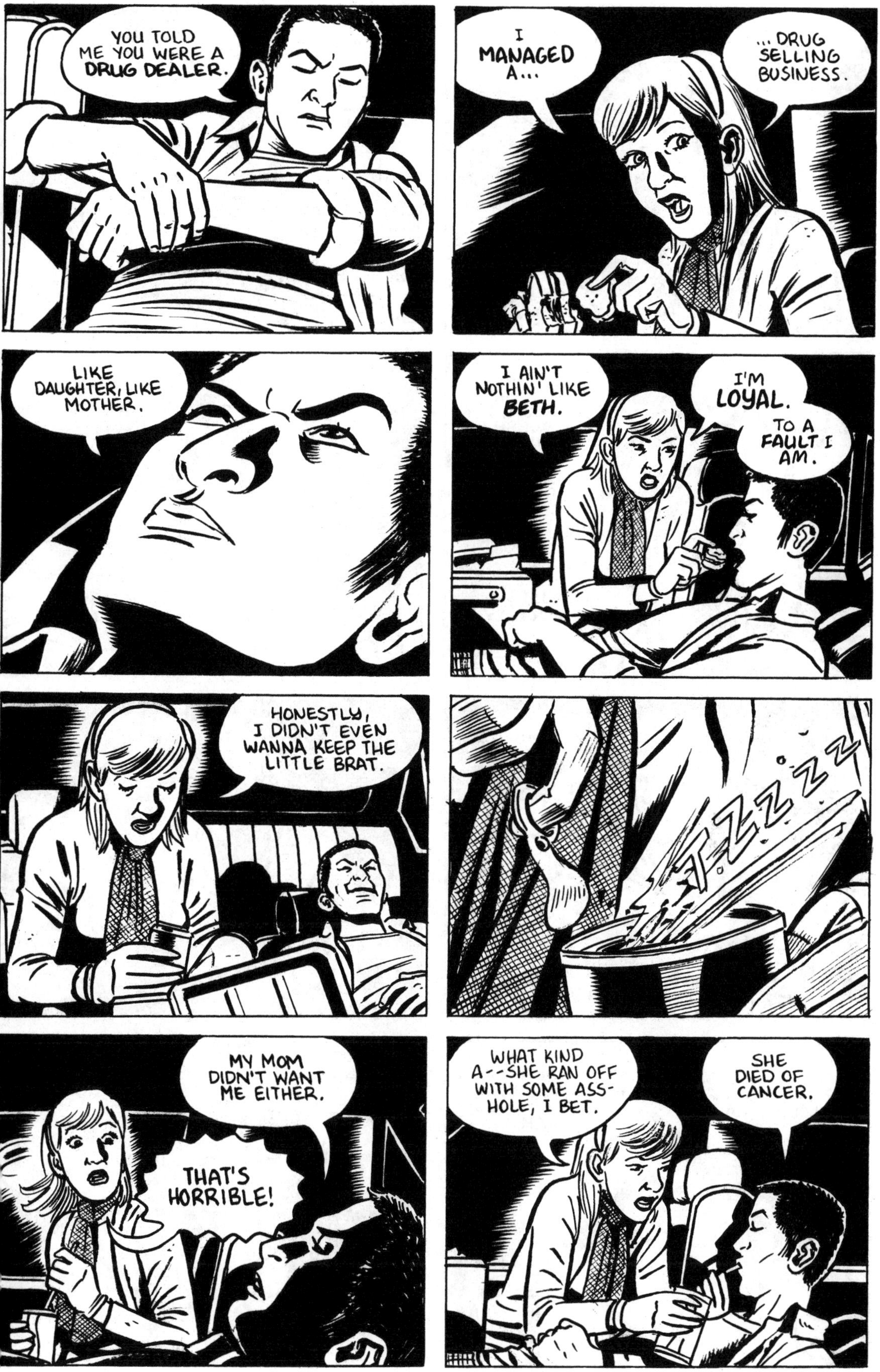
YOU TOLD ME YOU WERE A DRUG DEALER.
I MANAGED A...
...DRUG SELLING BUSINESS.
LIKE DAUGHTER, LIKE MOTHER.
I AIN'T NOTHIN' LIKE BETH.
I'M LOYAL.
TO A FAULT I AM.
HONESTLY, I DIDN'T EVEN WANNA KEEP THE LITTLE BRAT.
TZZZZZ
MY MOM DIDN'T WANT ME EITHER.
THAT'S HORRIBLE!
WHAT KIND A--SHE RAN OFF WITH SOME ASS-HOLE, I BET.
SHE DIED OF CANCER.

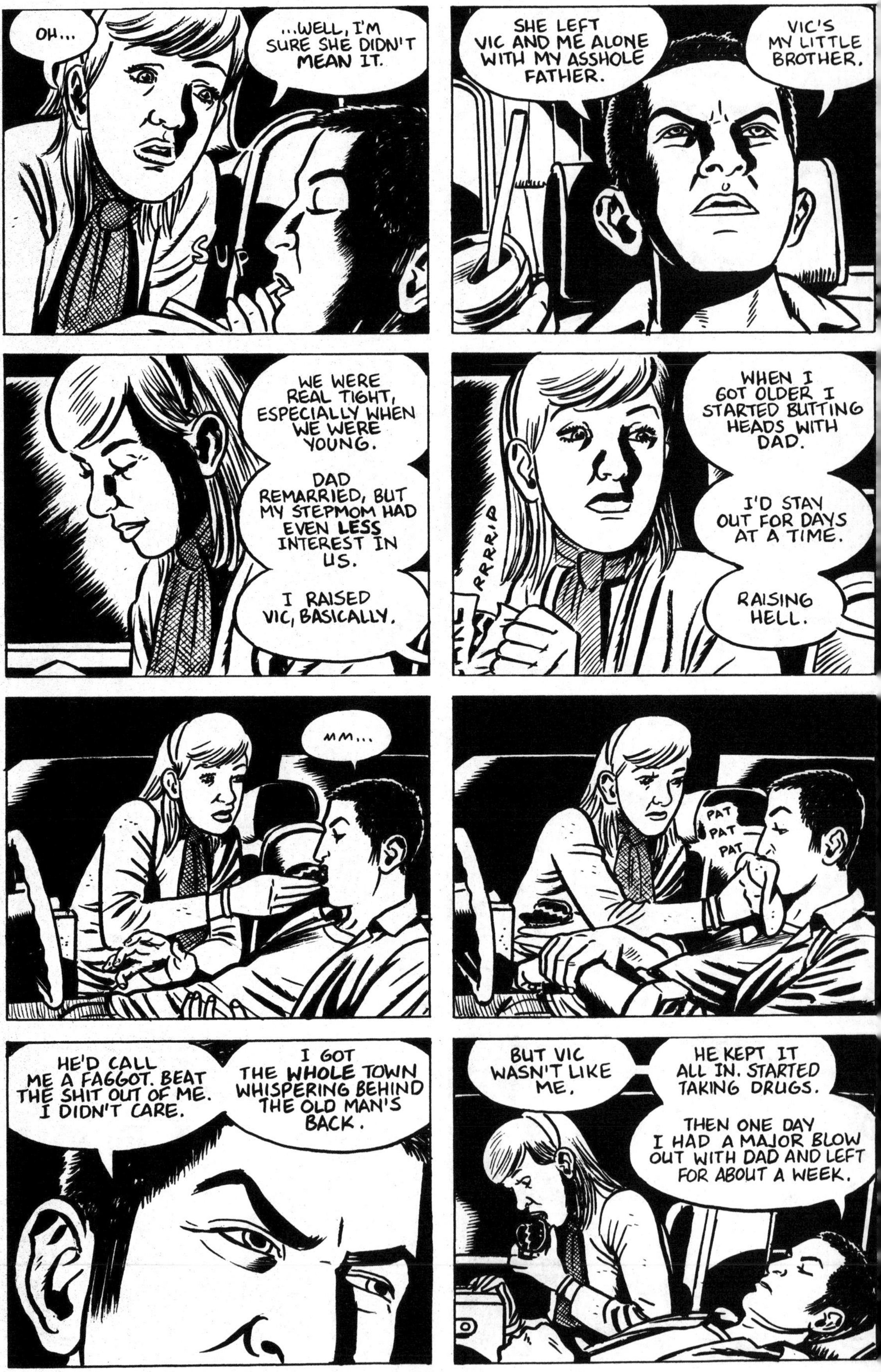

OH...
...WELL, I'M SURE SHE DIDN'T MEAN IT.
SUP
SHE LEFT VIC AND ME ALONE WITH MY ASSHOLE FATHER.
VIC'S MY LITTLE BROTHER.
WE WERE REAL TIGHT, ESPECIALLY WHEN WE WERE YOUNG.
DAD REMARRIED, BUT MY STEPMOM HAD EVEN LESS INTEREST IN US.
I RAISED VIC, BASICALLY.
RRRRIP
WHEN I GOT OLDER I STARTED BUTTING HEADS WITH DAD.
I'D STAY OUT FOR DAYS AT A TIME.
RAISING HELL.
MM...
PAT PAT PAT
HE'D CALL ME A FAGGOT. BEAT THE SHIT OUT OF ME. I DIDN'T CARE.
I GOT THE WHOLE TOWN WHISPERING BEHIND THE OLD MAN'S BACK.
BUT VIC WASN'T LIKE ME.
HE KEPT IT ALL IN. STARTED TAKING DRUGS.
THEN ONE DAY I HAD A MAJOR BLOW OUT WITH DAD AND LEFT FOR ABOUT A WEEK.

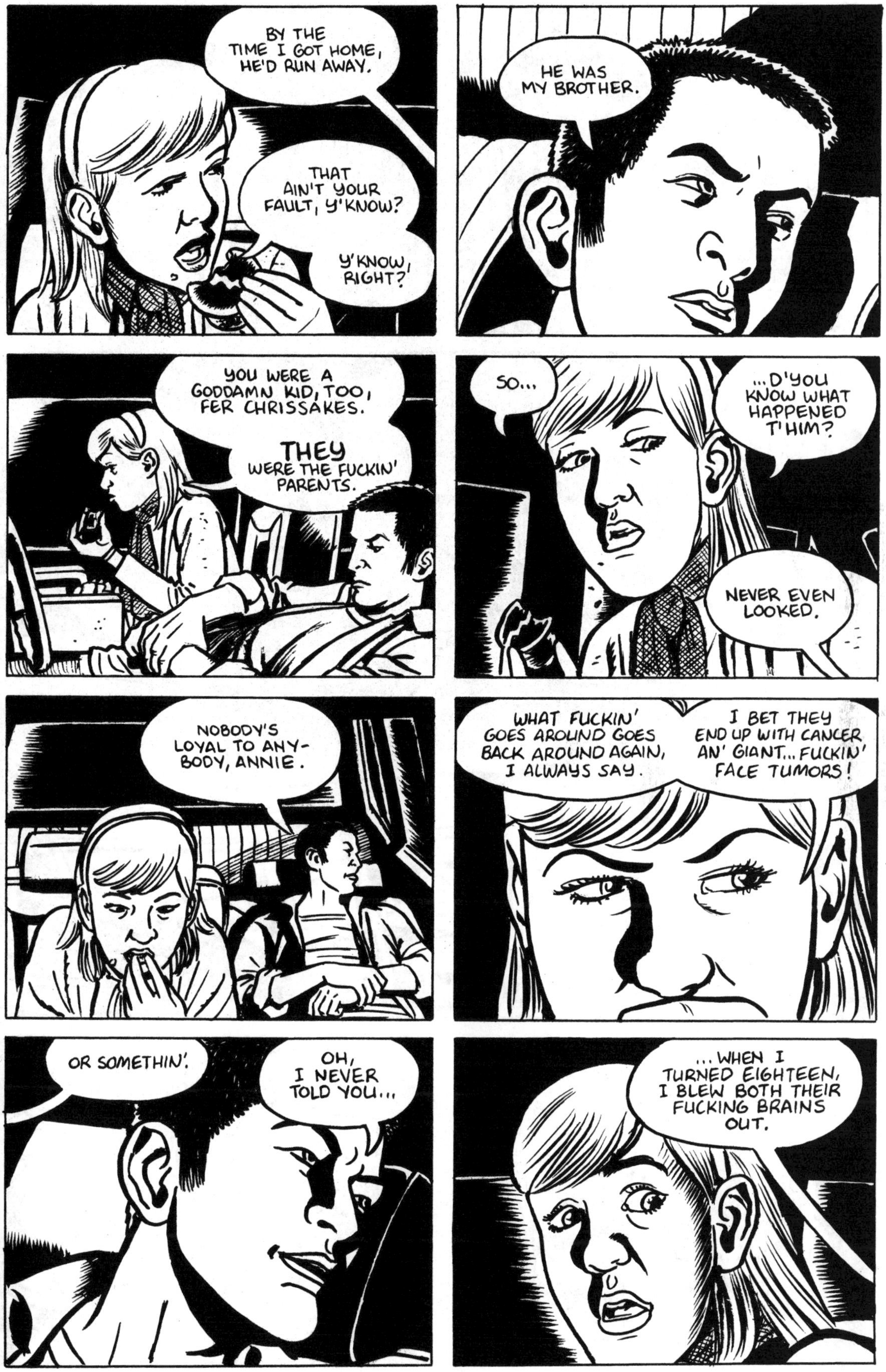
BY THE TIME I GOT HOME, HE'D RUN AWAY.
THAT AIN'T YOUR FAULT, Y'KNOW?
Y'KNOW, RIGHT?
HE WAS MY BROTHER.
YOU WERE A GODDAMN KID, TOO, FER CHRISSAKES.
THEY WERE THE FUCKIN' PARENTS.
SO...
...D'YOU KNOW WHAT HAPPENED T'HIM?
NEVER EVEN LOOKED.
NOBODY'S LOYAL TO ANY-BODY, ANNIE.
WHAT FUCKIN' GOES AROUND GOES BACK AROUND AGAIN, I ALWAYS SAY.
I BET THEY END UP WITH CANCER AN' GIANT... FUCKIN' FACE TUMORS!
OR SOMETHIN'.
OH, I NEVER TOLD YOU...
...WHEN I TURNED EIGHTEEN, I BLEW BOTH THEIR FUCKING BRAINS OUT.

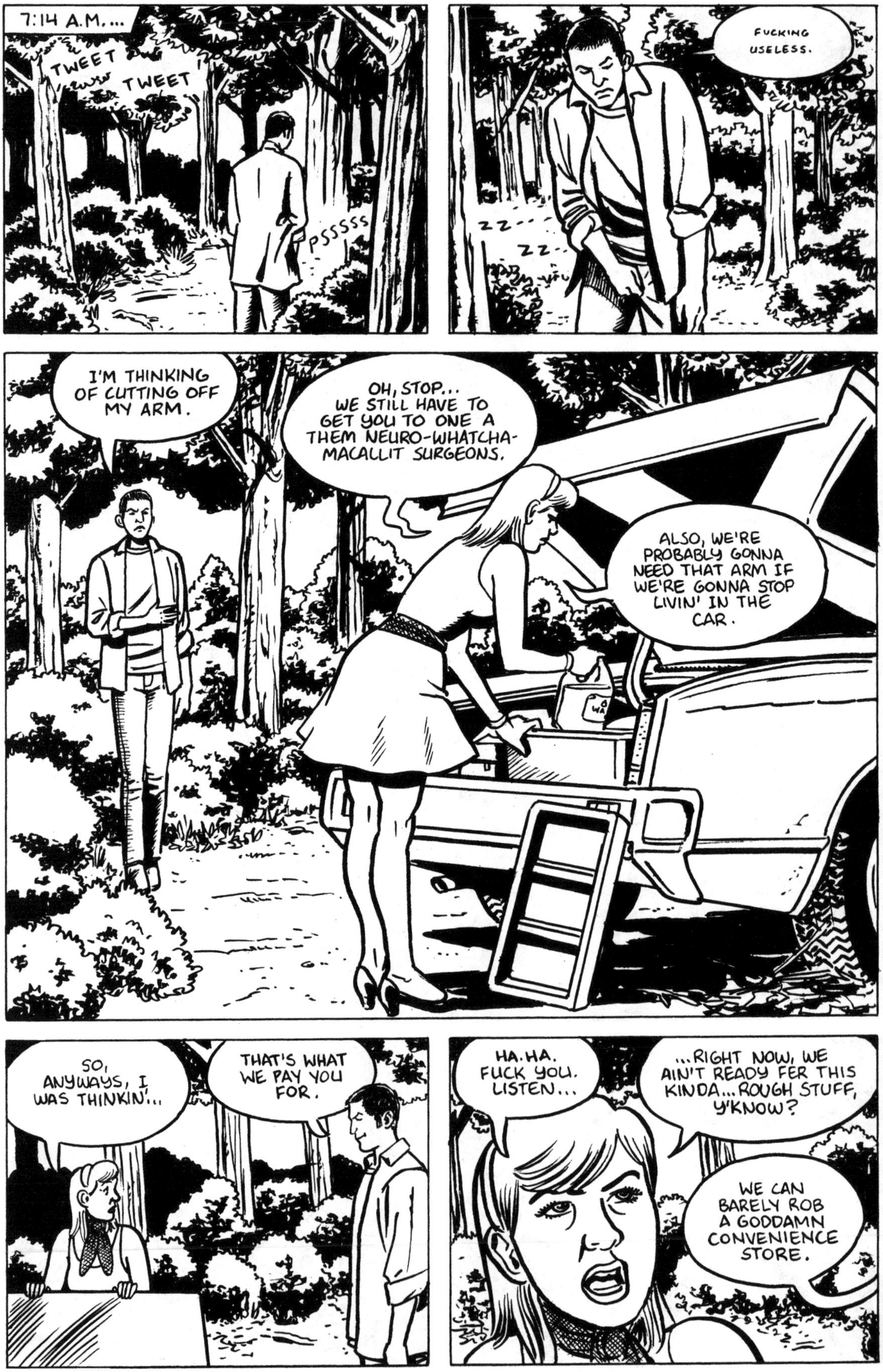
7:14 A.M. ...
TWEET
TWEET
PSSSSS
FUCKING USELESS.
ZZ
ZZ
I'M THINKING OF CUTTING OFF MY ARM.
OH, STOP... WE STILL HAVE TO GET YOU TO ONE A THEM NEURO-WHATCHA-MACALLIT SURGEONS.
ALSO, WE'RE PROBABLY GONNA NEED THAT ARM IF WE'RE GONNA STOP LIVIN' IN THE CAR.
SO, ANYWAYS, I WAS THINKIN'...
THAT'S WHAT WE PAY YOU FOR.
HA. HA. FUCK YOU. LISTEN...
...RIGHT NOW, WE AIN'T READY FER THIS KINDA... ROUGH STUFF, Y'KNOW?
WE CAN BARELY ROB A GODDAMN CONVENIENCE STORE.

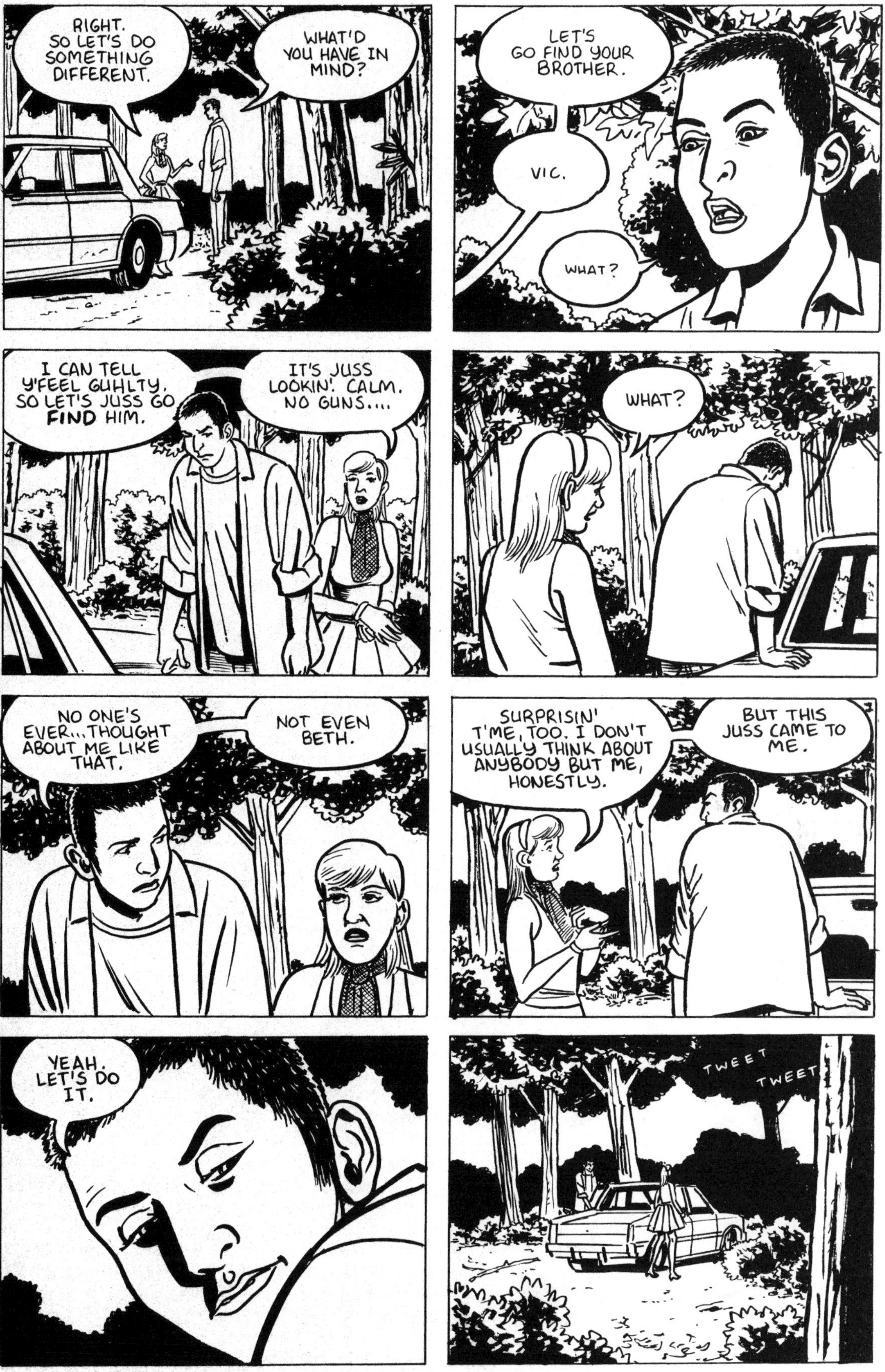
RIGHT. SO LET'S DO SOMETHING DIFFERENT.
WHAT'D YOU HAVE IN MIND?
LET'S GO FIND YOUR BROTHER.
VIC.
WHAT?
I CAN TELL Y'FEEL GUHLTY. SO LET'S JUSS GO **FIND** HIM.
IT'S JUSS LOOKIN'. CALM. NO GUNS....
WHAT?
NO ONE'S EVER...THOUGHT ABOUT ME LIKE THAT.
NOT EVEN BETH.
SURPRISIN' T'ME, TOO. I DON'T USUALLY THINK ABOUT ANYBODY BUT ME, HONESTLY.
BUT THIS JUSS CAME TO ME.
YEAH. LET'S DO IT.
TWEET
TWEET

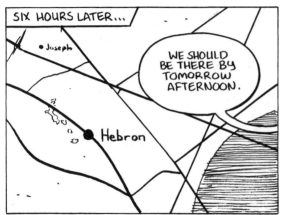

SIX HOURS LATER...

Joseph

Hebron

WE SHOULD BE THERE BY TOMORROW AFTERNOON.

FOR ALL I KNOW, VIC'S BACK HOME WITH A WIFE AND SIX KIDS.

YOU'VE NEVER EVEN CHECKED?

ONCE I STARTED DOWN THIS ROAD, DIDN'T SEEM TO BE MUCH POINT.

USA MAP

SO... WHAT'S HEBRON LIKE?

ACTUALLY, WE LIVED IN AN EVEN SMALLER DICKWATER TOWN...

...CALLED JOSEPH.

MAIN STREET ISN'T EVEN PAVED.

THE GENERAL STORE'S ALSO THE POST OFFICE AND BUS STATION AND FEED STORE.

WE SHARED A SCHOOL WITH THE NEXT SHITHOLE OVER.

MY AUNT OWNS THE ONLY RESTAURANT, THE COUNTRY KITCHEN.

WE HAVE TWO CHURCHES AND-- I LOVE THIS-- THREE BARS.

AND... THAT'S ABOUT IT.

FUCK POPPIN' YER PARENTS.

AFTER EIGHTEEN YEARS OF THAT, HOW DID YOU NOT SHOOT YERSELF.

2:19 A.M. ...

MOTEL

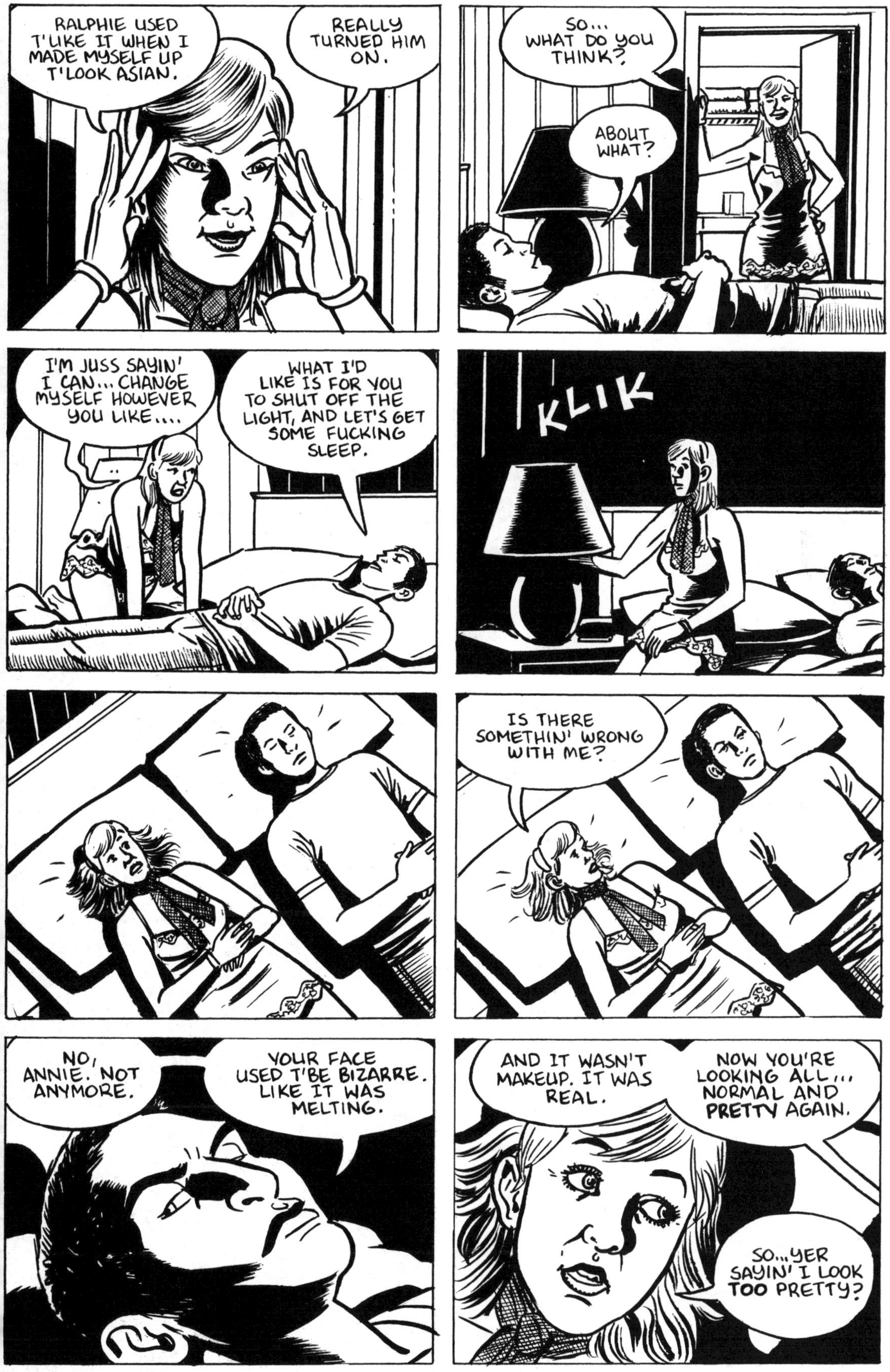

RALPHIE USED T'LIKE IT WHEN I MADE MYSELF UP T'LOOK ASIAN.
REALLY TURNED HIM ON.
SO... WHAT DO YOU THINK?
ABOUT WHAT?
I'M JUSS SAYIN' I CAN... CHANGE MYSELF HOWEVER YOU LIKE....
WHAT I'D LIKE IS FOR YOU TO SHUT OFF THE LIGHT, AND LET'S GET SOME FUCKING SLEEP.
KLIK
IS THERE SOMETHIN' WRONG WITH ME?
NO, ANNIE. NOT ANYMORE.
YOUR FACE USED T'BE BIZARRE. LIKE IT WAS MELTING.
AND IT WASN'T MAKEUP. IT WAS REAL.
NOW YOU'RE LOOKING ALL... NORMAL AND PRETTY AGAIN.
SO... YER SAYIN' I LOOK TOO PRETTY?

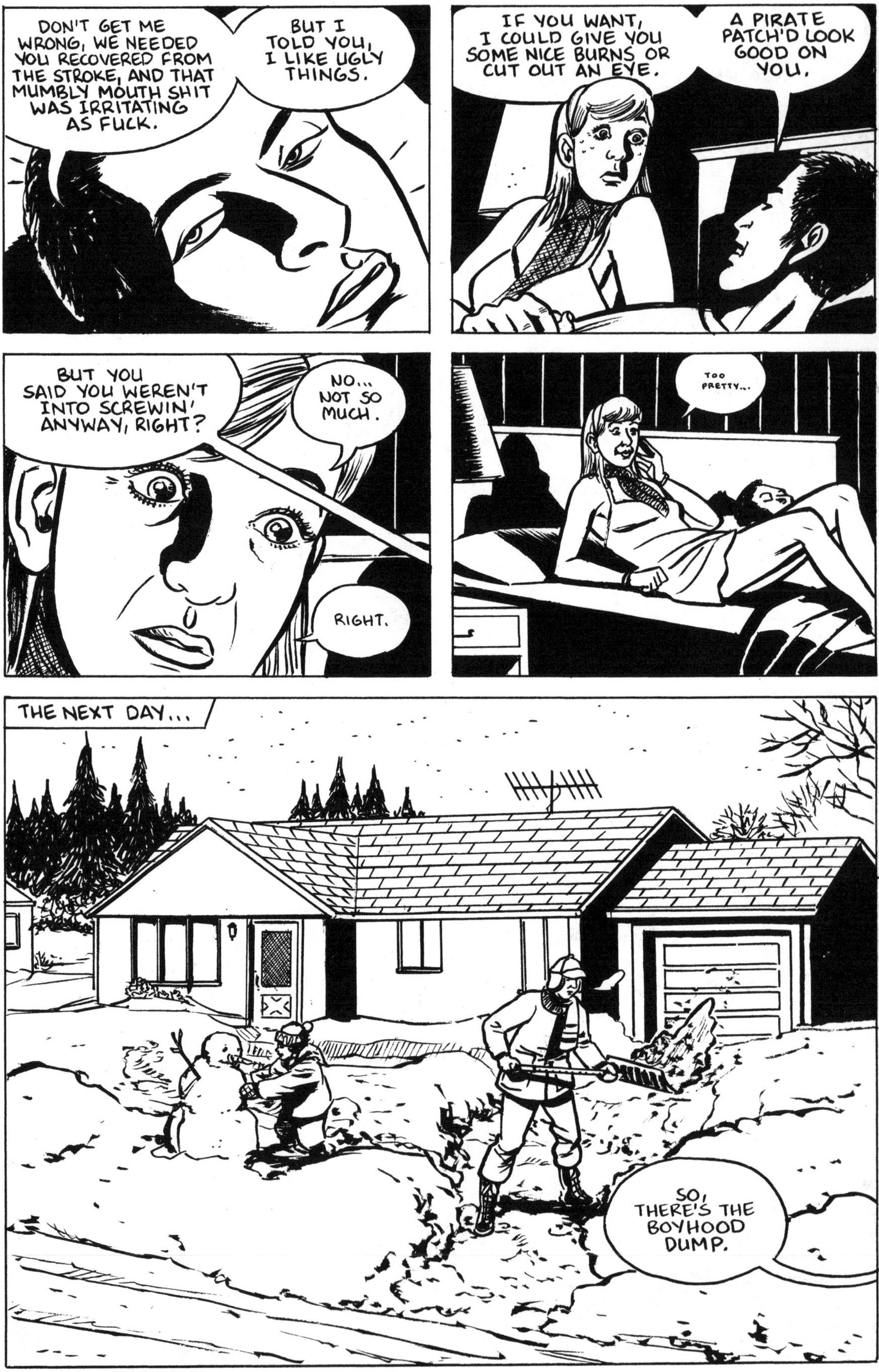
DON'T GET ME WRONG, WE NEEDED YOU RECOVERED FROM THE STROKE, AND THAT MUMBLY MOUTH SHIT WAS IRRITATING AS FUCK.
BUT I TOLD YOU, I LIKE UGLY THINGS.
IF YOU WANT, I COULD GIVE YOU SOME NICE BURNS OR CUT OUT AN EYE.
A PIRATE PATCH'D LOOK GOOD ON YOU.
BUT YOU SAID YOU WEREN'T INTO SCREWIN' ANYWAY, RIGHT?
NO... NOT SO MUCH.
RIGHT.
TOO PRETTY...
THE NEXT DAY...
SO, THERE'S THE BOYHOOD DUMP.

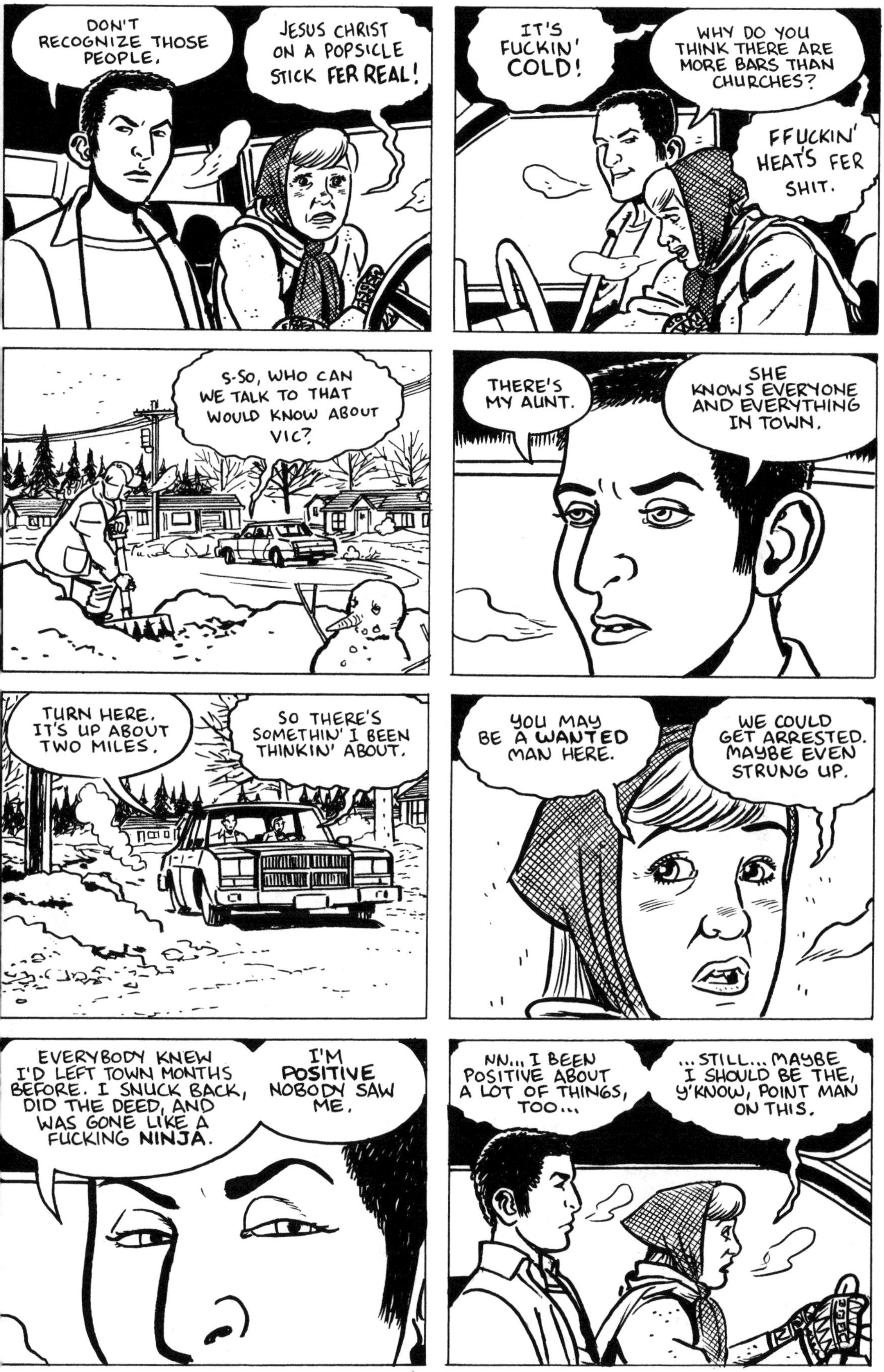
DON'T RECOGNIZE THOSE PEOPLE.
JESUS CHRIST ON A POPSICLE STICK FER REAL!
IT'S FUCKIN' COLD!
WHY DO YOU THINK THERE ARE MORE BARS THAN CHURCHES?
FFUCKIN' HEAT'S FER SHIT.
S-SO, WHO CAN WE TALK TO THAT WOULD KNOW ABOUT VIC?
THERE'S MY AUNT.
SHE KNOWS EVERYONE AND EVERYTHING IN TOWN.
TURN HERE. IT'S UP ABOUT TWO MILES.
SO THERE'S SOMETHIN' I BEEN THINKIN' ABOUT.
YOU MAY BE A WANTED MAN HERE.
WE COULD GET ARRESTED. MAYBE EVEN STRUNG UP.
EVERYBODY KNEW I'D LEFT TOWN MONTHS BEFORE. I SNUCK BACK, DID THE DEED, AND WAS GONE LIKE A FUCKING NINJA.
I'M POSITIVE NOBODY SAW ME.
NN... I BEEN POSITIVE ABOUT A LOT OF THINGS, TOO...
...STILL... MAYBE I SHOULD BE THE, Y'KNOW, POINT MAN ON THIS.

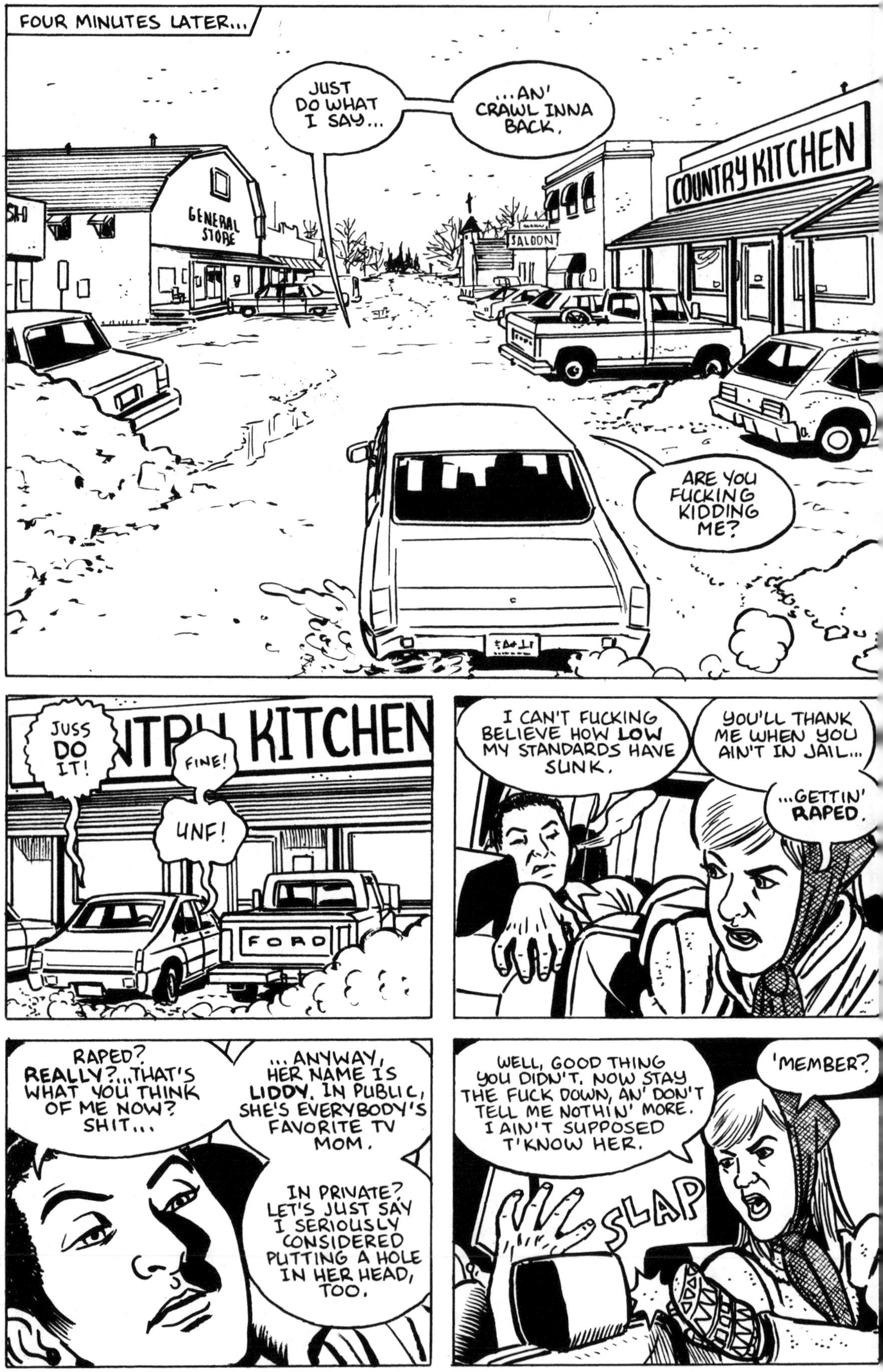
FOUR MINUTES LATER...
JUST DO WHAT I SAY...
...AN' CRAWL INNA BACK.
GENERAL STORE
SALOON
COUNTRY KITCHEN
ARE YOU FUCKING KIDDING ME?
JUSS DO IT!
FINE!
UNF!
FORD
I CAN'T FUCKING BELIEVE HOW LOW MY STANDARDS HAVE SUNK.
YOU'LL THANK ME WHEN YOU AIN'T IN JAIL...
...GETTIN' RAPED.
RAPED? REALLY?...THAT'S WHAT YOU THINK OF ME NOW? SHIT...
...ANYWAY, HER NAME IS LIDDY. IN PUBLIC, SHE'S EVERYBODY'S FAVORITE TV MOM.
IN PRIVATE? LET'S JUST SAY I SERIOUSLY CONSIDERED PUTTING A HOLE IN HER HEAD, TOO.
WELL, GOOD THING YOU DIDN'T. NOW STAY THE FUCK DOWN, AN' DON'T TELL ME NOTHIN' MORE. I AIN'T SUPPOSED T'KNOW HER.
'MEMBER?
SLAP

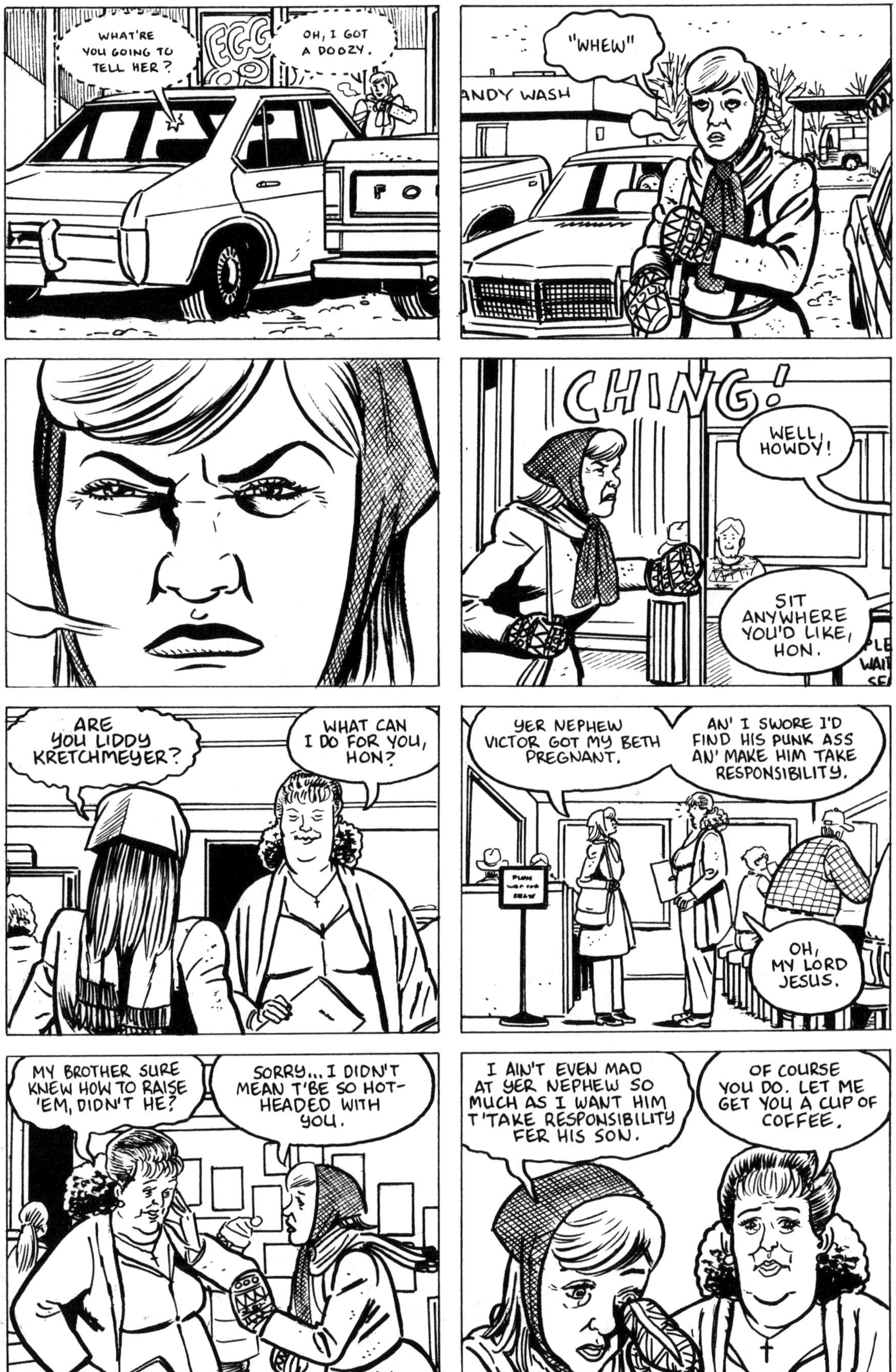
WHAT'RE YOU GOING TO TELL HER?
OH, I GOT A DOOZY.
EGG
"WHEW"
ANDY WASH
CHING!
WELL, HOWDY!
SIT ANYWHERE YOU'D LIKE, HON.
ARE YOU LIDDY KRETCHMEYER?
WHAT CAN I DO FOR YOU, HON?
YER NEPHEW VICTOR GOT MY BETH PREGNANT.
AN' I SWORE I'D FIND HIS PUNK ASS AN' MAKE HIM TAKE RESPONSIBILITY.
OH, MY LORD JESUS.
MY BROTHER SURE KNEW HOW TO RAISE 'EM, DIDN'T HE?
SORRY... I DIDN'T MEAN T'BE SO HOT-HEADED WITH YOU.
I AIN'T EVEN MAD AT YER NEPHEW SO MUCH AS I WANT HIM T'TAKE RESPONSIBILITY FER HIS SON.
OF COURSE YOU DO. LET ME GET YOU A CUP OF COFFEE.

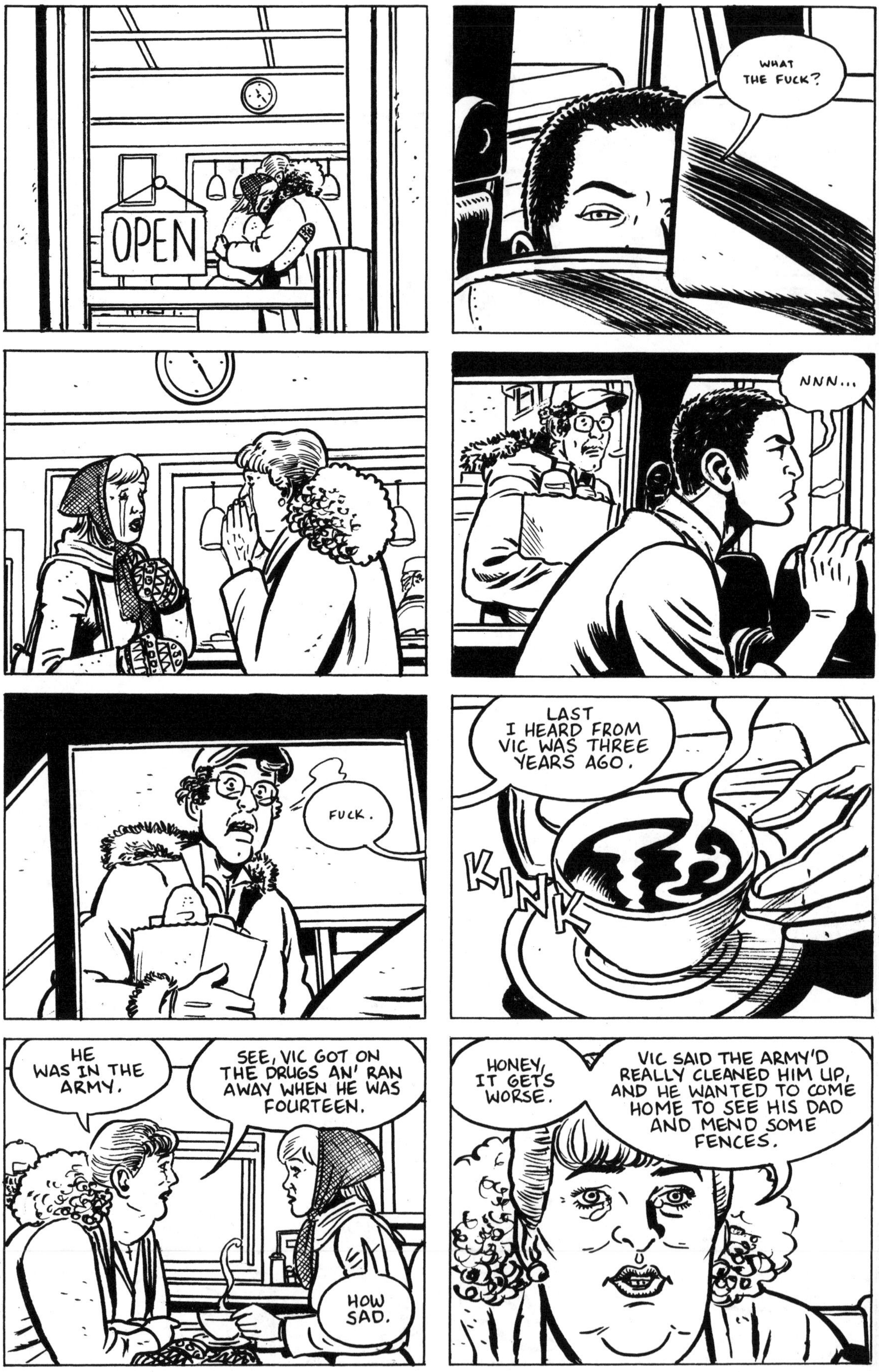
OPEN
WHAT THE FUCK?
NNN...
FUCK.
LAST I HEARD FROM VIC WAS THREE YEARS AGO.
KINK
HE WAS IN THE ARMY.
SEE, VIC GOT ON THE DRUGS AN' RAN AWAY WHEN HE WAS FOURTEEN.
HOW SAD.
HONEY, IT GETS WORSE.
VIC SAID THE ARMY'D REALLY CLEANED HIM UP, AND HE WANTED TO COME HOME TO SEE HIS DAD AND MEND SOME FENCES.

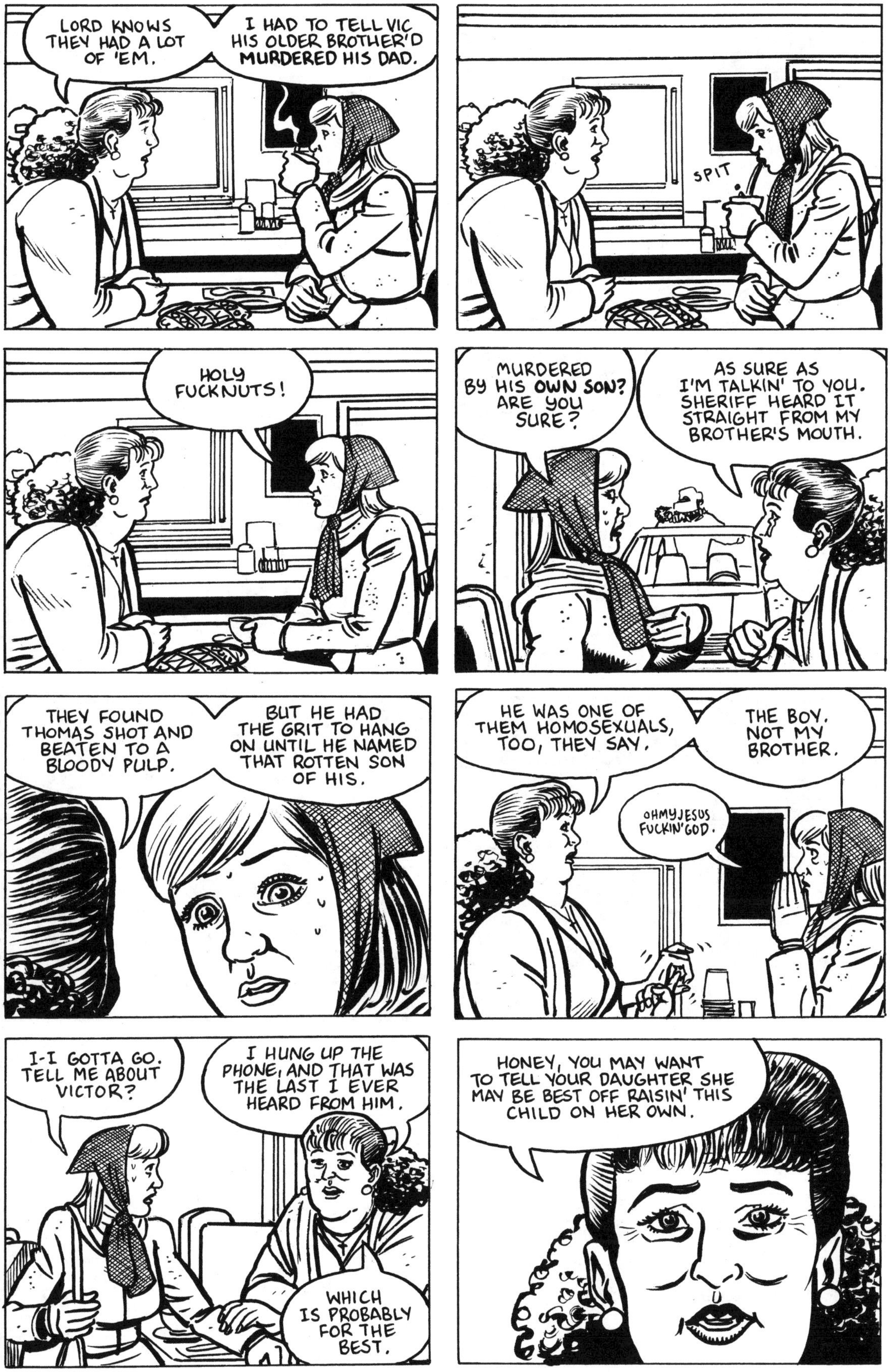
LORD KNOWS THEY HAD A LOT OF 'EM.
I HAD TO TELL VIC HIS OLDER BROTHER'D **MURDERED** HIS DAD.
SPIT
HOLY FUCKNUTS!
MURDERED BY HIS **OWN SON**? ARE YOU SURE?
AS SURE AS I'M TALKIN' TO YOU. SHERIFF HEARD IT STRAIGHT FROM MY BROTHER'S MOUTH.
THEY FOUND THOMAS SHOT AND BEATEN TO A BLOODY PULP.
BUT HE HAD THE GRIT TO HANG ON UNTIL HE NAMED THAT ROTTEN SON OF HIS.
HE WAS ONE OF THEM HOMOSEXUALS, TOO, THEY SAY.
THE BOY. NOT MY BROTHER.
OHMYJESUS FUCKIN'GOD.
I-I GOTTA GO. TELL ME ABOUT VICTOR?
I HUNG UP THE PHONE, AND THAT WAS THE LAST I EVER HEARD FROM HIM.
WHICH IS PROBABLY FOR THE BEST.
HONEY, YOU MAY WANT TO TELL YOUR DAUGHTER SHE MAY BE BEST OFF RAISIN' THIS CHILD ON HER OWN.

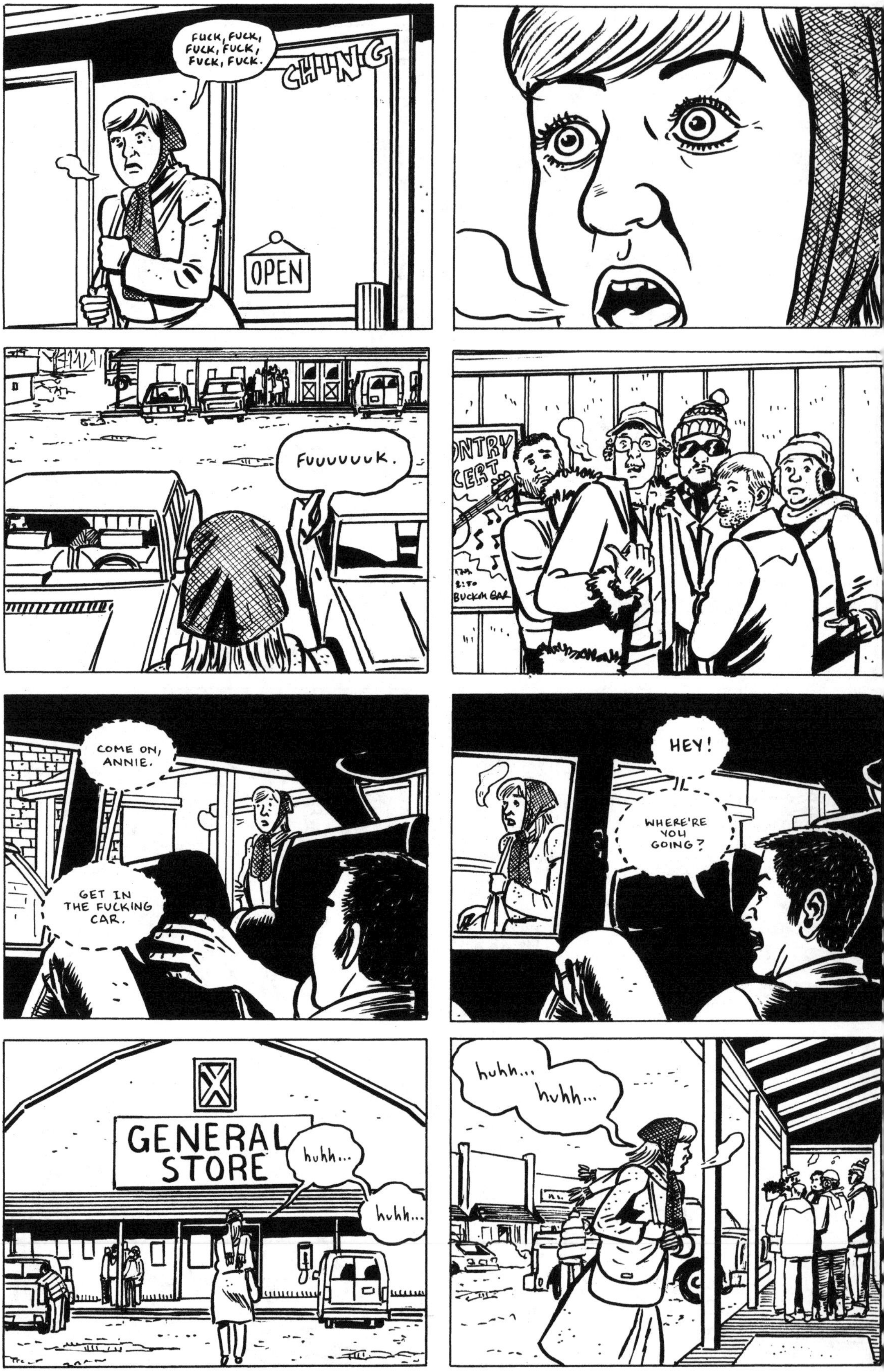
FUCK, FUCK, FUCK, FUCK, FUCK, FUCK.
CHING
OPEN
FUUUUUUK.
COME ON, ANNIE.
GET IN THE FUCKING CAR.
HEY!
WHERE'RE YOU GOING?
GENERAL STORE
huhh...
huhh...
huhh...
huhh...

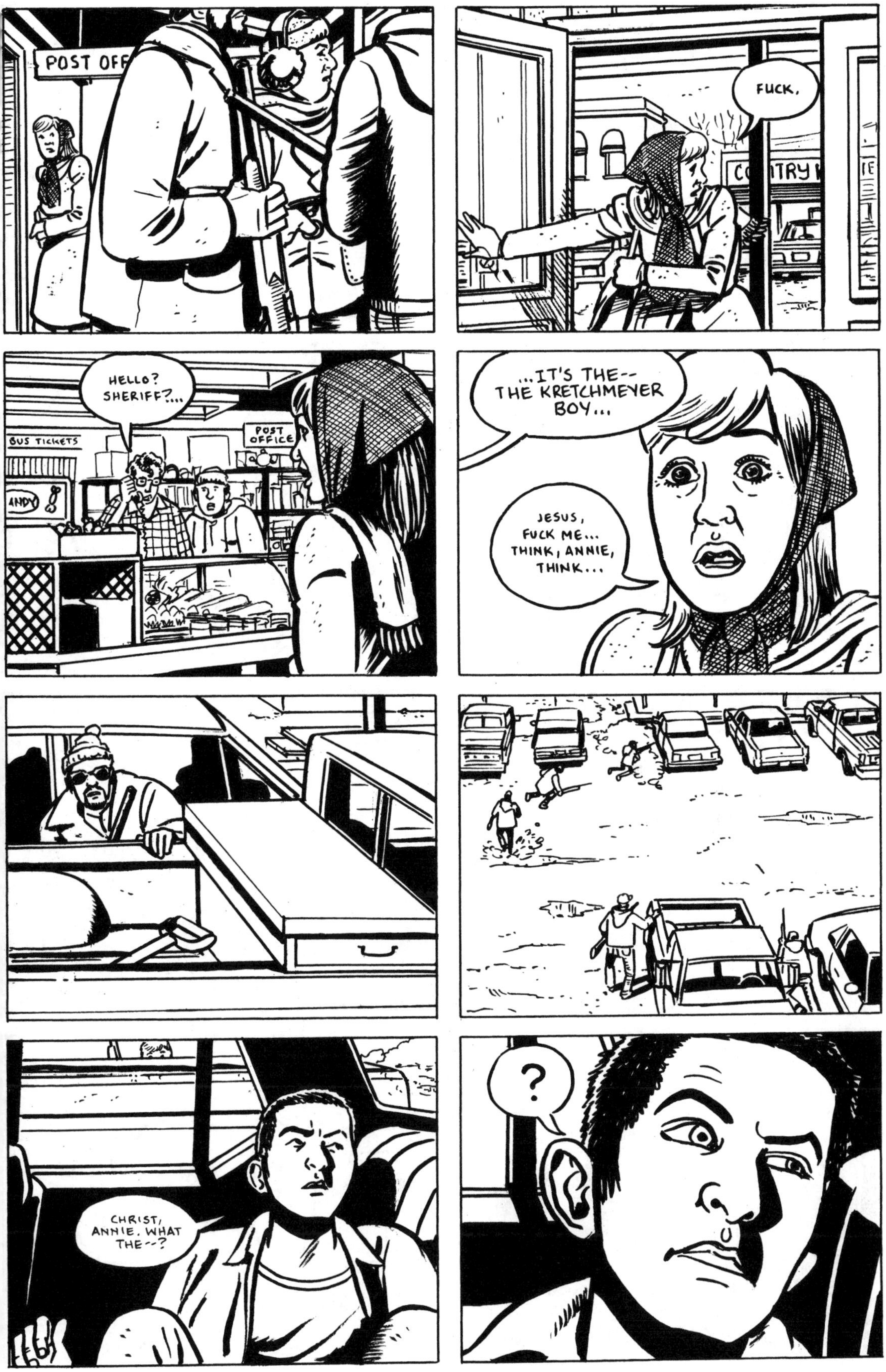
POST OFF
FUCK.
CO TRY
HELLO? SHERIFF?...
BUS TICKETS
POST OFFICE
...IT'S THE-- THE KRETCHMEYER BOY...
JESUS, FUCK ME... THINK, ANNIE, THINK...
CHRIST, ANNIE. WHAT THE--?
?

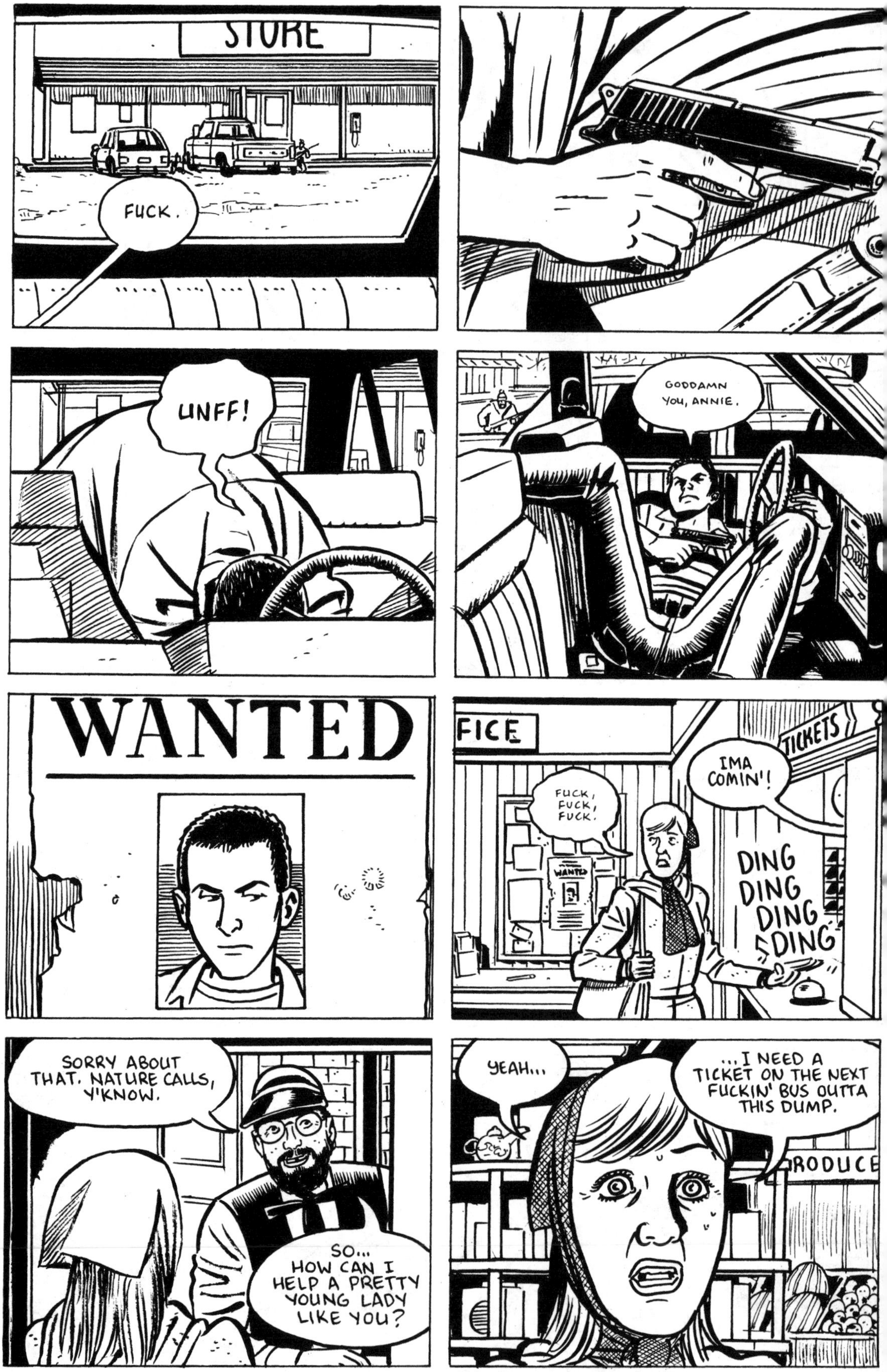
STORE
FUCK.
UNFF!
GODDAMN YOU, ANNIE.
WANTED
FICE
TICKETS
FUCK, FUCK, FUCK.
IMA COMIN'!
WANTED
DING DING DING DING
SORRY ABOUT THAT. NATURE CALLS, Y'KNOW.
SO... HOW CAN I HELP A PRETTY YOUNG LADY LIKE YOU?
YEAH...
...I NEED A TICKET ON THE NEXT FUCKIN' BUS OUTTA THIS DUMP.
RODUCE

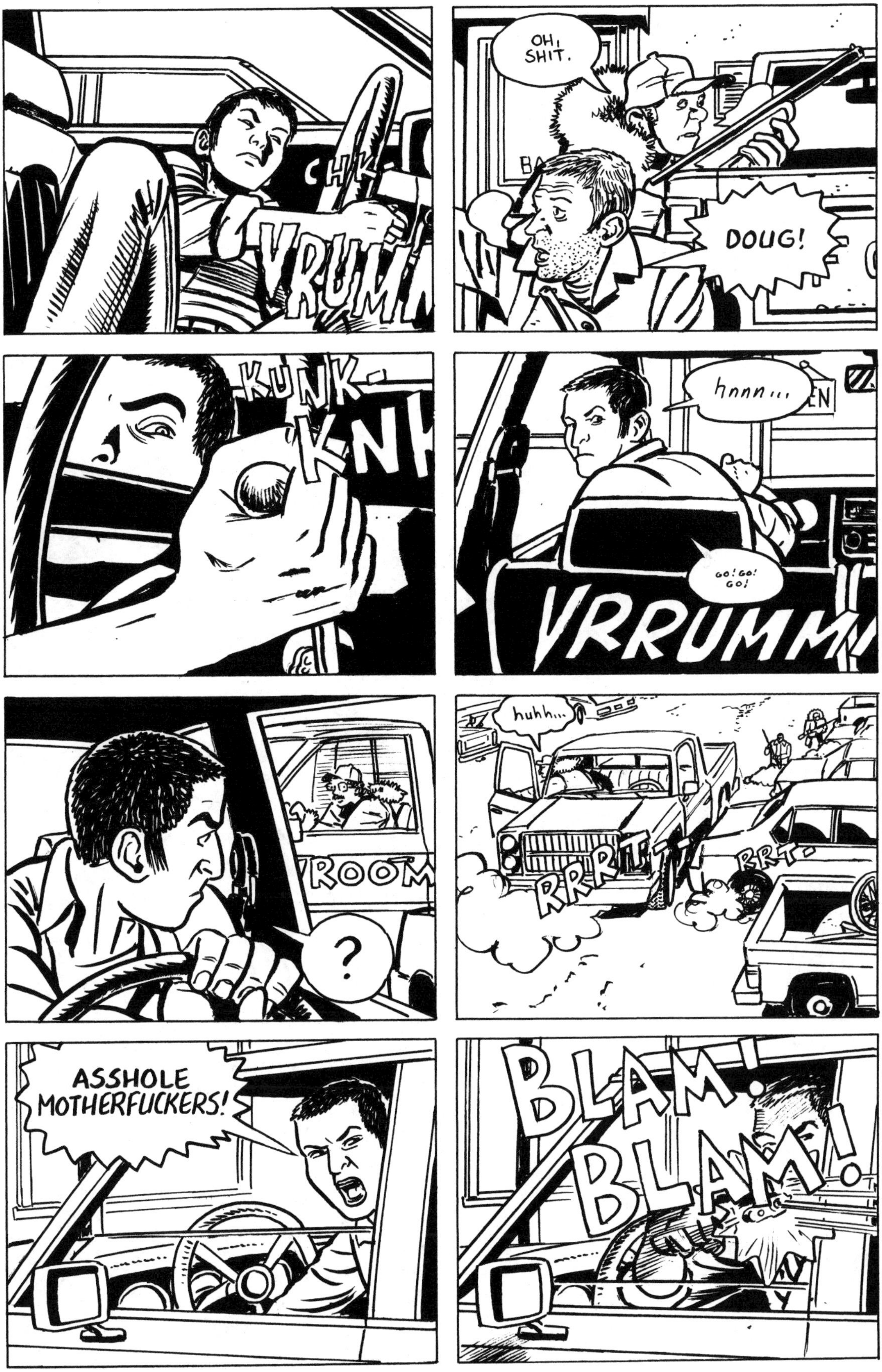
CHK-
VRUMM
OH, SHIT.
DOUG!
KUNK-
KNK
hnnn...
GO! GO! GO!
VRRUMM
ROOM
?
huhh...
RRRT-
RRT-
ASSHOLE MOTHERFUCKERS!
BLAM!
BLAM!

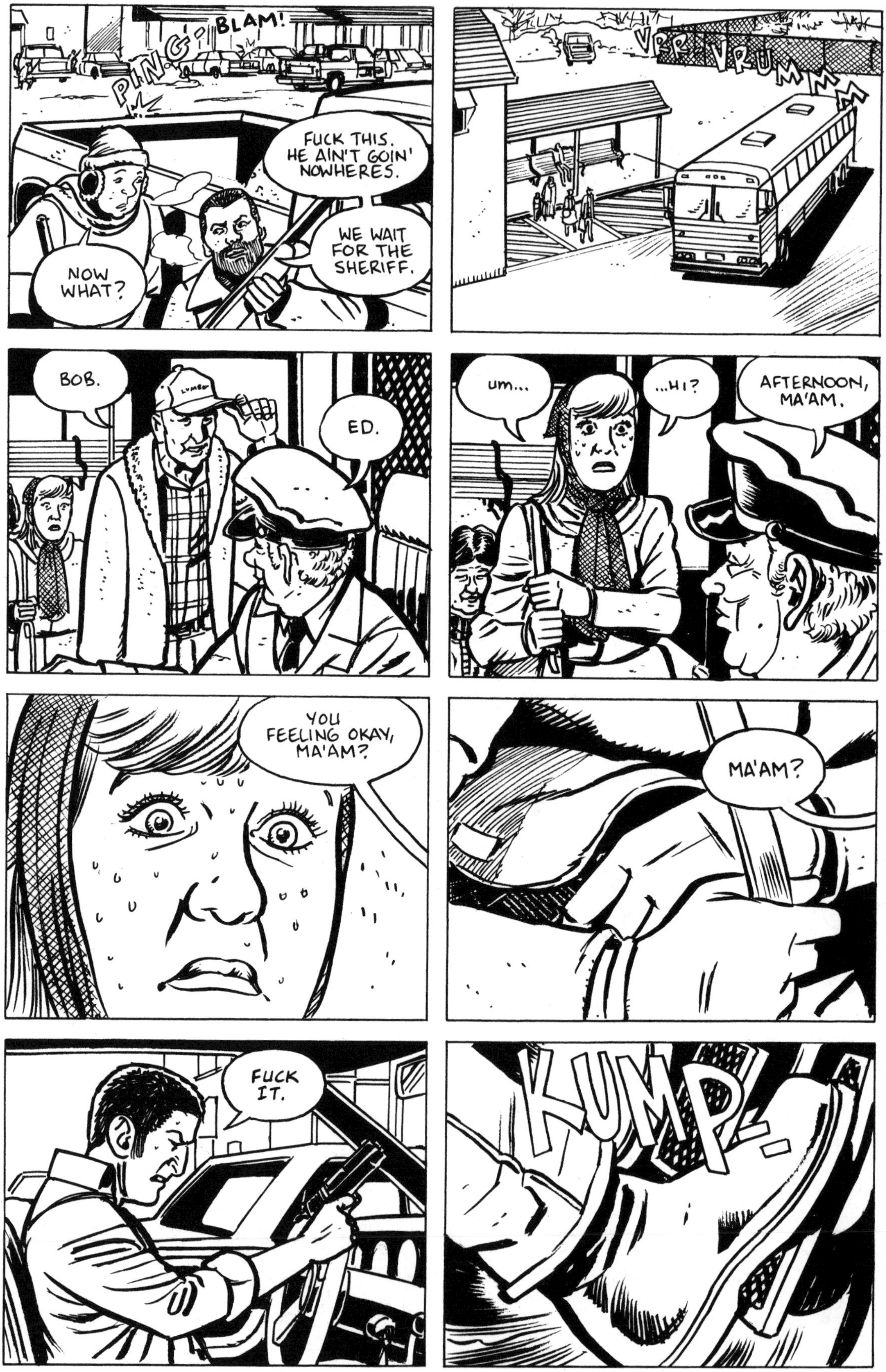
PING!
BLAM!
FUCK THIS. HE AIN'T GOIN' NOWHERES.
NOW WHAT?
WE WAIT FOR THE SHERIFF.
VRR-VRUMMMM
BOB.
ED.
um...
...HI?
AFTERNOON, MA'AM.
YOU FEELING OKAY, MA'AM?
MA'AM?
FUCK IT.
KUMP

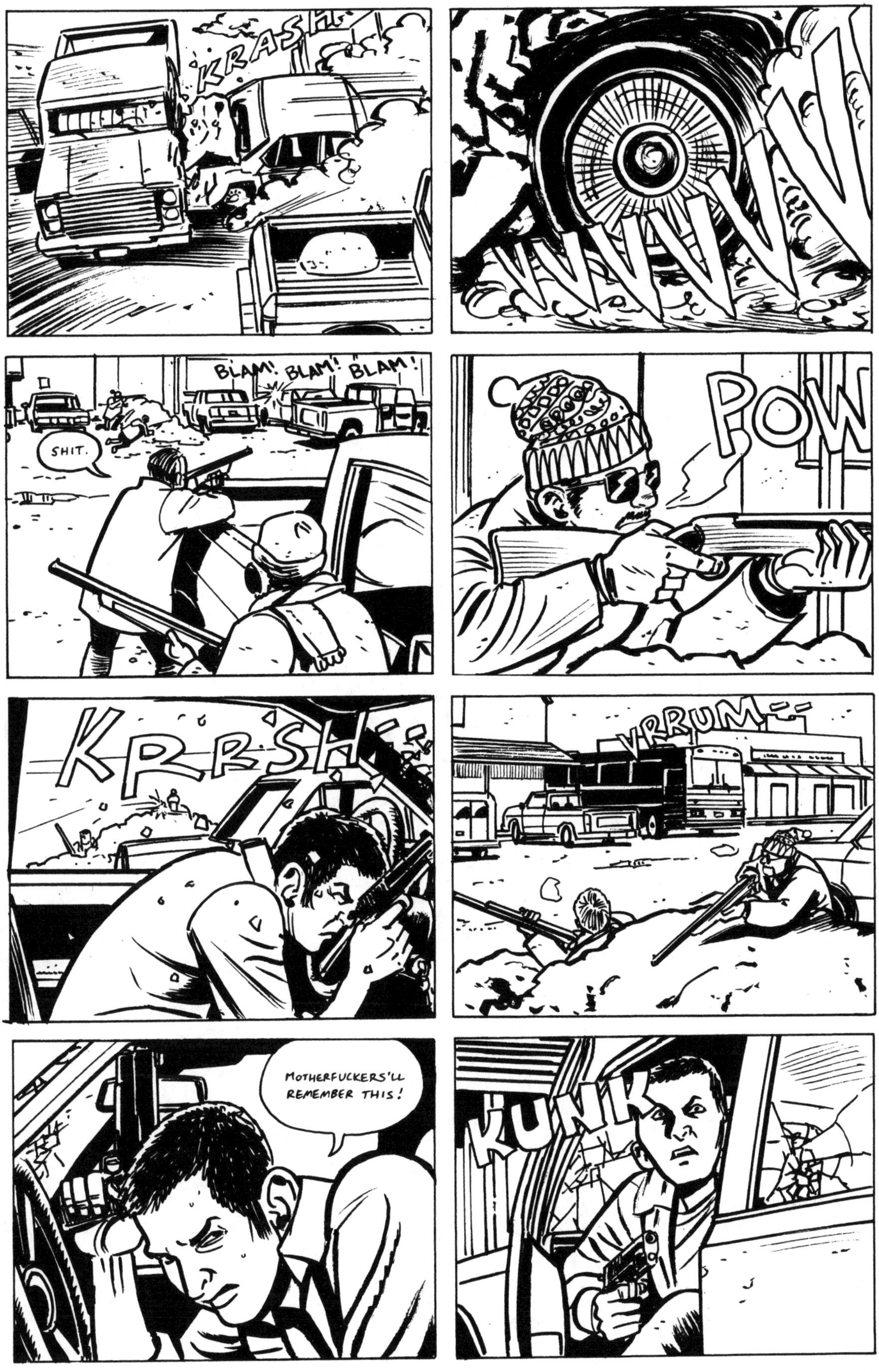

KRASH
VVVVV
BLAM! BLAM! BLAM!
SHIT.
POW
KRRSH
VRRUM
MOTHERFUCKERS'LL REMEMBER THIS!
KUNK

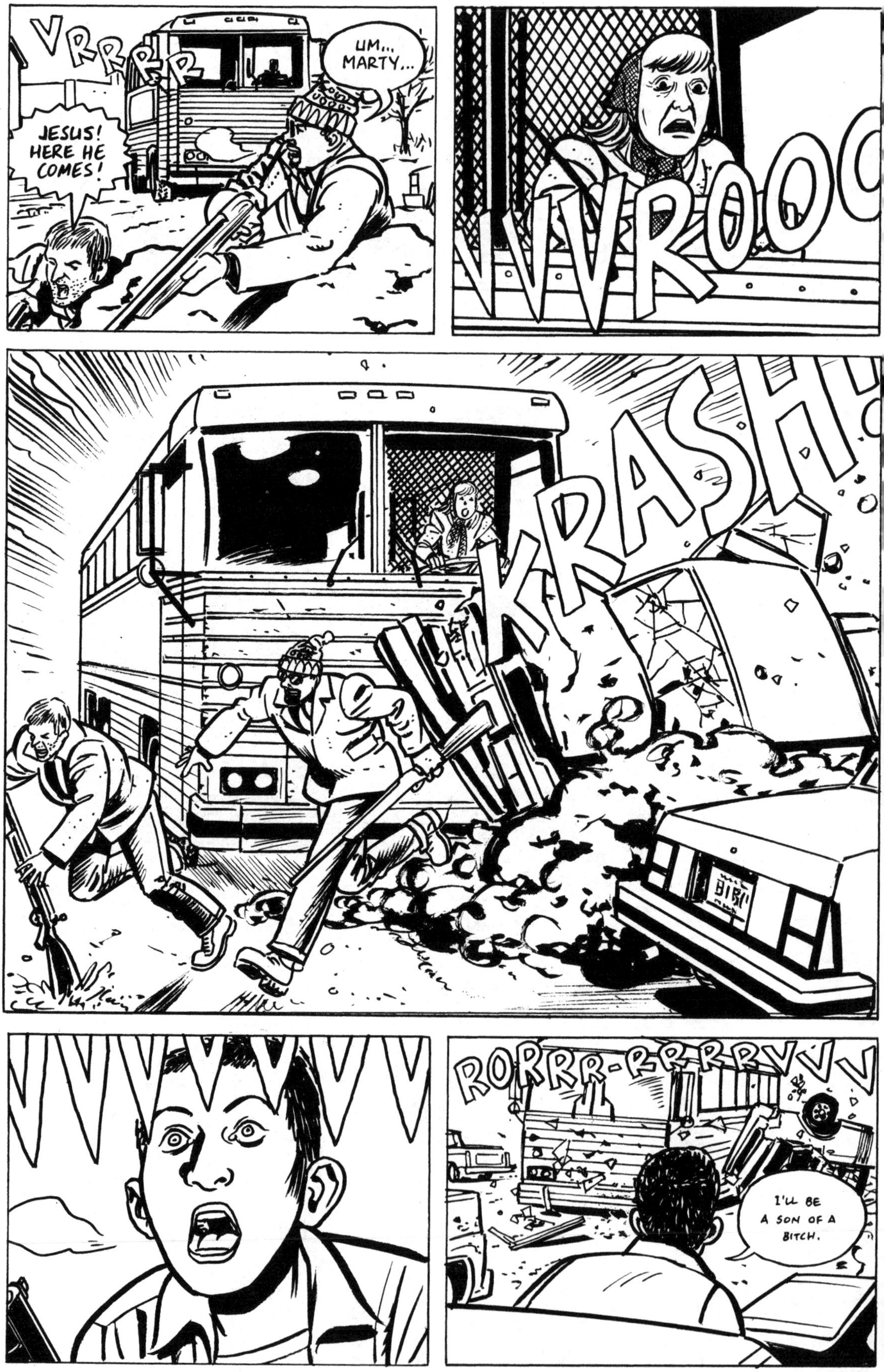
VRRRRR
JESUS! HERE HE COMES!
UM... MARTY...
VVVROOO
KRASH!
VVVVVVVVV
RORRR-RRRRVVV
I'LL BE A SON OF A BITCH.

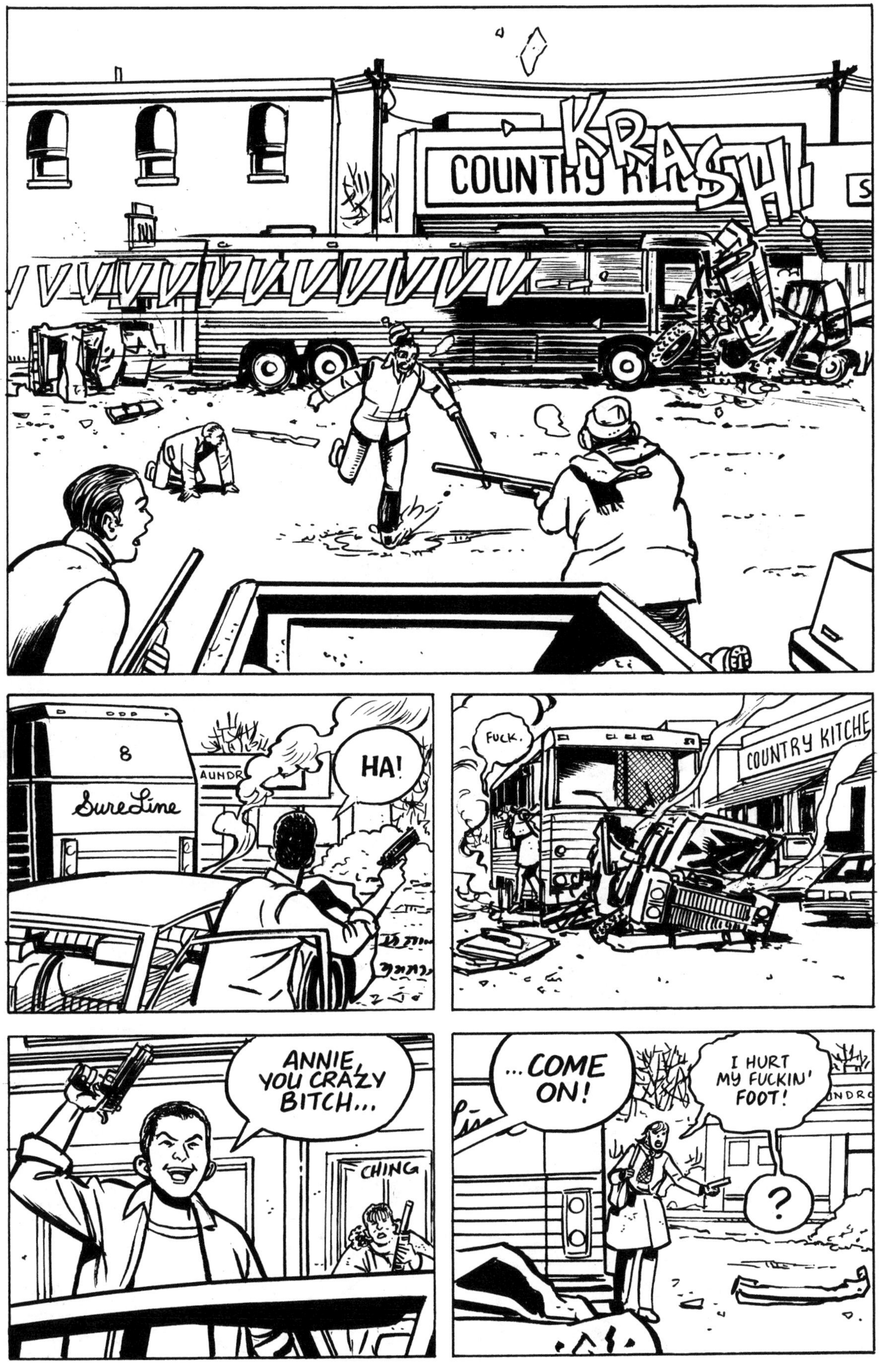

KRASH!
COUNTRY
VVVVVVVVVVVVVVVV
8
SureLine
AUNDR
HA!
FUCK.
COUNTRY KITCHE
ANNIE, YOU CRAZY BITCH...
CHING
...COME ON!
I HURT MY FUCKIN' FOOT!
?

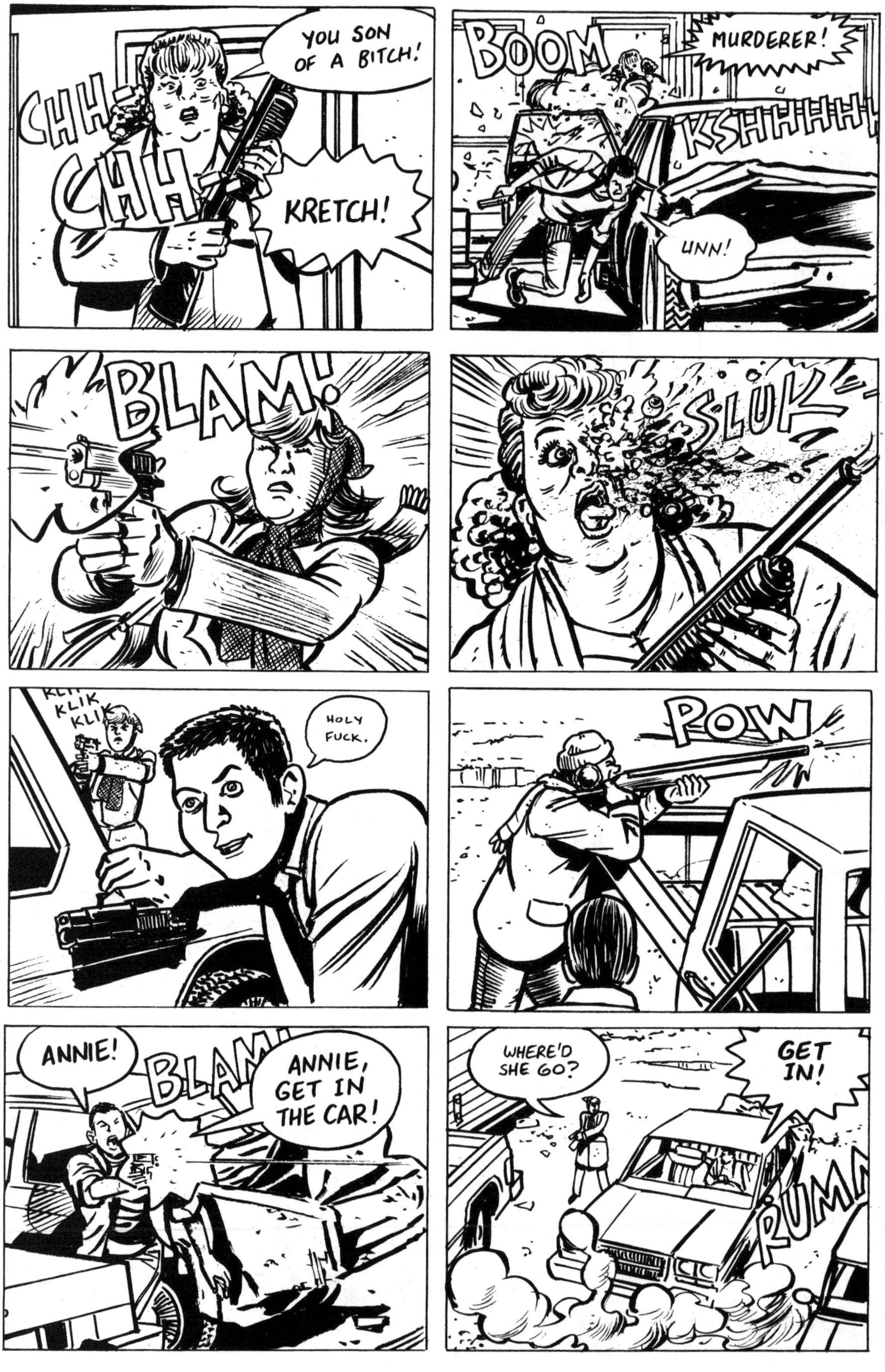
YOU SON OF A BITCH!
CHH-
CHH-
KRETCH!
BOOM
MURDERER!
KSHHHHH
UNN!
BLAM!
SLUK
KLIK
KLIK
HOLY FUCK.
POW
ANNIE!
ANNIE, GET IN THE CAR!
WHERE'D SHE GO?
GET IN!

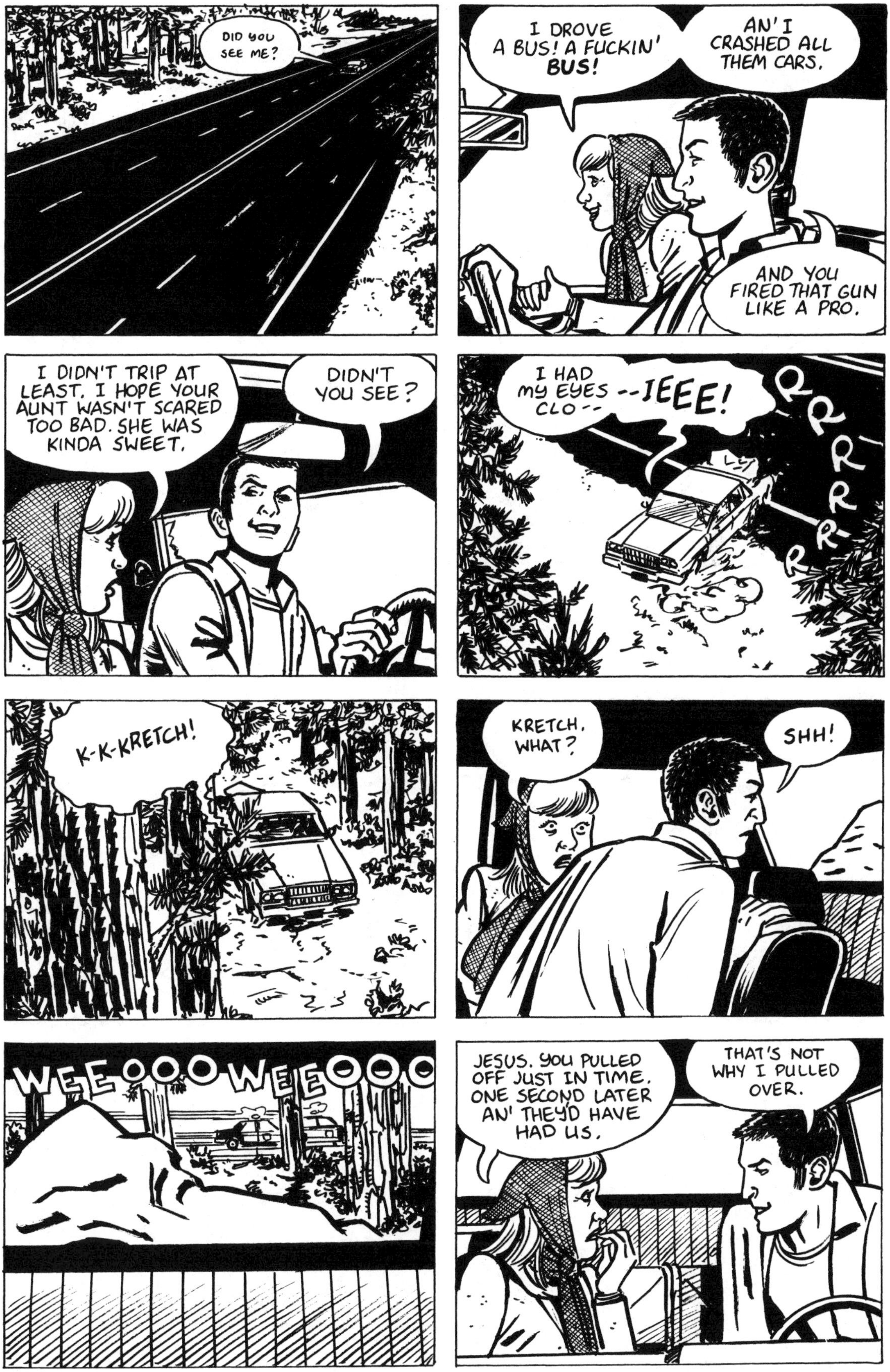
DID YOU SEE ME?
I DROVE A BUS! A FUCKIN' BUS!
AN' I CRASHED ALL THEM CARS.
AND YOU FIRED THAT GUN LIKE A PRO.
I DIDN'T TRIP AT LEAST. I HOPE YOUR AUNT WASN'T SCARED TOO BAD. SHE WAS KINDA SWEET.
DIDN'T YOU SEE?
I HAD MY EYES CLO--
--IEEE!
RRRRRRR
K-K-KRETCH!
KRETCH. WHAT?
SHH!
WEEOOOWEEOOO
JESUS. YOU PULLED OFF JUST IN TIME. ONE SECOND LATER AN' THEY'D HAVE HAD US.
THAT'S NOT WHY I PULLED OVER.

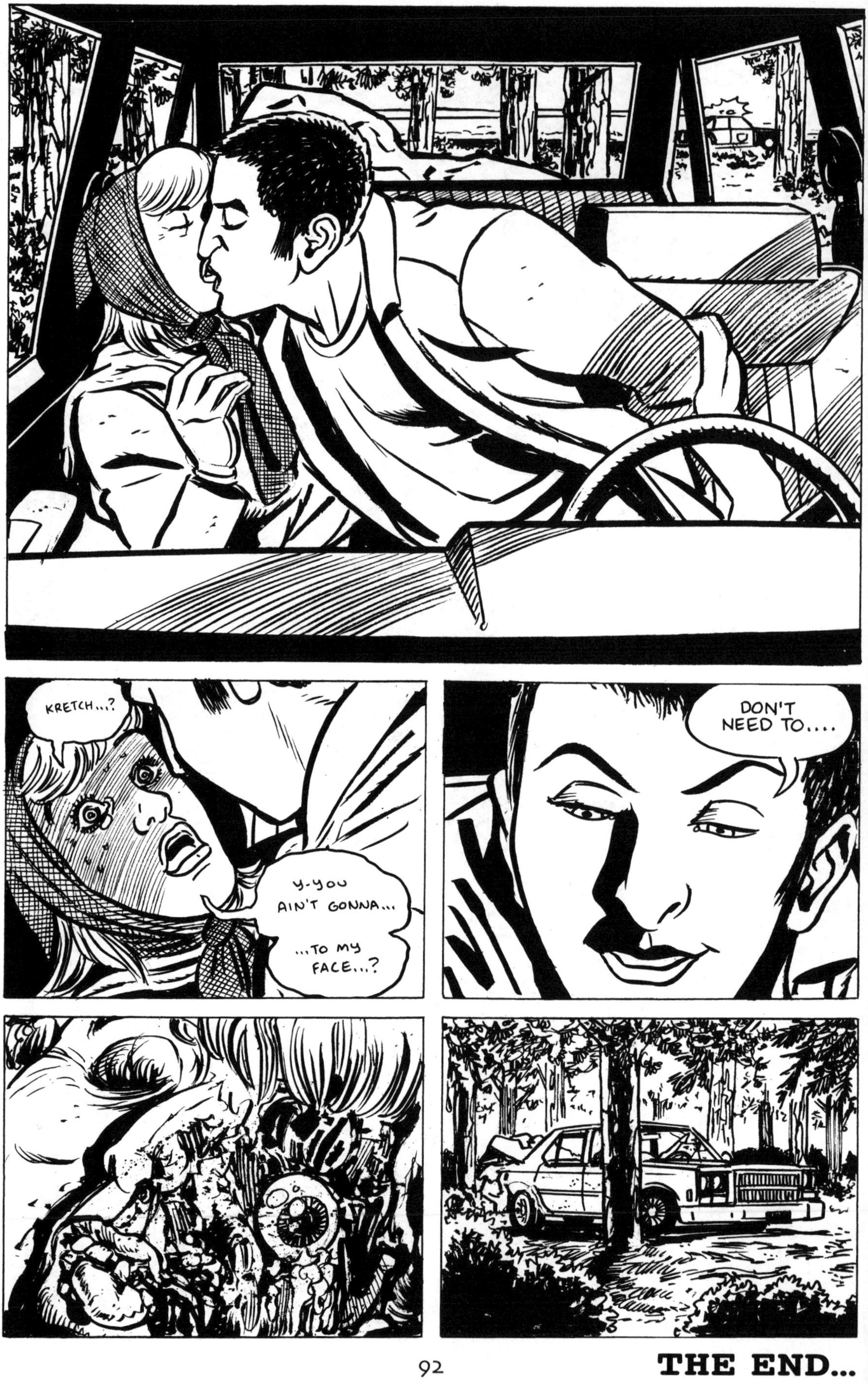
KRETCH...?
Y-YOU AIN'T GONNA...
...TO MY FACE...?
DON'T NEED TO....

THE END...

4

"MAGIC BANANA"

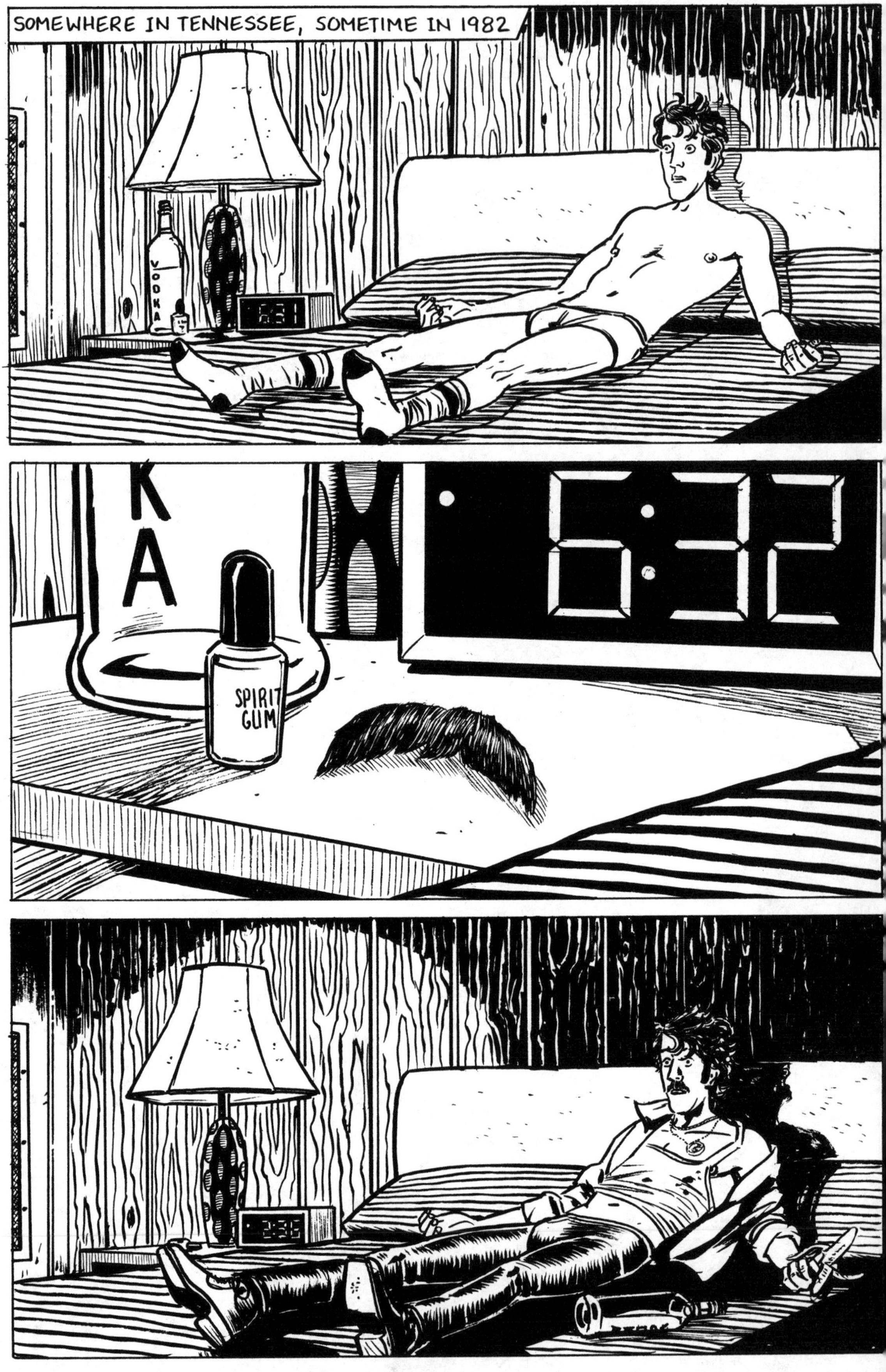
SOMEWHERE IN TENNESSEE, SOMETIME IN 1982
VODKA
KA
SPIRIT GUM

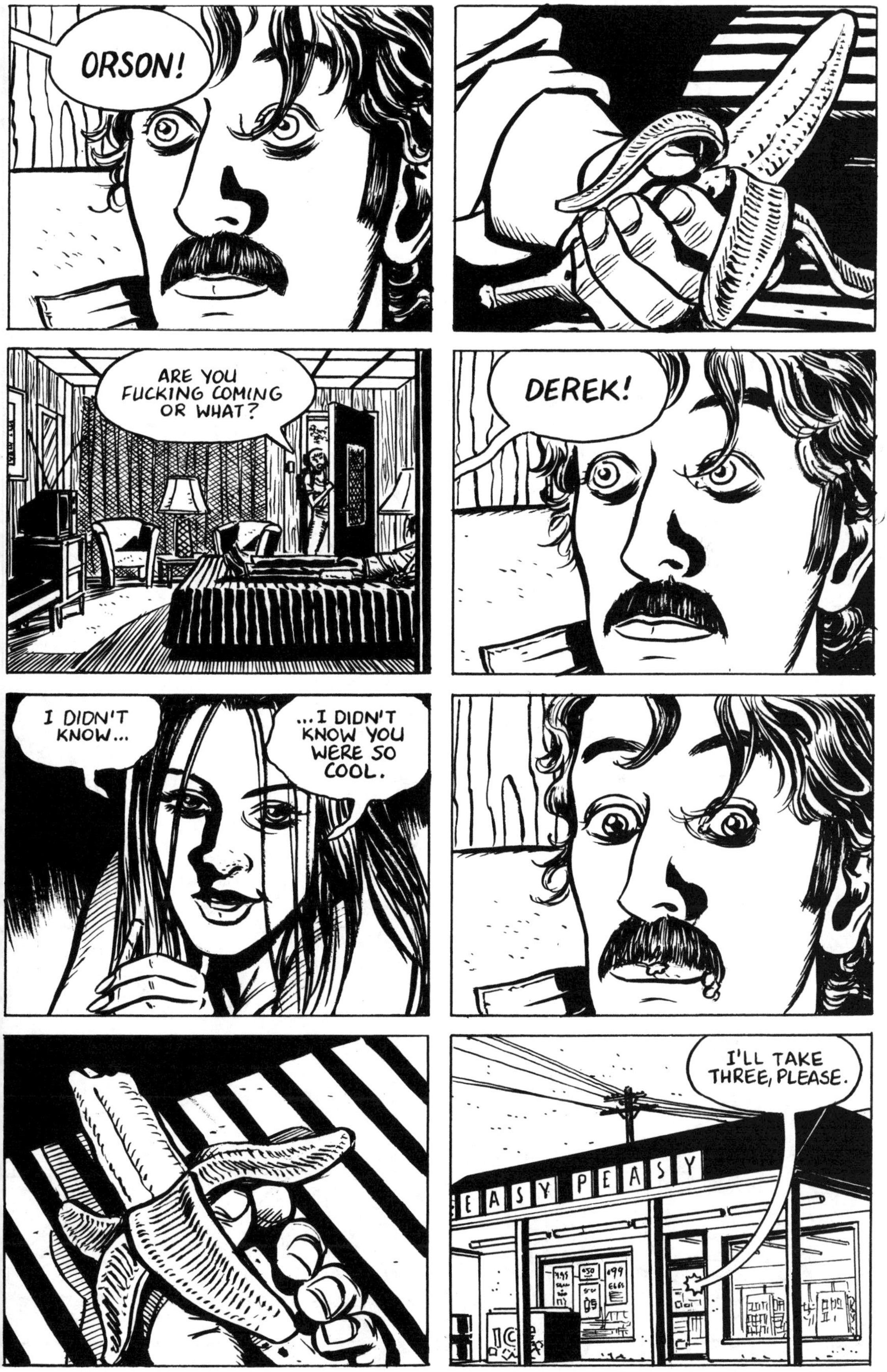
ORSON!
ARE YOU FUCKING COMING OR WHAT?
DEREK!
I DIDN'T KNOW...
...I DIDN'T KNOW YOU WERE SO COOL.
EASY PEASY
I'LL TAKE THREE, PLEASE.

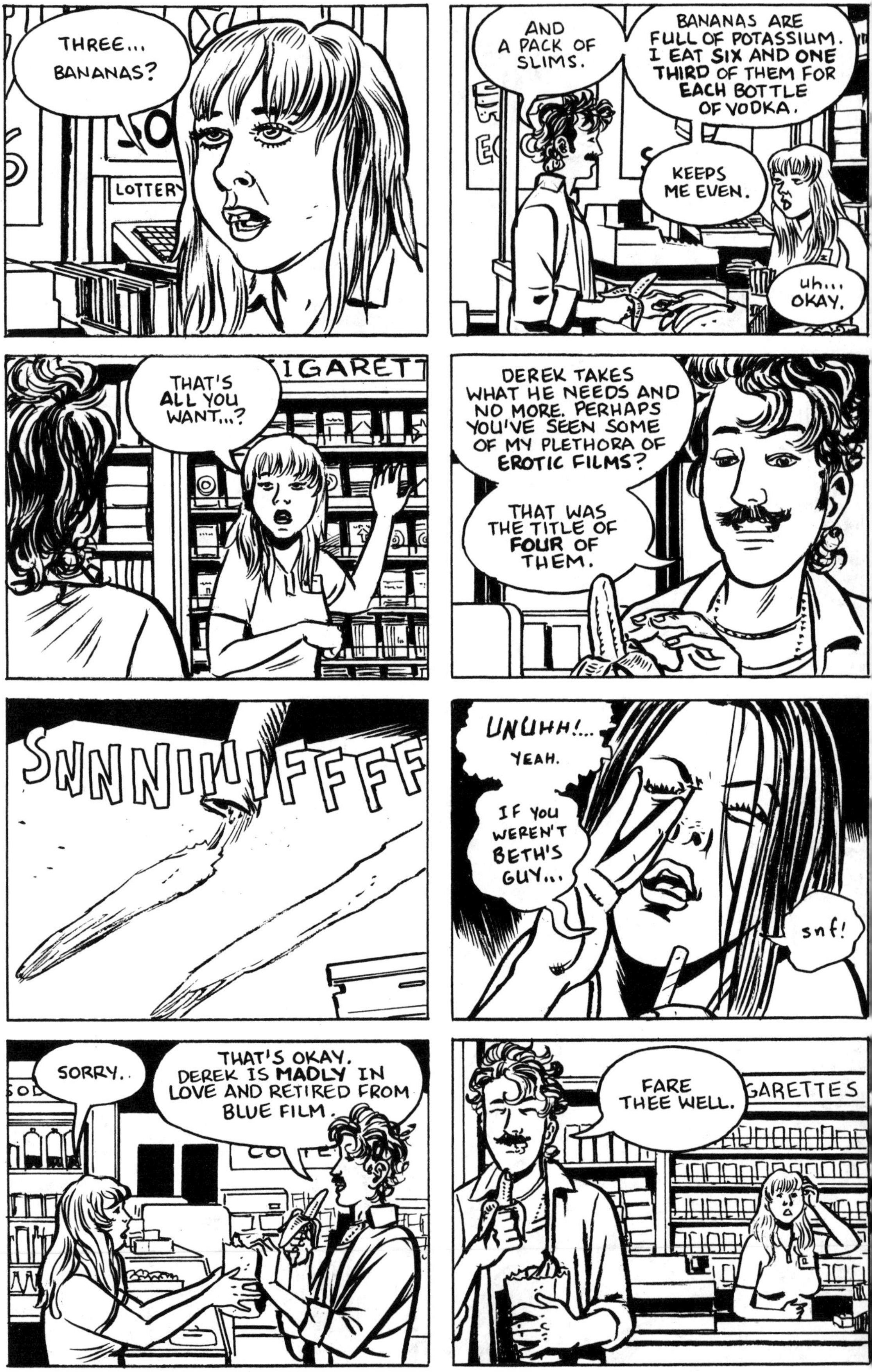
THREE... BANANAS?
LOTTERY
AND A PACK OF SLIMS.
BANANAS ARE FULL OF POTASSIUM. I EAT SIX AND ONE THIRD OF THEM FOR EACH BOTTLE OF VODKA.
KEEPS ME EVEN.
uh... OKAY.
THAT'S ALL YOU WANT...?
DEREK TAKES WHAT HE NEEDS AND NO MORE. PERHAPS YOU'VE SEEN SOME OF MY PLETHORA OF EROTIC FILMS?
THAT WAS THE TITLE OF FOUR OF THEM.
SNNNIIIIFFFF
UNUHH!...
YEAH.
IF YOU WEREN'T BETH'S GUY...
snf!
SORRY.
THAT'S OKAY. DEREK IS MADLY IN LOVE AND RETIRED FROM BLUE FILM.
FARE THEE WELL.
GARETTES

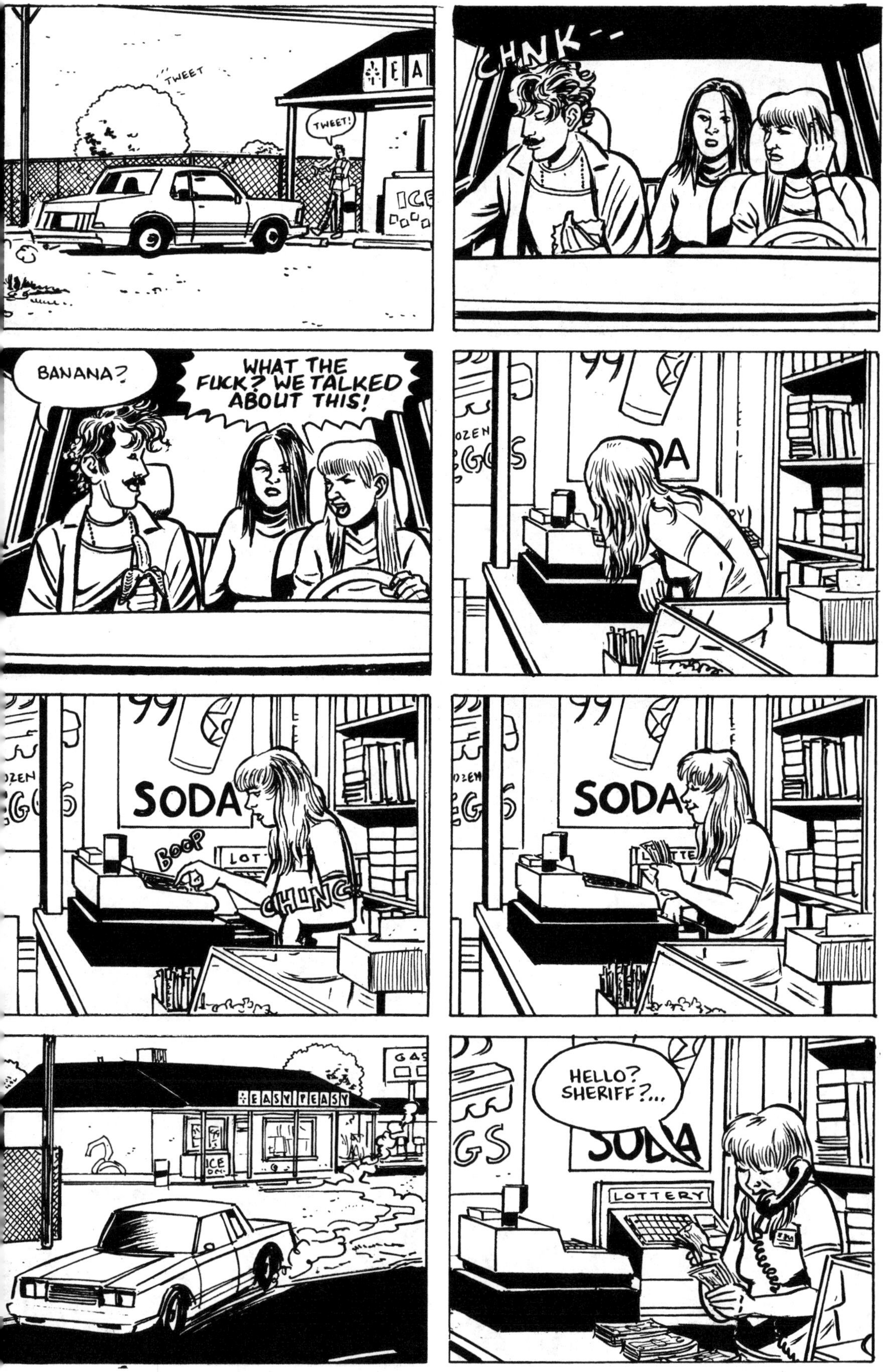
TWEET
TWEET!
CHNK--
BANANA?
WHAT THE FUCK? WE TALKED ABOUT THIS!
SODA
BOOP
CHING
SODA
EASY PEASY
HELLO? SHERIFF?...
LOTTERY

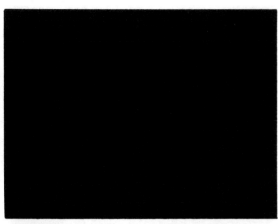

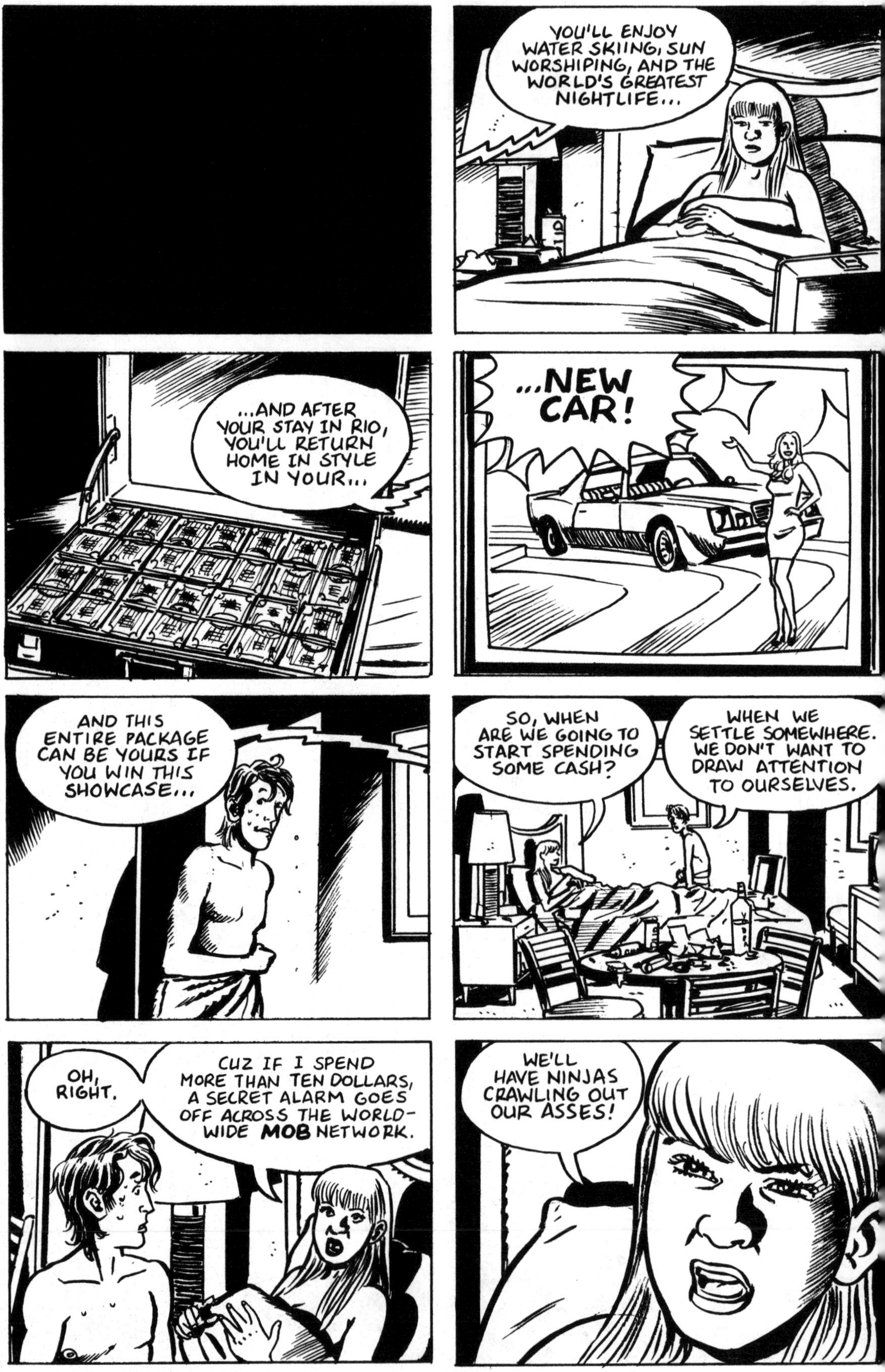
YOU'LL ENJOY WATER SKIING, SUN WORSHIPING, AND THE WORLD'S GREATEST NIGHTLIFE...
...AND AFTER YOUR STAY IN RIO, YOU'LL RETURN HOME IN STYLE IN YOUR...
...NEW CAR!
AND THIS ENTIRE PACKAGE CAN BE YOURS IF YOU WIN THIS SHOWCASE...
SO, WHEN ARE WE GOING TO START SPENDING SOME CASH?
WHEN WE SETTLE SOMEWHERE. WE DON'T WANT TO DRAW ATTENTION TO OURSELVES.
OH, RIGHT.
CUZ IF I SPEND MORE THAN TEN DOLLARS, A SECRET ALARM GOES OFF ACROSS THE WORLD-WIDE MOB NETWORK.
WE'LL HAVE NINJAS CRAWLING OUT OUR ASSES!

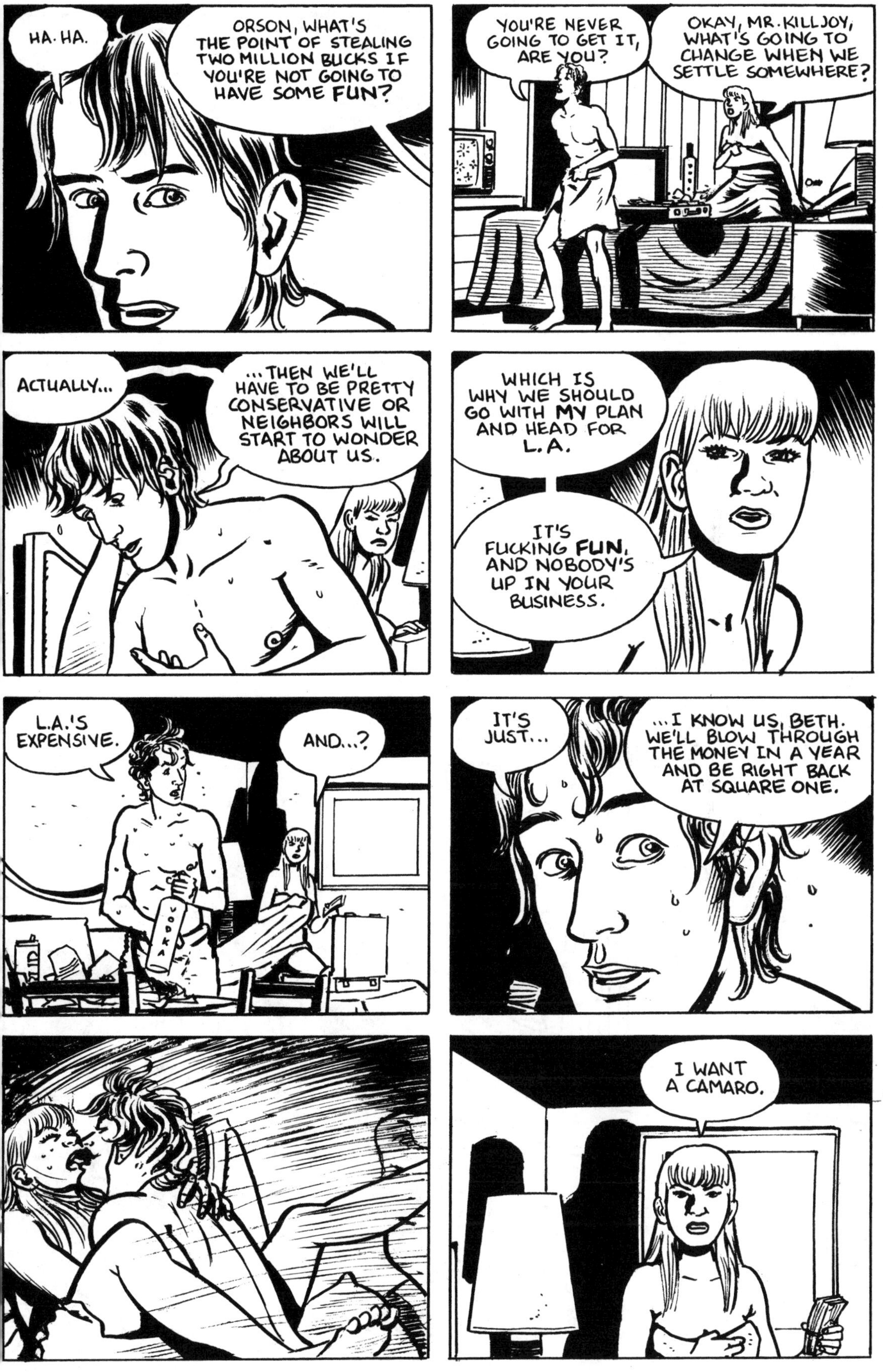
HA. HA.
ORSON, WHAT'S THE POINT OF STEALING TWO MILLION BUCKS IF YOU'RE NOT GOING TO HAVE SOME FUN?
YOU'RE NEVER GOING TO GET IT, ARE YOU?
OKAY, MR. KILLJOY, WHAT'S GOING TO CHANGE WHEN WE SETTLE SOMEWHERE?
ACTUALLY...
...THEN WE'LL HAVE TO BE PRETTY CONSERVATIVE OR NEIGHBORS WILL START TO WONDER ABOUT US.
WHICH IS WHY WE SHOULD GO WITH MY PLAN AND HEAD FOR L.A.
IT'S FUCKING FUN, AND NOBODY'S UP IN YOUR BUSINESS.
L.A.'S EXPENSIVE.
AND...?
VODKA
IT'S JUST...
...I KNOW US, BETH. WE'LL BLOW THROUGH THE MONEY IN A YEAR AND BE RIGHT BACK AT SQUARE ONE.
I WANT A CAMARO.

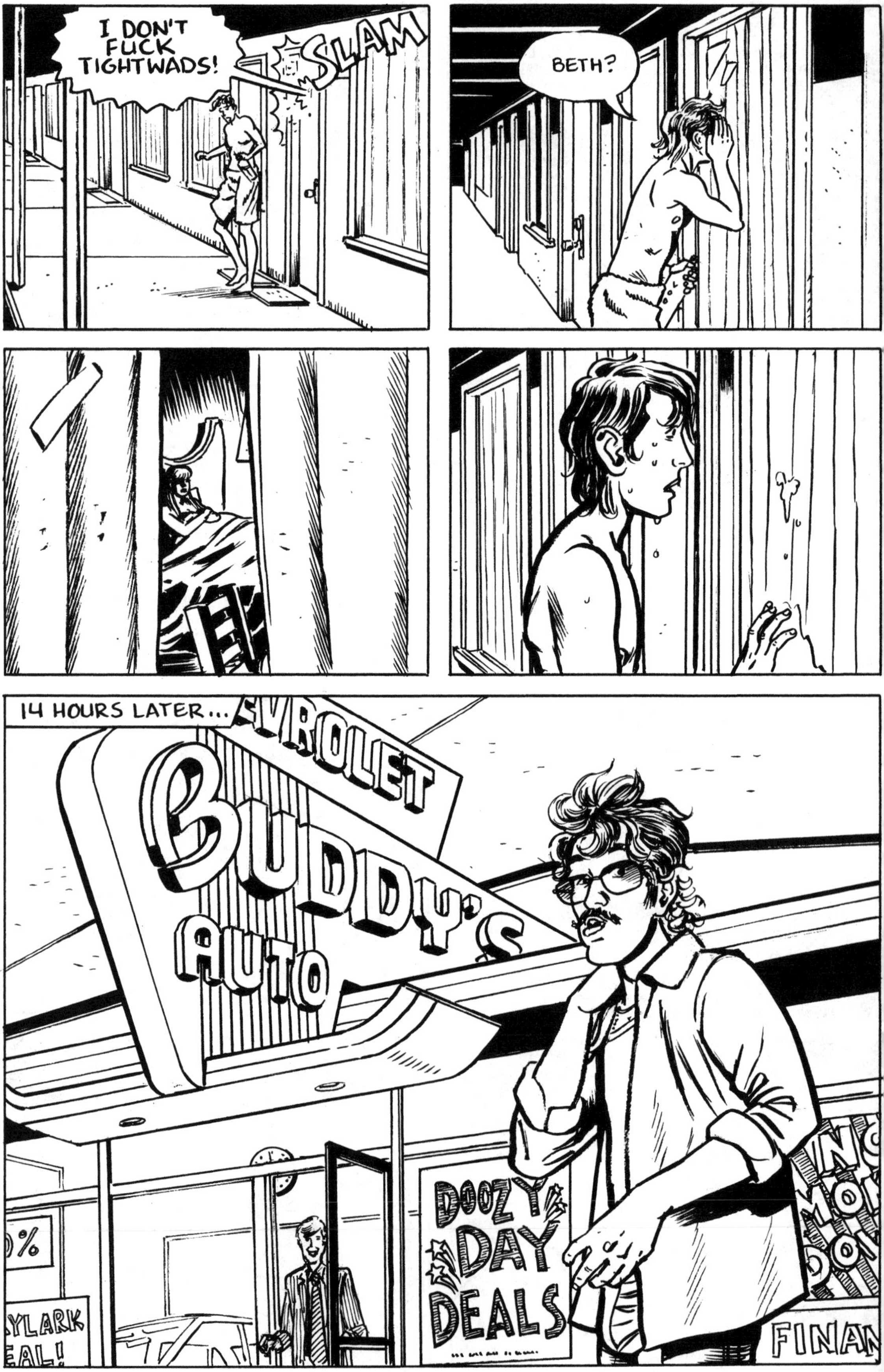
I DON'T FUCK TIGHTWADS!
SLAM
BETH?
14 HOURS LATER...
BUDDY'S AUTO
DOOZY DAY DEALS

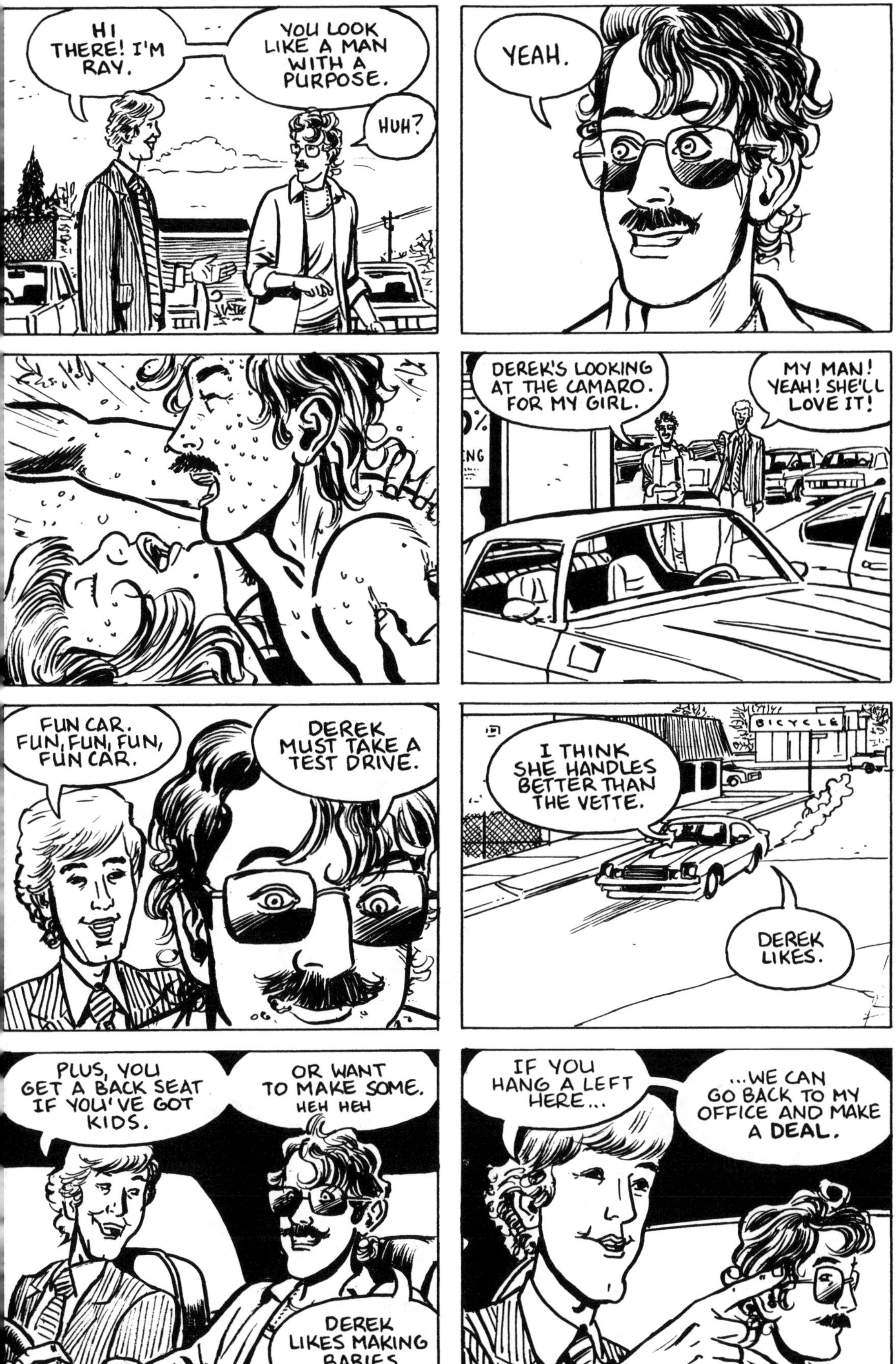
HI THERE! I'M RAY.
YOU LOOK LIKE A MAN WITH A PURPOSE.
HUH?
YEAH.
DEREK'S LOOKING AT THE CAMARO. FOR MY GIRL.
MY MAN! YEAH! SHE'LL LOVE IT!
FUN CAR. FUN, FUN, FUN, FUN CAR.
DEREK MUST TAKE A TEST DRIVE.
BICYCLE
I THINK SHE HANDLES BETTER THAN THE VETTE.
DEREK LIKES.
PLUS, YOU GET A BACK SEAT IF YOU'VE GOT KIDS.
OR WANT TO MAKE SOME. HEH HEH
DEREK LIKES MAKING BABIES.
IF YOU HANG A LEFT HERE...
...WE CAN GO BACK TO MY OFFICE AND MAKE A DEAL.

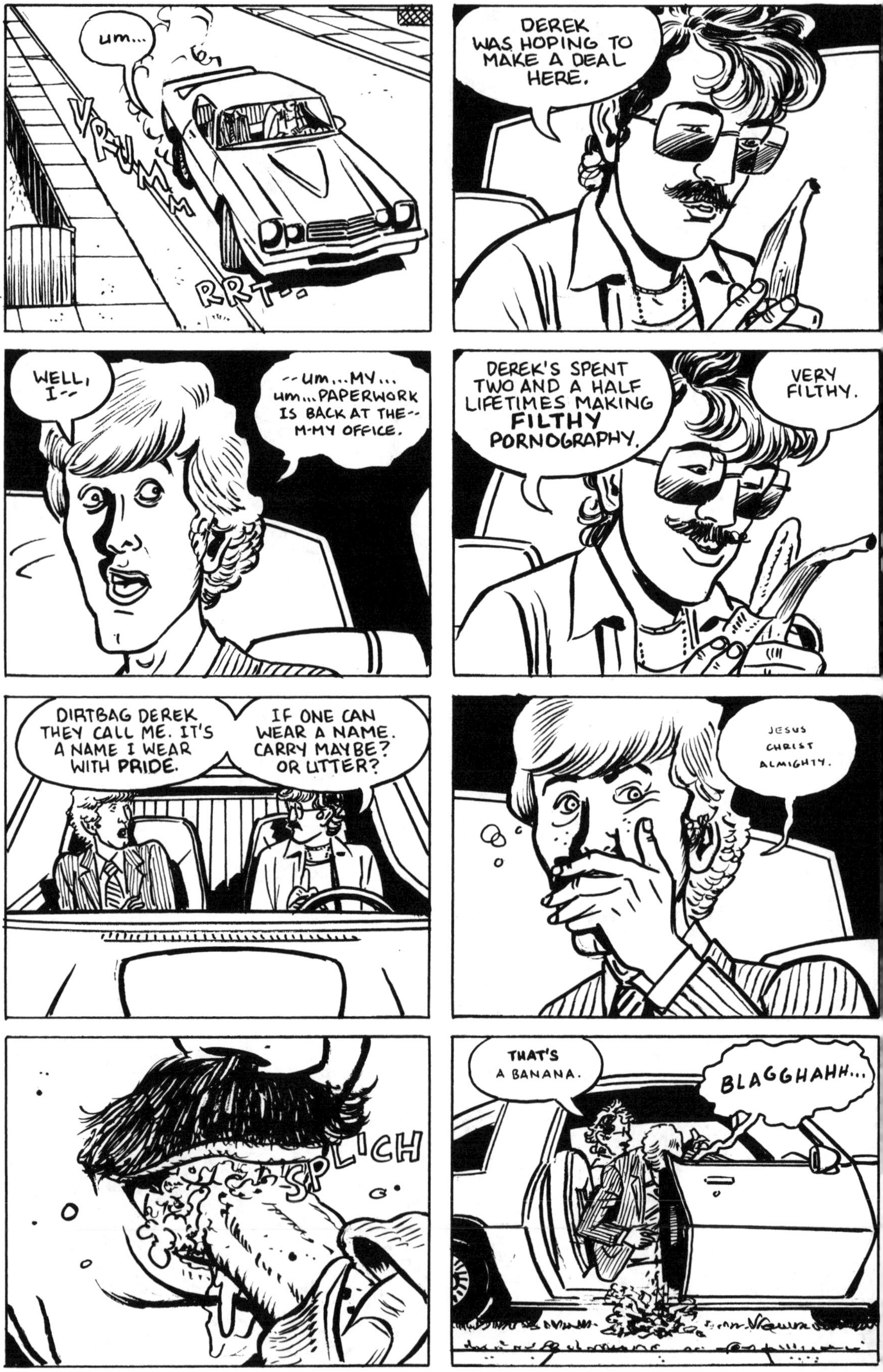
um...
VRUMMM
RRT--
DEREK WAS HOPING TO MAKE A DEAL HERE.
WELL, I--
--um...MY... um...PAPERWORK IS BACK AT THE-- M-MY OFFICE.
DEREK'S SPENT TWO AND A HALF LIFETIMES MAKING FILTHY PORNOGRAPHY.
VERY FILTHY.
DIRTBAG DEREK THEY CALL ME. IT'S A NAME I WEAR WITH PRIDE.
IF ONE CAN WEAR A NAME. CARRY MAYBE? OR UTTER?
JESUS CHRIST ALMIGHTY.
SPLICH
THAT'S A BANANA.
BLAGGHAHH...

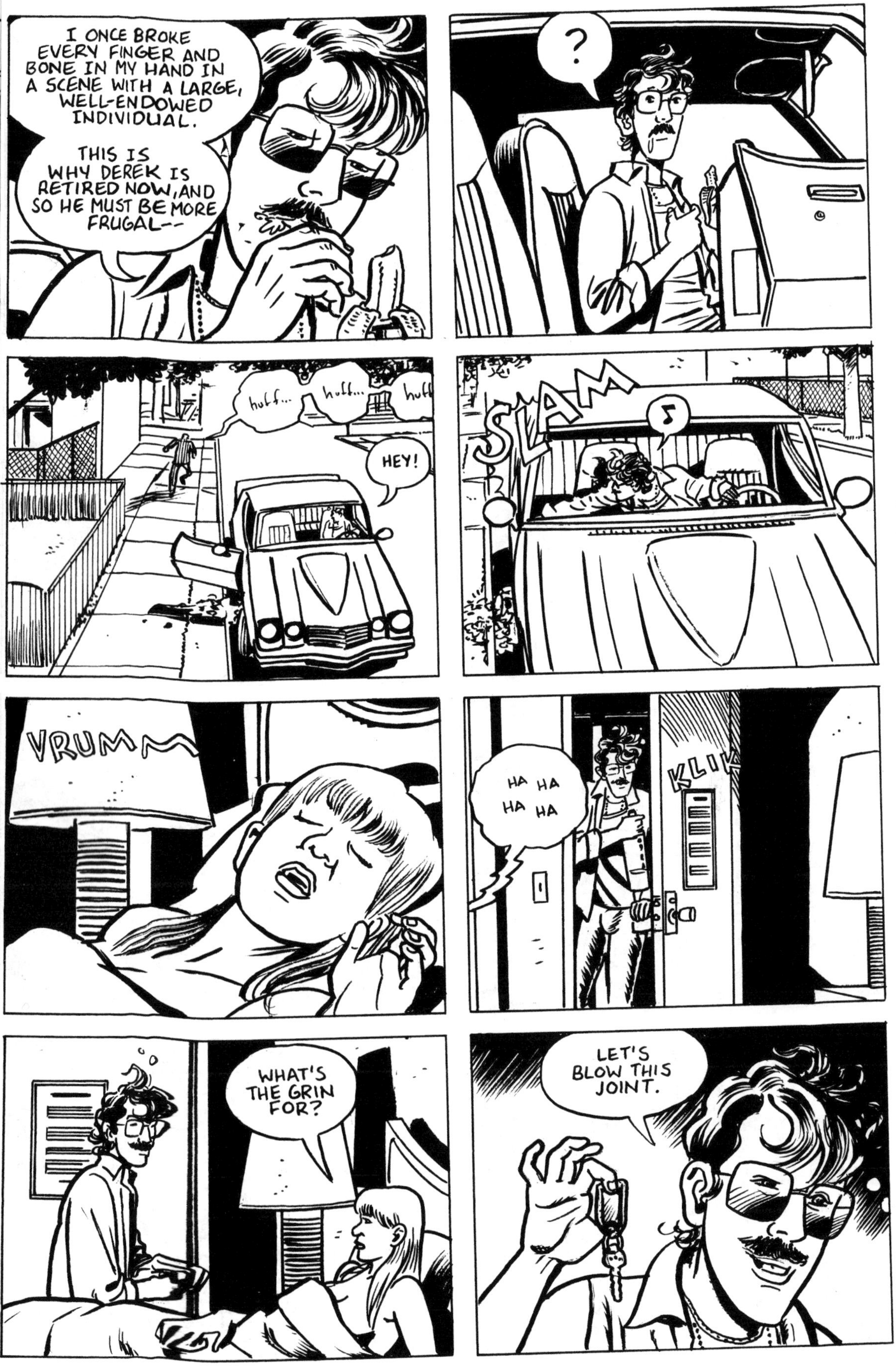
I ONCE BROKE EVERY FINGER AND BONE IN MY HAND IN A SCENE WITH A LARGE, WELL-ENDOWED INDIVIDUAL.
THIS IS WHY DEREK IS RETIRED NOW, AND SO HE MUST BE MORE FRUGAL--
?
huff... huff... huff
HEY!
SLAM
VRUMM
HA HA HA HA
KLIK
WHAT'S THE GRIN FOR?
LET'S BLOW THIS JOINT.

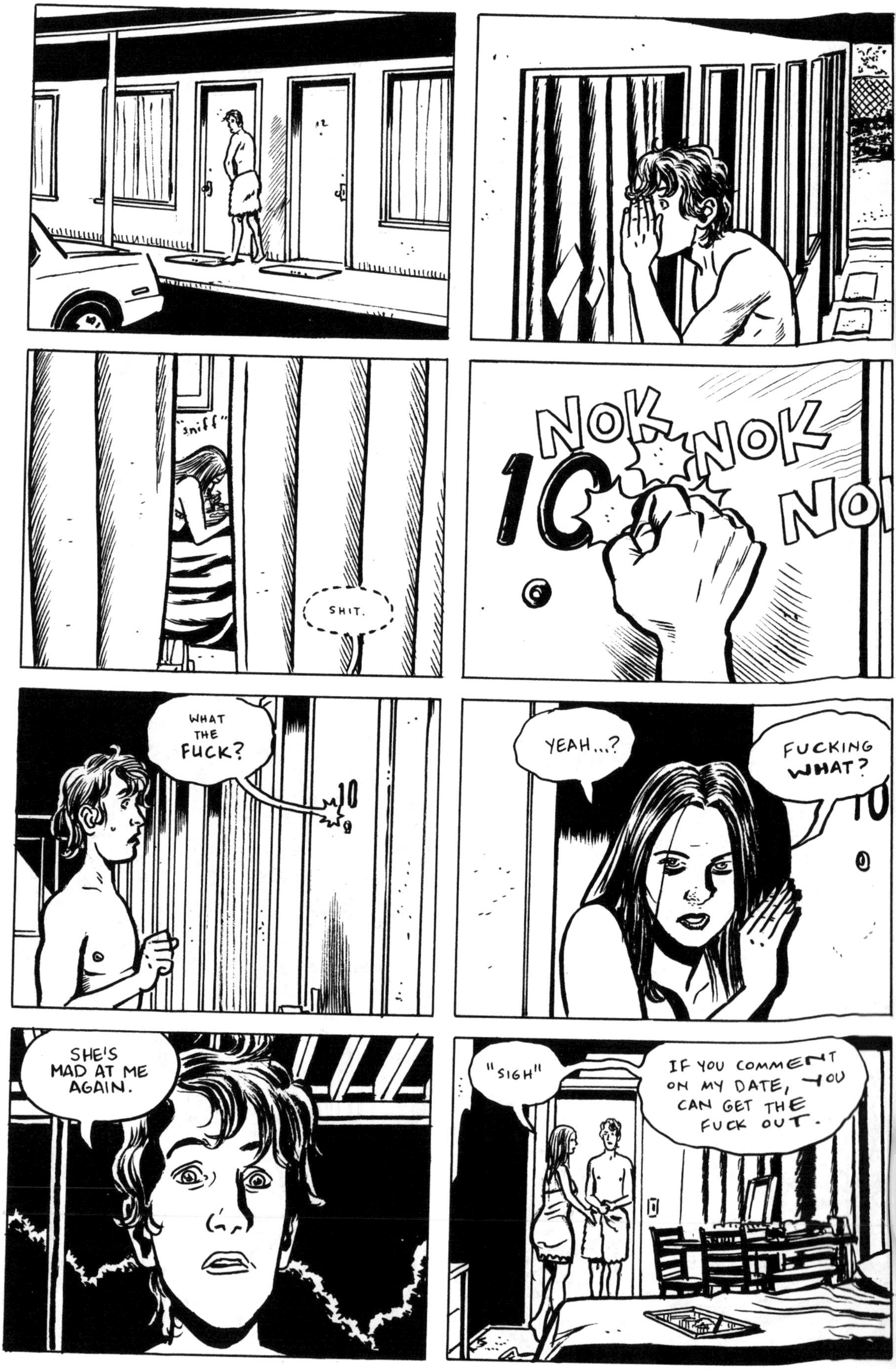
"sniff"
SHIT.
NOK NOK NO
10
WHAT THE FUCK?
YEAH...?
FUCKING WHAT?
SHE'S MAD AT ME AGAIN.
"SIGH"
IF YOU COMMENT ON MY DATE, YOU CAN GET THE FUCK OUT.

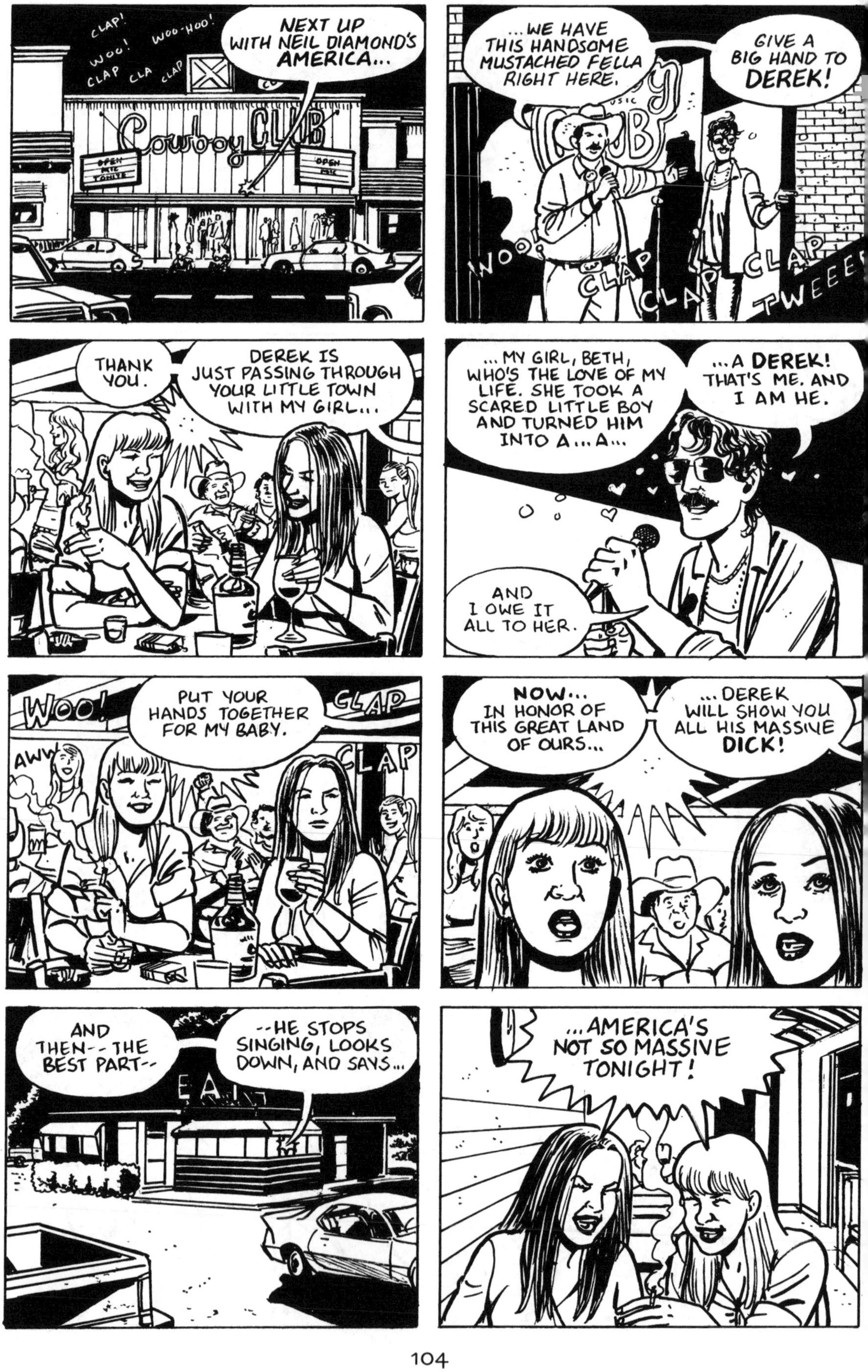
CLAP!
WOO!
WOO-HOO!
CLAP CLA CLAP
NEXT UP WITH NEIL DIAMOND'S AMERICA...
Cowboy CLUB
OPEN MIC TONITE
...WE HAVE THIS HANDSOME MUSTACHED FELLA RIGHT HERE.
GIVE A BIG HAND TO DEREK!
WOO!
CLAP CLAP CLAP CLAP
TWEEEE
THANK YOU.
DEREK IS JUST PASSING THROUGH YOUR LITTLE TOWN WITH MY GIRL...
...MY GIRL, BETH, WHO'S THE LOVE OF MY LIFE. SHE TOOK A SCARED LITTLE BOY AND TURNED HIM INTO A...A...
...A DEREK! THAT'S ME. AND I AM HE.
AND I OWE IT ALL TO HER.
WOO!
PUT YOUR HANDS TOGETHER FOR MY BABY.
CLAP
AWW
CLAP
NOW... IN HONOR OF THIS GREAT LAND OF OURS...
...DEREK WILL SHOW YOU ALL HIS MASSIVE DICK!
AND THEN--THE BEST PART--
--HE STOPS SINGING, LOOKS DOWN, AND SAYS...
...AMERICA'S NOT SO MASSIVE TONIGHT!

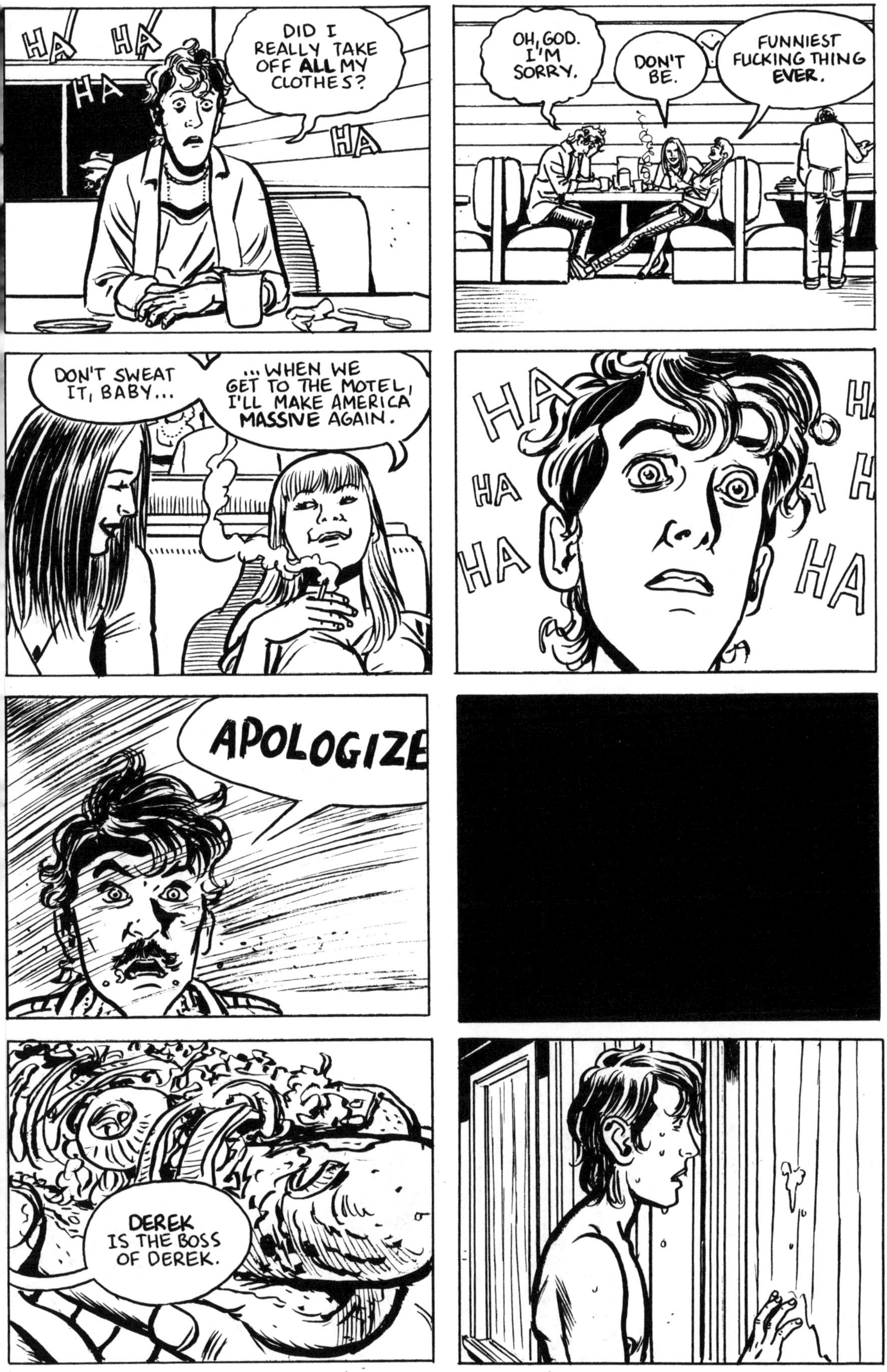
HA HA HA
DID I REALLY TAKE OFF ALL MY CLOTHES?
HA
OH, GOD. I'M SORRY.
DON'T BE.
FUNNIEST FUCKING THING EVER.
DON'T SWEAT IT, BABY...
...WHEN WE GET TO THE MOTEL, I'LL MAKE AMERICA MASSIVE AGAIN.
HA HA HA HA
APOLOGIZE
DEREK IS THE BOSS OF DEREK.

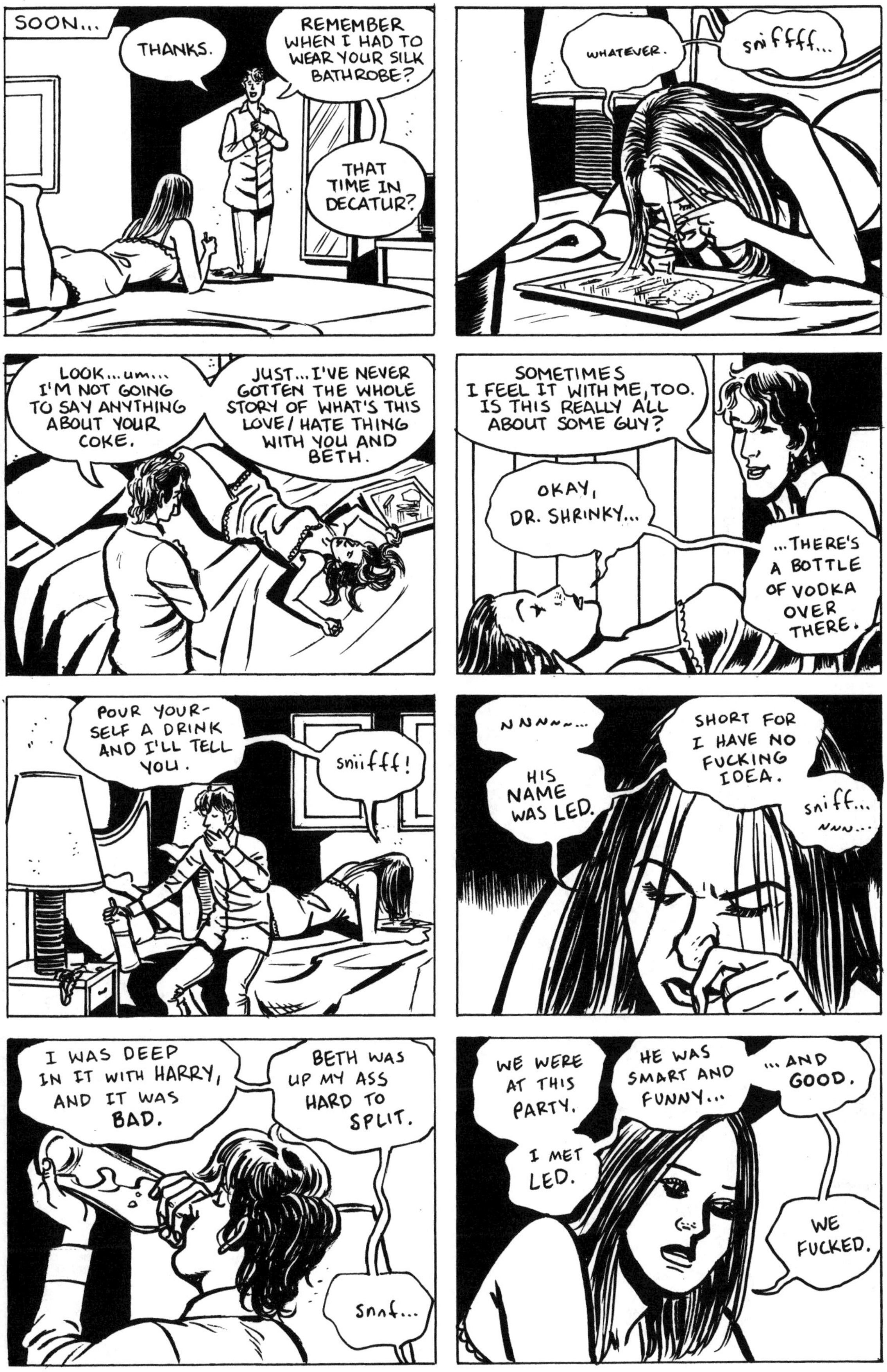
SOON...
THANKS.
REMEMBER WHEN I HAD TO WEAR YOUR SILK BATHROBE?
THAT TIME IN DECATUR?
WHATEVER.
sniffff...
LOOK...um... I'M NOT GOING TO SAY ANYTHING ABOUT YOUR COKE.
JUST...I'VE NEVER GOTTEN THE WHOLE STORY OF WHAT'S THIS LOVE/HATE THING WITH YOU AND BETH.
SOMETIMES I FEEL IT WITH ME, TOO. IS THIS REALLY ALL ABOUT SOME GUY?
OKAY, DR. SHRINKY...
...THERE'S A BOTTLE OF VODKA OVER THERE.
POUR YOURSELF A DRINK AND I'LL TELL YOU.
sniifff!
NNNnn...
HIS NAME WAS LED.
SHORT FOR I HAVE NO FUCKING IDEA.
sniff...
NNN...
I WAS DEEP IN IT WITH HARRY, AND IT WAS BAD.
BETH WAS UP MY ASS HARD TO SPLIT.
snnf...
WE WERE AT THIS PARTY.
I MET LED.
HE WAS SMART AND FUNNY...
...AND GOOD.
WE FUCKED.

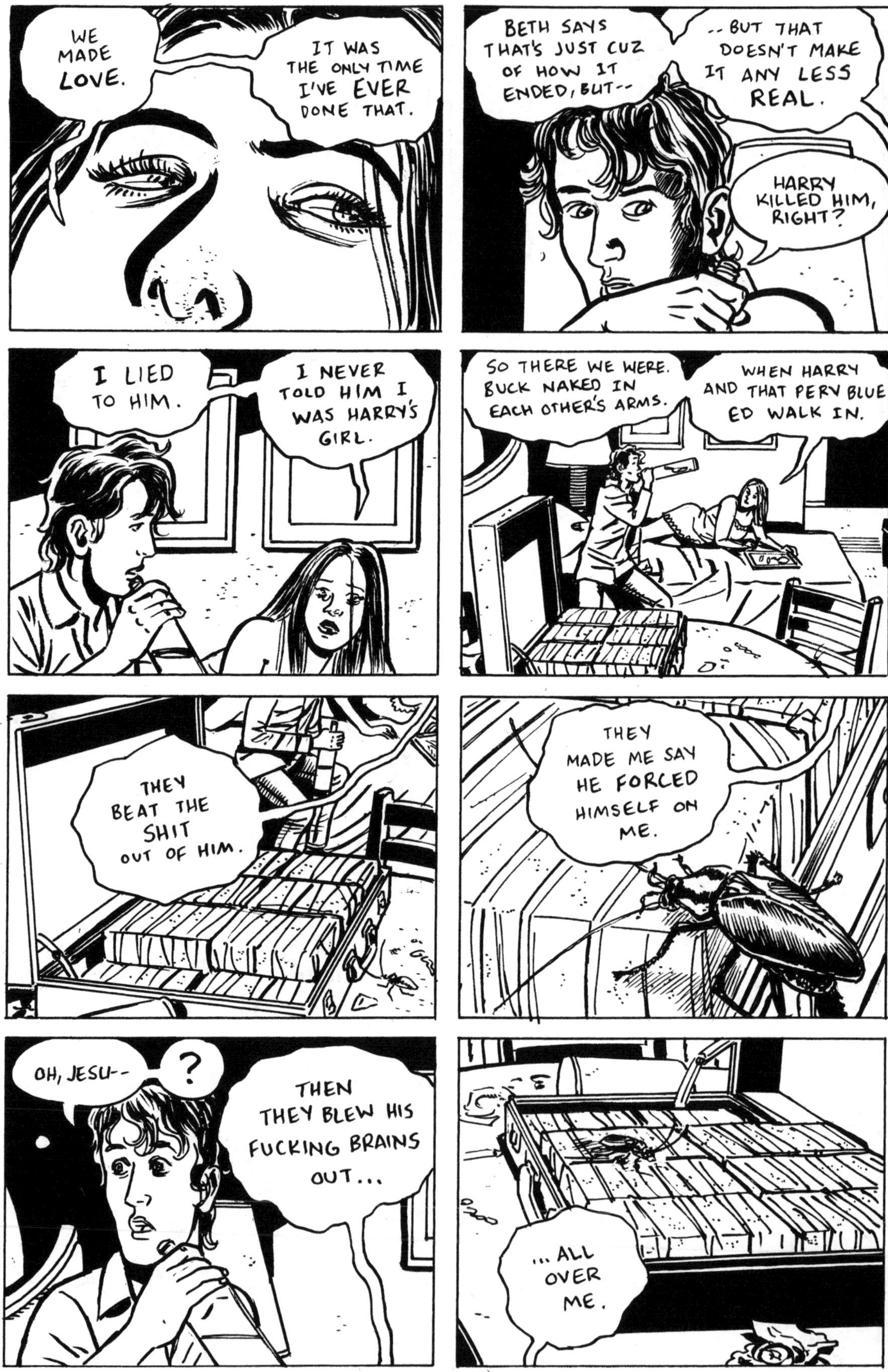
WE MADE LOVE.
IT WAS THE ONLY TIME I'VE EVER DONE THAT.
BETH SAYS THAT'S JUST CUZ OF HOW IT ENDED, BUT--
--BUT THAT DOESN'T MAKE IT ANY LESS REAL.
HARRY KILLED HIM, RIGHT?
I LIED TO HIM.
I NEVER TOLD HIM I WAS HARRY'S GIRL.
SO THERE WE WERE. BUCK NAKED IN EACH OTHER'S ARMS.
WHEN HARRY AND THAT PERV BLUE ED WALK IN.
THEY BEAT THE SHIT OUT OF HIM.
THEY MADE ME SAY HE FORCED HIMSELF ON ME.
OH, JESU--
?
THEN THEY BLEW HIS FUCKING BRAINS OUT...
...ALL OVER ME.

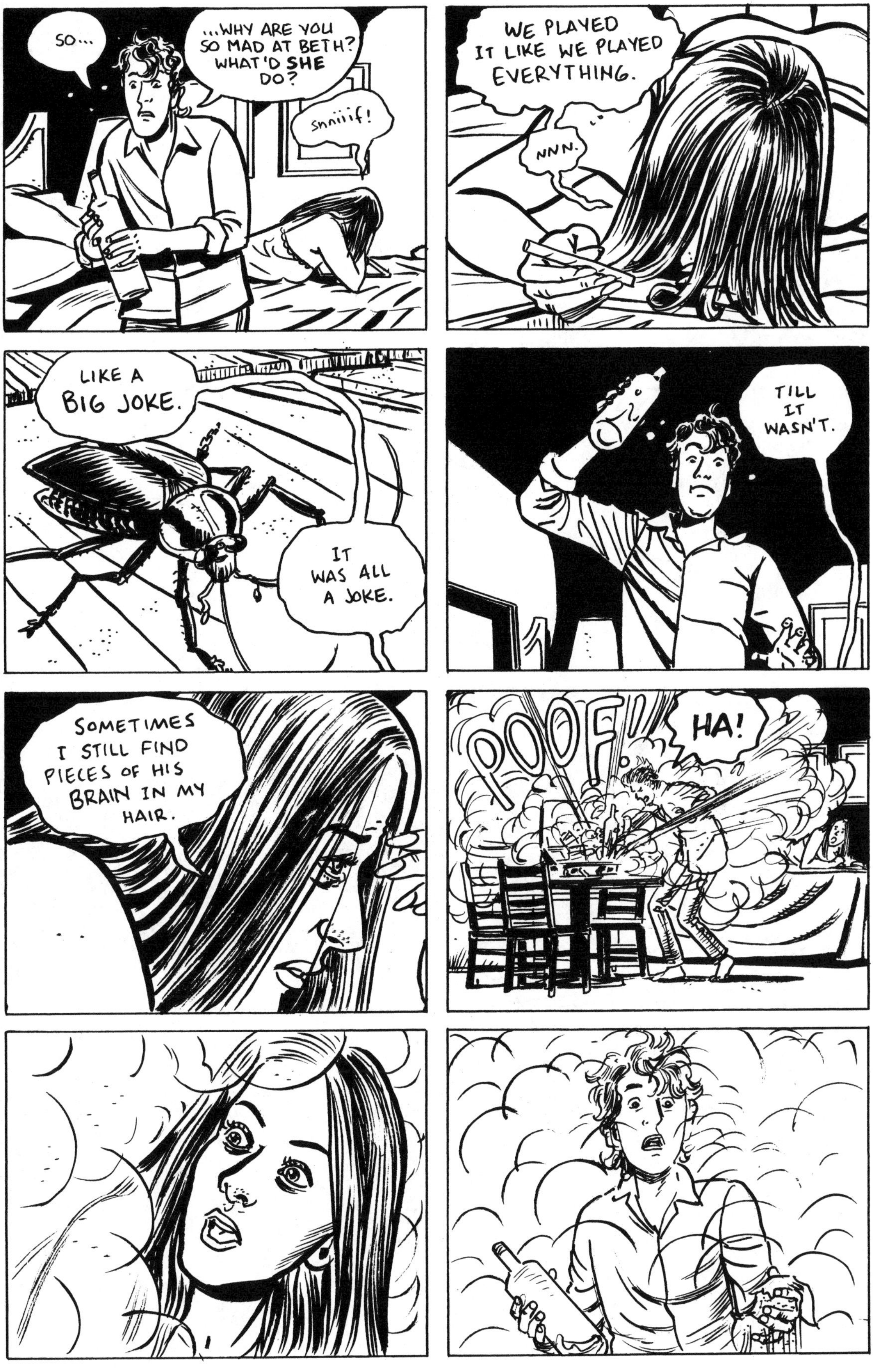

SO...
...WHY ARE YOU SO MAD AT BETH? WHAT'D SHE DO?
Snniiif!
WE PLAYED IT LIKE WE PLAYED EVERYTHING.
NNN.
LIKE A BIG JOKE.
IT WAS ALL A JOKE.
TILL IT WASN'T.
SOMETIMES I STILL FIND PIECES OF HIS BRAIN IN MY HAIR.
POOF!!
HA!

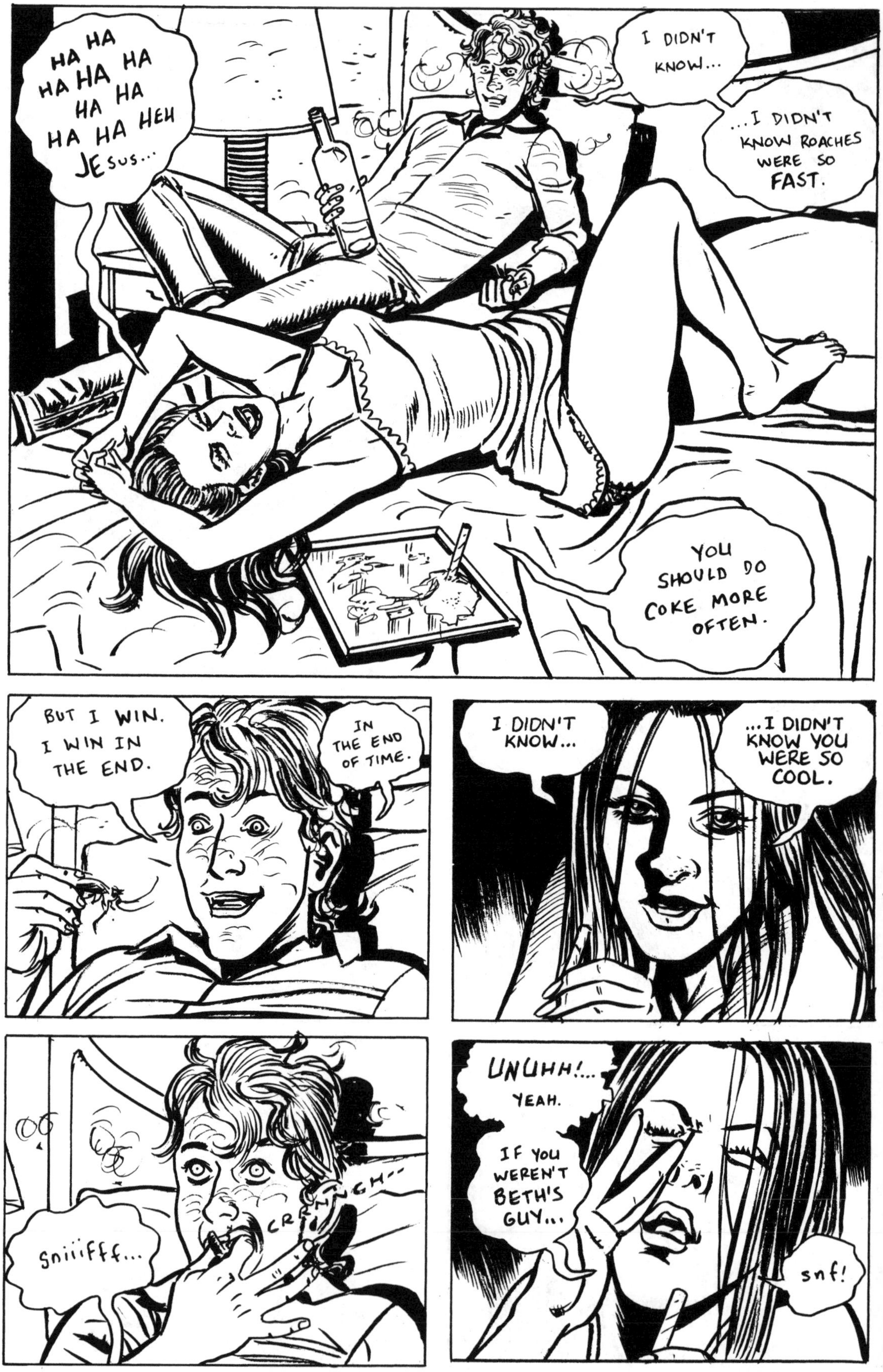
HA HA HA HA HA HA HA HA HA HA HEH JESUS...
I DIDN'T KNOW...
...I DIDN'T KNOW ROACHES WERE SO FAST.
YOU SHOULD DO COKE MORE OFTEN.
BUT I WIN. I WIN IN THE END.
IN THE END OF TIME.
I DIDN'T KNOW...
...I DIDN'T KNOW YOU WERE SO COOL.
sniiifff...
CRNNGH--
UNUHH!... YEAH.
IF YOU WEREN'T BETH'S GUY...
snf!

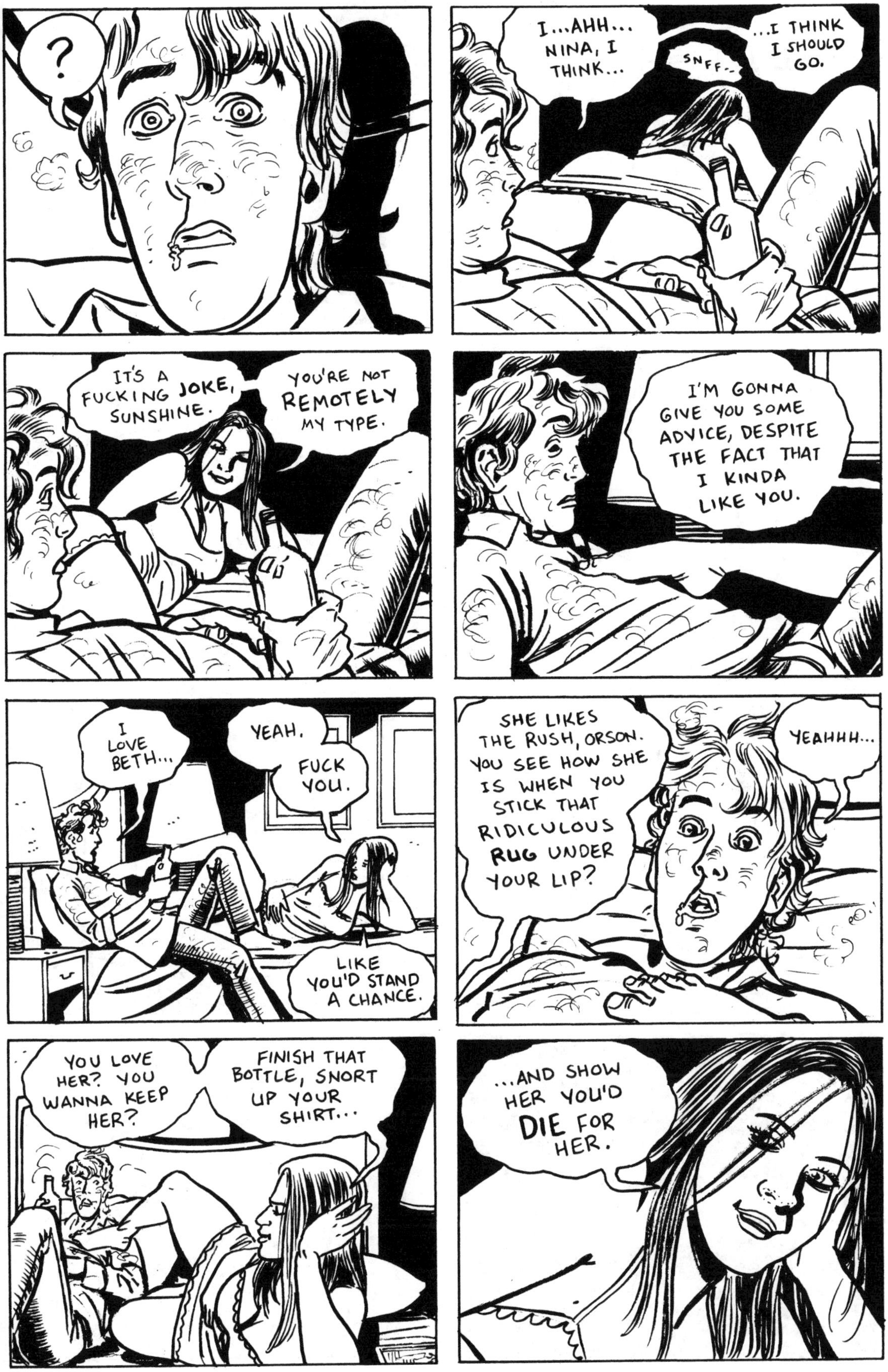
?
I...AHH... NINA, I THINK...
SNFF..
...I THINK I SHOULD GO.
IT'S A FUCKING JOKE, SUNSHINE.
YOU'RE NOT REMOTELY MY TYPE.
I'M GONNA GIVE YOU SOME ADVICE, DESPITE THE FACT THAT I KINDA LIKE YOU.
I LOVE BETH...
YEAH.
FUCK YOU.
LIKE YOU'D STAND A CHANCE.
SHE LIKES THE RUSH, ORSON. YOU SEE HOW SHE IS WHEN YOU STICK THAT RIDICULOUS RUG UNDER YOUR LIP?
YEAHHH...
YOU LOVE HER? YOU WANNA KEEP HER?
FINISH THAT BOTTLE, SNORT UP YOUR SHIRT...
...AND SHOW HER YOU'D DIE FOR HER.

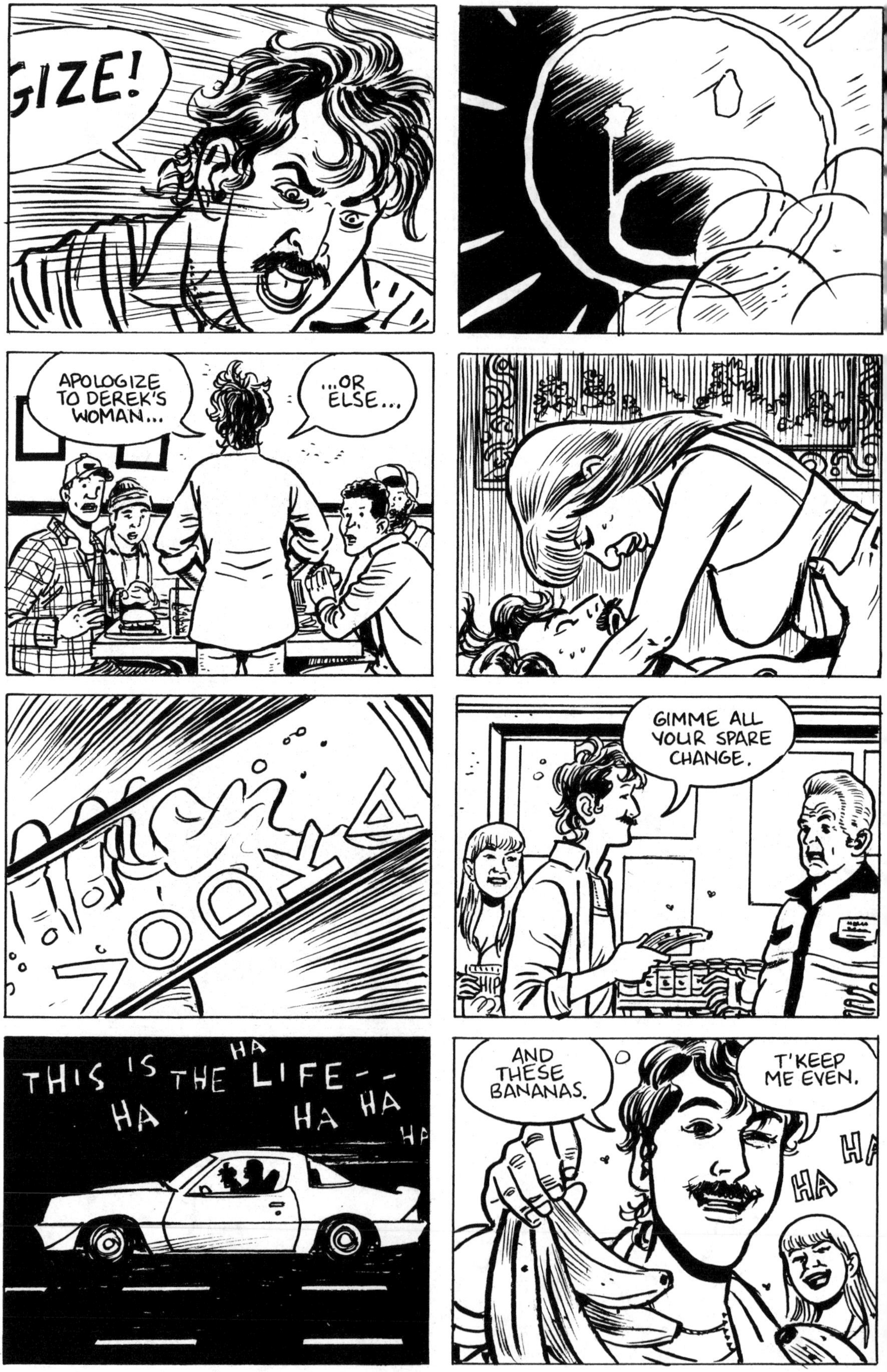
GIZE!
APOLOGIZE TO DEREK'S WOMAN...
...OR ELSE...
VODKA
GIMME ALL YOUR SPARE CHANGE.
THIS IS THE LIFE--
HA
HA
HA HA
HA
AND THESE BANANAS.
T'KEEP ME EVEN.
HA
HA

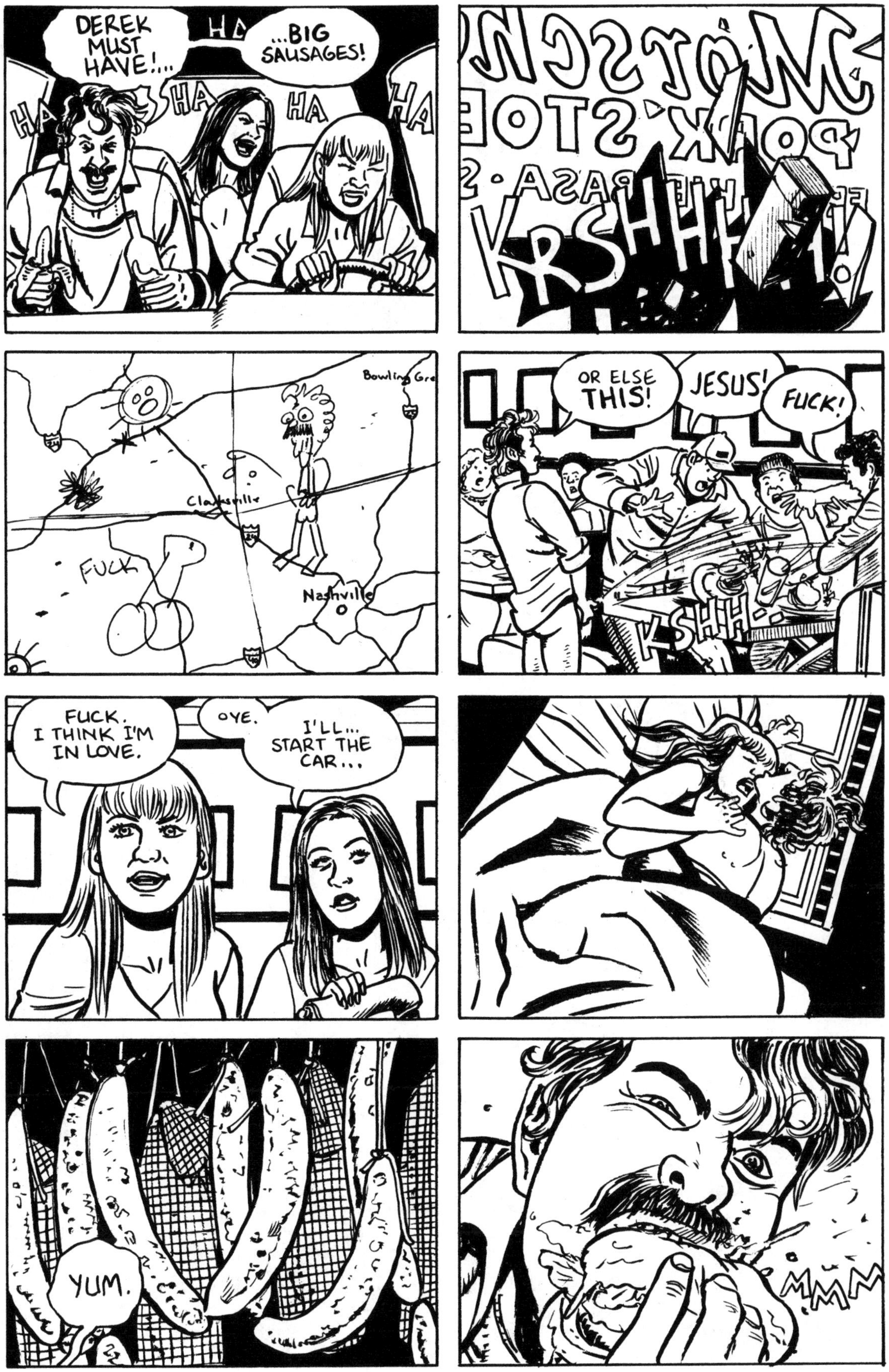
DEREK MUST HAVE!...
...BIG SAUSAGES!
HA HA HA HA HA
Bowling Gre
Clarksville
FUCK
Nashville
OR ELSE THIS!
JESUS!
FUCK!
FUCK. I THINK I'M IN LOVE.
OYE.
I'LL... START THE CAR...
YUM.
MMM

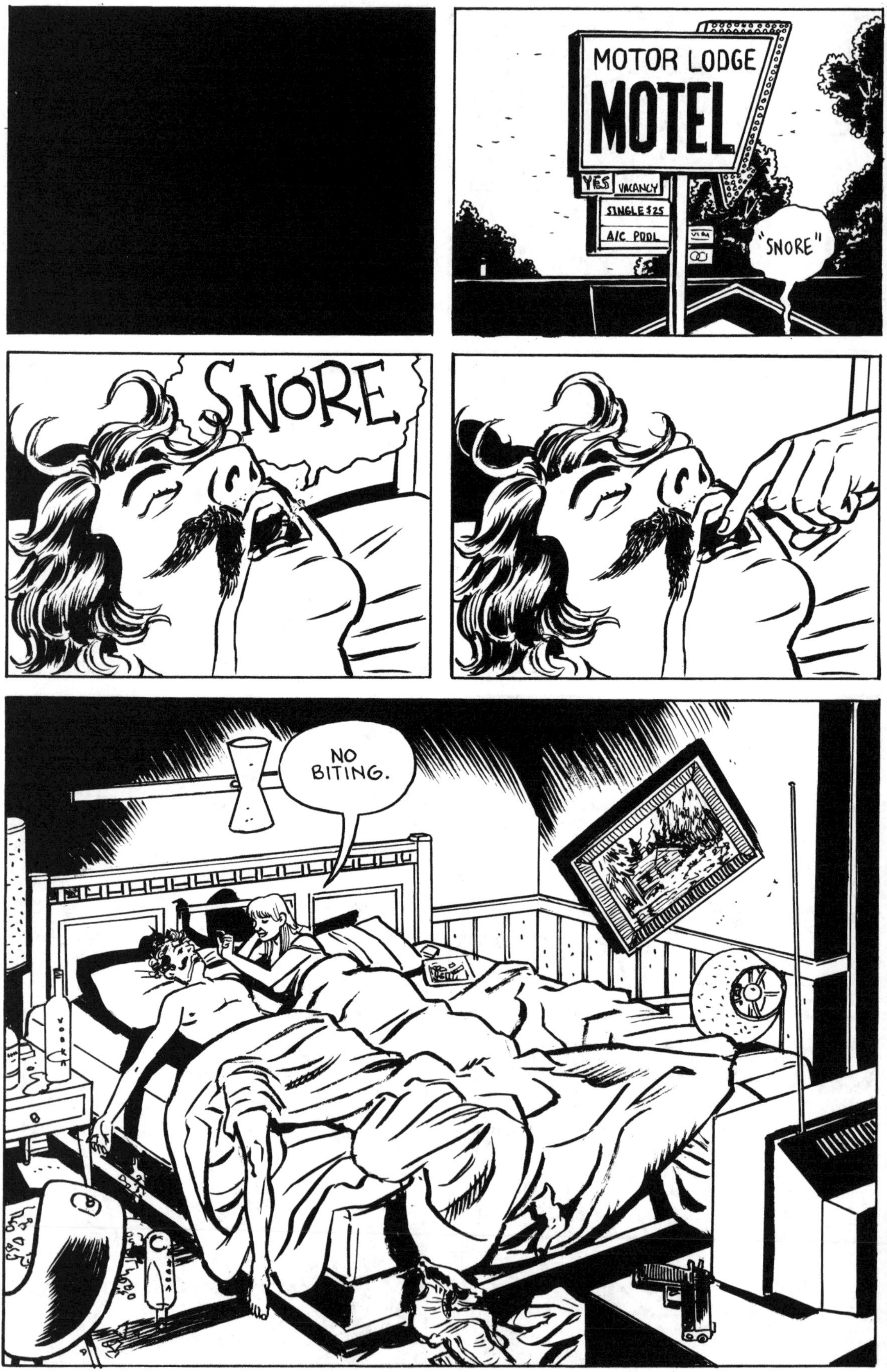
MOTOR LODGE
MOTEL
YES VACANCY
SINGLE $25
A/C POOL
VISA
"SNORE"
SNORE
NO BITING.

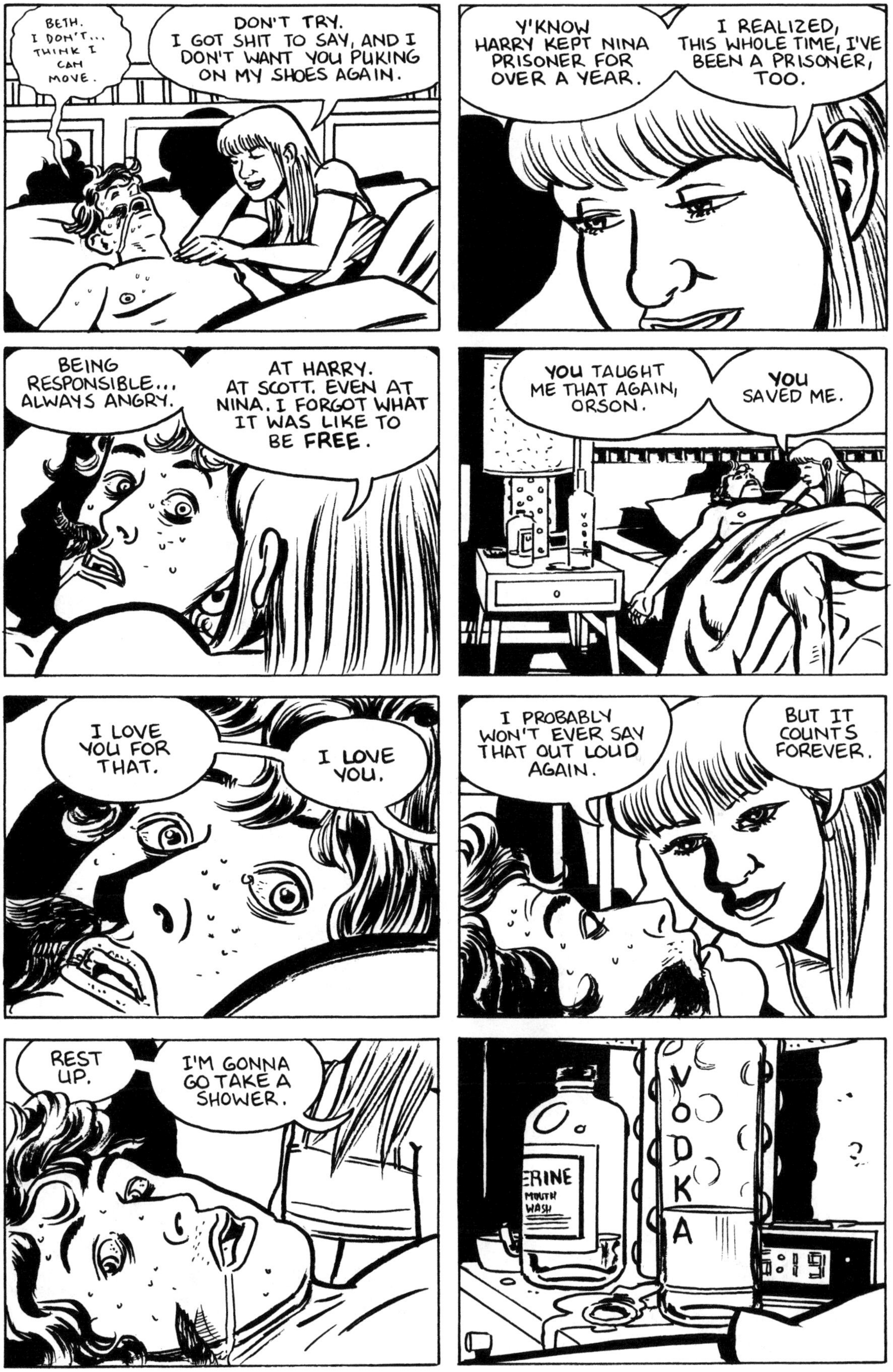
BETH. I DON'T... THINK I CAN MOVE.
DON'T TRY. I GOT SHIT TO SAY, AND I DON'T WANT YOU PUKING ON MY SHOES AGAIN.
Y'KNOW HARRY KEPT NINA PRISONER FOR OVER A YEAR.
I REALIZED, THIS WHOLE TIME, I'VE BEEN A PRISONER, TOO.
BEING RESPONSIBLE... ALWAYS ANGRY.
AT HARRY. AT SCOTT. EVEN AT NINA. I FORGOT WHAT IT WAS LIKE TO BE FREE.
YOU TAUGHT ME THAT AGAIN, ORSON.
YOU SAVED ME.
I LOVE YOU FOR THAT.
I LOVE YOU.
I PROBABLY WON'T EVER SAY THAT OUT LOUD AGAIN.
BUT IT COUNTS FOREVER.
REST UP.
I'M GONNA GO TAKE A SHOWER.
ERINE MOUTH WASH
VODKA
5:19

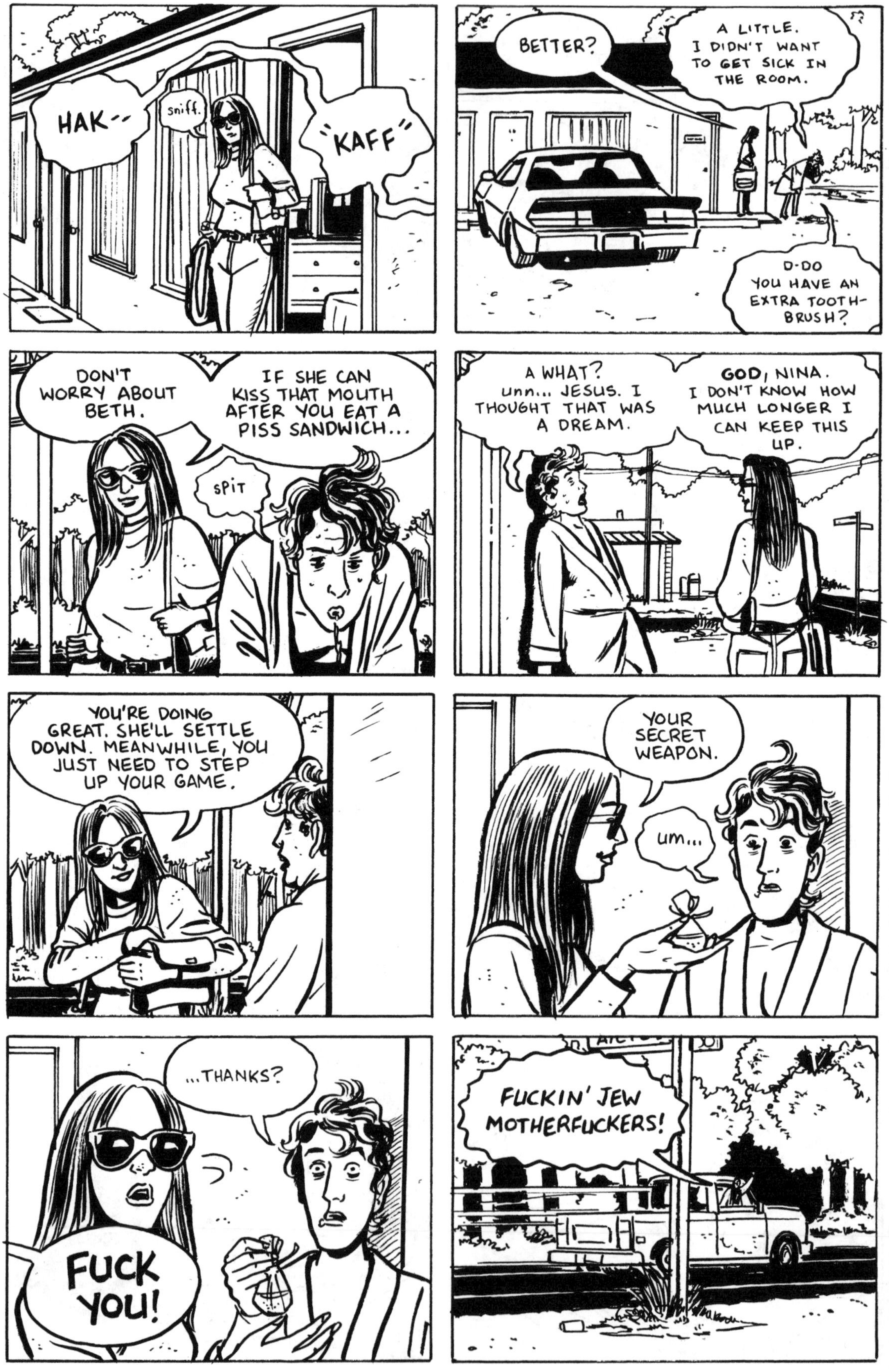
HAK--
sniff.
KAFF
BETTER?
A LITTLE. I DIDN'T WANT TO GET SICK IN THE ROOM.
D-DO YOU HAVE AN EXTRA TOOTH-BRUSH?
DON'T WORRY ABOUT BETH.
IF SHE CAN KISS THAT MOUTH AFTER YOU EAT A PISS SANDWICH...
SPIT
A WHAT? unn... JESUS. I THOUGHT THAT WAS A DREAM.
GOD, NINA. I DON'T KNOW HOW MUCH LONGER I CAN KEEP THIS UP.
YOU'RE DOING GREAT. SHE'LL SETTLE DOWN. MEANWHILE, YOU JUST NEED TO STEP UP YOUR GAME.
YOUR SECRET WEAPON.
um...
...THANKS?
FUCK YOU!
FUCKIN' JEW MOTHERFUCKERS!

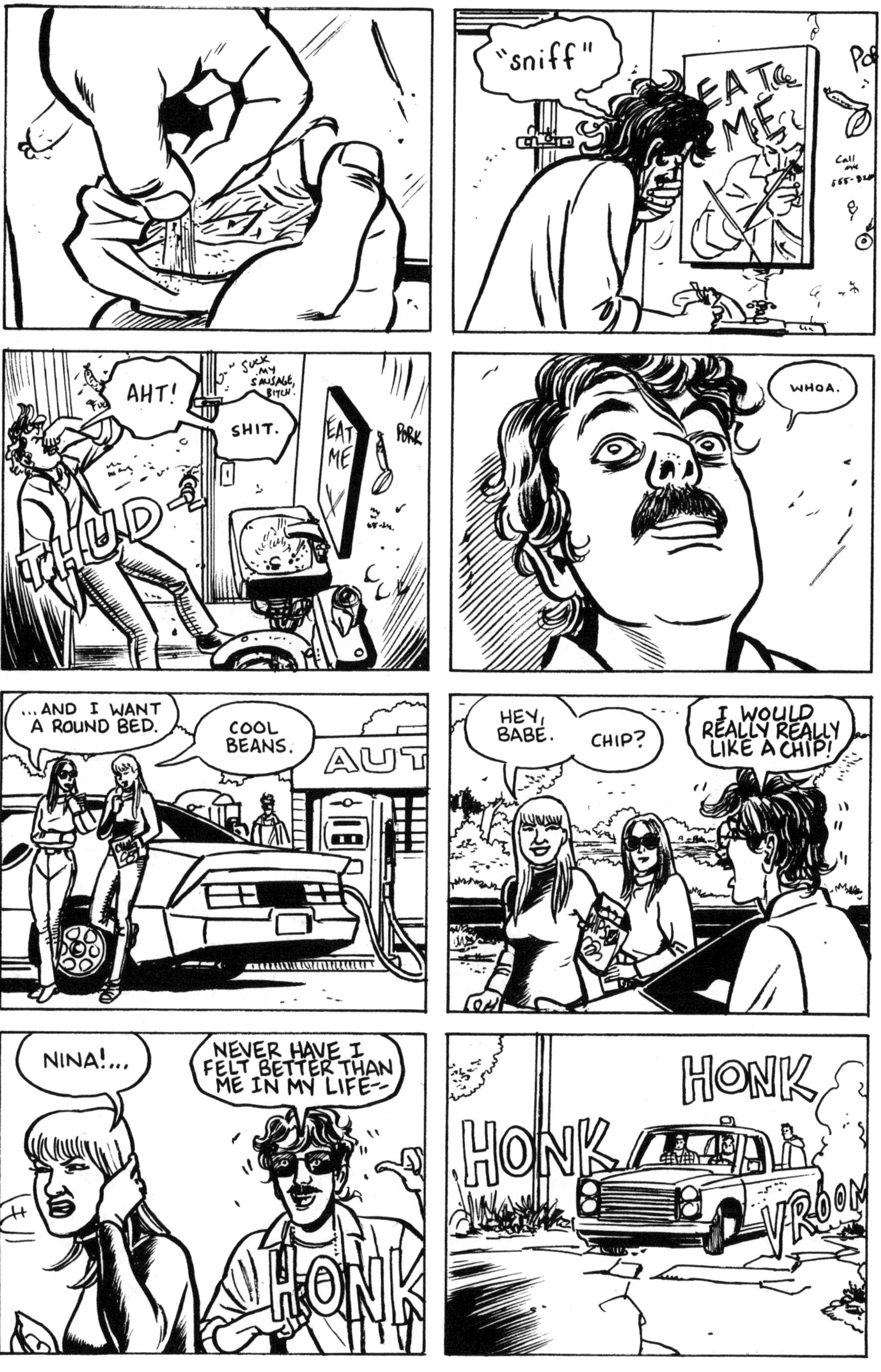
"sniff"
EAT ME
AHT!
SUCK MY SAUSAGE, BITCH
SHIT.
THUD
EAT ME
PORK
WHOA.
...AND I WANT A ROUND BED.
COOL BEANS.
HEY, BABE.
CHIP?
I WOULD REALLY REALLY LIKE A CHIP!
NINA!...
NEVER HAVE I FELT BETTER THAN ME IN MY LIFE--
HONK
HONK
HONK
VROOM

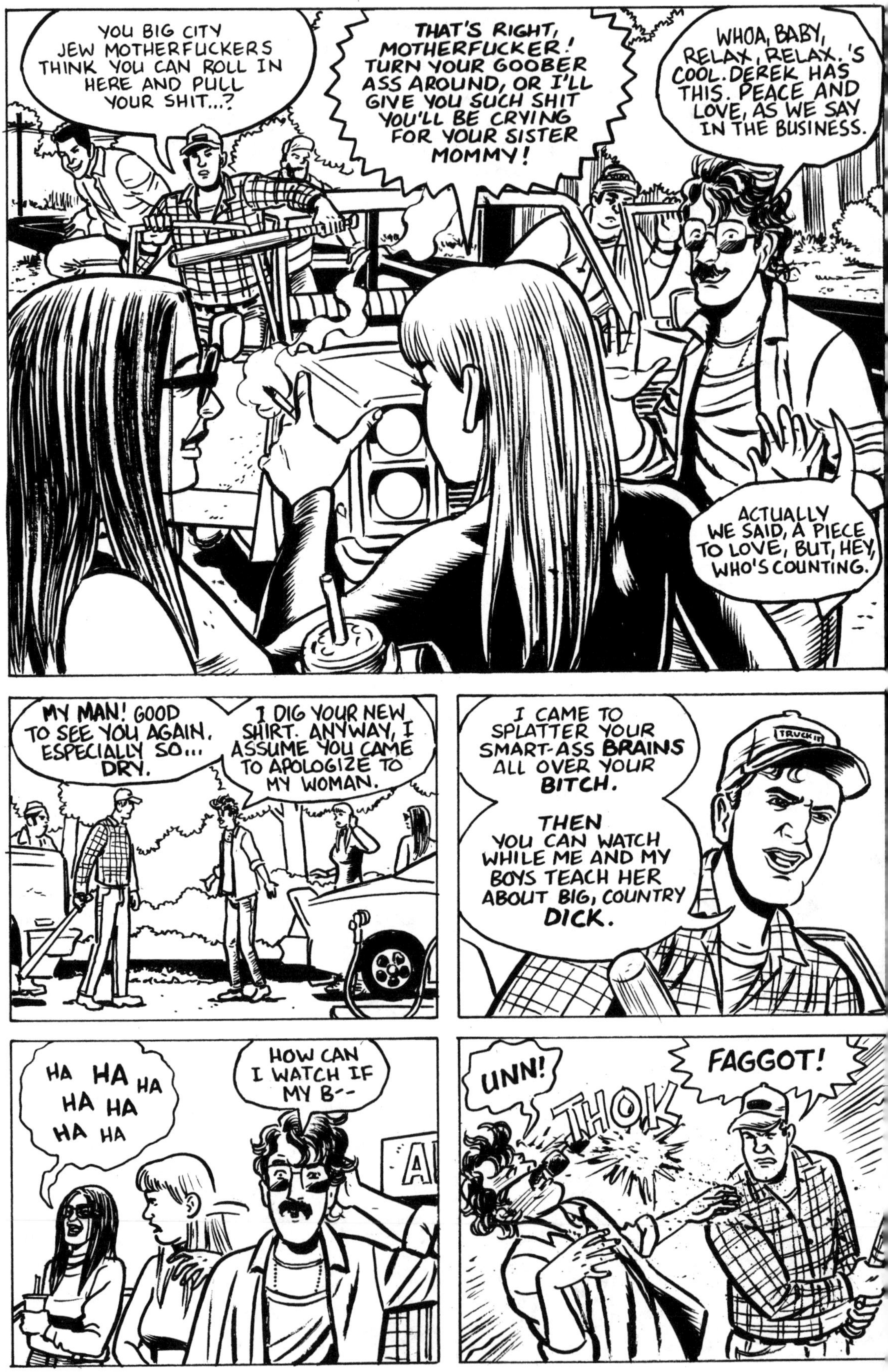
YOU BIG CITY JEW MOTHERFUCKERS THINK YOU CAN ROLL IN HERE AND PULL YOUR SHIT...?
THAT'S RIGHT, MOTHERFUCKER! TURN YOUR GOOBER ASS AROUND, OR I'LL GIVE YOU SUCH SHIT YOU'LL BE CRYING FOR YOUR SISTER MOMMY!
WHOA, BABY, RELAX, RELAX. 'S COOL. DEREK HAS THIS. PEACE AND LOVE, AS WE SAY IN THE BUSINESS.
ACTUALLY WE SAID, A PIECE TO LOVE, BUT, HEY, WHO'S COUNTING.
MY MAN! GOOD TO SEE YOU AGAIN. ESPECIALLY SO... DRY.
I DIG YOUR NEW SHIRT. ANYWAY, I ASSUME YOU CAME TO APOLOGIZE TO MY WOMAN.
I CAME TO SPLATTER YOUR SMART-ASS BRAINS ALL OVER YOUR BITCH.
THEN YOU CAN WATCH WHILE ME AND MY BOYS TEACH HER ABOUT BIG, COUNTRY DICK.
TRUCK IT
HA HA HA HA HA HA HA
HOW CAN I WATCH IF MY B--
UNN!
THOK
FAGGOT!

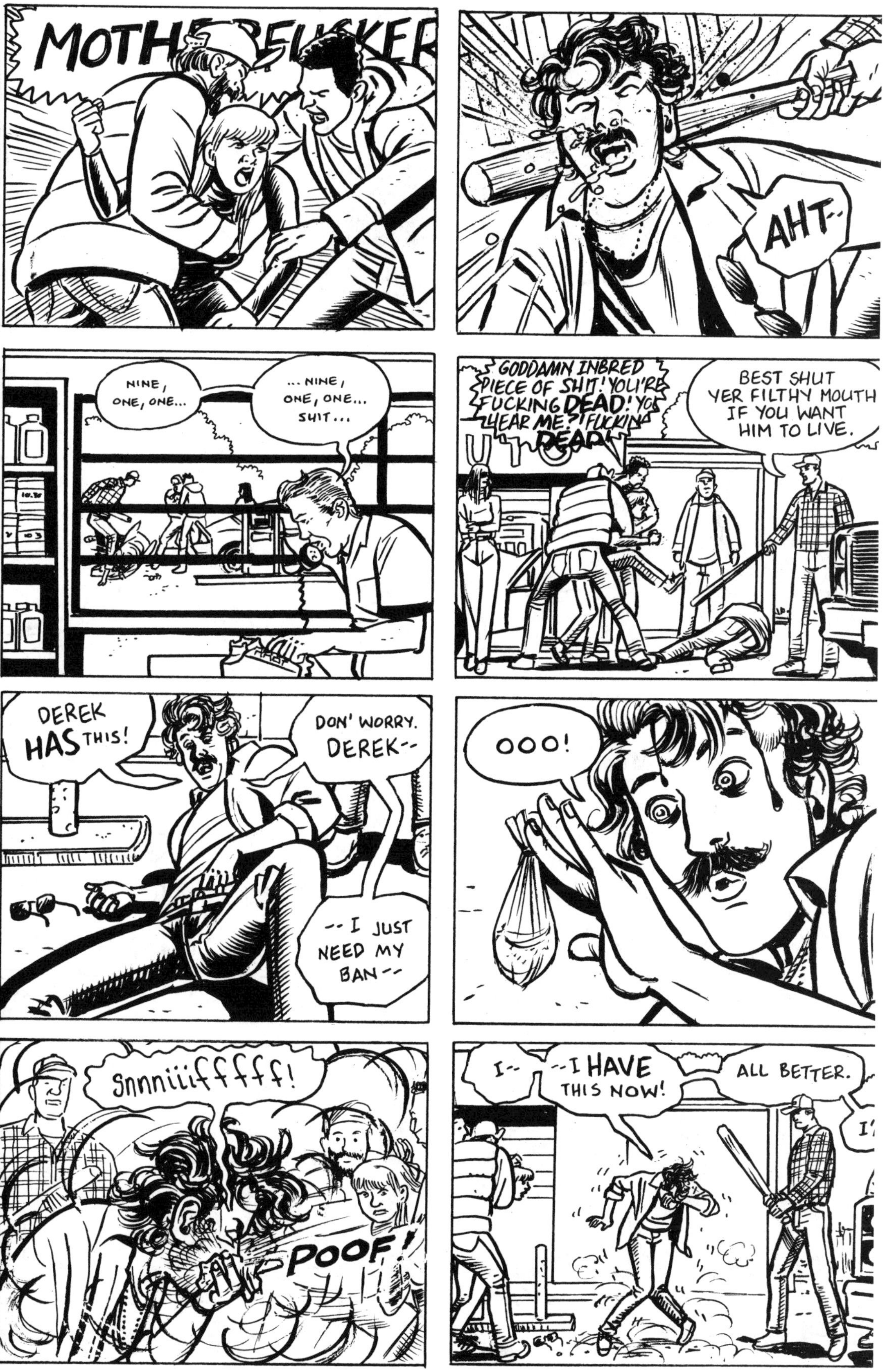
MOTHE
UCKER
AHT--
NINE, ONE, ONE...
...NINE, ONE, ONE... SHIT...
GODDAMN INBRED PIECE OF SHIT! YOU'RE FUCKING DEAD! YO HEAR ME? FUCKIN DEAD!
BEST SHUT YER FILTHY MOUTH IF YOU WANT HIM TO LIVE.
DEREK HAS THIS!
DON' WORRY. DEREK--
--I JUST NEED MY BAN--
OOO!
Snnniiiffffff!
POOF!
I--
--I HAVE THIS NOW!
ALL BETTER.
I'

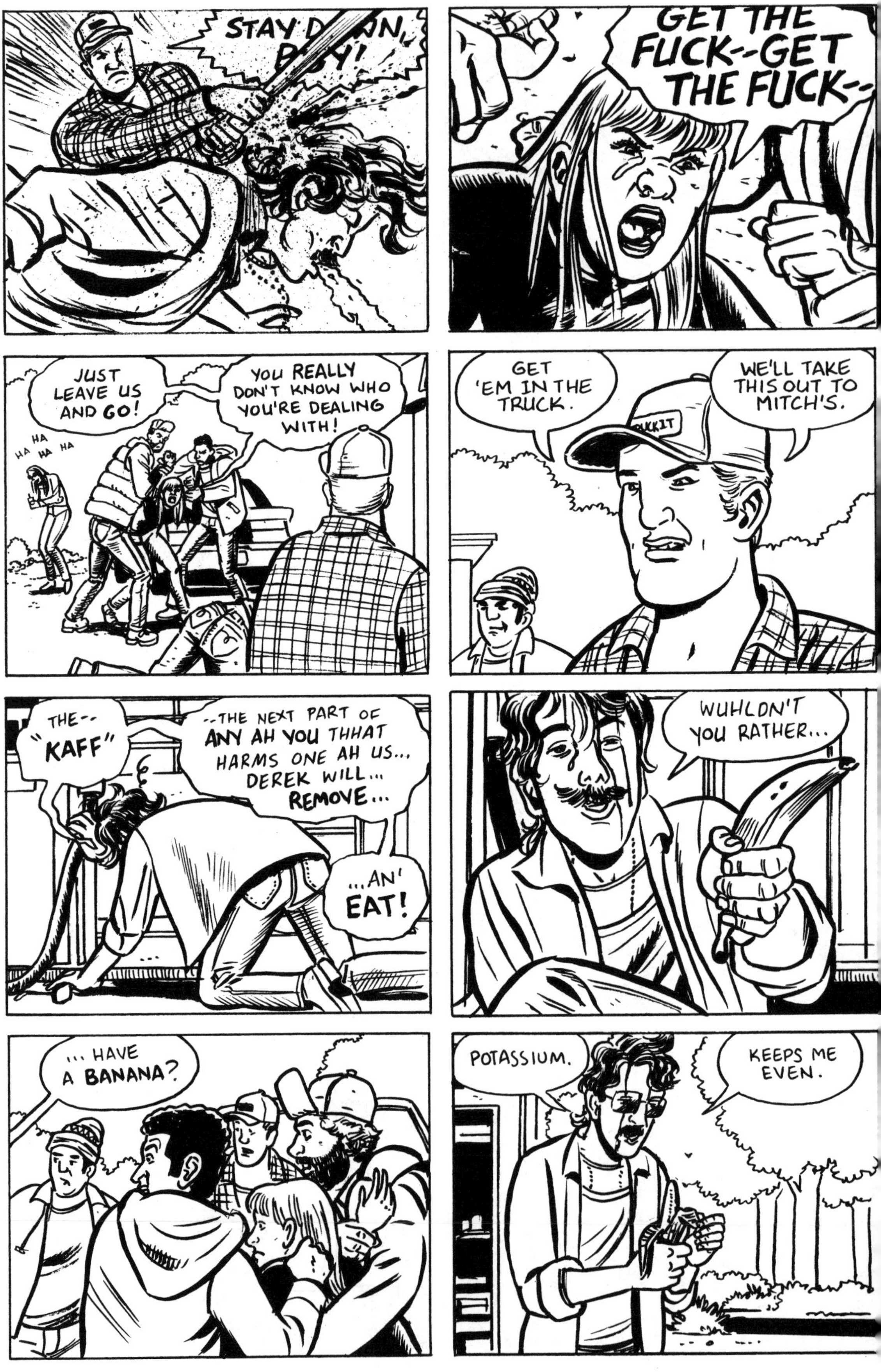
STAY DOWN, BOY!
GET THE FUCK--GET THE FUCK--
JUST LEAVE US AND GO!
YOU REALLY DON'T KNOW WHO YOU'RE DEALING WITH!
HA HA HA HA HA
GET 'EM IN THE TRUCK.
WE'LL TAKE THIS OUT TO MITCH'S.
THE-- "KAFF"
--THE NEXT PART OF ANY AH YOU THHAT HARMS ONE AH US... DEREK WILL... REMOVE...
...AN' EAT!
WUHLDN'T YOU RATHER...
... HAVE A BANANA?
POTASSIUM.
KEEPS ME EVEN.

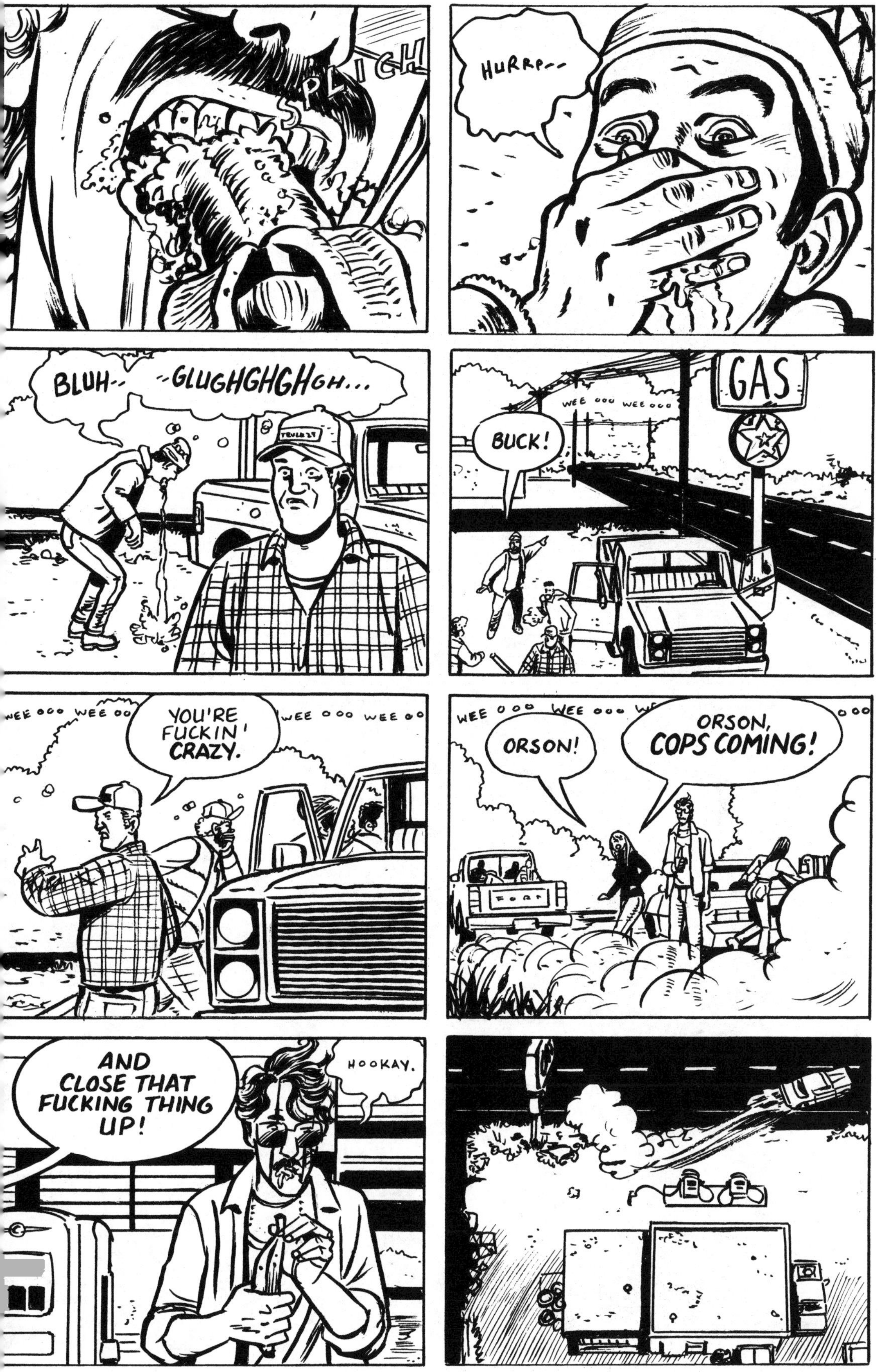
SPLICH
HURRP...
BLUH... ...GLUGHGHGHGH...
BUCK!
WEE OOO WEE OOO
WEE OOO WEE OO
YOU'RE FUCKIN' CRAZY.
WEE OOO WEE OO
WEE OOO WEE OOO
ORSON!
ORSON, COPS COMING!
AND CLOSE THAT FUCKING THING UP!
HOOKAY.

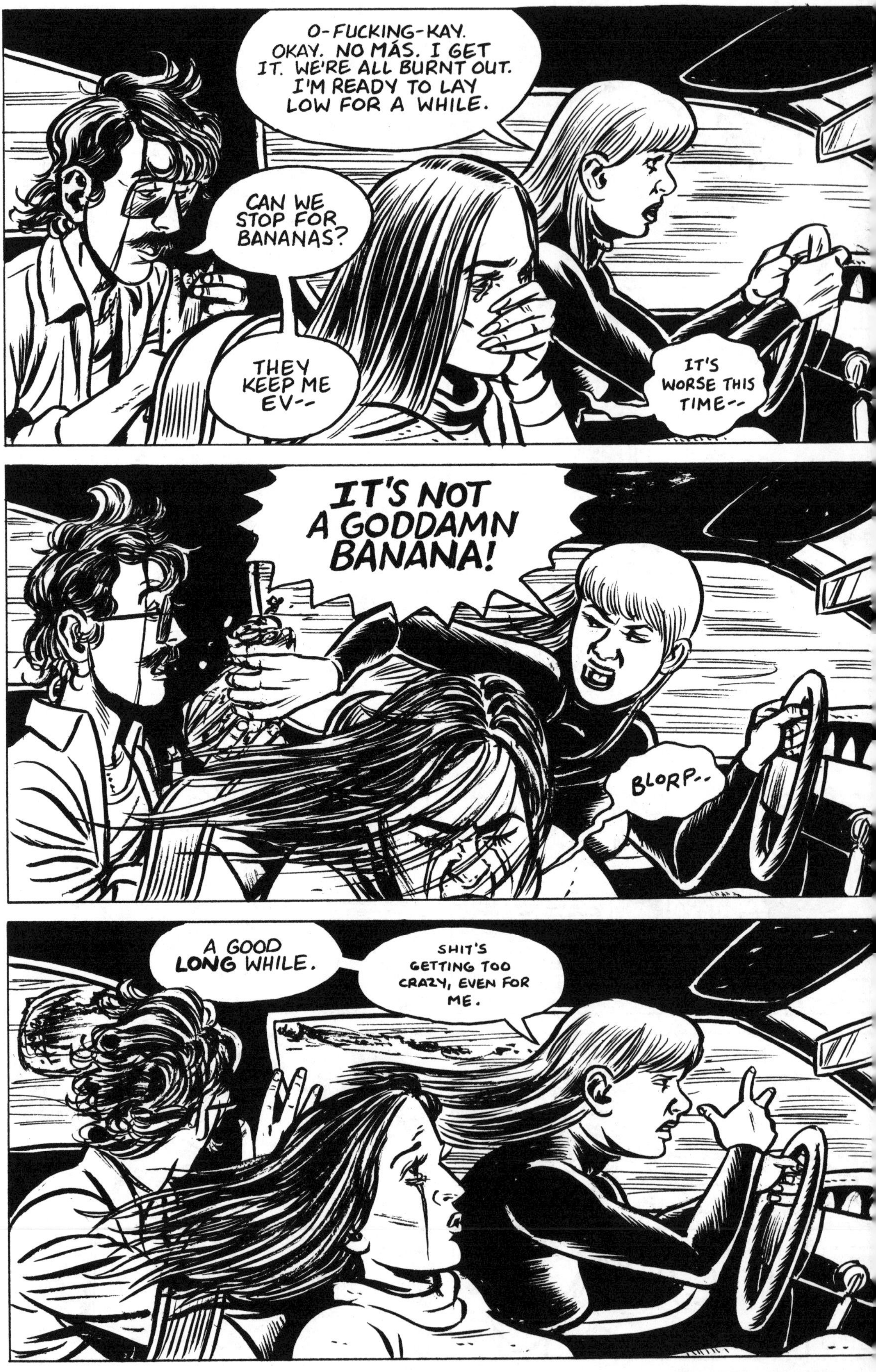
O-FUCKING-KAY. OKAY. NO MÁS. I GET IT. WE'RE ALL BURNT OUT. I'M READY TO LAY LOW FOR A WHILE.
CAN WE STOP FOR BANANAS?
THEY KEEP ME EV--
IT'S WORSE THIS TIME--
IT'S NOT A GODDAMN BANANA!
BLORP..
A GOOD LONG WHILE.
SHIT'S GETTING TOO CRAZY, EVEN FOR ME.

THE END...

5

"TO TWEET AND TWEET AGAIN"

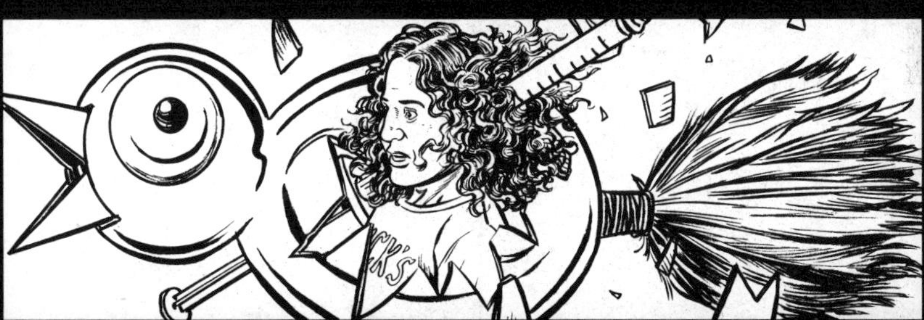

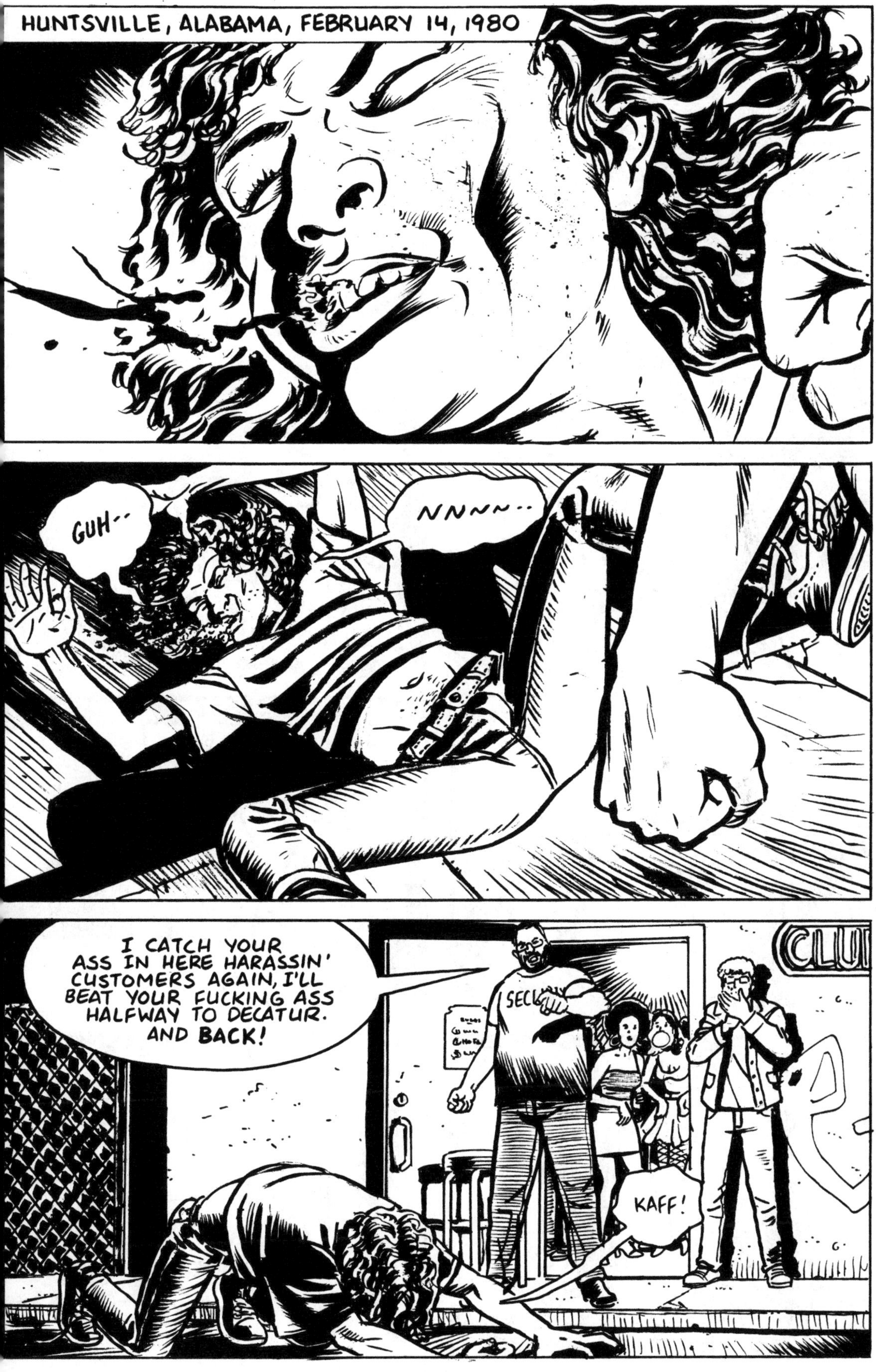
HUNTSVILLE, ALABAMA, FEBRUARY 14, 1980
GUH--
NNNN--
I CATCH YOUR ASS IN HERE HARASSIN' CUSTOMERS AGAIN, I'LL BEAT YOUR FUCKING ASS HALFWAY TO DECATUR. AND **BACK!**
KAFF!

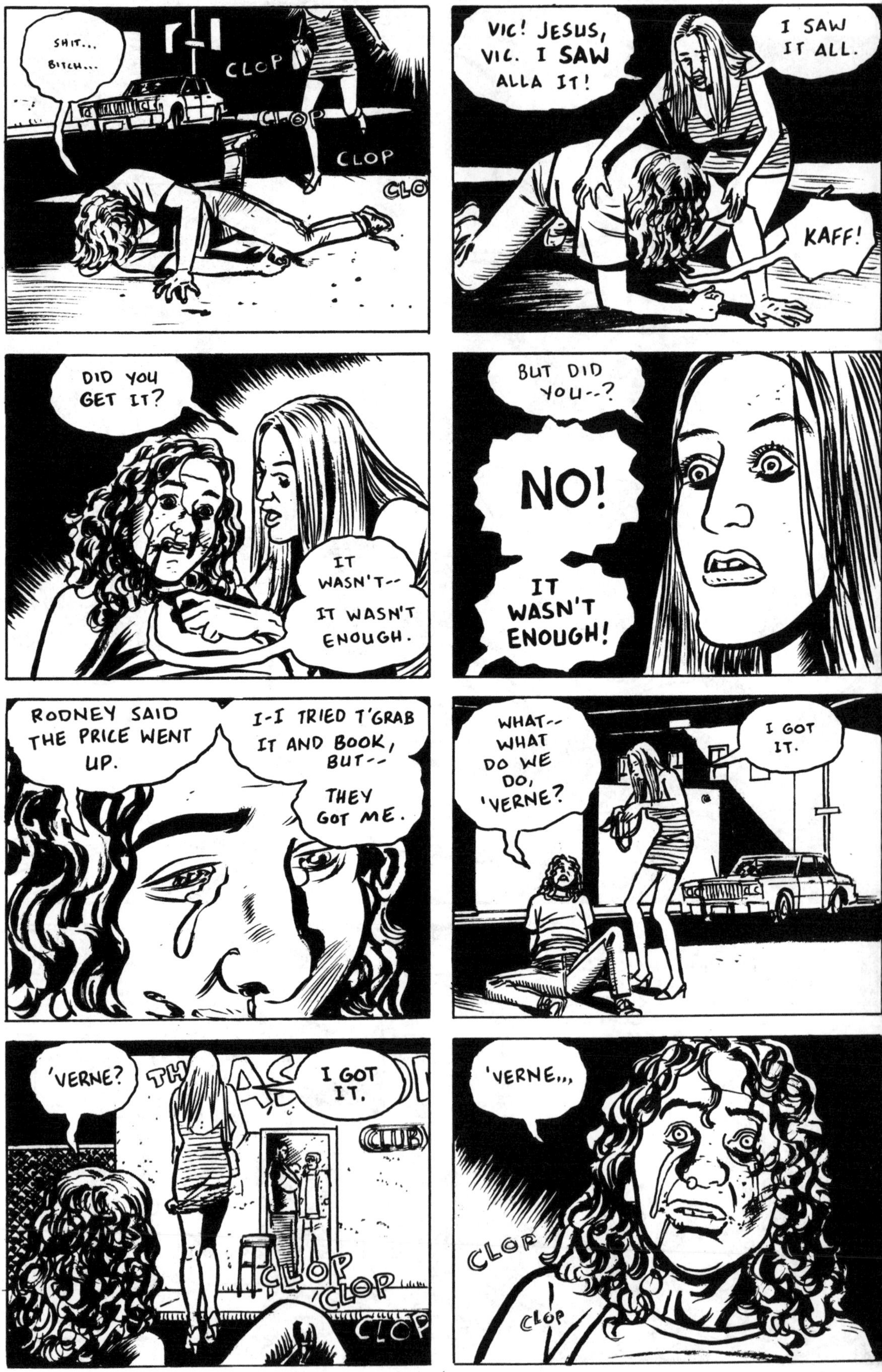
SHIT... BITCH...
CLOP
CLOP
CLOP
CLO
VIC! JESUS, VIC. I SAW ALLA IT!
I SAW IT ALL.
KAFF!
DID YOU GET IT?
IT WASN'T--
IT WASN'T ENOUGH.
BUT DID YOU--?
NO!
IT WASN'T ENOUGH!
RODNEY SAID THE PRICE WENT UP.
I-I TRIED T'GRAB IT AND BOOK, BUT--
THEY GOT ME.
WHAT-- WHAT DO WE DO, 'VERNE?
I GOT IT.
'VERNE?
I GOT IT.
CLUB
CLOP
CLOP
CLOP
'VERNE...
CLOP
CLOP

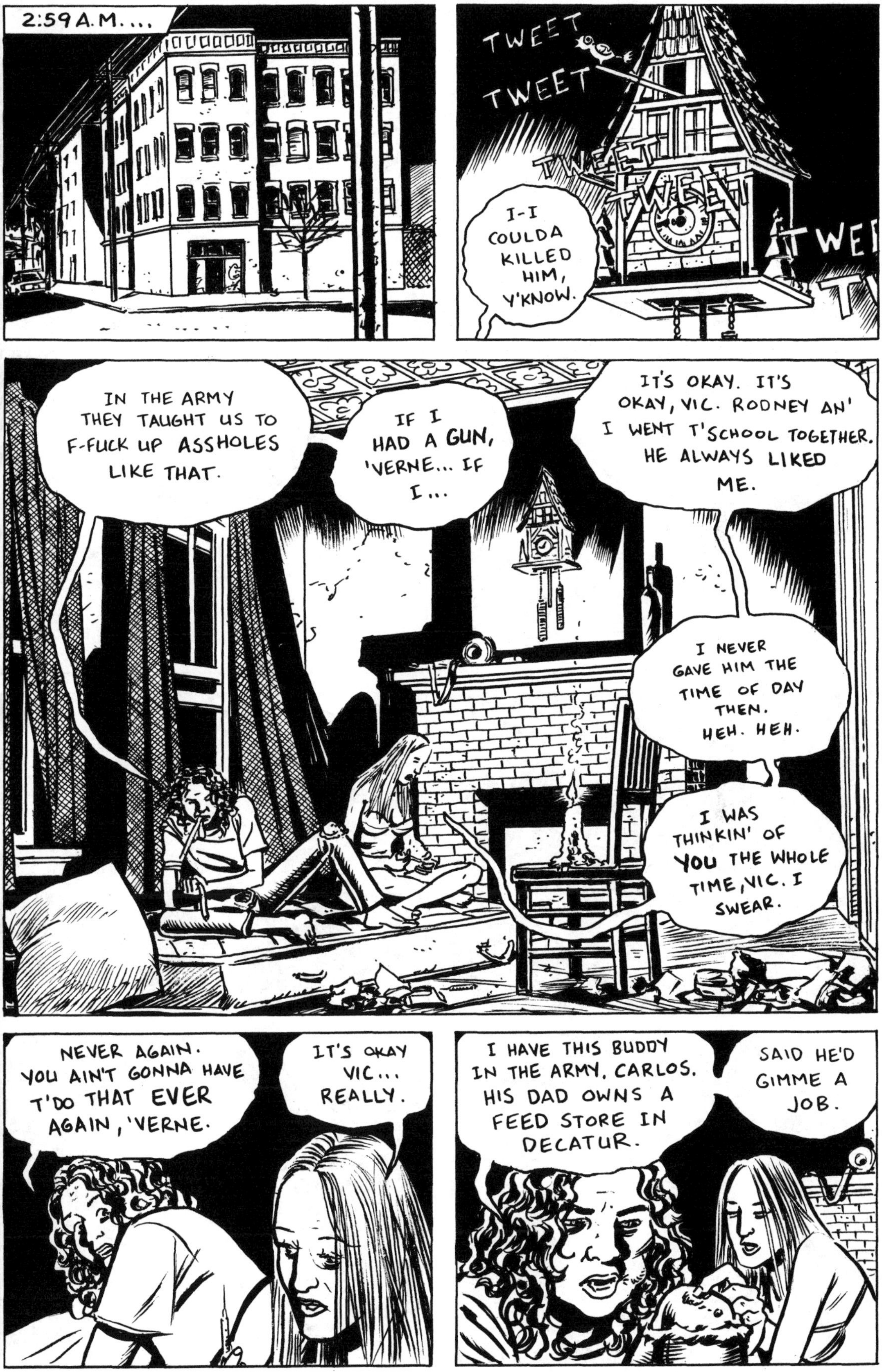
2:59 A.M. ...
TWEET TWEET
I-I COULDA KILLED HIM, Y'KNOW.
IN THE ARMY THEY TAUGHT US TO F-FUCK UP ASSHOLES LIKE THAT.
IF I HAD A GUN, 'VERNE... IF I...
IT'S OKAY. IT'S OKAY, VIC. RODNEY AN' I WENT T'SCHOOL TOGETHER. HE ALWAYS LIKED ME.
I NEVER GAVE HIM THE TIME OF DAY THEN. HEH. HEH.
I WAS THINKIN' OF YOU THE WHOLE TIME, VIC. I SWEAR.
NEVER AGAIN. YOU AIN'T GONNA HAVE T'DO THAT EVER AGAIN, 'VERNE.
IT'S OKAY VIC... REALLY.
I HAVE THIS BUDDY IN THE ARMY, CARLOS. HIS DAD OWNS A FEED STORE IN DECATUR.
SAID HE'D GIMME A JOB.

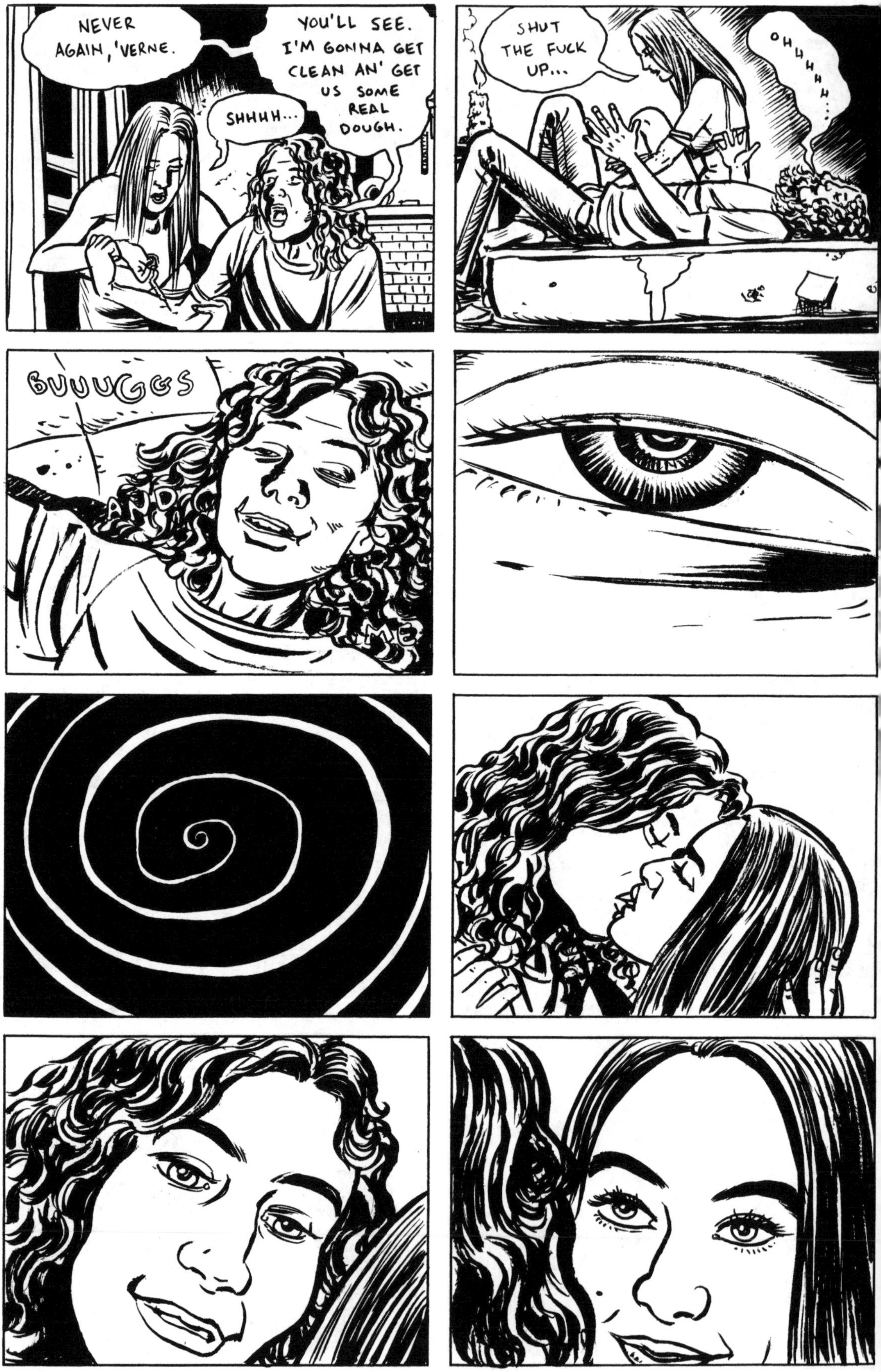
NEVER AGAIN, 'VERNE.
YOU'LL SEE. I'M GONNA GET CLEAN AN' GET US SOME REAL DOUGH.
SHHHH...
SHUT THE FUCK UP...
OHHHHH...
BUUUGGS

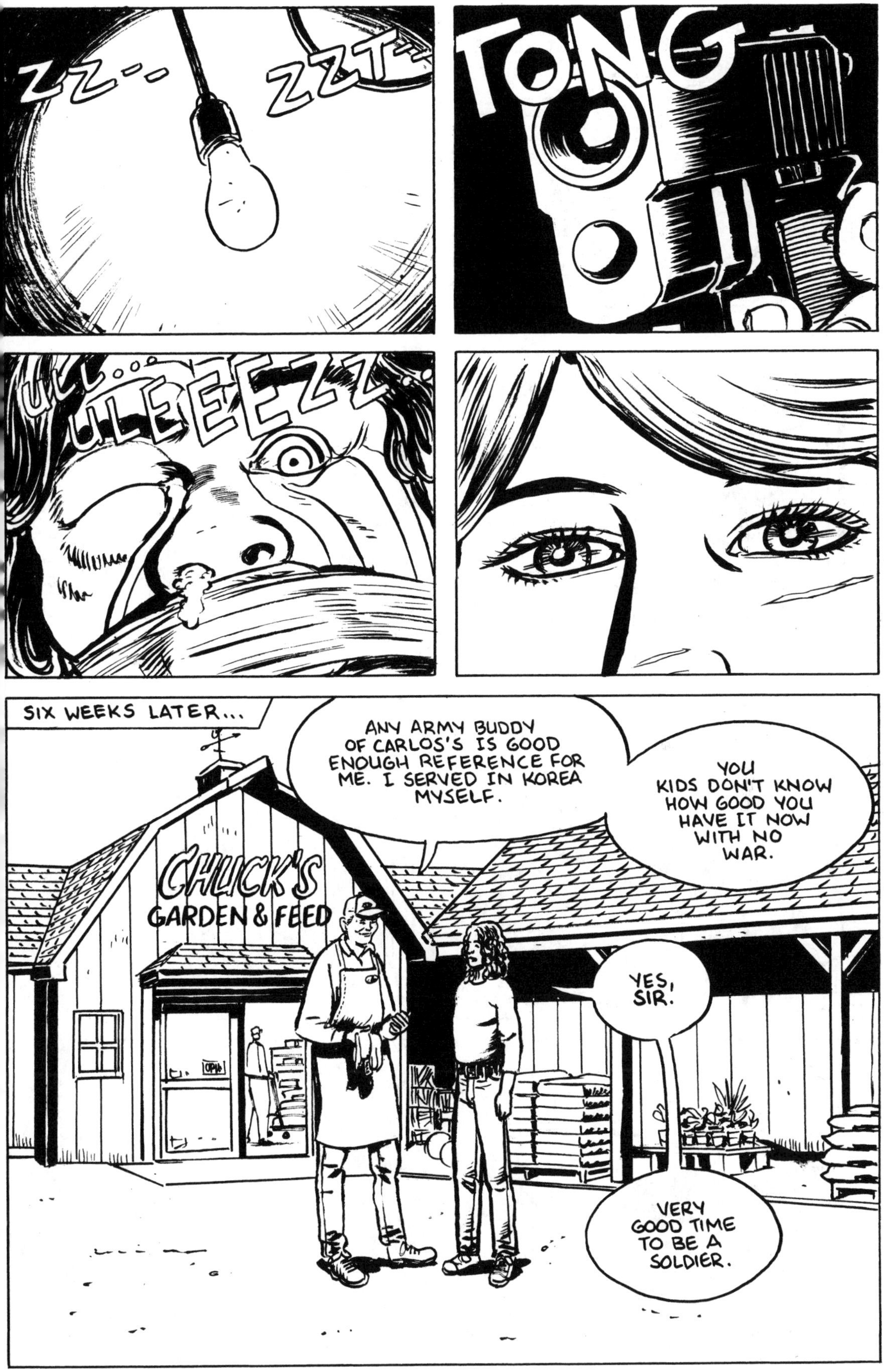
ZZ-..
ZZT-
TONG
ULEEEZZ
SIX WEEKS LATER...
ANY ARMY BUDDY OF CARLOS'S IS GOOD ENOUGH REFERENCE FOR ME. I SERVED IN KOREA MYSELF.
YOU KIDS DON'T KNOW HOW GOOD YOU HAVE IT NOW WITH NO WAR.
CHUCK'S GARDEN & FEED
YES, SIR.
VERY GOOD TIME TO BE A SOLDIER.

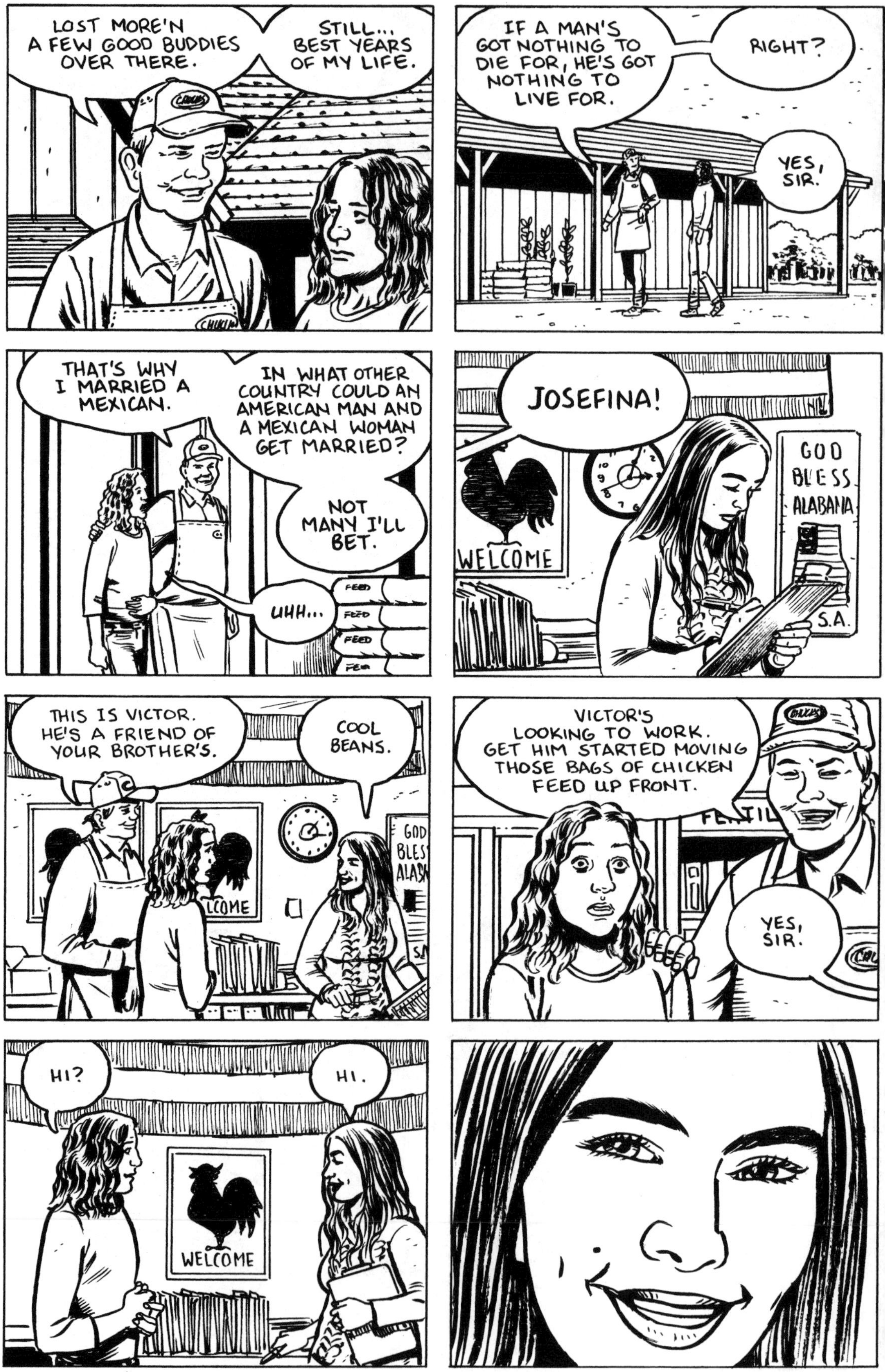
LOST MORE'N A FEW GOOD BUDDIES OVER THERE.
STILL... BEST YEARS OF MY LIFE.
IF A MAN'S GOT NOTHING TO DIE FOR, HE'S GOT NOTHING TO LIVE FOR.
RIGHT?
YES, SIR.
THAT'S WHY I MARRIED A MEXICAN.
IN WHAT OTHER COUNTRY COULD AN AMERICAN MAN AND A MEXICAN WOMAN GET MARRIED?
NOT MANY I'LL BET.
UHH...
FEED
FEED
FEED
JOSEFINA!
WELCOME
GOD BLESS ALABAMA
THIS IS VICTOR. HE'S A FRIEND OF YOUR BROTHER'S.
COOL BEANS.
VICTOR'S LOOKING TO WORK. GET HIM STARTED MOVING THOSE BAGS OF CHICKEN FEED UP FRONT.
YES, SIR.
HI?
HI.
WELCOME

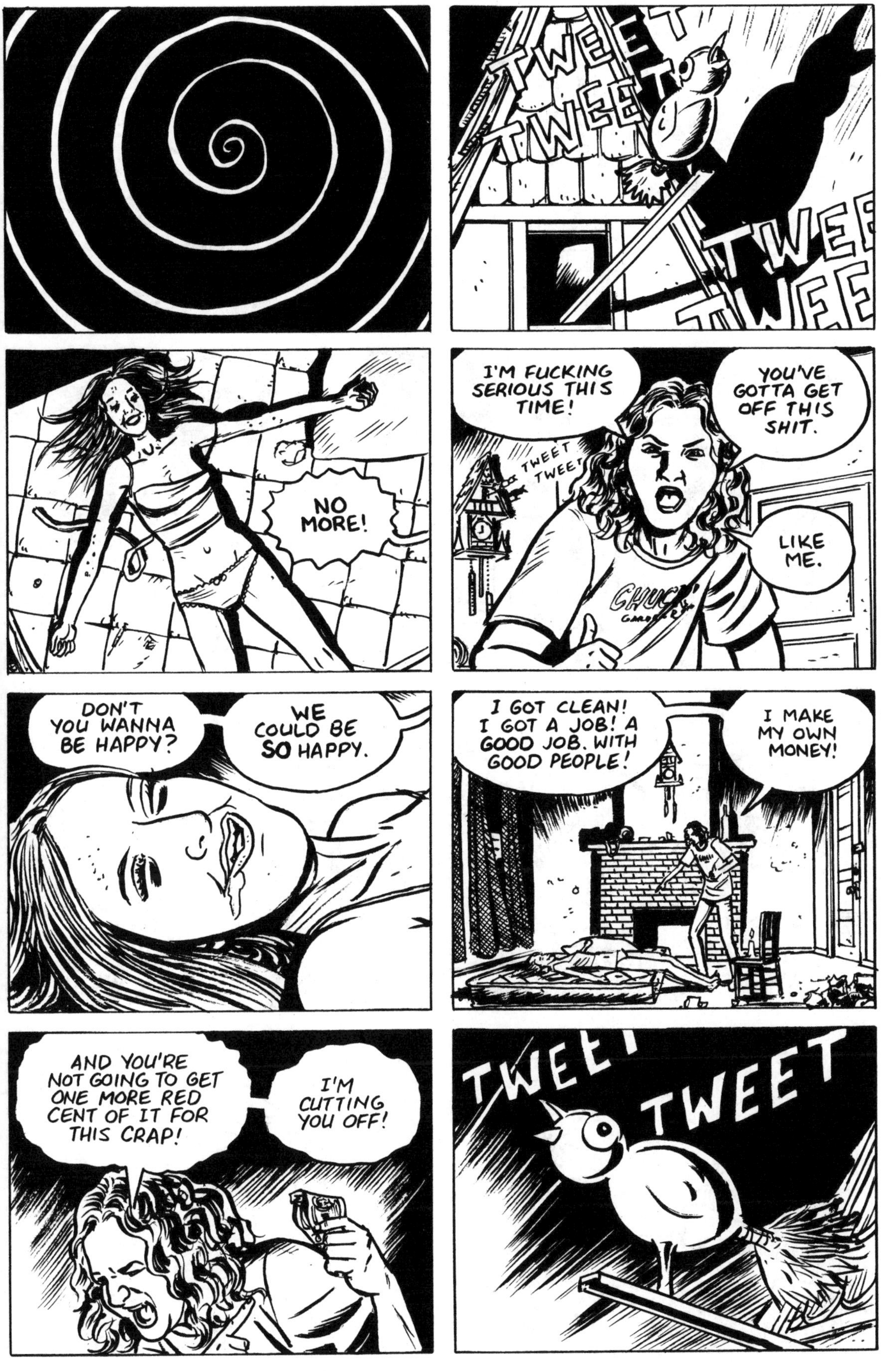
TWEET
TWEET
TWEE
TWEE
NO MORE!
I'M FUCKING SERIOUS THIS TIME!
YOU'VE GOTTA GET OFF THIS SHIT.
TWEET TWEET
LIKE ME.
DON'T YOU WANNA BE HAPPY?
WE COULD BE SO HAPPY.
I GOT CLEAN! I GOT A JOB! A GOOD JOB. WITH GOOD PEOPLE!
I MAKE MY OWN MONEY!
AND YOU'RE NOT GOING TO GET ONE MORE RED CENT OF IT FOR THIS CRAP!
I'M CUTTING YOU OFF!
TWEET
TWEET

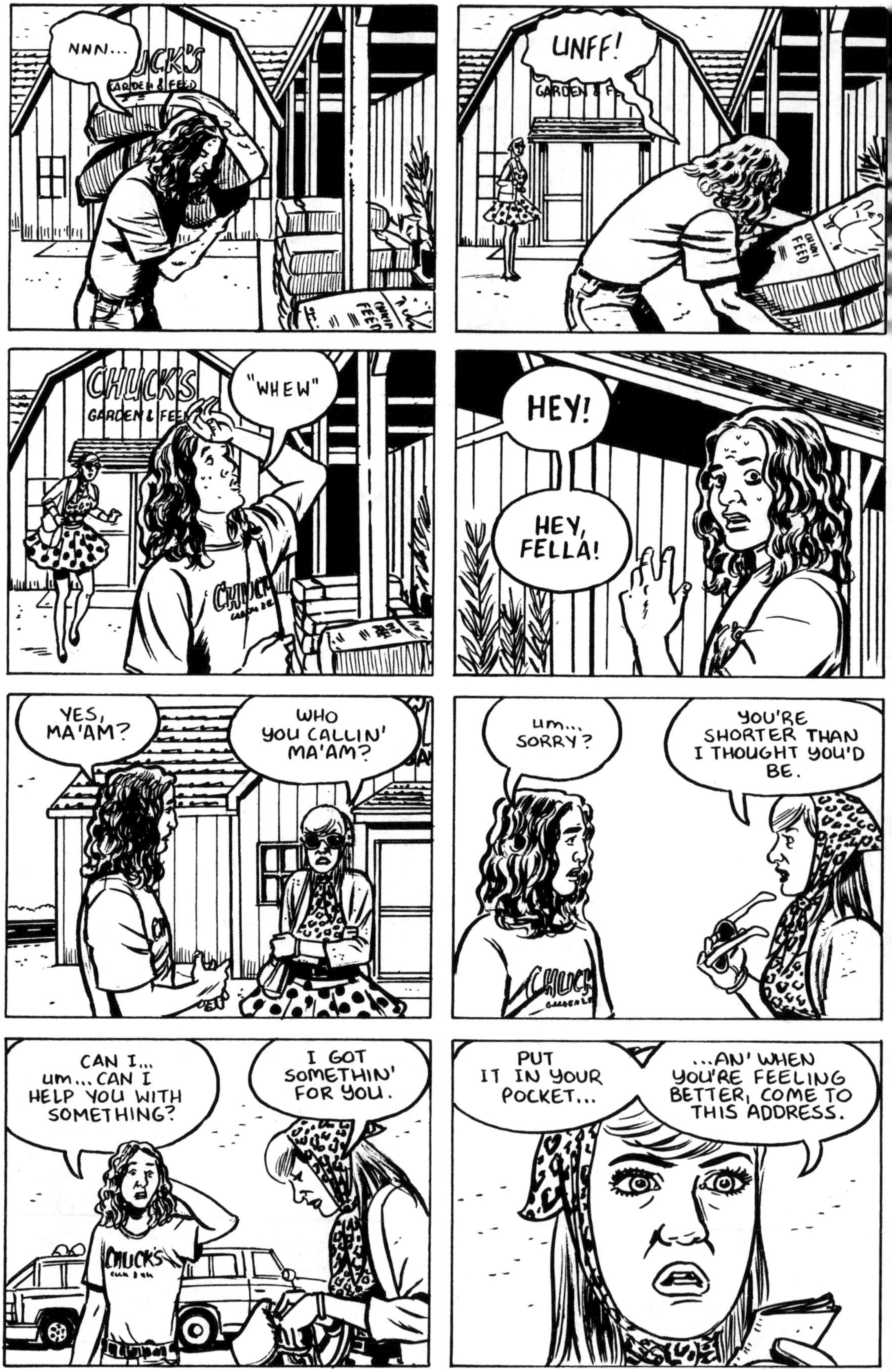
NNN...
UNFF!
"WHEW"
HEY!
HEY, FELLA!
YES, MA'AM?
WHO YOU CALLIN' MA'AM?
um... SORRY?
YOU'RE SHORTER THAN I THOUGHT YOU'D BE.
CAN I... um... CAN I HELP YOU WITH SOMETHING?
I GOT SOMETHIN' FOR YOU.
PUT IT IN YOUR POCKET...
...AN' WHEN YOU'RE FEELING BETTER, COME TO THIS ADDRESS.

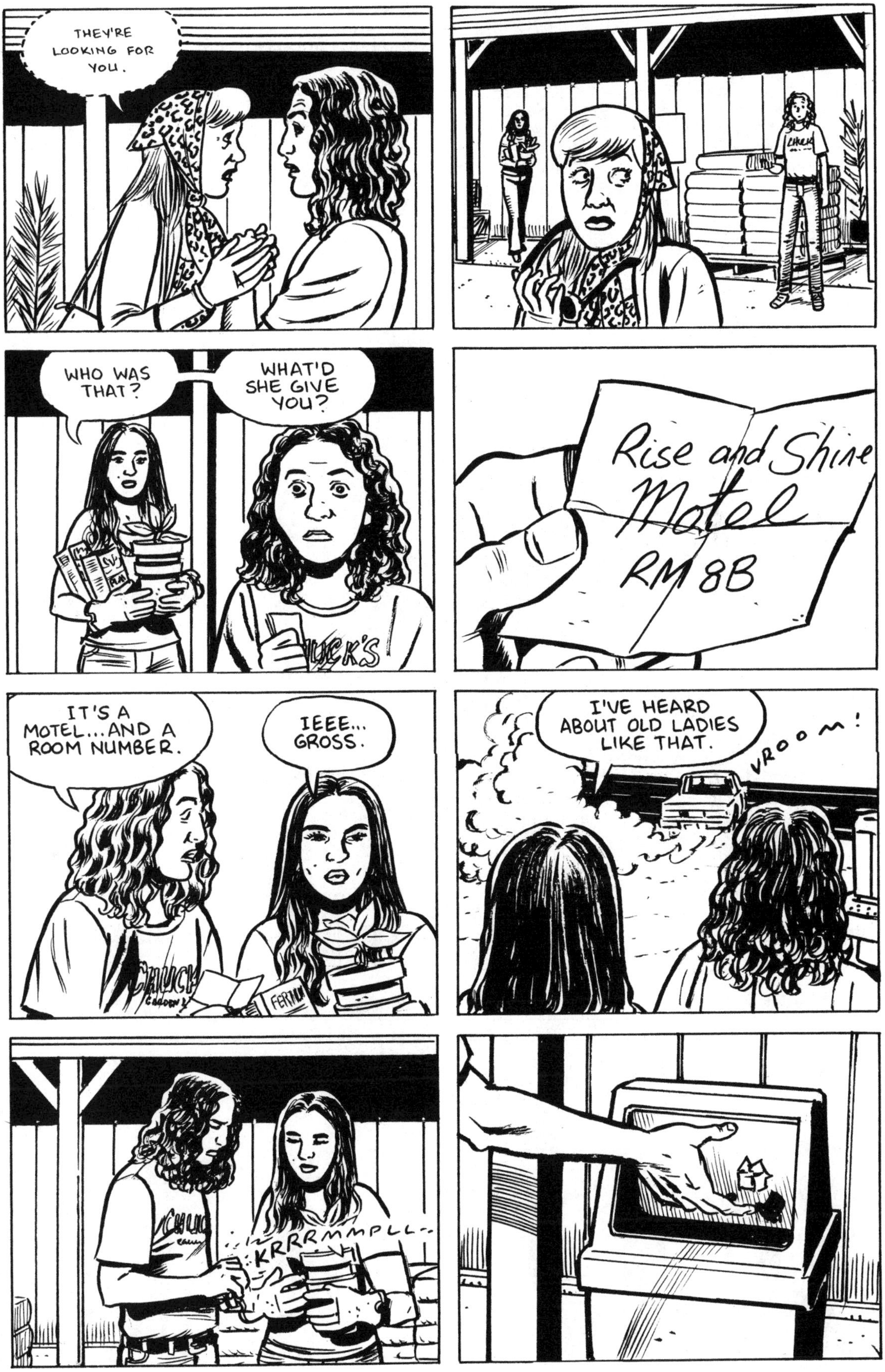
THEY'RE LOOKING FOR YOU.
WHO WAS THAT?
WHAT'D SHE GIVE YOU?
Rise and Shine Motel RM 8B
IT'S A MOTEL...AND A ROOM NUMBER.
IEEE... GROSS.
I'VE HEARD ABOUT OLD LADIES LIKE THAT.
VROOM!
KRRRMMPLL

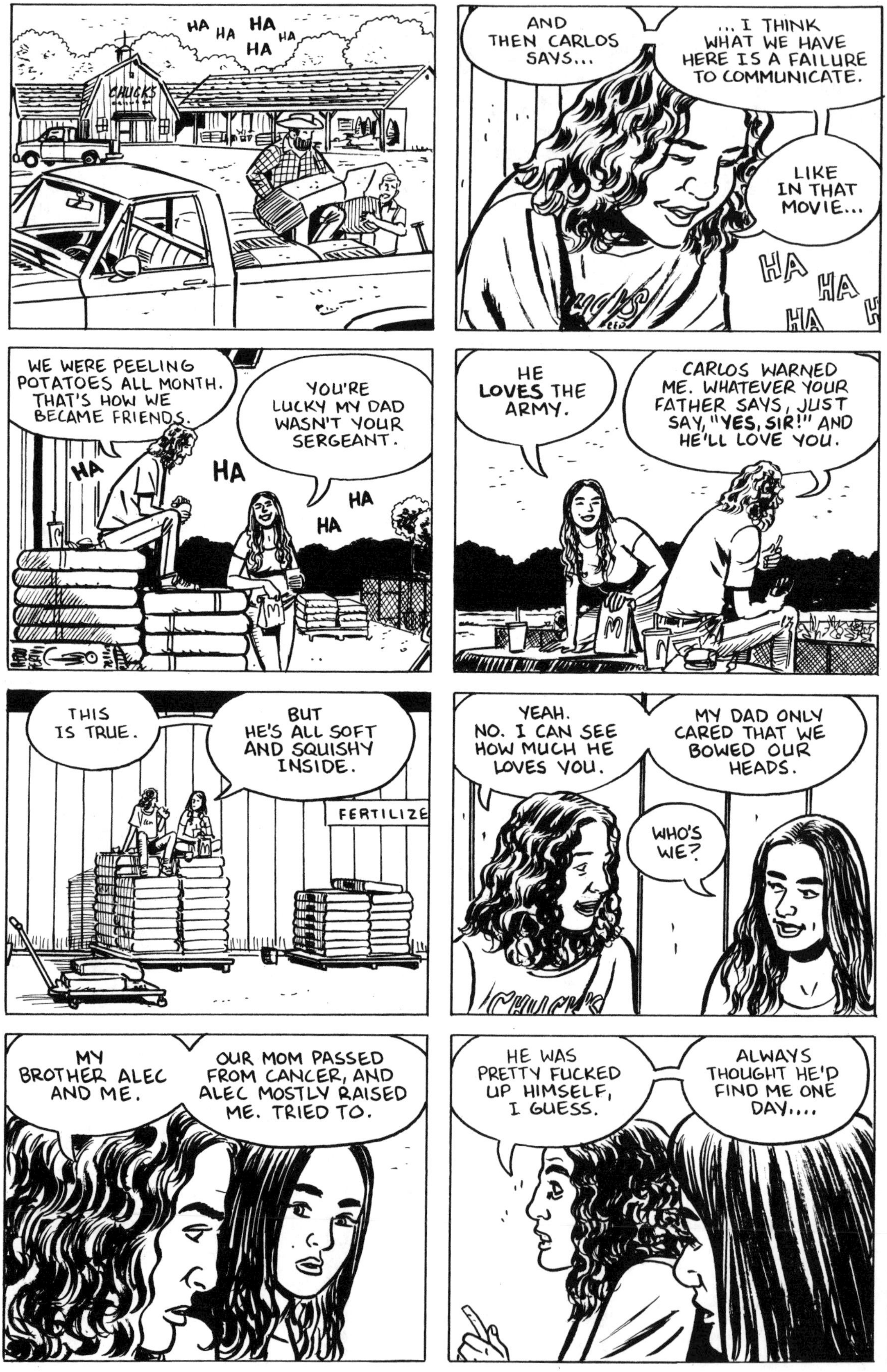
HA HA HA HA HA
AND THEN CARLOS SAYS...
... I THINK WHAT WE HAVE HERE IS A FAILURE TO COMMUNICATE.
LIKE IN THAT MOVIE...
HA HA HA
WE WERE PEELING POTATOES ALL MONTH. THAT'S HOW WE BECAME FRIENDS.
HA HA
YOU'RE LUCKY MY DAD WASN'T YOUR SERGEANT.
HA HA
HE **LOVES** THE ARMY.
CARLOS WARNED ME. WHATEVER YOUR FATHER SAYS, JUST SAY, "**YES, SIR!**" AND HE'LL LOVE YOU.
THIS IS TRUE.
BUT HE'S ALL SOFT AND SQUISHY INSIDE.
FERTILIZE
YEAH. NO. I CAN SEE HOW MUCH HE LOVES YOU.
MY DAD ONLY CARED THAT WE BOWED OUR HEADS.
WHO'S WE?
MY BROTHER ALEC AND ME.
OUR MOM PASSED FROM CANCER, AND ALEC MOSTLY RAISED ME. TRIED TO.
HE WAS PRETTY FUCKED UP HIMSELF, I GUESS.
ALWAYS THOUGHT HE'D FIND ME ONE DAY....

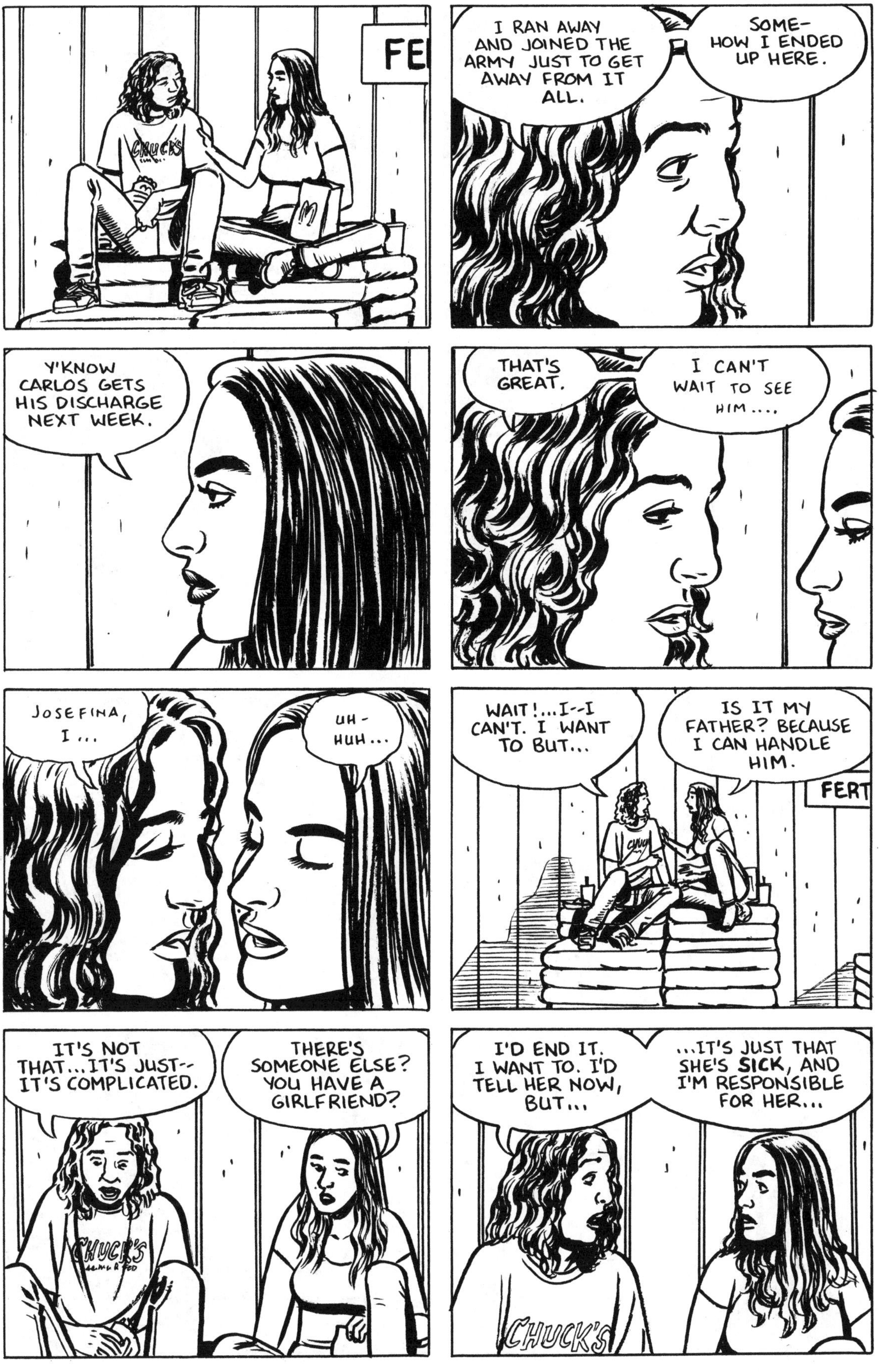
FE
I RAN AWAY AND JOINED THE ARMY JUST TO GET AWAY FROM IT ALL.
SOME-HOW I ENDED UP HERE.
Y'KNOW CARLOS GETS HIS DISCHARGE NEXT WEEK.
THAT'S GREAT.
I CAN'T WAIT TO SEE HIM....
JOSEFINA, I...
UH-HUH...
WAIT!...I--I CAN'T. I WANT TO BUT...
IS IT MY FATHER? BECAUSE I CAN HANDLE HIM.
FERT
IT'S NOT THAT...IT'S JUST--IT'S COMPLICATED.
THERE'S SOMEONE ELSE? YOU HAVE A GIRLFRIEND?
I'D END IT. I WANT TO. I'D TELL HER NOW, BUT...
...IT'S JUST THAT SHE'S **SICK**, AND I'M RESPONSIBLE FOR HER...
CHUCK'S

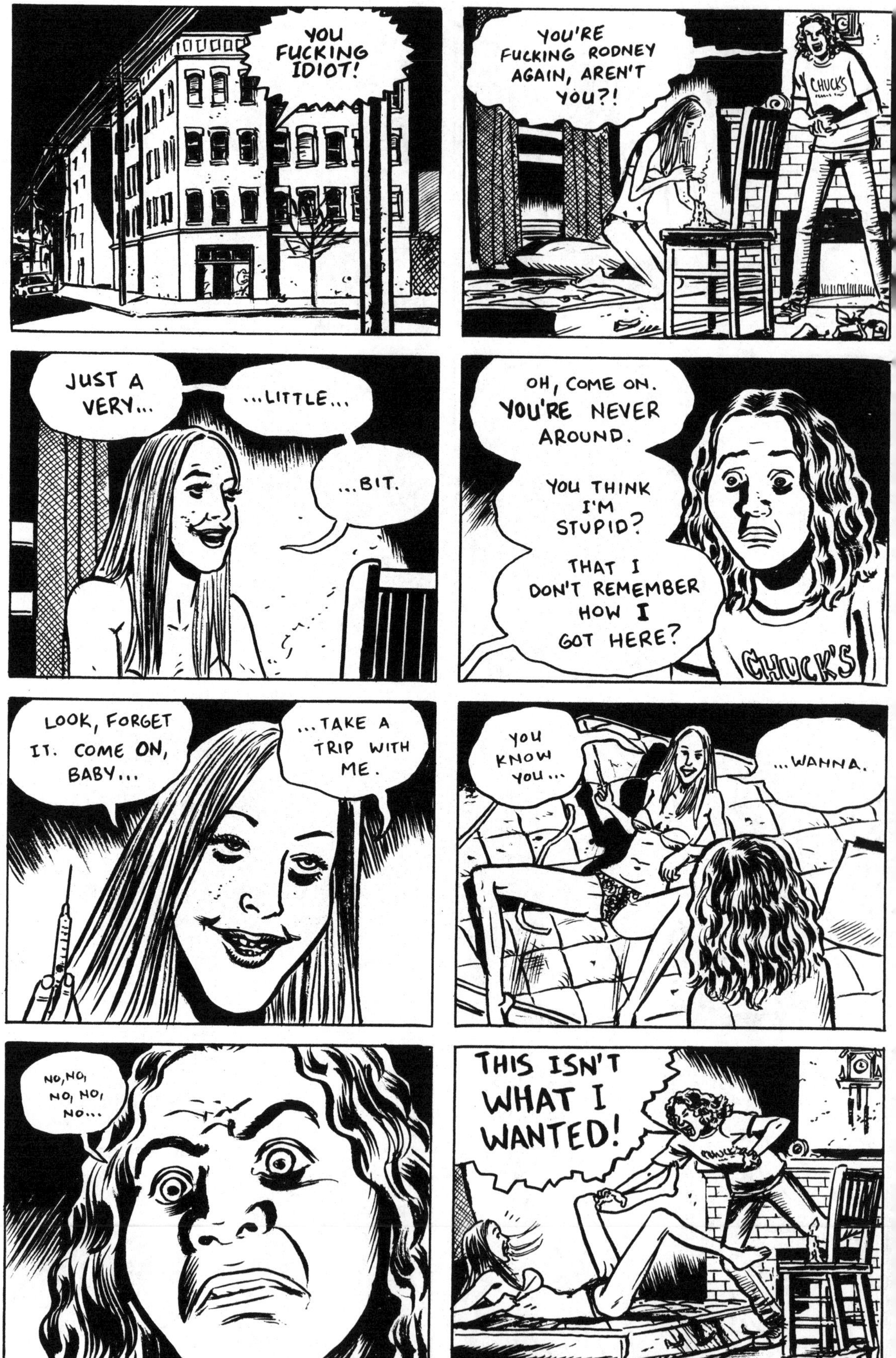
YOU FUCKING IDIOT!
YOU'RE FUCKING RODNEY AGAIN, AREN'T YOU?!
CHUCK'S
JUST A VERY...
...LITTLE...
...BIT.
OH, COME ON. YOU'RE NEVER AROUND.
YOU THINK I'M STUPID?
THAT I DON'T REMEMBER HOW I GOT HERE?
CHUCK'S
LOOK, FORGET IT. COME ON, BABY...
...TAKE A TRIP WITH ME.
YOU KNOW YOU...
...WANNA.
NO, NO, NO, NO, NO...
THIS ISN'T WHAT I WANTED!

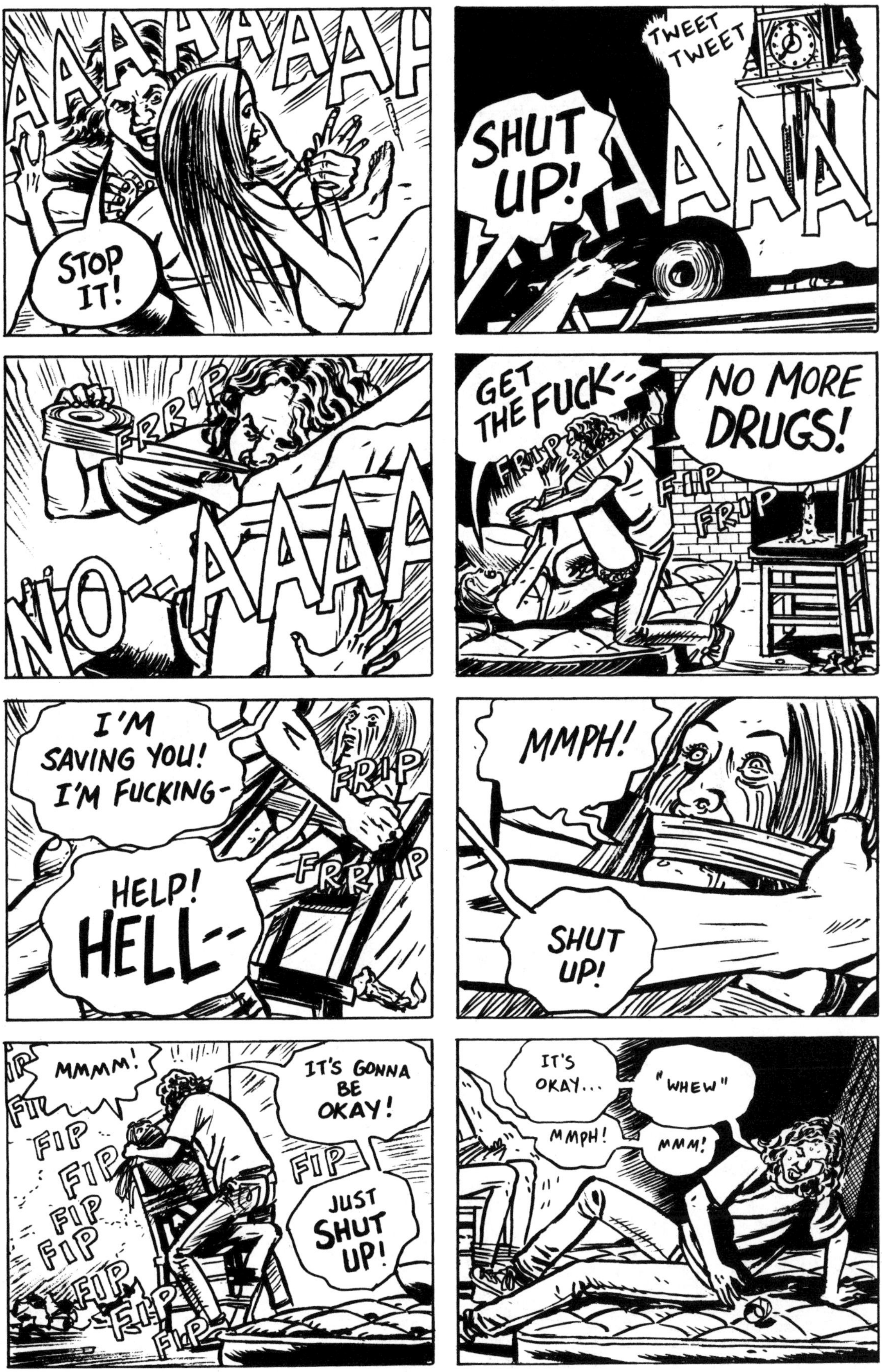
AAAAAAA
STOP IT!
TWEET TWEET
SHUT UP!
AAAAA
FRRIP
NO--AAAA
GET THE FUCK--
NO MORE DRUGS!
FRIP
FIP
FRIP
I'M SAVING YOU! I'M FUCKING-
FRIP
HELP! HELL--
FRRIP
MMPH!
SHUT UP!
MMMM!
IT'S GONNA BE OKAY!
FIP
FIP
FIP
FIP
FIP
FIP
FIP
FIP
JUST SHUT UP!
IT'S OKAY...
"WHEW"
MMPH!
MMM!

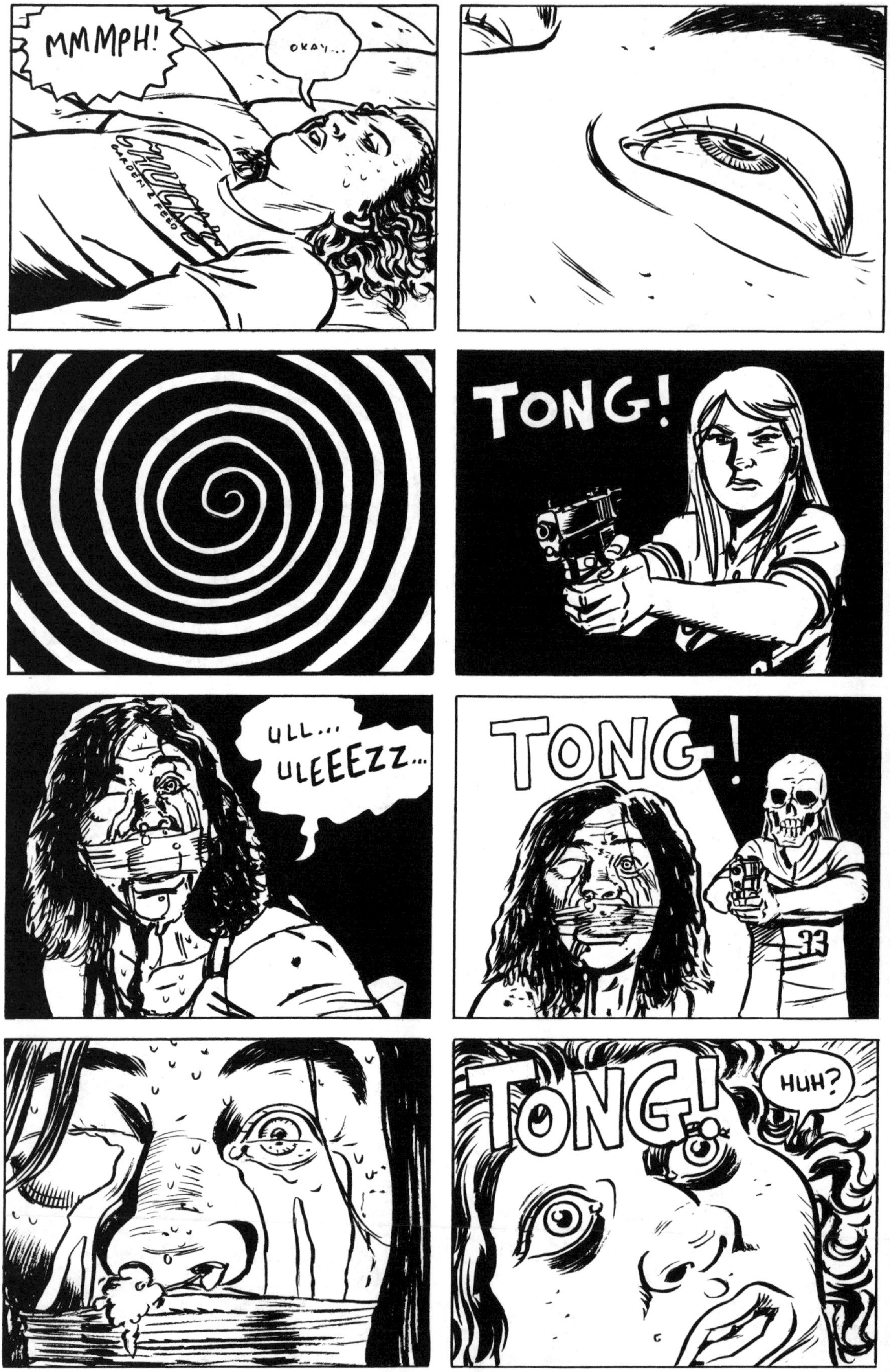
MMMPH!
OKAY...
TONG!
ULL... ULEEEZZ...
TONG!
33
TONG!
HUH?

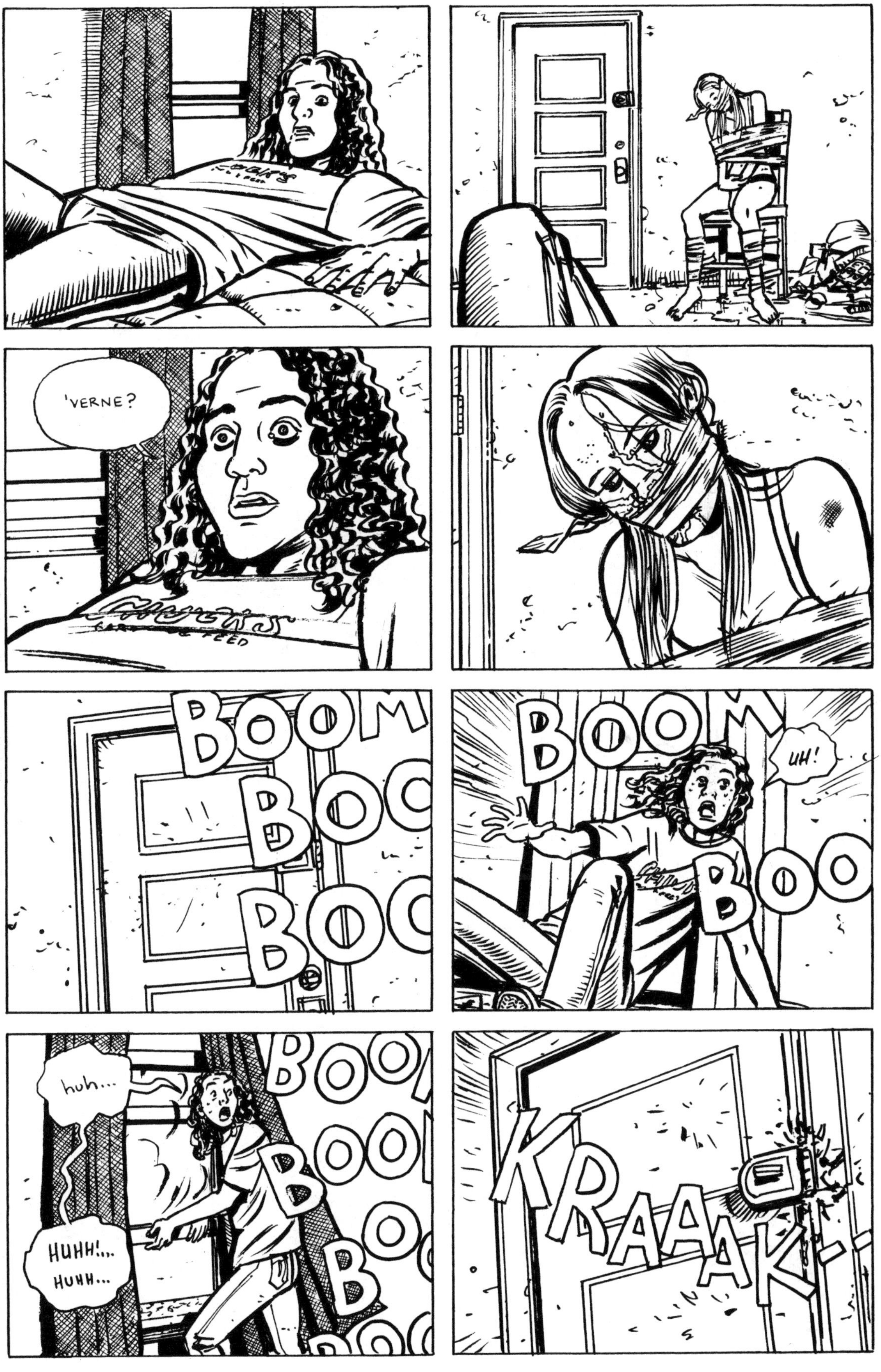
'VERNE?
BOOM
BOO
BOO
BOOM
UH!
BOO
huh...
HUHH!...
HUHH...
BOO
BOO
B
BOO
B
KRAAAK-

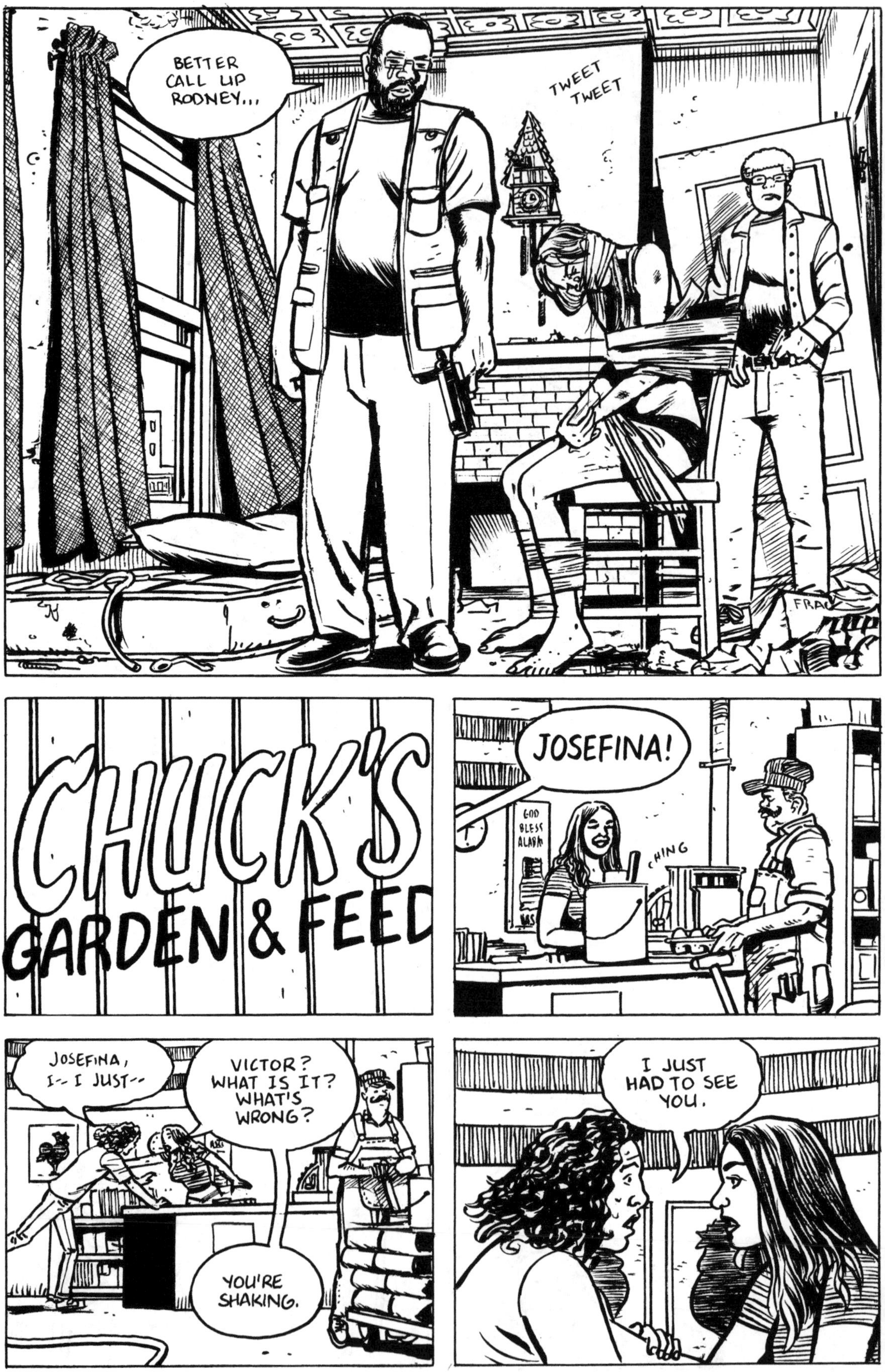
BETTER CALL UP RODNEY...
TWEET TWEET
CHUCK'S GARDEN & FEED
JOSEFINA!
GOD BLESS ALABA
CHING
JOSEFINA, I-- I JUST--
VICTOR? WHAT IS IT? WHAT'S WRONG?
YOU'RE SHAKING.
I JUST HAD TO SEE YOU.

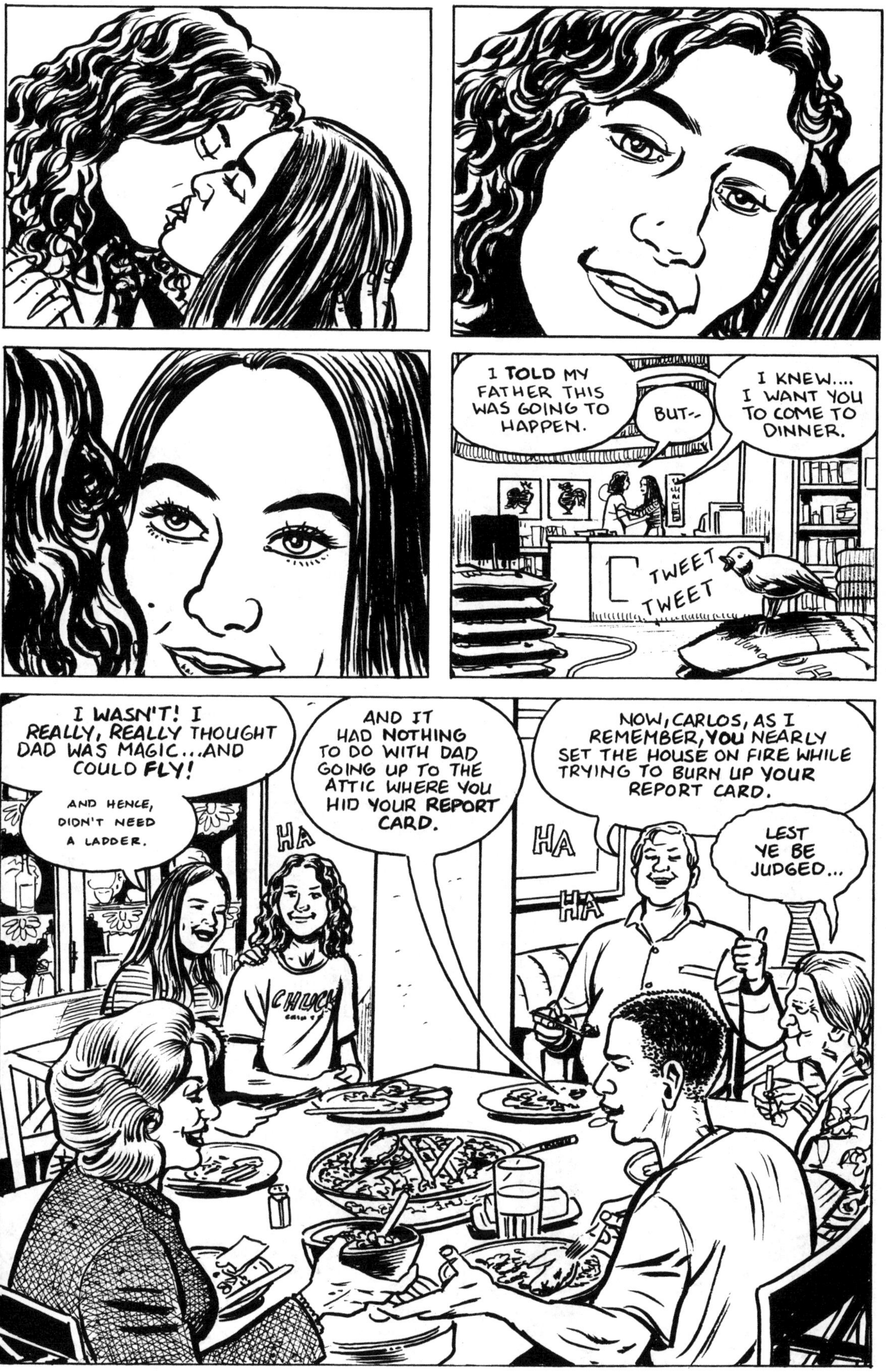
I TOLD MY FATHER THIS WAS GOING TO HAPPEN.
BUT-
I KNEW.... I WANT YOU TO COME TO DINNER.
TWEET TWEET
I WASN'T! I REALLY, REALLY THOUGHT DAD WAS MAGIC...AND COULD FLY!
AND HENCE, DIDN'T NEED A LADDER.
AND IT HAD NOTHING TO DO WITH DAD GOING UP TO THE ATTIC WHERE YOU HID YOUR REPORT CARD.
HA
HA
HA
NOW, CARLOS, AS I REMEMBER, YOU NEARLY SET THE HOUSE ON FIRE WHILE TRYING TO BURN UP YOUR REPORT CARD.
LEST YE BE JUDGED...
CHUCK

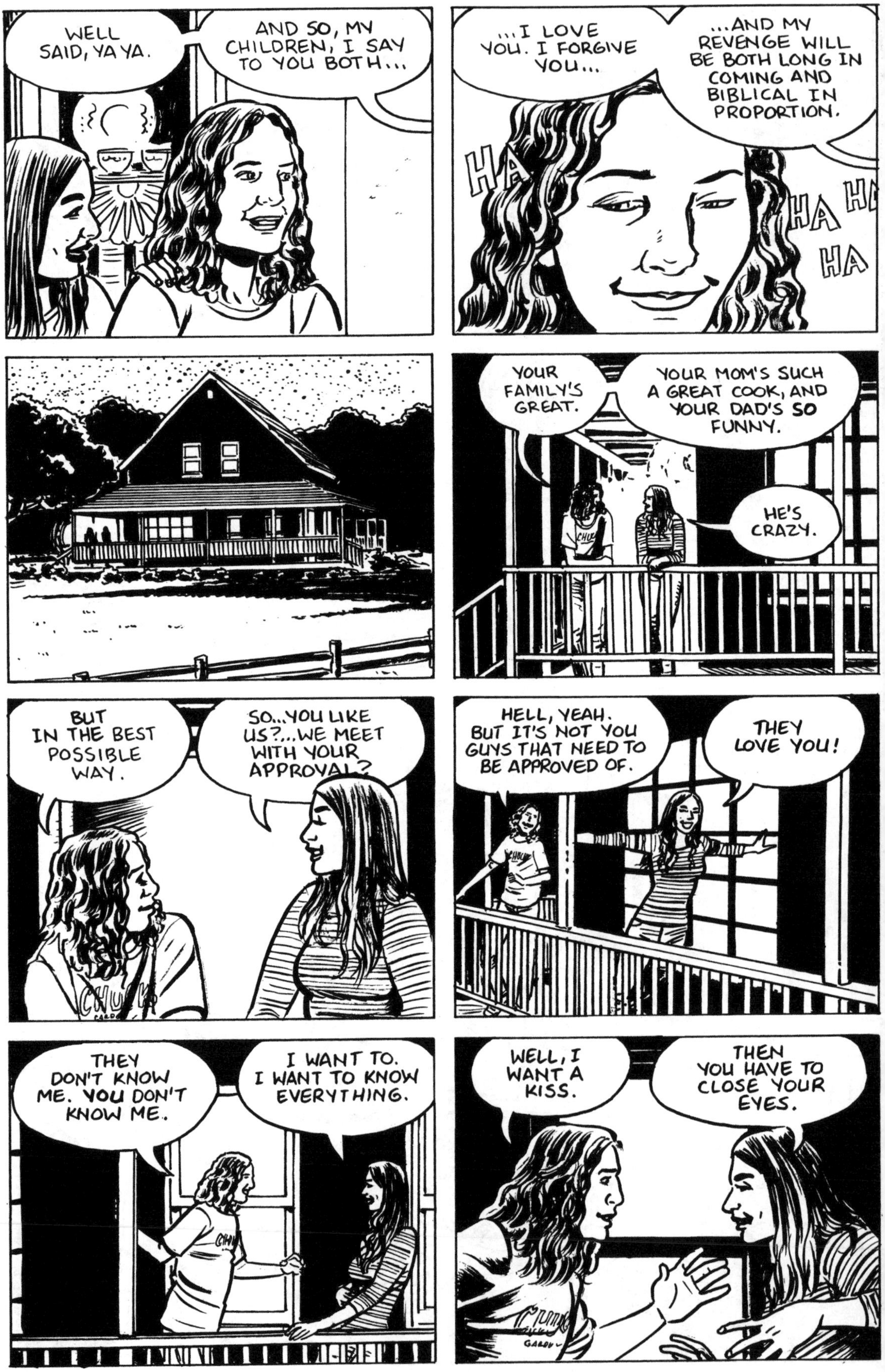
WELL SAID, YA YA.
AND SO, MY CHILDREN, I SAY TO YOU BOTH...
...I LOVE YOU. I FORGIVE YOU...
...AND MY REVENGE WILL BE BOTH LONG IN COMING AND BIBLICAL IN PROPORTION.
HA
HA
HA
YOUR FAMILY'S GREAT.
YOUR MOM'S SUCH A GREAT COOK, AND YOUR DAD'S SO FUNNY.
HE'S CRAZY.
BUT IN THE BEST POSSIBLE WAY.
SO...YOU LIKE US?...WE MEET WITH YOUR APPROVAL?
HELL, YEAH. BUT IT'S NOT YOU GUYS THAT NEED TO BE APPROVED OF.
THEY LOVE YOU!
THEY DON'T KNOW ME. YOU DON'T KNOW ME.
I WANT TO. I WANT TO KNOW EVERYTHING.
WELL, I WANT A KISS.
THEN YOU HAVE TO CLOSE YOUR EYES.

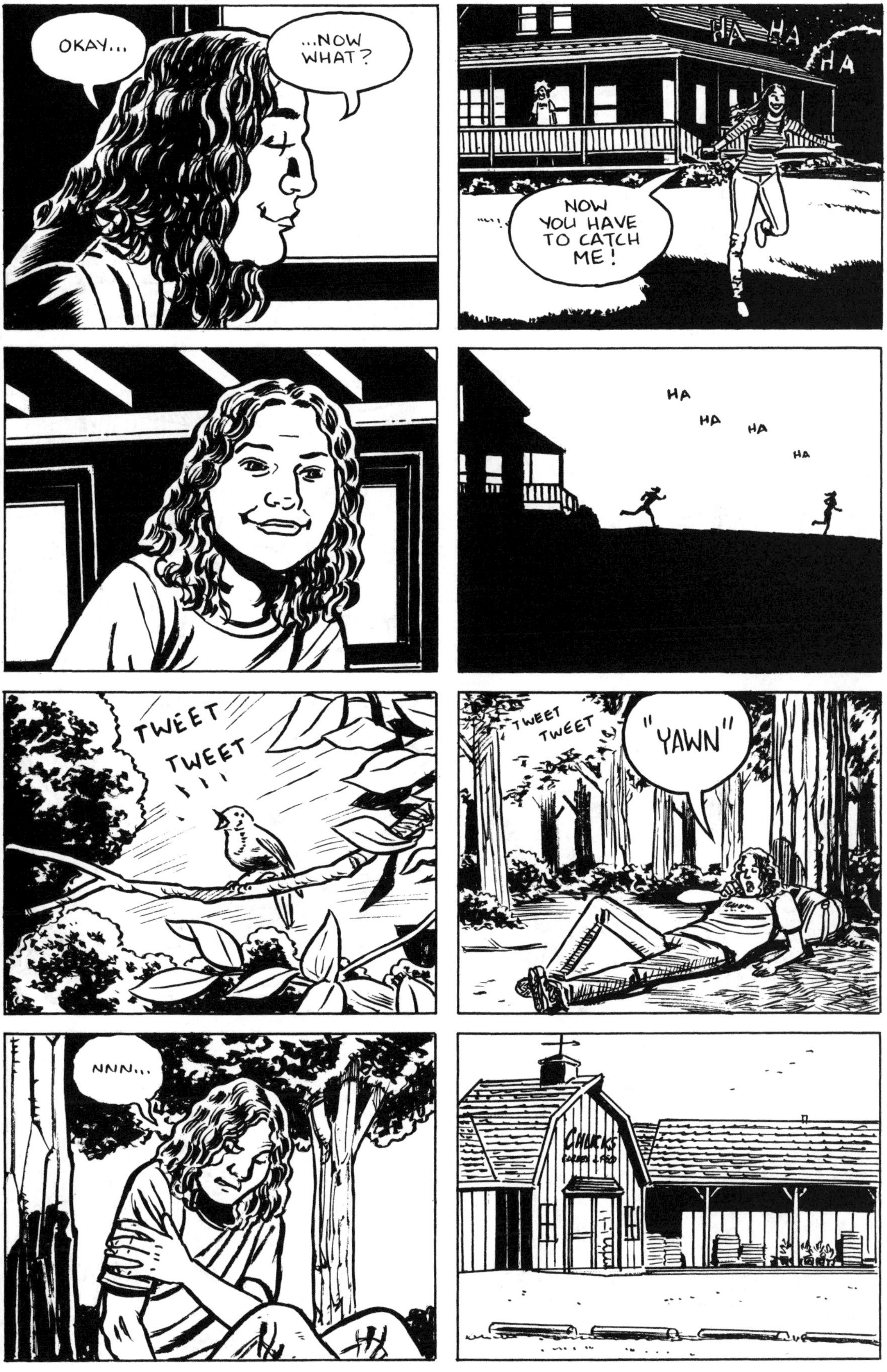
OKAY...
...NOW WHAT?
HA HA HA
NOW YOU HAVE TO CATCH ME!
HA
HA
HA
HA
TWEET
TWEET
TWEET TWEET
"YAWN"
NNN...

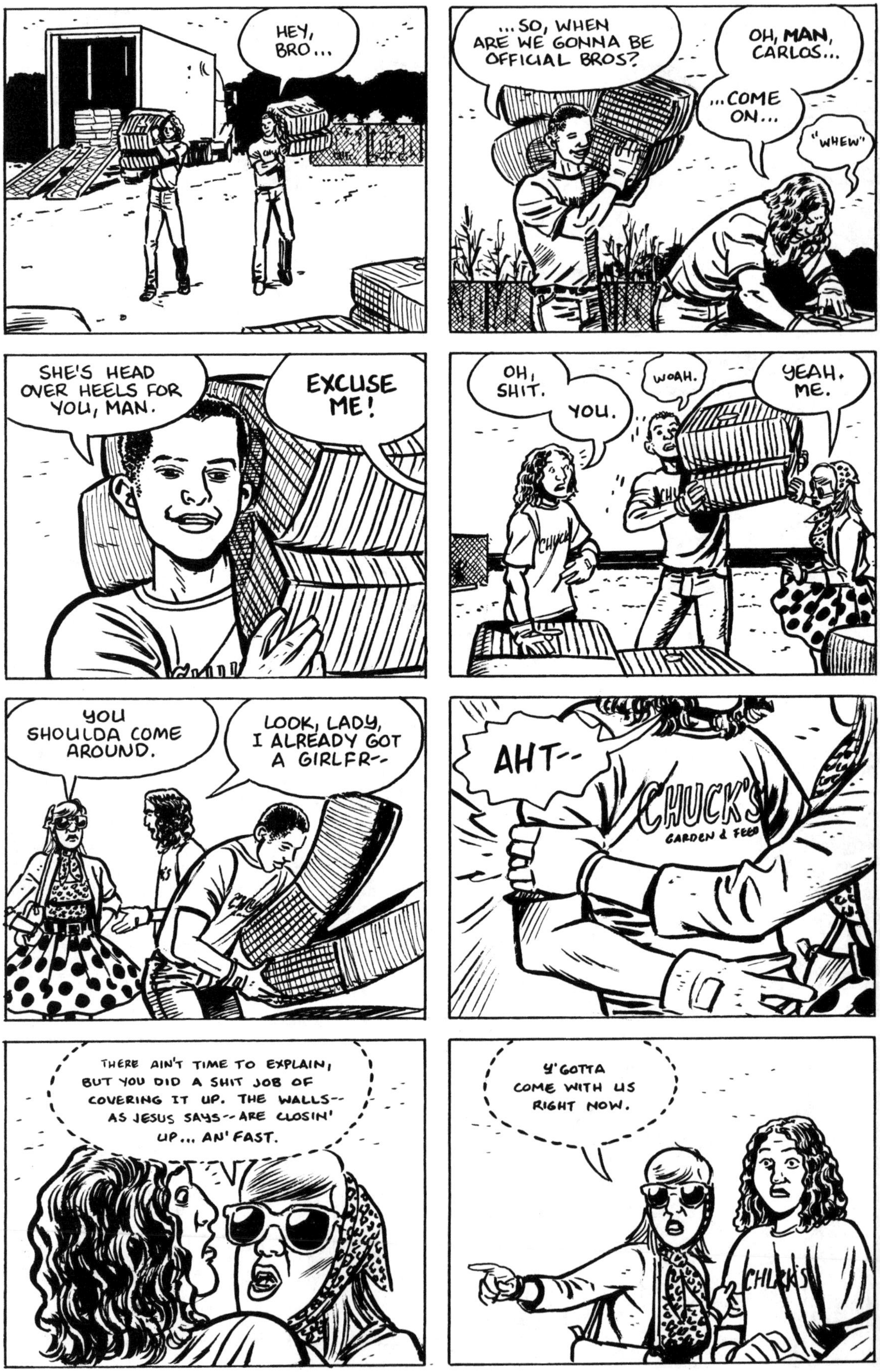
HEY, BRO...
...SO, WHEN ARE WE GONNA BE OFFICIAL BROS?
OH, MAN, CARLOS...
...COME ON...
"WHEW"
SHE'S HEAD OVER HEELS FOR YOU, MAN.
EXCUSE ME!
OH, SHIT.
YOU.
WOAH.
YEAH. ME.
YOU SHOULDA COME AROUND.
LOOK, LADY, I ALREADY GOT A GIRLFR--
AHT--
CHUCK'S
GARDEN & FEED
THERE AIN'T TIME TO EXPLAIN, BUT YOU DID A SHIT JOB OF COVERING IT UP. THE WALLS-- AS JESUS SAYS--ARE CLOSIN' UP... AN' FAST.
Y'GOTTA COME WITH US RIGHT NOW.

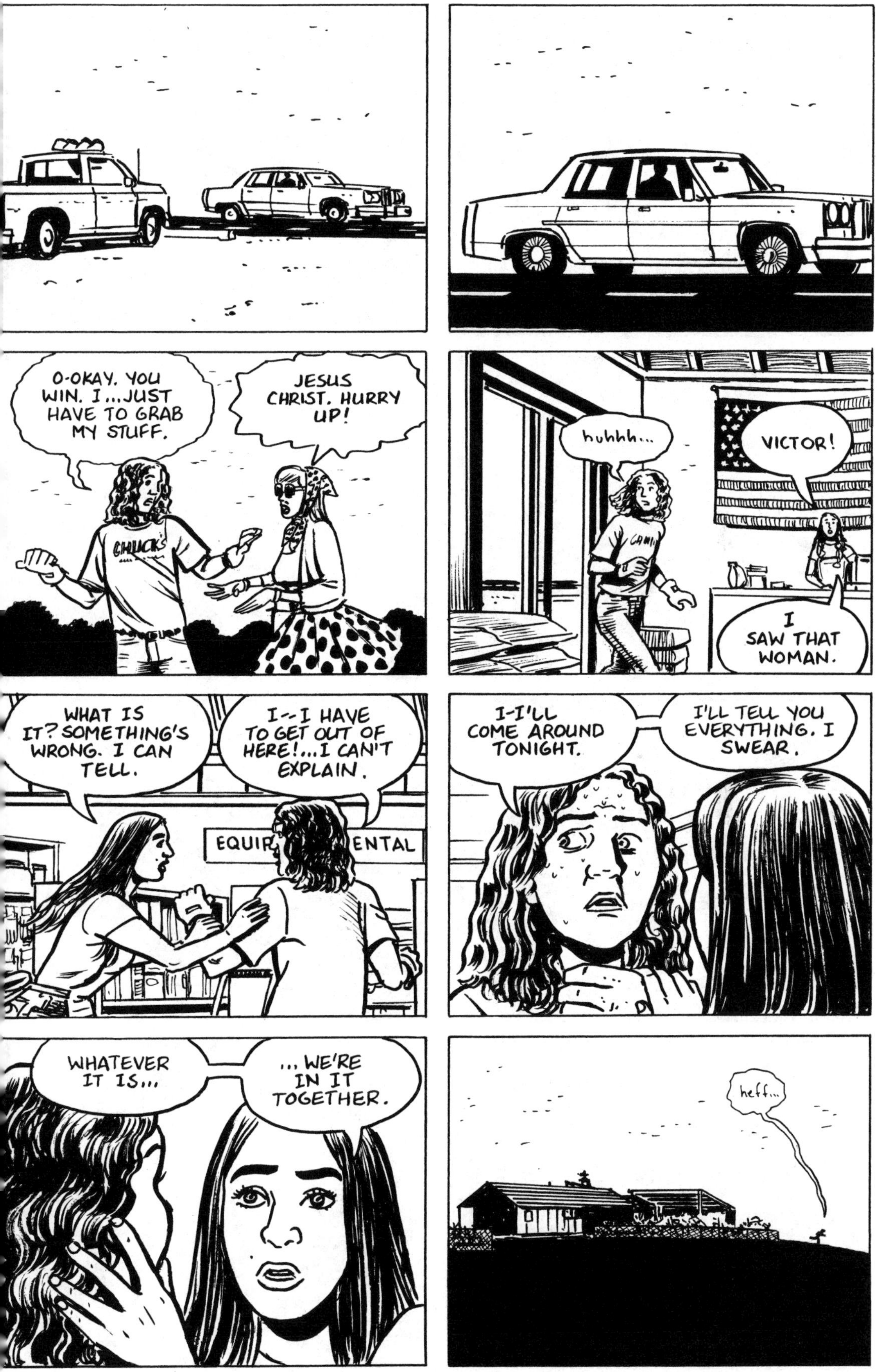

O-OKAY. YOU WIN. I...JUST HAVE TO GRAB MY STUFF.
JESUS CHRIST. HURRY UP!
CHUCK'S
huhhh...
VICTOR!
I SAW THAT WOMAN.
WHAT IS IT? SOMETHING'S WRONG. I CAN TELL.
I--I HAVE TO GET OUT OF HERE!...I CAN'T EXPLAIN.
EQUIP ENTAL
I-I'LL COME AROUND TONIGHT.
I'LL TELL YOU EVERYTHING. I SWEAR.
WHATEVER IT IS...
...WE'RE IN IT TOGETHER.
heff...

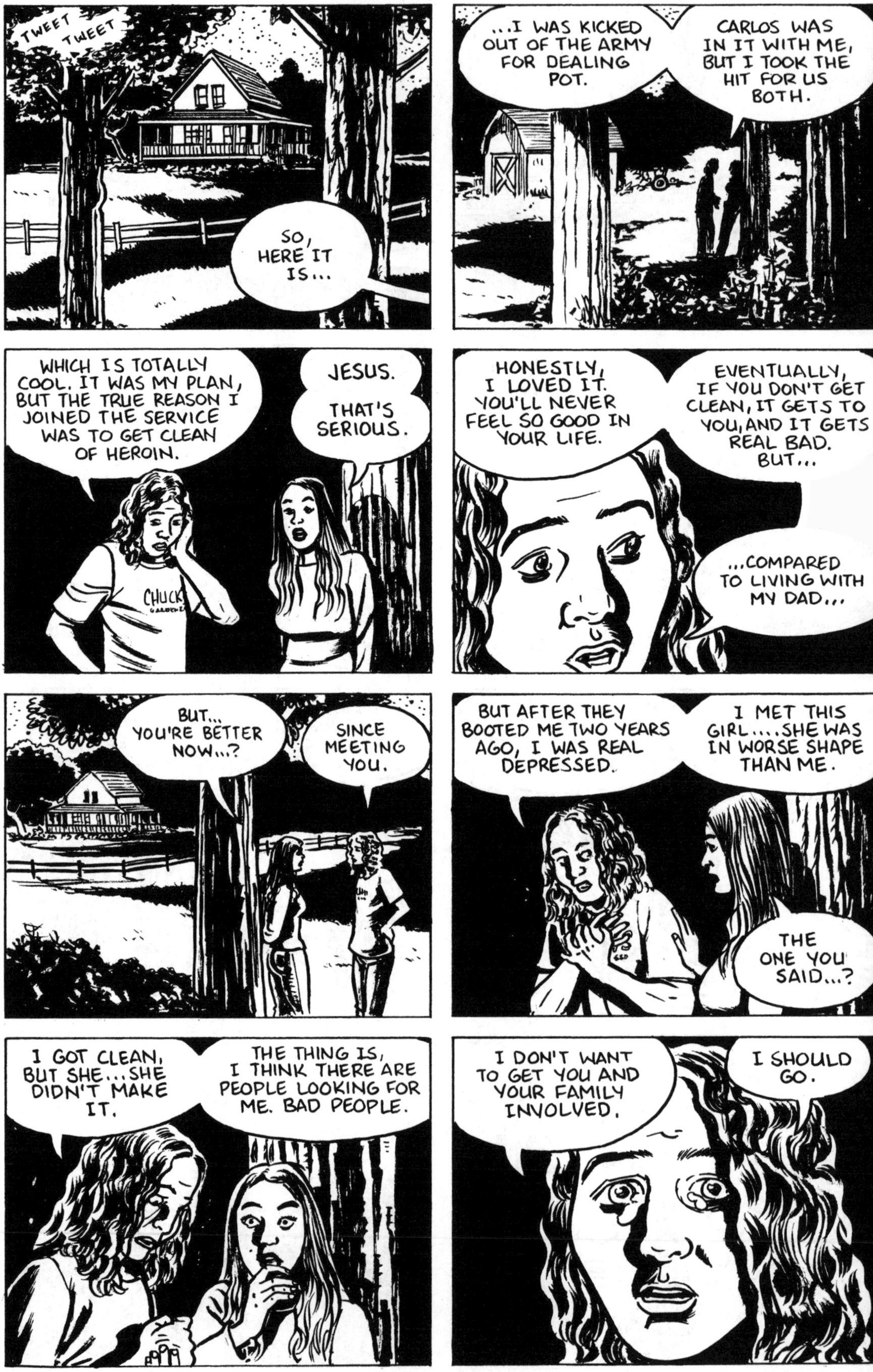
TWEET TWEET
SO, HERE IT IS...
...I WAS KICKED OUT OF THE ARMY FOR DEALING POT.
CARLOS WAS IN IT WITH ME, BUT I TOOK THE HIT FOR US BOTH.
WHICH IS TOTALLY COOL. IT WAS MY PLAN, BUT THE TRUE REASON I JOINED THE SERVICE WAS TO GET CLEAN OF HEROIN.
JESUS.
THAT'S SERIOUS.
CHUCK
HONESTLY, I LOVED IT. YOU'LL NEVER FEEL SO GOOD IN YOUR LIFE.
EVENTUALLY, IF YOU DON'T GET CLEAN, IT GETS TO YOU, AND IT GETS REAL BAD. BUT...
...COMPARED TO LIVING WITH MY DAD...
BUT... YOU'RE BETTER NOW...?
SINCE MEETING YOU.
BUT AFTER THEY BOOTED ME TWO YEARS AGO, I WAS REAL DEPRESSED.
I MET THIS GIRL....SHE WAS IN WORSE SHAPE THAN ME.
THE ONE YOU SAID...?
I GOT CLEAN, BUT SHE...SHE DIDN'T MAKE IT.
THE THING IS, I THINK THERE ARE PEOPLE LOOKING FOR ME. BAD PEOPLE.
I DON'T WANT TO GET YOU AND YOUR FAMILY INVOLVED.
I SHOULD GO.

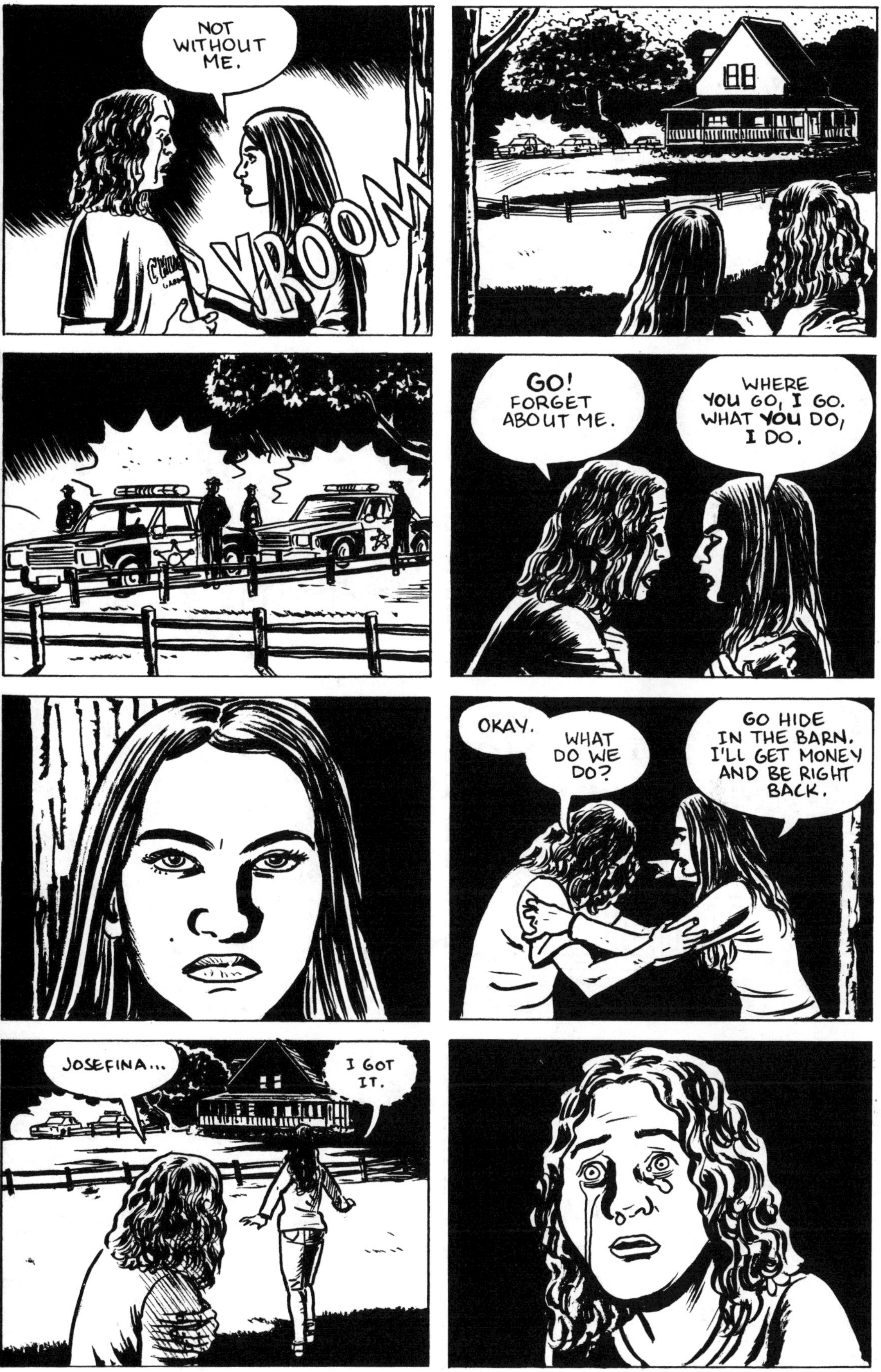

NOT WITHOUT ME.
VROOM
GO! FORGET ABOUT ME.
WHERE YOU GO, I GO. WHAT YOU DO, I DO.
OKAY.
WHAT DO WE DO?
GO HIDE IN THE BARN. I'LL GET MONEY AND BE RIGHT BACK.
JOSEFINA...
I GOT IT.

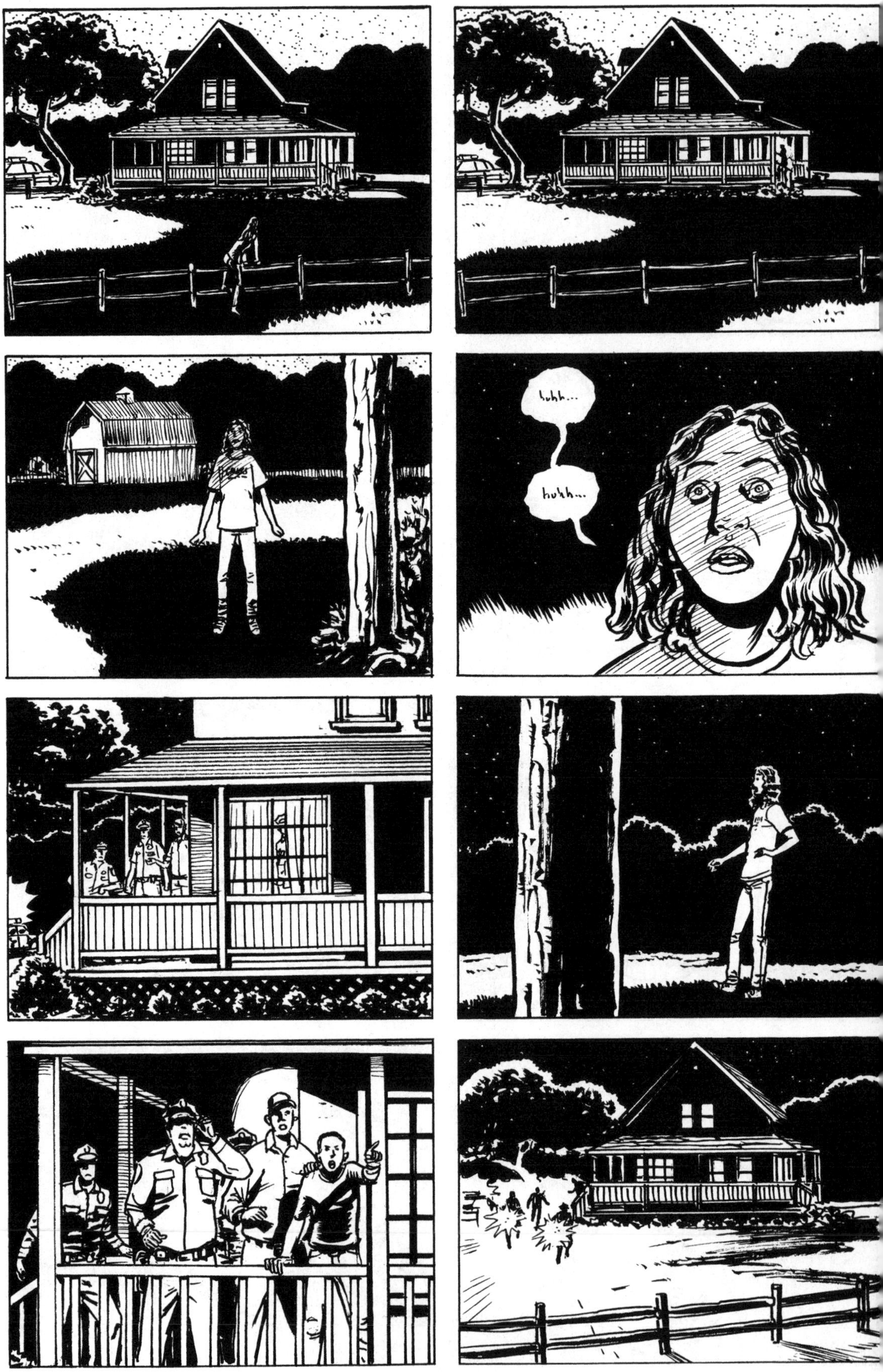
huhh...
huhh...

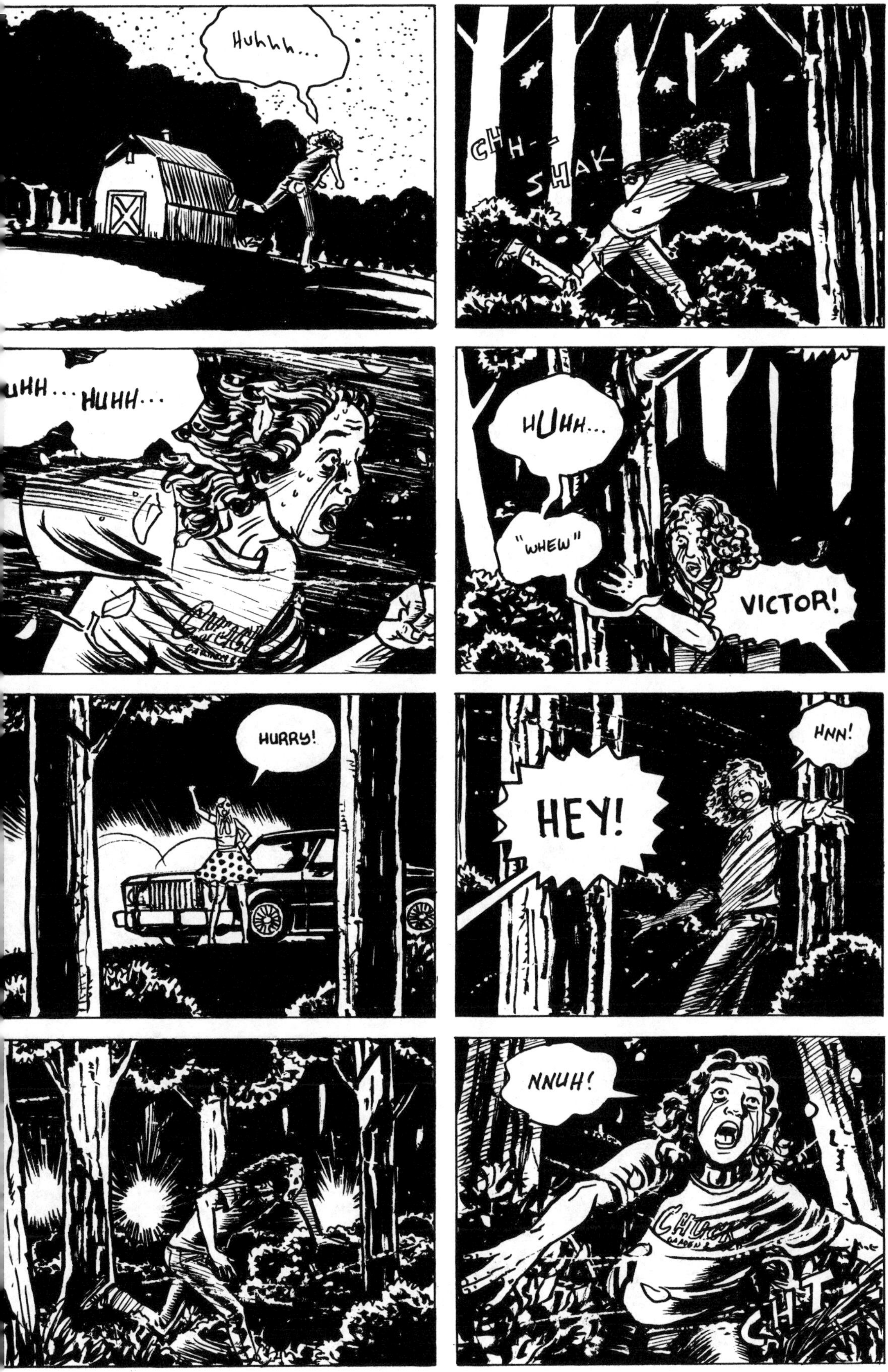
Huhhh...
CHH--SHAK
UHH... HUHH...
HUHH...
"WHEW"
VICTOR!
HURRY!
HNN!
HEY!
NNUH!
CHT

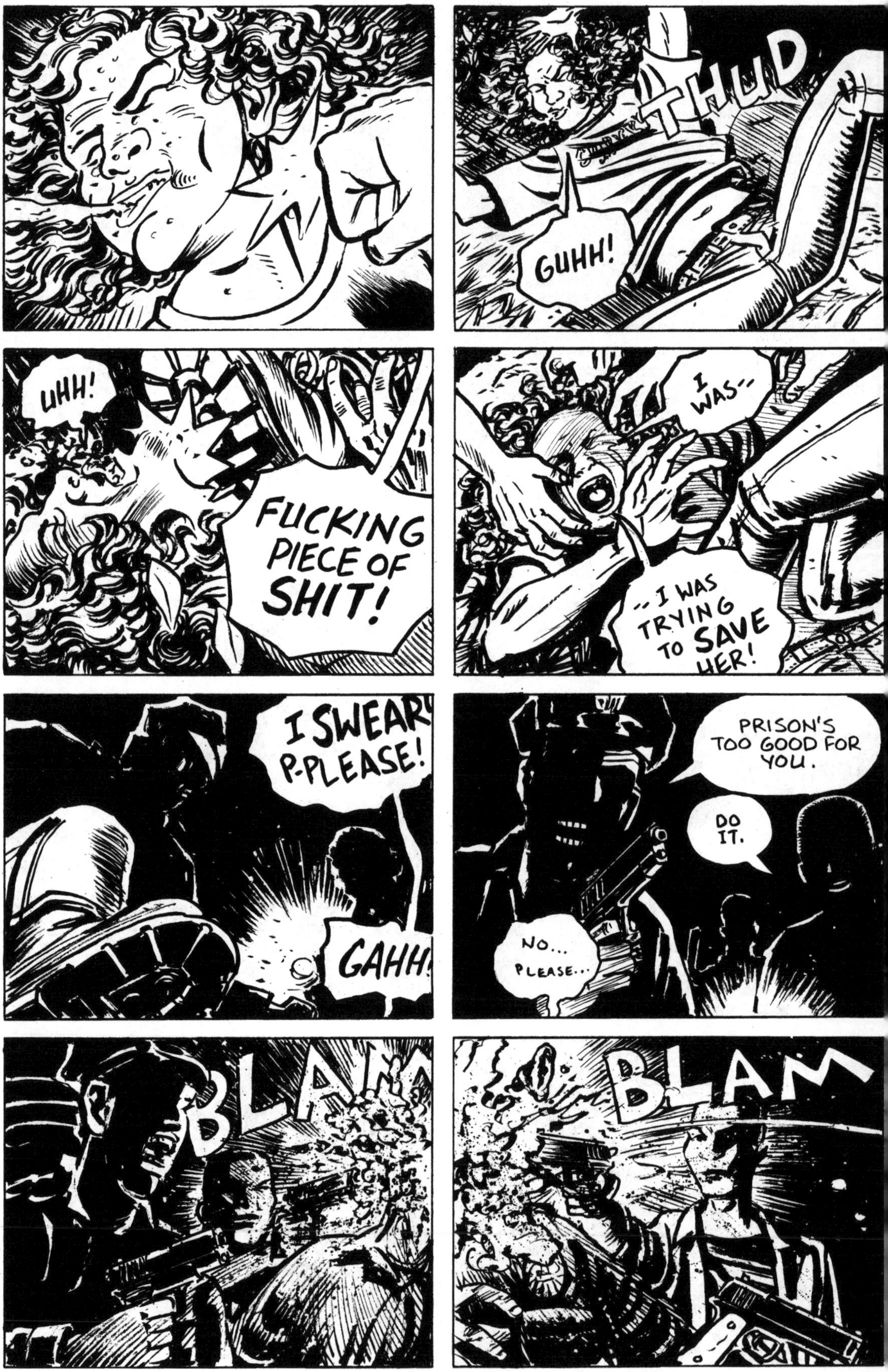
THUD
GUHH!
UHH!
FUCKING PIECE OF SHIT!
I WAS..
.. I WAS TRYING TO SAVE HER!
I SWEAR P-PLEASE!
GAHH!
PRISON'S TOO GOOD FOR YOU.
DO IT.
NO... PLEASE...
BLAM
BLAM

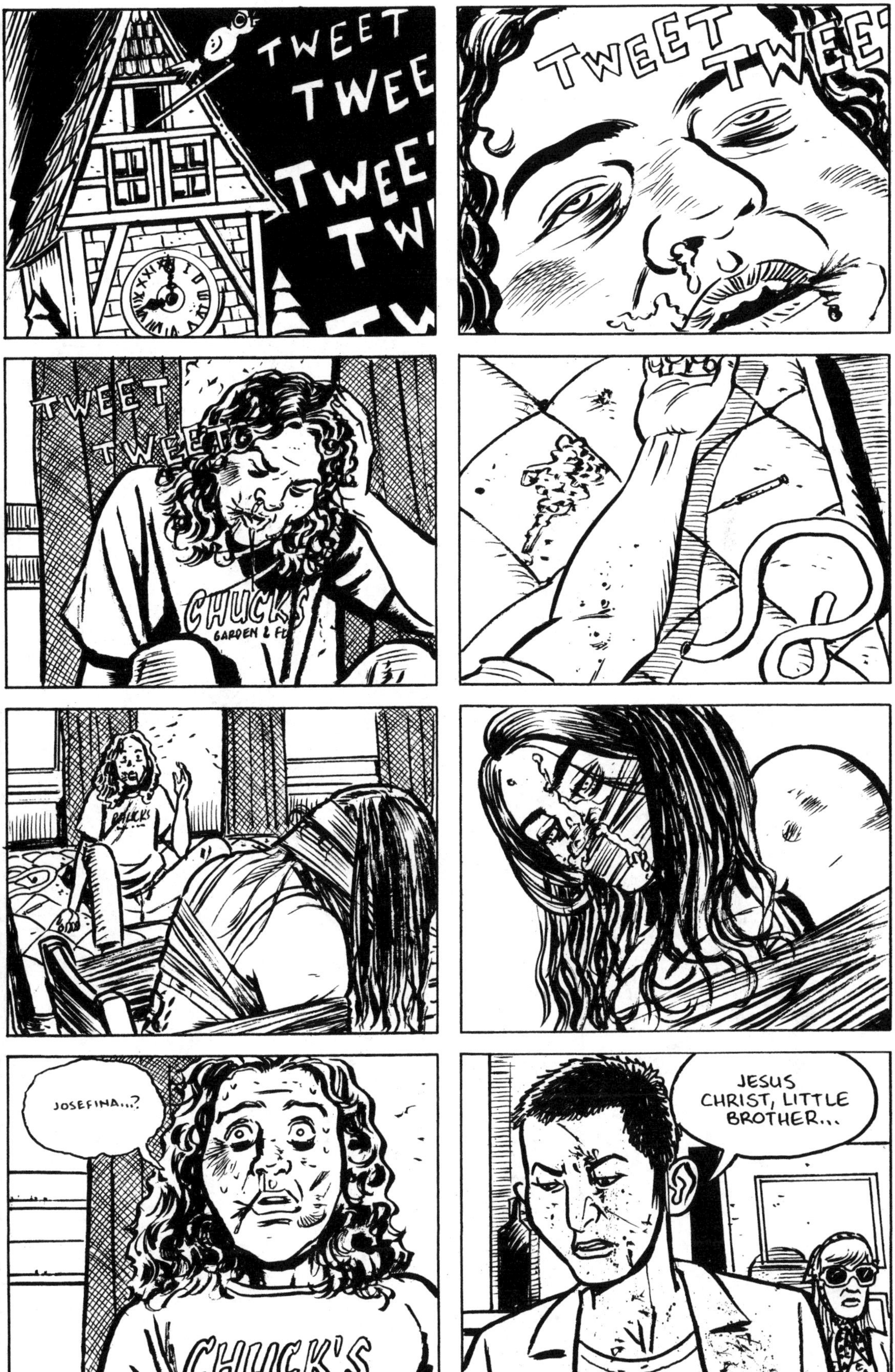
TWEET
TWEE
TWEE
TW
TWEET
TWEE
TWEET
TWEET
CHUCK'S
GARDEN & F
JOSEFINA...?
CHUCK'S
JESUS CHRIST, LITTLE BROTHER...

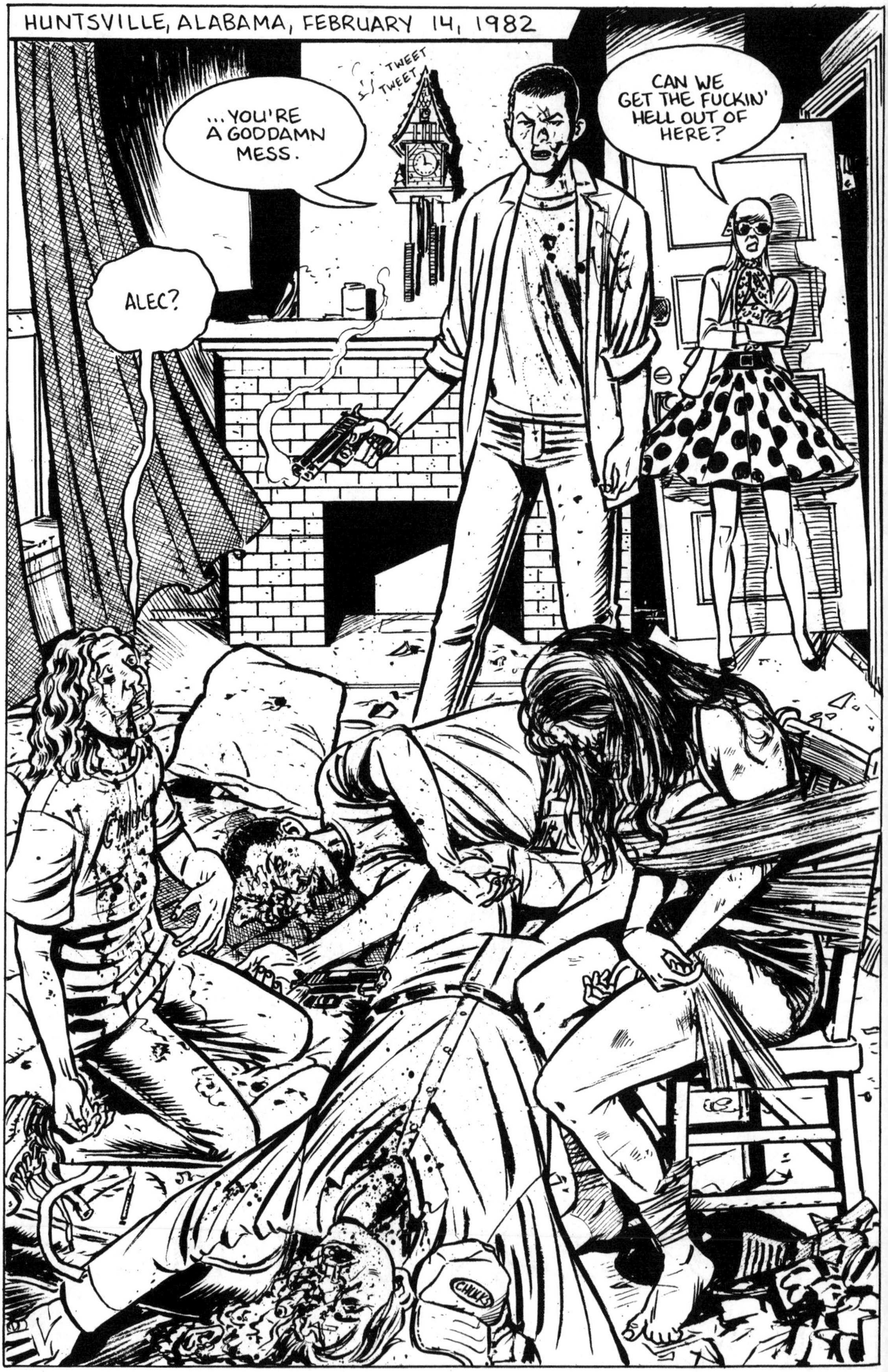
HUNTSVILLE, ALABAMA, FEBRUARY 14, 1982
TWEET TWEET
...YOU'RE A GODDAMN MESS.
CAN WE GET THE FUCKIN' HELL OUT OF HERE?
ALEC?

THE END...

"DETENTION FOREVER"

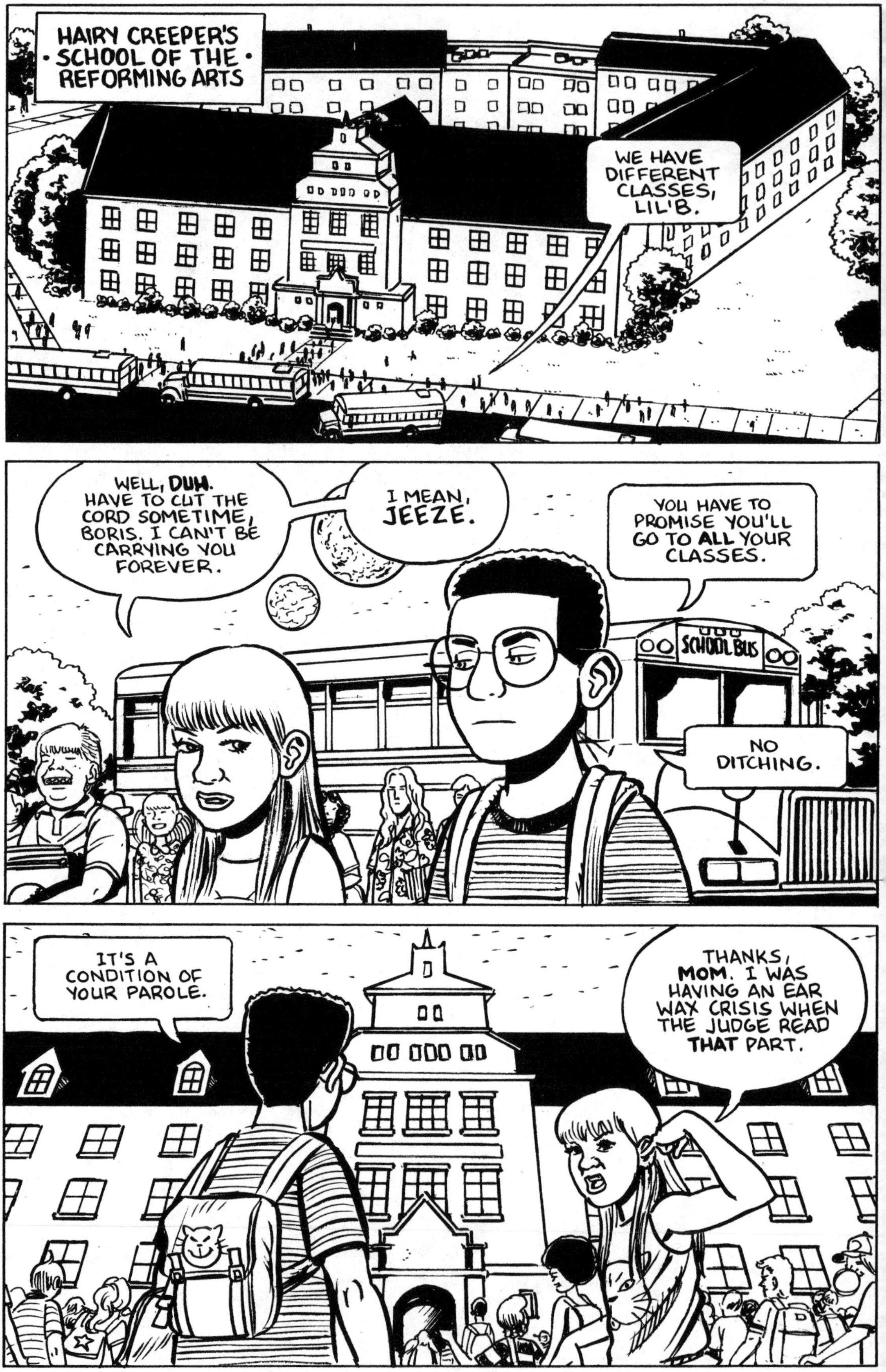
HAIRY CREEPER'S
• SCHOOL OF THE •
REFORMING ARTS
WE HAVE DIFFERENT CLASSES, LIL'B.
WELL, **DUH**. HAVE TO CUT THE CORD SOMETIME, BORIS. I CAN'T BE CARRYING YOU FOREVER.
I MEAN, **JEEZE**.
YOU HAVE TO PROMISE YOU'LL GO TO **ALL** YOUR CLASSES.
SCHOOL BUS
NO DITCHING.
IT'S A CONDITION OF YOUR PAROLE.
THANKS, **MOM**. I WAS HAVING AN EAR WAX CRISIS WHEN THE JUDGE READ **THAT** PART.

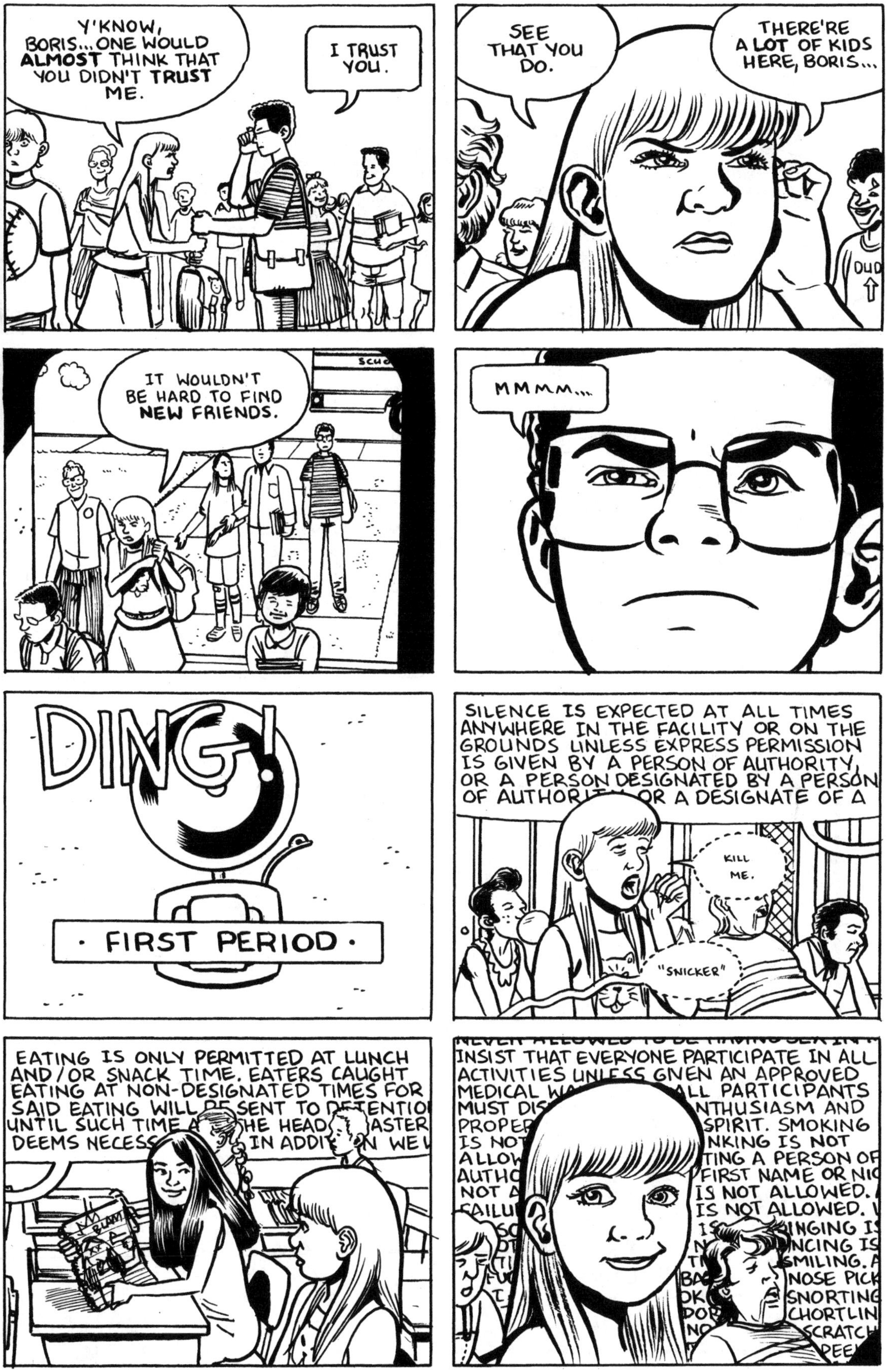
Y'KNOW, BORIS... ONE WOULD ALMOST THINK THAT YOU DIDN'T TRUST ME.
I TRUST YOU.
SEE THAT YOU DO.
THERE'RE A LOT OF KIDS HERE, BORIS...
DUD
IT WOULDN'T BE HARD TO FIND NEW FRIENDS.
MMMM...
DING!
· FIRST PERIOD ·
SILENCE IS EXPECTED AT ALL TIMES ANYWHERE IN THE FACILITY OR ON THE GROUNDS UNLESS EXPRESS PERMISSION IS GIVEN BY A PERSON OF AUTHORITY, OR A PERSON DESIGNATED BY A PERSON OF AUTHORI OR A DESIGNATE OF A
KILL ME.
"SNICKER"
EATING IS ONLY PERMITTED AT LUNCH AND/OR SNACK TIME. EATERS CAUGHT EATING AT NON-DESIGNATED TIMES FOR SAID EATING WILL BE SENT TO DETENTIO UNTIL SUCH TIME A HE HEAD ASTER DEEMS NECESS IN ADDI N WE
INSIST THAT EVERYONE PARTICIPATE IN ALL ACTIVITIES UNLESS GIVEN AN APPROVED MEDICAL W ALL PARTICIPANTS MUST DIS NTHUSIASM AND PROPER SPIRIT. SMOKING IS NOT NKING IS NOT ALLOW TING A PERSON OF AUTHO FIRST NAME OR NI NOT A IS NOT ALLOWED. FAILU IS NOT ALLOWED.
NGING IS
NCING IS
SMILING.
NOSE PICK
SNORTING
CHORTLIN
SCRATCH

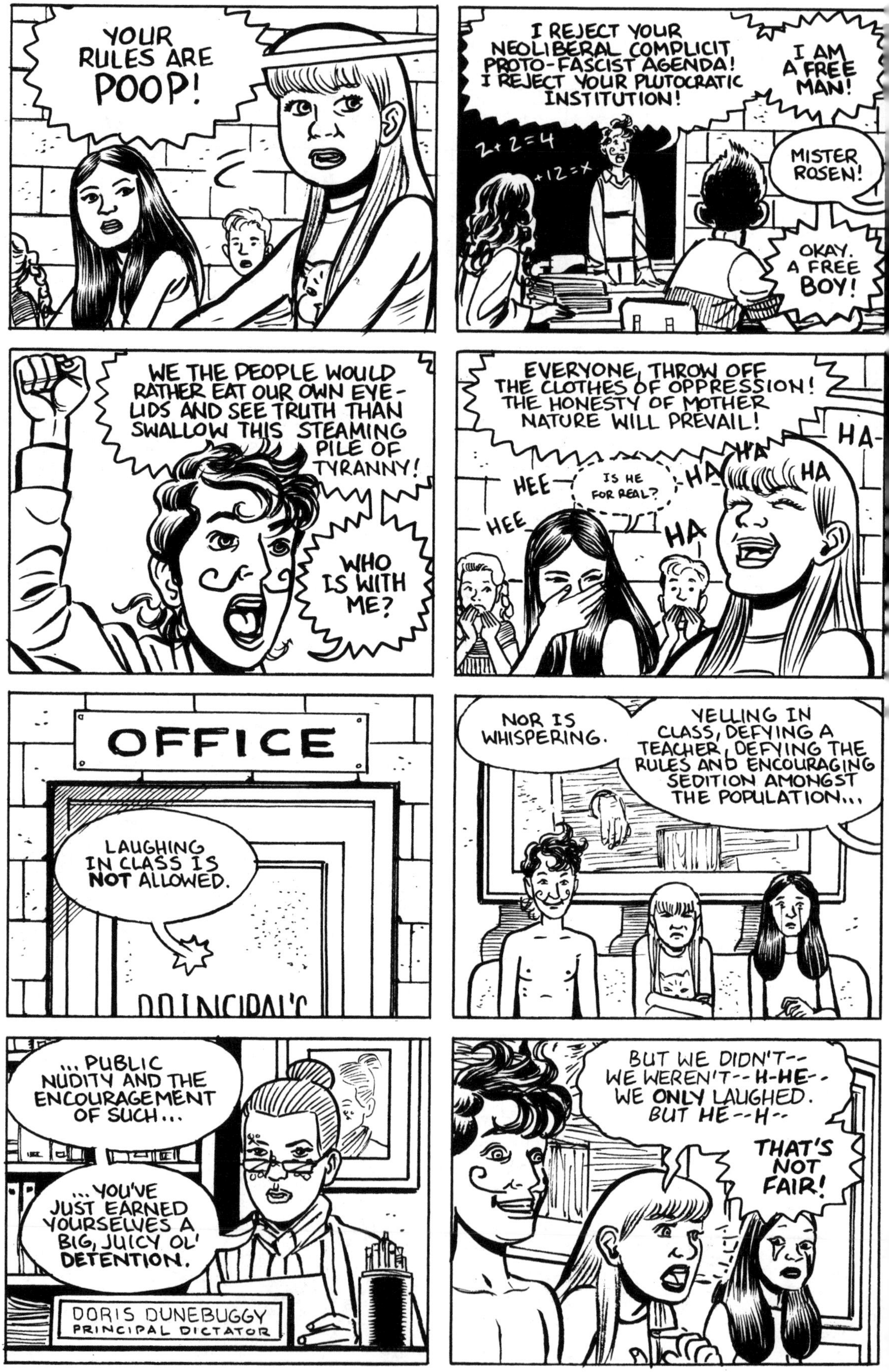
YOUR RULES ARE POOP!
I REJECT YOUR NEOLIBERAL COMPLICIT PROTO-FASCIST AGENDA! I REJECT YOUR PLUTOCRATIC INSTITUTION!
I AM A FREE MAN!
2+2=4
+12=X
MISTER ROSEN!
OKAY. A FREE BOY!
WE THE PEOPLE WOULD RATHER EAT OUR OWN EYE-LIDS AND SEE TRUTH THAN SWALLOW THIS STEAMING PILE OF TYRANNY!
WHO IS WITH ME?
EVERYONE, THROW OFF THE CLOTHES OF OPPRESSION! THE HONESTY OF MOTHER NATURE WILL PREVAIL!
HA-
HEE
IS HE FOR REAL?
HA
HA
HA
HEE
HA
OFFICE
LAUGHING IN CLASS IS NOT ALLOWED.
NOR IS WHISPERING.
YELLING IN CLASS, DEFYING A TEACHER, DEFYING THE RULES AND ENCOURAGING SEDITION AMONGST THE POPULATION...
...PUBLIC NUDITY AND THE ENCOURAGEMENT OF SUCH...
...YOU'VE JUST EARNED YOURSELVES A BIG, JUICY OL' DETENTION.
DORIS DUNEBUGGY
PRINCIPAL DICTATOR
BUT WE DIDN'T-- WE WEREN'T--H-HE-- WE ONLY LAUGHED. BUT HE--H--
THAT'S NOT FAIR!

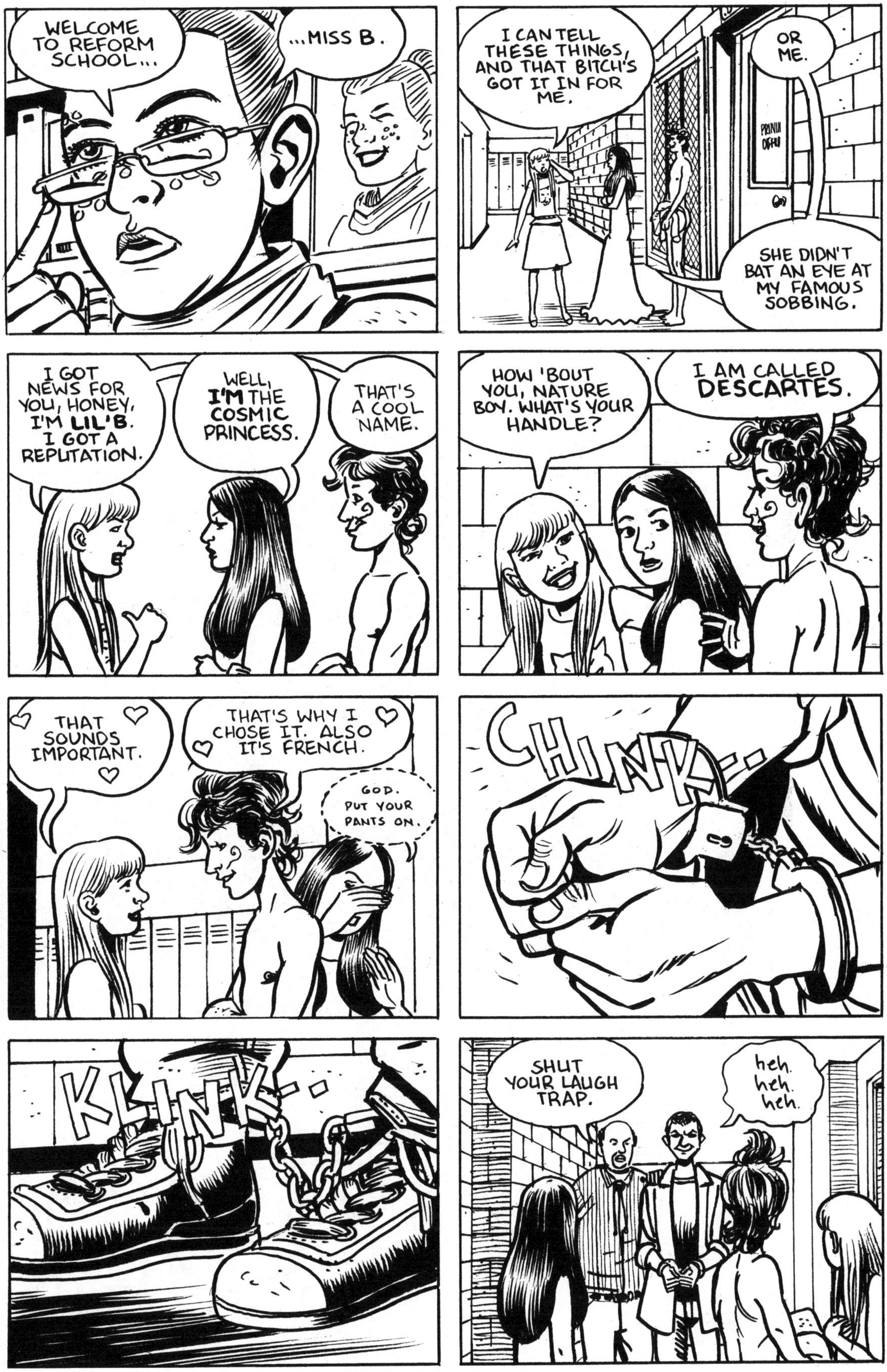
WELCOME TO REFORM SCHOOL...
...MISS B.
I CAN TELL THESE THINGS, AND THAT BITCH'S GOT IT IN FOR ME.
OR ME.
SHE DIDN'T BAT AN EYE AT MY FAMOUS SOBBING.
I GOT NEWS FOR YOU, HONEY, I'M LIL'B. I GOT A REPUTATION.
WELL, I'M THE COSMIC PRINCESS.
THAT'S A COOL NAME.
HOW 'BOUT YOU, NATURE BOY. WHAT'S YOUR HANDLE?
I AM CALLED DESCARTES.
THAT SOUNDS IMPORTANT.
THAT'S WHY I CHOSE IT. ALSO IT'S FRENCH.
GOD. PUT YOUR PANTS ON.
CHINK..
KLINK..
SHUT YOUR LAUGH TRAP.
heh. heh. heh.

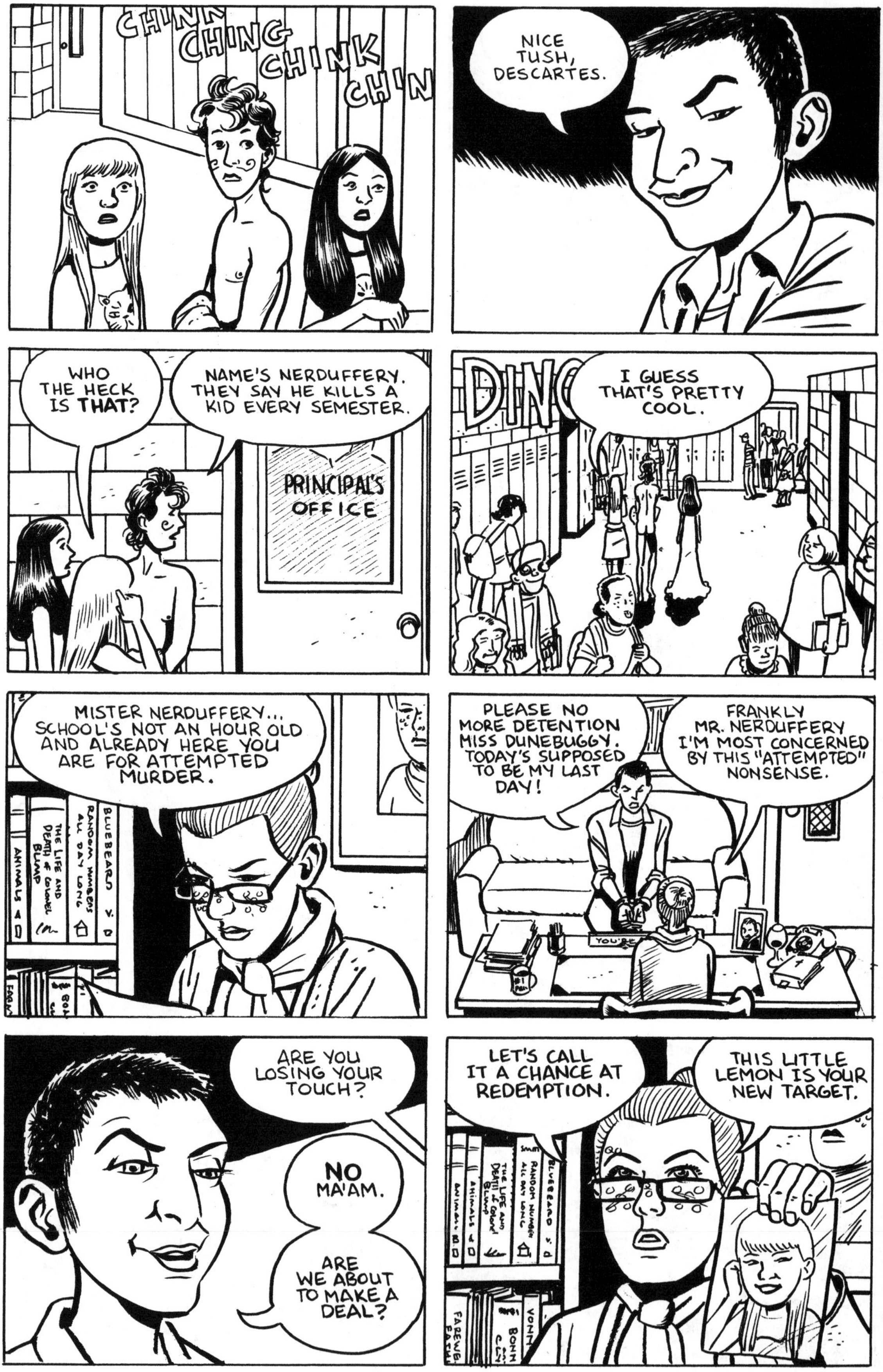
CHINK
CHING
CHINK
CHIN
NICE TUSH, DESCARTES.
WHO THE HECK IS **THAT**?
NAME'S NERDUFFERY. THEY SAY HE KILLS A KID EVERY SEMESTER.
PRINCIPAL'S OFFICE
I GUESS THAT'S PRETTY COOL.
MISTER NERDUFFERY... SCHOOL'S NOT AN HOUR OLD AND ALREADY HERE YOU ARE FOR ATTEMPTED MURDER.
BLUEBEARD V.D
RANDOM NUMBERS ALL DAY LONG
THE LIFE AND DEATH of COLONEL BLUMP
ANIMALS A
PLEASE NO MORE DETENTION MISS DUNEBUGGY. TODAY'S SUPPOSED TO BE MY LAST DAY!
FRANKLY MR. NERDUFFERY I'M MOST CONCERNED BY THIS "ATTEMPTED" NONSENSE.
ARE YOU LOSING YOUR TOUCH?
NO MA'AM.
ARE WE ABOUT TO MAKE A DEAL?
LET'S CALL IT A CHANCE AT REDEMPTION.
THIS LITTLE LEMON IS YOUR NEW TARGET.

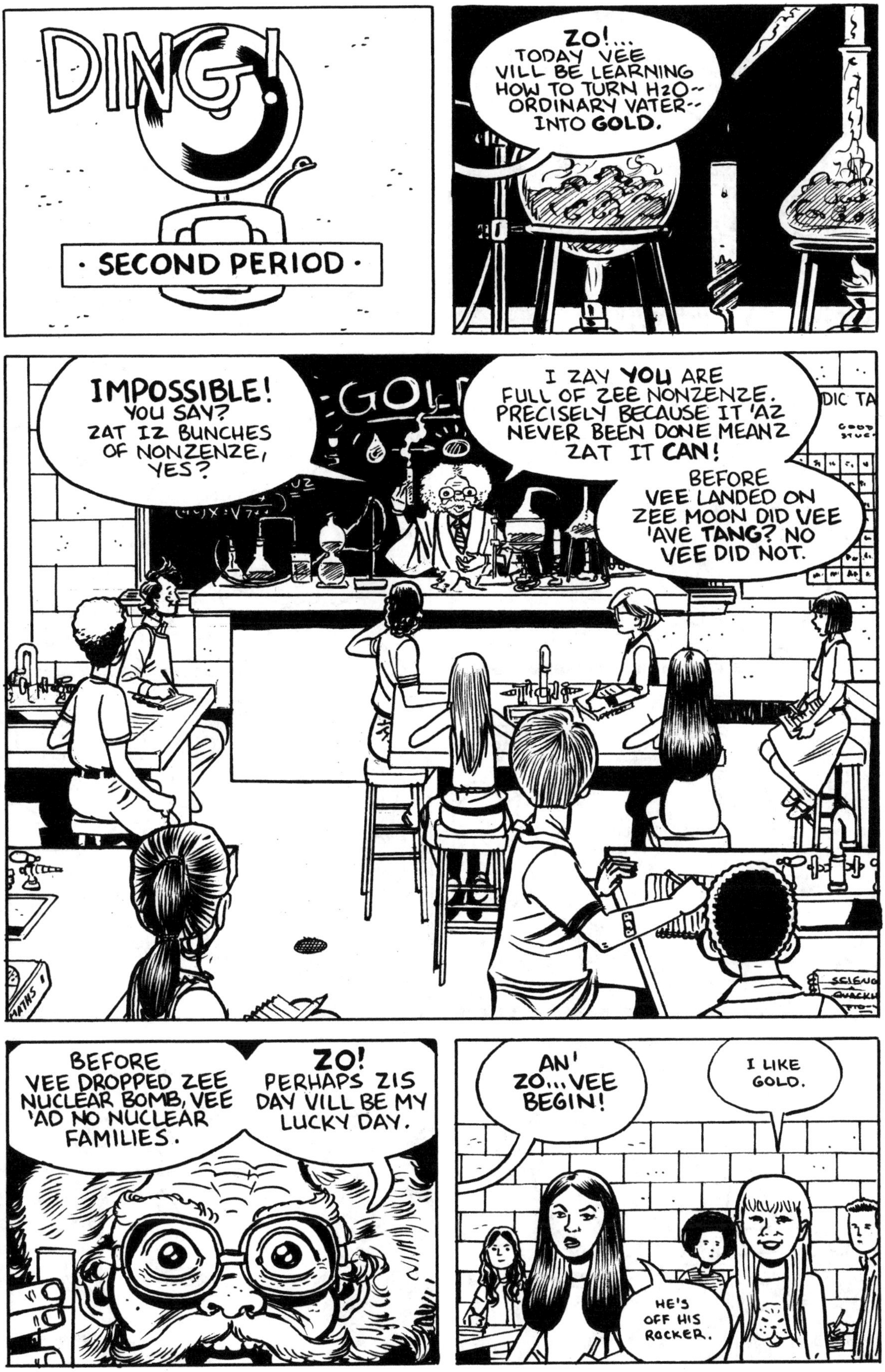
DING!
· SECOND PERIOD ·
ZO!... TODAY VEE VILL BE LEARNING HOW TO TURN H2O-- ORDINARY VATER-- INTO GOLD.
IMPOSSIBLE! YOU SAY? ZAT IZ BUNCHES OF NONZENZE, YES?
I ZAY YOU ARE FULL OF ZEE NONZENZE. PRECISELY BECAUSE IT 'AZ NEVER BEEN DONE MEANZ ZAT IT CAN!
BEFORE VEE LANDED ON ZEE MOON DID VEE 'AVE TANG? NO VEE DID NOT.
BEFORE VEE DROPPED ZEE NUCLEAR BOMB, VEE 'AD NO NUCLEAR FAMILIES.
ZO! PERHAPS ZIS DAY VILL BE MY LUCKY DAY.
AN' ZO... VEE BEGIN!
I LIKE GOLD.
HE'S OFF HIS ROCKER.

AND ELSEWHERE...

HEADS DOWN AND EYES ON YOUR OWN PAPER AT ALL TIMES.

FAILURE TO FOLLOW THESE RULES WILL RESULT IN DETENTION.

ENGLISH CLASSW—
① WRITE THE "A" IN THE DICTI—
② WR
③ DRAW P TO DEM UNDERS
④ DO THIS THREE

AND BELIEVE ME, YOU DO NOT WANT DETENTION. THERE'S A NINETEEN PERCENT **MORTALITY** RATE AND IT'S GOING **UP.**

"COUGH" SHEEP!

heh...

MAMA'S GOTTA HOT DATE TONIGHT.

MISS TINA, I NEED A FAVOR.

SIT DOWN, MISTER NERDUFFERY.

I NEED A HALL PASS.

DON'T BE RIDICULOUS. DO YOU KNOW THE PAPERWORK I'D HAVE TO FILL OUT?

WH-WHAT ARE YOU DOING...?

YOU KNOW YOU'RE VERY SEXY WHEN YOU'RE MAD?...

I-I'M YOUR TEACHER.

YOU'VE BEEN MY TEACHER FOR TWELVE YEARS...

...TINA.

I THINK IT'S TIME FOR OUR RELATIONSHIP TO **EVOLVE....**

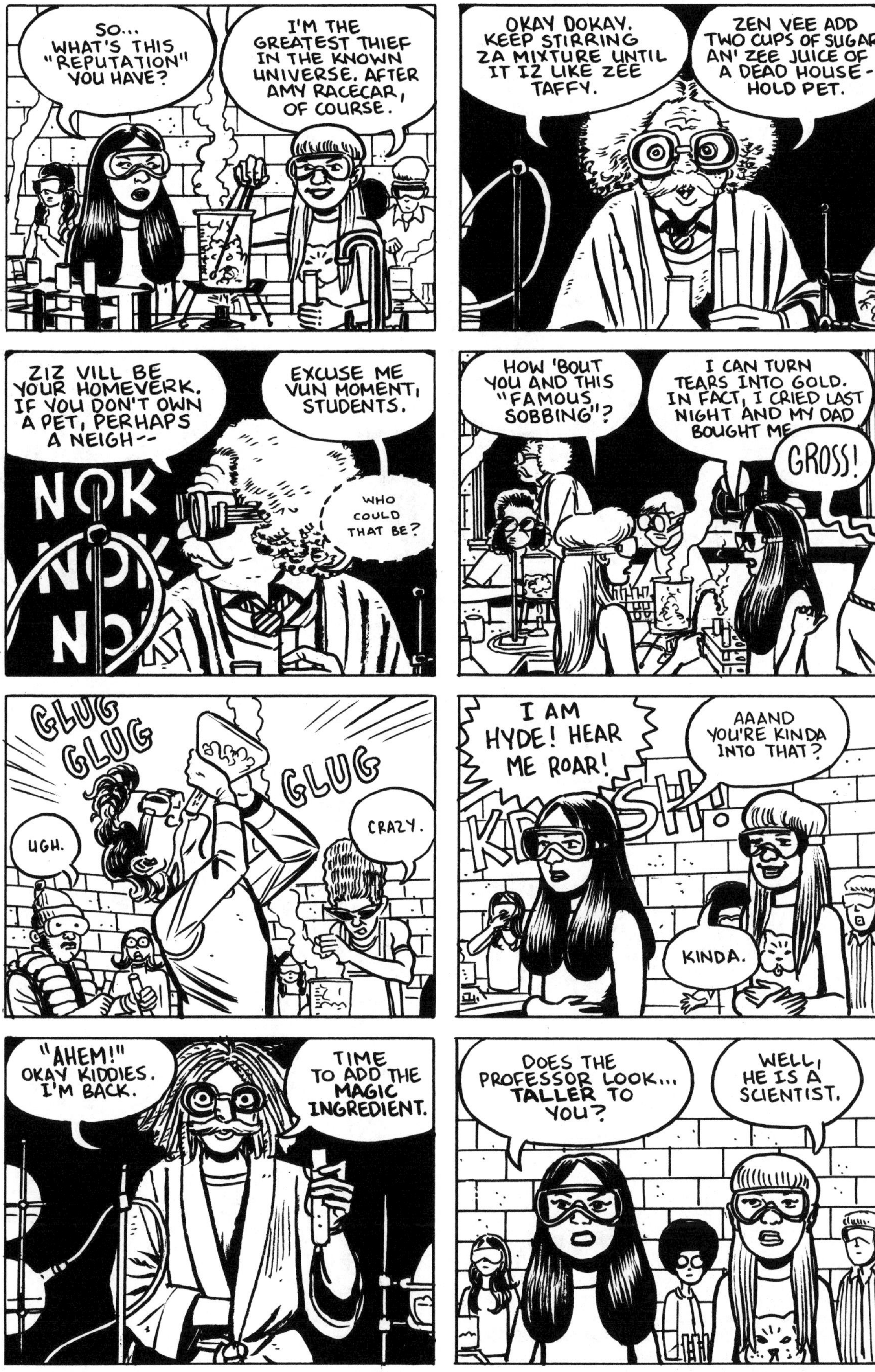

SO... WHAT'S THIS "REPUTATION" YOU HAVE?
I'M THE GREATEST THIEF IN THE KNOWN UNIVERSE. AFTER AMY RACECAR, OF COURSE.
OKAY DOKAY. KEEP STIRRING ZA MIXTURE UNTIL IT IZ LIKE ZEE TAFFY.
ZEN VEE ADD TWO CUPS OF SUGAR AN' ZEE JUICE OF A DEAD HOUSE-HOLD PET.
ZIZ VILL BE YOUR HOMEVERK. IF YOU DON'T OWN A PET, PERHAPS A NEIGH--
NOK NOK NOK
EXCUSE ME VUN MOMENT, STUDENTS.
WHO COULD THAT BE?
HOW 'BOUT YOU AND THIS "FAMOUS SOBBING"?
I CAN TURN TEARS INTO GOLD. IN FACT, I CRIED LAST NIGHT AND MY DAD BOUGHT ME
GROSS!
GLUG GLUG
GLUG
UGH.
CRAZY.
I AM HYDE! HEAR ME ROAR!
AAAND YOU'RE KINDA INTO THAT?
KINDA.
"AHEM!" OKAY KIDDIES. I'M BACK.
TIME TO ADD THE MAGIC INGREDIENT.
DOES THE PROFESSOR LOOK... TALLER TO YOU?
WELL, HE IS A SCIENTIST.

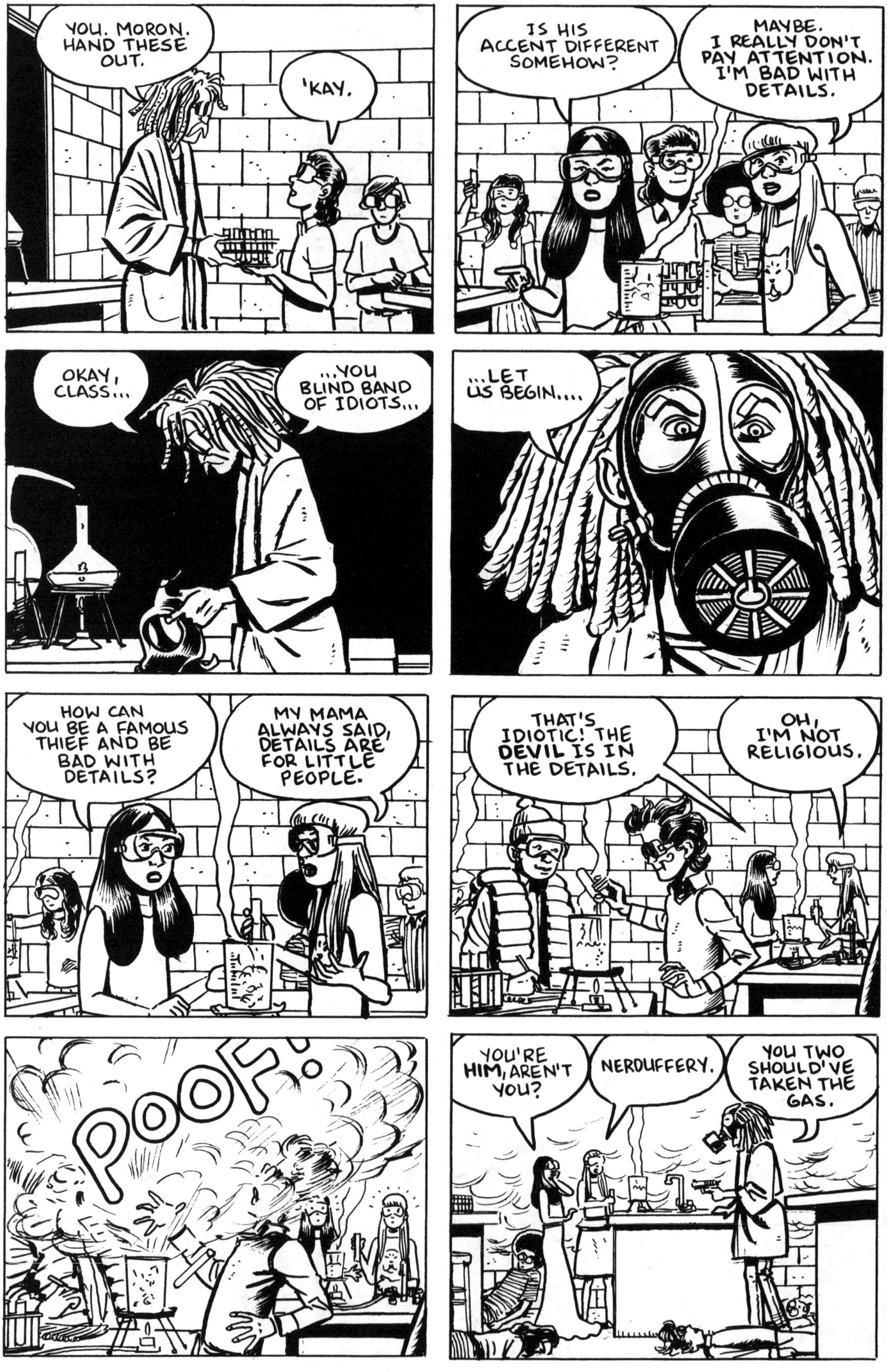
YOU. MORON. HAND THESE OUT.
'KAY.
IS HIS ACCENT DIFFERENT SOMEHOW?
MAYBE. I REALLY DON'T PAY ATTENTION. I'M BAD WITH DETAILS.
OKAY, CLASS...
...YOU BLIND BAND OF IDIOTS...
...LET US BEGIN....
HOW CAN YOU BE A FAMOUS THIEF AND BE BAD WITH DETAILS?
MY MAMA ALWAYS SAID, DETAILS ARE FOR LITTLE PEOPLE.
THAT'S IDIOTIC! THE DEVIL IS IN THE DETAILS.
OH, I'M NOT RELIGIOUS.
POOF!
YOU'RE HIM, AREN'T YOU?
NERDUFFERY.
YOU TWO SHOULD'VE TAKEN THE GAS.

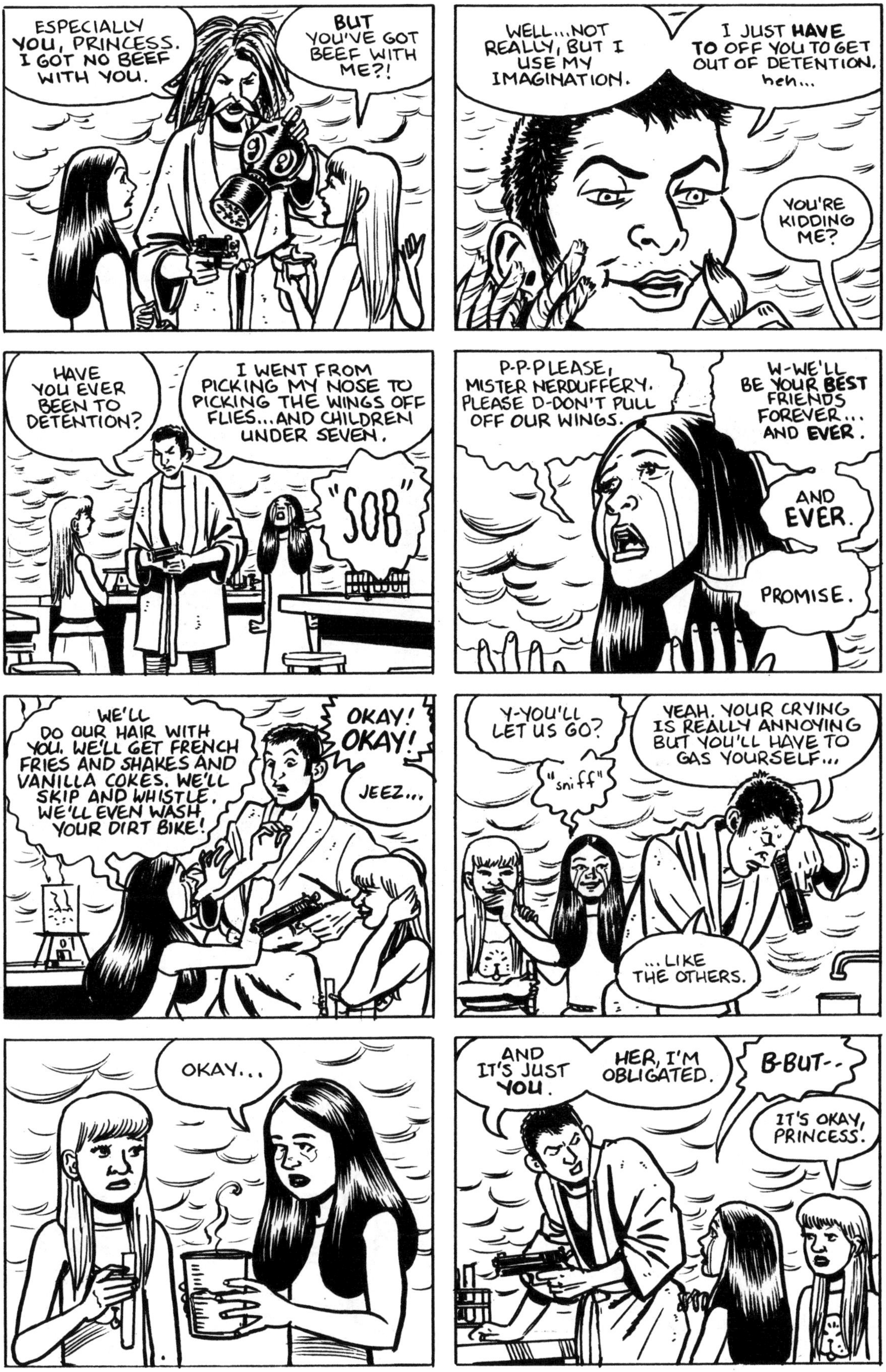
ESPECIALLY YOU, PRINCESS. I GOT NO BEEF WITH YOU.
BUT YOU'VE GOT BEEF WITH ME?!
WELL...NOT REALLY, BUT I USE MY IMAGINATION.
I JUST HAVE TO OFF YOU TO GET OUT OF DETENTION. heh...
YOU'RE KIDDING ME?
HAVE YOU EVER BEEN TO DETENTION?
I WENT FROM PICKING MY NOSE TO PICKING THE WINGS OFF FLIES...AND CHILDREN UNDER SEVEN.
"SOB"
P-P-PLEASE, MISTER NERDUFFERY. PLEASE D-DON'T PULL OFF OUR WINGS.
W-WE'LL BE YOUR BEST FRIENDS FOREVER... AND EVER.
AND EVER.
PROMISE.
WE'LL DO OUR HAIR WITH YOU. WE'LL GET FRENCH FRIES AND SHAKES AND VANILLA COKES. WE'LL SKIP AND WHISTLE. WE'LL EVEN WASH YOUR DIRT BIKE!
OKAY! OKAY!
JEEZ...
Y-YOU'LL LET US GO?
"sniff"
YEAH. YOUR CRYING IS REALLY ANNOYING BUT YOU'LL HAVE TO GAS YOURSELF...
...LIKE THE OTHERS.
OKAY...
AND IT'S JUST YOU.
HER, I'M OBLIGATED.
B-BUT--
IT'S OKAY, PRINCESS.

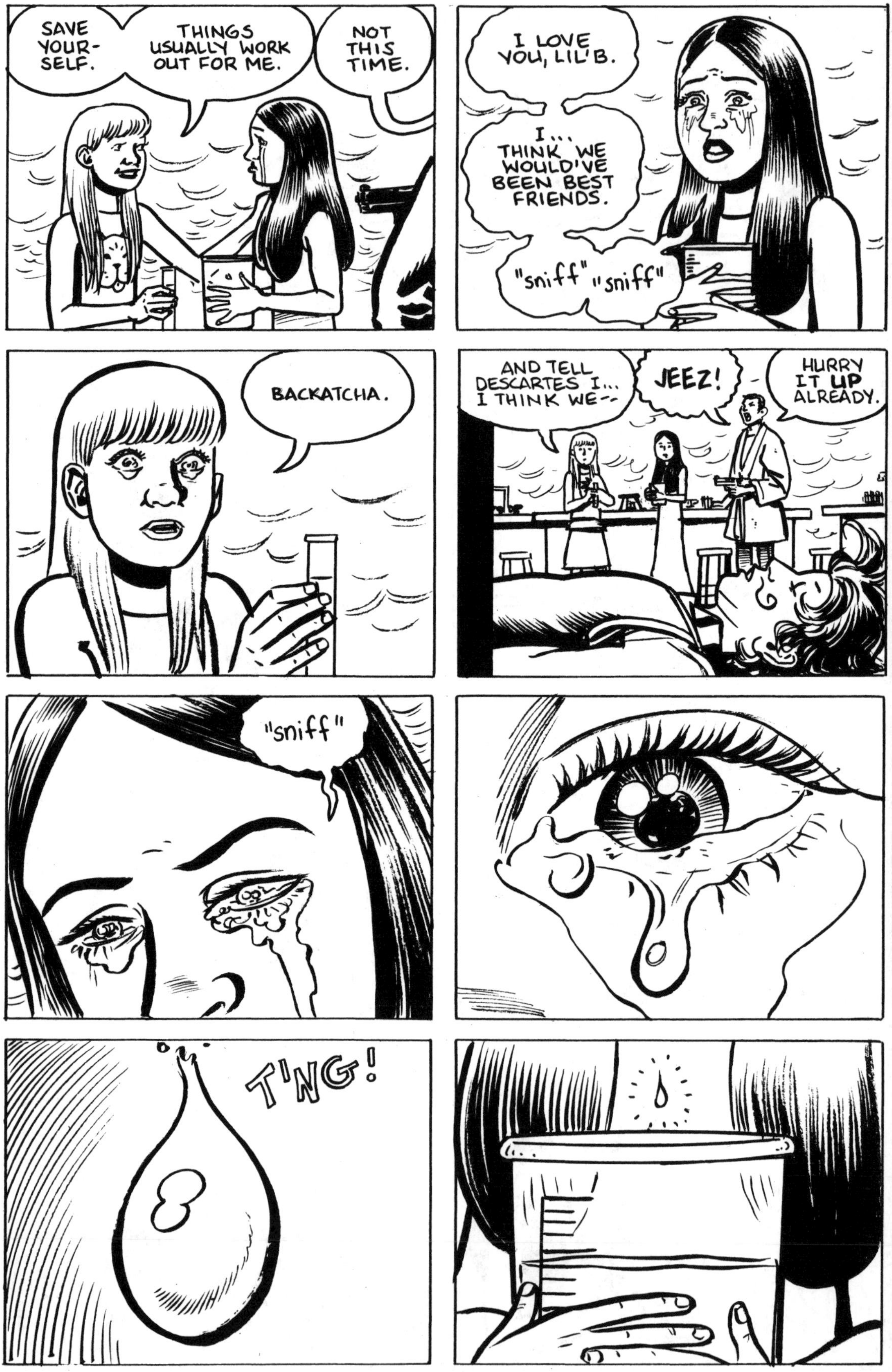
SAVE YOUR-SELF.
THINGS USUALLY WORK OUT FOR ME.
NOT THIS TIME.
I LOVE YOU, LIL'B.
I... THINK WE WOULD'VE BEEN BEST FRIENDS.
"sniff" "sniff"
BACKATCHA.
AND TELL DESCARTES I... I THINK WE--
JEEZ!
HURRY IT UP ALREADY.
"sniff"
T'NG!

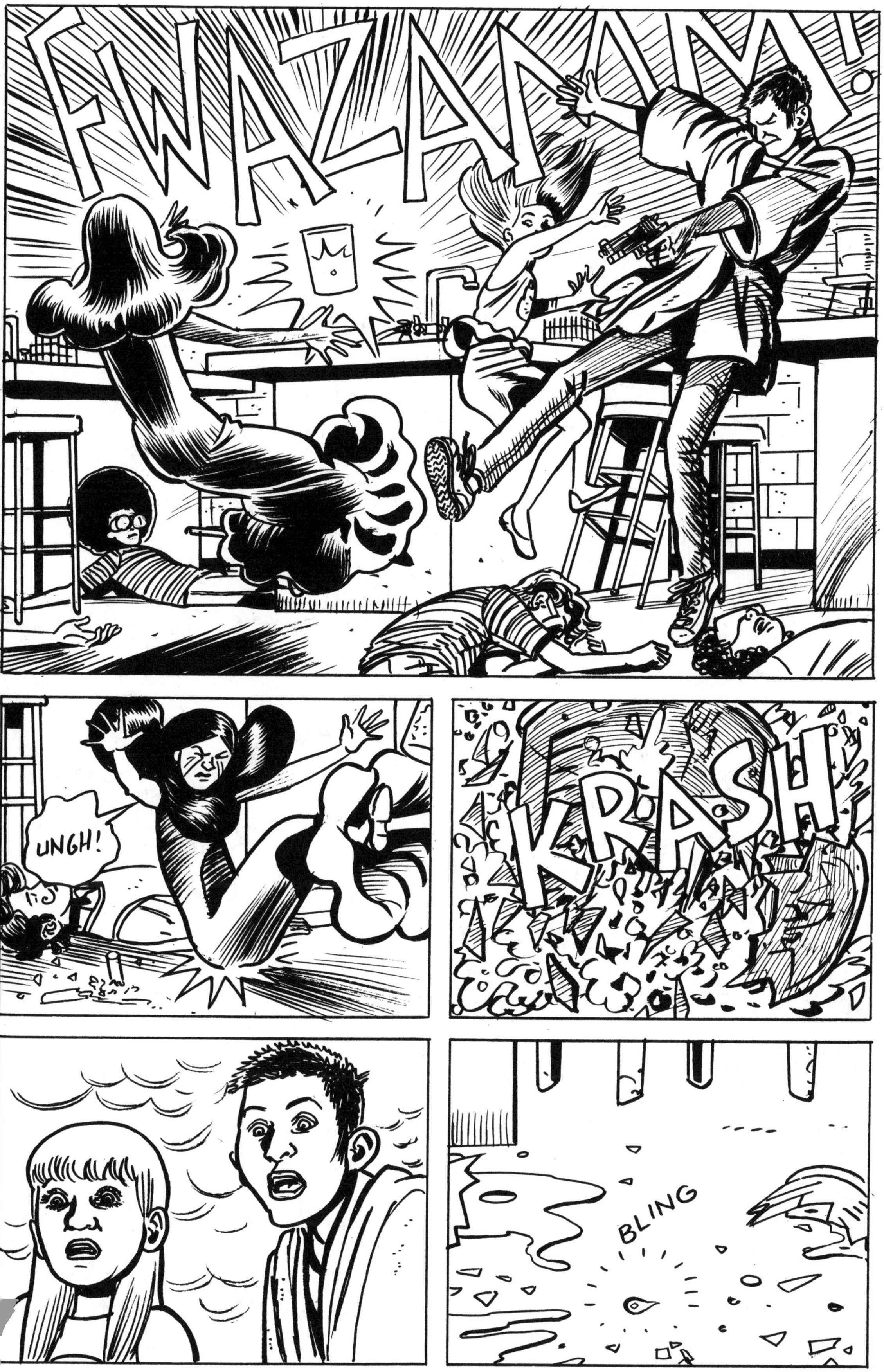
FWAZAAM!
UNGH!
KRASH
BLING

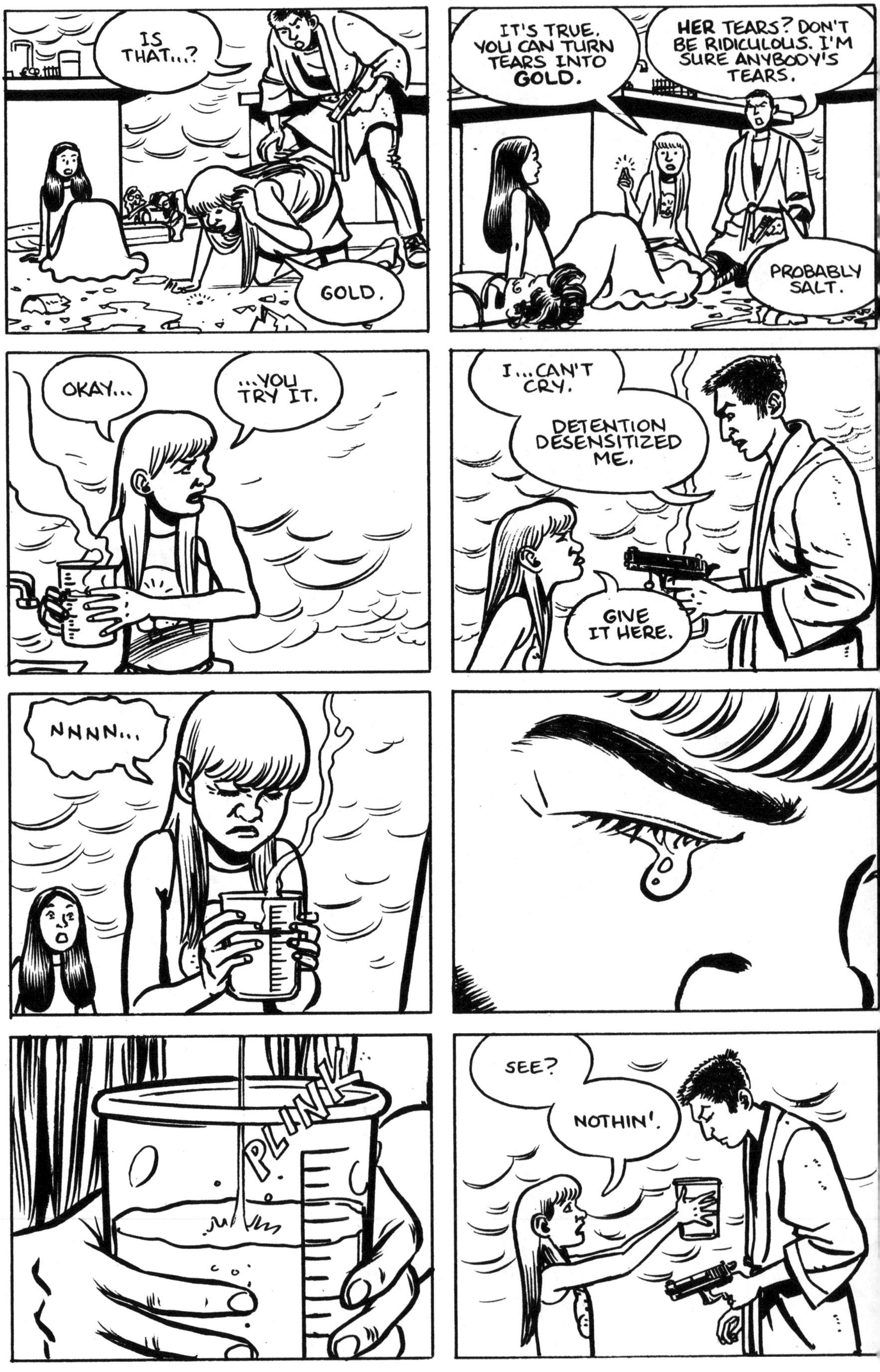
IS THAT...?
GOLD.
IT'S TRUE. YOU CAN TURN TEARS INTO GOLD.
HER TEARS? DON'T BE RIDICULOUS. I'M SURE ANYBODY'S TEARS.
PROBABLY SALT.
OKAY...
...YOU TRY IT.
I...CAN'T CRY.
DETENTION DESENSITIZED ME.
GIVE IT HERE.
NNNN...
PLINK
SEE?
NOTHIN'!

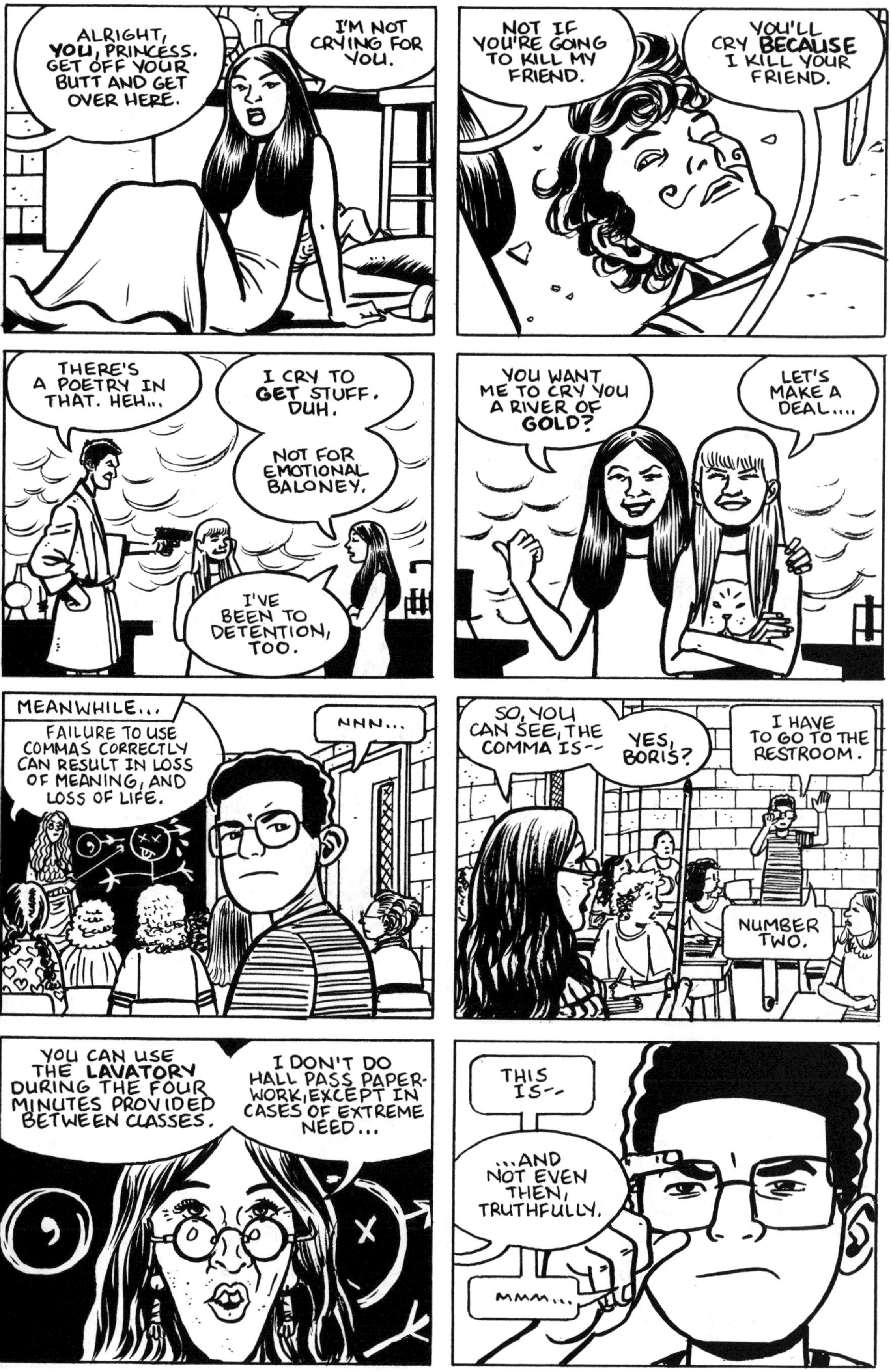
ALRIGHT, **YOU**, PRINCESS. GET OFF YOUR BUTT AND GET OVER HERE.
I'M NOT CRYING FOR YOU.
NOT IF YOU'RE GOING TO KILL MY FRIEND.
YOU'LL CRY **BECAUSE** I KILL YOUR FRIEND.
THERE'S A POETRY IN THAT. HEH...
I CRY TO **GET** STUFF. DUH.
NOT FOR EMOTIONAL BALONEY.
I'VE BEEN TO DETENTION, TOO.
YOU WANT ME TO CRY YOU A RIVER OF **GOLD?**
LET'S MAKE A DEAL....
MEANWHILE...
FAILURE TO USE COMMAS CORRECTLY CAN RESULT IN LOSS OF MEANING, AND LOSS OF LIFE.
NNN...
SO, YOU CAN SEE, THE COMMA IS--
YES, BORIS?
I HAVE TO GO TO THE RESTROOM.
NUMBER TWO.
YOU CAN USE THE **LAVATORY** DURING THE FOUR MINUTES PROVIDED BETWEEN CLASSES.
I DON'T DO HALL PASS PAPER-WORK, EXCEPT IN CASES OF EXTREME NEED...
THIS IS--
...AND NOT EVEN THEN, TRUTHFULLY.
MMM...

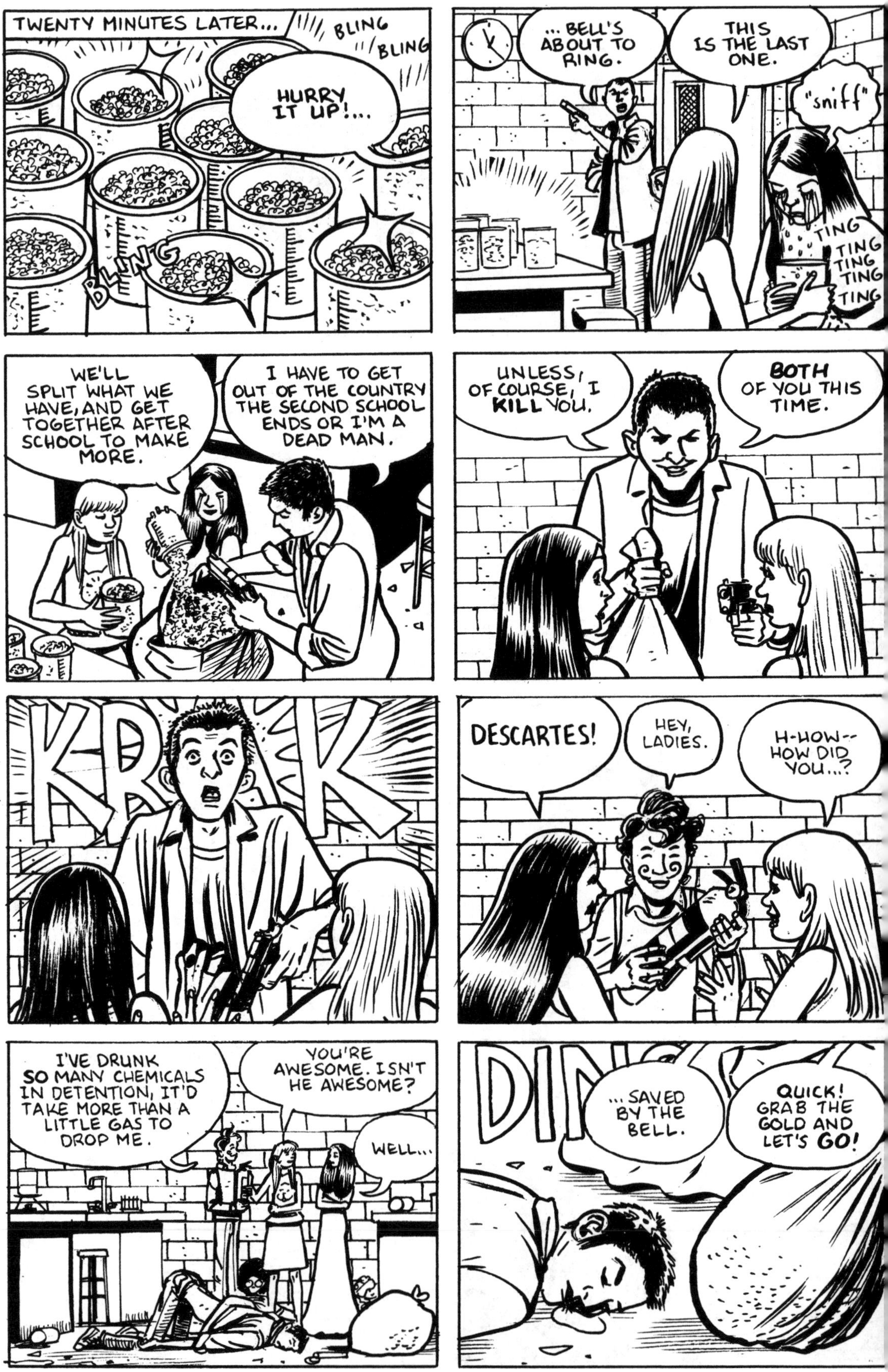
TWENTY MINUTES LATER...
BLING
BLING
HURRY IT UP!...
BLING
...BELL'S ABOUT TO RING.
THIS IS THE LAST ONE.
"sniff"
TING
TING
TING
TING
TING
WE'LL SPLIT WHAT WE HAVE, AND GET TOGETHER AFTER SCHOOL TO MAKE MORE.
I HAVE TO GET OUT OF THE COUNTRY THE SECOND SCHOOL ENDS OR I'M A DEAD MAN.
UNLESS, OF COURSE, I KILL YOU.
BOTH OF YOU THIS TIME.
KRAK
DESCARTES!
HEY, LADIES.
H-HOW-- HOW DID YOU...?
I'VE DRUNK SO MANY CHEMICALS IN DETENTION, IT'D TAKE MORE THAN A LITTLE GAS TO DROP ME.
YOU'RE AWESOME. ISN'T HE AWESOME?
WELL...
...SAVED BY THE BELL.
QUICK! GRAB THE GOLD AND LET'S GO!

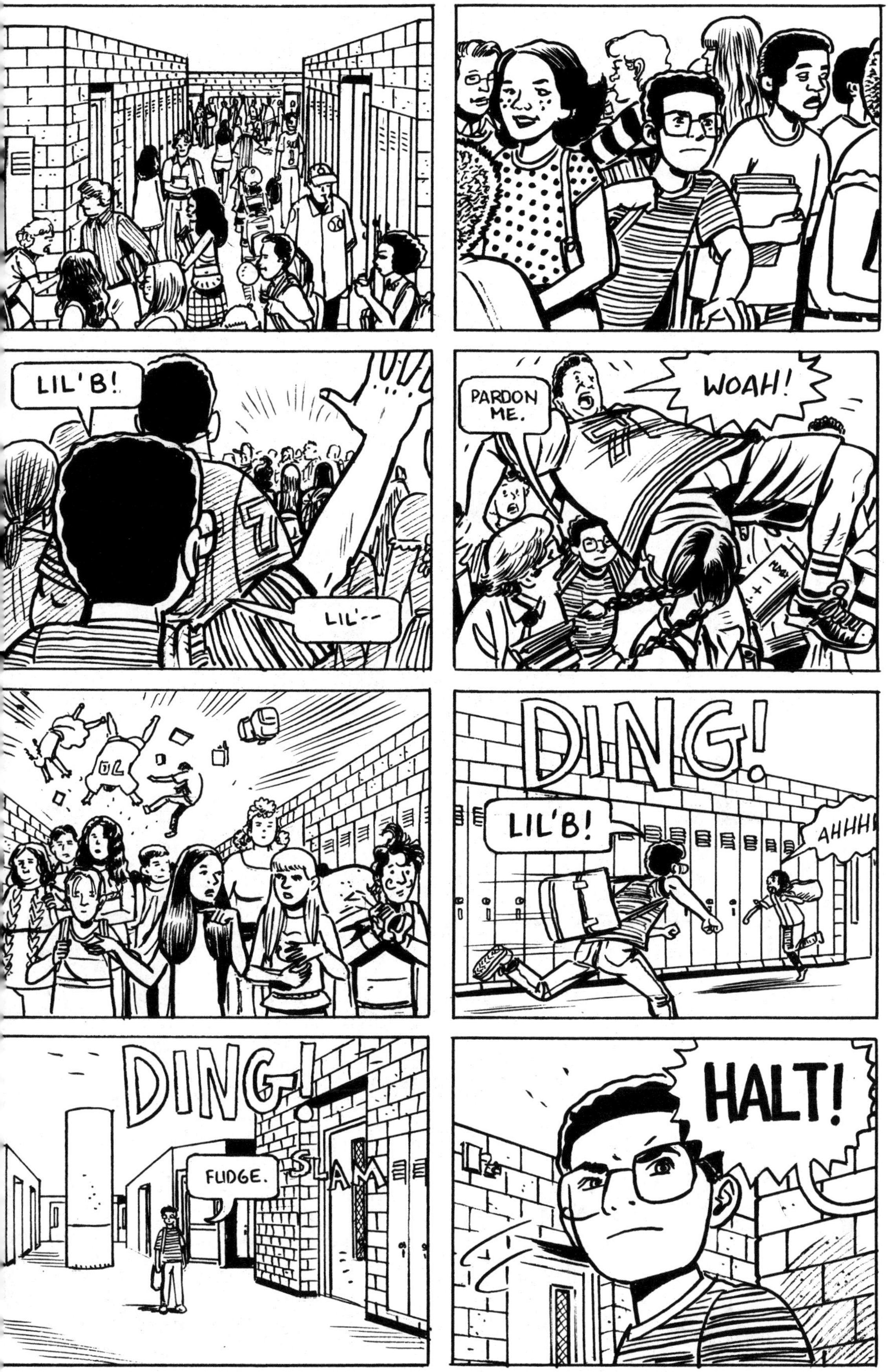
LIL'B!
LIL'--
PARDON ME.
WOAH!
DING!
LIL'B!
AHHH
DING!
FLIDGE.
SLAM
HALT!

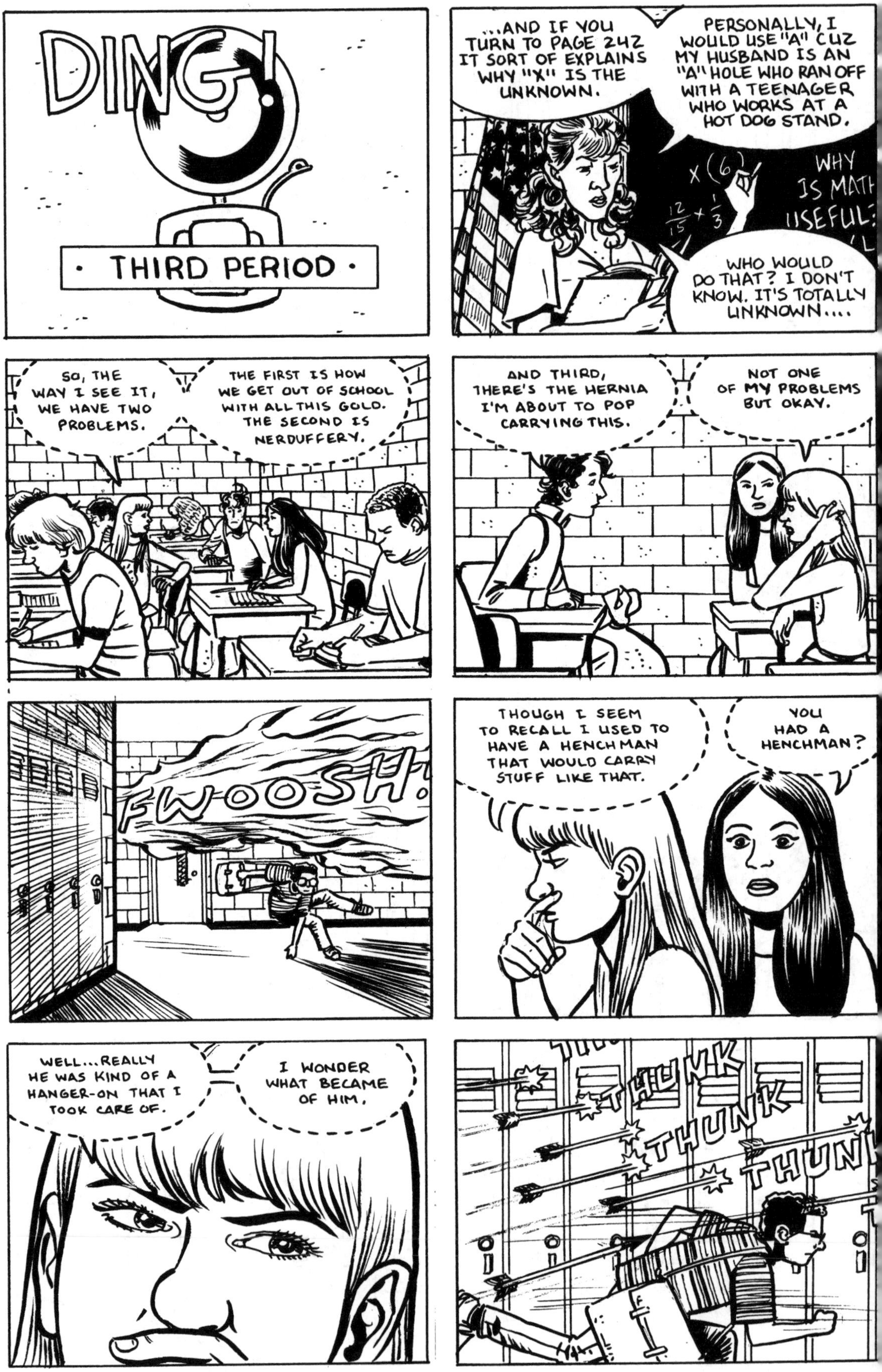
DING!
• THIRD PERIOD •
...AND IF YOU TURN TO PAGE 242 IT SORT OF EXPLAINS WHY "X" IS THE UNKNOWN.
PERSONALLY, I WOULD USE "A" CUZ MY HUSBAND IS AN "A" HOLE WHO RAN OFF WITH A TEENAGER WHO WORKS AT A HOT DOG STAND.
WHY IS MATH USEFUL?
WHO WOULD DO THAT? I DON'T KNOW. IT'S TOTALLY UNKNOWN....
SO, THE WAY I SEE IT, WE HAVE TWO PROBLEMS.
THE FIRST IS HOW WE GET OUT OF SCHOOL WITH ALL THIS GOLD. THE SECOND IS NERDUFFERY.
AND THIRD, THERE'S THE HERNIA I'M ABOUT TO POP CARRYING THIS.
NOT ONE OF MY PROBLEMS BUT OKAY.
FWOOSH!
THOUGH I SEEM TO RECALL I USED TO HAVE A HENCHMAN THAT WOULD CARRY STUFF LIKE THAT.
YOU HAD A HENCHMAN?
WELL...REALLY HE WAS KIND OF A HANGER-ON THAT I TOOK CARE OF.
I WONDER WHAT BECAME OF HIM.
THUNK
THUNK
THUNK

I'M...um... A NEW STUDENT.

HMMM... THE SECOND OF THE DAY. I MUST'VE BEEN ASLEEP WHEN ZA PAPERWORK CAME IN.

VELL, VIND A SEAT UND A PAIR OF GOGGLES.

TODAY, AS VEE DO EVERY DAY, VEE ARE FAILING TO MAKE ZEE GOLD.

UND TODAY VEE VILL BE ADDING EXPLOSIVE AGENTS TO HELP ZA BON...

MIND IF I...?

ARE YOU A YAPPER?

NO.

OKAY.

...AND NONE OF THIS INCLUDES MY SON'S BRACES, MY DAUGHTER'S SOCCER CAMP, AND MY PRESCRIPTIONS! WHO THE HAIRY SHIT CAN AFFORD THIS?!

UNKNOWN! ALL UNKNOWN!

FOR MORTGAGE
ELECTRICITY
TOILET PAPER
ASPIRIN
ROMANCE NOV
CATS, CATS, C
"A" HOLE
FUCKED

WE'RE GOING TO HAVE TO MAKE IT UNTIL THE END OF THE DAY.

HE'S RIGHT. DUNEBUGGY KEEPS THE SCHOOL ON LOCK-DOWN, AND THERE ARE DEATH TRAPS.

PLUS THE DOORS ARE LOCKED.

THE GOOD NEWS IS THAT THERE'S NO WAY NERDUFFERY GETS EVERY TEACHER TO GIVE HIM A HALL PASS.

SO WE'LL ONLY HAVE TO AVOID HIM BETWEEN CLASSES.

DING!

Before
· FOURTH PERIOD ·

171

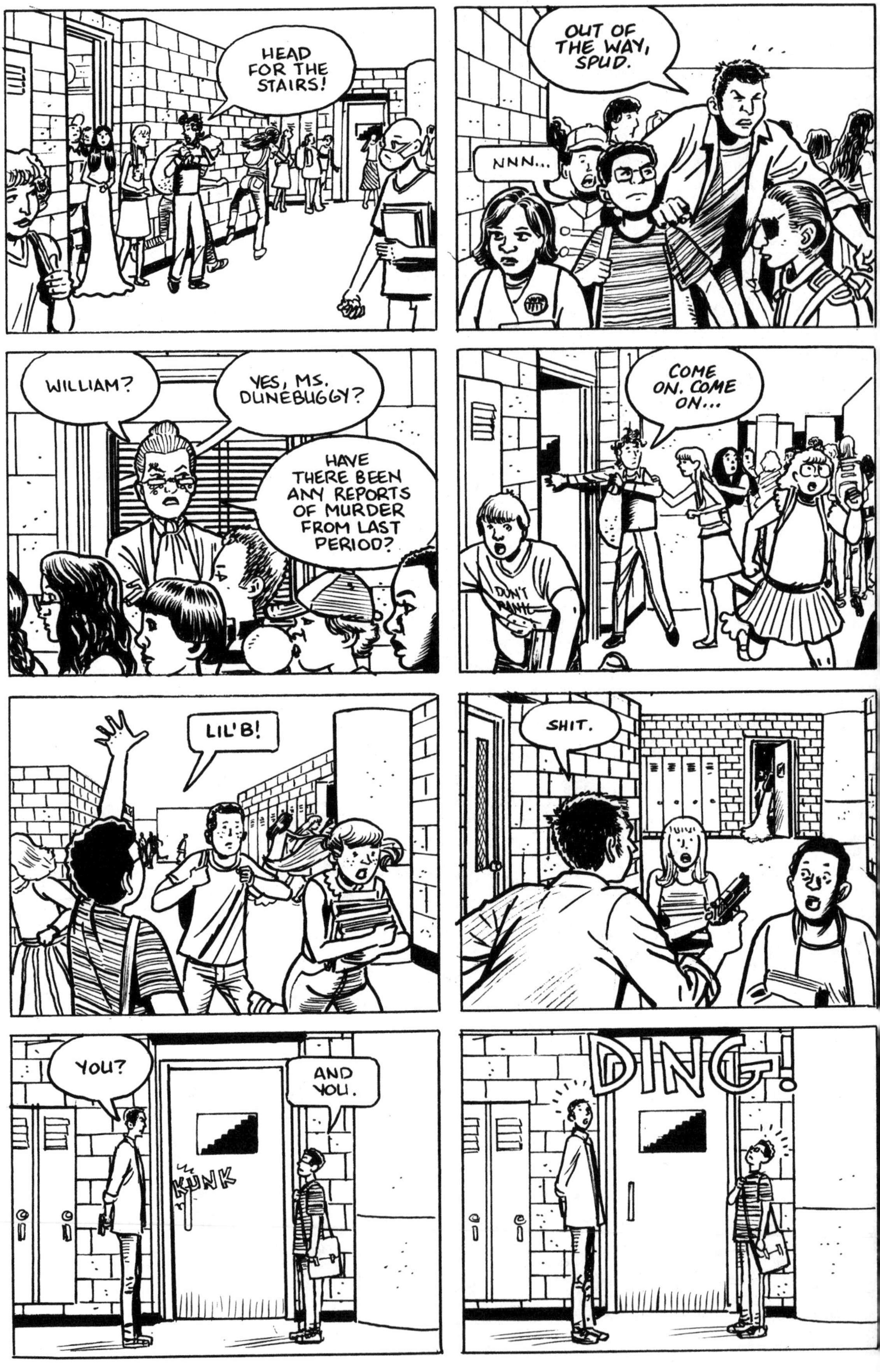
HEAD FOR THE STAIRS!
OUT OF THE WAY, SPUD.
NNN...
WILLIAM?
YES, MS. DUNEBUGGY?
HAVE THERE BEEN ANY REPORTS OF MURDER FROM LAST PERIOD?
COME ON. COME ON...
LIL'B!
SHIT.
YOU?
KUNK
AND YOU.
DING!

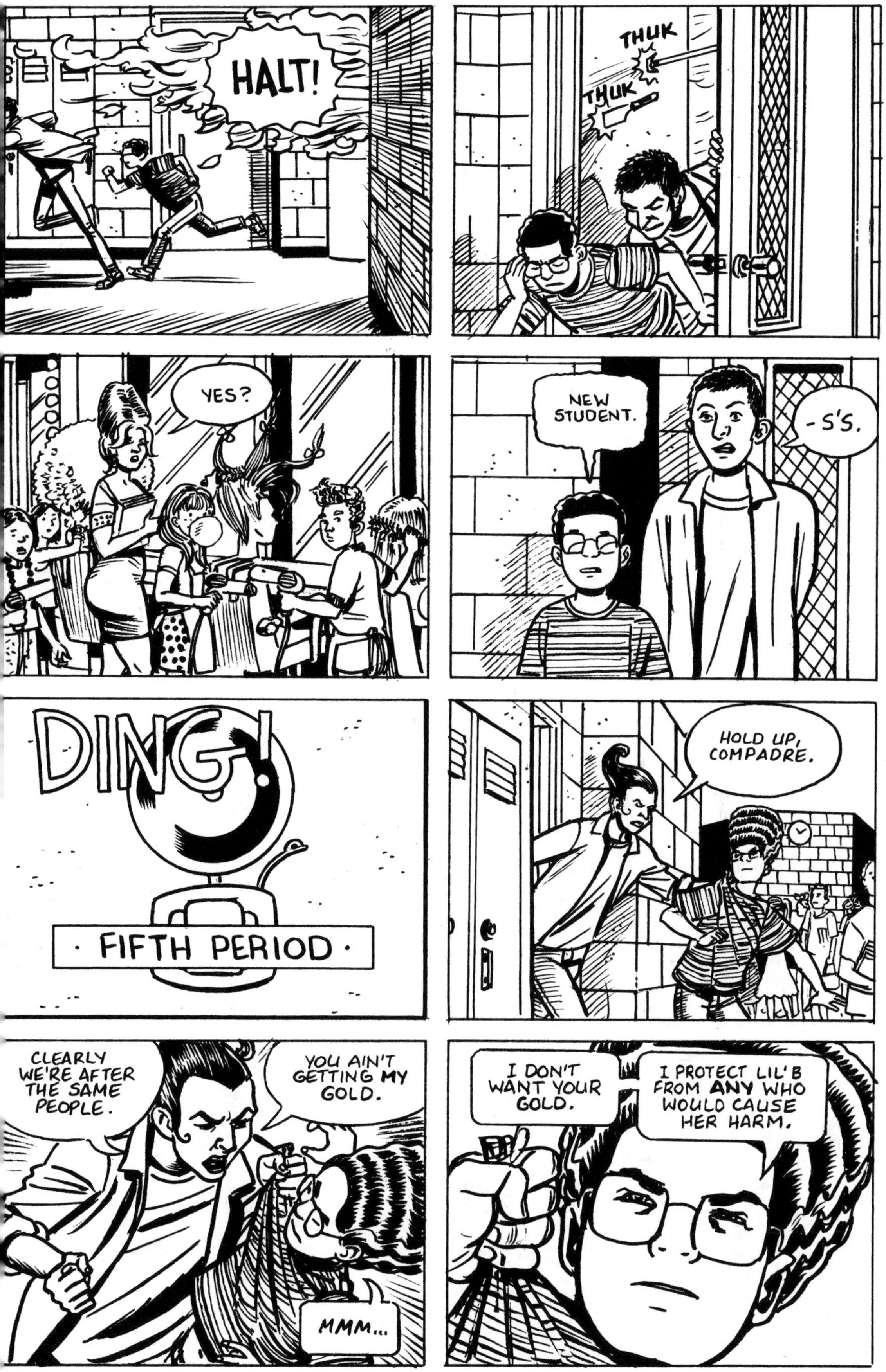
HALT!
THUK
THUK
YES?
NEW STUDENT.
-S'S.
DING!
FIFTH PERIOD
HOLD UP, COMPADRE.
CLEARLY WE'RE AFTER THE SAME PEOPLE.
YOU AIN'T GETTING MY GOLD.
MMM...
I DON'T WANT YOUR GOLD.
I PROTECT LIL'B FROM ANY WHO WOULD CAUSE HER HARM.

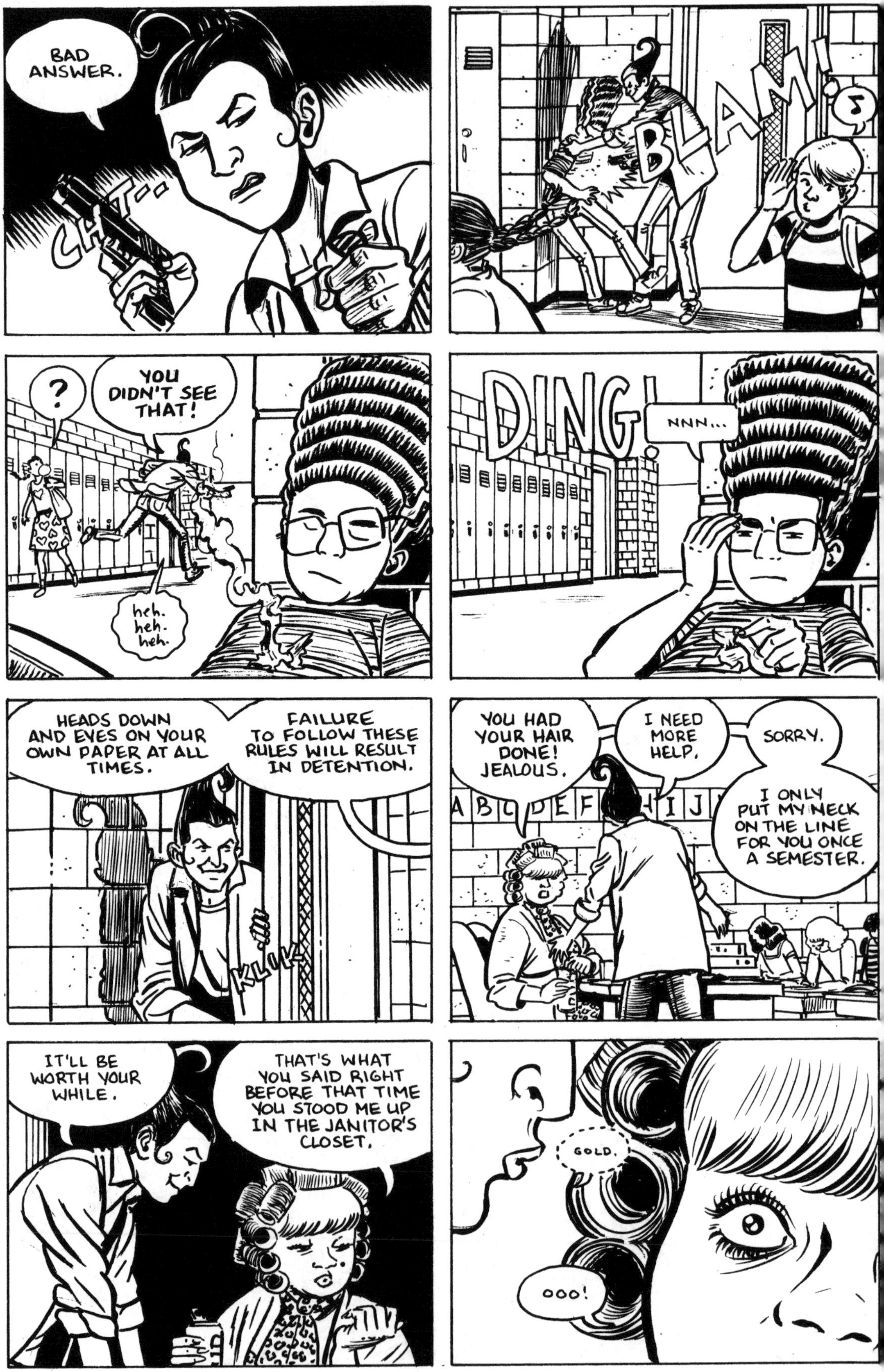
BAD ANSWER.
CHK-T-o
BLAM!
?
YOU DIDN'T SEE THAT!
heh. heh. heh.
DING!
NNN...
HEADS DOWN AND EYES ON YOUR OWN PAPER AT ALL TIMES.
FAILURE TO FOLLOW THESE RULES WILL RESULT IN DETENTION.
KLIK
YOU HAD YOUR HAIR DONE! JEALOUS.
I NEED MORE HELP.
SORRY.
I ONLY PUT MY NECK ON THE LINE FOR YOU ONCE A SEMESTER.
IT'LL BE WORTH YOUR WHILE.
THAT'S WHAT YOU SAID RIGHT BEFORE THAT TIME YOU STOOD ME UP IN THE JANITOR'S CLOSET.
GOLD.
OOO!

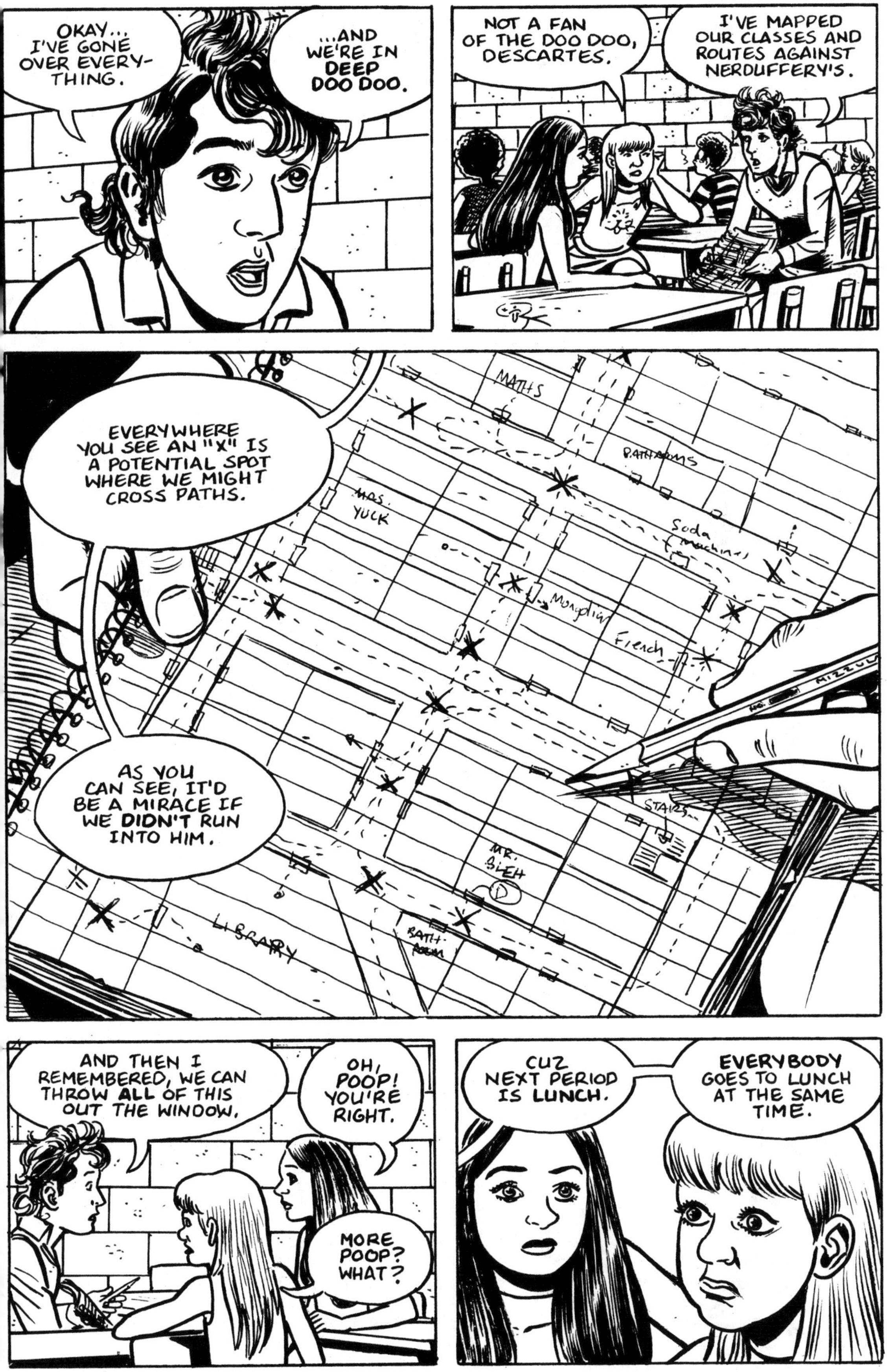
OKAY... I'VE GONE OVER EVERYTHING.
...AND WE'RE IN DEEP DOO DOO.
NOT A FAN OF THE DOO DOO, DESCARTES.
I'VE MAPPED OUR CLASSES AND ROUTES AGAINST NERDUFFERY'S.
EVERYWHERE YOU SEE AN "X" IS A POTENTIAL SPOT WHERE WE MIGHT CROSS PATHS.
MATHS
BATHROOMS
MRS. YUCK
Soda machines
Mongolian
French
STAIRS
MR. SIEH
LIBRARY
BATHROOM
AS YOU CAN SEE, IT'D BE A MIRACE IF WE DIDN'T RUN INTO HIM.
AND THEN I REMEMBERED, WE CAN THROW ALL OF THIS OUT THE WINDOW.
OH, POOP! YOU'RE RIGHT.
MORE POOP? WHAT?
CUZ NEXT PERIOD IS LUNCH.
EVERYBODY GOES TO LUNCH AT THE SAME TIME.

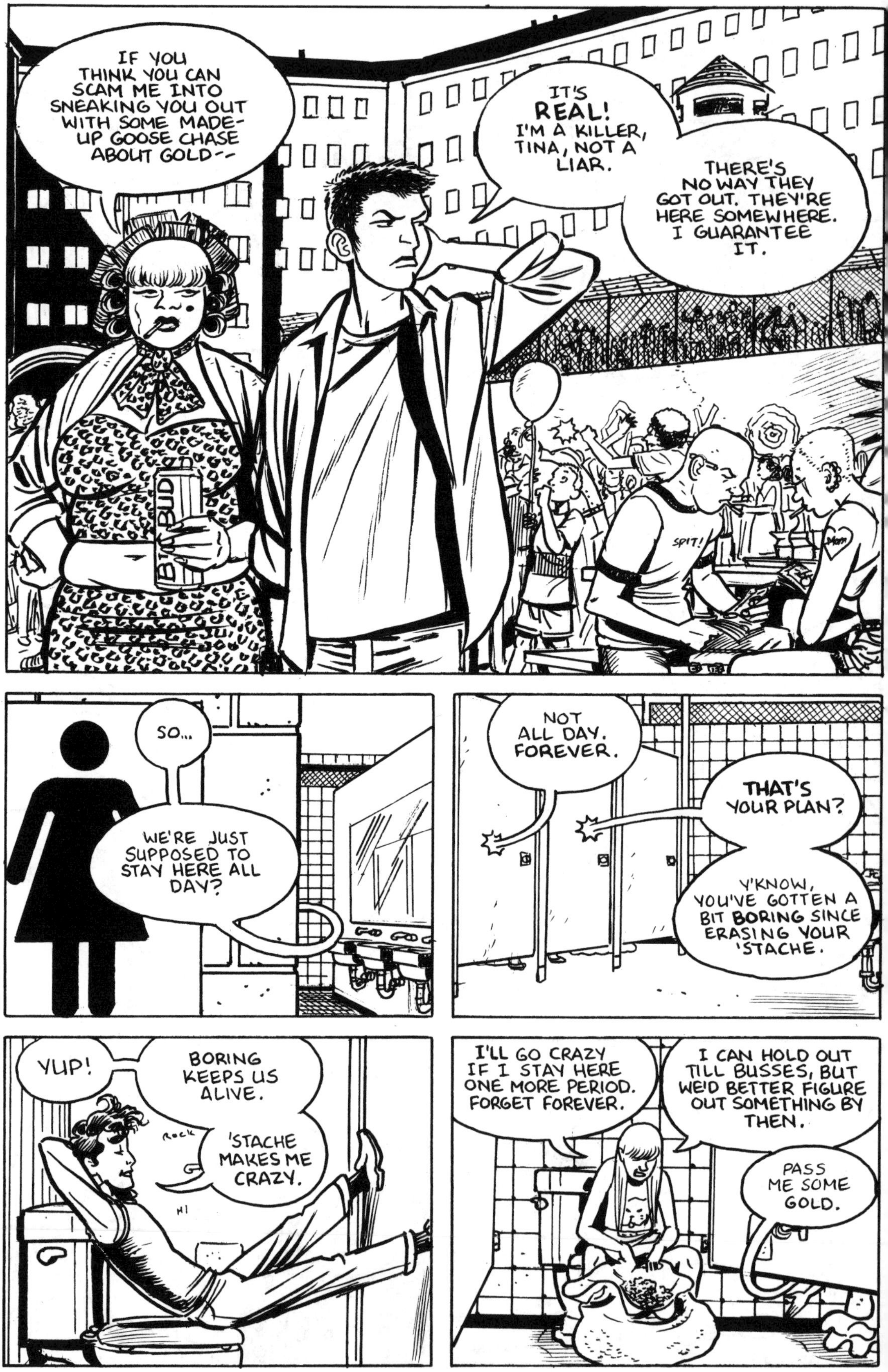

IF YOU THINK YOU CAN SCAM ME INTO SNEAKING YOU OUT WITH SOME MADE-UP GOOSE CHASE ABOUT GOLD--
IT'S **REAL!** I'M A KILLER, TINA, NOT A LIAR.
THERE'S NO WAY THEY GOT OUT. THEY'RE HERE SOMEWHERE. I GUARANTEE IT.
SPIT!
SO...
WE'RE JUST SUPPOSED TO STAY HERE ALL DAY?
NOT ALL DAY. FOREVER.
THAT'S YOUR PLAN?
Y'KNOW, YOU'VE GOTTEN A BIT **BORING** SINCE ERASING YOUR 'STACHE.
YUP!
BORING KEEPS US ALIVE.
ROCK
'STACHE MAKES ME CRAZY.
HI
I'LL GO CRAZY IF I STAY HERE ONE MORE PERIOD. FORGET FOREVER.
I CAN HOLD OUT TILL BUSSES, BUT WE'D BETTER FIGURE OUT SOMETHING BY THEN.
PASS ME SOME GOLD.

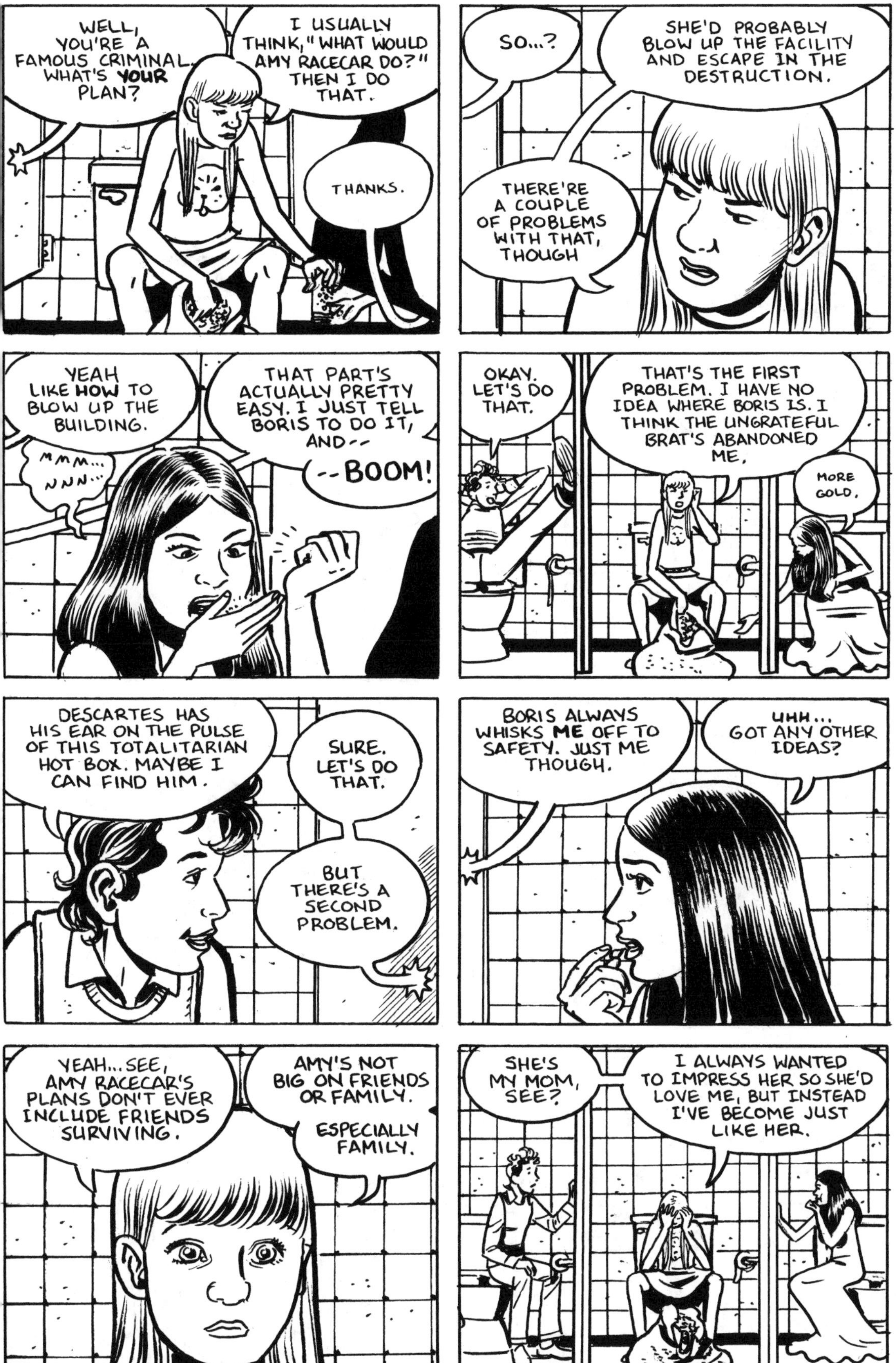
WELL, YOU'RE A FAMOUS CRIMINAL. WHAT'S **YOUR** PLAN?
I USUALLY THINK, "WHAT WOULD AMY RACECAR DO?" THEN I DO THAT.
THANKS.
SO...?
SHE'D PROBABLY BLOW UP THE FACILITY AND ESCAPE IN THE DESTRUCTION.
THERE'RE A COUPLE OF PROBLEMS WITH THAT, THOUGH
YEAH LIKE **HOW** TO BLOW UP THE BUILDING.
MMM... NNN...
THAT PART'S ACTUALLY PRETTY EASY. I JUST TELL BORIS TO DO IT, AND--
--BOOM!
OKAY. LET'S DO THAT.
THAT'S THE FIRST PROBLEM. I HAVE NO IDEA WHERE BORIS IS. I THINK THE UNGRATEFUL BRAT'S ABANDONED ME.
MORE GOLD.
DESCARTES HAS HIS EAR ON THE PULSE OF THIS TOTALITARIAN HOT BOX. MAYBE I CAN FIND HIM.
SURE. LET'S DO THAT.
BUT THERE'S A SECOND PROBLEM.
BORIS ALWAYS WHISKS **ME** OFF TO SAFETY. JUST ME THOUGH.
UHH... GOT ANY OTHER IDEAS?
YEAH...SEE, AMY RACECAR'S PLANS DON'T EVER INCLUDE FRIENDS SURVIVING.
AMY'S NOT BIG ON FRIENDS OR FAMILY.
ESPECIALLY FAMILY.
SHE'S MY MOM, SEE?
I ALWAYS WANTED TO IMPRESS HER SO SHE'D LOVE ME, BUT INSTEAD I'VE BECOME JUST LIKE HER.

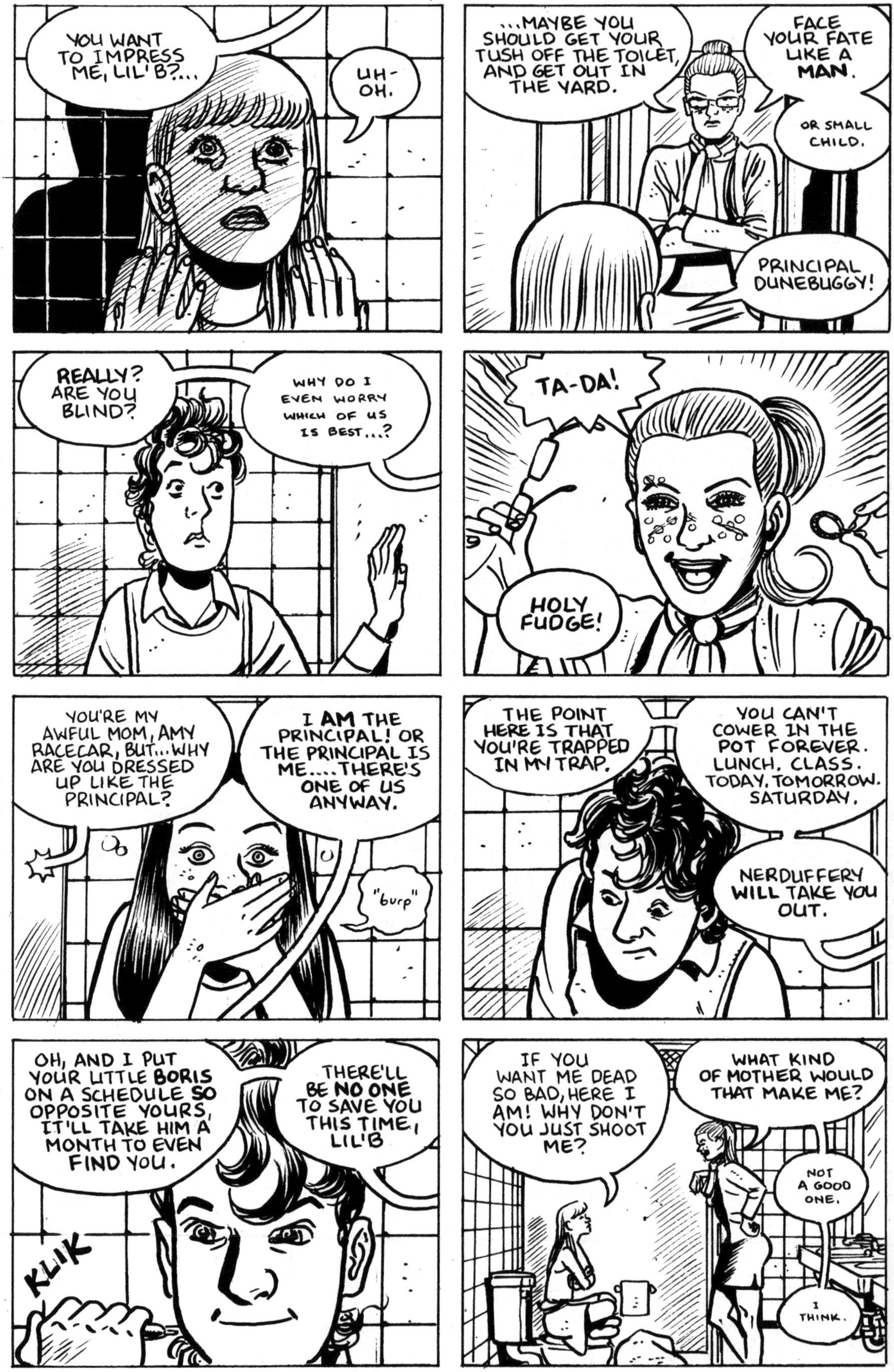
YOU WANT TO IMPRESS ME, LIL' B?...
UH-OH.
...MAYBE YOU SHOULD GET YOUR TUSH OFF THE TOILET, AND GET OUT IN THE YARD.
FACE YOUR FATE LIKE A MAN.
OR SMALL CHILD.
PRINCIPAL DUNEBUGGY!
REALLY? ARE YOU BLIND?
WHY DO I EVEN WORRY WHICH OF US IS BEST...?
TA-DA!
HOLY FUDGE!
YOU'RE MY AWFUL MOM, AMY RACECAR, BUT... WHY ARE YOU DRESSED UP LIKE THE PRINCIPAL?
I AM THE PRINCIPAL! OR THE PRINCIPAL IS ME.... THERE'S ONE OF US ANYWAY.
"burp"
THE POINT HERE IS THAT YOU'RE TRAPPED IN MY TRAP.
YOU CAN'T COWER IN THE POT FOREVER. LUNCH. CLASS. TODAY. TOMORROW. SATURDAY.
NERDUFFERY WILL TAKE YOU OUT.
OH, AND I PUT YOUR LITTLE BORIS ON A SCHEDULE SO OPPOSITE YOURS, IT'LL TAKE HIM A MONTH TO EVEN FIND YOU.
THERE'LL BE NO ONE TO SAVE YOU THIS TIME, LIL'B
KLIK
IF YOU WANT ME DEAD SO BAD, HERE I AM! WHY DON'T YOU JUST SHOOT ME?
WHAT KIND OF MOTHER WOULD THAT MAKE ME?
NOT A GOOD ONE.
I THINK.

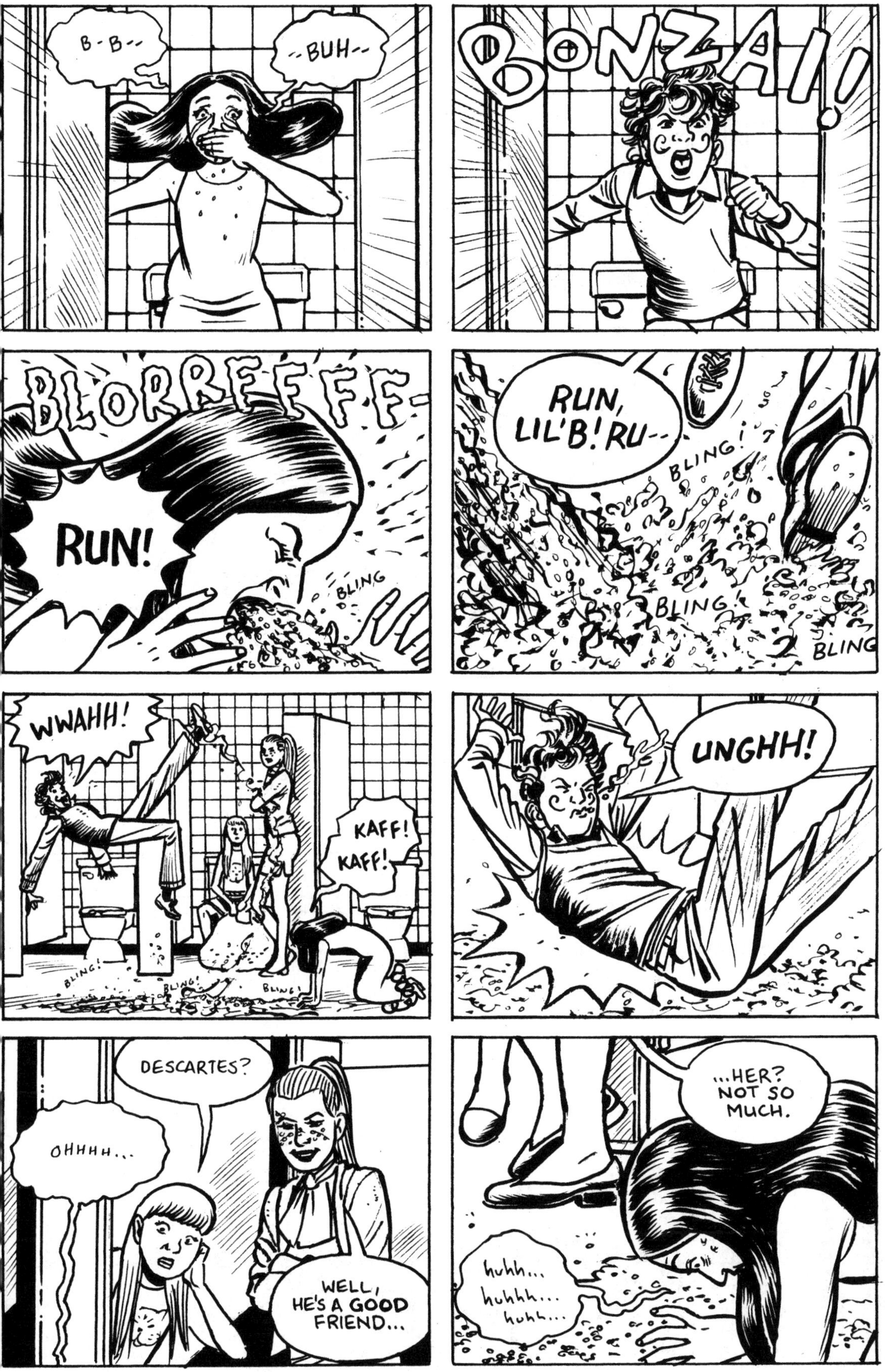
B-B--
--BUH--
BONZAI!
BLORRFFFF-
RUN!
BLING
RUN, LIL'B! RU--
BLING!
BLING!
BLING
WWAHH!
KAFF! KAFF!
BLING!
BLING!
BLING!
UNGHH!
DESCARTES?
OHHHH...
WELL, HE'S A GOOD FRIEND...
...HER? NOT SO MUCH.
huhh... huhhh... huhh...

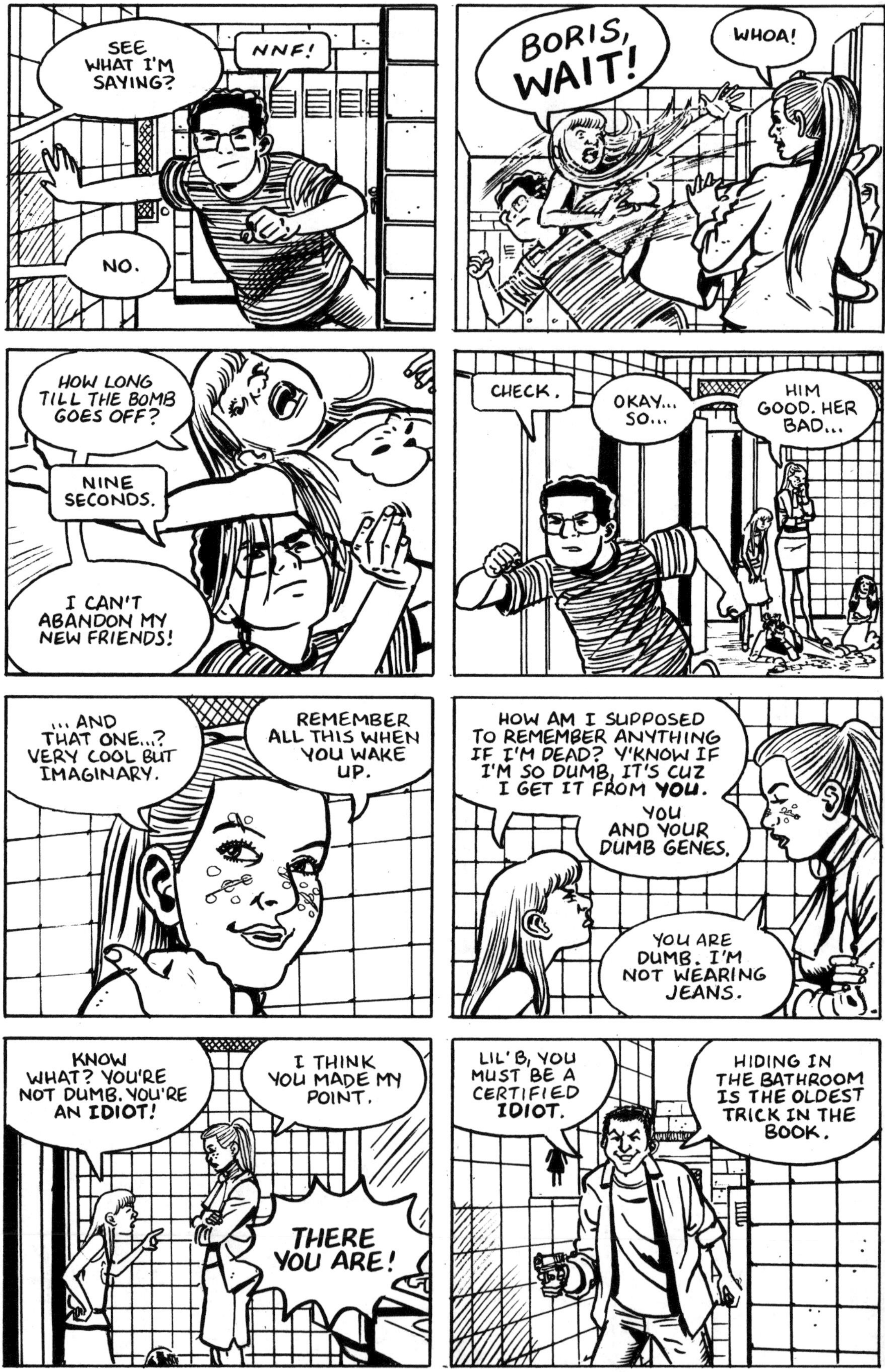
SEE WHAT I'M SAYING?
NNF!
NO.
BORIS, WAIT!
WHOA!
HOW LONG TILL THE BOMB GOES OFF?
NINE SECONDS.
I CAN'T ABANDON MY NEW FRIENDS!
CHECK.
OKAY... SO...
HIM GOOD. HER BAD...
...AND THAT ONE...? VERY COOL BUT IMAGINARY.
REMEMBER ALL THIS WHEN YOU WAKE UP.
HOW AM I SUPPOSED TO REMEMBER ANYTHING IF I'M DEAD? Y'KNOW IF I'M SO DUMB, IT'S CUZ I GET IT FROM **YOU**.
YOU AND YOUR DUMB GENES.
YOU ARE DUMB. I'M NOT WEARING JEANS.
KNOW WHAT? YOU'RE NOT DUMB. YOU'RE AN **IDIOT**!
I THINK YOU MADE MY POINT.
THERE YOU ARE!
LIL' B, YOU MUST BE A CERTIFIED **IDIOT**.
HIDING IN THE BATHROOM IS THE OLDEST TRICK IN THE BOOK.

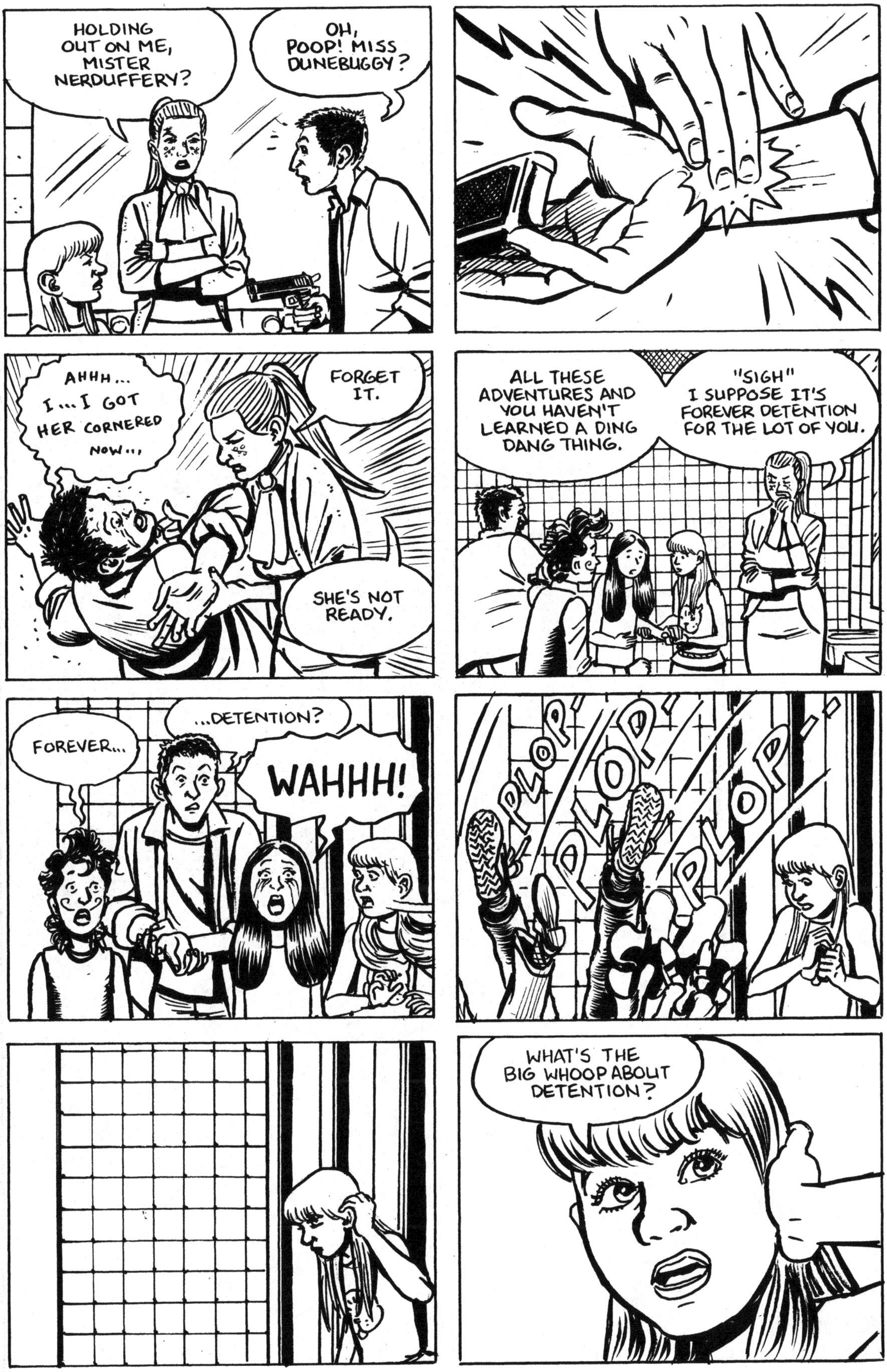
HOLDING OUT ON ME, MISTER NERDUFFERY?
OH, POOP! MISS DUNEBUGGY?
AHHH... I... I GOT HER CORNERED NOW...,
FORGET IT.
SHE'S NOT READY.
ALL THESE ADVENTURES AND YOU HAVEN'T LEARNED A DING DANG THING.
"SIGH" I SUPPOSE IT'S FOREVER DETENTION FOR THE LOT OF YOU.
FOREVER...
...DETENTION?
WAHHH!
PLOP
PLOP
PLOP
PLOP--
WHAT'S THE BIG WHOOP ABOUT DETENTION?

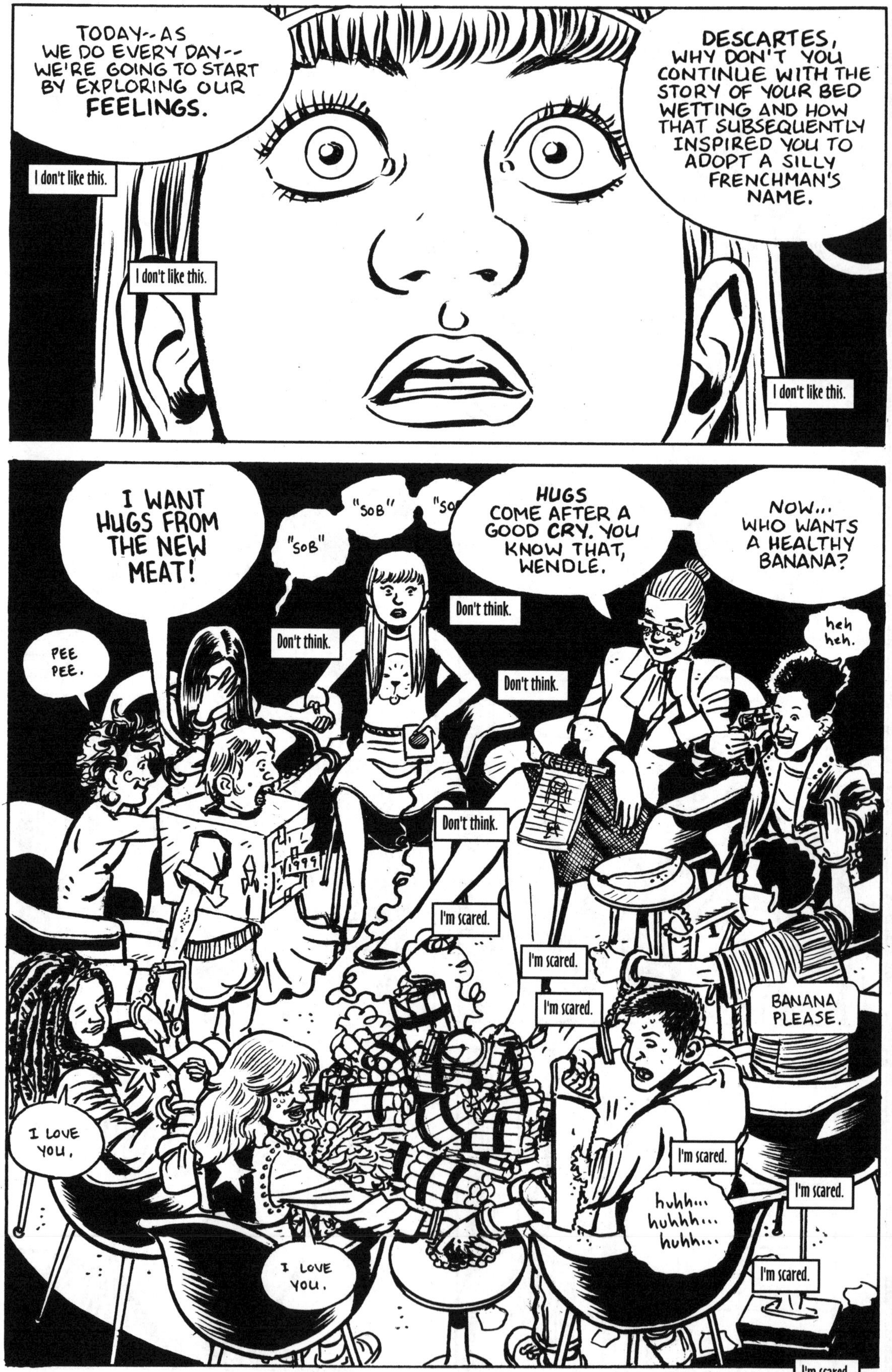

TODAY--AS WE DO EVERY DAY--WE'RE GOING TO START BY EXPLORING OUR FEELINGS.
I don't like this.
I don't like this.
DESCARTES, WHY DON'T YOU CONTINUE WITH THE STORY OF YOUR BED WETTING AND HOW THAT SUBSEQUENTLY INSPIRED YOU TO ADOPT A SILLY FRENCHMAN'S NAME.
I don't like this.
I WANT HUGS FROM THE NEW MEAT!
"SOB"
"SOB"
HUGS COME AFTER A GOOD CRY. YOU KNOW THAT, WENDLE.
NOW... WHO WANTS A HEALTHY BANANA?
PEE PEE.
Don't think.
Don't think.
Don't think.
heh heh.
Don't think.
1999
I'm scared.
I'm scared.
I'm scared.
BANANA PLEASE.
I LOVE YOU.
I'm scared.
I'm scared.
huhh... huhhh... huhh...
I LOVE YOU.
I'm scared.
I'm scared.

THE END...

7

"THE RAINBOW CONNECTION"

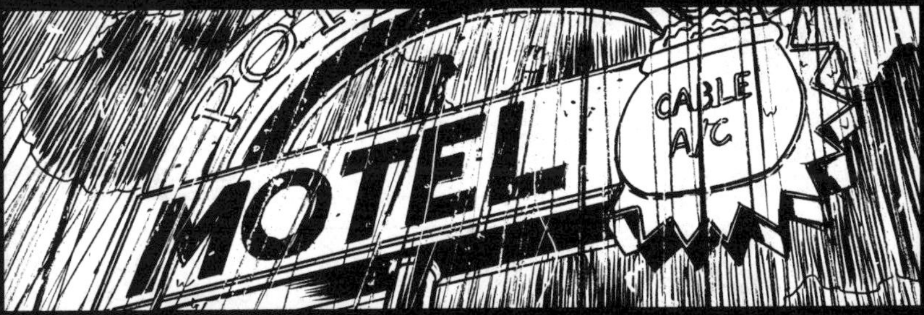
MOTEL
CABLE
A/C

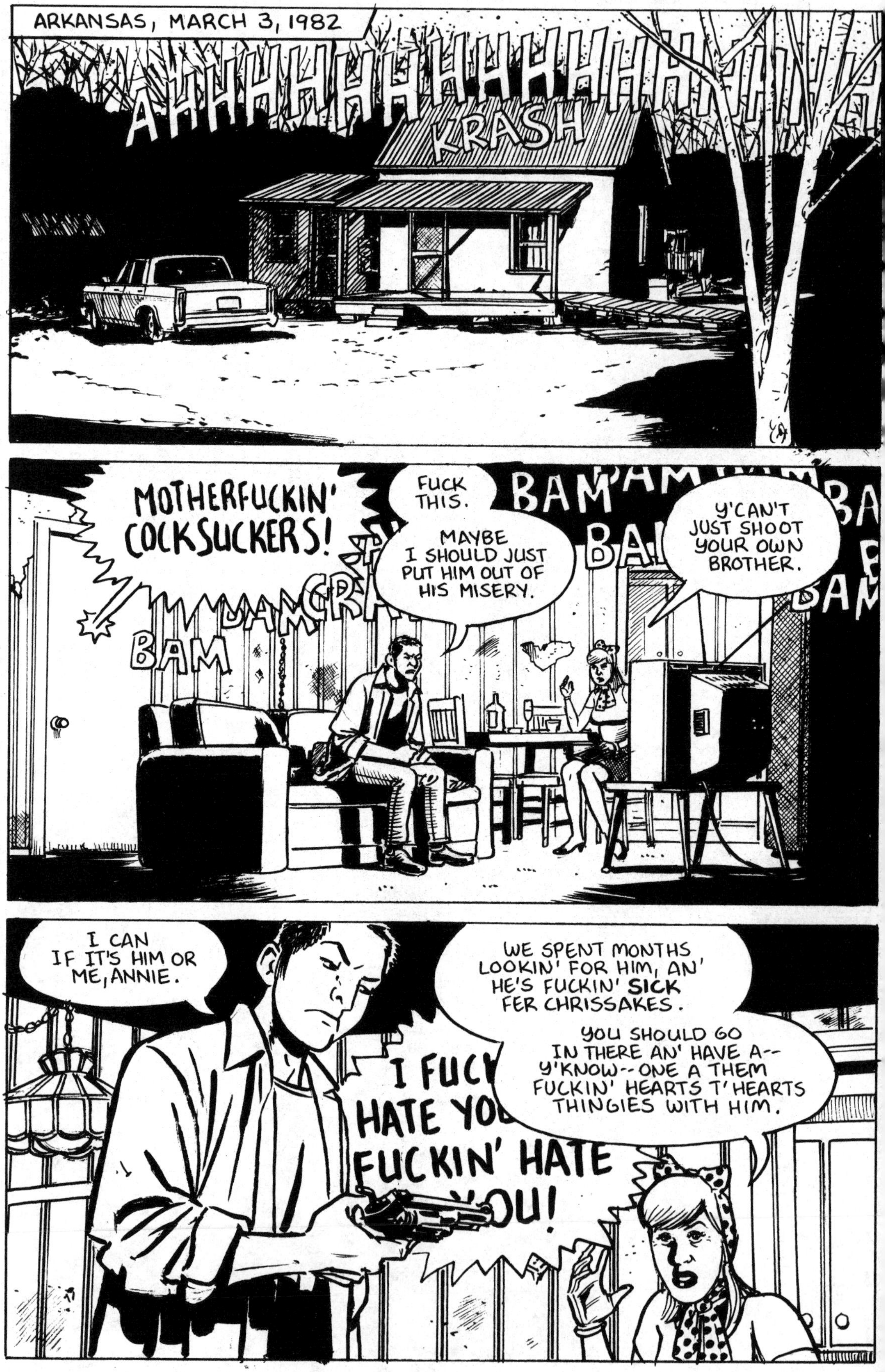
ARKANSAS, MARCH 3, 1982
KRASH
MOTHERFUCKIN' COCKSUCKERS!
BAM
FUCK THIS.
MAYBE I SHOULD JUST PUT HIM OUT OF HIS MISERY.
Y'CAN'T JUST SHOOT YOUR OWN BROTHER.
I CAN IF IT'S HIM OR ME, ANNIE.
WE SPENT MONTHS LOOKIN' FOR HIM, AN' HE'S FUCKIN' **SICK** FER CHRISSAKES.
YOU SHOULD GO IN THERE AN' HAVE A--Y'KNOW--ONE A THEM FUCKIN' HEARTS T' HEARTS THINGIES WITH HIM.
FUCKIN' HATE

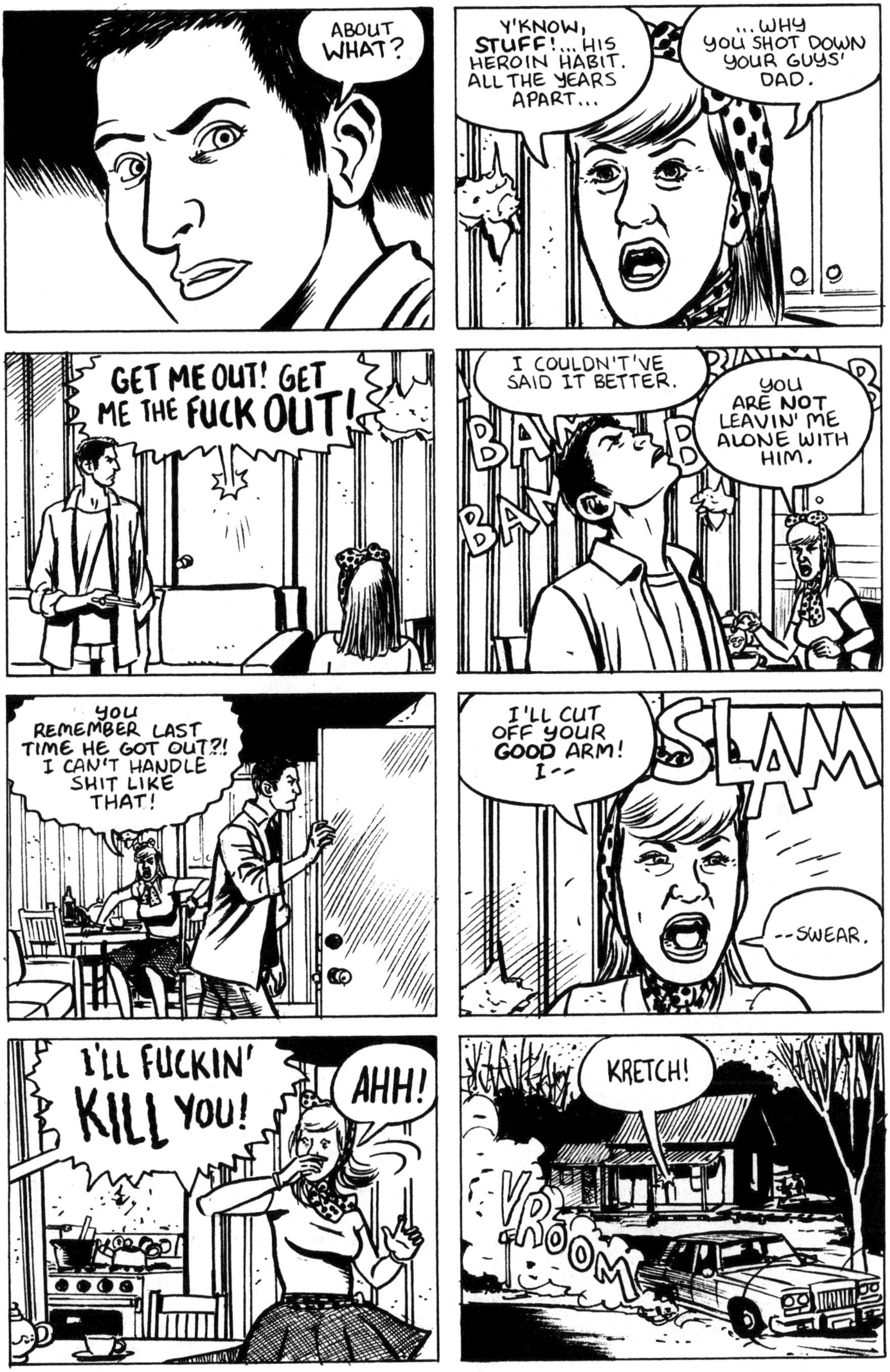
ABOUT WHAT?
Y'KNOW, STUFF!... HIS HEROIN HABIT. ALL THE YEARS APART...
...WHY YOU SHOT DOWN YOUR GUYS' DAD.
GET ME OUT! GET ME THE FUCK OUT!
I COULDN'T'VE SAID IT BETTER.
BAM
BAM
BAM
YOU ARE NOT LEAVIN' ME ALONE WITH HIM.
YOU REMEMBER LAST TIME HE GOT OUT?! I CAN'T HANDLE SHIT LIKE THAT!
I'LL CUT OFF YOUR GOOD ARM! I--
SLAM
--SWEAR.
I'LL FUCKIN' KILL YOU!
AHH!
KRETCH!
VROOM

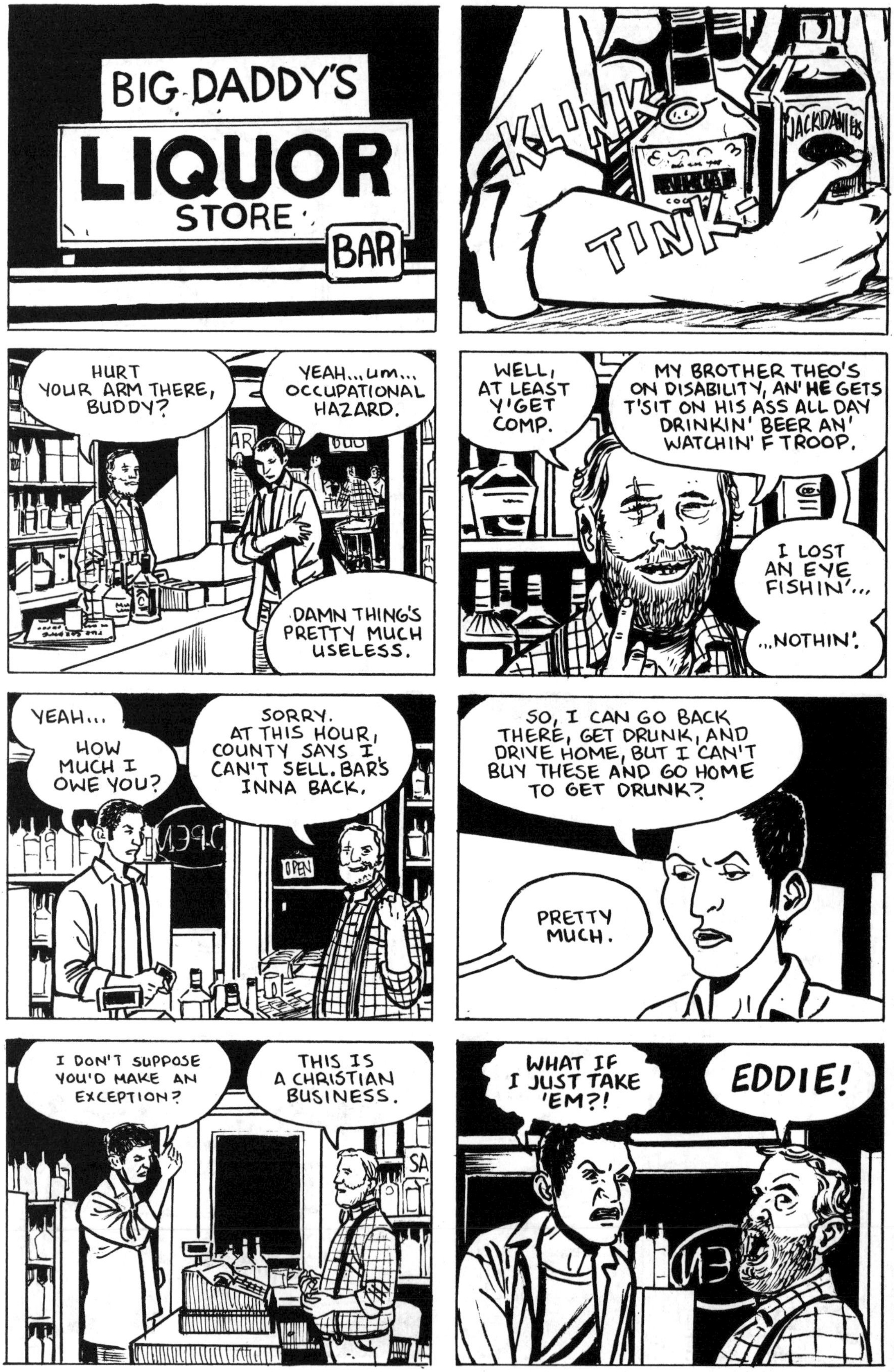

BIG DADDY'S
LIQUOR STORE
BAR
KLINK
TINK-
JACK DANIEL'S
HURT YOUR ARM THERE, BUDDY?
YEAH...um... OCCUPATIONAL HAZARD.
DAMN THING'S PRETTY MUCH USELESS.
WELL, AT LEAST Y'GET COMP.
MY BROTHER THEO'S ON DISABILITY, AN' **HE** GETS T'SIT ON HIS ASS ALL DAY DRINKIN' BEER AN' WATCHIN' F TROOP.
I LOST AN EYE FISHIN'...
...NOTHIN'.
YEAH...
HOW MUCH I OWE YOU?
SORRY. AT THIS HOUR, COUNTY SAYS I CAN'T SELL. BAR'S INNA BACK.
OPEN
SO, I CAN GO BACK THERE, GET DRUNK, AND DRIVE HOME, BUT I CAN'T BUY THESE AND GO HOME TO GET DRUNK?
PRETTY MUCH.
I DON'T SUPPOSE YOU'D MAKE AN EXCEPTION?
THIS IS A CHRISTIAN BUSINESS.
WHAT IF I JUST TAKE 'EM?!
EDDIE!

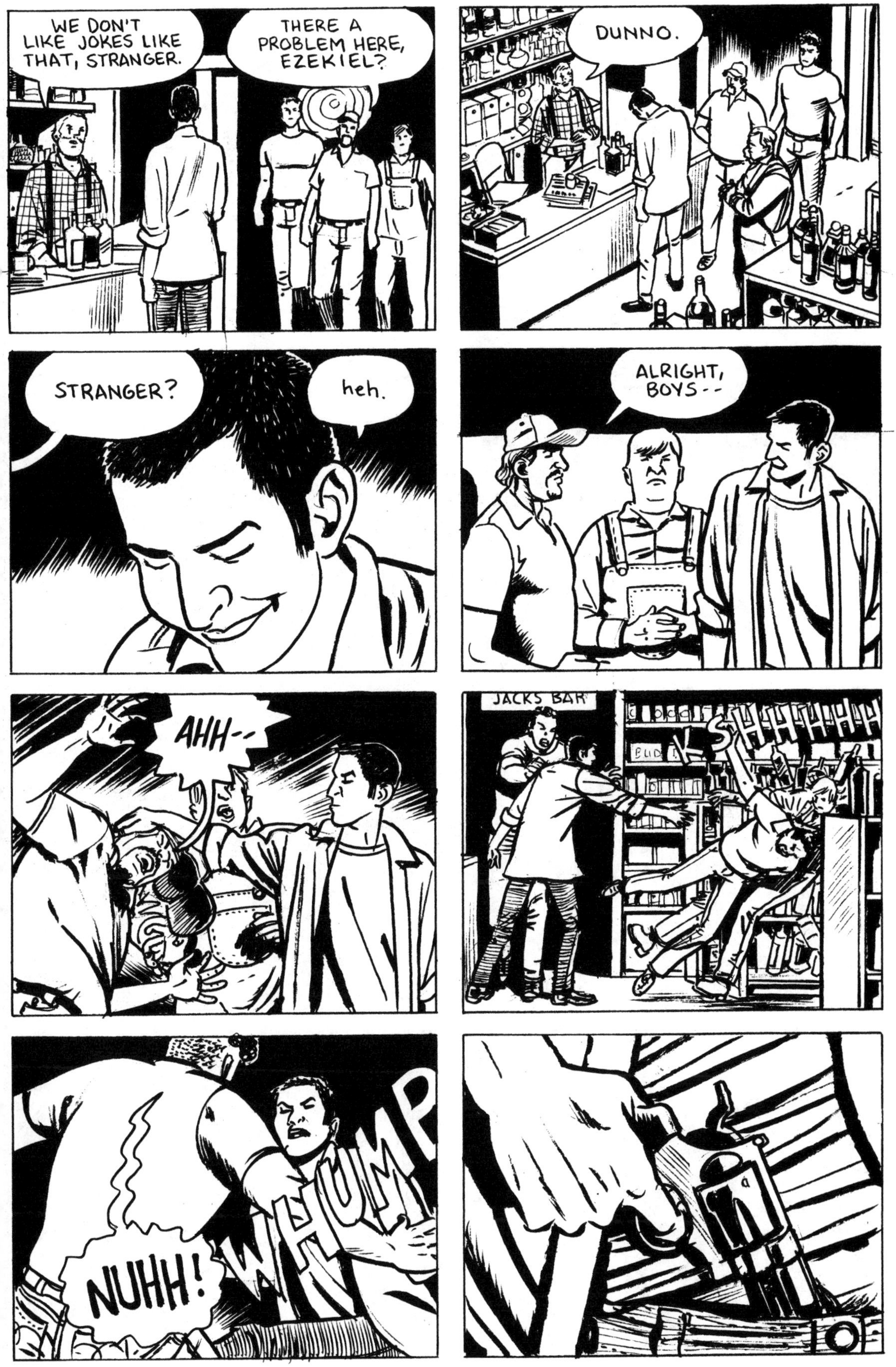
WE DON'T LIKE JOKES LIKE THAT, STRANGER.
THERE A PROBLEM HERE, EZEKIEL?
DUNNO.
STRANGER?
heh.
ALRIGHT, BOYS--
AHH--
JACKS BAR
SHHHHHHH
NUHH!
WHUMP

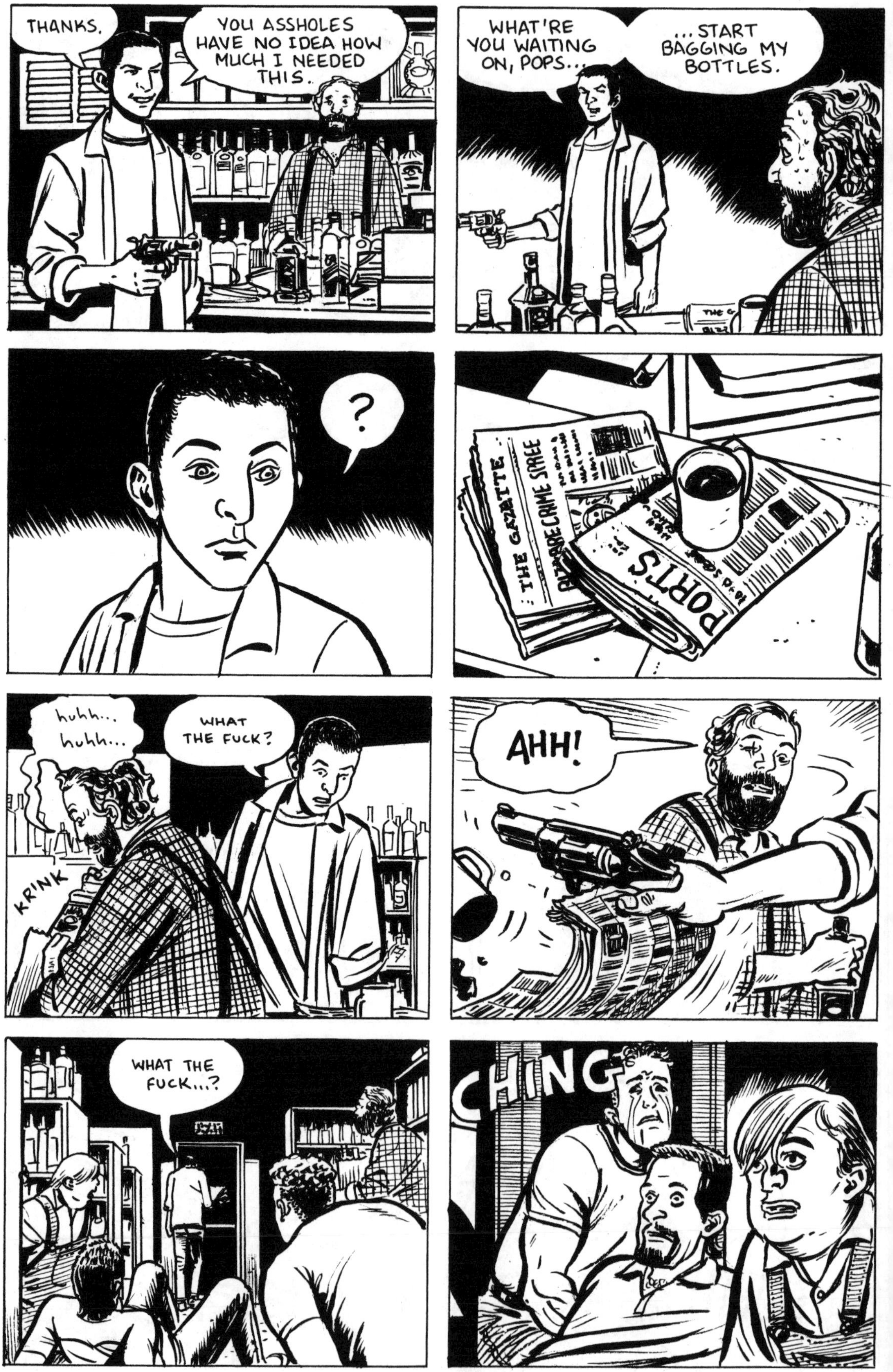
THANKS.
YOU ASSHOLES HAVE NO IDEA HOW MUCH I NEEDED THIS.
WHAT'RE YOU WAITING ON, POPS...
...START BAGGING MY BOTTLES.
?
THE GAZETTE
PORTS
huhh... huhh...
WHAT THE FUCK?
KR'NK
AHH!
WHAT THE FUCK...?
CHING

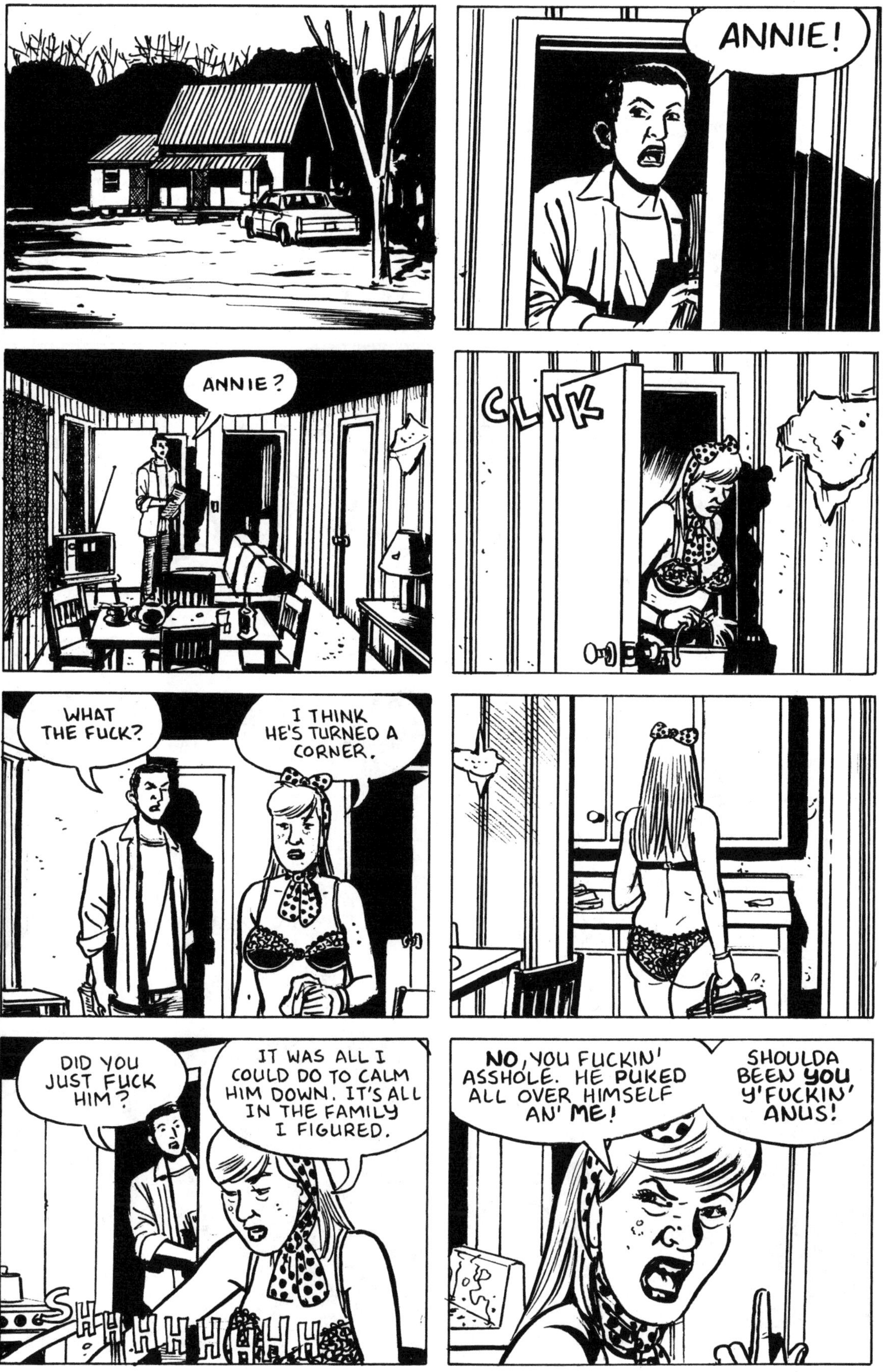
ANNIE!
ANNIE?
CLIK
WHAT THE FUCK?
I THINK HE'S TURNED A CORNER.
DID YOU JUST FUCK HIM?
IT WAS ALL I COULD DO TO CALM HIM DOWN. IT'S ALL IN THE FAMILY I FIGURED.
SHHHHHHHHH
NO, YOU FUCKIN' ASSHOLE. HE PUKED ALL OVER HIMSELF AN' ME!
SHOULDA BEEN YOU Y'FUCKIN' ANUS!

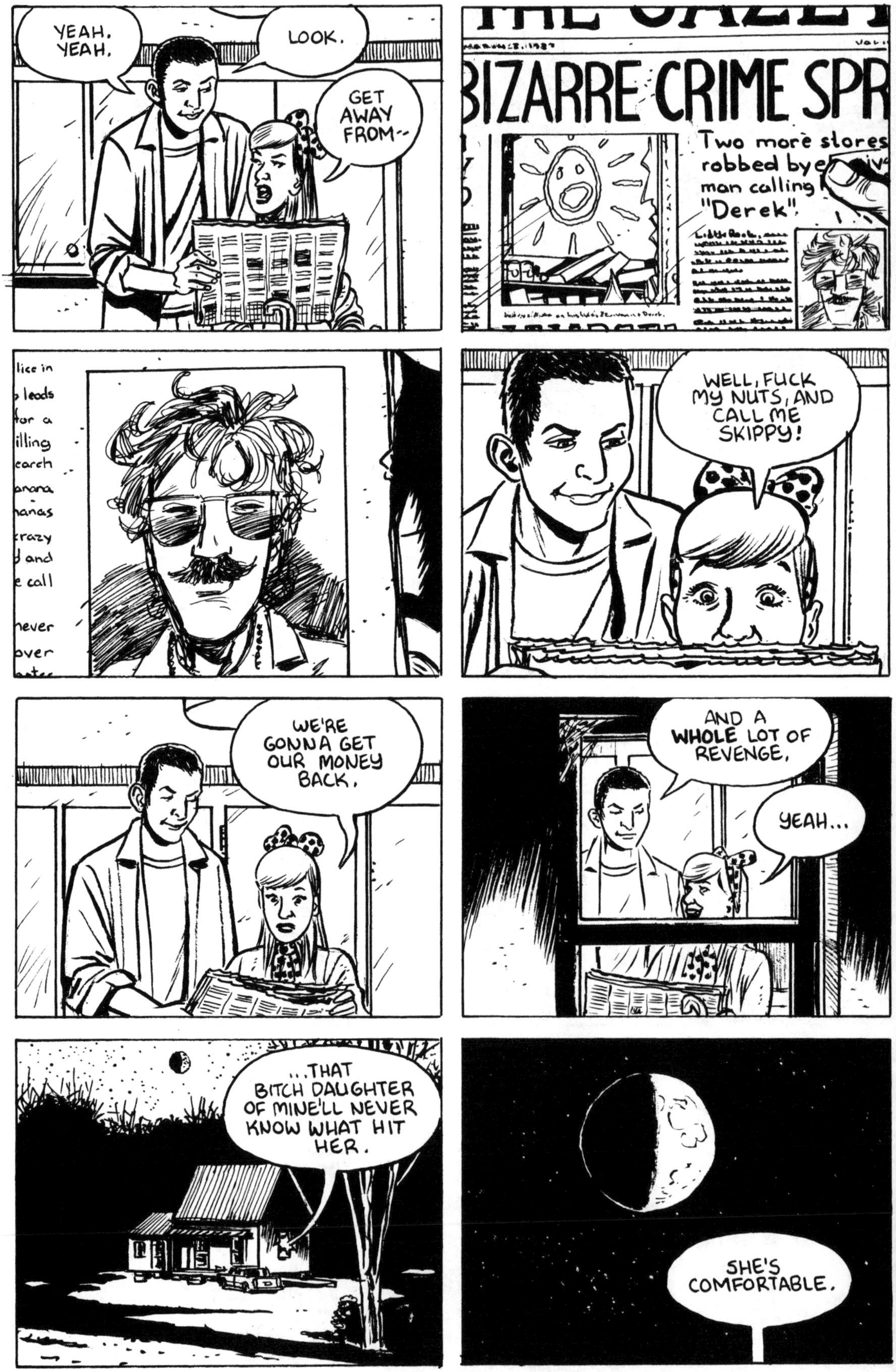
YEAH. YEAH.
LOOK.
GET AWAY FROM--
BIZARRE CRIME SPR
Two more stores
robbed by e
man calling
"Derek"
WELL, FUCK MY NUTS, AND CALL ME SKIPPY!
WE'RE GONNA GET OUR MONEY BACK.
AND A **WHOLE** LOT OF REVENGE.
YEAH...
..THAT BITCH DAUGHTER OF MINE'LL NEVER KNOW WHAT HIT HER.
SHE'S COMFORTABLE.

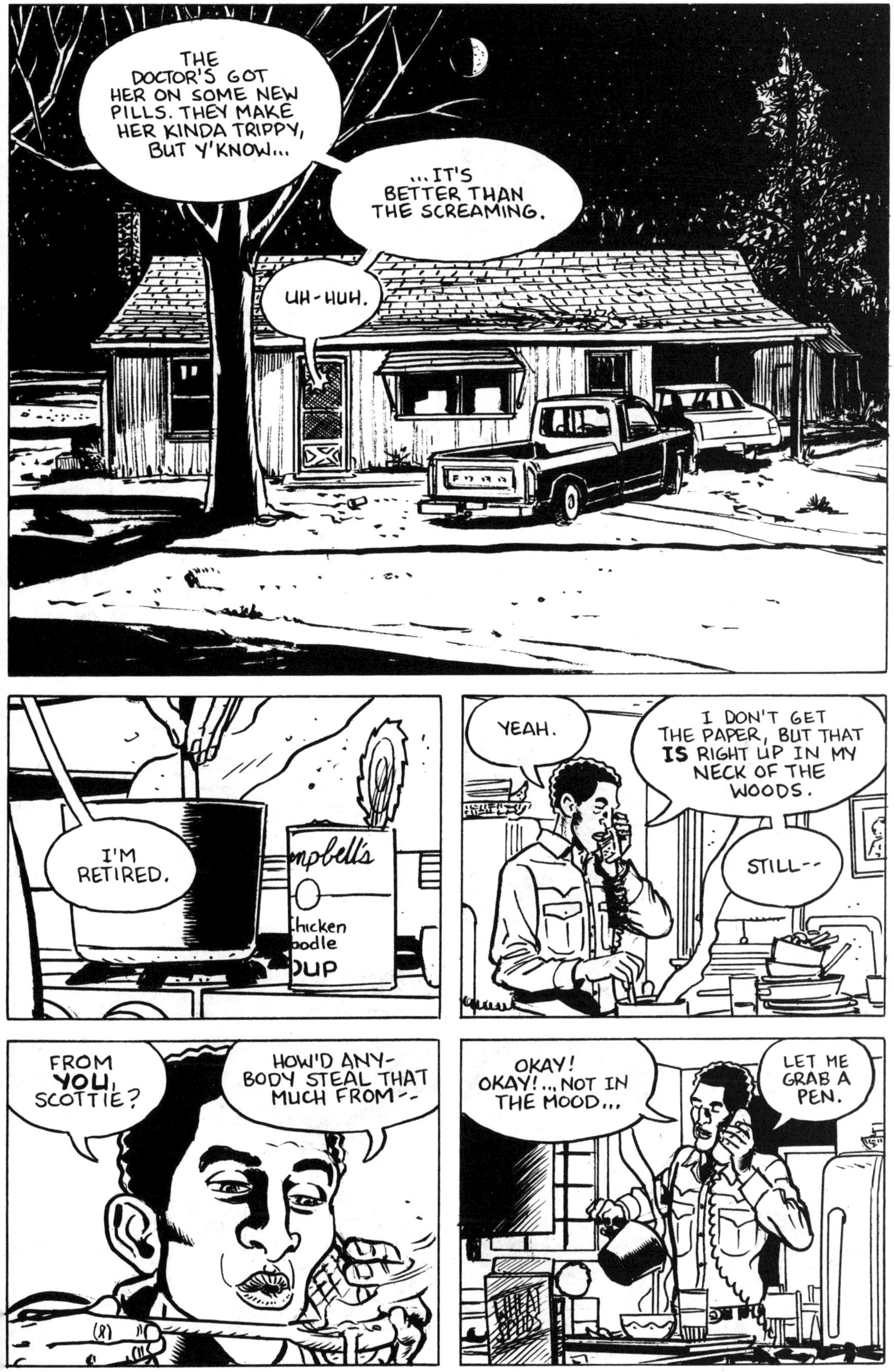
THE DOCTOR'S GOT HER ON SOME NEW PILLS. THEY MAKE HER KINDA TRIPPY, BUT Y'KNOW...
...IT'S BETTER THAN THE SCREAMING.
UH-HUH.
FORD
I'M RETIRED.
mpbell's
Chicken oodle OUP
YEAH.
I DON'T GET THE PAPER, BUT THAT **IS** RIGHT UP IN MY NECK OF THE WOODS.
STILL--
FROM **YOU**, SCOTTIE?
HOW'D ANYBODY STEAL THAT MUCH FROM--
OKAY! OKAY!... NOT IN THE MOOD...
LET ME GRAB A PEN.
WHEAT PUFFS

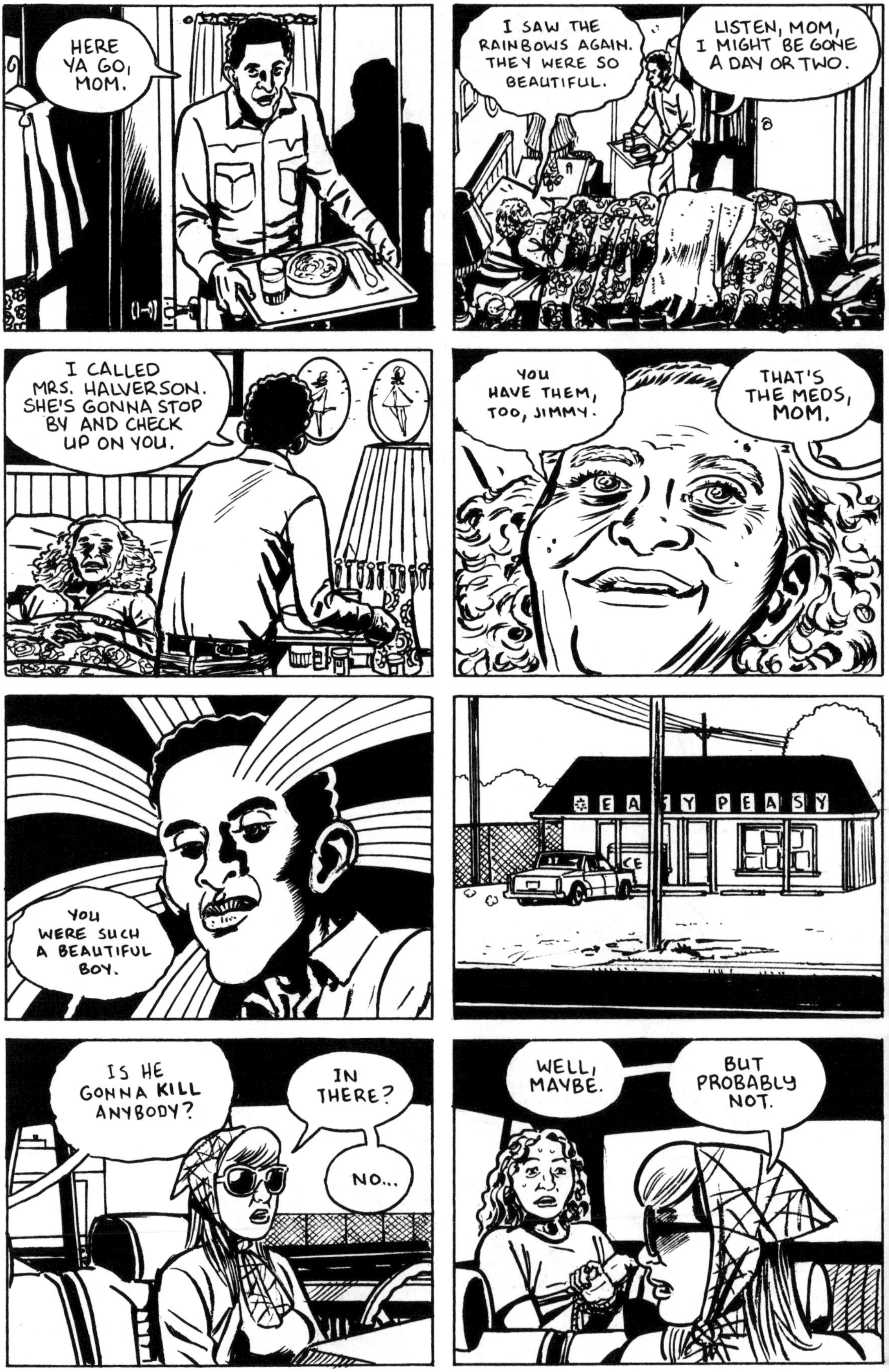
HERE YA GO, MOM.
I SAW THE RAINBOWS AGAIN. THEY WERE SO BEAUTIFUL.
LISTEN, MOM, I MIGHT BE GONE A DAY OR TWO.
I CALLED MRS. HALVERSON. SHE'S GONNA STOP BY AND CHECK UP ON YOU.
YOU HAVE THEM, TOO, JIMMY.
THAT'S THE MEDS, MOM.
YOU WERE SUCH A BEAUTIFUL BOY.
EASY PEASY
IS HE GONNA KILL ANYBODY?
IN THERE?
NO...
WELL, MAYBE.
BUT PROBABLY NOT.

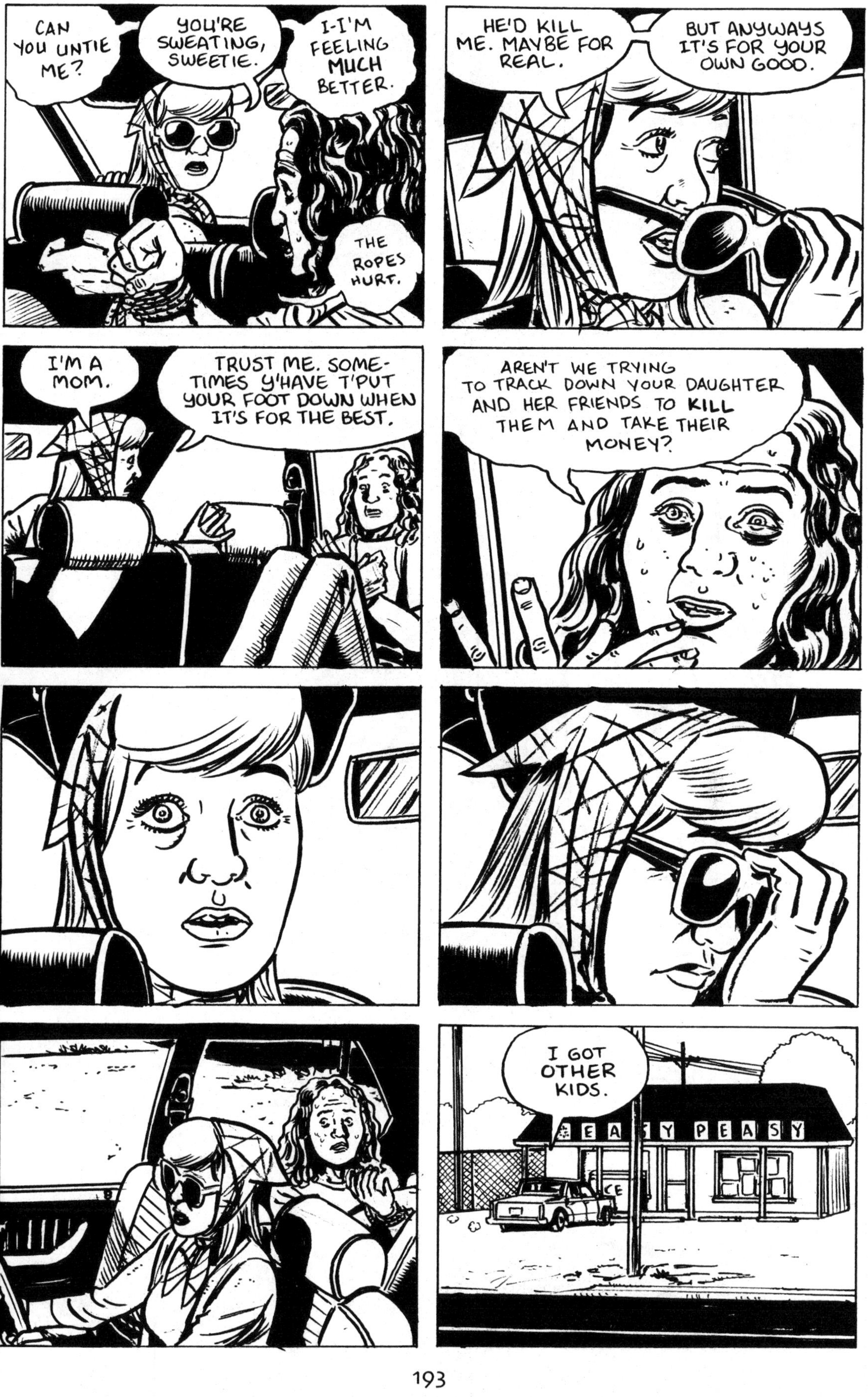
CAN YOU UNTIE ME?
YOU'RE SWEATING, SWEETIE.
I-I'M FEELING MUCH BETTER.
THE ROPES HURT.
HE'D KILL ME. MAYBE FOR REAL.
BUT ANYWAYS IT'S FOR YOUR OWN GOOD.
I'M A MOM.
TRUST ME. SOME-TIMES Y'HAVE T'PUT YOUR FOOT DOWN WHEN IT'S FOR THE BEST.
AREN'T WE TRYING TO TRACK DOWN YOUR DAUGHTER AND HER FRIENDS TO KILL THEM AND TAKE THEIR MONEY?
I GOT OTHER KIDS.
EASY PEASY

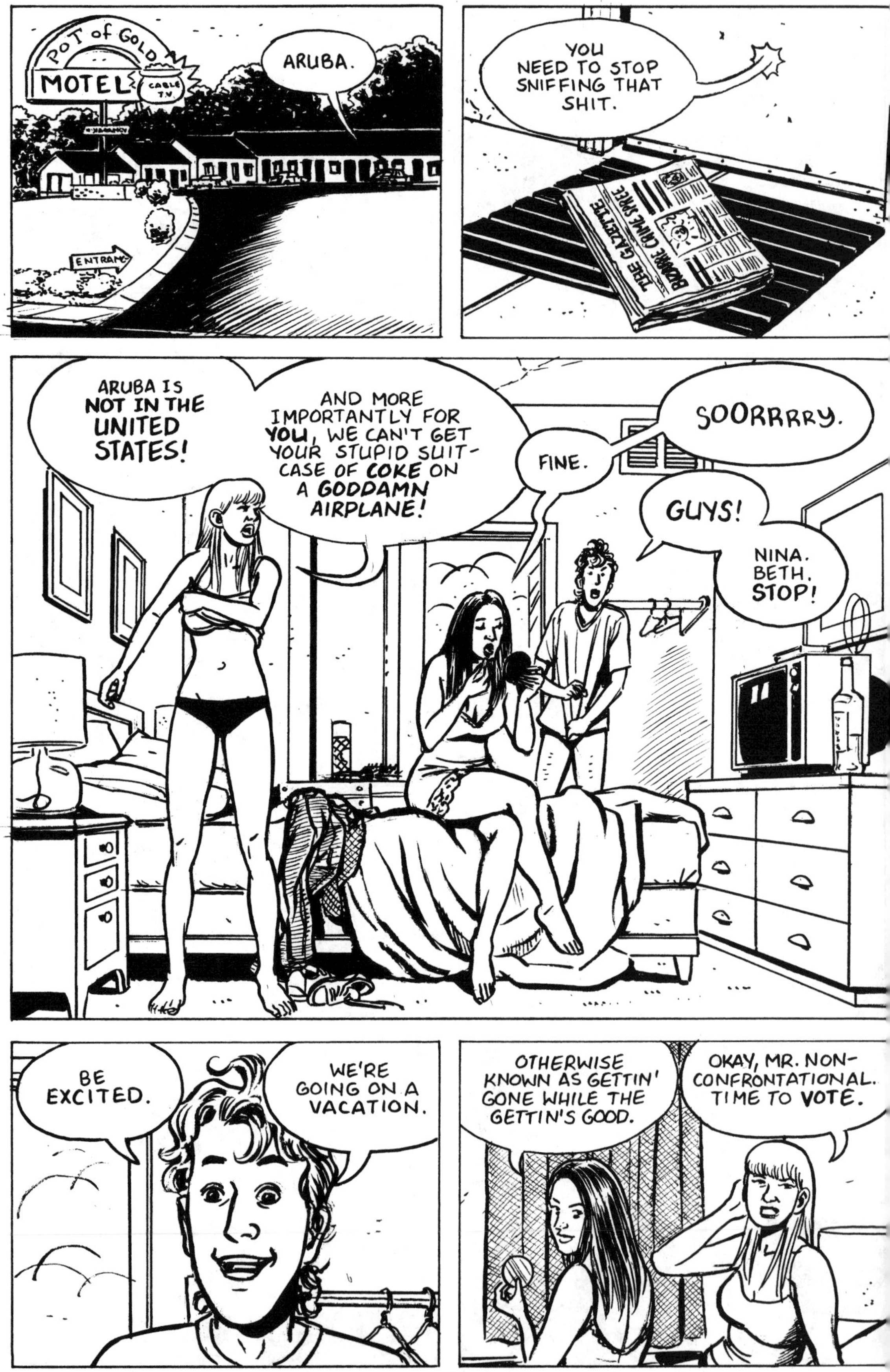

POT of GOLD
MOTEL
CABLE T.V.
ARUBA.
YOU NEED TO STOP SNIFFING THAT SHIT.
THE GAZETTE
ARUBA IS NOT IN THE UNITED STATES!
AND MORE IMPORTANTLY FOR YOU, WE CAN'T GET YOUR STUPID SUIT-CASE OF COKE ON A GODDAMN AIRPLANE!
FINE.
SOORRRRRY.
GUYS!
NINA. BETH. STOP!
BE EXCITED.
WE'RE GOING ON A VACATION.
OTHERWISE KNOWN AS GETTIN' GONE WHILE THE GETTIN'S GOOD.
OKAY, MR. NON-CONFRONTATIONAL. TIME TO VOTE.

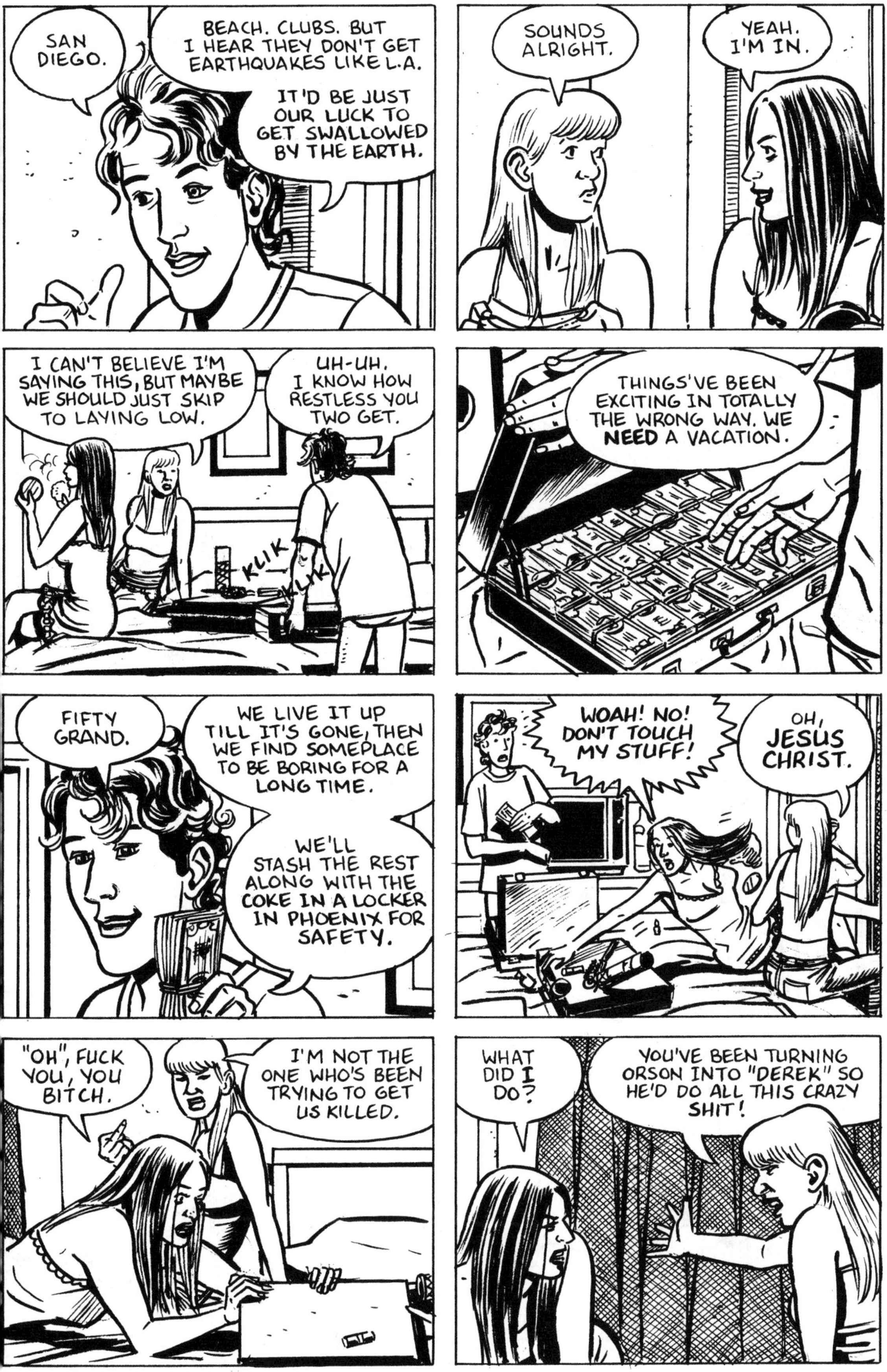
SAN DIEGO.
BEACH. CLUBS. BUT I HEAR THEY DON'T GET EARTHQUAKES LIKE L.A.
IT'D BE JUST OUR LUCK TO GET SWALLOWED BY THE EARTH.
SOUNDS ALRIGHT.
YEAH. I'M IN.
I CAN'T BELIEVE I'M SAYING THIS, BUT MAYBE WE SHOULD JUST SKIP TO LAYING LOW.
UH-UH. I KNOW HOW RESTLESS YOU TWO GET.
KLIK
KLIK
THINGS'VE BEEN EXCITING IN TOTALLY THE WRONG WAY. WE NEED A VACATION.
FIFTY GRAND.
WE LIVE IT UP TILL IT'S GONE, THEN WE FIND SOMEPLACE TO BE BORING FOR A LONG TIME.
WE'LL STASH THE REST ALONG WITH THE COKE IN A LOCKER IN PHOENIX FOR SAFETY.
WOAH! NO! DON'T TOUCH MY STUFF!
OH, JESUS CHRIST.
"OH", FUCK YOU, YOU BITCH.
I'M NOT THE ONE WHO'S BEEN TRYING TO GET US KILLED.
WHAT DID I DO?
YOU'VE BEEN TURNING ORSON INTO "DEREK" SO HE'D DO ALL THIS CRAZY SHIT!

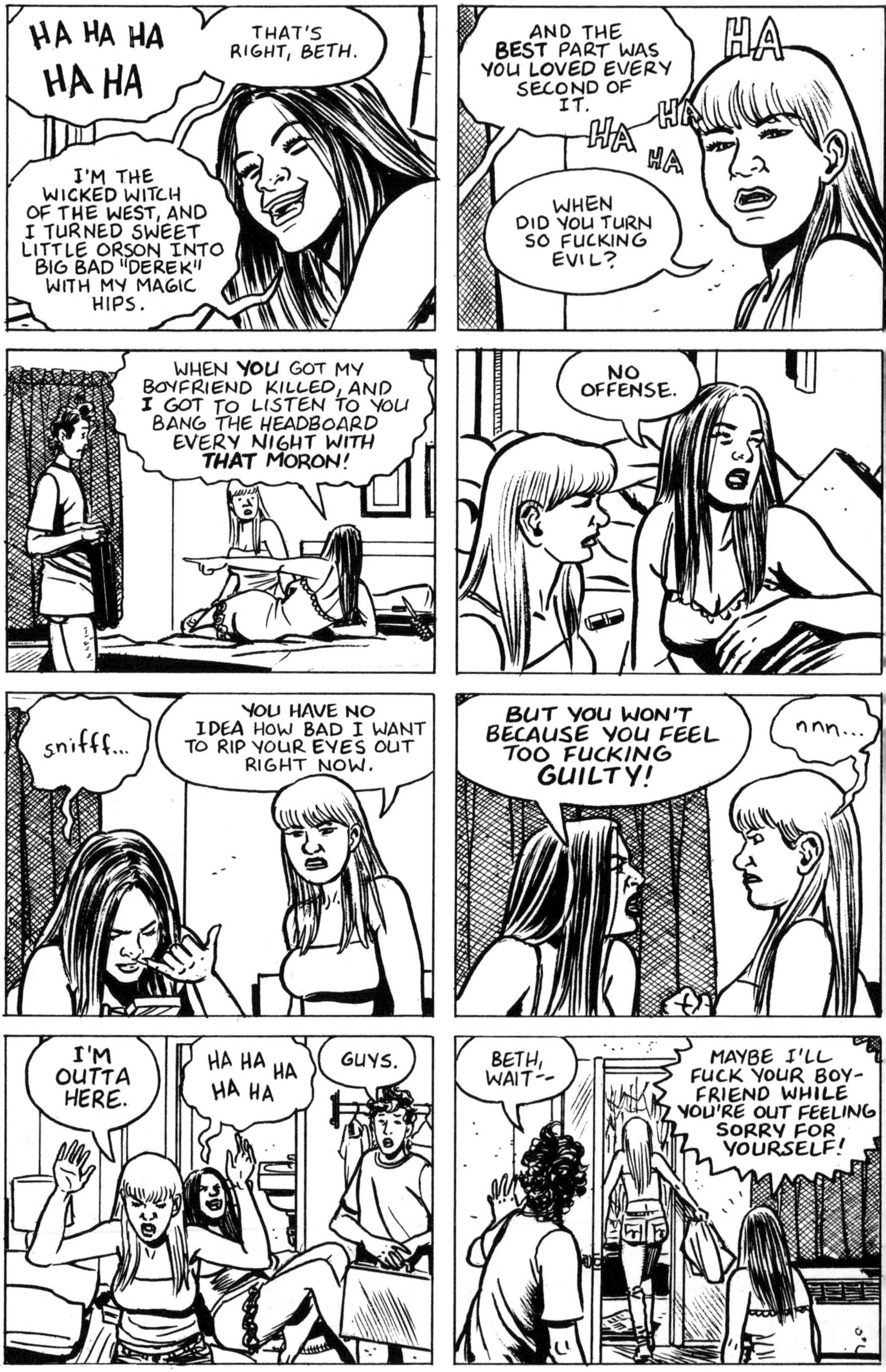
HA HA HA
HA HA
THAT'S RIGHT, BETH.
I'M THE WICKED WITCH OF THE WEST, AND I TURNED SWEET LITTLE ORSON INTO BIG BAD "DEREK" WITH MY MAGIC HIPS.
AND THE **BEST** PART WAS YOU LOVED EVERY SECOND OF IT.
HA
HA
HA
HA
WHEN DID YOU TURN SO FUCKING EVIL?
WHEN **YOU** GOT MY BOYFRIEND KILLED, AND **I** GOT TO LISTEN TO YOU BANG THE HEADBOARD EVERY NIGHT WITH **THAT** MORON!
NO OFFENSE.
sniffff...
YOU HAVE NO IDEA HOW BAD I WANT TO RIP YOUR EYES OUT RIGHT NOW.
BUT YOU WON'T BECAUSE YOU FEEL TOO FUCKING **GUILTY**!
nnn...
I'M OUTTA HERE.
HA HA HA HA HA
GUYS.
BETH, WAIT--
MAYBE I'LL FUCK YOUR BOY-FRIEND WHILE YOU'RE OUT FEELING SORRY FOR YOURSELF!

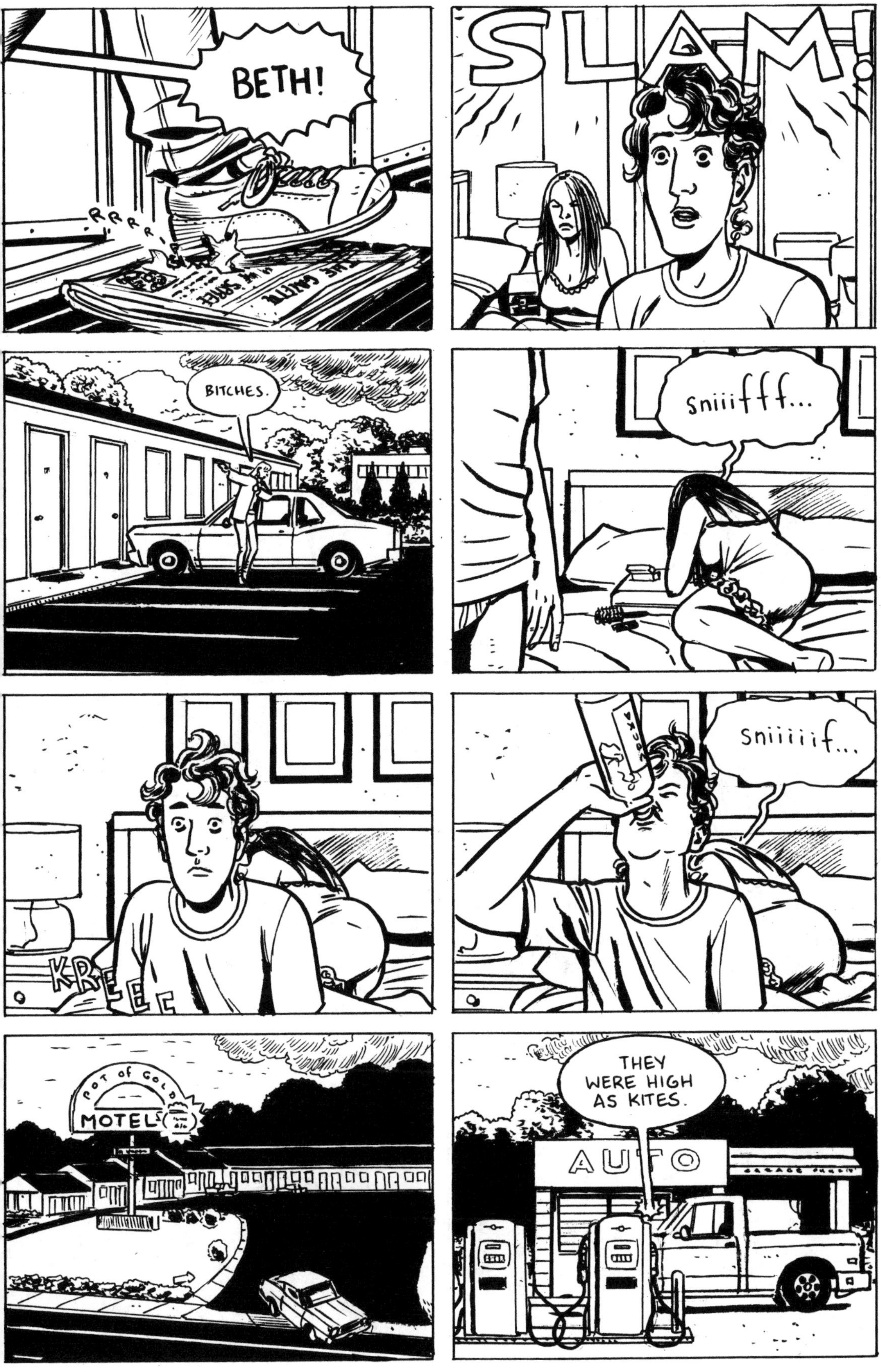
BETH!
RRRRR
SLAM!
BITCHES.
sniiifff...
KREEE
sniiiiif...
POT OF GOLD
MOTEL
THEY WERE HIGH AS KITES.
AUTO

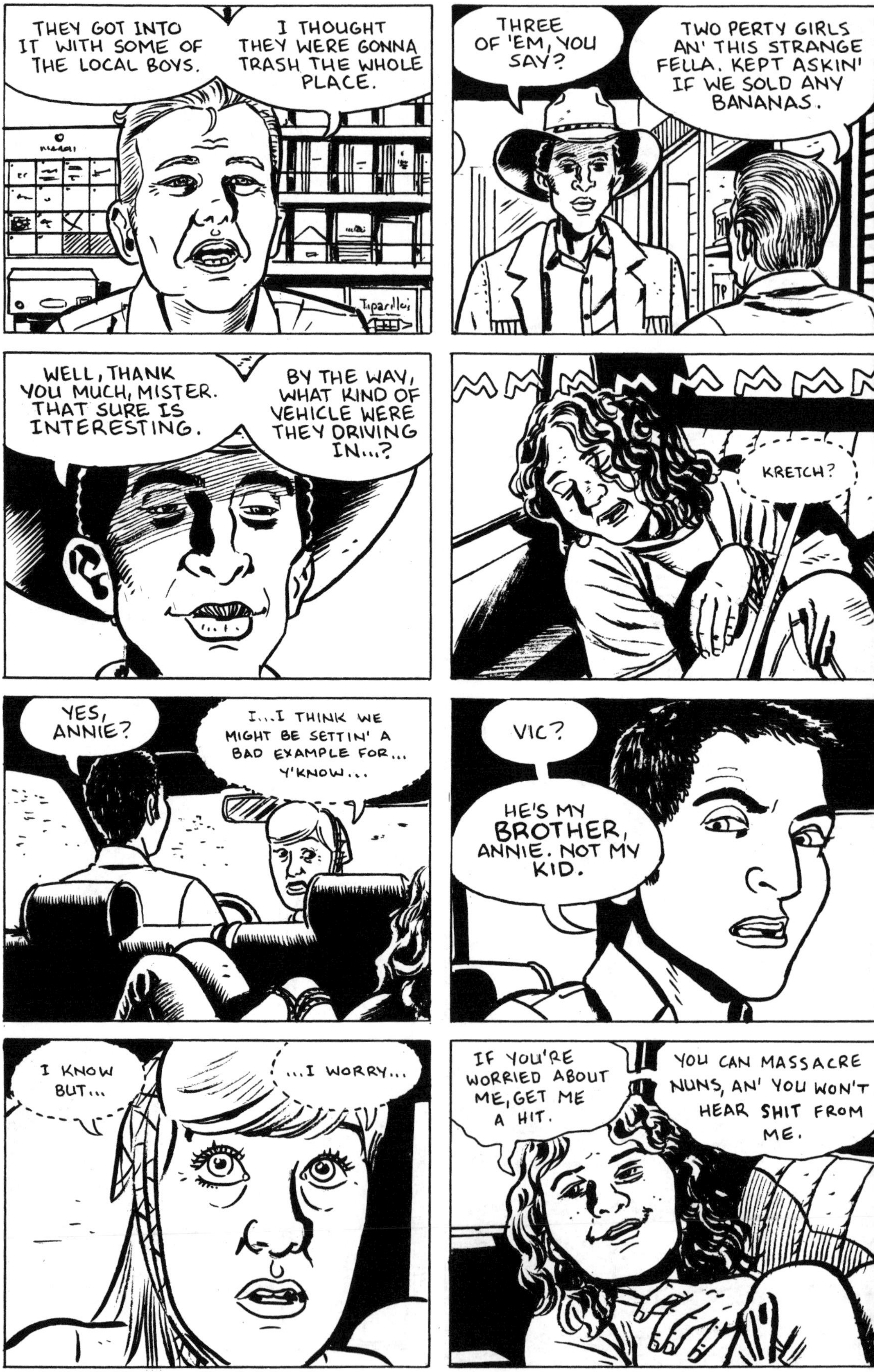
THEY GOT INTO IT WITH SOME OF THE LOCAL BOYS.
I THOUGHT THEY WERE GONNA TRASH THE WHOLE PLACE.
THREE OF 'EM, YOU SAY?
TWO PERTY GIRLS AN' THIS STRANGE FELLA. KEPT ASKIN' IF WE SOLD ANY BANANAS.
WELL, THANK YOU MUCH, MISTER. THAT SURE IS INTERESTING.
BY THE WAY, WHAT KIND OF VEHICLE WERE THEY DRIVING IN...?
MMMMMMMMM
KRETCH?
YES, ANNIE?
I...I THINK WE MIGHT BE SETTIN' A BAD EXAMPLE FOR... Y'KNOW...
VIC?
HE'S MY BROTHER, ANNIE. NOT MY KID.
I KNOW BUT...
...I WORRY...
IF YOU'RE WORRIED ABOUT ME, GET ME A HIT.
YOU CAN MASSACRE NUNS, AN' YOU WON'T HEAR SHIT FROM ME.

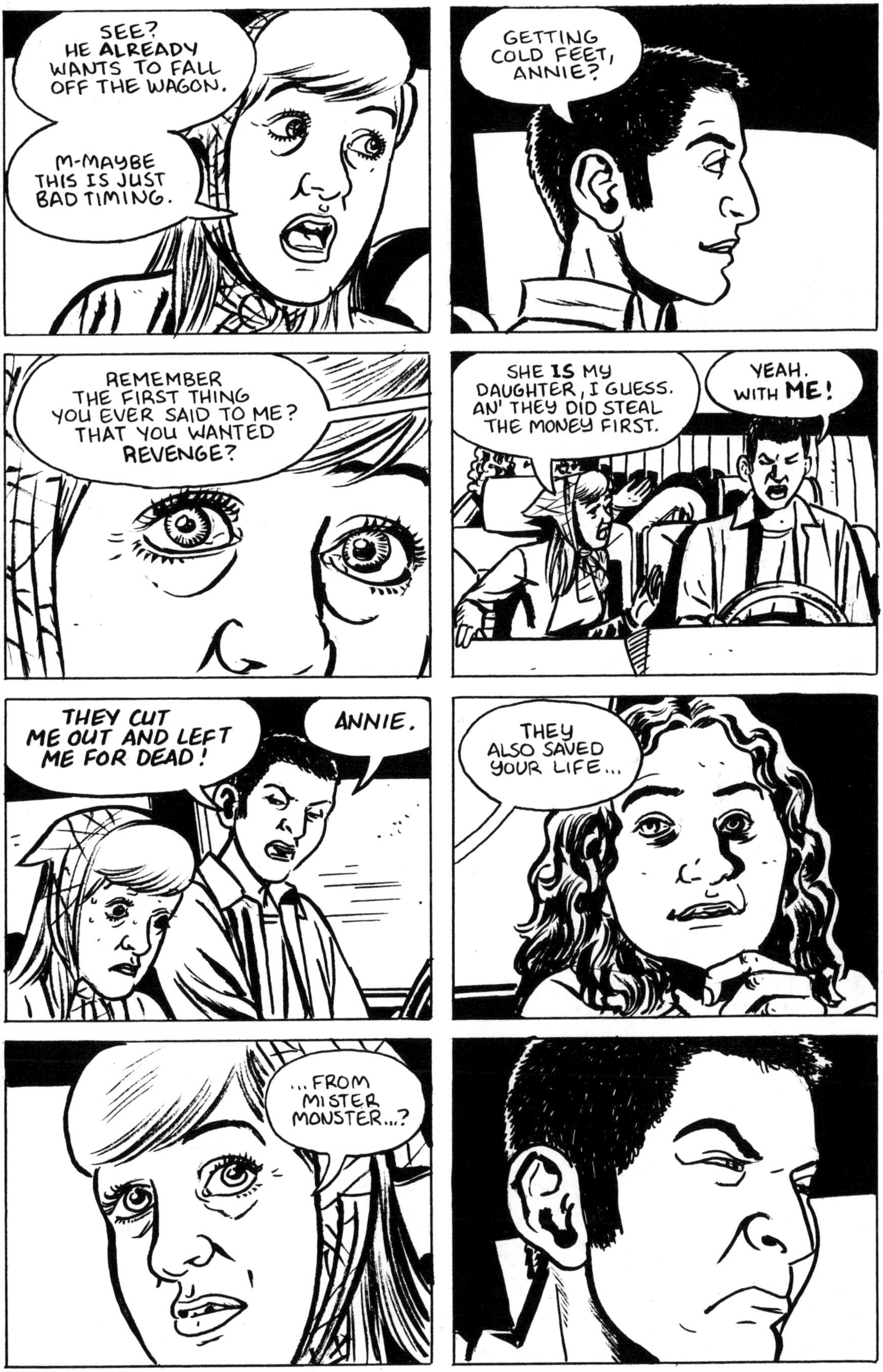

SEE? HE ALREADY WANTS TO FALL OFF THE WAGON.
M-MAYBE THIS IS JUST BAD TIMING.
GETTING COLD FEET, ANNIE?
REMEMBER THE FIRST THING YOU EVER SAID TO ME? THAT YOU WANTED REVENGE?
SHE IS MY DAUGHTER, I GUESS. AN' THEY DID STEAL THE MONEY FIRST.
YEAH. WITH ME!
THEY CUT ME OUT AND LEFT ME FOR DEAD!
ANNIE.
THEY ALSO SAVED YOUR LIFE...
...FROM MISTER MONSTER...?

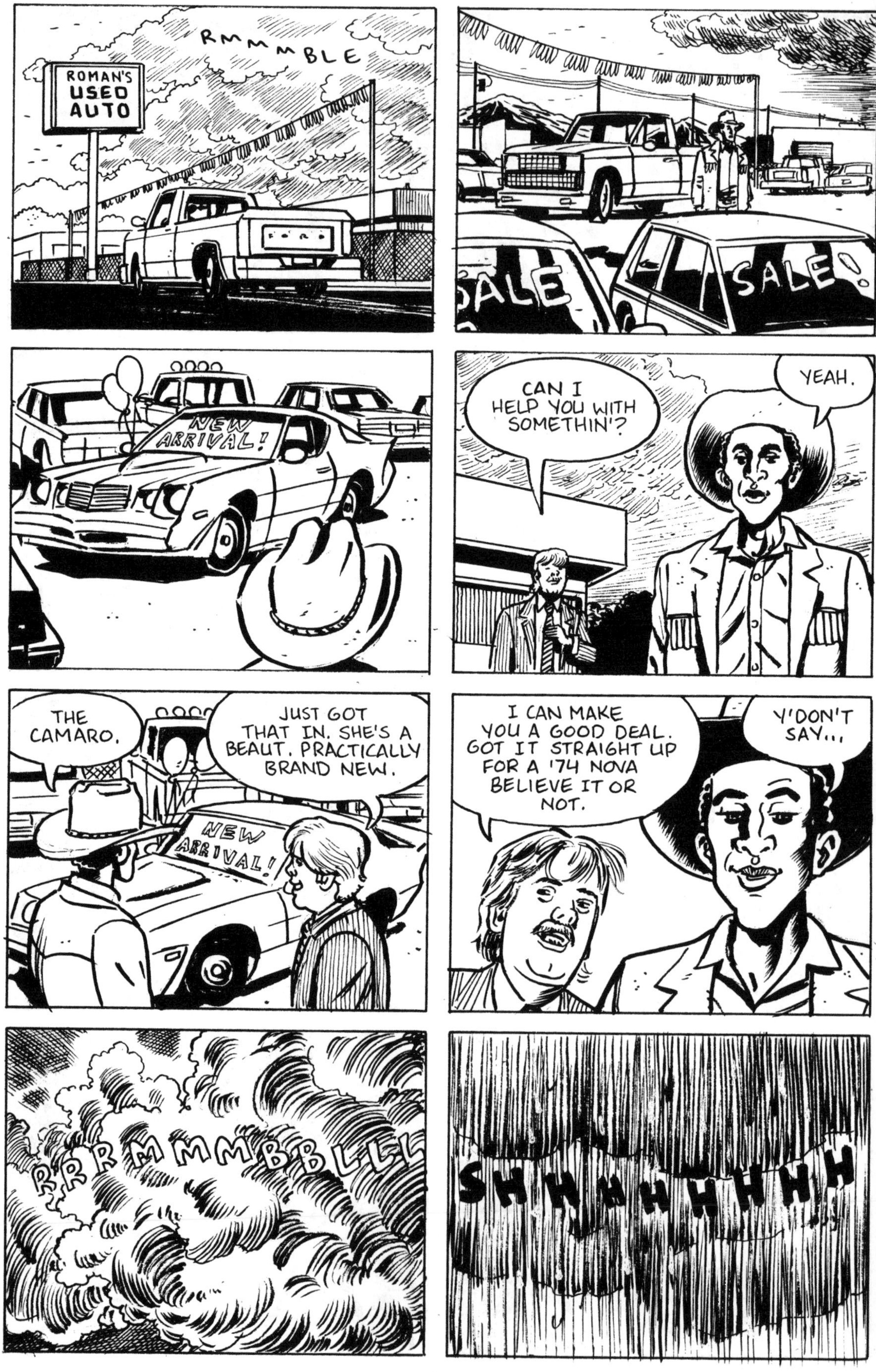

RMMMMBLE
ROMAN'S USED AUTO
SALE
SALE!
NEW ARRIVAL!
CAN I HELP YOU WITH SOMETHIN'?
YEAH.
THE CAMARO.
JUST GOT THAT IN. SHE'S A BEAUT. PRACTICALLY BRAND NEW.
NEW ARRIVAL!
I CAN MAKE YOU A GOOD DEAL. GOT IT STRAIGHT UP FOR A '74 NOVA BELIEVE IT OR NOT.
Y'DON'T SAY...
RRRMMMMBBLLL
SHHHHHHHH

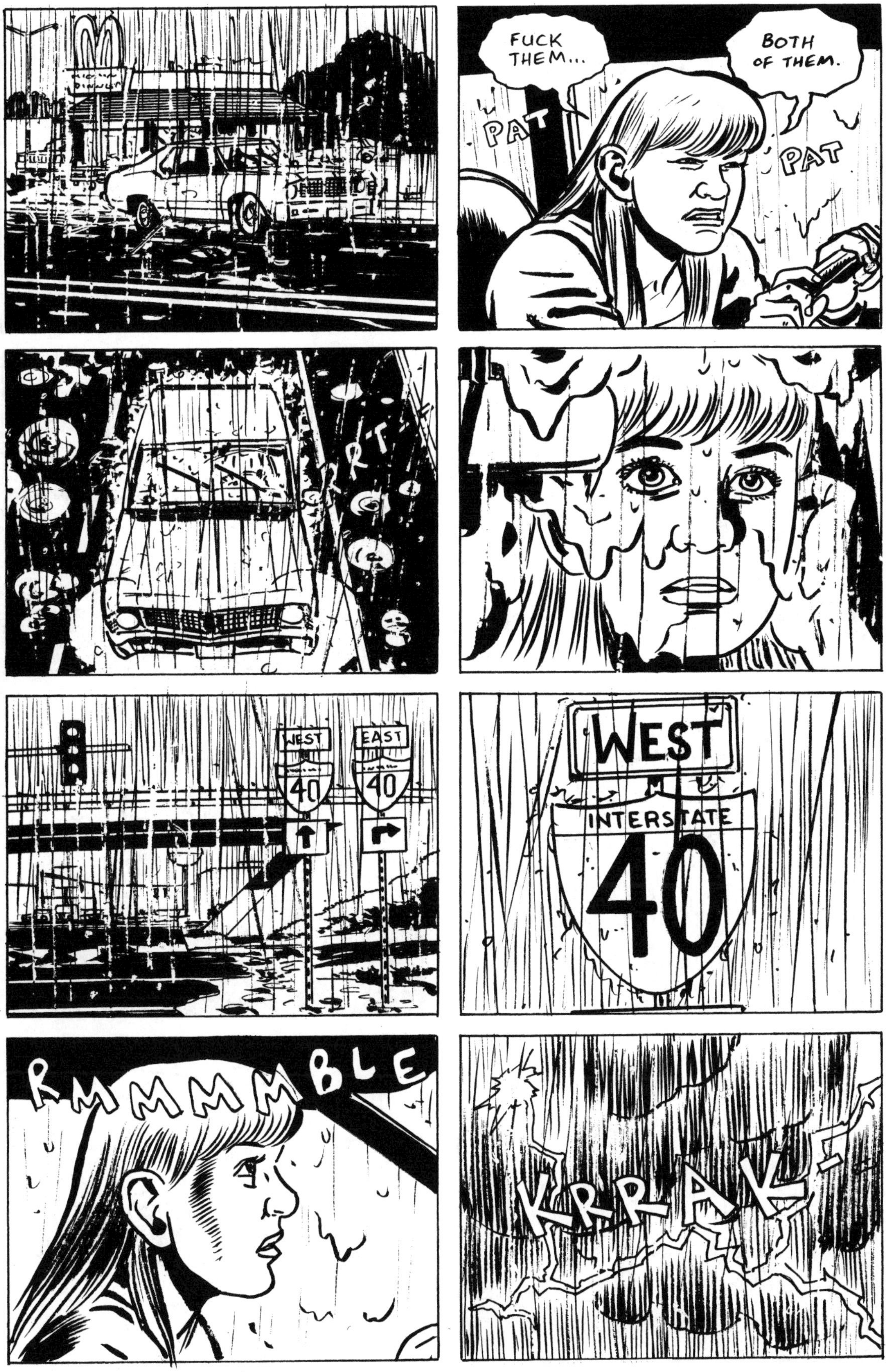
FUCK THEM...
BOTH OF THEM.
PAT
PAT
WEST
40
EAST
40
WEST
INTERSTATE
40
RMMMMBLE
KRRAK

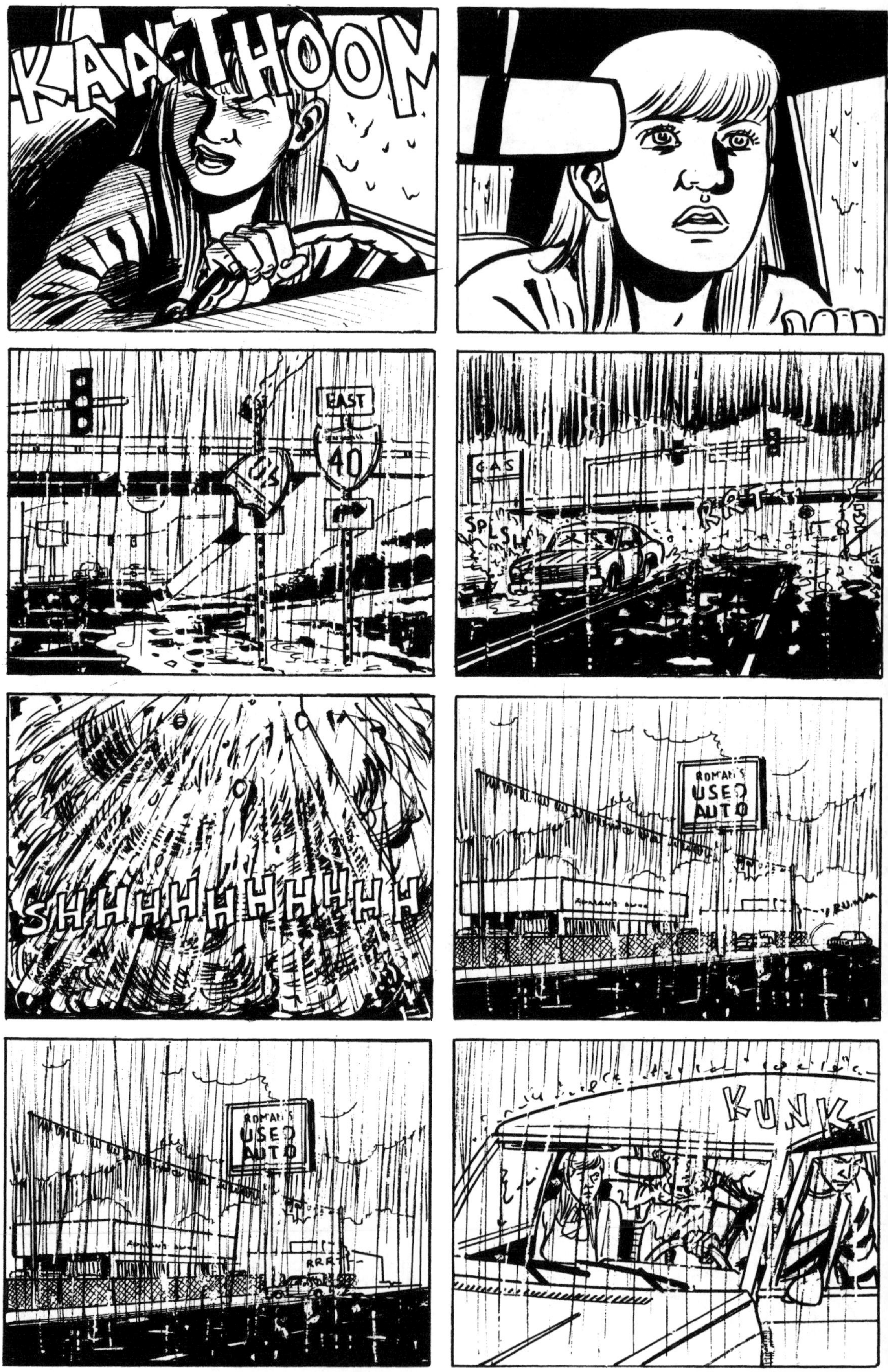
KAA-THOOM
EAST
40
GAS
SPLSH
RRRT
SHHHHHHHHHH
ROMAN'S
USED
AUTO
ROMAN'S
USED
AUTO
RRRT
KUNK

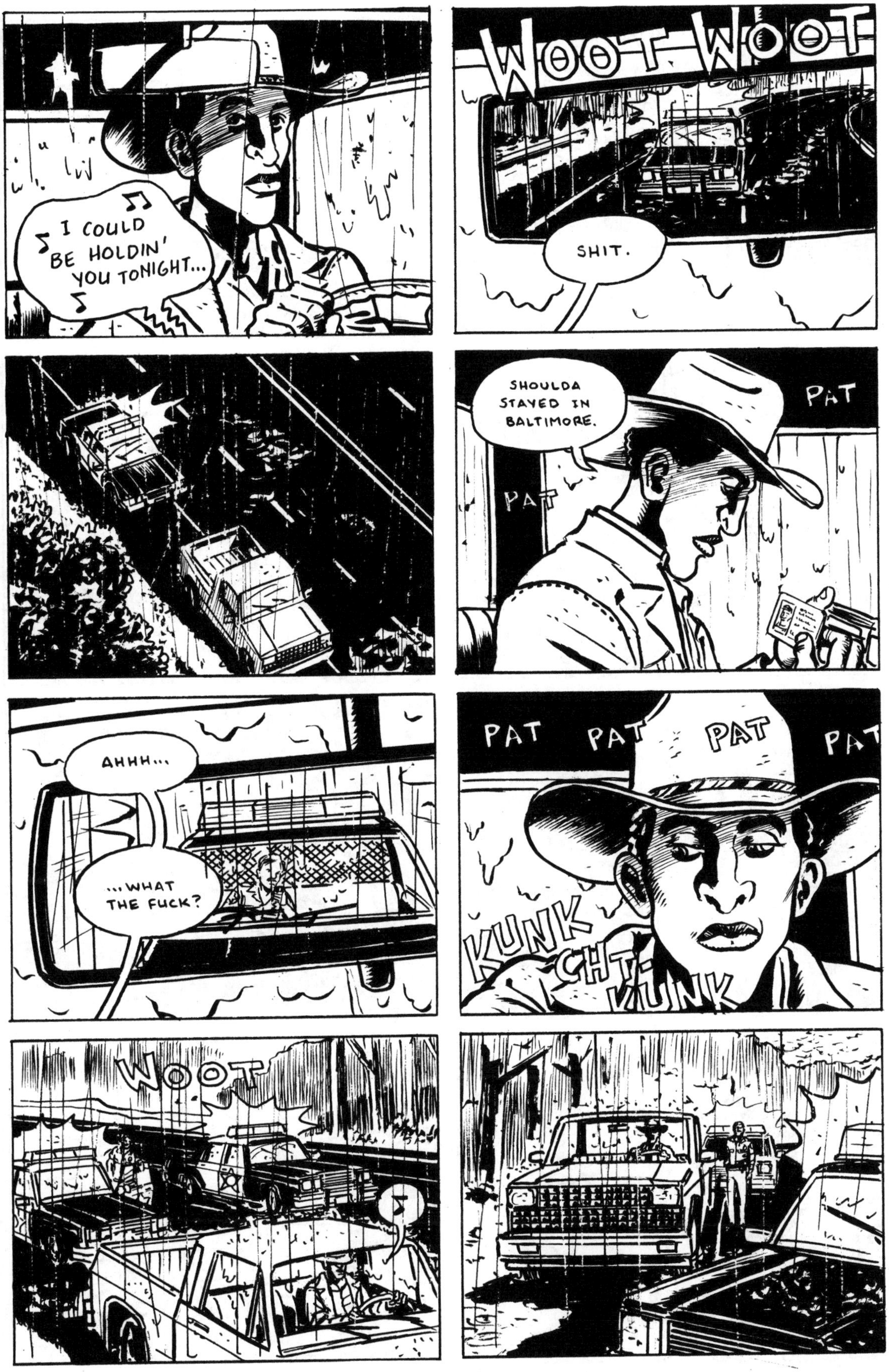
I COULD BE HOLDIN' YOU TONIGHT...
WOOT WOOT
SHIT.
SHOULDA STAYED IN BALTIMORE.
PAT
PAT
AHHH...
...WHAT THE FUCK?
PAT PAT PAT PAT
KUNK
CHT-KUNK
WOOT

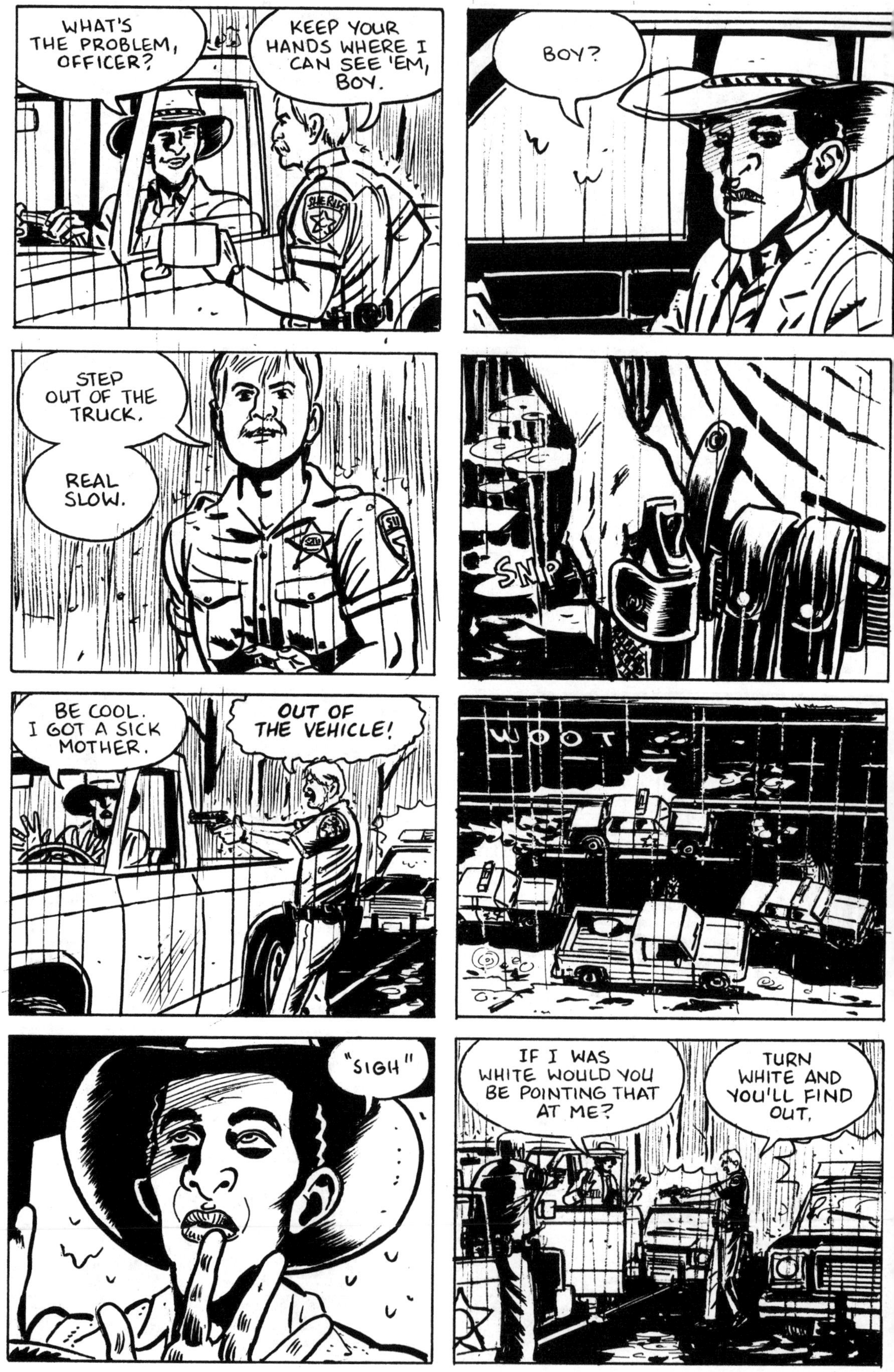
WHAT'S THE PROBLEM, OFFICER?
KEEP YOUR HANDS WHERE I CAN SEE 'EM, BOY.
BOY?
STEP OUT OF THE TRUCK.
REAL SLOW.
SNP
BE COOL. I GOT A SICK MOTHER.
OUT OF THE VEHICLE!
"SIGH"
IF I WAS WHITE WOULD YOU BE POINTING THAT AT ME?
TURN WHITE AND YOU'LL FIND OUT.

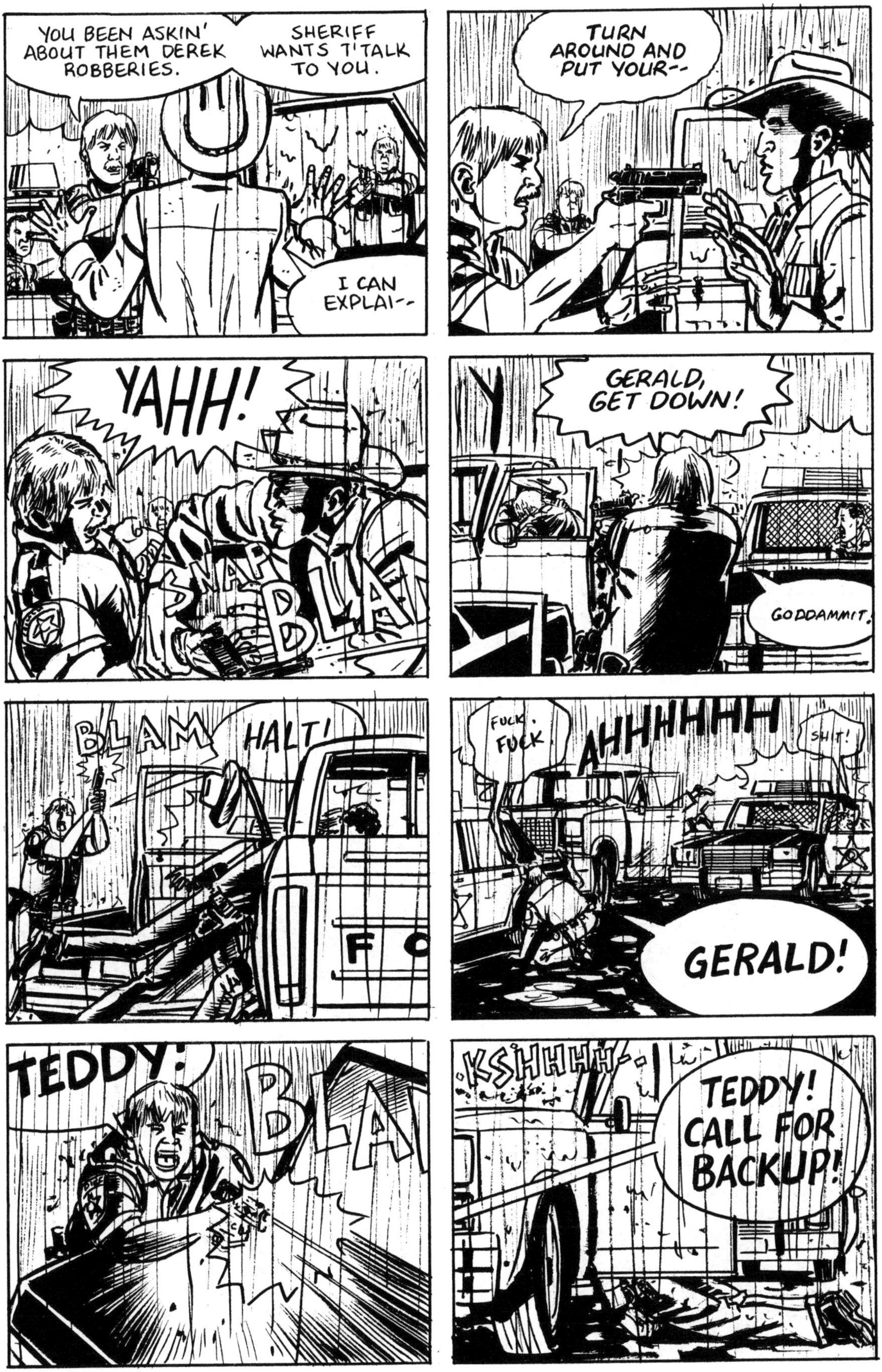

YOU BEEN ASKIN' ABOUT THEM DEREK ROBBERIES.
SHERIFF WANTS T'TALK TO YOU.
I CAN EXPLAI--
TURN AROUND AND PUT YOUR--
YAHH!
SNAP
BLAM
GERALD, GET DOWN!
GODDAMMIT.
BLAM
HALT!
FUCK. FUCK
AHHHHHH
SHIT!
GERALD!
TEDDY!
BLAM
KSHHHH--!
TEDDY! CALL FOR BACKUP!

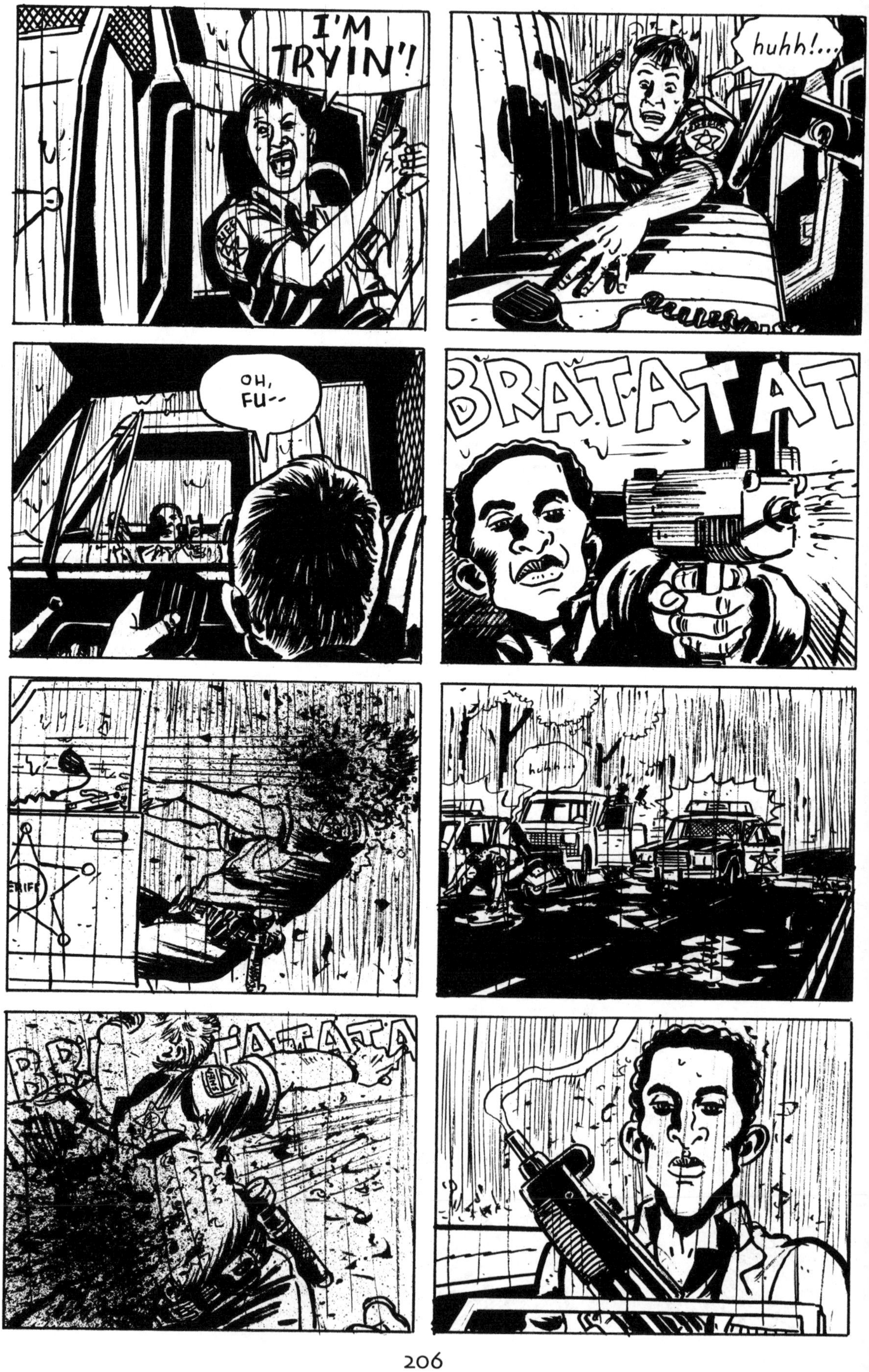
I'M TRYIN'!
huhh!...
OH, FU--
BRATATAT
huhh...
TATATA

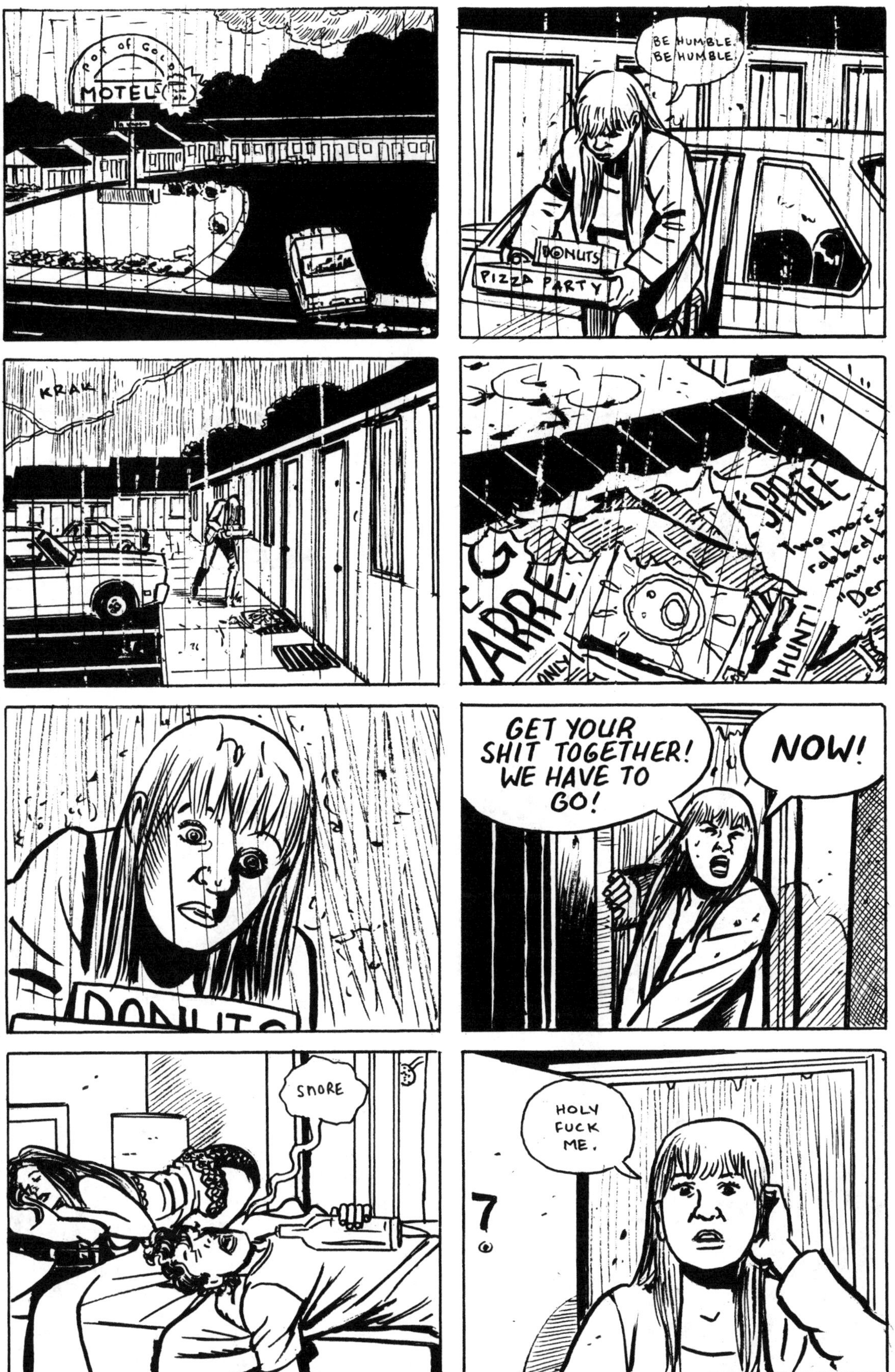
MOTEL
BE HUMBLE. BE HUMBLE.
DONUTS
PIZZA PARTY
KRAK
GET YOUR SHIT TOGETHER! WE HAVE TO GO!
NOW!
SNORE
HOLY FUCK ME.
7

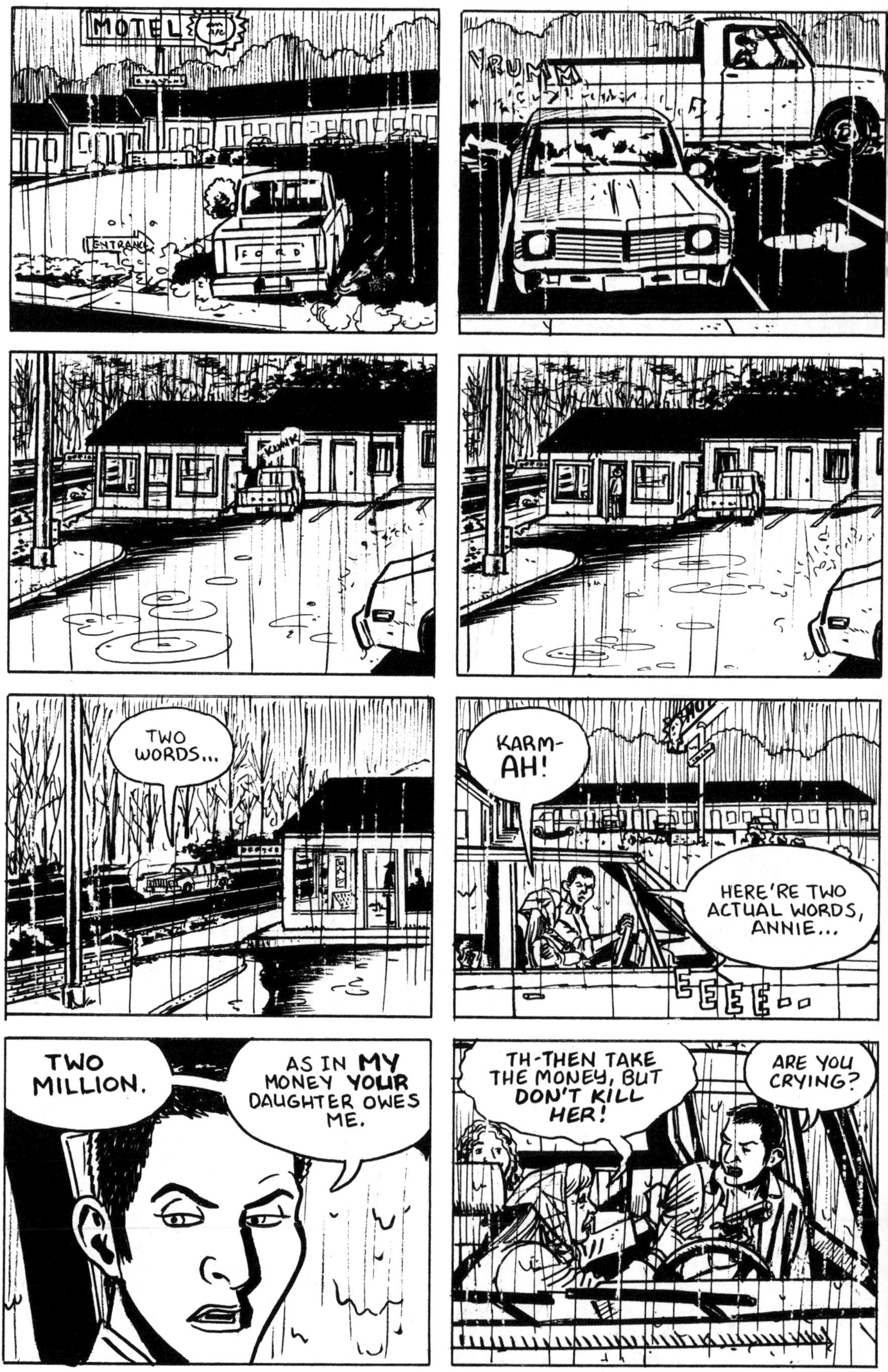
MOTEL
ENTRANCE
FORD
VRUMM
TWO WORDS...
KARM-AH!
HERE'RE TWO ACTUAL WORDS, ANNIE...
EEEE..
TWO MILLION.
AS IN MY MONEY YOUR DAUGHTER OWES ME.
TH-THEN TAKE THE MONEY, BUT DON'T KILL HER!
ARE YOU CRYING?

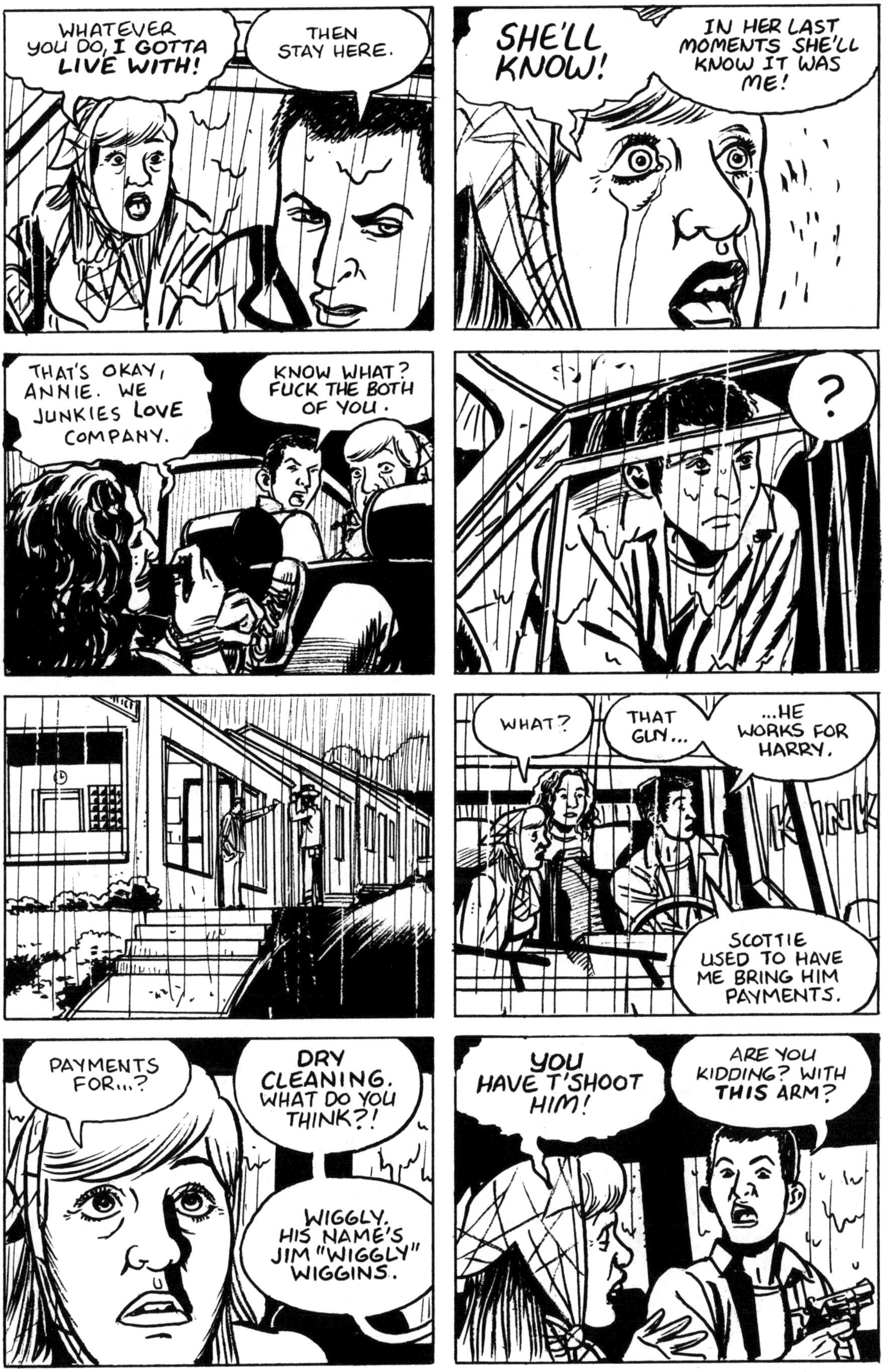
WHATEVER YOU DO, I GOTTA LIVE WITH!
THEN STAY HERE.
SHE'LL KNOW!
IN HER LAST MOMENTS SHE'LL KNOW IT WAS ME!
THAT'S OKAY, ANNIE. WE JUNKIES LOVE COMPANY.
KNOW WHAT? FUCK THE BOTH OF YOU.
?
WHAT?
THAT GUY...
...HE WORKS FOR HARRY.
KLINK
SCOTTIE USED TO HAVE ME BRING HIM PAYMENTS.
PAYMENTS FOR...?
DRY CLEANING. WHAT DO YOU THINK?!
WIGGLY. HIS NAME'S JIM "WIGGLY" WIGGINS.
YOU HAVE T'SHOOT HIM!
ARE YOU KIDDING? WITH THIS ARM?

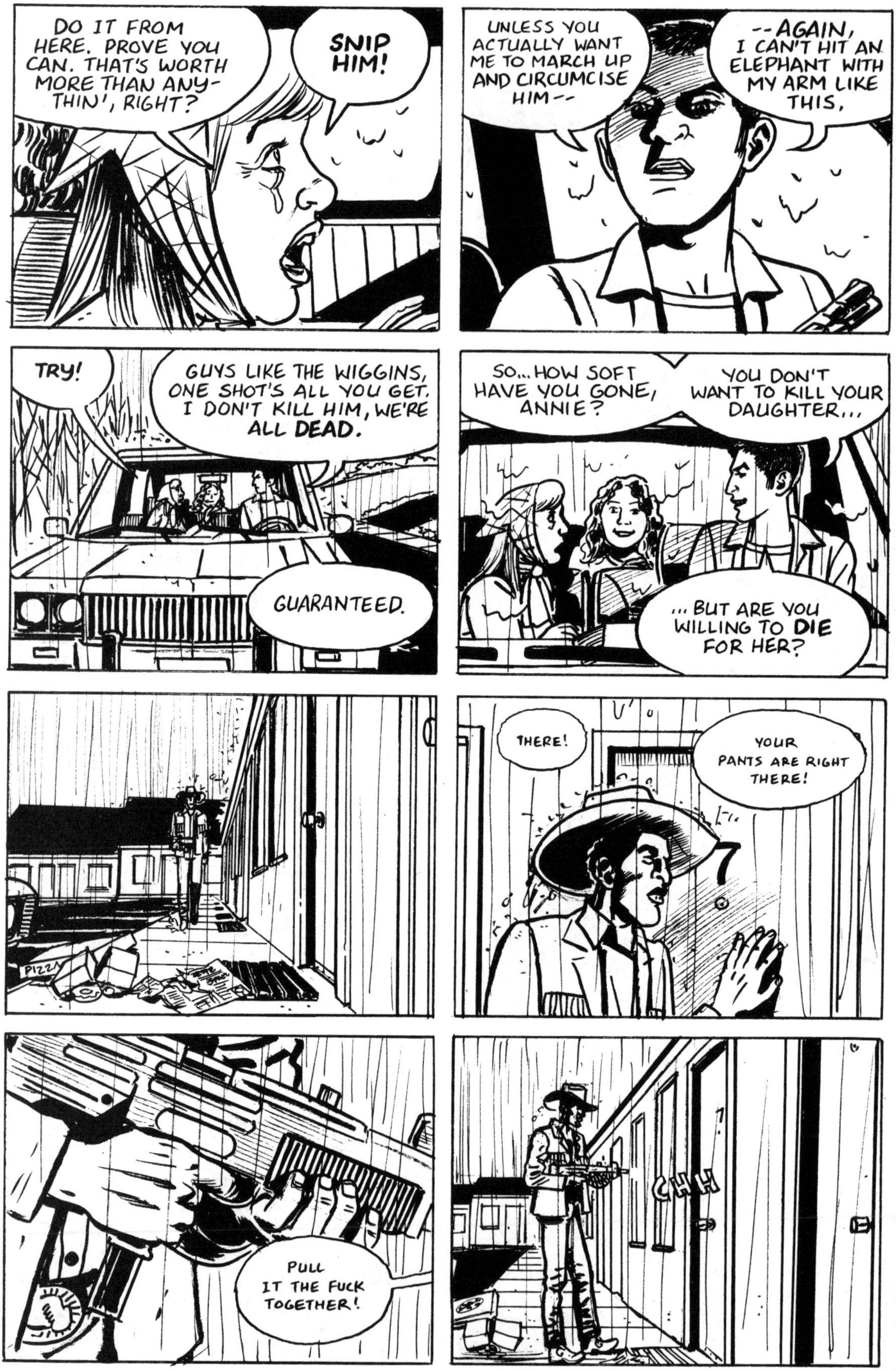
DO IT FROM HERE. PROVE YOU CAN. THAT'S WORTH MORE THAN ANY-THIN', RIGHT?
SNIP HIM!
UNLESS YOU ACTUALLY WANT ME TO MARCH UP AND CIRCUMCISE HIM--
--AGAIN, I CAN'T HIT AN ELEPHANT WITH MY ARM LIKE THIS.
TRY!
GUYS LIKE THE WIGGINS, ONE SHOT'S ALL YOU GET. I DON'T KILL HIM, WE'RE ALL DEAD.
GUARANTEED.
SO... HOW SOFT HAVE YOU GONE, ANNIE?
YOU DON'T WANT TO KILL YOUR DAUGHTER...
...BUT ARE YOU WILLING TO DIE FOR HER?
PIZZA
THERE!
YOUR PANTS ARE RIGHT THERE!
PULL IT THE FUCK TOGETHER!
CHH

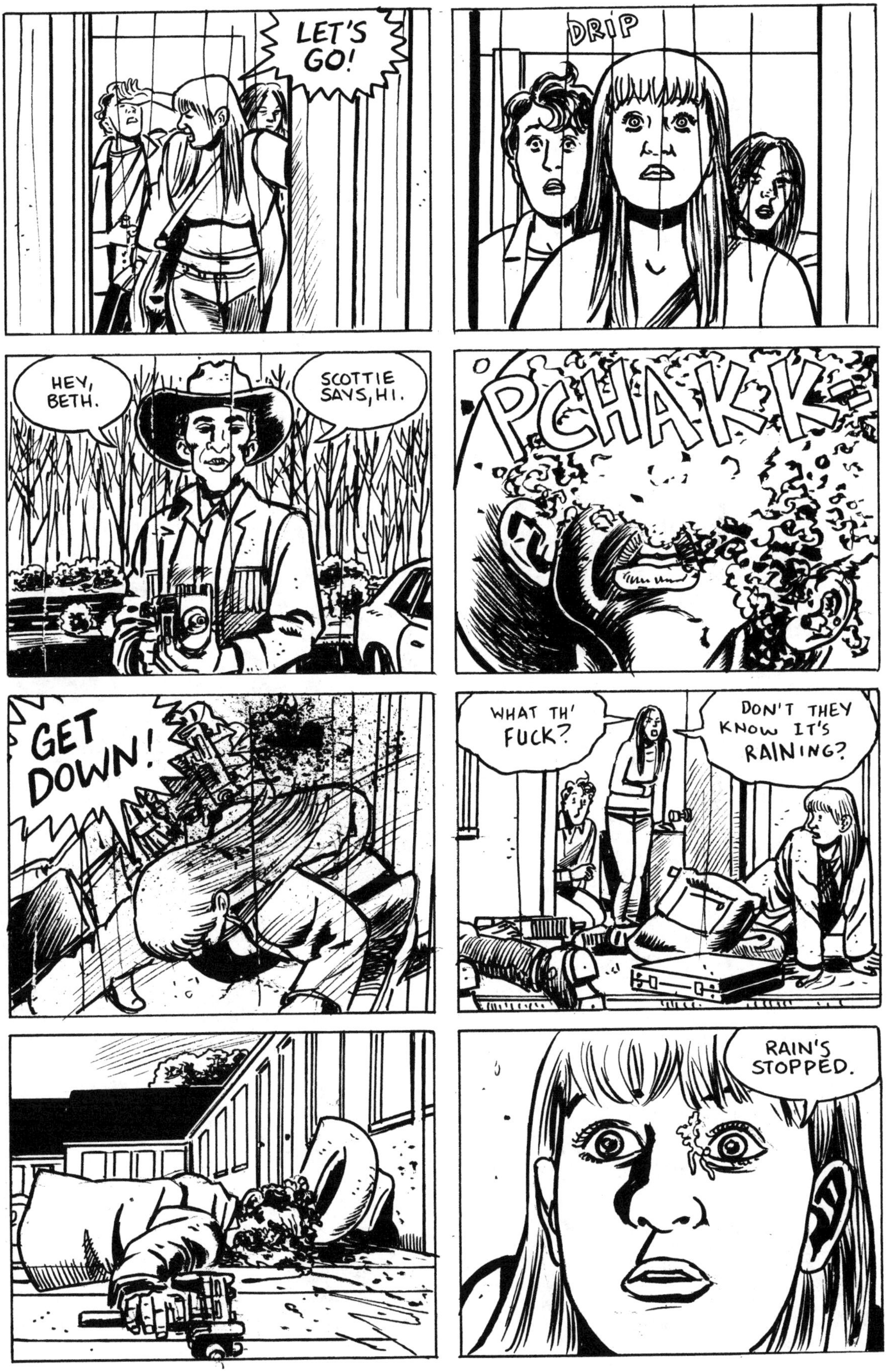
LET'S GO!
DRIP
HEY, BETH.
SCOTTIE SAYS, HI.
PCHAKK-
GET DOWN!
WHAT TH' FUCK?
DON'T THEY KNOW IT'S RAINING?
RAIN'S STOPPED.

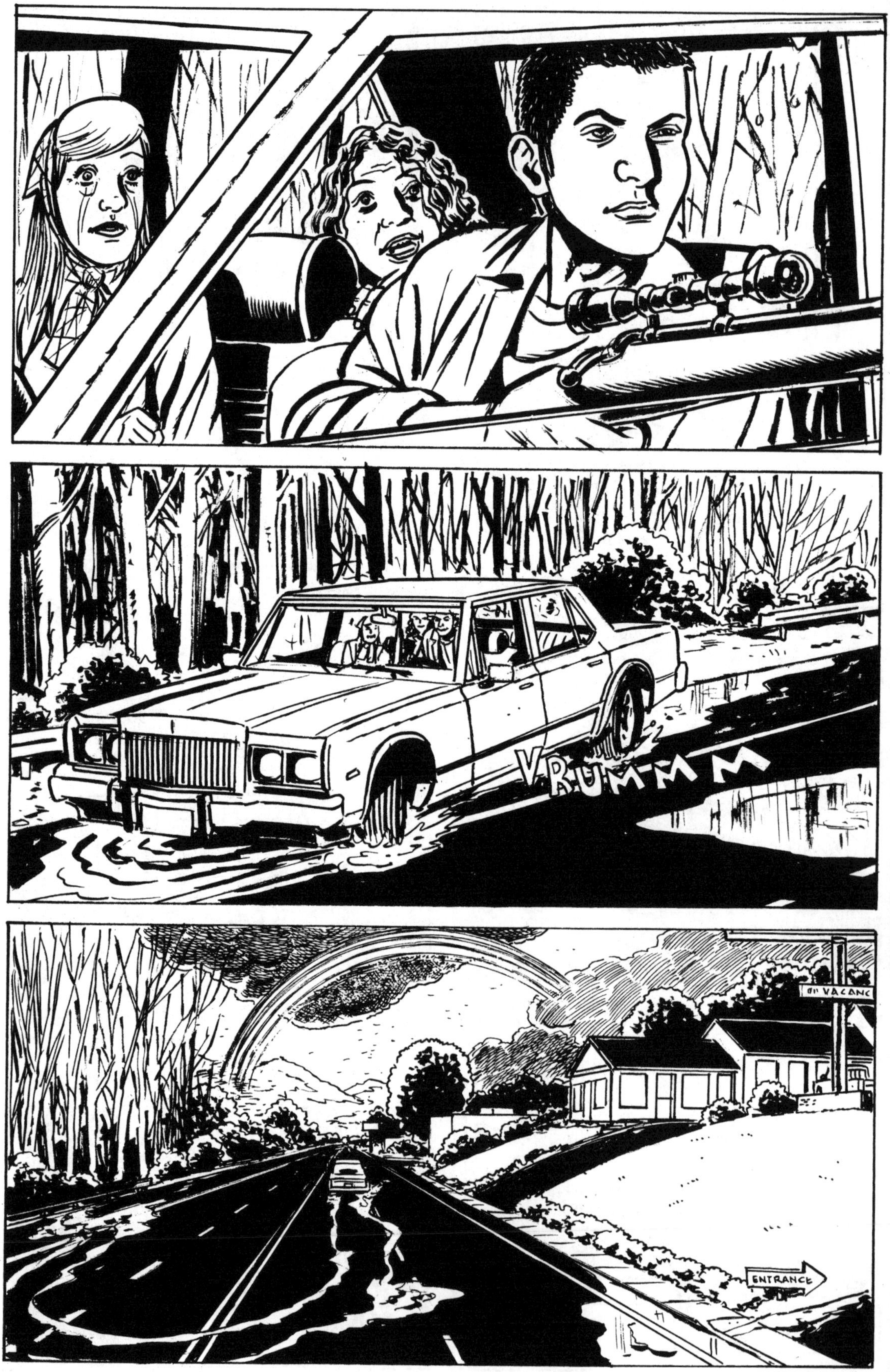
VRUMMM
ENTRANCE

THE END...

8

"MOJO AND DONUTS"

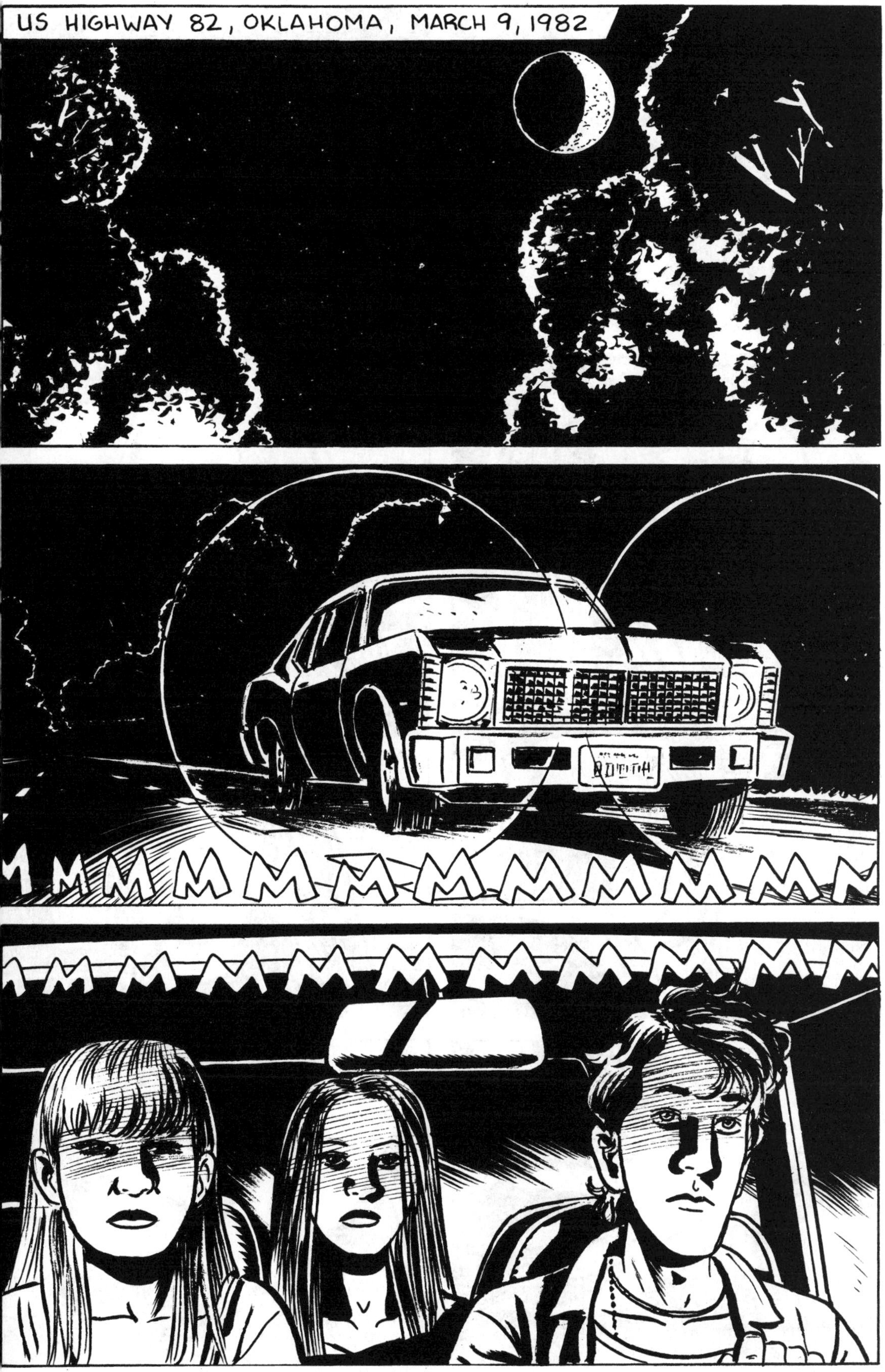
US HIGHWAY 82, OKLAHOMA, MARCH 9, 1982
MMMMMMMMMMMM
MMMMMMMMMMMM

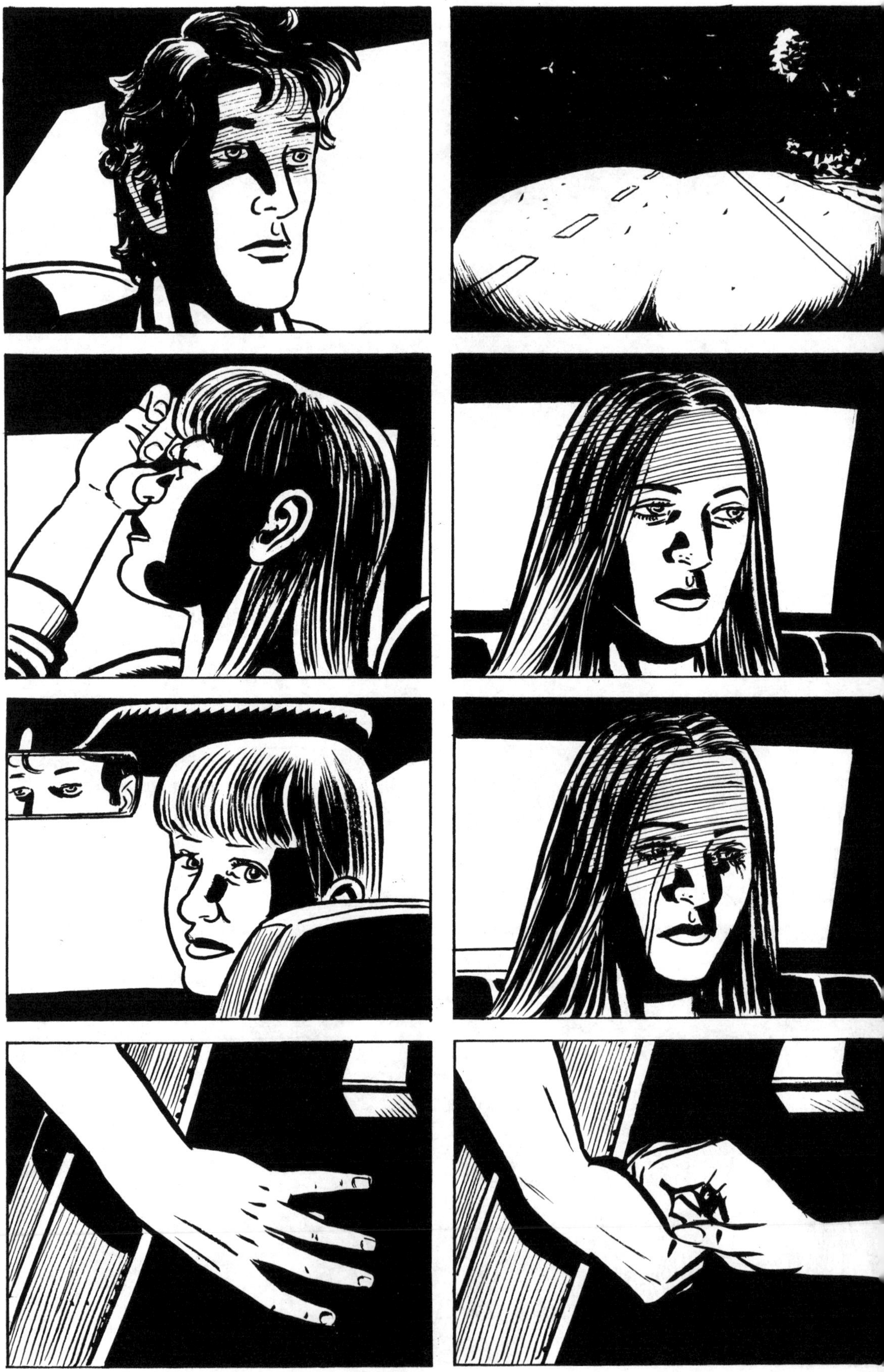

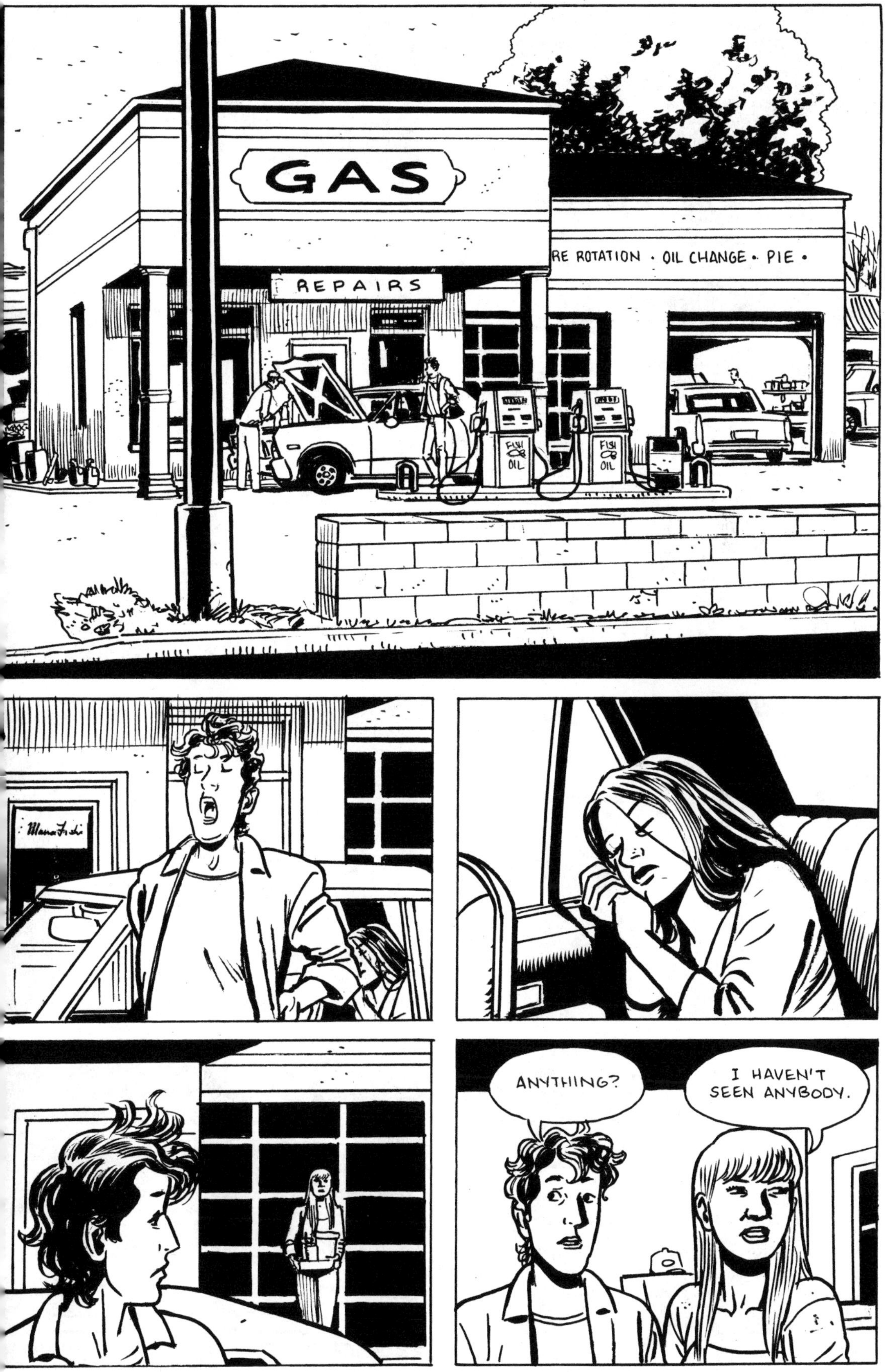
GAS
REPAIRS
RE ROTATION · OIL CHANGE · PIE ·
FISH OIL
FISH OIL
ANYTHING?
I HAVEN'T SEEN ANYBODY.

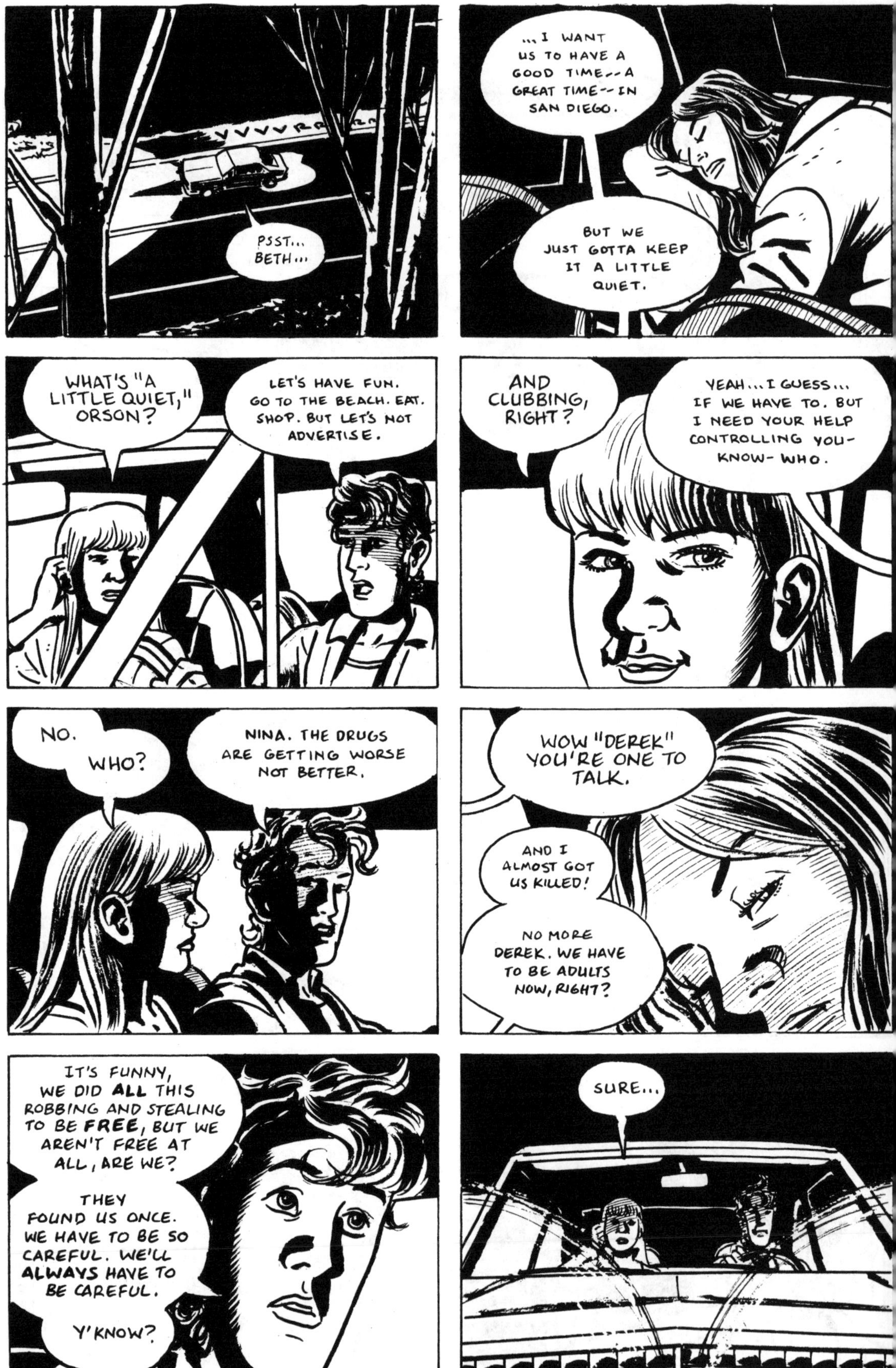
PSST... BETH...
...I WANT US TO HAVE A GOOD TIME--A GREAT TIME--IN SAN DIEGO.
BUT WE JUST GOTTA KEEP IT A LITTLE QUIET.
WHAT'S "A LITTLE QUIET," ORSON?
LET'S HAVE FUN. GO TO THE BEACH. EAT. SHOP. BUT LET'S NOT ADVERTISE.
AND CLUBBING, RIGHT?
YEAH... I GUESS... IF WE HAVE TO. BUT I NEED YOUR HELP CONTROLLING YOU-KNOW-WHO.
NO.
WHO?
NINA. THE DRUGS ARE GETTING WORSE NOT BETTER.
WOW "DEREK" YOU'RE ONE TO TALK.
AND I ALMOST GOT US KILLED!
NO MORE DEREK. WE HAVE TO BE ADULTS NOW, RIGHT?
IT'S FUNNY, WE DID **ALL** THIS ROBBING AND STEALING TO BE **FREE**, BUT WE AREN'T FREE AT ALL, ARE WE?
THEY FOUND US ONCE. WE HAVE TO BE SO CAREFUL. WE'LL **ALWAYS** HAVE TO BE CAREFUL.
Y'KNOW?
SURE...

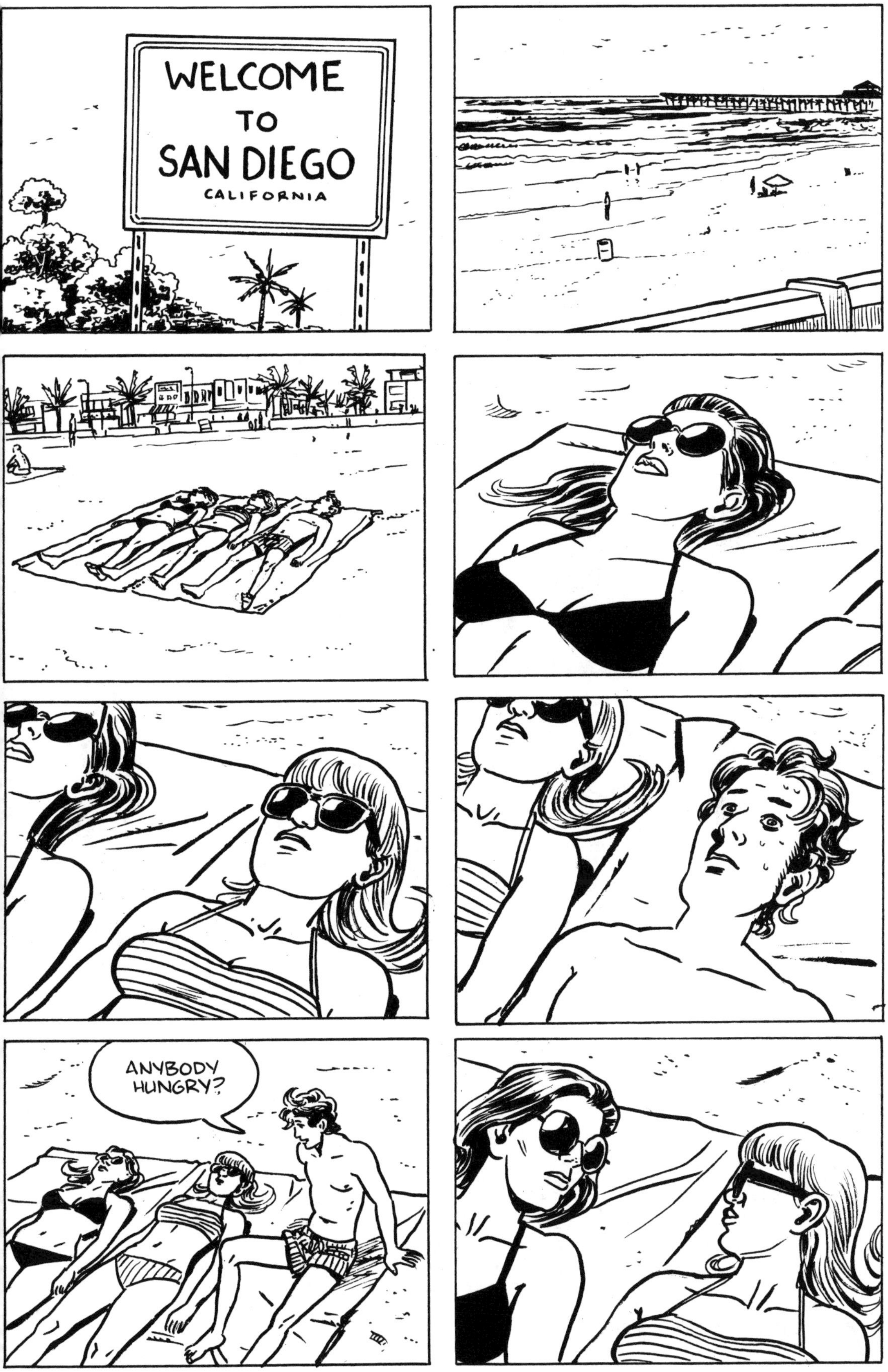
WELCOME
TO
SAN DIEGO
CALIFORNIA
ANYBODY HUNGRY?

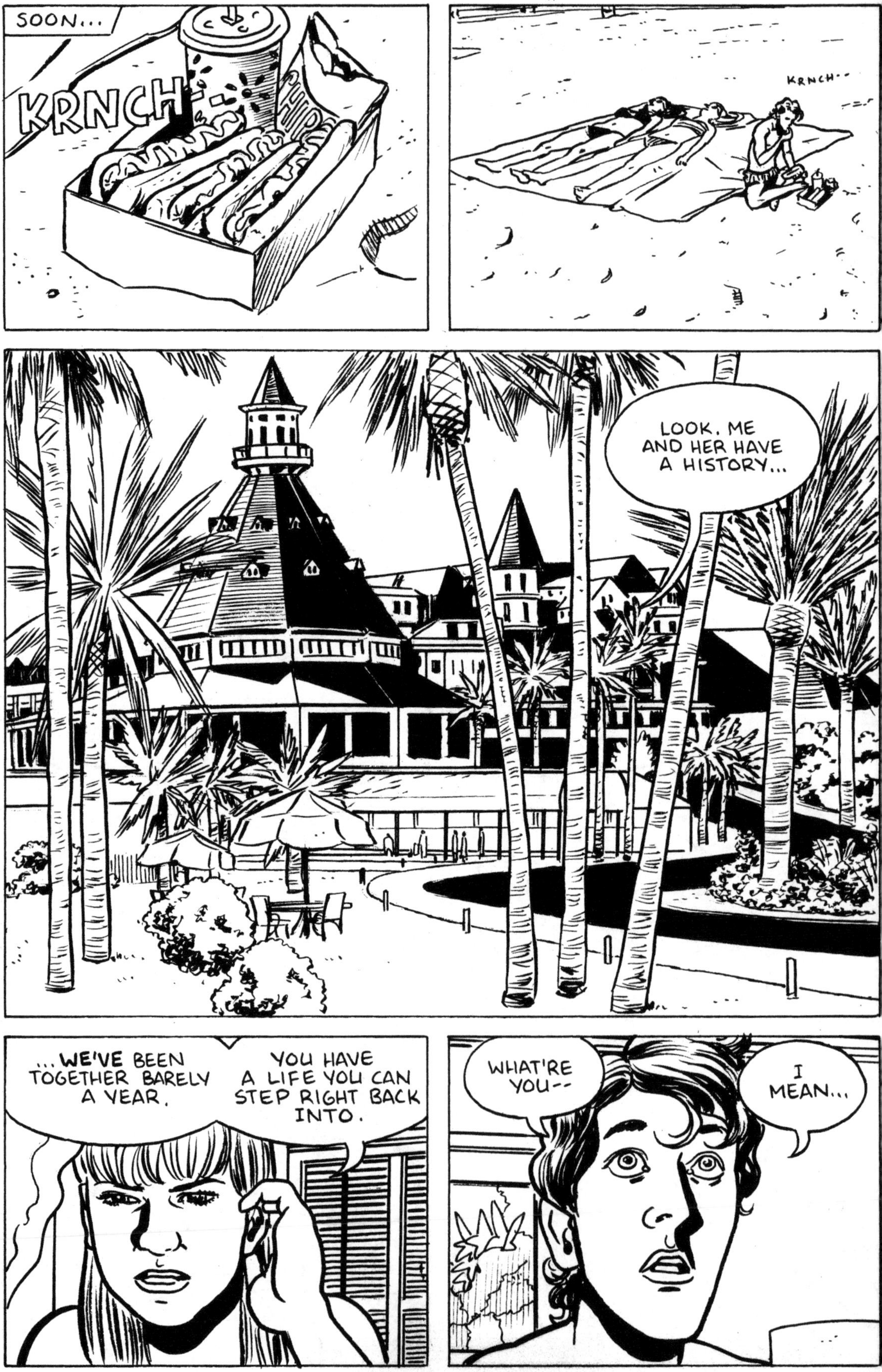
SOON...
KRNCH-
KRNCH--
LOOK. ME AND HER HAVE A HISTORY...
...WE'VE BEEN TOGETHER BARELY A YEAR.
YOU HAVE A LIFE YOU CAN STEP RIGHT BACK INTO.
WHAT'RE YOU--
I MEAN...

I'M SAYING IT'S TIME FOR YOU TO GO HOME.

YOU'LL GET YOUR SHARE.

CHRIST.

YOU'RE SUCH A GODDAMN BABY.

HERE'S A FUCKING TICKET!

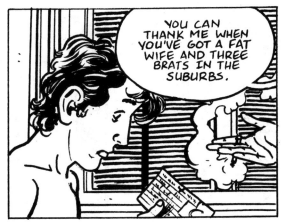

YOU CAN THANK ME WHEN YOU'VE GOT A FAT WIFE AND THREE BRATS IN THE SUBURBS.

MARYLAND...

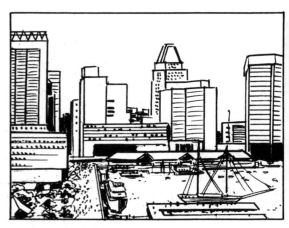

MOTE

...SUNNY WITH A HIGH OF FIFTY-EIGHT...

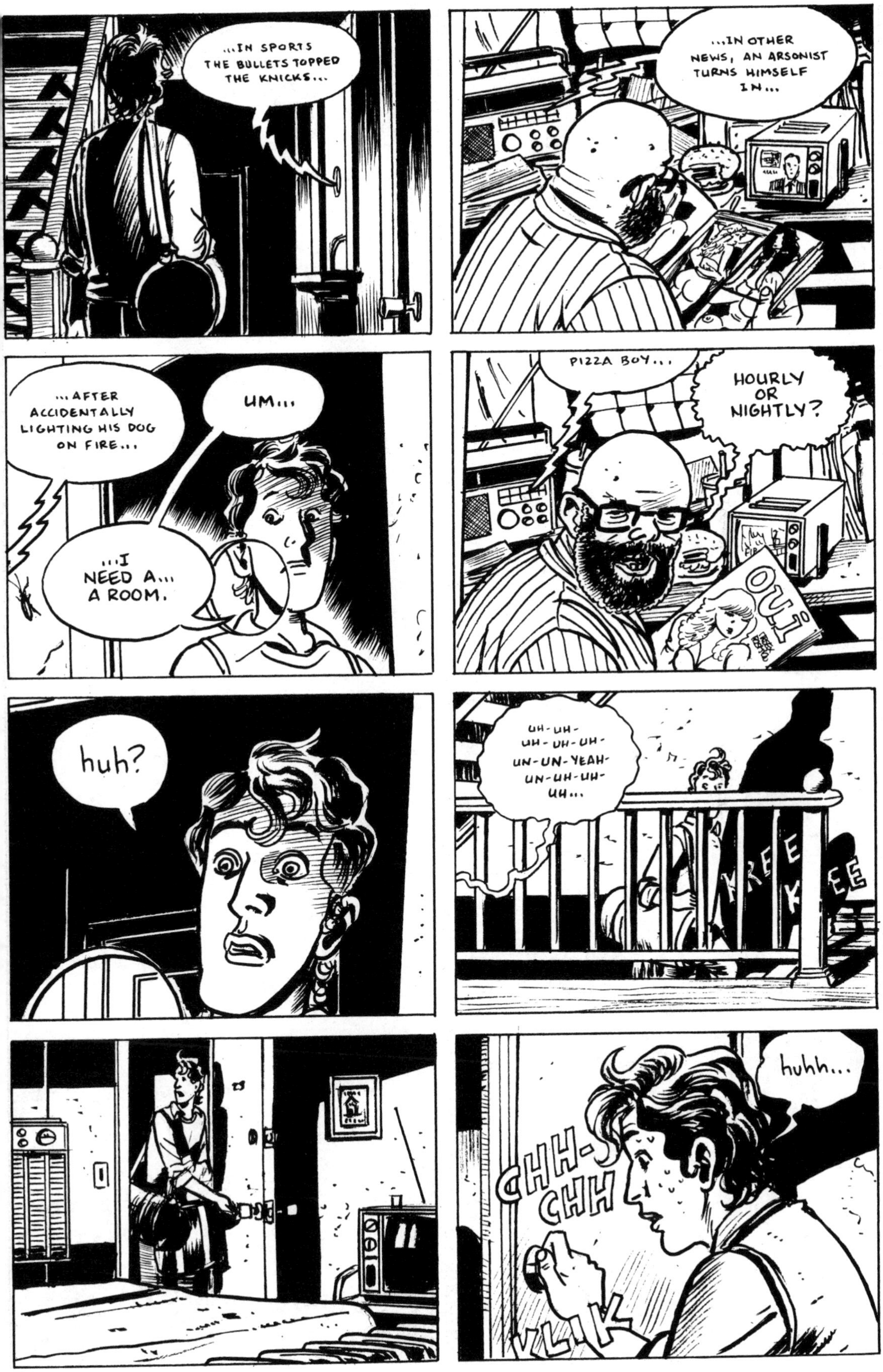
...IN SPORTS THE BULLETS TOPPED THE KNICKS...
...IN OTHER NEWS, AN ARSONIST TURNS HIMSELF IN...
...AFTER ACCIDENTALLY LIGHTING HIS DOG ON FIRE...
UM...
...I NEED A... A ROOM.
PIZZA BOY...
HOURLY OR NIGHTLY?
OUT
huh?
UH-UH-UH-UH-UH-UN-UN-YEAH-UN-UH-UH-UH...
KREE
KEE
huhh...
CHH-CHH
KLIK

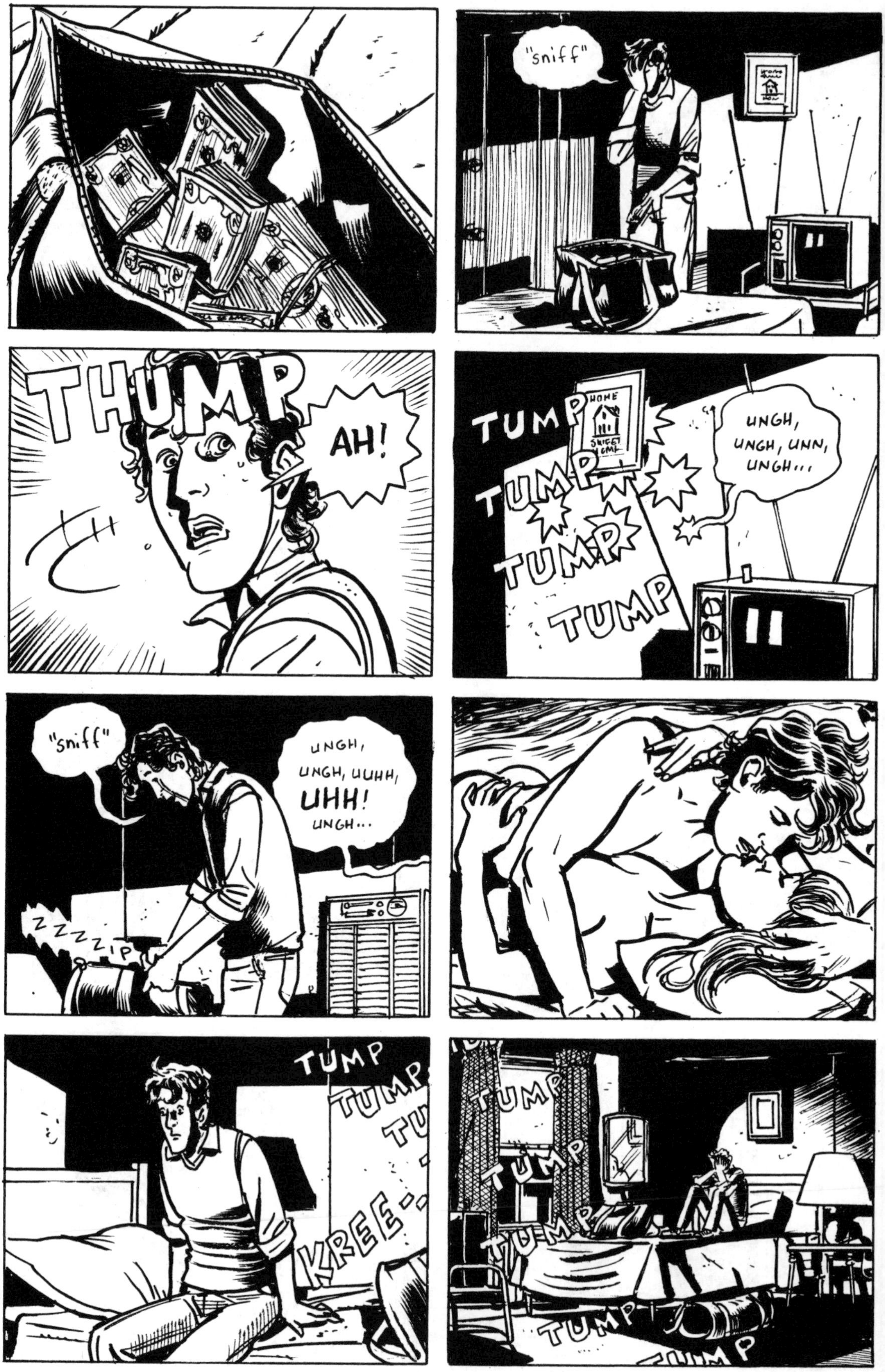
"sniff"
THUMP
AH!
TUMP
TUMP
TUMP
TUMP
UNGH, UNGH, UNN, UNGH...
"sniff"
UNGH, UNGH, UUHH, UHH! UNGH...
ZZZZZIP
TUMP
TUMP
TU
KREE..
TUMP
TUMP
TUMP
TUMP

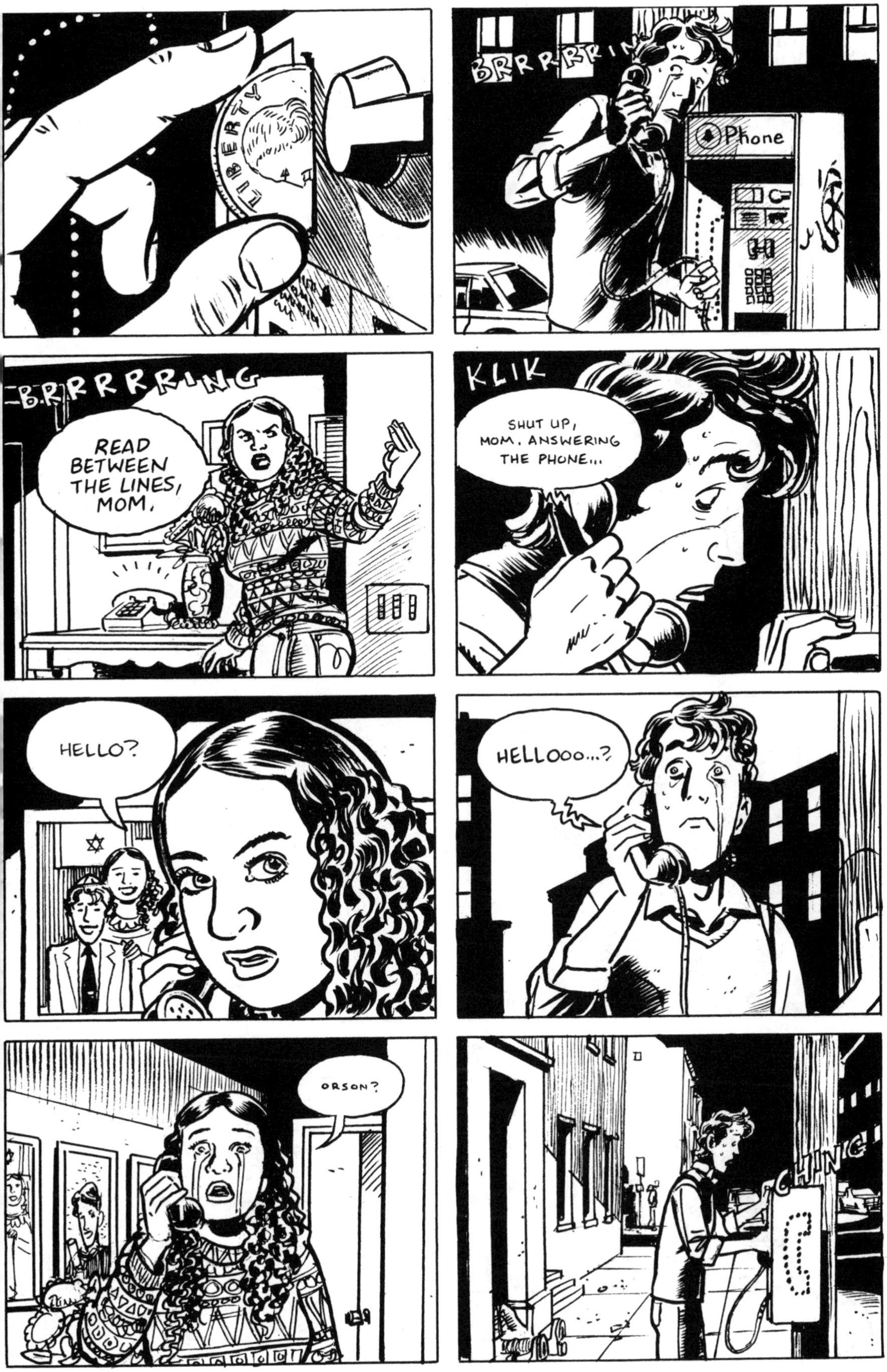
LIBERTY
BRRRRRING
Phone
BRRRRRING
READ BETWEEN THE LINES, MOM.
KLIK
SHUT UP, MOM. ANSWERING THE PHONE...
HELLO?
HELLOoo...?
ORSON?
CHING

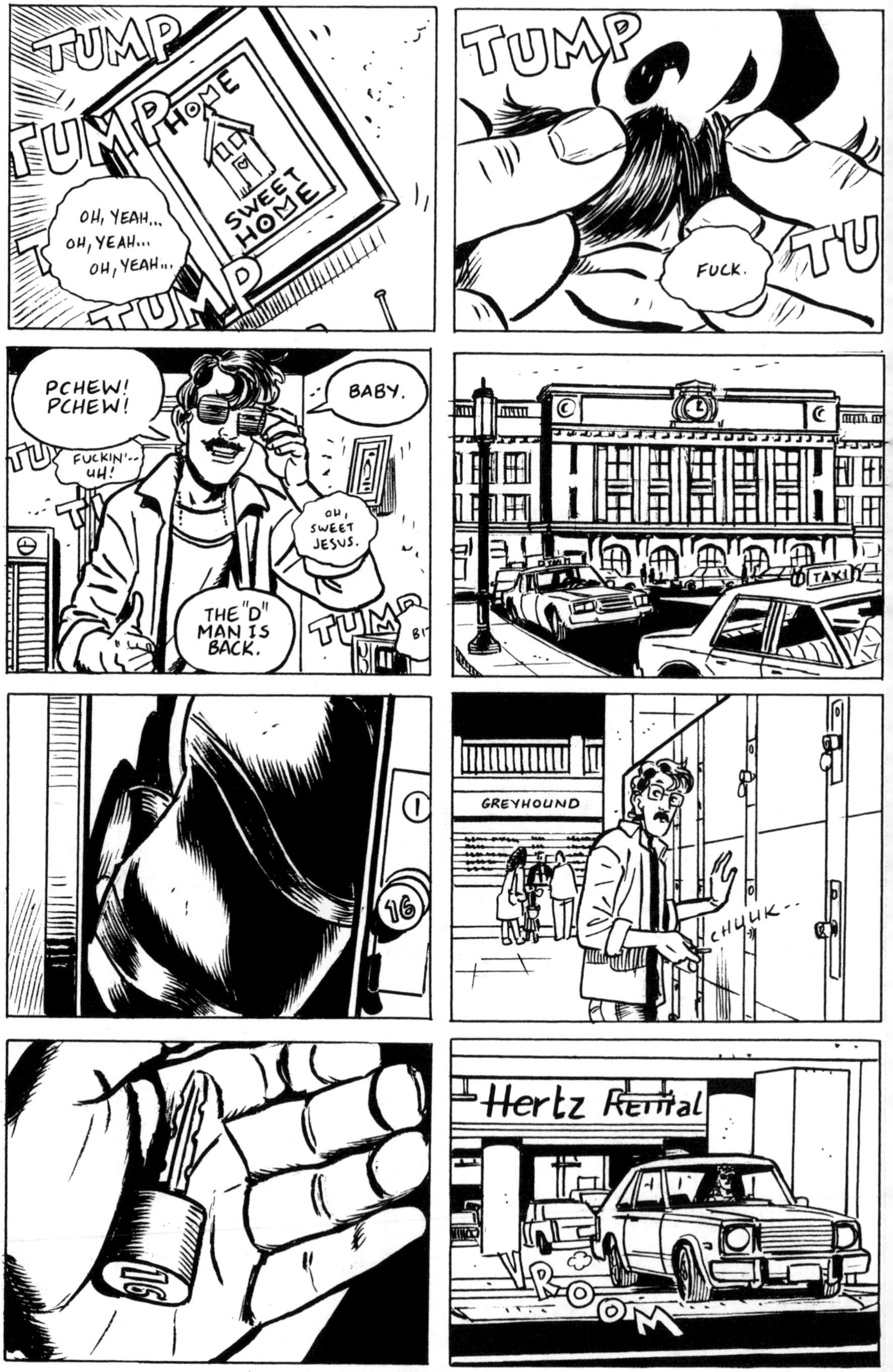
TUMP
TUMP
HOME SWEET HOME
OH, YEAH...
OH, YEAH...
OH, YEAH...
TUMP
TUMP
FUCK.
TU
PCHEW! PCHEW!
FUCKIN'... UH!
BABY.
OH, SWEET JESUS.
THE "D" MAN IS BACK.
TUMP
TAXI
GREYHOUND
CHUUK...
Hertz Rental
VROOM

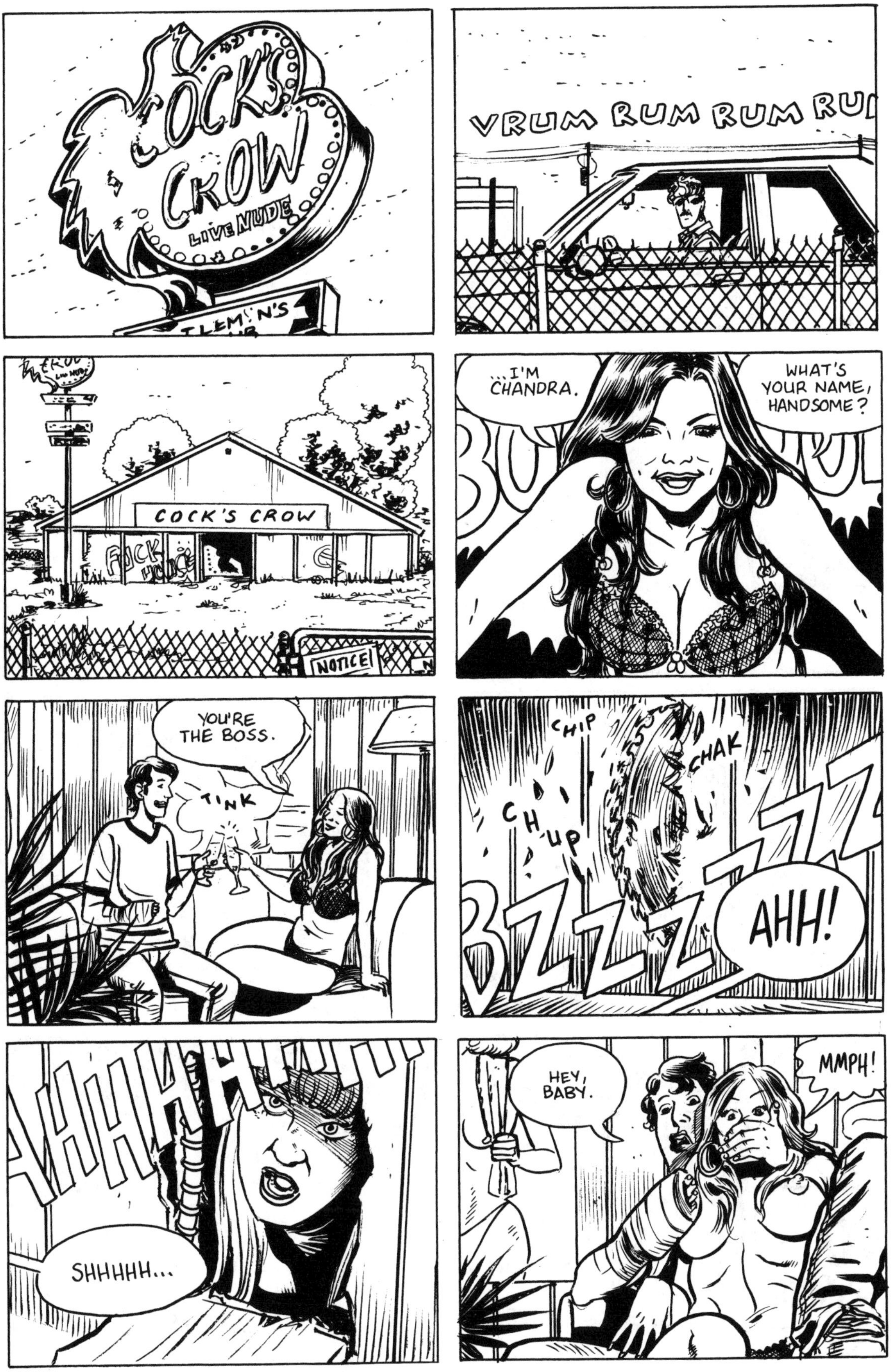
COCK'S CROW
LIVE NUDE
VRUM RUM RUM RU
COCK'S CROW
FUCK HOUSE
NOTICE
...I'M CHANDRA.
WHAT'S YOUR NAME, HANDSOME?
YOU'RE THE BOSS.
TINK
CHIP
CHAK
CHUP
BZZZZZ
AHH!
SHHHHH...
HEY, BABY.
MMPH!

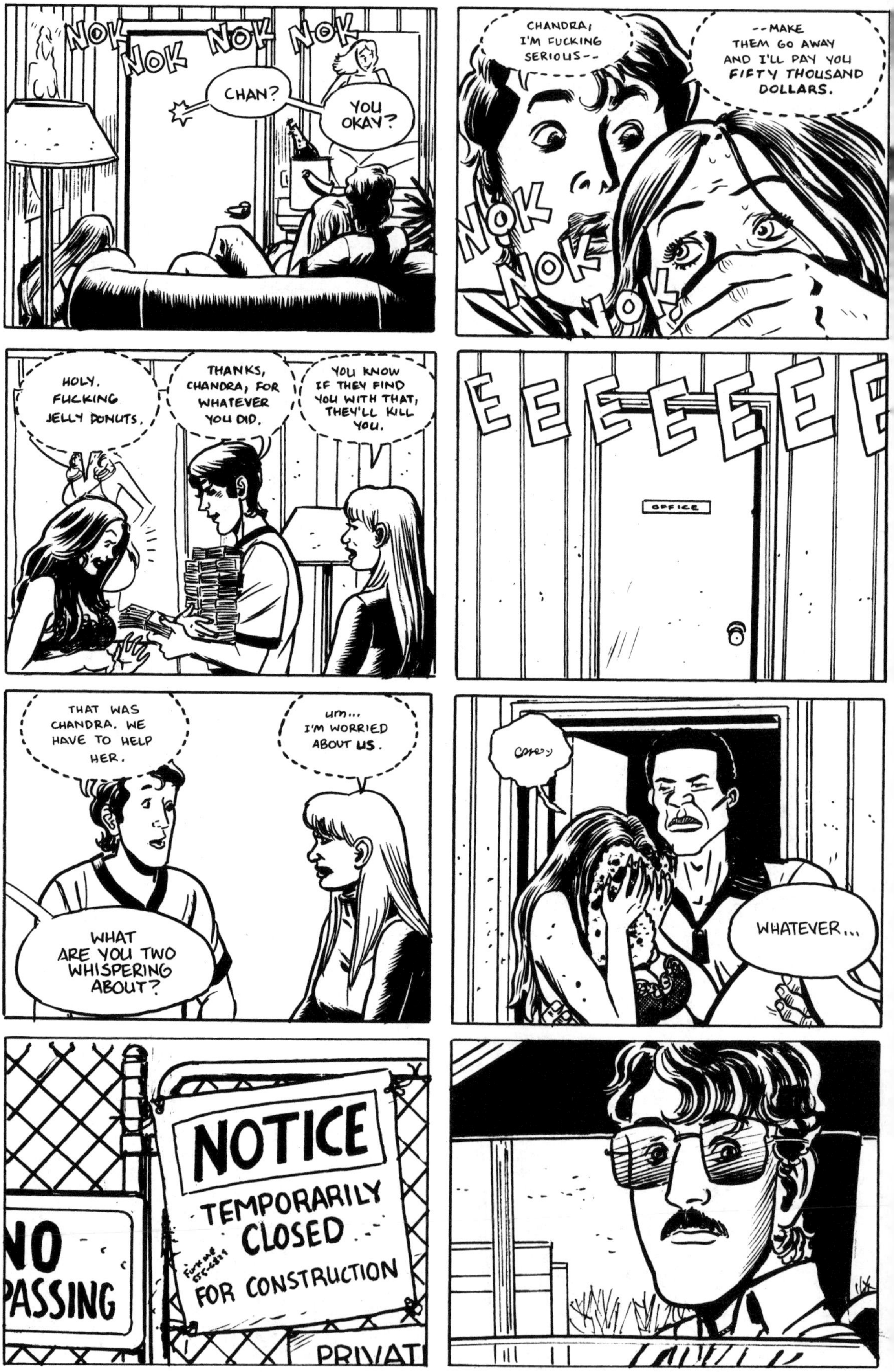
NOK NOK NOK NOK
CHAN?
YOU OKAY?
CHANDRA, I'M FUCKING SERIOUS--
--MAKE THEM GO AWAY AND I'LL PAY YOU FIFTY THOUSAND DOLLARS.
NOK NOK NOK
HOLY, FUCKING JELLY DONUTS.
THANKS, CHANDRA, FOR WHATEVER YOU DID.
YOU KNOW IF THEY FIND YOU WITH THAT, THEY'LL KILL YOU.
EEEEEEE
OFFICE
THAT WAS CHANDRA. WE HAVE TO HELP HER.
UM... I'M WORRIED ABOUT US.
WHAT ARE YOU TWO WHISPERING ABOUT?
WHATEVER...
NO
PASSING
NOTICE
TEMPORARILY CLOSED
FOR CONSTRUCTION
PRIVAT

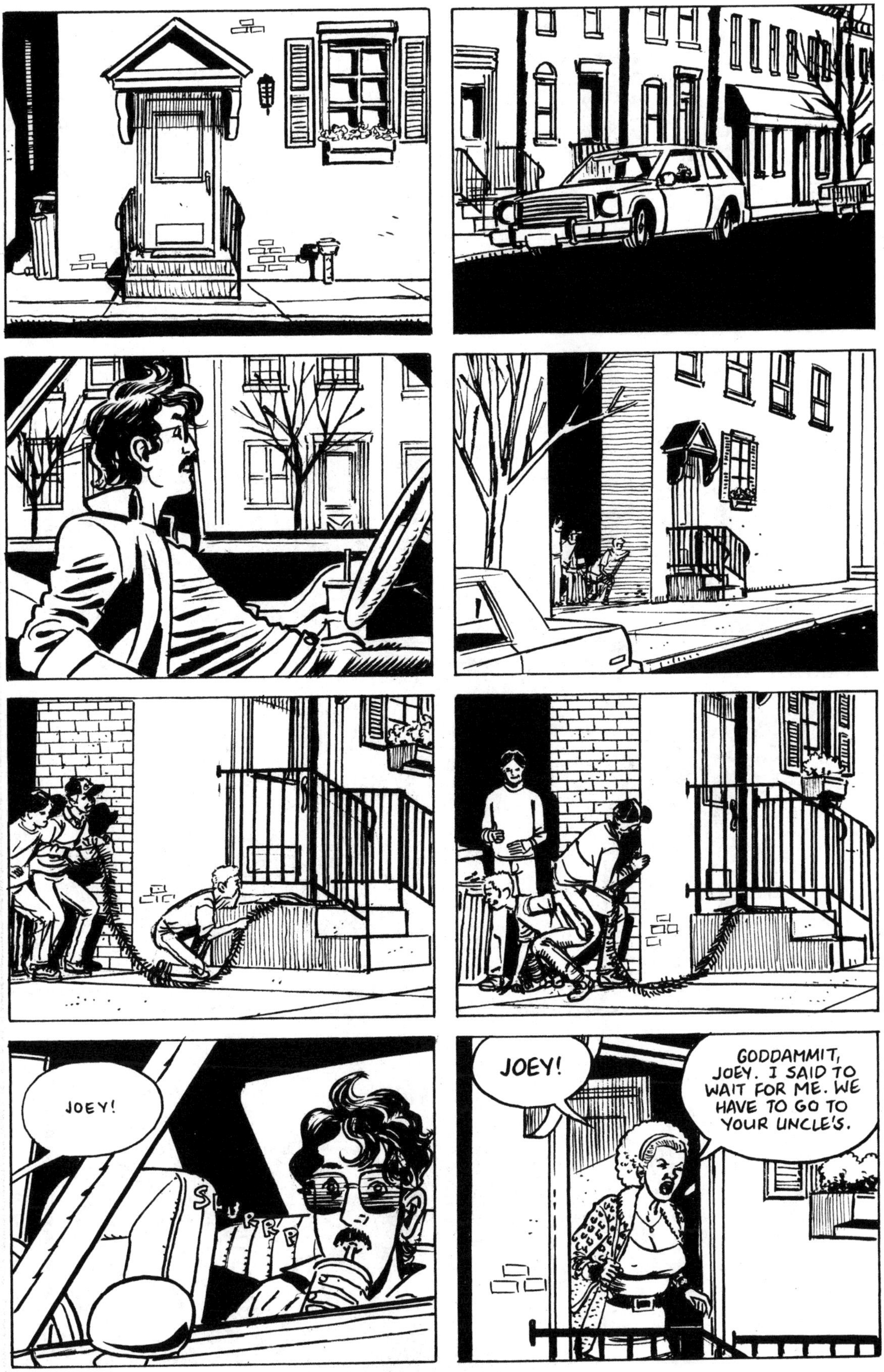
JOEY!
SLURRP
JOEY!
GODDAMMIT, JOEY. I SAID TO WAIT FOR ME. WE HAVE TO GO TO YOUR UNCLE'S.

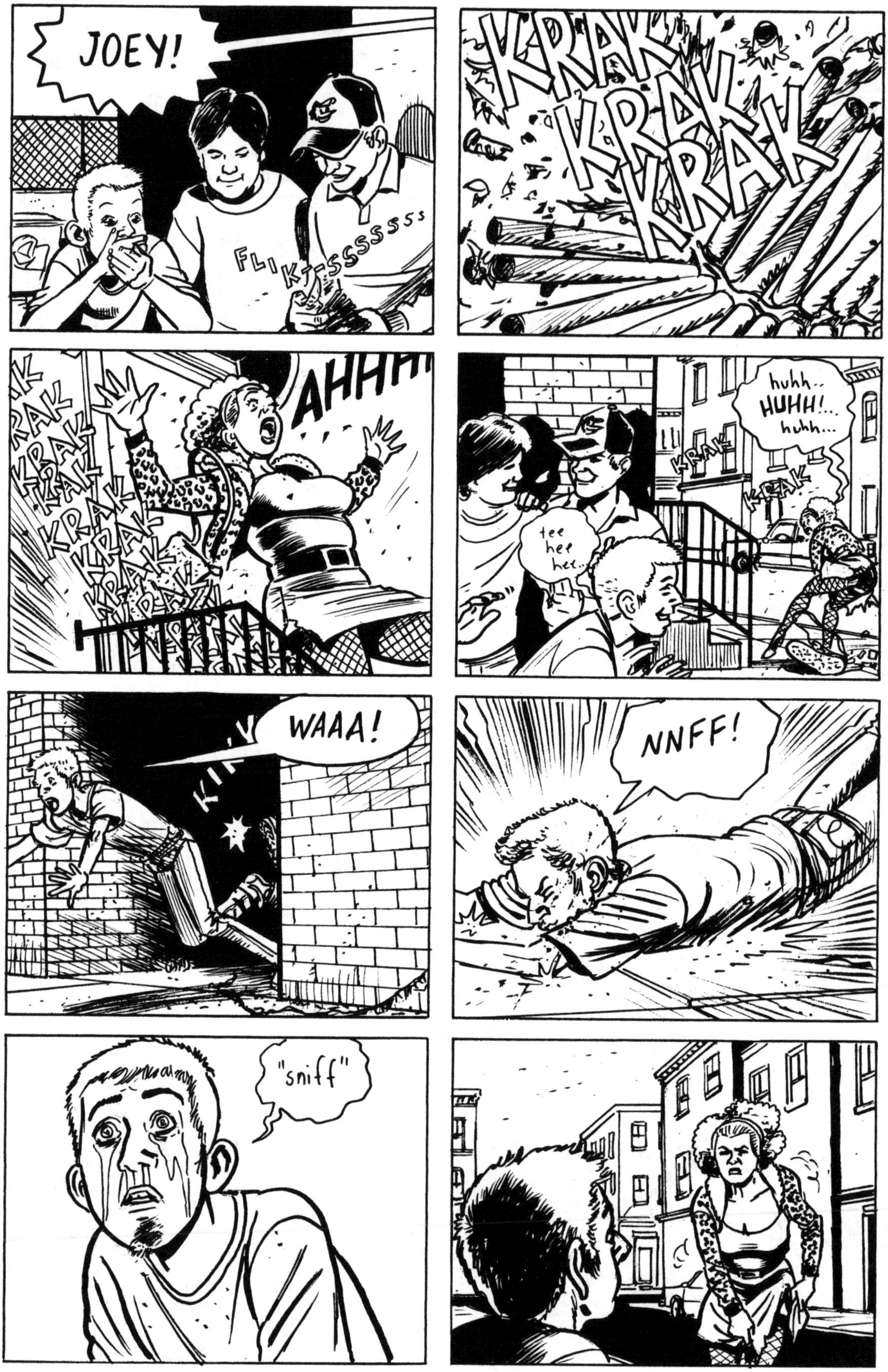
JOEY!
FLIK-SSSSSSSS
KRAK KRAK KRAK
AHHH
huhh..
HUHH!...
huhh...
tee hee hee...
WAAA!
NNFF!
"sniff"

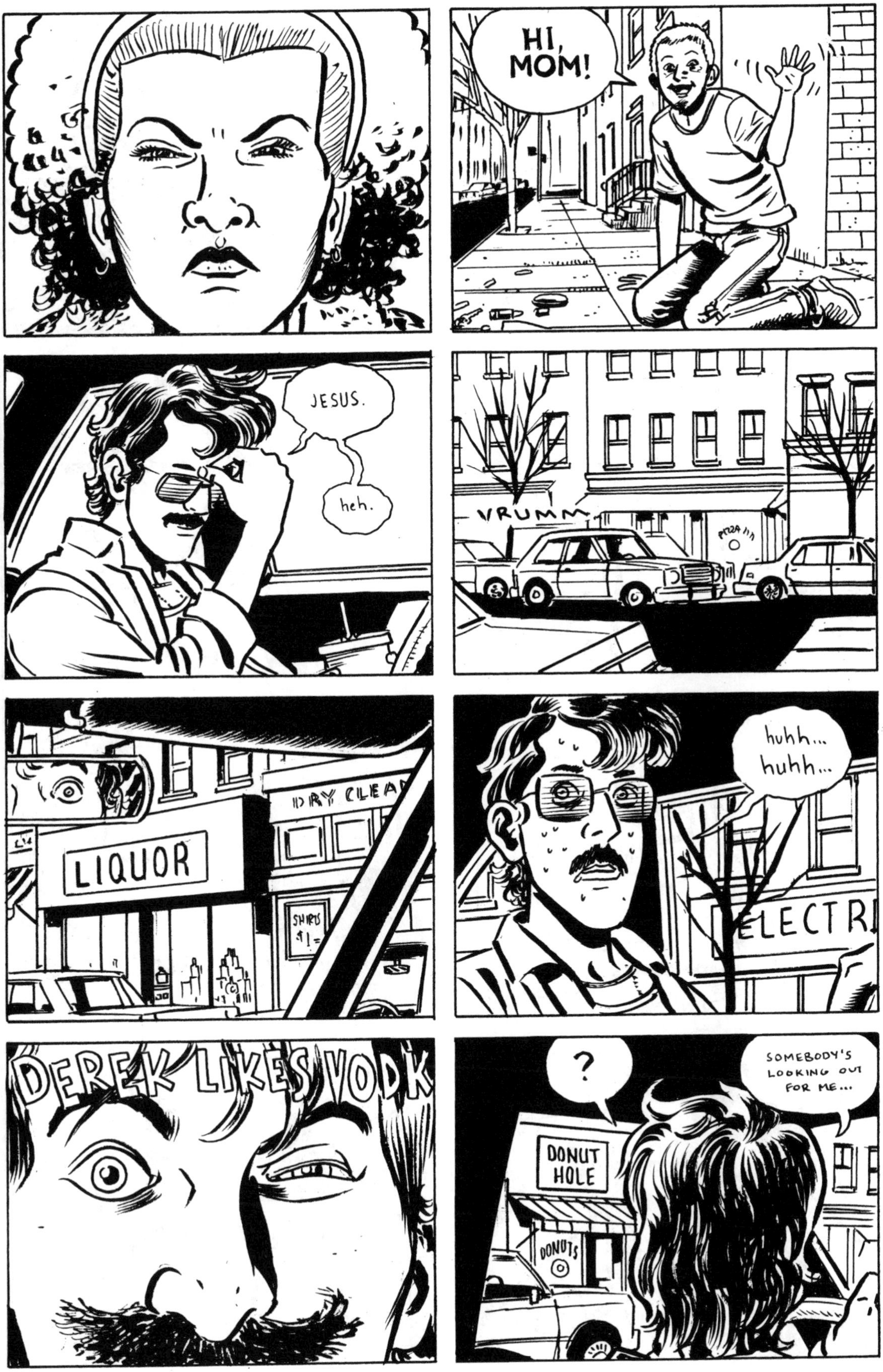
HI, MOM!
JESUS.
heh.
VRUMM
LIQUOR
DRY CLEA
huhh... huhh...
ELECTR
DEREK LIKES VODK
?
SOMEBODY'S LOOKING OUT FOR ME...
DONUT HOLE
DONUTS

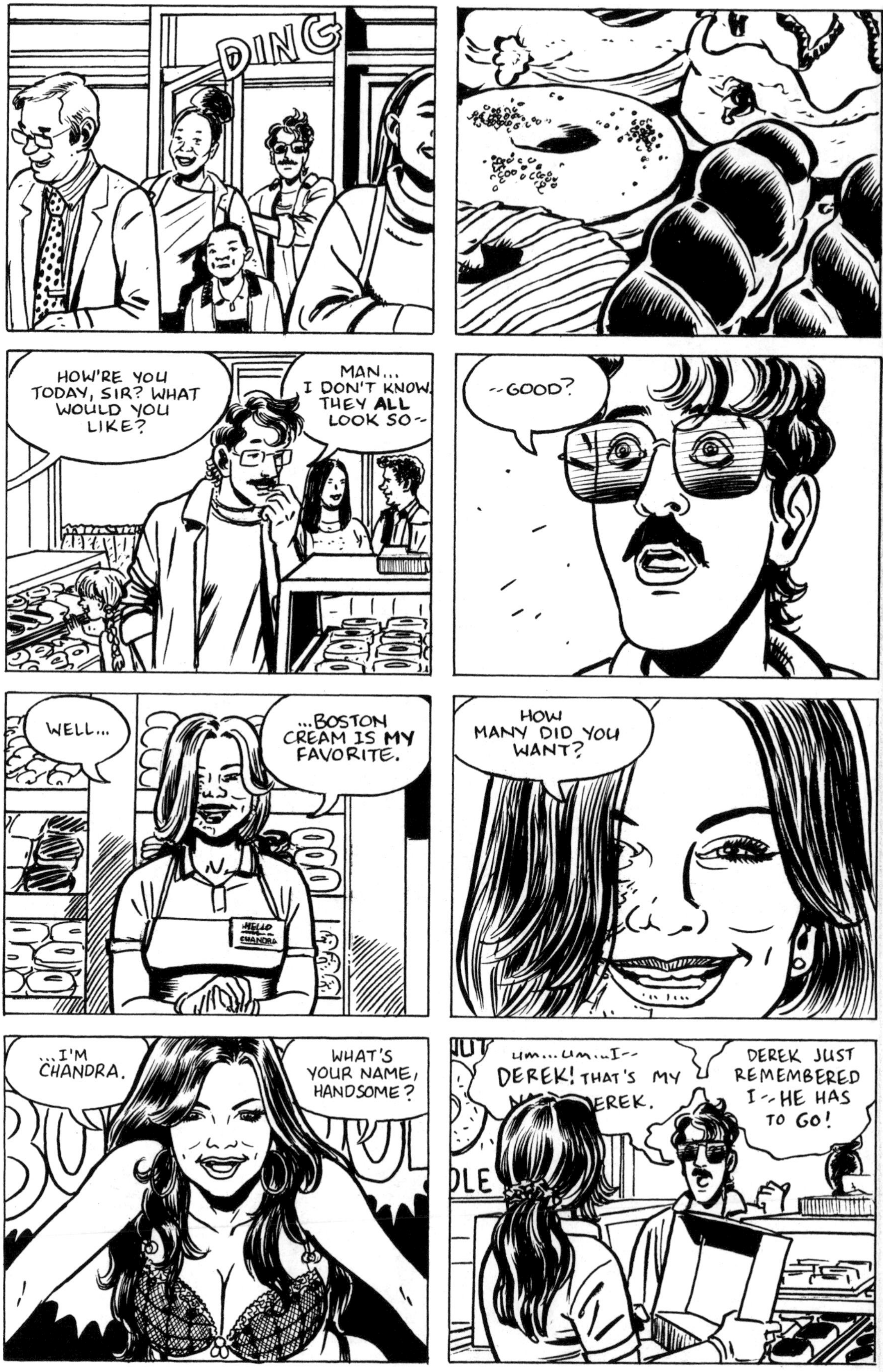
DING
HOW'RE YOU TODAY, SIR? WHAT WOULD YOU LIKE?
MAN... I DON'T KNOW. THEY **ALL** LOOK SO--
--GOOD?
WELL...
...BOSTON CREAM IS **MY** FAVORITE.
HELLO CHANDRA
HOW MANY DID YOU WANT?
...I'M CHANDRA.
WHAT'S YOUR NAME, HANDSOME?
um...um...I--
DEREK! THAT'S MY
EREK.
DEREK JUST REMEMBERED I--HE HAS TO GO!

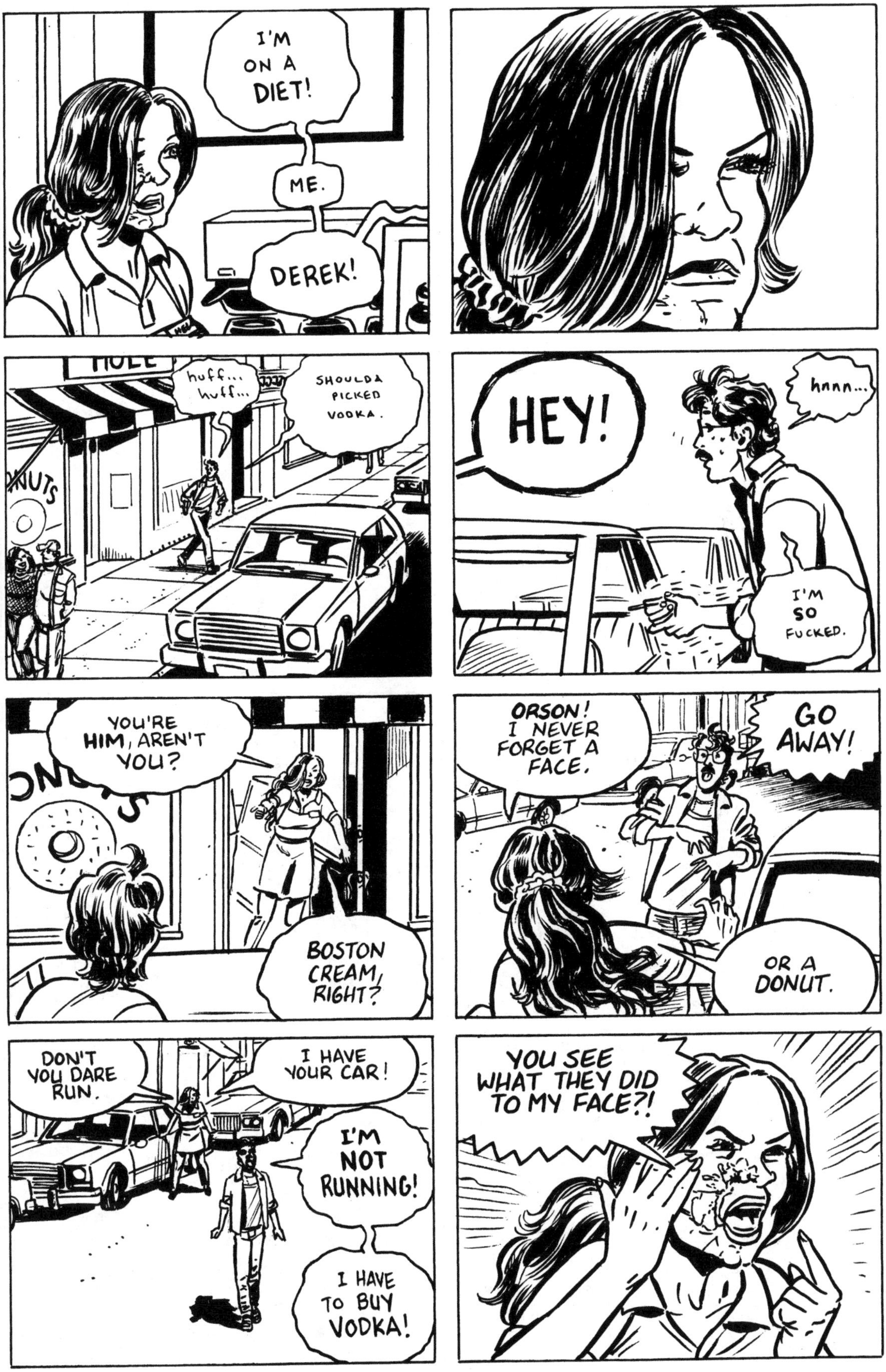

I'M ON A DIET!
ME.
DEREK!
huff... huff...
SHOULDA PICKED VODKA.
HEY!
hnnn...
I'M SO FUCKED.
YOU'RE HIM, AREN'T YOU?
BOSTON CREAM, RIGHT?
ORSON! I NEVER FORGET A FACE.
GO AWAY!
OR A DONUT.
DON'T YOU DARE RUN.
I HAVE YOUR CAR!
I'M NOT RUNNING!
I HAVE TO BUY VODKA!
YOU SEE WHAT THEY DID TO MY FACE?!

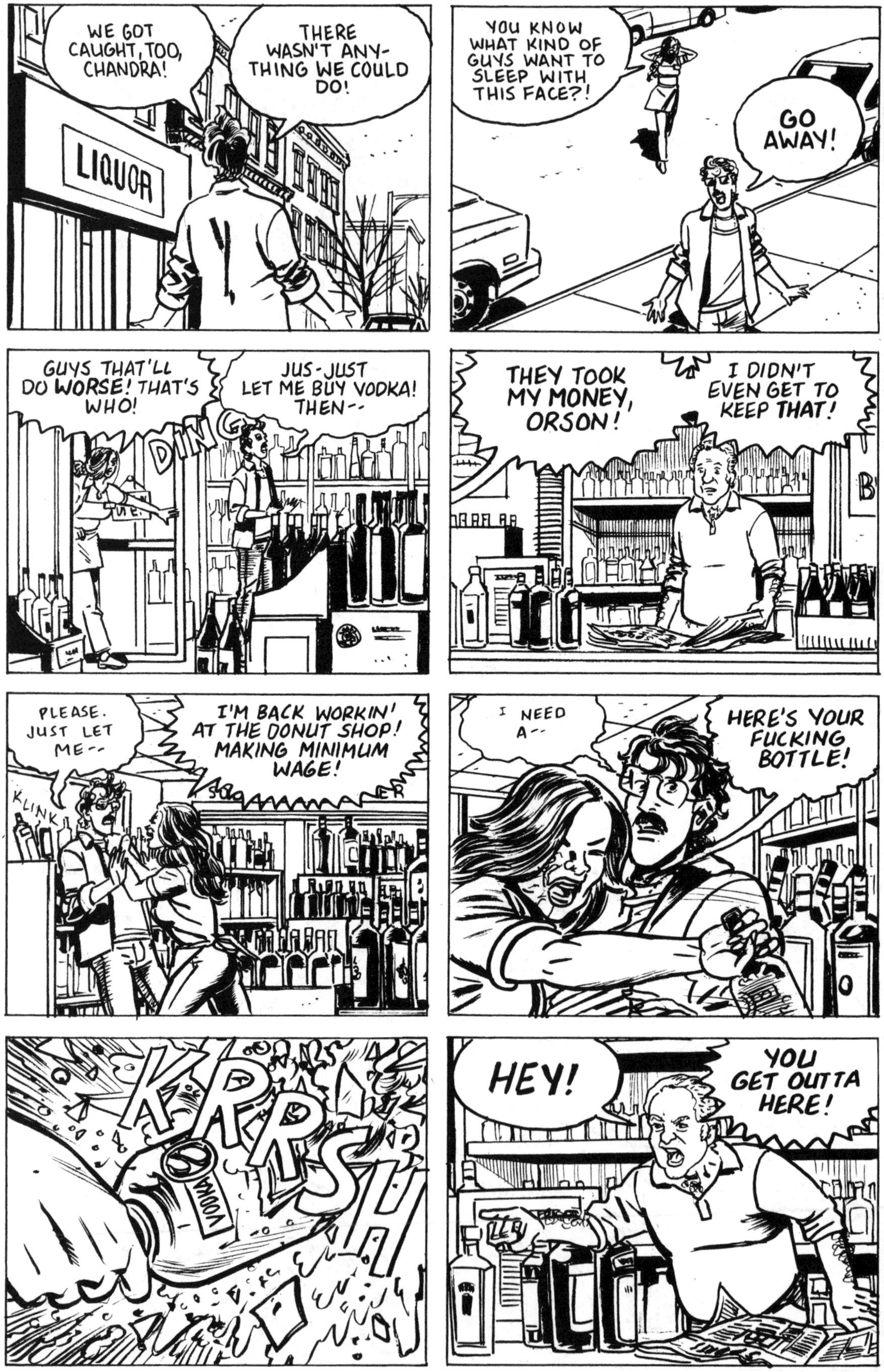
WE GOT CAUGHT, TOO, CHANDRA!
THERE WASN'T ANYTHING WE COULD DO!
LIQUOR
YOU KNOW WHAT KIND OF GUYS WANT TO SLEEP WITH THIS FACE?!
GO AWAY!
GUYS THAT'LL DO WORSE! THAT'S WHO!
JUS-JUST LET ME BUY VODKA! THEN--
DING
THEY TOOK MY MONEY, ORSON!
I DIDN'T EVEN GET TO KEEP THAT!
PLEASE. JUST LET ME--
I'M BACK WORKIN' AT THE DONUT SHOP! MAKING MINIMUM WAGE!
KLINK
I NEED A--
HERE'S YOUR FUCKING BOTTLE!
KRRSH
VODKA
HEY!
YOU GET OUTTA HERE!

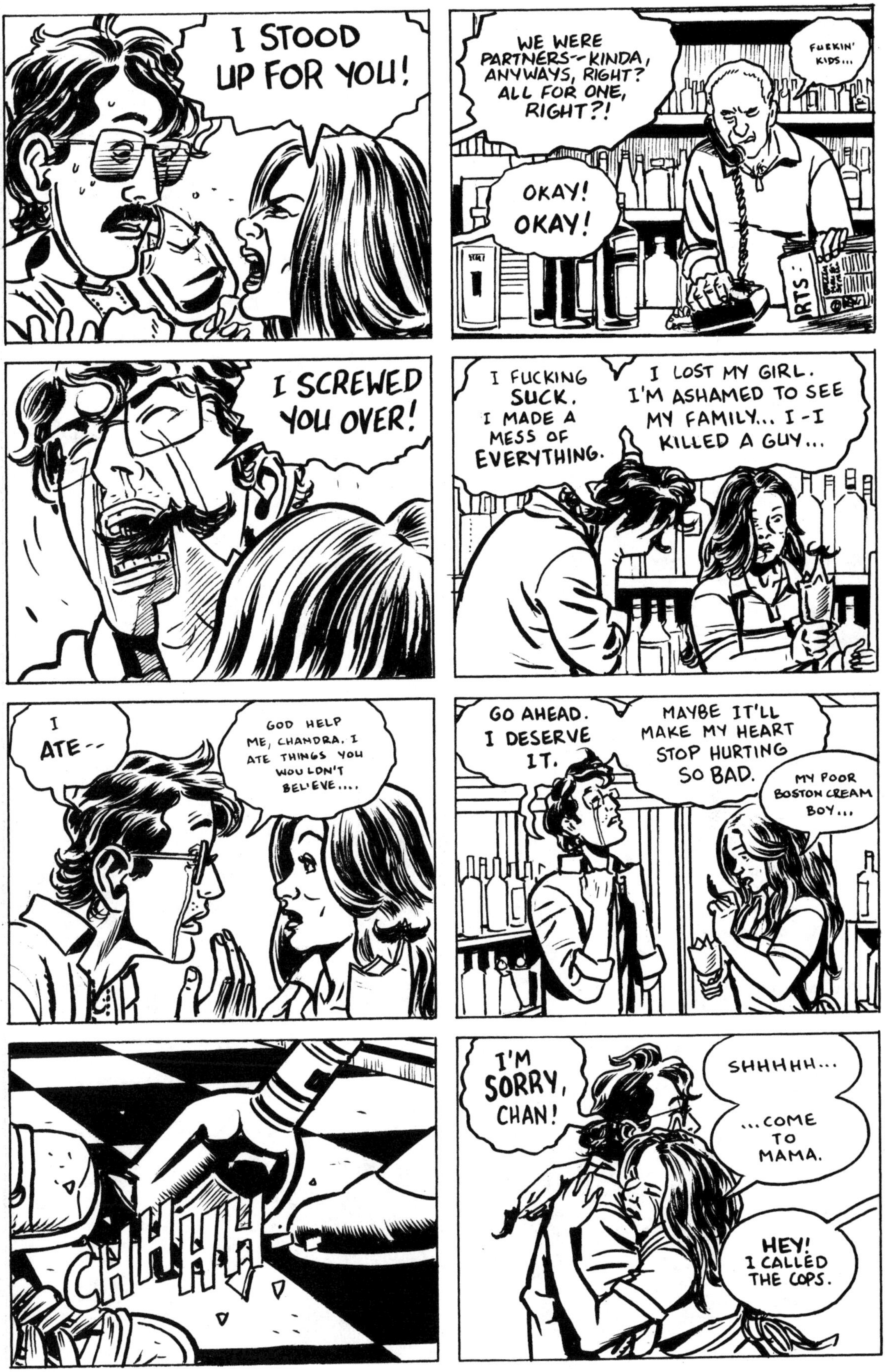
I STOOD UP FOR YOU!
WE WERE PARTNERS--KINDA, ANYWAYS, RIGHT? ALL FOR ONE, RIGHT?!
FUCKIN' KIDS...
OKAY! OKAY!
I SCREWED YOU OVER!
I FUCKING SUCK. I MADE A MESS OF EVERYTHING.
I LOST MY GIRL. I'M ASHAMED TO SEE MY FAMILY... I-I KILLED A GUY...
I ATE--
GOD HELP ME, CHANDRA. I ATE THINGS YOU WOULDN'T BELIEVE....
GO AHEAD. I DESERVE IT.
MAYBE IT'LL MAKE MY HEART STOP HURTING SO BAD.
MY POOR BOSTON CREAM BOY...
CHHHH
I'M SORRY, CHAN!
SHHHHH...
...COME TO MAMA.
HEY! I CALLED THE COPS.

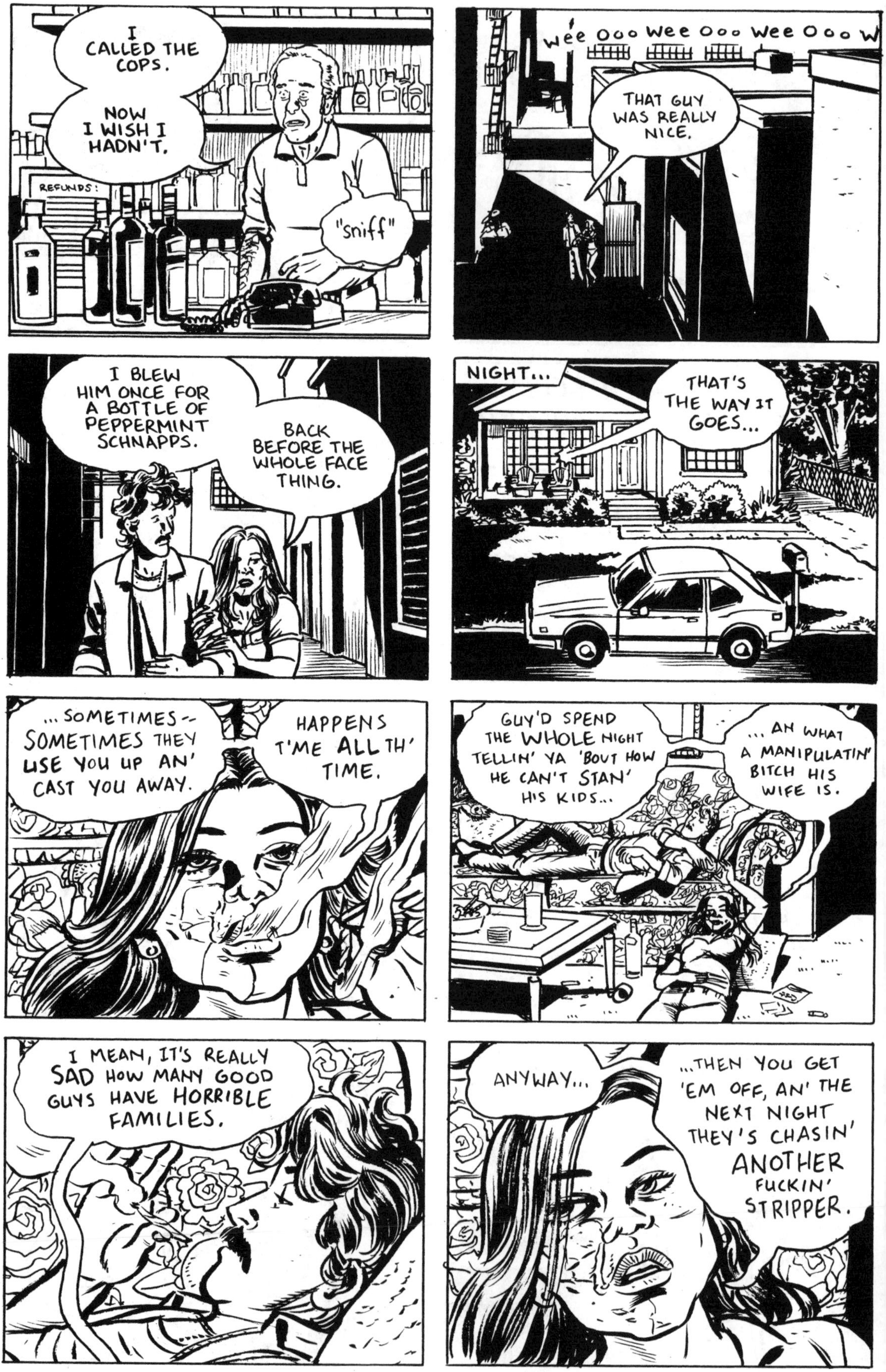
I CALLED THE COPS.
NOW I WISH I HADN'T.
REFUNDS:
"sniff"
wee ooo wee ooo wee ooo w
THAT GUY WAS REALLY NICE.
I BLEW HIM ONCE FOR A BOTTLE OF PEPPERMINT SCHNAPPS.
BACK BEFORE THE WHOLE FACE THING.
NIGHT...
THAT'S THE WAY IT GOES...
...SOMETIMES-- SOMETIMES THEY USE YOU UP AN' CAST YOU AWAY.
HAPPENS T'ME ALL TH' TIME.
GUY'D SPEND THE WHOLE NIGHT TELLIN' YA 'BOUT HOW HE CAN'T STAN' HIS KIDS...
...AN WHAT A MANIPULATIN' BITCH HIS WIFE IS.
I MEAN, IT'S REALLY SAD HOW MANY GOOD GUYS HAVE HORRIBLE FAMILIES.
ANYWAY...
...THEN YOU GET 'EM OFF, AN' THE NEXT NIGHT THEY'S CHASIN' ANOTHER FUCKIN' STRIPPER.

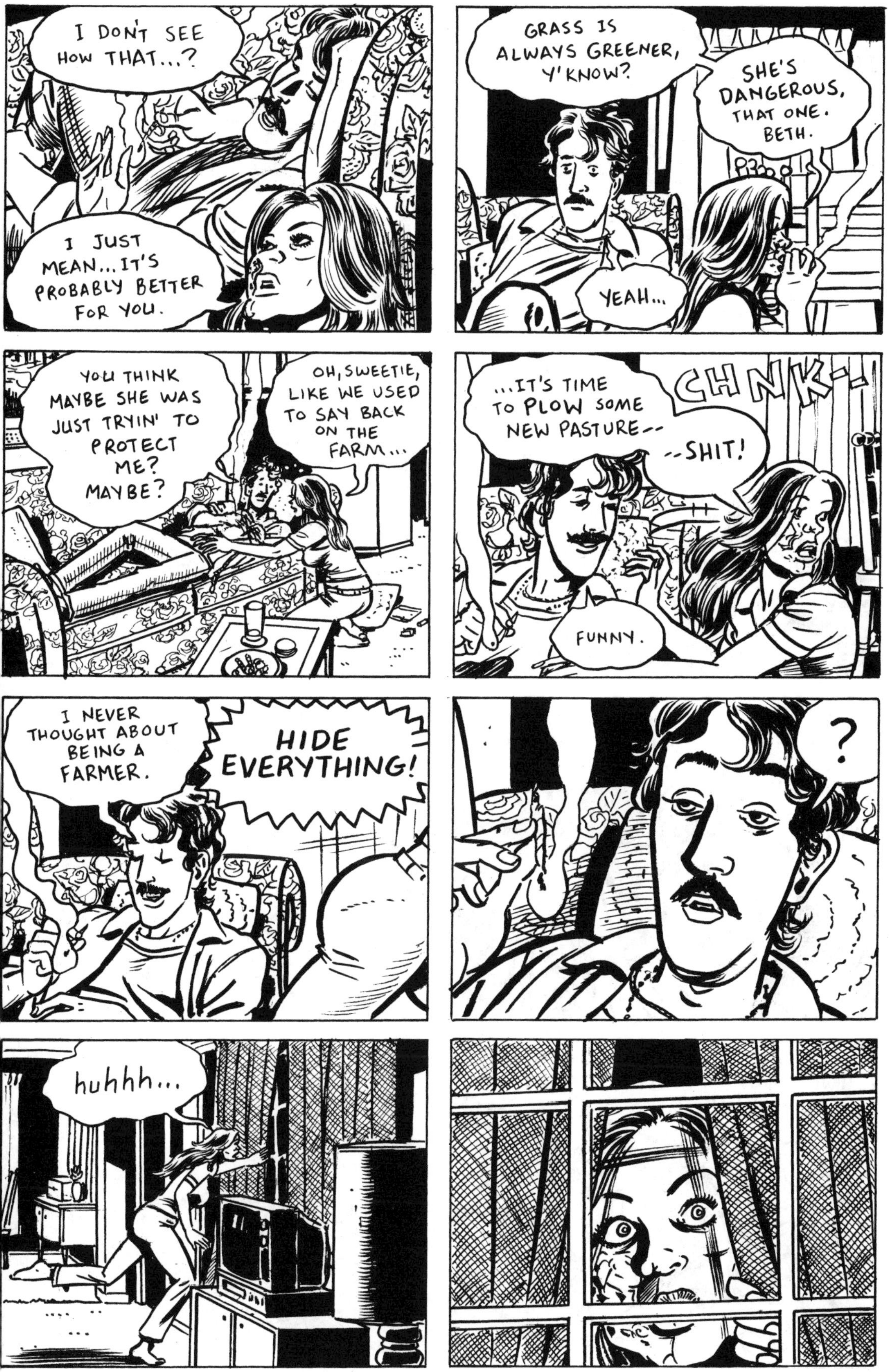
I DON'T SEE HOW THAT...?
I JUST MEAN... IT'S PROBABLY BETTER FOR YOU.
GRASS IS ALWAYS GREENER, Y'KNOW?
SHE'S DANGEROUS, THAT ONE. BETH.
YEAH...
YOU THINK MAYBE SHE WAS JUST TRYIN' TO PROTECT ME? MAYBE?
OH, SWEETIE, LIKE WE USED TO SAY BACK ON THE FARM...
...IT'S TIME TO PLOW SOME NEW PASTURE--
CHNK--
--SHIT!
FUNNY.
I NEVER THOUGHT ABOUT BEING A FARMER.
HIDE EVERYTHING!
?
huhhh...

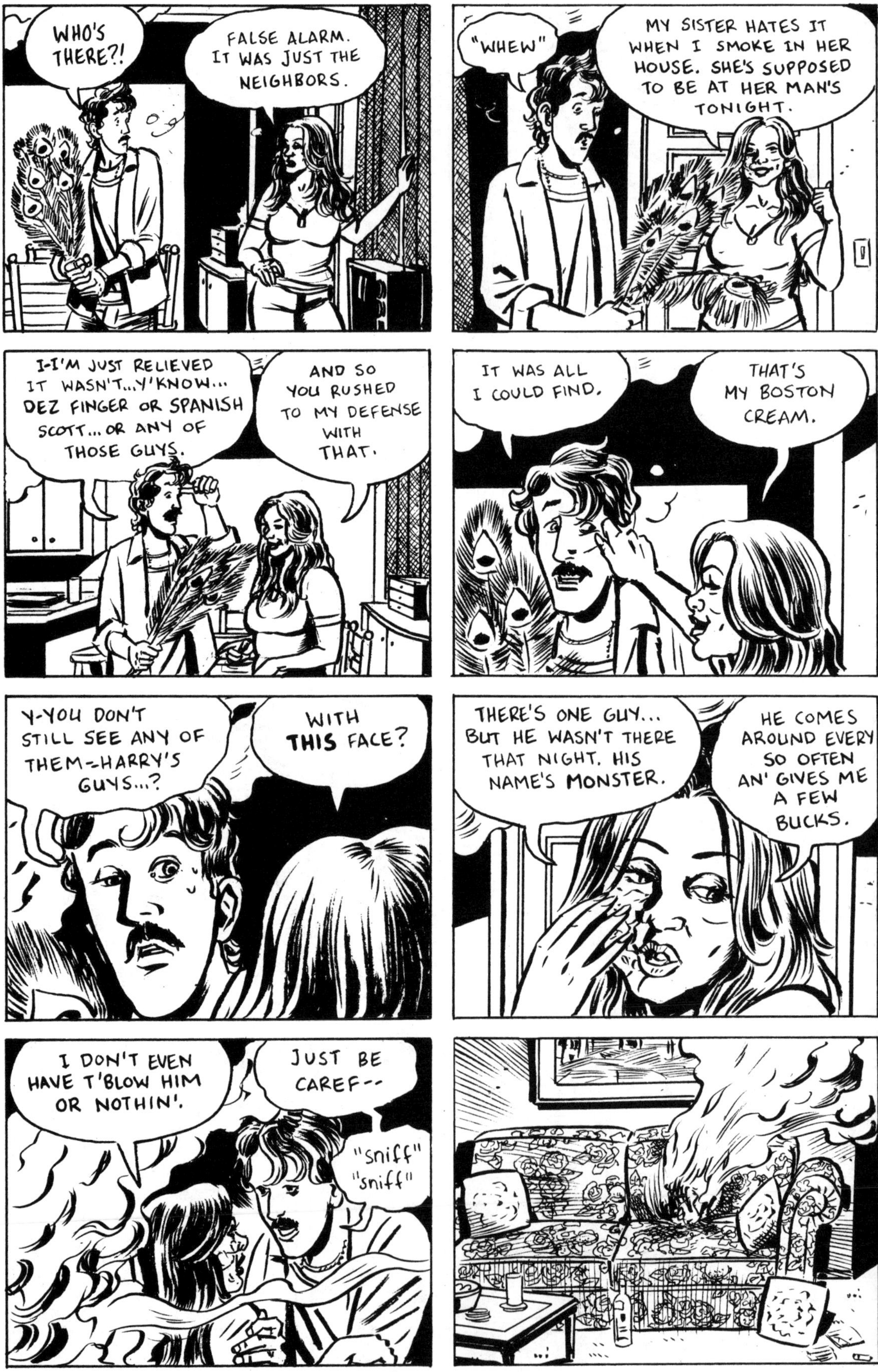
WHO'S THERE?!
FALSE ALARM. IT WAS JUST THE NEIGHBORS.
"WHEW"
MY SISTER HATES IT WHEN I SMOKE IN HER HOUSE. SHE'S SUPPOSED TO BE AT HER MAN'S TONIGHT.
I-I'M JUST RELIEVED IT WASN'T...Y'KNOW... DEZ FINGER OR SPANISH SCOTT... OR ANY OF THOSE GUYS.
AND SO YOU RUSHED TO MY DEFENSE WITH THAT.
IT WAS ALL I COULD FIND.
THAT'S MY BOSTON CREAM.
Y-YOU DON'T STILL SEE ANY OF THEM--HARRY'S GUYS...?
WITH THIS FACE?
THERE'S ONE GUY... BUT HE WASN'T THERE THAT NIGHT. HIS NAME'S MONSTER.
HE COMES AROUND EVERY SO OFTEN AN' GIVES ME A FEW BUCKS.
I DON'T EVEN HAVE T'BLOW HIM OR NOTHIN'.
JUST BE CAREF--
"sniff" "sniff"

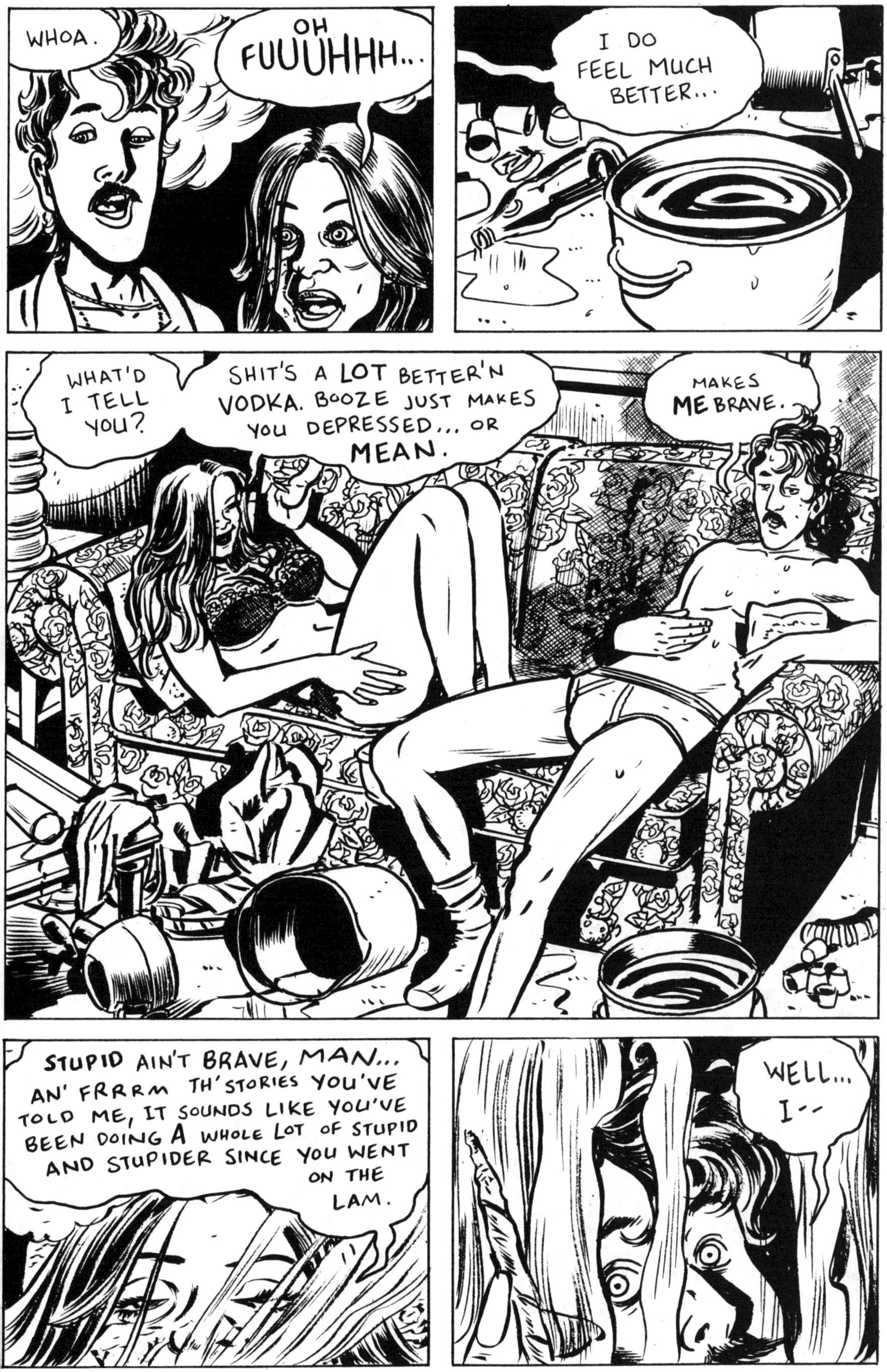
WHOA.
OH FUUUHHH...
I DO FEEL MUCH BETTER...
WHAT'D I TELL YOU?
SHIT'S A LOT BETTER'N VODKA. BOOZE JUST MAKES YOU DEPRESSED... OR MEAN.
MAKES ME BRAVE.
STUPID AIN'T BRAVE, MAN... AN' FRRRM TH' STORIES YOU'VE TOLD ME, IT SOUNDS LIKE YOU'VE BEEN DOING A WHOLE LOT OF STUPID AND STUPIDER SINCE YOU WENT ON THE LAM.
WELL... I--

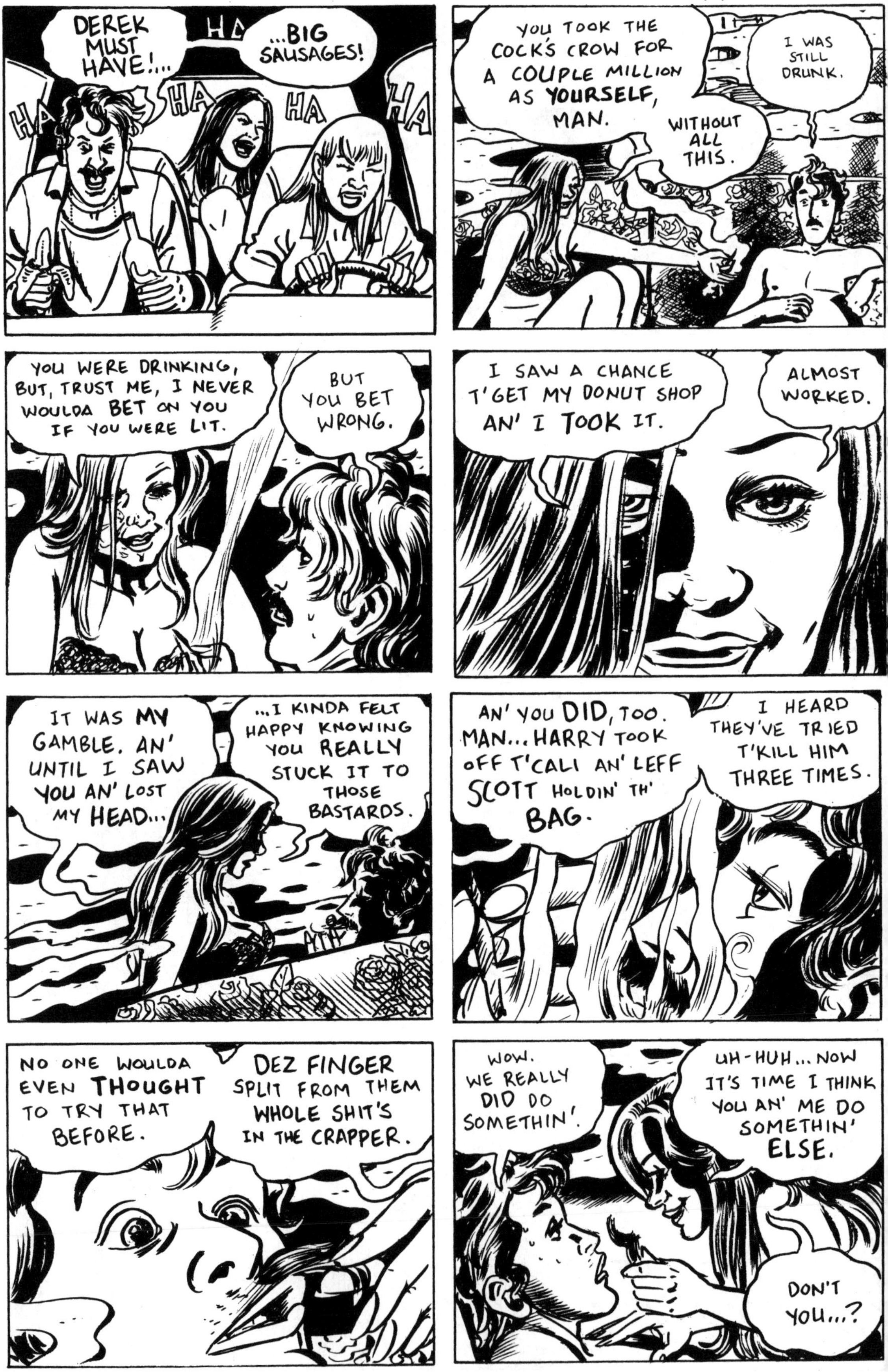
DEREK MUST HAVE!...
HA
...BIG SAUSAGES!
HA HA HA HA
YOU TOOK THE COCK'S CROW FOR A COUPLE MILLION AS YOURSELF, MAN.
WITHOUT ALL THIS.
I WAS STILL DRUNK.
YOU WERE DRINKING, BUT, TRUST ME, I NEVER WOULDA BET ON YOU IF YOU WERE LIT.
BUT YOU BET WRONG.
I SAW A CHANCE T'GET MY DONUT SHOP AN' I TOOK IT.
ALMOST WORKED.
IT WAS MY GAMBLE. AN' UNTIL I SAW YOU AN' LOST MY HEAD...
...I KINDA FELT HAPPY KNOWING YOU REALLY STUCK IT TO THOSE BASTARDS.
AN' YOU DID, TOO. MAN... HARRY TOOK OFF T'CALI AN' LEFF SCOTT HOLDIN' TH' BAG.
I HEARD THEY'VE TRIED T'KILL HIM THREE TIMES.
NO ONE WOULDA EVEN THOUGHT TO TRY THAT BEFORE.
DEZ FINGER SPLIT FROM THEM WHOLE SHIT'S IN THE CRAPPER.
WOW. WE REALLY DID DO SOMETHIN'.
UH-HUH... NOW IT'S TIME I THINK YOU AN' ME DO SOMETHIN' ELSE.
DON'T YOU...?

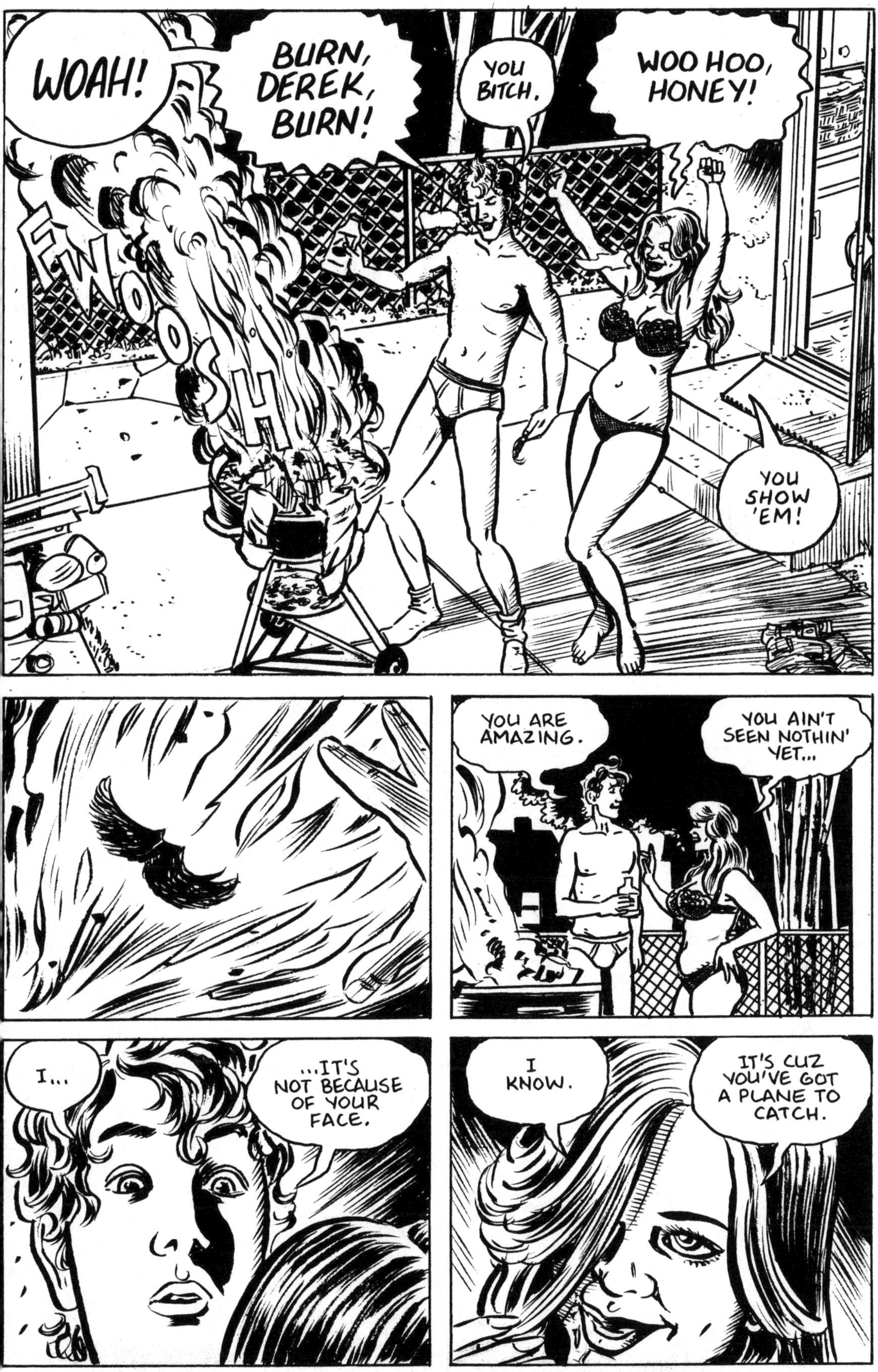
WOAH!
BURN, DEREK, BURN!
YOU BITCH.
WOO HOO, HONEY!
FWOOOSH
YOU SHOW 'EM!
YOU ARE AMAZING.
YOU AIN'T SEEN NOTHIN' YET...
I...
...IT'S NOT BECAUSE OF YOUR FACE.
I KNOW.
IT'S CUZ YOU'VE GOT A PLANE TO CATCH.

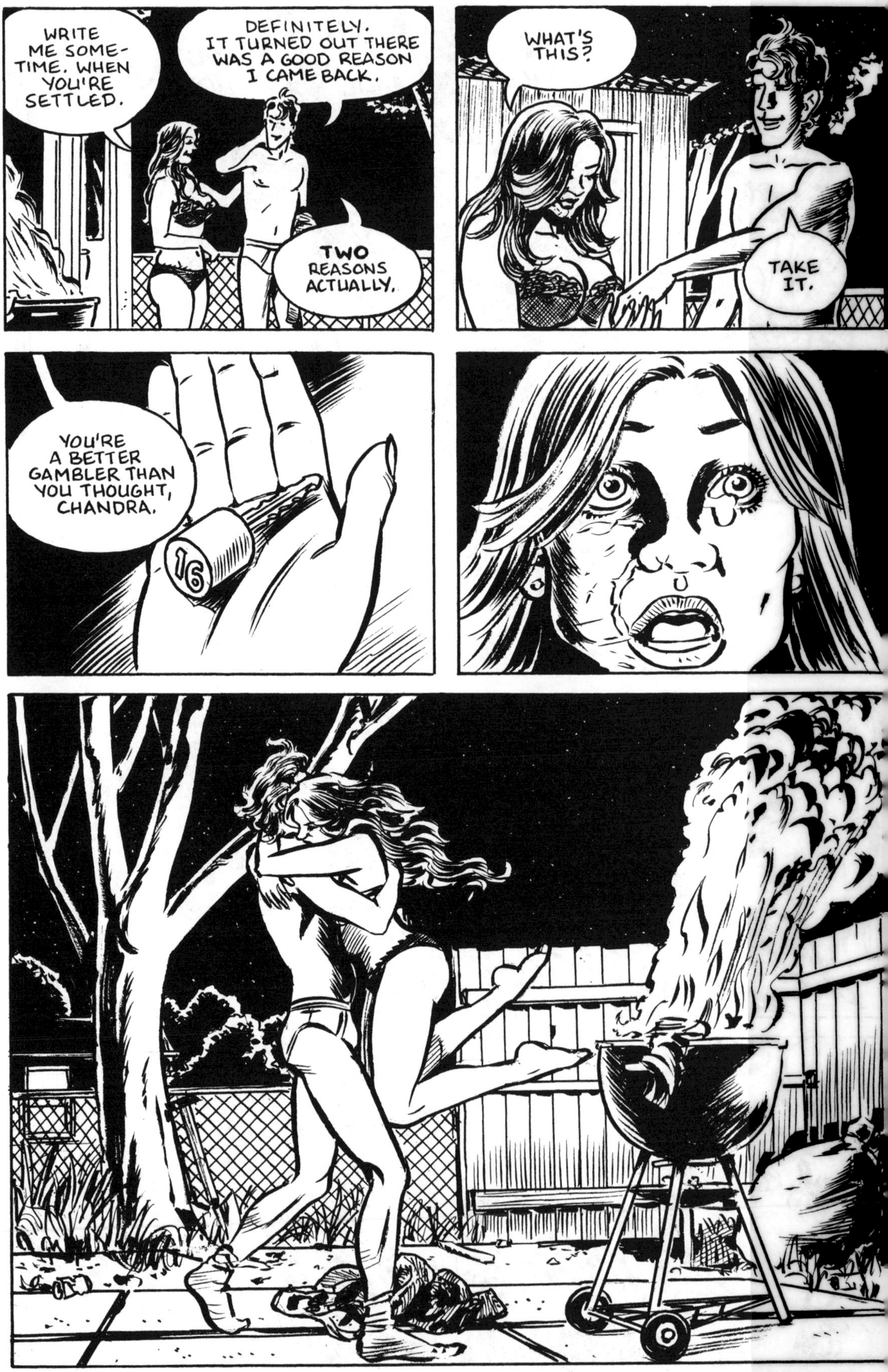
WRITE ME SOME-TIME. WHEN YOU'RE SETTLED.
DEFINITELY. IT TURNED OUT THERE WAS A GOOD REASON I CAME BACK.
TWO REASONS ACTUALLY.
WHAT'S THIS?
TAKE IT.
YOU'RE A BETTER GAMBLER THAN YOU THOUGHT, CHANDRA.
16

THE END...